A
Garland Series

VICTORIAN
FICTION

NOVELS OF FAITH
AND DOUBT

A collection of 121 novels
in 92 volumes, selected by
Professor Robert Lee Wolff,
Harvard University,
with a separate introductory volume
written by him
especially for this series.

MOSTLY FOOLS

Edmund Randolph

Three volumes in one

Garland Publishing, Inc., New York & London

1976

Bibliographical note:

this facsimile has been made from a copy in the
British Museum
(12636.g.16)

Library of Congress Cataloging in Publication Data

Randolph, Edmund.
  Mostly fools.

  (Victorian fiction : Novels of faith and doubt)
  Reprint of the 1886 ed. published by S. Low, Marston,
Searle & Rivington, London.
  I. Title. II. Series.
PZ3.R1597Mo7   [PR5209.R15]   823'.8   75-461
ISBN 0-8240-1539-8

Printed in the United States of America

MOSTLY FOOLS.

A Romance of Civilization.

BY

Mr. RANDOLPH,

AUTHOR OF "ONE OF US."

" . . . We arrive at the undeniable, but unexpected conclusion, that eminently
gifted men are raised as much above mediocrity as idiots are depressed below it."

FRANCIS GALTON.

IN THREE VOLUMES.

VOL. I.

London:

SAMPSON LOW, MARSTON, SEARLE, & RIVINGTON,

CROWN BUILDINGS, 188, FLEET STREET.

1886.

LONDON:
PRINTED BY GILBERT AND RIVINGTON, LIMITED,
ST. JOHN'S SQUARE.

TO MY ADVERSARIES.

INTRODUCTION.

I HAD been a member of the Psychical Society
for at least three weeks; but had not as yet
seen the ghost of a ghost. To say that I was
disappointed would be too strong a term. I
merely experienced the feelings common to
mortals who have recently joined anything; a
church, a wife, or a club, no matter what.

Although I had realized that even under the
new conditions of my environment, ghosts were
not to be as blackberries, I had not therefore ceased to be on the alert, and when
one morning, seated at my study writing-table,
I heard a voice different and easily distinguish-
able from that of man, I at once responded
to it, with no deeper sensation than a mild and
agreeable surprise. The hour was unusual,
and the manner of communication was no less
so. But this was all the better.

The expression, " heard a voice," is perhaps
open to the objection that it is strictly in-
accurate in its usual sense. If I had seen an
apparition with my eyes, and heard him speak
with my ears, I should have at once suspected

him (or myself). Every schoolgirl knows that sight and hearing are merely a succession of nervous shocks, and anything in the nature of a nervous shock must necessarily militate greatly against that calm spirit of judicial inquisition in which such a matter should be approached. No; I neither saw nor heard him. Thank Heaven! no such palpable objection can ever be raised to my remarkable visitant. The presence conversed with me *inwardly*, and this, as every fair-minded person will admit, must preclude the possibility of mistake, while I realized his meaning by some process that I am quite unable to understand, and consequently to explain. If there was some difficulty in doing this at first, it soon passed away, and I was shortly able to speak to him as plainly as a man does to his wife. My notes, taken at the time, run as follows :—

"Who are you?" question by myself.

Reply inarticulate, but sounding like, "Nobody," and a groan.

"In one sense I had concluded as much. I should say rather, 'Who *were* you?'"

"I never was anybody!" A deep-drawn sigh.

This curious answer took me by surprise, and I blurted out naturally enough, "Then you are not a common ghost?"

"Very much the reverse." A groan.

"You groan a good deal. May I ask why? What are you doing?"

"Waiting."

" What for ? "

" To be embodied."

" O-oh !   I think I understand.   Pray sit down."

" *Hélas !* " he responded in French, perhaps from motives of delicacy, " I am like the rest of us, *Je n'ai pas de quoi.*"

" Well, well, do make yourself at home.   I should like to ask a few things.   This is a subject that interests me much.   Pray have you waited long ? "

" Ever since the life-germs first came into existence, some hundred millions of ages back. I have really lost count.   They were all created together, you know."

" No, I don't ; but I should like to know, exceedingly.   I wish you would make yourself comfortable for a chat.   Pray are there many like you ? "

" We are countless."

My informant no longer sighed, he was brightening up under the influence of our conversation, although he still spoke with a certain sullenness.

" But," said I, in a consolatory manner, " here you are on earth, at any rate.   Your chance must come very shortly.   Surely six months or so can't make much difference after waiting so long.   You look out for your bodily affinity while it is still in embryo, watch your opportunity, and then slip in at the right moment.   I believe that's the way it's done, isn't it ? "

He smiled contemptuously. How is it possible to express the way in which that smile and its accentuation were brought home to me? I know not, yet I felt it.

"Crude—crude—very. Yes, something like that; a mere man can't be expected to know better. No, I can't do it quite so easily, I wish I could. I wish we all could. But," here he looked me full in the face, though of course I did not see him, "there's been a mistake, an awful mistake. The fact is," he seized me by the button-hole, "my generation *missed its turn.*"

"Good gracious!"

"Yes;" and he added, sternly, "*you* are the mistake."

"I have sometimes thought so," I answered, recovering my composure, "but, still, anything I can do—pray—"

"Pooh!" he retorted, sharply, "I mean you and your entire race of to-day. You can't do anything. But it's a monstrous shame you should be here out of your turn, and when ours may come round again, Heaven only knows."

"But surely you can—you can—my biology is rather shaky—start fresh and work up again."

"Start fresh and work up again?" he almost screamed. "Oh! yes," and he laughed a laugh of withering sarcasm. "Oh! by all means—yes, you can do that, go back and be the primordial promise of a protoplasm, anybody—I mean any life-germ can do that, if he cares about it. Why, sir, are you aware," he said, turning on me fiercely, " that working up, as you facetiously express it, it took me exactly twenty-seven million years to become a caterpillar—a mere miserable, every-day caterpillar, sir, that you squash, squash, sir, between your thumb and forefinger ? "

This was not my way of exterminating caterpillars, but I allowed it to pass. He appeared so excited, that I gave him a minute to cool before I answered.

" I beg your pardon. I spoke without thinking or even knowing. Twenty-seven million of years, you said " (I made an entry in my note book). " That is excessively interesting."

" Oh ! excessively," he retorted, "especially when you are working up. However, after all, perhaps it's no such loss. Primitive man," and here he shot a scathing glance at me, "appears to be a poor thing after all. A few millions of years hence, and he may develop into something decent."

" Primitive man," I repeated after him, annoyed by his manner, " I am at a loss to understand your meaning. I have no doubt the individual you allude to, *was* a very queer specimen, but in these latter days—"

The expression seemed to tickle him, indeed he was fairly convulsed.

" Come, come," he said, not unkindly; I see we are out of your depths; by primitive man, I was referring to yourselves of to-day."

"I beg your pardon," I said, suppressing a gasp; "the idea was new to me, ha! ha! I rather like it, now I come to think of it, but I should be glad to know exactly how you make it out."

"Well, it's tolerably plain, I should think, even to a nineteenth-century intellect. How long do you suppose man has walked the earth?"

"Oh! a few thousand years."

"Precisely; a few beggarly thousands. To an advanced life-germ like myself, who has the power of looking back, it seems hardly more than yesterday; and how long do you suppose the 'life period' of this rather paltry planet, to which you and I happen to have been posted, extends?"

"Oh! into millions."

"Exactly. Hundreds of millions; and into those hundreds of millions, the race of man, in some shape or other, has certainly to go."

"Whew! Well, possibly—I—I begin to see what you mean. Then you think we need not expect the end of the world the day after to-morrow, as I was taught at school?"

To this rather idle question, he gave no direct answer.

"Nature does not work in spasm," he went on. "Man is evolving, like the rest, in the tremendous procession of the ages; his seed blazed in the fire mists of the beginning, no knowing what he may come to; he will be a different thing in even a million years. I shan't lose by it after all;" this he said as if to himself.

"There certainly is breadth in your views," I admitted, slowly considering the new position. "You give me hope. I always thought time was so short. Why, all our difficulties—Ireland, the lunacy laws, the Thames drainage, Egypt, religion—should be met and conquered in that time. But, by the way, at our present rate of progression, what will our beliefs be in a hundred million years? The test will be a trifle severe."

"Facts will stand much as before," he answered drily; "but I may as well tell you that the great cosmic facts are not to be expressed in any language yet known to man."

"Ah! I'm sorry in anticipation for the schoolboy of the period. What an awful thing history will be!"

"Awful. But we are wandering; after all, it's one's own time that interests one most, and that's why, I suppose, I cannot get over the feeling which has brought me here to talk to you. You see, you took my place. I am your unborn brother."

"Oh!!"

"Do you understand?"

"Not quite; but I feel sure it's all right," I added, civilly; "perhaps you can give me some little explanation."

"It's all wrong," he replied, gruffly. "You will allow, I suppose, that you and everything about you, are the result of an apparently chance concourse of innumerable accidents, the slightest alteration in any one of which would have made you and them entirely different from what you really are. Well, one day it so happened that a hitch *did* occur, it twisted the world a hairbreadth out of its groove, and there you are—where *we* ought to be. That hair-breadth caused you and all your circumstances. You and they, if I may so express it, are our alternatives, if you hadn't happened we should have happened, and vice versa. That hitch changed everything, not that the change was perceptible in the least. Everything was just different, yet the general concourse of results was almost identical, as both phases were evolved from the same antecedents. It was a simple shuffle of the cards; take it all round, I think we did better than you, we made our mistakes—should have made them, I mean—but I doubt whether we bungled *quite* so much. The questions of the day were the same, but on the whole we gave them, I think, more satisfactory answers. Events ripened somewhat more quickly with us—a more intelligent manipulation, you see."

"Just so. Yet I should have imagined that the average of intellect would remain unchanged under the circumstances you mention; still I am glad to listen to your views. Then, so I understand,—you and your people are—were—would have been—(really I am a little mixed)—a precise parallel to ourselves in our conditions?"

" You describe it exactly."

" My dear sir, it's the very thing I've been wishing to come across for years."

" I am your man, then," he said with some eagerness, and, as if recollecting himself, " I mean, that is a matter I can help you in, and I shall be glad to do so. We germs have a keen delight in evoking the phantoms of the existence that should have been ours; in this way we, as it were, lead that potential life. You must clearly realize my position," he continued with some haughtiness. " It is true I would put on flesh if I could, but the germ or soul (pardon so hackneyed and misguiding a term), is an essential individuality, and as such infinitely superior to any mere composite man. Man, poor devil, does not really know if he has an ego of his own at all, he cannot strictly call his thumb his own, much less his soul ! Man is a mere aggregation of cells which condescend to work more or less together on some kind of vague instinct of self-interest or self-defence. Still it is in this semi-bestial shape the true ego finds its best chances of promotion, although in most ways the step is retrograde and it is handicapped with almost unbearable conditions. However " — he shrugged his shoulders—" one must take the roughs with the smooths, I suppose."

" I suppose so; but before we discuss that, tell me. If these things haven't happened, how can you describe them ? "

" Dear me ! " he said, impatiently, " if you

don't know the alphabet of existence, how on earth am I to explain the system? Put your old notions out of your head. Time, space, matter, and so forth, are essential nonentities, and are *nil* to the spirit until he has once fallen under the spell of embodiment, then I admit they become serious questions. In my present half-and-half state, fact and fiction become virtually identical. You are not more real, not a bit," he insisted, "than the things that should have been; their circumstances were ready cut and dried for them, just as yours are for you; but as all visible phenomena are the out-put of the invisible, you are hardly qualified to form an opinion."

"If you could give me some slight sketch," I hazarded, fearing we should shortly be out of my depth altogether.

"I will," he said, heartily; "I will."

"Just a few leading persons and features—religious, social, political, of this alternative generation which we so curiously replaced. The study should be of interest to ourselves."

"You have certainly claims upon me. As your *alter ego*, and occupying the same relative place, I see things from your point of view. Write. I will inspire you with the story of the Times."

An author's ghost, I mused; something new. "You are aware," I said aloud, "that ghosts sometimes get into trouble. There was once a sculptor who—"

"Don't be afraid," he interrupted. "*I* shan't get into trouble by describing the people and things among which I was so fortunate as to find myself. I won't promise so much for you, ha! ha!" Here he seemed to die away in a species of ill-natured chuckle.

So ended the interview. It was the first and last; and during the progress of the work which resulted from it, there were times when I was tempted to doubt the presence of any inspiration whatever! But it is obvious, from what has been said, that it is absolutely beyond, perhaps it should be said above, criticism. Under its conditions no single character or incident could by any possibility have been drawn from life. It appeared to have something in it; therefore I have set it down, and if the phantoms conjured up are grotesque, or flippant, or false to their own principles, or to the principles of fiction, they must be left to fight it out. Any attempt to lay the responsibility of them upon human shoulders must necessarily fail.

MOSTLY FOOLS.

CHAPTER I.

A YOUNG man stood on the threshold of life, and he was goodly to see. He looked forth upon a goodly prospect of hill, and dale, and wood, in whose gentle bosom lay a vast pile of fair building—tower and turret, cloister and church—amid swelling lawns and running streams. She was the Alma Mater that lay before him in the valley, more dear now in the parting hour than ever he had thought her, much as he had always loved the spot. With a sigh he turned away. This college was the lineal descendant of those famous schools, the old Eton and Winchester, a nursery of English Catholicism from out of the days of the penal laws ; and if it lacked something of the dignity of age, nevertheless its shorter history was one of honourable struggle and of triumph over difficulties. Here, unchanged, the old religion of England found its embodiment. Here no cuckoo sat in the nest builded by better birds, and such dignity as the original has over the copy, at least was its inheritance. Now these schooldays were over. The boy is the father of the man. What was the augury of this one's boyhood? He re-cast the long file of days since first he had set foot in those halls. He had been like other boys, save that in his ambition he overstepped his fellows, often to failure. He remembered it all perfectly, and as the past rose before him in a series of pictures, he could not but laugh, though he was sad at heart. Every boy's life is a terribly serious comedy. Let us look back with him, and see whether the British schoolboy within these walls was different from what he was elsewhere.

The story, then, of Roland Tudor's schooldays may be said to have begun at the following point.

*　　*　　*　　*　　*　　*　　*

The major was lying in bed, and why the deuce should not the major be lying in bed? If a gentleman with several hundreds a year to spend, and nothing to do in this vacuous world but to kick his heels all the day long, may not lie in bed until half-past eleven in the morning, who may, pray? The fact may be insignificant in itself, but it serves the purpose of a fitting introduction, not only to this gentleman, but to two other individuals with whom we are concerned.

There was a knock at the door : at this unearthly hour, no wonder the major only flung it a half-articulate curse, and continued to sleep the sleep of the just. The knock, not alto-

gether the respectful knock of well-domesticated
servitude, but one which might be called a
thump, came again. The major was short-
tempered, especially at this time ; he started
up and glared round. He flung his night-cap
against the offending panel, and as this did
not produce appreciable effect, he followed it
yet more impetuously with his handkerchief ;
but the failure of that missile was more palpable
still, for it did not reach halfway ; then, driven
to desperation, he stooped once more, dragged
from under the bed an open bootjack, and sent
it about its mission fairly and squarely. In so
far it was not to be found fault with ; after
this he turned over with a determined snore.

Any really unprejudiced observer will admit
that the bootjack was intended as a deterrent,
and herein only was it unsuccessful. The door
responded cheerfully, and burst open with a
scrimmage. There entered a little black, long-
haired dog, who had evidently taken in the joke
from the first, and was only waiting to show
his thorough enjoyment of it. He bounded
from the floor to the chair, from the chair to
the bed (ye gods !), from the bed to the washing-
stand, from thence on the dressing-table, where
he threw over a pot of pretty red stuff, and he
took up a final position on the top of a neatly-
brushed and folded pile of dress clothes. I
don't pretend to know what the owner's feelings
were, he had such peculiar feelings at times,
such odd fancies ; and he had had only a
couple of brandies and sodas as yet this

morning, there stood the two long glasses
empty, and he—well—he was sitting up in
bed, blue and gibbering. But a second visitor
followed the first, and put things right in a
trice. He caught the dog by his tail, and
cast him not unkindly into the empty fire-
place. The little dog, stricken with a mighty
awe, gave one yelp of disheartened penitence,
and lay down among the fire-irons, acquiescing
in the justice of his sentence. His per-
emptory master was Roland Tudor, the hero of
this history, then but a small sturdy Englishman
of fourteen, with hair almost golden, and
straight-cut features of singular charm and
strength.

"It's me, uncle," he said, going up to the
bed and putting out his hand; for he felt that
things had gone askew, "I'm sorry about the
dog, but when there's a row in a fellow's room,
he always goes and does that. He thought
you banged the door on purpose."

The major gasped.

"But never mind, I'll teach him; I've my
notions about discipline, and he knows it."

Hereupon the master glanced at the fender
with an eye so terrific, that it elicited a melancholy howl (though withal resigned). The lad's
appearance and explanation had a wonderful
effect upon the old man, who, still shaking with
his fright, sank back upon the pillow and
clutched his nephew's hand.

"Good G—d, Roly! what made you come in
upon your poor old uncle like that? I thought

it was the devil. Oh dear! oh, Lord! I mean, what did you bring that infernal, dirty, stinking, beastly brute in here for? For Heaven's sake don't touch the thing, he'll make your hands smell; whew!" and five feeble, jewelled fingers gave a deprecatory wave from under the bed-clothes.

The boy bridled.

"No he won't, uncle; I wash him myself twice a week, and he's had the best education of any dog I know; I've trained him myself. You should see him with a rat."

"A rat," groaned his uncle, "Ugh! well, there are none here, at any rate."

"I daresay there's something here," said the lad coolly, looking round. Cockchafers, now, he's A 1 at cockchafers."

"There, Roly," said the old man, with despair in his voice, "I've nothing of that sort, 'pon my soul I haven't. You won't be hard on your old uncle, Roly, will you? A poor old Guffin like me, stranded on the sands of life. Let him be; pull up the blind, and let me have a look at you."

The boy did as he was bid, a little reluctantly; and the dog, grovelling on the floor in the most abject depths of sham humility, crawled under the bed. It will be observed, even thus early, that the major's utterances, though they evidently sprang from his heart, were contradictory; and why was this?

The explanation lay in the following circumstances. Major Lickpenny was in truth

very much what he tersely described himself to
be—" a poor old Guffin, stranded on the sands
of life." His life had been a failure, deep,
blank, dead, as every day proved to him now
more clearly. He had been what might be
termed a professional pusher, but he had
never pushed beyond the drawing-rooms of the
'elegant' and 'select' type (to their owners),
and a first-rate second-rate club. Perhaps he
would have stayed content, but that these
minor mercies were becoming shadowy.
Such popularity as the useful and subservient
'tame cat' of early days had been able to
achieve, was long since gone from the padded
and saturnine old fellow, who bored men and
women alike with attentions they had no wish
for. More serious still, even his modest stipend,
the 'few hundreds' that he was ever bitterly
alluding to, as though they were a sort of curse
in themselves, these even would one day be
dependent on the good will and pleasure of this
only nephew of his, to whom he has been left
guardian. For the nephew was the coming
king (happily for himself); had it been otherwise, the major would probably long since have
tried negotiations with a baby-farmer, and the
relations of the two would have been different.
As it was, however, he was gradually breaking
himself in to the task of paying court to the
boy; it was not always easy—the outrage to
his feelings on the present occasion had been
tremendous; no uncle but would have broken
out under such a provocation, but he luckily

remembered, and pulled himself up just in time to become maudlin and abject before he had gone too far.

The boy took in most things, and did not let them go in a hurry. Of his uncle's two moods, he infinitely preferred the former, but he said nothing, and the major went on to lick the dust before the power that was to be. Never was anything so preposterous in real life ; but then this book deals only with those who have been unfairly ousted from the procession of the ages. Whether they were very different from ourselves, wherein they were better, in what they were worse, it aims at setting forth.

The boy it has been said was the heir, but he had already imbibed some quaint notions for an heir. He was a small mathematician, and had one day reckoned that as his family counted from the conquest, he ought to be able to claim over sixteen millions of direct ancestors at that period. This, if it staggered him at first, effectually laid the " family " fallacy to rest at once and for ever. He felt what every British boy should feel, that in his own veins ran the blood of all England, and already there was burning within him some inkling of a career. His father was dead and his mother; he had no near relation but this maternal uncle, his guardian, and so it came about that whatever there was left of fame, of honour, and of land to this name, which so many generations back had played a recognized part in the making of the national history, centred round his solitary figure. That he already felt this keenly, and that the responsibilities it implied were often in his thoughts, though he never spoke of it, was certainly a fact. Strange to say, with it all was inherent an idea of the very opposite; the lad was at heart a radical and a democrat. These terms may somewhat overstate the case, but it was to a refined and ideal equality that his spirit leaned. At fourteen there is a haze over all these things. But to revert.

"Oh! you lucky young beggar," said the major; "so I have got to take you to college, have I? When is it to be?"

"Thursday, sir," answered Roland, failing to see altogether where the "luck" was.

"What would I have given to have gone to college with such an allowance as you; and you're to go to this Roman place. You'll be a howling swell among the holy Romans. Well! religion don't matter much; all my father did for me was to kick me out of the house, and tell me I ought to be thankful for existing at all—curse him! I think he was about the most pious man I ever met."

In justice it should be told that Major Lickpenny's father had been one of those facile individuals, who do the not very hard work of populating the world, and of evolving children, whom they are well aware they can by no earthly possibility ever bring up, trusting to some charitable person to do it for them; or, failing this, to sickness, emigration, or early

death to relieve them from the responsibilities
of a position which they themselves have made
intolerable.   He was one of those who openly
and aloud bewail before their children the hardship they entail upon them, as if these luck-
less beings were responsible for their own
existence; and, being a pious man, as the
major had said, so far as his lights went, he
was fond of quoting the Bible in laudation of
his own position; and his whole duty to
God and man was, he considered, fulfilled by
bringing into being as many half-crippled
paupers, male and female, as was possible.
They were a rickety race, as he well knew, yet
he was fond of assuring them that no family
could be freer from taint of any sort, moral or
physical; and really it was their own fault if,
despite want of food and education, they did
not grow up into magnificent specimens of men
and women. So he lived and so he died, founding,
no doubt, upon all the misery he had left behind, unanswerable claims to eternal happiness.

If any man could have been a contrast to this
one, Roland's father, the major's brother-in-law,
also a Roland Tudor, was.   He had met, by an
odd chance, one of the unfortunate female waifs
of the ill-starred family—the fifth, the sixth, the
seventh—heaven knows where she came on
the list.   By the time he met her, one had disappeared altogether, one had died in the work-
house; there was no counting them exactly.
The girl had become a Catholic, and this at least
would have kept her father at the other end of

heaven from her had she died; but her fate was to live. She could not go as a governess, she knew nothing; and, dazed with struggle and starvation, she was on the point of entering a poverty-stricken convent as a lay sister or servant, when she was met by Roland Tudor. In plain words, she was sent to his house to beg, not for herself, but for the support of her future home. Mr. Tudor was still a young man; he was a great student of character. The girl's person was attractive—wondrously so, considering her lot—by some extraordinary freak of Nature's, she was every inch a lady. Mr. Tudor became at once interested; enquiry disclosed the whole of her painful history. The man's entire heart was stirred at the knowledge. She went into a convent, it is true, immediately after—not as a lay sister, but as a pupil—not into the East of London, but into the West, and into the best that could be found. Three years after, when she came out, as the prize scholar and star of the school, he married her, and then was fructified that germ of romance which through so many generations lay deep in the hearts of all the Tudors.

She died, of course; such a story means no long lingering in a world like this. The boy was her only child, and when, presently, and before his time, the father came to die also, although he himself was no believer, he held sacred the religion of the woman he loved, as he held sacred everything that belonged to her. He directed that the child should be brought

up with all strictness in her faith, and he constituted her only surviving brother the boy's guardian.   For her sake, he had long since lifted
this brother out of the gutter and made a gentleman of him, or rather tried to do so, by giving
him a commission; and so it happens that the
major has his several hundreds a year, and that
nothing in this world is half good enough for him.

"What do you intend to be?" asked he of
his nephew, after surveying him from top to toe.

"I intend to be a representative man,"
answered the boy, with great gravity.

His uncle burst into a guffaw.   "Well! you
start as a fairly good type of your time.   Your
father was an excellent atheist, your mother
was a red-hot Roman, and your guardian is
a first-rate Protestant, a d—d good Protestant, sir, though he says it that shouldn't,
and going to hell as fast as he can!"   This
ludicrous idea so tickled the major that he
laughed till he half-choked himself.   The
boy's face stirred not a muscle, but a curious
look came upon it; however, he made no remark.

"Gad!" said his uncle, recovering himself
and changing the subject, "You must make a
start in society.   We've got two days; we'll
go to the de Robinsons to-night, and I think I
can manage to take you to the duchess to-
morrow."   For the major had a duchess of his
own (a lady of foreign title).   Roland was
whistling.

"I don't care about the duchess."

" WHAT ? "

" I dislike her," said Roland, simply and decisively.

" You young cub, you ! " said the major, losing all patience.

" I like my dog's company best." (Stoutly.)

" Capital society," jeered his uncle, " yawning, sniffing, and scratching about like that. Quiet, you cur ! "

" The duchess yawns—more than he does, and—" continued the boy, with an imperturbable malice twinkling in his eye, " as for sniffing, didn't she just sniff when you took me up to her, and told her who I was, and about poor mamma. She scratches, too, now and then ; I've seen her. Dog's not had the opportunities she's had, and take it all round, I think he's better mannered."

The major sat up like one transfixed. What he had to say on this subject will never be known, for at this moment the small animal, in whose brain had been implanted an inextinguishable thirst for inquiry, emerged from a corner, bearing aloft triumphantly a prize. What it was it is impossible to say, but he seemed pleased with it, and joyously entangled himself in a few yards of cord that dangled from it.

The bruised worm turned at last, and with a yell sprang from its bed, disclosing in the action a pair of withered shanks which, like the rest of the major, stood in sorest need of making-up. One of these he directed with incredible ferocity at the dog, and having

opened the door, actually kicked him a yard
or two down the passage. Then, turning on
his nephew, he dealt him such a box on the
ear as nearly threw himself over, without doing
Roland any appreciable damage. However,
the boy took the hint, and vanished; the major
found himself again alone, while peals of
Homeric laughter came up out of the distance.

Thus it fell out that, during his two days
in London, poor Roland was deprived of the
fostering care of his uncle and guardian. The
major had, however, taken the precaution of
providing him with board and lodging at an old
servant's, when he had sent for him from the
private school at which his education had
begun.

The boy spent the time well, wandering
about with his dog at his heels the whole of
that day and the whole of the next, and the
sights he saw in those two days made them an
era in his life, and influenced it to the end.
The actual knowledge, too, of the general
life of the great city that he picked up, was
astonishing. The novelty of all he saw left
on the fresh young mind vivid impressions
never to be effaced, and the mystery of its
wondrous humanity sank into his heart. He
did not go to see many sights, but hung about
the streets, the wharves, and the river, and he
only got into one small difficulty, when, havng
persuaded a waterman to allow him to take an
oar in his boat to the other side, he tendered
him half-a-crown in payment.

" Wot's this 'ere ?" said the man.

Roland explained, perhaps rather unneces-
sarily, that it was half-a-crown. The man
retorted that if it were not for this explanation
and the evidence of his senses, he couldn't
have believed it, and that he'd never knowed a
gentleman what had taken an oar in his boat,
offer him less than a suv'rin for it, which
was probably true enough; adding, that he
wouldn't have asked, but that he'd seed one in
his purse. Roland squared himself, and hinted
that he was welcome to try and take it, while
his dog fell into a paroxysm of fury. The man
changed his tone, and said he had only mentioned it in a casual way. And, as the two
went off, Roland flinging him another shilling,
he overheard the fellow mutter, " Well I'm
blanked, if that ain't the blankest pair of bull
pups that I iver kimed across;" this was a
gross libel on one of them at least, for he was
a Skye terrier.

It may be doubted whether, if his uncle had
not boxed his ears, Roland would have gone
near him again; but a grain or two of respect
still lingered in his heart, simply because of
this very fact, in which there was a latent
spark of manhood which for many a long day
saved his uncle's position. When the day
came, he presented himself at the appointed
time, with his best clothes and best behaviour
obtrusively put on, and the two journeyed
down together under a species of armed
neutrality clause, understood but not expressed,

to the great school where the boy was to make his *début* in public life.

The major did not half like the task he had before him ; in the first place, he had to play the respectable, heavy father and beneficent guardian in one or two days at least, and as he well knew, his respectability never lasted intact for more than five consecutive minutes. Then he was venturing on ground altogether unknown to him. He had a vague idea that it was etiquette to kiss the Lord Abbot fellow's great toe, that every guest being presented on entry with a discipline, was required to scourge himself in public three times a day, and then to lay it about his neighbours. He did not know whether it was not their idiotic custom in these places to go to bed at seven, rise again at midnight, and worship the saints in one of their infernal chapels until three in the morning. All this sort of thing was out of his line, and the whole way down he sat wording apologies and excuses for future use, which, with the exception of a slip here and there, were highly creditable to his ingenuity. He had settled down a little into the grim humour of the situation, and he had even begun to twit Roland facetiously on the subject, when he observed that three youthful fellow-passengers began to eye him suspiciously. These were three young gentlemen, whose ages may have ranged from sixteen to twenty. They had been discussing some apparently abstruse questions on the nature of philosophy and rhetoric.

"It is only since I entered philosophy—in fact, since I became a philosopher—that I have realised what an incredible pull we have over you rhetoricians," observed one of them, a pale youth with a wild blue eye, who wore a coat of semi-clerical cut.

"Humph!" grunted the gentleman addressed, "if it weren't for the extra prog, I'd just as soon be in bounds."

Terse rhetoric that, mused the major.

"You rhetoricians certainly stand on delicate ground," continued the philosopher, "belonging neither to the upper nor the lower, you—"

"Oh! dash it all," said the personage addressed as a rhetorician, "I don't see that a year makes any difference, except for the extra side you can clap on; does it, Jenkins?" appealing to the third. Mr. Jenkins expressed his opinion in a prolonged and emphatic negative. Philosophy and rhetoric were silenced.

"Pray, sir," said the major, who had been listening, turning to the one who had last spoken, for explanation, "are you one of these gentlemen?"

"Oh, no," he disclaimed generously, "I am merely a poet."

"Merely a poet!" said the major, lifting his eyebrows, "I wish I was half as much myself, in these hard times. I dare say you make a good thing of it."

The poet, however, hinted that his position was nothing to boast of, but he hoped that something might be done for them—i.e., for

poets in general, which would effect a permanent
improvement. Then, when it was presently
discovered that they were all bound for the
some destination—viz., for St. Augustine's,
they became very friendly. The poet detailed
his past experiences, and enlarged, rather
prosily it must be admitted, on commonplace
topics. The rhetorician sat silent, and the
young philosopher gave Roland much good
advice on his future in collegiate life. As for
the latter, he could hardly believe his senses at
his good fortune in meeting so early, and in so
friendly a way, with three such distinguished
individuals—men, who by each others' admission, occupied such important and unusual positions in that new world to which he was
hurrying. He might have thought less of it had
he known that the names were merely those of
the classes to which they belonged—philosophy,
poetry, rhetoric—in lieu of sixth form, fifth
form, &c.

When at length the party were set down at
their station, it had grown pitch dark and had
begun to snow. The three collegians were
here joined by a fourth, who had come by the
same train, a gentleman in "humanities," as
the visitors were privately informed, and the
four having carefully secured the one cranky
fly in waiting, packed themselves in with great
cheerfulness and alacrity; the philosopher just
stopping to say politely to the major and Roland
something about "sorry he couldn't offer them
a lift, but after all, difficulties were made to be

overcome," and expressing a hope that they might meet again.

Here was a state of things which Roland settled after his own fashion. Leaving his uncle storming in the waiting-room, he walked off through the gloom into the village, and in less than an hour returned, driving a light cart, with a lad in it as guide. This was better than nothing, at any rate. The uncle, the baggage, the dog, were hoisted in, and they got away as fast as the roads and the light would allow them. They had already gone some distance, when, at the bottom of a dell, they became aware of a blockade ahead. The unlucky cab, after being, as its owner subsequently admitted, sixty years upon the road, had selected this unhallowed time and spot for the finish of its career. The feeble glimmer of the single lamp disclosed it on its side in the water of a stream which crossed the highway. Seated on a bursten box, dabbling his feet in the water, as though it were midsummer, without his hat, and wringing his hands, was the philosopher; soaked to the skin, plainly, but not so plainly facing his fate. By him stood the rhetorician, speechless. A sounding torrent of abuse which proceeded out of the darkness ahead proved that the poet was endeavouring to arrive at conclusions with the cabman; while the student in humanities had seized the reins, and was belabouring the unfortunate beast with an oaken cudgel. A semi-contemptuous pity arose in Roland's breast for the poor philosopher, who seemed less capable than the others of taking care of himself. By sitting with a portmanteau on his knee for the rest of the way, it was just possible to make room in the cart for one more, and this he did. The philosopher was got up behind, his legs were hung over the rail, so that the little jets of water from the toe of each boot could play freely into the road; a rug was thrown over him, under cover of which he reposed in a corpse-like silence, but for his teeth, which rattled like castanets. In this guise the party reached the college.

St. Augustine's was an imposing edifice to come upon at any hour of the day or night. Its extent was enormous, the buildings covered some acres of ground (a little city in itself), and this being still Christmas time, it was brilliantly lit up within, and the twinkle of hundreds of lights played upon tower, buttress, pinnacle, and roof, in seemingly endless succession.

The history of the establishment had been characteristic. Founded in penal times as quite a small place, it still retained an odd whiff of them here and there in its ways and customs. It had started from a simple Jacobean manor-house, which had been bought by a great monastic order for a secluded house of refuge, when it first ventured back again on English soil—an order to which the country owes its most glorious ecclesiastical monuments. Things were highly classic in those early days, and when it had developed into a school, by immense exertions, a stone portico was raised in severe Doric as the entrance.

Then came the invention of Gothic—or what was supposed to be Gothic—in 1825, and with it a prior who decided that Alma Mater was to be Gothic, if she was to be anything at all. Gothic architecture was Catholic architecture, and it was absurd to suppose that the heretic ever would or ever could build in this inspired style. The prior was a man of curious research, as the astonishing character of his building proved. He had unearthed, some said invented, an obscure saint of his own, out of some remote Irish bog or Scotch highland, a certain St. Finnan Haddie, to whom he modestly attributed all his successes. He built, among other things, thirteen machicolated turrets in honour of the thirteen virgins who had been the associates of the holy man (or holy woman, so uncertain was the story) in all his or her labours; but even he never had the audacity to light upon a relic of his patron. Whether this omission brought disaster, I know not. The good man, having exhausted his own private fortune, having drained the resources of the foundation to the last penny, having broken the hearts of two bishops, his spiritual chiefs —died, swamped in an overwhelming ocean of bankruptcy. The place went to pieces and was sold. It became first an asylum for idiots, and afterwards a blacking manufactory.

Whether the saint relented, who can say? He

or she was blazoned in a dozen "lights," utterly
out of joint in the execrable glass of the period,
and probably felt himself (or herself) out of
place amidst the blacking and the idiots—or
perhaps the faith and the piety of the true,
simple-hearted man who was gone, triumphed
at last. The estate was bought up for a few
thousands, and given to another religious order
free, without let or hindrance. It was given by
an outsider, a man of no religion, to be raised
afresh as a monument to his dead wife, and
the giver was Roland Tudor, the father of my
hero.

Once reset upon its foundations, all went
merrily as a marriage-bell. They chose a new
patron of unquestionable antecedents ; and of
as much accuracy as is to be expected in
saintly history. Subscriptions were raised, and
with them new buildings by a great pioneer architect of modern Gothic. These, though good in
parts, were poor and gimcrack in others ; but
so far had the science advanced, that a quarter
of a century later the community themselves,
with but little professional aid, were able to design a magnificent range of collegiate buildings
in the most perfect style of the Gothic Renaissance, and to carry them out with their own
labourers and stone-masons, under their own
supervision, after the good old fashion of their
fathers. It would take a volume to enumerate
the several parts of the edifice. There was an
immense church and nine smaller chapels, five
libraries, three refectories, six dormitories, a

museum, an observatory, a theatre, a gaso-
meter, four racquet-courts, a bathing-basin and
a guest-house. The establishment was almost
entirely self-supporting, growing its own meat
and corn, and consuming them; it numbered
several hundreds; from little boys of ten in
one wing, to middle-aged men, or men of any
age, in the other; some of those, perhaps, who
had come late into the fold, and were going
through a course of divinity previous to entering the priesthood.

Judge then what was the reception which
awaited Roland and his uncle at St. Augustine's!

A small boy was the first to perceive their
arrival. He was dressed in a scarlet cassock
and biretta and was only about four feet high,
but looked so wonderfully imposing, that the
major rubbed his eyes, thinking it must be the
Lord Abbot himself. This delusion was dispelled at once, however, by his precipitate retreat, and the very audible exclamation,—

"Hullo! here's a lot of new pals."

The porter made his appearance in due time,
and they were taken to the guest-house, a
building standing a little apart from the rest,
where, during the day, the friends and relatives of the students were entertained with all
hospitality; ladies however, at the striking of
nine o'clock, were bound to retire from the
college precincts to quarters secured for them
in the neighbouring village. In five minutes
came the great man, whose official title was the

Lord Rector. He was a magnificent person, over six feet in height, the picture of all that he should be, and he received them with graceful enthusiasm, which set the major fairly at his ease again. Then came in another high official, and another, and Roland found himself the object of a kindly but rather embarassing curiosity. They were toasting themselves comfortably over the fire, when the booming of a great bell made itself heard, and the trampling of feet in the passages and rooms above them grew most alarming. The rector opened the door, and there were beheld legions of black figures hurrying mysteriously through the dim lights of the colonnades and arches, all in one direction.

"Come," said he cheerily, "you'll want some tea after your journey; we shall find some in the refectory."

And then they went out and walked through at least a mile of stone corridors—as it seemed to Roland. These were very cold and very draughty, and the major hobbled along, looking heartily sorry for himself. As they went on, fresh figures dropped in, coming from all quarters; and presently two lines formed in regular procession, and it was noticeable that while the elders went through the corridors independently, the smaller fry marched in single file along the walls in dead silence; and every one, great and small, managed to take a furtive glance at Roland, who found himself much more interesting to the public than his uncle.

The great refectory was a splendid Gothic hall, not unlike one of the larger ones at the Universities; rows of open tables stretched from end to end, and in the bay beyond, which was lit by two large oriels, was the high table, where Roland and his uncle found themselves placed at the right hand of the rector. As symbolism obtained to a large extent at St. Augustine's, this was a very high compliment indeed, sufficient to set the whole college agog, as it did.

Had the major been aware of this, he would perhaps have borne his fate with better grace; he had, however, as much idea of these things as a tax collector or policeman; and when, after the benedicite, an elaborate grace, chanted by one of the infernal black fellows, as he mentally defined them, he sat down at last to a repast of the weakest of tea and of dry bread only (for it was the vigil of a feast, and consequently a fast), his inward wrath nearly burst its frail tenement. He was about to speak but, oddly enough, nobody said a word; silence had settled like a pall over the whole assembly, and in a minute another black fellow got up into a species of pulpit and began to read a chapter from the Bible.

" Holy Maria ! " exclaimed the major huskily, under his breath, " what next ?"

This was the mildest and most pious phrase he could think of, it was not profane at any rate, and the rector, who overheard it, thought it was merely an ave Maria, and asked him in

D 2

a whisper, seeing something was wrong, whether he would like another lump of sugar in his tea. His guest sputtered out a word, luckily indistinguishable, but an obvious negative, and making a plunge, asked if he could have some cold meat and beer. The rector looked surprised, even pained, but after a moment of thought, whispered that supper was being got ready for a party in the guest-house (a party of heretics and schismatics, by the way), and that he could join them in a few minutes. The radiance that came out upon the major's face at this information was little short of celestial; he looked like a fallen spirit suddenly beatified; Roland too pricked up his ears with scarcely less joy, but he by no means omitted to finish his bread and tea. The meal was not such an infliction after all; it lasted exactly eight minutes; and then the man in the pulpit gave out the proverb,—

"As cold waters to a thirsty soul, so is good news from a far country,"

and the myriads rose and went trampling back on their separate ways. As for the terrier, lucky dog, the rector had despatched him at once, with an almost suspicious precipitancy, to the kitchen, where, fasts and feasts being alike to him, he had not hesitated to partake of each separate delicacy offered to him by the couple of dozen odd servants about the place, until he fell into a torpor of indigestion, from which he did not properly recover for a week.

On their return to the guest-house, the travellers were ushered into a room full of company, where the major, to his great delectation, found a capital cold supper on the table, and a petticoat or two, with whose antecedents, i.e., a grandmother or great aunt (he knew a large number of those relations), he happened to be acquainted. This brought him out at his best, he grew almost too flattering to his fair companions, told innumerable anecdotes of the British aristocracy in the days of William the Fourth, nudged the Lord Rector in the ribs, and asked him whether they didn't reckon Mrs. Dash a d—d fine woman? He knew (with a wink) they had a reputation for taste, but he had hardly expected anything so good as this; though, 'pon his soul, when he came to think of it, she really was not a patch on her grandmother.

Small wonder that the august head of the college shook in his shoes, and, rising hastily, proposed, if they had finished their wine, that they should adjourn to the palace.

CHAPTER II.

THE word " palace " requires explanation.

It had been the custom, from time immemorial, to elect from among the students one who, at each Christmastide, was crowned as "king." How the custom originated, has not been recorded. It dated back well into penal times, and probably the germ had existed in some shape or other at one of the old French colleges, which for so many years fed the English mission—perhaps at Douai or St. Omer. St. Augustine's had grown out of its continental prototypes by the natural law of child from parent; and much of its strength, and not a little of its weakness, was derived from the traditionary policy of those great schools, which in their day have done such yeoman service for the Roman Church in England, supplying her with a stream of confessors, and, when need arose, of martyrs, with no let or hindrance to the flow through all the long, dark days of persecution. No doubt there were things in the system which militated against the educational instincts of Englishmen, and this, in Roland's time, was beginning to be dimly felt. Although the changes required would not have been difficult, little or no effort had as yet been made in that direction, and the standard of the institution was consequently not what it might have been.

The king, however, represented one of the most agreeable of the hereditary usages. It was not the custom—odd as it must sound to alien ears—for the students to return to their homes more than once a year, and this was at midsummer; the king consequently held his court with undiminished splendour during the Christmas revels.

The office was elective, he and his officers were chosen by the free vote of the whole community; during the fortnight he reigned, his word was law. A great hall, at all times and in consequence called the palace, was set apart for him, and here in the evening plays were performed, feasts and junketings were held, and music and song resounded before the king and court and all his loyal subjects assembled.

To this potentate Roland was accordingly introduced, and took the oath of allegiance. Long years after he was heard to confess, that though he had conversed with every kind and condition of man, and had waited on popes and emperors, never had human greatness seemed to him so truly personified as in the person of the College King at St. Augustine's. His majesty's name alone survives, the records of his reign are long since forgotten. But to-night, being in the zenith of his power, he summoned one of his minions, whom he placed at Roland's disposal, with orders that the new subject should be well entertained. The minion, who was no other than the little boy in the red cassock, which he had since exchanged for a black one, walked him off, elated at the prospect of doing the honours.

Something of a pessimist was this guide, and he began with,—

"You're one of the lot that came to-night, I suppose?"

"Yes; I suppose I am."

"Well, one must begin, but it's a fearful life for the new lot; I remember what it was in my time. I suppose you'll be in the 'Fourth of Rudiments,' and here's the Rudiments' play-room."

The play-room was decidedly rudimentary, and what little furniture it contained was equally so. Looking at the building from the outside, it was difficult to imagine such a room within. The floor was stone paved and highly irregular; there was a set of cupboards round the wall with the doors mostly broken. What had been a table, dragged out a precarious existence with the aid of two benches and the skeleton of a chair. The only ornament in the room was a plaster statue of the Madonna and Child, standing in a niche high up; and it was noticeable that while the walls were scarred in every direction, this was quite untouched, and there was a little bunch of fresh winter flowers lying at the feet. Roland's heart sank slightly;

the private school at which he had been, was very different from this.

"What do you do here?" he asked.

"Well, we usually storm forts, and in the long evenings sometimes we have one of the fifteen decisive battles of the world."

The new boy brightened.

"There's hardly anything left to make a fort with now," said the little ecclesiastic gloomily, looking at the *débris* of the table; "but there's the fire-place," and he pointed to an immense cage, "where they have the penances, and sometimes, you know, a martyrdom. When a fellow's done anything very bad, they roast him; once they roasted a fellow to death—you're sure to be roasted—new fellows always are; and here's the place where they've the public kickings. You're placed in the centre, and the head of the school comes up and knocks you down on the floor, then all the others rush upon you and kick you everywhere they can, as hard as they like."

"Gracious!" said Roland, blanching at this terrific picture; "does this happen often?"

"Well, no," admitted his guide, "*not* often. I believe the last was forty-five years ago; but it's still the law, you know, and might happen any day."

"Oh! ah! just so," replied Roland with a breath of relief.

"Here's the corridor where the big fellows make you run the gauntlet, and pin you with racquet-balls; and, you see, there's the washhouse down there, so handy to wash up the blood when you're knocked over. And that's where they've the fights; they say two fellows fought there for seven hours once, and one was killed— but that was before I came. It's curious how fashions change, they don't fight so much now, it's gone out. Last year thumb-screws came in, and this year it's beating with brushes, the bristly side, you know; and when you've got no clothes on, doesn't it hurt! Jobkins of ours was the best at it, he could make a hole with every bristle every stroke. Last term he made thirty-two hundred holes in one new fellow one morning—now he's gone," and he sighed heavily; "but Rawes, who sleeps in our dormitory, where you'll be, is nearly as good."

Round the corner, at this point, came a benevolent, elderly gentleman, in a purple cassock, who patted Roland's shoulder, asked him his name, and said he hoped they were taking care of him and making it pleasant.

"Uncommonly so, sir," said Roland with a slight mental reservation.

"Ah," you'll be as happy as a sand-boy, my lad," said the monsignore going off, " we all are here."

The guide shook his head wearily, as one who knew more of his world, but somehow the appalling visions he had evoked, flitted from Roland's brain and returned no more.

After this they went back to the palace, where he was shown to a seat, by the side of a small youth with large blue eyes, and a very serious expression, who was introduced to him as the head of the " Fourth Rudiments," by the name of John Mark.

" You'll remember that," said its owner, smiling, " it's very rare for a fellow to be able to claim a patron saint for each name—and such patrons; fancy! two of the Apostles, St. John and St. Mark. I'm the only one in the lower school who can do it; Jimmy Petre pretends, but that's all bosh, you know, the Petre is quite different."

The first boy apparently thought this frivolous hair-splitting was not to be encouraged, for he put his hands in his pockets, and walked away whistling, with his biretta stuck jauntily at the side of his head, after the way of a miniature life-guardsman.

John Mark was a grave and earnest little boy, he had come to the college a mere mite, and, being on the foundation, had never left it, but he had very decided views as to the life outside and in, with its aims and duties. He possessed a treble that might have been a seraph's, and was the star of the college choir. While all the world talked of his singing, he never spoke about it, but went about always curiously diffident and retiring; and the poor fellow had some reason, for in the space of a few months his voice broke and he never recovered it. There was a quaint little ascetic spirit in everything he said and did, and even at this time it was not difficult to predict that he would live to be one day a devoted priest, a prop and pillar of the Church.

"You come straight out of the world, I suppose," he said to Roland; "how glad you must be to get here and feel safe. You know " (in an undertone), "I'm always thinking that the Day of Judgment is close by. I thought it would have come this winter, but it's been so mild; of course, it's not likely to come in the summer, with the vacations and all that. Revelation says it will be winter, and a bad winter; but as this is a mild one, there's the more chance of a bad one next year. I do hope it won't come before I'm ordained, but that'll be ten years at least, and the world's awfully wicked. Do you know, there was a sacrilege even here the other night. One of the chapel windows was broken by a ball; and the worst of it is, no one's owned to it. I should have thought any fellow would have been only too glad to give himself up, and take his penance for such a thing as that. I wonder how he sleeps. By the way, did you hear that the Prince of Wales told the Archbishop of Canterbury last week, that he had vowed to make England swim with Catholic blood before he'd been six months on the throne?"

Roland had heard nothing of this, and thought there must have been some misunderstanding; but Mark grew graver than before, and added,—

"Ah! you'll see Tower Hill and Tyburn back again; the only thing is to be ready for it." And the small Confessor looked as happy as if he had been ordered out to instant execution.

"How did you get on with Ridley?" he asked presently, changing the subject.

Ridley was the first boy, who had departed to seek more congenial society, and who was now to be seen at the top of the back benches, his biretta more than ever awry, eating and drinking surreptitiously from some hidden store, and passing audible comments on the performance, mostly of an unfavourable and personal nature. There was a concert going on at this end of the palace, where a little amphitheatre of benches was arranged; other amusements were in process in other parts of the building, order being kept by the two bounds' masters, who were young divines, named Mr. Bellamy and Mr. Challis. Unless disorder became flagrant, the boys were allowed to go their own way; indeed, it was Mr. Bellamy's stock phrase, and it saved him some trouble, that he could not believe harm of anybody, and that he tried to think equally well of all. It is needless to add that there were criminals so hardened that they took advantage of this. As for Mr. Challis, he was a studious man, and liked to work alone in his rooms, and he openly bemoaned the fate which consigned him to keeping order in the unruly court of the reigning monarch, albeit his life was spent in a " palace."

"The worst of Ridley," continued Mark, "is that he's such an undisciplined mind."

At that moment, Roland happened to look

up, and to catch Master Ridley in the act of furtively jerking walnut-shells down on the heads of the performers; he found no difficulty, therefore, in giving assent to this proposition.

"Only the other day, he actually called his majesty by his proper name; of course he got a jolly good fine for it; it's half-a-crown, while he reigns, to call him by his name. And as for the rubrics, he knows nothing about them, and he says he hates the Gothic seats in the chapel. Do you know, he actually boasts that he comes from Bishop Ridley, and says he means to be a reformer all his life! I'm sure he doesn't know what self-denial is, and he makes fellows fag for him that are twice as big as he is. But he's awfully clever; they confiscated his tool-box because he nailed up all the fellows' cupboards one evening; and, do you know, the very next day, he made a bow and arrows without any hammer or nails at all.

"And he's so awfully irreverent. What do you think he said to the Prefect, at supper, after lauds, last Holy Week? He told him it was a case of long lauds in the chapel, and short commons in the refectory. I can't imagine why they didn't give him "pandies," but they didn't; they only laughed, and that encourages him. It's a shame to put him among the Church boys, he ought to have been a lay-fellow."

It should be stated that there was a considerable lay element in the college, composed of lads wearing the hat and coat of every-day life, and this composite character was one of the curious features of the establishment. The lay boys had separate play-rooms, but attended the same classes as the Church boys up to a certain age ; in other respects they had rather an easier time of it. They rose half an hour later, had half an hour less chapel, butter with their tea, and enjoyed other small and equally inscrutable indulgences.

"I tell you what I've decided to do," said Roland's confidant, lowering his voice, and glancing uneasily to where the subject of their conversation was treating himself and his neighbours to a series of semi-fiendish antics ; "and I advise you to do it too, cross yourself whenever he comes near you, and I tell you why," still more mysteriously. "Only last week he mesmerized young Timmins into a trance, and then he wouldn't get him out again ; and when the bell rang he just laughed and hooked it: and they had to take young Timmins to the pump and put him under it for three minutes before they woke him up, and they were all late, and all got penances."

This tale completely miscarried in its effect, for Roland burst into a roar of laughter, which he only stopped on seeing how shocked his friend looked.

"Ah!" exclaimed the latter, "I forgot, of course you're a lay boy; but we're all apt to be led away. I can imagine what the world must be. Why even all the lights and music here, and the pleasure, is a sort of temptation, isn't it? don't you feel it so?" looking earnestly at Roland, who was aching with sitting so long on the hard and backless benches. They were in what was termed by courtesy the pit, two or three of the footlights still burning in front, half blinded them, the shades having proved failures; one of the lamps, which had expired a quarter of an hour before, had been emitting ever since a curl of poisonous smoke, which seemed to have wreathed itself permanently about their heads. As for the music, the college band having finished its selection, the ground had been left free to a few amateurs, most of whom, with a marvellous unanimity, had seized upon the big drum; and, as there was no lack of room on the instrument, were "playing" it all at once. Roland reviewed these circumstances in detail, and then said that, taking it all in all, he thought the temptations to be found in the world were worse; but the chapel bell sounding at this moment, he found himself carried away in the crowd to night prayers, whence he was marched, with a number of others, by a dark and corkscrew staircase, straight to bed.

Meanwhile, Major Lickpenny had been escorted to his room—a luxurious, old-fashioned apartment, panelled with black oak, and draped with crimson hangings. He had quite recovered his spirits; in fact, as was his wont at this time of the evening, he had become a trifle noisy, and the rector led him up, not sorry to be rid of him.

" I daresay you will like to attend chapel in the morning; our services are thought—"

" No, thank you, my lord;" said the major, feeling for his host in the ribs, " I think I'll go to perdition my own way, and let you go yours. Every one to his taste."

The rector had seen much of the world, but this experience had something novel in it, and he said, " Good night," trembling as to how much of the uncle would have to be eradicated from the nephew.

Roland's sleeping-place was in one of the long dormitories—a tiny cell, with wooden walls, and the prefect, who slept at one end, in charge, came to look at him, and asked him kindly whether there was anything he wanted? This personage was an immense man, in the prime of life, who with great difficulty kept up a semblance of tremendous severity; secretly his heart of hearts warmed to the forlorn little waifs that staggered in alone, for the first time, on the public stage of college life. Whatever Roland may have felt, he was cool and self-possessed enough; so much so, that he rather amused the prefect; but when the latter was gone, the boy sat down upon the little truckle-bed and leant against the frail wooden wall, feeling very solitary indeed. He did not attempt to undress, but gave himself up to his dreams, which were all of the future, and looked far beyond the boyhood that still stretched before him.

Suddenly an intensely sharp, shooting pain

seized him in the shoulder ; he jumped from the
bed with a cry, and looking round, saw the
bright revolving point of a gimlet making its
way through the panel.

Then came a suppressed voice, which he
thought he recognized : " Hullo ! you new lot, I
wish you wouldn't lean against the point of my
gimlet, you'll blunt it all to pieces," followed
by smothered laughter.

Revenge was clearly impossible, as the point
was already withdrawn ; so, after registering a
promise with his antagonist to be even with
him some day, Roland turned in and fell asleep.

The contrasts of college life are often defined
with singular sharpness. He had been in bed
but an hour or two, it seemed to him, when the
strains of a familiar hymn came borne faintly
to his cell. " Alma Redemptoris Mater ! " he
knew the Christmas anthem well, which the
community were chanting at their office in the
cold church thus early. The soft symphonies
mingled with his dreams, and lingered there
like pleasant memories, when instantaneously,
and without warning, burst out a din that
might be described as little short of infernal.
The boy started from his sleep, every pulse in
his body beating like a sledge hammer. His
first idea was that the whole building was
falling in upon him ; but even this would have
been a quiet incident by comparison ; and the
awful sound, whatever it was, was plainly flying
down the dormitory past his door. The reader
will imagine better than can be described the

appalling effect of a huge watchman's rattle
suddenly sprung in the stillness under the long,
echoing vault of the roof. It ceased as it had
begun, and a great voice, like an organ-pipe,
broke forth in a resounding chant—

> " Laudate pueri Dominum,
> Laudate nomen Domini.
> Sit nomen Domini benedictum
> Ex hoc nunc et usque in sæculum.
> A solis ortu ad occasum
> Laudabile nomen Domini,"

and so on to the end of the psalm.

The activity that supervened upon this in
the cells was beyond belief, and was testified to
by the knocking and bumping of numberless
heads, elbows, and shoulders, against the shaky
panelling all down the line. Tradition affirms
positively, that only five minutes was allowed at
this juncture, but when the time was up (this
was announced by an angry spurt on the part
of the rattle), Roland found himself with
little more than his stockings on, and could
hardly believe his eyes when he saw boy
after boy flying towards the stairs completely
dressed. The washing and finishing, it turned
out, were all to be done in the stone washhouse
below ; this seemed, at first sight, a curious
arrangement, and was an abominably cold
one.

Major Lickpenny, also, was awakened at the
same hour, but in a different way. He had
slept well, as he always did,—such is the
reward of a good conscience even in this

world,—when there came the distant sound of a bell. It was the dinner bell, of course, he turned sleepily, and his toothless gums watered. The sound continued until it came up to his door, where it grew somewhat over-powering, and succeeded in convincing him that the summons was not for dinner. Then came a knock, and a gruff voice ejaculated, " Benedicamus Domino."

The major sat up in terror, threw off his night-cap, pulled his one wisp of hair out of curl paper, reached for a row of front teeth that were under the pillow, fixed them, jerked a cashmere shawl round his shoulders, and wheezed, " Come in."

" Benedicamus Domino," repeated the voice outside the door, in a tone not to be trifled with, accompanying it with a thump.

Now " Deo gratias " was the proper answer; one which would have very imperfectly described the major's feelings, even had he known the words and the meaning of them. This sort of thing made him downright ill, and it was the second time during the week it had happened ; so he wheezed again, more testily than before, " Oh! blank you, blank you, come in."

But the stern lay brother outside the door had his orders, and these were to get his answer, and no doubt crossed him but that he had to deal with a pious but ultra somnolent son of Mother Church. Therefore, opening the door, he went in, and raising his bell to excruciation, he enunciated, more loudly and sternly than ever, " Benedicamus Domino."

" Oh ! my good man, by all means," groaned the victim, putting his fingers to his ears, " I'll do anything in the world you like, if you'll only take yourself off and that infernal bell ; there's five shillings for you, there's ten," and with his toe he indicated where the money lay upon the table. But that was not the sort of stuff the lay brother was made of ; his work was done, and with a final clang of his bell and a scornful glance at the bed, he went out, and was heard blessing the Lord far away into the distance.

There was a long spell of early chapel for the church boys, far too much for any boys, it ran from an hour and a quarter to an hour and three ; this every day and before breakfast. The chapel was not perceptibly warmed, even at this time of year, and when the poor shivering wretches were at last released, they were hurried to a schoolroom to study, or " spiritual reading," for yet another half hour before the welcome summons came for the refectory. Strong boys thrived well enough under this Spartan system, but weaker ones frequently carried its effects away with them for the rest of their lives. Breakfast for the younger lads consisted of bowls of weak tea, and bread without butter ; but the elder, for some undefined reason, were treated more liberally. The commissariat may be described, in general, as bad to the verge of immorality.

Roland and his uncle did not meet for some time, as the authorities wished to wean him gradually from worldly things, and, rather to his surprise, he was informed that he would have to be examined publicly after breakfast, to ascertain his qualifications. There was nothing that struck such dismay into the breast of the newcomer as this ordeal. The immense room, with its long baize-covered table, heaped with folios and papers, the row of a dozen chairs on the one side, and the single one facing upon the other, reserved for the trembling neophyte. The rows of eager faces of the boys, who crowded the raised benches at the further end, the subdued whisper and hushed laugh, made the experience a terrible one.

The new boy was led in by the two bounds' masters and up to the table, where he was left, the solitary centre of the huge circle. He did not like it; he tried to look unconcerned, and to whistle (mentally, of course), but this was a dismal failure. Presently a door opened, and the examiners swept slowly in. They appeared to be elderly, rather undersized men, and their long robes trailed upon the floor; each bowed gravely to Roland as he took his seat. The one who seemed to be the chief, an aged man, whose white beard and flowing locks lent him a dignity which would otherwise have been wanting, then stood up in the midst, and, taking a folio volume, opened the proceedings.

"My dear young friend," he said, " pray dismiss once and for all the natural alarm with which you must regard us. We are merely here to ascertain that vast number of qualifications which you do not possess ; and if some day, as we all hope, your career will lead you to the altar" (the reverend gentleman said 'halter'), " you will then be grateful to us for the attempt we make to-day to place your feet in the right road for it. The college curricle runs to many matters, it embraces many objects ; and you, being such an object, we should gladly embrace you if time allowed."

Here arose a most unaccountable tittering from the audience, sternly repressed on the spot by authority. The line of professors was much disturbed, and Roland heard the order given for a culprit among the spectators to be then and there marched out for five hundred " ferulas." Now, the maximum at his former school had been twenty-four, and this made his blood run cold. This was progress with a vengeance.

" Now, sir," said the professor, assuming a different tone, and one of quite uncalled-for severity, " you shall not detain us long ; we shall ask you a few questions, and if you cannot answer them, it is one of the proud traditions of St. Augustine's, that in that case, the examinee should examine the examiner. Do you understand ? "

Roland did not. It had been Greek to him from the first, nor had he an inkling of the truth.

" Now, my little man," resumed the Professor, what exercises have you been used to ; what can you do best ? "

" The sword exercise," blurted out Roland desperately. Thunders of applause from the gallery, suppressed, as before.

" Very good ! You have, of course, studied the culinary art; and as you are no doubt well acquainted with book-keeping, I presume that you could cook an account in really first-rate style, eh ? And may I inquire if you have studied logic ? Can you prove that the drunkard must infallibly go to heaven ? "

" I—I—hardly know, sir."

" Dear me ! dear me ! Your early training has been sadly neglected. Dr. Wiggins, as professor of logic, will you kindly prove this simple matter ? "

A shrunken little man, whose robes hung about him in voluminous folds, here rose, and in a quavering voice, said the idea of any difficulty on that point had never occurred to him before, but the explanation, if required, was as follows :—

> He who drinketh deeply, sleepeth soundly ;
> He who sleepeth soundly, doeth no evil ;
> He who doeth no evil, goeth to Heaven.

" Now, sir, attend," said the first examiner, for Roland was hopelessly dazed; " I trust you understand that the drunkard *must* go to heaven, whether he likes it or not. My learned friend here, on the right, will now examine you in elocution."

Hereupon another professor arose and inquired of the victim whether he knew any piece for recitation. Roland said he knew "Trafalgar's Bay."

"Good again. Just stand up there on your head and recite it. Don't be nervous. Your ordinary voice and gesture will do very well."

"Sir!" stammered Roland, his brain reeling, "I beg your pardon, I—"

Here one of the professors whispered to the examiner that the boy was perhaps accustomed to recite the other way up, and if he preferred it, there was really no reason why he should not try it that way; this, on being put to the vote, was agreed to, and, standing on the chair, Roland commenced a laboured version of that celebrated ditty. When it came to the chorus, there was a general cry of "sing it, sing it," and the professors themselves joined in heartily, considering their age and infirmities, and stamped the floor with their feet.

"So so," said the examiner. "Now for the next verse; but your action is very imperfect, deficient in vigour; you want help, and you shall have it if we can give it you. Here, Mr. Spouter," calling down from the gallery the identical rhetorician of the day before; "this is in your line, be good enough to put our friend up to it."

Roland began the second verse, and as he did so his arms were pinioned from behind and suddenly shot out and about in the most surprising and emphatic manner.

"Perfect; quite too perfect," chimed in the whole ring of professors, clapping their hands.

By this time even the victim was aware that all
was not as it should be; to what extent the joke
had been carried he would hardly have known,
but that at this moment arose some slight
difference of opinion between the two reverend
and elderly fathers in the centre. High words
were followed by a scuffle, and, to Roland's
amazement, the gentleman with the white
beard, suddenly seized upon the folio volume,
and brought it down with crushing force upon
the other's biretta, whereupon that other flew
at him, knocked off his assailant's wig and tore
out his white beard and whiskers by handfuls,
disclosing to Roland's astonished gaze the infuriated features of Ridley the Reformer. Most
of the professors jumped upon the other two,
until quite a pile of them was raised, the
meeting broke up in the wildest confusion, and,
amid the hooting and the yelling, Roland was
hustled outside, a happier and a wiser boy than
he had been half an hour before.

Shortly after this the rector sent for him to
his own rooms, and had a short but kindly conversation with him; and it is not too much to
say that at the close, he was the more impressed of the two, although he did not choose
to show it. He had resolved, very properly,
that no difference should be made between
Roland and any other lad under his care, and
he hinted as much, at the same time that
he spoke gracefully of the deep obligation of
the community to Roland's father. In consequence, however, of his being founder's

kin, he was to be allowed the unprecedented
privilege of keeping his dog, such a thing
having been previously quite unknown in all
the annals of the junior school, though the
rector admitted that in pre-historic times a
student had once kept a monkey. This
favoured animal had led a most disreputable
course and had justly come to a bad end: the
rector concluded by hoping that the terrier's
career would be very different.

" He has been well educated, my lord, I've
done it myself; I think a great deal of education."

" Do you, my boy? So do we," laughed the
great man; " and now you may go."

Major Lickpenny's first appearance was not
until near midday, his usual hour. He had
breakfasted very comfortably in bed, and felt
that, by this time, he would be safe, for, as he
mentally observed, they had been at it since
five in the morning, and their confounded
psalm-singing would be over and done.

He was stepping gingerly down the slippery
oaken stairs, when he perceived a small knot
of the guests and others standing talking under
an archway. Most of them held prayer-books,
but he felt no fear on this score, and as he saw
his lady friend of the night before, looking
more monstrously fine than ever in a set of
sable tail, he had no hesitation in joining them,
with the purpose of absorbing as much as possible of her company. The siren was very much
accustomed to her magnetic power, and roguishly
inclined to the full use of it. She archly de-

manded the gallant soldier's protection, and gave him her muff to hold and her smelling-salts. Suddenly an acolyte pushed through a swing-door, and thrust into the hands of all the company a wax taper.

"What's this?" stuttered the major. "What in the name of the Dickens is this?" holding the obnoxious thing out, as if it were a serpent; but the boy was gone.

"Come," said the temptress, seeing that he hesitated, "you'll not desert *me*, I am sure."

The party passed through the archway, and the doors closed behind them; retreat was cut off. They were in the transept of the great church, and in and out through the pillars of the nave wound a long procession. First came the choir with banners, then the community in their robes, then the students, after them the guests fell in behind, and last of all the servants. The major had just had his candle lit, and a playful draught was guttering the wax in three separate streams, through his fingers and on to his trousers and boots, when up came a gentleman in a cassock, no less than the master of ceremonies himself, very hot and flustered.

"There *must* be a banner here, we *always* reserve a banner here. One of our guests has an inalienable claim to the privilege" (looking round), "which one is it to be on this occasion?"

There were not many men among the guests; one was stout and apoplectic, another had his arm in a sling,—the brawny major, of course.

"My *dear* sir," said the M.C., with enthusiasm, "the very man;" and he took the candle from him, replacing it with the pole.

"There! mind the tassels, it undoes quite easily," and he flapped the silk. "So very, very kind of you, I'm sure, *so* indebted," and with a fervent hand clasp, he hurried off to the other end of the procession, nearly a quarter of a mile away. They were singing a hymn in front, but the distance was so great and the windings so many, that here behind they were trudging along in dead silence, which, from the major's point of view, made the proceeding more hopelessly idiotic.

It is to be hoped the lady in sables was as deep in her devotions as she appeared to be; she walked on holding her candle very demurely, but her face was buried in her prayer-book, and the tips of her ears were exceedingly red. She, at least, was comfortable in her long furs, but the major, of course, was hatless and without his overcoat. The rage in his breast was too great for words, he could not have expressed it then, had he had the opportunity; as it was, it gave him a topic of conversation for the term of his natural life. "Mercy! if Jones or any of the fellows from town should see me like this, or even hear of it!" was his one thought, and although his teeth were chattering, the great drops rolled from his forehead.

The procession passed through several bitterly cold stone corridors, round the unglazed cloisters, where the draughts struck like daggers,

and finally emerged into the open air making
for a statue of a saint in the grounds. It was
a lovely January morning, and from a distance,
no doubt, the scene looked exceedingly well.
A brilliant sun shone on the crisp light-fallen
snow, upon the banners, scarlet cassocks and
white surplices, as they trailed through the
frost-festooned shrubberies. But the wind was
high. The major's green banner flapped awk-
wardly, and every now and again took an ugly
twist, from which he had some difficulty in re-
storing it. He was much fatigued, and in
mortal terror of actually breaking down, when
he found they had come round again to the
church. There he dropped the pole like a hot
coal, and, more dead than alive, stumbled up to
his room, where a wood fire was sputtering
hospitably in the grate. He sank down before
it and seized a time-table, to look out the
next train for town. It was intolerable, it was
diabolical, the whole lot of it—the whole lot of
them—and that blanked Mrs. Dash was the
worst. He must end this foolery. Still, appearances must be kept up. He packed his portmanteau, rang the bell, ordered a fly, and, pulling together all his powers, went down into the
guest-room with a very creditable stride. The
carriage drove round to the great portico, and
there, upon the steps, in the presence of the
rector, the vice, and a number of the professors
and guests, he called aloud for Roland, who
was brought up. Then, with a courtly grace,
he shook hands with the ladies, and, hat in

hand, thanked the community for their hospitality; and, holding Roland by the shoulder, he said,—

"Take care of him, my lord, and make a man of him. You know what he must represent to me. Good-bye, Roland Tudor; be a good boy, and I am sure you will be a happy one." He placed his hand, as though in blessing, on his nephew's head. Again he raised his hat. It was magnificent; but who would have thought, five minutes after, that that cowering figure, collapsed in one corner of the carriage like a pricked wind-bag, could have done it all?

CHAPTER III.

THE boy just launched at college, is the veriest
atom in the aggregate, the smallest thing conceivable; and there was a healthy democratic spirit in
the lower school, which prevented even a Roland
Tudor from receiving more notice than was
good for him. A few, very few, of the boys
ransacked their English histories, and a work on
the collateral branches of the royal family was
disinterred from a back shelf in the poets'
library, where it had lain an inch deep in dust;
but its extreme dryness, together with the dust,
choked off inquirers, and it was presently re-
buried. One or two of the "divines," who
knew what was what, and who had that eye to
the future and to scenic effect which is sometimes to be found even among divines, looked
up the pedigree, and it eventually became one
of the stock subjects to be mentioned when a
visitor came to the college, and as much an
institution in its way as the clock, or the king,
or the rector himself.

In the course of a few days, the boy found
his level without difficulty—a lowish one, it
occurred to him, but he soon picked up a friend

or two ; and in the second week after his arrival, when he stood up to Ridley in return for a practical joke, and had bestowed upon him a reminder which made him see darkness with one eye, and sparks to illuminate it with the other, that worthy dropped his arms, and metaphorically embraced him as a man and a brother. This, with other important events which shortly took place in the microcosm of the Rudiments' room, speedily lifted him into notice.

Master Ridley was at this period of his career a great man, and one of whom it was good to make a friend. He was not so much a reformer as a revolutionist, pure and simple, and he was always hatching plots, or rather, laying and addling them—good, healthy plots, too, which should have turned out excellently. In consequence of his unquestioned ability, he was a leader among the juniors, and had won the battle of Waterloo—a favourite battle—seven times, chiefly by his own prowess in the playroom. He was of opinion that authority was to be sapped rather by indirect, than by direct aggression. A good cry was a capital thing for men to march to; but he wanted something more for his followers—a song, or many songs, a " Marseillaise," for instance—which would put spirit into them ; and he would quote Béranger as to letting other fellows make the laws, if he could only make the songs of the people. All this he confided to Roland before the holidays were over, casting, like others of his mould in other places, a gloss of con-

stitutional reform over the whole. The two
bounds' masters were the powers most aimed
at, in consequence of the insulting amount of
surveillance they thought it necessary to exercise over the juniors.

Roland opined that if it was a matter of
standing up for their rights, instant steps were
imperative, and long consultations took place as
to the best mode of procedure. Now the play-
room was at this time exceptionally fortunate,
in that it possessed a live author, who had once
had a thing in actual print! This gentleman,
one Brabant by name, was rather older than
the others—his studies having been interfered
with by weak health, which, however, had
not prevented him from expending his restless
energies in ways which lay open to him; he
had a certain cynical form about him which,
in spite of his delicacy, made him a force to
be reckoned with among his fellows. Ridley,
having one day called him into council, admitted
before his face, with the utmost *sangfroid*, that
he didn't " truck " much with weaklings of this
sort; but he recommended him to Roland's
favourable consideration as an undoubted poet,
and one whose brain-power, to some extent,
made amends for the absence of the more
valuable muscular article. He was by no means
one of that high-up and far-away order of gen-
tleman-poets, but the " pukka " thing, turned
straight out of Nature's own factory; and he
(Ridley) diffidently confessed that he had some
ideas of his own as to melody—" not the theory

of double bass, you know, and all that, but just what was wanted, and there you were."

Brabant, with some veiled intellectual scorn, as became a leader and fashioner of public opinion, promised his support; and, after sitting with a wet towel round his head alone in a class-room for an afternoon, he perfected an effort in verse, of which the two following only survive :—

> Oh! Mr. Bellamy,
> Don't you tell o' me,
> Try to think well o' me,
>   If you can.
>
> And you, Mr. Challis,
> Who live in a palace,
> I say without malice,
>   Are a fortunate man!

Meanwhile the two other conspirators had, with the help of that moribund institution, the junior piano, composed a melody. It was rather sing-song, but with the instrumental strength of the junior play-room brought to bear upon it, went with rattling effect. There was nothing in the trifle, it merely expressed in a poetic form, and with a touch of poetic license, the well-known sentiments of Mr. Bellamy, and the lamentations of Mr. Challis; and yet there must have been a hidden fang somewhere, for, after an unprecedented success of three nights—it being started with overwhelming vigour whenever one of these gentlemen showed his face—it was suddenly suppressed by edict from the crown. But a portion, at least, of its purpose was accomplished. Ridley, Tudor, and Brabant were henceforth looked upon as rising and representative men, and took the lead in their room, and sometimes out of it. By the way, it should be noted that St. Augustine's being a college, and an institution of much magnitude, it was customary always to speak of the students as "men," from the highest divines down to the veriest imps.

The holidays passed away, and Roland soon fell into the routine of work. It was not hard, though in one sense it was more thorough and satisfactory than that of the upper classes. This was the weak point of the establishment; the grounding was good, but in higher education the deficiency was lamentable. The fact that it had to depend upon a stray convert here and there to obtain a professor with any University training at all, and that there was hardly a man of really first-rate scholarly attainment in the place, made high-class education for the upper schools an impossibility.

This only appeared in its true force when boys going out from the college, and leaving the comfortable system under which they had perhaps carried off prize after prize, encountered the stern competition of the outer world. There, they found themselves hopelessly handicapped; then, at the eleventh hour, the distracted parents flew about in search of a coach or crammer who could promise them a chance of success in the professions. To one of these the boy had invariably to go if he was to do anything at all for himself. So far as decency and morality went, many of the houses kept by these persons were sinks of iniquity—little hells upon earth; the best were not good; and, even if the lad's moral stamina was such as to resist the strain, he frequently broke down physically under the pressure of work; being required to cram into a few months all that had been spread through half the term of their education for the others. This was a very ordinary course for Catholic boys, and it must be remembered that while this ordeal was forced upon them, the great Universities, with all their learning, discipline, and lingering spirit of the Faith, were absolutely closed to them, not by the law of the land, but by their own authorities.

But how, it will be asked, did great schools like St. Augustine's get out of this difficulty? Thus: there was always some phenomenal youth, as there could hardly fail to be out of such a number, who saved the college honour in the hour of need; some one or two, upon whom the whole forces of the establishment were turned, when their ability had been recognised. No Derby favourite was ever nursed with greater care than such a one; and the results were apparent on the great day when Llewellyn Phibbs passed direct from St. Augustine's first, second, or third, into the something or other; and Henry Bosher, from the same celebrated school, eighth, or ninth, or tenth. Then came the exasperated parent of the average, wooden-headed boy, remembering only that his own son had failed, and asking how it was.

" But, my dear sir, have you seen the lists ? Do you know where young Phibbs of ours was placed ? are you aware of what was done by little Bosher on that occasion ? "

And the Phibbs, and the Boshers, who were not too common, often stood thus as figure-heads for half a generation of schoolboys, until a second Phibbs arose, or the rays of a new Bosher illuminated the horizon.

It is impossible to estimate the loss to Catholicism at this period, from want of good public schools, and proper University training. The fatal error that prevented boys, and in consequence men, from competing on equal terms with their fellow men, either had not been discerned or was treated with contemptuous indifference. There existed even a fanatical section who boasted that the learning of this world was dross to them, and openly rejoiced in their ignorance. Many years had elapsed since emancipation, and while the numerical increase of the body had been great, the influence of those numbers was in inverse ratio. No name of eminence had yet arisen among pure bred Catholics in this country, nor under such a system was it likely to do so. That the Church numbered illustrious names was true, but these, without exception, were those of converts to the faith. This fact, if noticed at all, sat lightly on its members ; but the lever thus supplied to its outside opponents, was the most powerful that could have been devised.

Brought up in a quaint and dangerous

asceticism of thought, both cleric and lay were
turned out upon a world of which they were as
ignorant as babes, and at an age when the
consequent revulsion of feeling was likely to
be greatest. If here and there scandals came
it was no wonder; the wonder was rather that
they did not come in scores. At St. Augustine's
the only breath that reached the students from
the outer world was through the illustrated
papers, the dailies were not admitted. Here
they found in detail the latest movements
of royalty, the latest arrangements in dress-
improvers, and so forth. The papers that
catered for women and children were, with the
exception of the religious prints that were
laid upon the table in the various libraries, the
only ones from which these boys and grown
men in leading-strings had to extract their
necessary knowledge of the world. Within the
walls, no hint as to a coming citizenship, no
hint as to the right of every man with a stake
in the country to raise his voice in the government of it; no suggestion as to a possibility of
any public usefulness, was ever dropped.

Yet it was an age of progress and reform unexampled; it was also an age of infidelity, and
it seems incredible that the church in England
of that day should have stood aside, praying
its prayers, lighting its candles, and painting
its sanctuaries, while the all-absorbing interests of the hour trembled in the balance.
What might have been done had religion stepped
in, while it was yet possible, to share in the

moral suasion of the people, can only be surmised. It did not, and the opportunity passed
away.

True, the church had to contend against
internal difficulty; she possessed an aristocracy
who were few, and a democracy who were
many, and these latter were mostly Irish and
mostly pauperized; of middle-class backbone
there was none at all. The gentleman, too, in
the full understanding of the word, was a
comparative rarity, and this made the mainte-
nance of the right tone and feeling, not only in
her colleges, but in the length and breadth of
her boundaries, a difficulty and, in some sets,
an impossibility. Perhaps the influence of the
true gentleman, the καλὸς κἀγαθός, was a trifle
underrated by a body of rulers who had not
had too much experience of him.

While the upper classes stood aloof entirely
from serious work, they were by no means
backwards in attending to the amusements and
frivolities of life. Debarred of their own free
will from public career, they ran greatly to
private hobby. One would take up church
decoration, another found in himself a more
fitting object for beautification, a third would
go to the bad merely for the want of something
better, a fourth would devote himself to his
nieces, the life-long labours of a fifth resulted
in a hundred and nineteen ways of saying the
" Salve Regina," and so on, through the whole
of Catholic society. Hence arose the idea
that if a man contributed to his schools,

raised a window in his parish church to the memory of his grandmother, or if, at any public meeting, he strung together half a dozen halting and ungrammatical sentences, in the right strain of a bitter and impossible fanaticism, such a one was " sound," the prototype of a lay nobility that fulfilled every precept of the law. These details are sufficiently dry, but are necessary for the full understanding of this history, which might otherwise be inconceivable to a reader of our generation, amid a state of things, as we all know, so totally and entirely different!

Roland was happily unconscious of the state of affairs, but keenly observant; as he grew up, some glimmering would come to him from time to time; there were no phenomena about him that he did not watch and note secretly; this was his nature, and he had already a crude theory of its use. He liked the college, he liked the games, which were pursued with infinite spirit, for the most part he liked his companions, and the long rambles through the woods, the miniature adventures by flood and fell, the battles with the snakes, the squirrel chases, the snaring of the hedgehogs, and the trapping of the birds. Well might he enjoy it all; he was never sick nor sorry, and many of the ordinary weak points of humanity seemed to be quite unknown to him. He was never tired, so said his fellows, and he had but very vague ideas as to pain or fear. When chastised, as he often was in these early days, he always declared he did not feel it, and, as he once told poor Brabant, who was pacing to and fro, his hands writhing in his pockets, while he trembled with the pain of half a dozen ferulas, and vainly tried to repress his sobs,—

"I can't make you out, Braby; you're not a bad fellow, and I know you're a plucky one, but you look shaken to pieces, man. When they thrash me, I feel inclined to laugh; it's like dusting my coat. I expect I'm made of leather, and they know it too, for there's not a master in the place would send me up for less than two dozen;" and he walked off, sympathetic, but puzzled with the puzzle the strong always find in the weak.

There was a fine broad savagery in the school punishments that would have done credit to a mediæval inquisition. The "ferula," as usually administered, was a sufficiently brutal instrument; the penance of kneeling in the middle of a stone floor was worse, because more dangerous in its after-effects, and the total deprivation of playtime for days together, which often fell to the lot of stupid or obstinate boys, was little short of criminal. The boy of the period had his notions of honour—he did not go whining home, and the average parent, who can scarcely be looked upon as a rational being where his children are concerned, seldom stooped to inquire into particulars. Public opinion, it might be imagined, would mitigate the evil, but in that small coterie—"the Catholic world"—there was little publicity, and certainly nothing approaching a coherent general opinion on any subject whatever. In spite of these drawbacks, the usual relations of master and pupil showed no lack of cordiality.

The "bounds," which were the ordinary recreation ground for all classes up to "philosophy," were cruelly small, and surrounded by a high wall; however, the lower boys usually got out on half holidays, and for cricket and other games they were allowed to go outside, where three or four excellent grounds had been laid down in the noble park in which the college nestled. In old days, the spirit of espionage, brought from France, had been carried to a great extent; but now a better one prevailed, the more English idea of putting boys upon their honour was growing into favour. So far had this now advanced, that the "invalids," boys who were not well, instead of being penned up day after day in the wretched, dark, unfurnished room, called the infirmary, were allowed to make a party and go into the country for an hour in the afternoon, the senior boy there exercising an unofficial supervision. What this innovation was, only those who remembered the old style could appreciate : it was a priceless boon to the boys, and there is no record that it was ever abused.

In Lent took place "the retreats." The big retreat, as it was called, was for the "church fellows," but was attended by all the seniors of the community, and was ordinarily given by some member of a religious order, celebrated for his piety and learning. Certainly no course of lectures could well have been more impressive to a young man with the life of the priesthood before him; and so popular was it, that many of the elder lay boys applied to go through the course, although the programme was such as at first sight almost to take one's breath away. It lasted ten days: prayer, lecture, and recreation, dividing the time about equally. During the entire space the strictest silence was observed, and it was wonderful how easily it came, even to the beginner.

The lower schools and the lay boys were under a different *régime*, and a much less severe. They had extra play time, were allowed to talk as much as they liked during it, and that year they were in charge of a jovial-looking friar, who dropped his h's about sadly. It was not very judicious to place a number of sharp youths in such hands for such a purpose, and plenty of harmless fun was made of him, but the good man's blunt, straightforward earnestness was so great, that by the end of the time, which was in this case only five days, he quite carried the boys with him, and they forgot to laugh.

One specimen culled from his discourses will give a notion of all. After the usual preliminary prayer, he sat down, and, with a very serious face, said that he had noticed amongst his congregation a tendency to laughter. Laughter was very bad in such a place, and he was not sure that it was very good anywhere. He didn't mean to say there was any sin in it, but he certainly wouldn't take upon himself to say

that there was not. He had looked up the early
Fathers about it; he had not found much, but
what he had found had frightened him (as well
it might do, for the good man was a great
offender). It was known, as an historical fact,
that the devils laughed, a fiendish laugh had
become a proverb, but no one ever heard of the
angels laughing, and so on.

After twenty minutes or so of this, he
changed the subject, and warned the boys, who
understood as much of it as the man in the
moon, not to be led away by "secret societies."
He gave a scathing denunciation of Freemasonry, which was so far comprehended by the
smaller fry that they had a fight in the play-
room that night, arising from a discussion as
to whether there were, or whether there were
not, inherent wickedness in the trade of a brick-
layer.

This done, he went on to another topic.

"Now, my boys," he said, "I want to put you
up to a dodge—dodge the devil, never get drunk."
He enlarged freely on this congenial subject,
and drew so horrible, so graphic, and, it must
be admitted, so truthful a picture of a drunkard
lying in the gutter, that his audience were in
fits; he even accompanied him home, and put
him safely to bed, amid the wailings of his wife
and the howlings of his children, and further
illustrated the vice by a quotation from St.
Augustine, who, he said, spoke of a young man
"of Africa." A suppressed guffaw from Roland,
hitherto one of the sedate, proved there were

limits to his capacity for gravity. The story was circumstantial. The young man had gone home in a fit of drunken fury, he had slain his brother in the passage, knocked his mother downstairs, cut his sister's throat on the landing, and strangled his father at the top. It was an irresistible opportunity for verse, into which Brabant turned it on the spot :—

> There was a young man of the Cape,[1]
> Who set all his neighbours agape,
> By slaying his mother, his sister, and brother,
> And knocking his dad out of shape.

To his credit, be it said, this was not published until after the lecture had broken up.

"Now, boys, I'll tell ye what I want ye to do before we finish," said the friar. "I want ye to sing me a song, and I'll teach ye how to do it. It's a very beautiful song that I'm going to teach ye, they say it's the finest known, and that this very song was taught to St. — by the angels, this identical thing, mind ye, as ye'll hear it from me."

Now it is impossible to say whether, in those byegone times, the musical education of the angels was defective, or had not attained such a pitch of excellence as is now supposed to be the case. Certain it is that the song of the angels was of the earth, earthy, and given

---

[1] "The Cape" appears to have been fixed upon, from the rather large margin left by St. Augustine, because at the time very remarkable stories from this locality were afloat.

forth with the bellowing of a bull, and with
scarcely more tune. It went flat, it went sharp,
it went anyhow, and the curious thing was
that each successive verse bore but a chance
resemblance to its predecessor. When the
boys tried to sing it, as they did very hard,
there arose pandemonium. And so the proceedings broke up; what levity there was, had
no vice in it, and was never carried within the
walls of church or chapel—in this respect,
Catholic boys probably stood alone.

The early days of Roland's school life fled
away like a shadow; they were uneventful and
differed in no way from those of any other
healthy lad. Yet, within himself, he was conscious of a feeling of singularity, though he
never took the trouble to analyse it. Boys
have scant respect for individuality, the rough
and tumble of their lives rubs off the odd
corners, but very few of his were rubbed
off, and long afterwards, when he reached manhood, he always said of himself, "I believe
my mind settled into its grooves when I was
three years old. I can recollect no change
of bias in all the course of its development."

He was at this time a thoughtful boy, who
walked much alone in musing; but he would,
as it were, wake up, and breaking out in a
moment, astonish his fellows by some unexpected and unpractised feat of strength or
endurance : these were so wonderful in the eyes
of his friends, that they began to speak of him

with bated breath, and to shake their heads
mysteriously. The philosophers, too, and the
divines, began also to take some notice of him,
and bestowed a little kindly patronage on him,
which was very good of them and very unusual on
their part. To all he was carelessly indifferent,
and went his own way until something turned
up to be done, when, forgetting his thoughts,
whatever they were, he would be the life and
soul of any chance enterprise, and carry it
through in a way that astonished all beholders.
What was most uncommon in a boy of his
physique was, that he read voraciously, and
the provoking thing to his neighbours was,
that his muscles appeared no whit the more
flabby for it, as was proved to his cost by a
personal enemy of the most aggravated type,
who, observing that for a whole month Roland
had scarcely left the library in play time,
challenged him to fight, and in the space of
two minutes and a half was doubled up, or to
speak more literally, as he himself admitted,
trebled and quadrupled. We have it from this
self-same authority, that he never felt anything like his opponent's peculiar knack of
" getting home," and as he was a professional,
who fought for mere glory and position, his
evidence is of weight. On his recovery, some
half an hour afterwards, he begged, in a most
amiable and gentleman-like way, that he might
be allowed the privilege of feeling his opponent's biceps : this was graciously accorded.
He said nothing at the time, but afterwards,

round the fire that night, was heard to compare it with the play-room poker, adding that there was a peculiar rigidness of muscular tension beneath the surface, which gave it an undoubted advantage over that fearful implement.

So Roland went back to his reading, and was never more molested. Everything that came in his way he devoured—a worshipper of the classics, he studied the day as closely, and he surreptitiously smuggled in the *Times* until it was discovered, when the rector was so struck with the idea, that he ordered an expurgated edition to be laid on the table in the divine's library from that day forward. So thus early it will be seen that he initiated reform, but, like most reformers, failed to derive the benefit of it himself.

Although fairly popular, he had few intimate friends. Ridley, as a thorough-going democrat, was one of the chief, and Brabant; in fact, this first triumvirate endured in some shape for several years.

The character of the last named had developed with unexpected force and intensity, to the detriment of a frame naturally not strong. So pronounced was this precocity, that Roland always felt, after a talk with Brabant, as if he had been speaking with a matured man of the world, and one whose knowledge and experience far distanced his own. This, while it drew them together, puzzled him mightily, and he was too young to see the possible explanation, and alas! as it proved, the true one.

He had another friend, an Anglo-American of Irish extraction; he too was delicate. This boy's name was not unknown in Irish history, and his soul was steeped in patriotism: waking and sleeping, Ireland, her rights and wrongs, were ever before him. He had been sufficiently well laughed at to hold his tongue in public, for there was a strong anti-Irish feeling among the " better " class of boys; but with Roland, and a few sympathizers of his own race, he poured himself forth. The subject was new to his hearer, who at first was callous and rather amused, but gradually his eyes were opened, and he confessed that had he been an Irishman, he would have been a patriot, although he could not but think that the profession was a poor one.

The composition of the college resulted in a curious mixture, which gave human nature an opportunity of cropping out. There was a county family set, and one even smaller and more select still, consisting generally of two or three honourables, who foregathered much, and were trained after the good old fashion, toadied and made donkeys of from the first. All were injured by it, some slightly, the majority irreparably; their virile force was hopelessly sapped. Naturally, these distinctions led to trouble at times, for the divergences were great; many boys, on going into the world, never showed again above the social horizon, although most of them found useful places in lower strata.

Among the weak points of the establishment should be noted much bullying, of a somewhat cowardly character, among the lower classes. It was, however, probably not more than went on contemporaneously in the great public schools. Then, too, sufficient attention was not paid to outward appearance, and the inculcation of good manners, for their own sake. A little more drill, the habit taught of holding themselves erect and looking the world in the face, would have been of untold advantage to these youths, more especially to such as were to become priests. As a rule, the nearer these latter approached to their ordination, the more slouching and even slovenly did they become. The motives of this carelessness may have been good, but were certain to be misunderstood in a country like England.

The life was a pleasant and a healthy one; to a boy of Roland's capacities the work was easy and the chapel not overpowering. Indeed, as he grew up, he found in some odd corner of his heart lay a special fondness for the offices of the church, for her chants and her litanies, which left an indelible impression upon him, and he discovered that when the major was not there to make it ridiculous, a procession might be a solemn and a beautiful thing.

All went like clock-work for some years, and as he grew up he decided that he would try the army as a career. At this time there was an entrance examination, and that was all; the system did not then extend to major-generals, and when his class-fellows passed into rhetoric, he took a private tutor, as his line of work necessarily diverged from theirs.

Under this new *régime*, he was thrown with an entirely new set, foreigners for the most part, and Frenchmen; young men of some means who had come to the college solely to learn English, and who were mostly scoundrels of a very finished type. Unhappily, St. Augustine's was sadly in want of funds, and these youths paid well. It was the rector's idea to place a series of saints in marble outside the building, but to achieve it, it was necessary to fill the inside with sinners in the flesh. Roland's eyes were speedily opened to things he had never heard nor dreamed of previously. Every liberty was given to these young men, who were under private tuition, and who rejoiced in the name of "philosophers." They received him with open arms, as a likely addition, but a few days' companionship showed him their hand; the sort of thing was not to his taste, and he quietly withdrew, marvelling less at the idiocy of these gentle youths than at the blindness of the authorities.

One fact should be recorded; if well-nigh incredible, it is true: until he reached this stage, he never heard an immoral word spoken through the whole of his college life.

But from henceforth his position became a warm one; in a thousand small ways they found

means to take revenge; no one of them cared
to venture upon open insult, but still there
were means of insinuating as much, and these
were put into force. For instance, the philosophers had a room of their own, where the conversation was usually of a lively character. If
Roland entered it dead silence instantly ensued,
or the talk would be changed to a whisper and
a nod. If he stayed, one after another would
get up and go, making a facetious excuse.

"I 'ave to see my granmuzzer buried." "Ze
Pope, he 'ave zent for me to make cardinal."
"Ve vill go to ze chapel to zing ze litany of ze
zaints; Alleluia!" "I am zo dry, and zere is
no holy vater left in ze bottle; I most go to get
zome to drink." And so forth.

He took no notice of these witticisms, and
whenever he passed through the room, stalked in
scornful silence through the midst, while a hail
of expletives rattled about his ears as he closed
the door. This was his first experience of continental Catholicism. There was not a man
in the set who was not a coward, as far as
he could judge, and, although much provoked
at times, he was unable to do anything, as his
persecutors were too clever to give him any
handle for retaliation. But, happily, an accident brought about a crisis.

His old friend the Skye-terrier, who was by
this time a middle-aged and sober-minded dog,
lived with others of his kind in a yard behind
the chapel. He had not been well for some
time; indeed, he had apparently been suffering

from acute dyspepsia, and Roland had ordered that no food should be given him except what he supplied himself. It so happened that M. le Baron Hellantomé, the most rascally of all the brotherhood, kept in the adjoining kennel a villainous black mongrel, which was popularly supposed to be his familiar spirit; and he, the baron, had been heard to remark, that the Skye would "just make von breakfast" for his favourite, and that he intended to fatten him for the purpose.

One day, as Roland was idly smoking his pipe by the open window (it was in the sweet summer time, just before the vacations), he saw the baron, who was feeding his own dog, stealthily throw the Skye a bone. This was an offence in itself; and Roland, being in his shirt-sleeves, went down, without troubling himself to put on his coat. The coast was clear, the baron was gone, and, to the dog's intense dissatisfaction, the bone went too. Roland took it up, examined it, and found a piece of slate pencil firmly wedged down the centre. Then he walked after the baron.

That gentleman happened to be strolling in the shrubbery, humming to himself, and smoking an excellent cigar. He heard a hurried footstep behind him, and turned a little uneasily, but always "*comme il faut.*" When— whiz! crack!—came something at the back of his head like a pistol-shot, and happy it was for that unfortunate nobleman that his cranium was of such abnormal thickness and strength; as it was, he staggered, half-stunned, into the laurels. Roland sauntered up, hands in pockets. He was whistling.

"You brutal bull!" screamed the Frenchman, recovering himself, and dancing out, mad with fury; "you pig-jobbing Johnny. You no genkleman; you nozzing at all, nozzing—yah!" Here he jumped two feet into the air, and plucked out a handful of his nascent whisker, causing the blood to stream down his cheek.

"Now, look here," said Roland, "I haven't quite decided what I'll do with you; but if you don't hold that, and keep a civil tongue, you shall eat that bone, and I'll see you do it, if I swing for it." Then he went on with his tune.

The baron burst into tears, and cowered down upon the ground.

"If you genkleman, my fren vait upon you, and you fight like genkleman, not like beast," he ejaculated, tumbling the words one on top of the other, and cracking his finger joints, as he twisted them in and out. Roland turned away, grinding his heel into the earth; there was very little nervous excitement about him, and he realised the unfairness of pitting himself against a man in such a state.

That evening, as he was tending his flowers, for he had established a window-garden, a tap came at the door of his room, and a sallow, played-out youth minced in upon his toes. He wore a very turndown collar, very wide bell cuffs, and a fly-away spotted bow as a tie, and his lank hair was brushed well off his clammy, yellow brow. He presented himself, with a profound bow, as "the friend." Roland recognised him as the latest foreign importation, one by name Delorme, and received him with a laugh which made his guest's blood curdle.

Truly the baron had been right. What bloody savagery in this gross Englishman, so calmly cutting off the heads of his geraniums, and with such a laugh for an affair of life and death. However, he swallowed his emotion, and politely asked Roland if he, as the other principal, happened to have such a thing as a friend about him.

"A friend?" said Roland dubiously, falling in mightily with the humour of the idea, and delicately arranging a moss-rose in his buttonhole. "My dear sir, I don't possess such a thing; they are not to be had for money. M. le Baron has indeed the advantage of me there," and he cast a glance over the seedy youth which almost withered him.

This was trifling, but the visitor did not find courage to hint at it. He ventured to remark that a friend was a mere form, a necessary etiquette.

"No," returned Roland, determined to inculpate nobody but himself, "I'll have nothing of that sort, altogether it's not quite in my line; but if M. le Baron wishes to try his skill upon me, he shall have the chance, and I shall defend myself. Do you understand? and I shall be alone."

The visitor bowed.

" Swords or pistols ?" he stammered. " Your
lordship (!) has, of course, ze choice."

" Oh! by Heaven! " said Roland, in no way
appeased by his new dignity, " *both*, mind that.
And look here : if he, or you, or any of the
herd, are not satisfied, when I've done with
him, I'll fight you all in turn—the whole d—d
lot of you, mind that! "

Here he tenderly sniffed the moss-rose.

His visitor gave a quailing glance, a tottering
bow, and hurried out. Oh! magnificent confidence of youth and strength, what in all this
world is like it, or its equal? No doubt ever
crossed Roland's mind as to the possibility
of fulfilling his threat, but perhaps he knew
his men sufficiently well to justify his self-
confidence.

It was a gorgeous summer morning, a few days
later, the half-earthly, half-divine light of the daybreak rested rosily on the calm face of Nature,
scarce yet awakened. Now and again a zephyr
played through the woods, and the great trees
shook themselves drowsily to life. Roland was
strolling through the lush wet grass, drinking
in the beauty of it all with indescribable enjoyment ; these early rambles were a habit of his,
now that he was so far his own master.

Suddenly, as he rounded the path into a
bosky dell, three figures emerged into the open.
He knew in an instant what it meant, and a
quick glee danced in his heart. It was un-
christian, and he was no sophist to make
excuses for himself; however, even now

he determined that the position should be forced upon him—he would take no initiative; older and wiser men than he have found themselves in a like predicament. So he walked on, and as he came up waved his hand, as if to say good-morning, and would have walked on, but he was stopped. A muttered exclamation reached his ears as he did so, and the sallow Frenchman, looking more bloodless than ever, but with a latent swagger, apparently induced by doubt, came up and placed a rapier in his hand.

"Monsieur vill, vizout doubt, defend himself?"

"Oh, yes; without doubt I will defend myself!" said Roland; and he turned to look at his adversary.

The baron had come up to time very creditably. He was deathly pale, but his jetty ringlets were curled jauntily over his forehead. He was dressed entirely in black, and wore a morning jacket, close-fitting and apparently without seam or button. His trousers were intensely, preternaturally tight, and displayed a leg by no means deficient—altogether he looked as if he meant business. Very fair for an amateur, thought Roland, as he took him in, point by point. The third individual who has been mentioned, was also a foreigner, and one of the "philosophers," a youth who had been, and indeed still was, a medical student in a Paris hospital; he carried a case of instruments, and looked highly professional—so much so, that

Roland with difficulty stifled a smile, which would have sadly marred the solemnity of the occasion. He had no objection to this man, rather liked him, on the contrary, for he was tarred with a better brush than his fellows.

" A pity to leave this world on such a lovely morning, Baron, isn't it ? " observed Roland, as he turned up his wristband.

The baron gave a stare and a shrug ; this sort of thing was odious, and he advanced a step, planting himself in readiness.

" Softly, my Baron," exclaimed Roland, " I perceive that if we stand thus, I shall just get the sun in my eyes. Pretty thing a sunrise, but I should like you to see a little of it as well—a leetle, eh ? just a leetle round to the left ; if we both stand sideways to it we shall get a charming effect."

This banter told perceptibly on the baron's overstrung nerves, every word addressed to himself he looked on as an additional insult. The ignorance of social etiquette displayed by his opponent was simply disgusting. As a fact, Roland understood it all far the better of the two ; the subject was one which had fascinated him by its singularity, and but a short time since he had amused himself by getting up the laws of the duello, little thinking they might come into practical use.

His adversary moved sulkily into his place, muttering " etiquette," between his teeth ; but Roland knew the type of man, and decided in his own mind that this was not an occasion for etiquette. This was not his idea of the reality of life, the affair must begin and end as a screaming farce.

Then he stood up and looked at his weapon. It was a fencing-foil of the finest finish; which had been tapered to a sharp point—a beautiful and dangerous little weapon. This way and that he tried it, and it sprang deliciously to his hand; anon they planted themselves, measured distance, and crossed swords, when Delorme, who stood at the side, dropped his handkerchief as the signal to begin.

CHAPTER IV.

THE Frenchman's onslaught was terrific; like many of his nation, he was an excellent fencer, and agile as a cat, he sprang and lunged, recovered, guarded, and lunged again like lightning. More than once Roland was touched, but he contented himself with steadily guarding the passes, knowing that his opponent's physique would not allow him to keep up the assault at this pace for long.

So it proved. After three or four minutes the latter began to show signs of distress; the imperturbability of his adversary troubled him, he saw a red spot spreading slowly upon Roland's sleeve, a minute since, and Delorme had cried, "First blood to the baron!" but neither paid any attention, and exhausted, he fell back, amusing himself with a feint or two. Roland still parried.

This went on for some time, when Hellantomé, thinking from his play that the latter dare not venture on closing with such an antagonist as himself, sprang forward anew like a wild cat, and furiously attempted to beat down his guard. Watching his opportunity, Roland, with a sudden turn of his powerful wrist, caught and twined the blade round his opponent's, jerked it from his hand, and sent it spinning with a twang (δεινὴ δὲ κλαγγὴ γένετ') into the boughs of the elms above, where it stayed. Then, stepping up to the Frenchman, who stood aghast, with his gaze on the clouds, and using his foil as a whip, he administered two sounding cuts on the rear of that gentleman's person, which gave him the exact sensation of being cut into three pieces.

The trick was one that he had spent a week in perfecting at a fencing-school during the long vacation.

The baron went well-nigh mad, he burst into a torrent of tears and curses, snatched up an empty pistol which lay by on the grass, and, after vainly trying to discharge it in Roland's face, flung it at his head, missing him by a hair breadth.

It was with difficulty that his two friends got him away under the trees, where they quieted him by proceeding to load the pistol as an earnest of vengeance to come. His injuries not being such as to require a surgeon, and yet to cause a difficulty in sitting down, he paced like a mad creature to and fro in the glade, while the victor stood calmly in his place and looked round to ascertain his hurts. A few drops were oozing leisurely from a puncture on his sword-arm, but this was cooling and pleasant, and he stanched them, whistling after his wont.

Presently Delorme came up with a pistol, it

was double-barrelled and highly finished, like
the rapier, a pretty thing, but not a very serious
one unless they were to fight across a handkerchief. Roland nodded that it would do, and
turned the cartridges into his hand, Delorme
standing by graver than ever, drops of moisture hanging from his long dank hair, and looking altogether very much like a man who is
sea-sick. This done they measured out twenty
paces upon the sward.

When M. Hellantomé stood up for the
second time, he was still shaking, but to do
him justice it was with rage not with fear.
Roland eyed him with ill-disguised contempt.
What the deuce was the man upset about, did
he imagine that he could hit a haystack in that
state ?

Again the handkerchief fell; one shot upon
another rang out crisply in the still air. Some
young leaves fluttered down, the ping of the
bullet sounded in Roland's ear high on the left.
The Frenchman staggered as if struck, but recovered himself in an instant, and they both
fired again simultaneously. This time the
baron fell backwards and lay motionless on the
grass. Roland put his pistol in his pocket, and
walked across to where the two others were
raising his antagonist in their arms.

Suddenly there was a gesture of confusion
and astonishment from the medico, who first
lifted him and as speedily let him drop. Roland saw Delorme's face change from the colour
of ashes to an unhealthy bloom. What could

it mean, was the fellow dead? and for the first time a pang crossed him, a spark of compassion kindled in his breast, and he sprang forward. To his astonishment Delorme faced him, crimson, and seized both his hands at once.

"Sare," he said, incoherent with agitation, "my fren is no more my fren. I spurn him viz my foots, he is pigs—g-r-r-r-r! ze life is save, and ze honour is loss; but ve, *nous autres*," here he thumped himself, and his eyes protruded half an inch from his head, "ve are not of zis *canaille*; if you doubt, sare, I vill bare my bosoms for fight myself."

The little man stood transfixed with passion, and tore open his waistcoat. It was a riddle to Roland, who, shaking him off, stepped up to the prostrate youth.

The baron lay on his back, his eyes closed, his face bloodless, in a dead faint. Over his heart his coat was ripped in a triangle, and a large piece was torn right away, disclosing beneath a metal breast-plate, looking suspiciously like an adapted dish-cover, upon which, at the distance of a couple of inches, were two slight indentations.

Happy it was for both that he had worn it; but the sight produced an instantaneous revulsion of feeling in his opponent.

"Heavens above!" exclaimed Roland, and stopped at the look of defiant misery in Delorme's eyes.

The medical student bent over his work,

head down, in silence. He was actually weeping over the disgrace of it. Unperceived, a fifth had emerged from the grove, and joined the group. When Roland looked up, his eyes encountered no other than those of the Lord Rector himself. Then he found his tongue, and the latter never forgot either the scene or the voice.

" Look, my lord," he said, " this is the sort of thing you and I have to deal with." With his foot, he half turned the prostrate form of his foe, and with a concentration of scorn, walked away in silence to the college; nor did the rector care to call him back.

So ended an affair of honour very celebrated in its time.

It would be quite impossible to analyse the feelings of the rector; who was tossed in many minds. By the purest accident he had come upon the scene, and the full significance of it, for the moment, overwhelmed him. From believing, good man, that the discipline and *morale* of the college were a pattern and model to the whole wide world, he rushed violently to the opposite extreme, and concluded that this was no more than an ordinary morning's amusement.

The fact was, he was too great a man; no subordinate ever dared to tell him anything but what was of the pleasantest. He stood more inhumanly alone than the captain of a man-of-war on his ship; and while every town and village, for twenty miles round, knew and appreciated the freaks of " the philosophers," he

remained in an ignorance which had in it something of sublimity.

If the affair should get wind, it was as much
as his place was worth; not that the place of
a Catholic head-master meant much of this
world's goods; still, there was an indefinable
something attaching to it. Then the other
colleges, which St. Augustine's fancied had
been considerably distanced in friendly rivalry,
how they would crow. What would be the
scorn of the immaculate philosophers of Stoney-
hurst, the grave pity of the sober men of
Ushaw, the laughter of the light-hearted monks
of Downside? What of Oscott and St. Edmund's? What would the Archbishop of Pimlico say? What would the Pope? The situation
was a grave one, and the rector made a very
bad breakfast that morning.

He had stayed upon the ground until the
baron was sufficiently recovered to find his legs
and slink away (never to return). He had sent
Delorme into the tree for the foil, and then
requested him and his other friend to go in
and help each other to pack their portmanteaux.
After that he had gathered up all the confiscated
weapons, which he did his best to conceal in
his robes, not altogether successfully, for, unknown to him, the blood-stained point of one
of the foils pierced the thin silk, and protruded
at least a foot and a half behind him.

Now it happened that he was met on his
entrance by the junior pot-boy; and that precocious youth took note, first, of the new and

unusual angles which his master's figure had suddenly developed, and secondly, of the awful apparition in the rear, which was by no means lost upon him. So important did he consider it, that he straightway gave up and forgot the business that he was about, and went back and confided to his senior, the boot-boy, who combined knives and windows with boots, as he did with pots, that he was "blowed if he didn't think the boss was up to zummat he was ashamed of, for he'd been out larkin' with the flosofers at five o'clock that morning."

Now, it was widely known that when a philosopher was out larking, no matter what the hour of the day or night, no good could be expected of it.

The senior pooh-poohed the idea. "Fotergraphs," he suggested curtly; for this was one of the rector's fads.

The imp put his fingers to his nose, "Pistols ain't fotergraphs, are they? Nor yet" (with sarcasm) "foils, with the points orf, all a-dripping with uman berlud?"

The senior was obliged to admit that these things did not generally come under the heading of photographs.

But his informant refused to go further, and contented himself with whispering, in a hoarse voice, "Gore! gore! gore! You'll see what'll come, yah! Sodom and Gomorrah was play to it." Which mysterious utterances so worked upon the boot-boy's brain, that he neither ate nor slept, or declared he did not, for three weeks afterwards.

What came about, however, was simply this. Although it was within a few days of exhibition time, i.e., the end of the half-year, all the philosophers who were foreigners found themselves called away, and left the college, urging in excuse to their friends, pretexts of an even more frivolous character than usual. And although, in due time, the Archbishop arrived in all the splendour of purple cassock, and what the shoe-boy, surely an authority, described as "brass boots;" although there were a dozen convert clergymen in his train, and many ladies, and flowers, and clouds of incense, and other beautiful things, nothing worse fell from the heavens or rose thither.

Roland was in his place, reserved, watchful, and fairly well amused; but he kept his own counsel, and to Brabant only was the story revealed.

Meantime many-tongued rumour ran wild as to the sudden disappearance of the philosophers. The college magazine, or rather its holiday number, "The Augustinian Oriel," was on the point of publication, and so remarkable an event could not be slurred over in a paragraph, but it was an intermittent magazine, and such was its literary solidity, that a leader took at least a week to write, and quite two to print.

The editor was tearing his hair, and even the scanty remnants of wall paper in his sanctum, when Brabant entered the office. He had been in labour with a sonnet on the subject the night before, and rising to the occasion had been safely delivered before morning. He looked haggard but triumphant, and the editor, who was a divine and junior professor, read it, and marvelling at the finish and cleverness of the production, promised him that his place in the world lay ready to his hand.

The poem gave no hint as to the real state of the case, but threw the required dust in the eyes of the public with the greatest ingenuity and humour. By superhuman exertions it was printed in time, and " The Oriel " shone forth not more than a week after.

Roland, needless to say, had had an interview with the rector, who received him with the utmost sternness, and in the most solemn state he could devise, the entire professional staff were assembled around him in a ring, and the air was heavy as with a thunder-storm. It burst, but far too violently to last; the great man spoke for ten minutes on the enormity of the case, then, pulling himself up, he demanded what Roland had to say for himself.

The delinquent had very little to say for himself, but a few incisive words on the subject of being forced into such company. This bit, and the ring was obviously moved. Again authority blustered, floundered a little, and discovering it, wisely ended with, " Well, sir, you may go."

Roland walked to the door and, as his hand was upon it, the same voice recalled him,—

"Stay, Mr. Tudor; I believe you have meant well, and, as you are about to leave us for good this half, I must ask you to allow me the pleasure of shaking hands with you."

So the sun of my hero's school career set in crimson and gold, for all the professors, with whom he was a general favourite, crowded round and followed the example of their chief.

This was on breaking-up day, when it was the custom with the younger members of the establishment to turn into the big quadrangle and shout for a whole hour. The hour was all but up when Roland emerged, and, although by this time the noise had dwindled, in consequence of utter exhaustion, into "shouting in a whisper," such a burst greeted him as would have done credit to the first five minutes, for the fact of the mysterious wigging had been coupled with the hazy rumours abroad, and the disappearance of the unpopular philosophers.

"Ah! Tudor," said Brabant, as he came up and took his arm; "I won't prophesy that you will be a great man, you *are* one. You have a gift over multitudes."

But, after all, it does not do to take what one's friends say for gospel!

It is on the evening of this day that we first saw him, and all these scenes that memory has called up are fading fast away, many of them are even now like shadows that were never realities. How impossible to see himself in the little fellow who had driven up with his uncle to those gates on the winter night so many years ago! His first friends of that date are almost all gone. Some are dead, a new generation of school-boys has grown up, and they are different. Yes, it is best to say good-bye now when it is time.

Throughout, the place had been " home " to him, and he had seldom had a holiday away from it, excepting for a little fishing in the summer, a day or two with his gun in the autumn, and perhaps a week's hunting on a scratch mount in the Christmas vacation, for all of which he was indebted to various relatives of his school friends, people who were glad to have him, and who, as a rule, knew far more of his antecedents and circumstances than he did himself. Latterly, he had had a run on the continent with a tutor, and now, for the first time for many years, he was to return to London and his uncle.

Major Lickpenny, to his nephew's great surprise, welcomed him back as an equal, almost as a superior. He was too old to be kept in leading strings any longer, and his venerable relative took him into a lengthy and imaginative confidence as regarded his place and prospects, of which more anon.

Time had dealt rather cruelly with the gallant soldier, who had grown decidedly rickety. The padding in his coats had become more glaring than ever, he was all over more obviously artificial. When the wind blew, a pitiful pair of spindle-shanks, which barely served to support the enfeebled frame, was made evident.

It was only when a pretty woman rounded the corner, that he plumed up for a moment, expanded his chest, planted his right foot firmly, and cocked his head with a knowing leer, but 'ere she was out of sight, the flame sank down into the ashes, his head dropped, his face fell, and he had to cling to the nearest friendly arm for support. Three was the uttermost he could enjoy, even on these moderate terms; if a fourth or a fifth passed, she saw only a broken-down old man hobbling along, his eye roving and watery, and a fixed crease in the corners of his mouth. Nathless in his own club, or seated among his own penates, who, by the way, were goddesses all, he was yet a delightful dog, the merriest and most light-hearted of good fellows.

The gaiety with which he received his nephew was quite charming, though it was considerably damped by the clothes in which the latter presented himself, a torn and patched tweed suit, which, with an inkling of malice, he had disdained to change. But the old man, although shocked, would not mar the festive occasion; he had prepared a *recherché* little luncheon, and opened his heart, together with a magnum of what he called dry champagne.

The luncheon was long and terribly tedious; the host sat and babbled on interminably, and, when at length it was over, linking his arm

with Roland's, he took him round and round
his rooms, inflicting a number of family relics
upon him, each with an uncommonly startling
history; until at last, halting before a "tall
boy," he pulled open a big drawer. Inside lay
piled, in reckless profusion, locks of hair, bows
of ribbon, satin shoes, ball cards, long soiled
gloves, odds and ends of lace, feathers, and
other female fripperies.

"Ah, my boy," said he, propping himself
against the drawers, his eye and mouth growing
tender and humid, "the spoils of a life time;
thank God, you've got yours before you."

Here he sniffed and extracted from the pile
a pink boot of no mean proportions; he stroked
it softly, laid it against his cheek, and finally
kissed it with feeling.

"Poor little Mimi," he murmured. "Oh,
Lord! oh, Lord!"

Now Roland's eye was like a hawk's for
form, and it struck him that even if little Mimi
had been six foot high, her *chaussure* need
hardly have pinched her. To him the boot
spoke as to his uncle, eloquently, it was but
one word—"corns." However, his command
of countenance would have done credit to a
red Indian, not a muscle stirred, yet the incident stamped itself on his mind ineffaceably,
as such a one, seen for the first time, is apt to
do.

Then the major pulled out from the heap, a
faded satin bonnet, much bedraggled, to which
was attached a wreath of unkempt ragged-edged

roses; this he gazed at long and fondly, with his head on one side, until his neck cricked, and a maudlin drop, which he hastily smeared away, fell on its creased strings.

"It was *her* bonnet," he said, "Oh, Lord! oh, Lord! I remember, *I* wore it, and she wore my chimney as we drove home, *that* night. Y'know, boy, *I* used to look doosid well in a bonnet once," and here the major stuck the relic awry on his wizened death's head, held the strings together under his lantern jaws, and ogled himself in the glass.

"Hah!" he said, tearing it off, "don't soot, lad, does it? Well! we must all come to this."

It did not "soot," he looked even more like a drunken satyr than usual.

"Well, boy, here are their pictures," and he opened another drawer.

There were fifty or more of them; photography, at that time, had not accomplished for female beauty what it has since kindly done; here were the women as nature had made them, untouched by art, a ghastly array, in the hideous old fashions they still displayed with the smirking pride of many dead years agone.

There was not a refined face among them all, except one, which was of an earlier date, a miniature on ivory. It was of a gentle-faced girl whom the gallant major had seduced at sixteen, and who, when she knew the meaning of it, had died straight away, "of love, sheer love, dear boy," as that pleasant gentleman now triumphantly related.

" Ah! well," he added, shutting up his collection, " I think you've seen enough to prove that I can show you a little bit of life. I'll put you up to a wrinkle; we'll go about together, old man, eh? you and I, you shall share my rooms, and we'll have a grand time yet."

With that he doubled up and collapsed into an arm-chair; but Roland had had enough for one day, and muttering an excuse, rushed downstairs into the open air, and found himself, for the second time in his life, a wanderer in the London streets.

How changed was this London from that of the days of his childhood, it was incredible to see, and the change was even then in progress. He had turned out of the Albany, and found himself tracing his steps through Berkeley Square into Mount Street. Without pretending that the men of this " alternative " generation were our superiors at every point, at least they had realized the value of Mount Street, which was now one of the finest thoroughfares in the metropolis. Where it abutted on the Park, instead of a row of rotten pill-boxes which might have disgraced Seven Dials, stood a range of splendid houses, the least of which brought in a rental of from eight hundred to a thousand a year. And elsewhere, the cramped, dingy city, with its monstrous congeries of filthy bricks, frightful in themselves, and hardly less so in their effects upon the wayfarer and the inhabitant, were rapidly giving way to admirable private residences and public palaces of marble and stone.

A furore of taste had seized upon the city and the nation, and enormous sacrifices were made to achieve beauty; at present the movement was only in the beginning, but the health, happiness, and moral well-being that accrued to the public in consequence of the change, was found to be so great, that the work was pushed on with all possible expedition.

The destruction of slums was naturally one of the first and leading features of the improvement, but westward an immense difference was also to be seen. Perhaps one of the loveliest of the new streets was Gower Street, where the architect had had a fine field to start with, but the change progressed very unequally, owing to leases and other causes, and Park Lane, being highly conservative, was one of the last to follow suit.

Quite early in the day it had occurred to a travelled nobleman, who had a house there and a hundred thousand a year on which to keep it up, that his London residence was not so very unlike a seaside lodging-house at a third-rate watering-place, at least so far as the outside went. There was the same narrow stuccoed front, the same feeble effort at a bay window running all the way up it, the same cast-iron balconies of execrable pattern, and the same pinched verandah, over which grew the identical mangy creeper.

His original mind gradually arrived at the

conclusion that there was even something
unsuitable in it, but he trembled at the thought
of the innovation which presented itself. Being
a determined man, however, he made up his
mind to follow it out, and, in spite of the
significant comments of his friends, bought up
at least half a dozen of these glorified pill-
boxes, with their strips of garden, and battered
them down, reducing them to their miserable
elements with inconceivable gusto.

Upon their site he built a single house, a
Pompeian villa in two storeys, and the fanatic
actually built it of white marble instead of
white brick—said he liked the material better,
forsooth! There was a verandah to it (called
by some preposterous Greek name), which was
supported by slender columns of translucent
Sicilian onyx, jasper, and other precious
marbles. In the front, facing the lane, was a
tesselated court and fountains, in the same
ridiculous stuff, which one looked upon through
a railing of gilt bronze; and all the world, as
it passed, noted the vases of rare stone filled
with rarer plants, the festoons of variegated
agate inlaid upon the walls, the tender-tinted
hues of the fern, and the flowers that were
slung at intervals in baskets of cunning metalwork beneath the colonnade.

The nobleman himself was an eccentricity,
at home he often wore a costume of his own
devising, of satin or velvet; and he had been
seen with lace ruffles at his throat and wrists,
after the fashion of a couple of centuries ago,

and, as he was young and still a very pretty
fellow, the ladies said they became him vastly;
but if you happened to call upon him, as likely
as not you would find him in shirt-sleeves and
apron, hoisted up on a scaffold, and picking
out one of his ceilings with flowers perhaps, or
with his own hand gilding a cornice, and almost
always with a knot of admiring fellow-workmen
round him whom he was leading through some
decorative difficulty.

His life had not been without a certain
interest.   Desperately fond of sport, as a youth
he had traversed half the known world in search
of it, and for some years had enjoyed his full
fling.   He had been a noted lion-slayer, had
yachted a bit, and had taken up the training and
running of horses.   Heaven knows what there
was in the way of intelligent sport at which he
had not tried his hand.   So far as he had gone
he had succeeded, but he had had over many
irons in the fire, and soon found that life was too
short to heat them all; at the age of thirty he
had pulled half of them out.   With some pangs
he gave up one after another, and now his time
was passed curiously enough.

He belonged to the local council, and as
there were a hundred thousand people whose
comfort had to be looked after, this absorbed a
certain amount of it; he was on the board of five
hospitals, and of at least a dozen charitable
institutes.

Being merely an Irish peer, he had gone into
Parliament, and was continually fighting elec-

tions, until lately, when he had become a representative one; and then, again, as a leading member of the Metropolitan Works, he was kept perpetually occupied.

He was a great club man, but the clubs that he mostly frequented were not to be found in Pall Mall; they lay in streets unknown to fame, and sometimes in a mews. And here his voice might be heard, night after night, lecturing to the great unwashed on some topic of the day. It interfered with the after-dinner cigar, indeed it often shortened dinner itself, or put it back to the unseemly hour of five; but he was young enough to make light of these things as trifles. All the same, if he had been a married man he might not have found it so easy.

Pall Mall was at first very hard on this kind of thing. "Deuced odd," "queer form," "young coxcomb," were some of the expressions hurled at him behind his back.

"Demnition! what could you expect from a fellow who would ride outside a 'bus, or wear a lace necktie. Could he be a man at all?"

The gentleman in question was inclined to believe he might be. When taken to task by his private friends, he urged that his and their respective ancestors wore satin and lace on suitable occasions, *bien entendu*, and were none the less men; further, that if they could behold their posterity and their ways, they would look upon them as a weakened and effeminatized race, in spite of their frightful clothes. Manhood lay in the ethics of life, not in the cut or fabric of a jacket; and, as his own was sufficiently proven on many a troublous field, his critics were constrained to admit that there was something in it.

The type most in favour at this period was like unto one we ourselves have known, and it fell into the name of " crusher." The world was ripe for him. No possible ending of the nineteenth century could have avoided him, or would have been otherwise complete. To the alternative generation he came, as he did to us, dropped like a plum, in the identical form, the latest splendid fruit of the procession of the ages. His collar, his straight waistcoat, his boots,— but why describe the indescribable, we all have known him. Now, will it be believed, this eccentric young nobleman refused to recognise the style as the embodiment of manly perfection, and declined to conform to it.

A certain code, of course, went with the clothes, and in this he found as little delight. In public, he declared he would dress inoffensively to others, if not to himself, as he wished to avoid remark; but in private, he would dress as he liked, work as he liked, think as he liked. And the climax came when he hinted that his way of taking life was more befitting a gentleman, and man of refinement and brains, than the ordinary course pursued by his fellows.

There was open revolt at this: brains and refinement were words not well understood of his class, and they had to be looked out in the dictionaries ; and much sarcastic comment ensued, particularly from one gentleman whom he had designated as " an empty-headed jackanapes."

" No, deah boy, it was not good form, it was rude, he is a boor ; but, you know, he wouldn't tell a lie to save his life."

This was all the consolation the injured one received from his friends. Thereupon, the gilded youths hugged themselves afresh, took their nips with renewed zest, and thanked heaven they were not such as this other.

One fine Sunday, however, Lord St. Maur, for this was his name, dispersed a riotous meeting in Hyde Park, and in the very same maroon velvet coat that had given such dire offence.

It was the style of thing we have seen. Police powerless, women crushed to death; railings torn down, flower-beds trampled out of existence, just as the present generation had it in '66, and just as they are going to have it again—it is difficult to predict the year exactly, but much too soon for the people who live near Park Lane. By some alchemy, he changed the howling of the mob into cheers, and they gave up their banners to him to make into pocket handkerchiefs, as he said he required them, and that the mottoes, " Down with everything," " Property is robbery," and so forth, would do him all the good in the world. Then the seething, surging crowds seized him, hoisted him upon their shoulders, and carried him triumphantly home.

" There, boys, pull that down, if you like," he said, as they neared his own gilt railings, " and make room for the people ; you are all welcome here; but leave the park alone, don't spoil your own property."

Oddly enough, not a finger was laid on his railings ; and he went in upon the marble balcony with only half a dozen followers, the people staying outside. And there he harangued them to their hearts' content, and, when that was done, they all went home to tea.

It was a fine thing, finely done, and the people understood it, though Pall Mall did not ; but henceforth the cloud was raised from over the house in Park Lane. It became a centre of attraction, enormous numbers of visitors flocked thither when its doors were flung open. Foreigners and Americans among others, who were not inexperienced in reckoning the up and down value of a thing in that day, any more than in this ; and as the owner was a lord, his sins were forgiven him, and he presently found himself at the head of a large following.

It was owing to him in great measure, that the movement in search of beauty took shape and form, and spread and developed, until it bid fair to transfigure the entire face of the country.

The alternative generation, like ourselves, had a knack of doubling their numbers every quarter of a century or so, and under these conditions the builder was a unit not to be sneezed at. " Take care of the builder," said St. Maur,

"and the buildings will take care of themselves."
Acting upon this principle he had founded a
college for this class, upon whom ever hangs
the weal or woe of the entire population.

Meantime he had been successful in pushing
through Parliament a bill of the most drastic
description, making penal the erection of buildings by uncertificated persons, and the result
was already prodigious. No longer did water
and soil pipe meander together in friendly
proximity whither they listed, upstairs and
down, leaving which was which to be fought
out at the pleasure of the occupant. They
were sternly relegated to their places. No
longer was Maria, " who always 'ad the heye
of the family," appealed to whenever a new
elevation was wanted for a church, a novel
façade for a mansion, or a nice fancy " summer-
'ouse " for anybody. No longer was the
" chastity " of a chimney-pot, or the " 'ansome-
ness " of a " ballerstrade " a matter for the
builder's own riotous imaginings, he had learnt
at any rate the rudiments of his art, and dared
not put up work that would have been the
laughing-stock of his fellows, even if it did not
fall under the ruthless ban of the surveyors.

This was an advance, but the matter did not
rest here, and men—gentlemen—began to study
style, and to design—of course with technical
help—their own houses ; and birth, blood, and
education, marvellous to say, competed not
unsuccessfully with the lack of it. It really
seemed as if the day was dawning when to be

an idle fool would no longer help a man in the social world.

The same principle began to be pushed in other directions, and ladies, upon whose schooling great sums had been lavished, began to have misgivings as to whether it was necessary or advisable that a number of illiterate shop-girls and half-bred milliners, living in two pair backs, or even in Bond Street fronts, should dictate taste and fashion to them. Hitherto such had been the well-springs of all dressing, but female education had latterly been pushed to a pitch verging on absolute intelligence, and a general revolt took place. Committees of ladies, self-appointed, organized themselves, and started competitive associations and exhibitions which, in spite of plenty of squabbling, paved the way to a very fair observance of good taste and good sense. Men, alas! were still trammelled as no woman had ever been: yet there were signs that the tyranny of their lot would not last for ever.

These were mere straws, but they and others pointed to the fact that society was internally and externally, morally, socially, and politically, entering upon the most radical change ever witnessed by human society since it was constituted. All that the most powerful thinker could hope to do, was to catch the drift of the main currents and so steer as at least to avoid shipwreck.

"Well, my lad, who taught you the right way of polishing a bronze?"

The question was addressed to Roland, who,

it may be remembered, was in his old school-clothes, prominent on which was a big patch upon the elbow.

When he had left his uncle's, it was with a vague idea of hunting up a tailor, but he had already forgotten all about that. Gazing upon the streets and their people, he had passed through tree-shaded Mount Street, lounged into the moss-grown churchyard, leading thence into South Audley Street, where the children were at play among the fountains and the flowers, and had come into Park Lane, where his steps arrested themselves before the mansion that has been told of.

He had stopped and stared, then walked on after a petticoat—the rascal!—a hundred yards, when, finding it a fraud, he had returned and looked again; form and colour, variety and idiosyncrasy, had at all times a fascination for him. He was greatly struck, and as critical as a youth of his years should be. At last going across, he began tenderly to rub with his hand the dimness away from the stern features of a bronze lion in the gateway; now the sun was striking upon it as upon a diamond, and the face was lightened up with a grim smile.

The question was addressed him by a well-looking artisan who was filing at the lock of the gate, and laughing, he answered him in his own tone,—

" Well, mate, it ain't such a bad way, is it ? "

" It's the only way," rejoined the other; " but the public's so pig-headed it won't see it, we ain't up to these things, we ain't," he went on as he continued his filing. "Tell yer wot I intends to do when they make's me 'Ome Secretary, which is a post where they wants a gentleman," and he laughed. " I means to get all the ragged lads in the place together, make 'em take off their boots, and swarm all over the public statooes in their greasy rags, a-polishing and a-rubbing like winking. I'd pay 'em a few coppers, and in a week every bronze in the metropolis 'ud be shining like the sun, as a bronze should do, and the saving to public property 'ud be thousands. But there! the hignorance of them hupper classes is sickening to behold. The last chap " (it is to be feared this referred to the Home Secretary) " 'as been a-painting of 'em all with some beastly varnish to preserve 'em. Painting bronze, good Lord ! "

It was Roland's turn to laugh.

" You're a radical, my friend, I suppose. Well, so am I, I believe ; but I ain't had your experience either in bronze or politics."

" Well, I ham, and I h'ain't," said the other, buckling afresh to his lock ; " but I likes to see a man fill 'is place, whether it's a big or a little 'un, that's wot I likes. Some of 'em tries. Now, there's this feller 'ere," and he jerked his file towards the villa, " 'e's one of that kidney, but it's a kind o' sort o' failure, don't cher know."

Roland knew nothing of London and its life except from report ; but this particular house

and its owner had been sufficiently lashed by
the press to make it unmistakable.

" I suppose this is Lord St. Maur's ? " he
said.

" Ay, that's he."

" It's very fine, it's magnificent. I'm an ig-
noramus at this sort of business; but it looks
a gentleman's shell, at any rate. After all
there's nothing like the Greek. Why, it'll stand
stucco and yet look decent ; but it's the only
style that will. Fancy Gothic in stucco, bah !
And what I like about this is, that you have
here the Greek forms in the materials for which
they were originally designed, in clouded jas-
pers and shot agates, in semi-transparent shafts
of old alabaster. I am sure, by its colour, some
of that has been buried, and you—"

Here his new friend lifted an astonished pair
of handsome blue eyes upon him. There was
a puzzled look in them, and they dubiously
surveyed Roland's patched elbow and torn
boots. The inspection reassured him apparently, for he smiled.

" Well, you ain't chucked your time away
for nothing, my lad, that's evident." (He
seemed to grow suddenly more careful of his
"h's.") " What's your line, eh? Out of a job?"

" Yes, very much so," laughed Roland.

" Well, tell you what " (mysteriously), " I'm
a good deal about this shop, and they knows
me well, and if you're that way, I don't mind
taking you in for a look round, and maybe, if
you're as neat-handed as you look, my lad, I

can find you a job. I'm sort of boss overseer here."

Nothing loth Roland followed. Once inside, his friend assumed a rather more patronizing tone, such as befitted his position as "boss."

The boy's keen enjoyment seemed to please him mightily, and although Roland could hardly help laughing in his sleeve all the time, he was more and more impressed with his guide. Evidently the latter was well known in the place, nobody stopped them. They passed the hall-porter snoozing in his chair, and several servants who were dawdling about. But the "boss" went to and fro, lifting aside the *portières*, opening the doors, and unlocking the cabinets as he liked. Then they went upstairs. As they entered one of the bedrooms a young housemaid in a self-coloured canvas garment piped with scarlet, fluttered by them, and dipped a profound curtsey. The guide frowned, turned red, and ran out after her, slamming the door. Certainly there was a to-do outside.

"Sweetheart?" asked Roland carelessly, as he re-entered.

"Oh! yes, sweetheart by all means, very much so," stammered the other, brightening up so obviously that Roland smelt a rat.

He looked at his guide. The boss was a very pretty fellow, his forehead was white like marble, upon it fell crisply short hyacinthine curls, his nose was slightly aquiline, and there was a play in his nostrils as in those of a high-bred horse. Under the fine arch of his brow was set a flashing blue eye, and his tawny moustache fell into a short pointed beard like a cavalier's.

"What sort of a man is this Lord St. Maur?" said Roland, turning upon him sharply.

"I—'pon my soul, I can't say—I've never," floundering, "ah—met him."

"Ah! well," laughed Roland, holding out his hand, "I fancy I have, and he seems," imitating the other's broad accent, "a rare lot, but not such a bad sort when you know him."

His lordship, whose delight it was to play Haroun al Raschid, was fairly caught, and burst into a fit of laughter.

"Well!" he said, "I don't know who you may be, but you're a man after my own heart anyhow."

He had the easy ways of the artist fraternity. When they left the room, it was arm in arm, and Roland stayed to dinner.

CHAPTER V.

It was a *tête-à-tête* dinner, and the two sat at the table (which by the way was a single slab of giallo antico) and talked far into the night.

Probably no more fortunate circumstance could have befallen Roland than his meeting with Lord St. Maur; a man who, although scarcely five-and-thirty, had already exercised no little influence upon his generation, as has been told. Finding that he could accomplish this, after his own fashion, he had not pushed forward in any particular line of politics or science (for both of which he had natural gifts) with the same energy that he bestowed upon the cause of general advancement. He had done much indirectly for his mother country, Ireland —for the aspirations of a nation towards nationality were ever sacred to him; and although circumstances prevented him from leading the fray himself, he had already had the satisfaction of bringing forward certain strong men into battle, and was regarded as a powerful, if occult, wire-puller in public life.

With all his *bonhomie*, he seldom took others

into his confidence, but worked out the problems which he set himself according to his own lights. Whatever the subject that he chose, he talked upon it with brilliancy and fascination ; and as the summer night wore late, Roland grew spellbound. It was as if he saw before him the Spirit of the Age embodied, the flash of whose eye, the gesture of whose hand, held him entranced ; and as he listened, his own youth and inexperience sat heavily upon his spirit.

Lord St. Maur came, like most of his contemporaries, of a mingled line. He himself was a nominal Anglican, who looked with approval on most forms of religious organization, and when he discovered the circumstances of his patched acquaintance, his interest redoubled.

Encouraged by this, young Tudor poured forth the long-pent thoughts of his boyhood's years, his searchings and speculations on life and its meaning, and his solution, so far as it went. He made it plain that he was no enthusiast. His host, on the other hand, in spite of his experience and many additional years, was ; and before they left the table, the latter had sketched out a career for him on a most generous scale.

He must go to one of the universities, without a doubt, not to prosecute his Greek and Latin, but to learn his world, and the men of it, and to pick up a few ornamental accomplishments. Then, since he wished it, the army, by all means, for a couple of years perhaps.

" Foreign service, another year or two. Oh, certainly; and then—why, Parliament, of course. No hurry, say at twenty-five." English constituencies were, here and there, admitting a stray Papist, but he thought Ireland would be best on the whole; there, there was always " the cause." The only possible Englishman for Ireland was one such as Roland : a gentleman to the backbone (one of actual kingly lineage), and yet absolutely democratic in his principles ; and then, with an independence, and his physique—why, the Cabinet at forty, an almost necessary sequence.

" Won't that do for you ? " he asked, as his guest looked more amused than impressed.

" I doubt it ; but we shall see. I confess to overwhelming ambitions, which I am quite unable to put into words. I have no notion where they will lead me, possibly to the gallows ; even if that is to be, I trust that they may so further the good of my race." He laughed. " I sometimes have a presentiment that destiny will fall so strong upon me, that I shall be a mere straw upon the waters, and as powerless."

St. Maur grew graver, " We have a belief in common," he said. " You have noticed that I have gone back to the Roman empire and the primitive Church for my surroundings."

This was the case ; here and there, among the superb emblems of the Cæsars, the eye caught some humble symbol of faith. Where should have stood the shrine of a god, was niched an emblem of the Good Shepherd, with an invocation, as if traced by some passer-by, upon the wall. Here were the crossed branches of a palm; there, a dove with an olive bough. Upon a tall candelabrum burned a lamp, in the handle of which was twined the sacred monogram of Christ.

"Well, like the early Christians, I have been unable to shake myself quite free of my pagan beliefs. Come! before you go, I will show you my oratory. I don't show it to everybody, most people would hardly understand it, but I fancy you will, and I have a feeling for you that I cannot explain. You shall see my skeleton cupboard." Saying which, he rose, and led Tudor to a doorway, which was almost concealed behind the heavy leafage of the palms.

This presently brought them into a bedroom, lit by an electric flower-chandelier; the ceiling was painted deep azure and sprinkled with gold stars, but the hangings were of the pale, faint blue of the morning, and every scrap of furniture was of mother-of-pearl. There were slippers about, and a coat was flung across a chair, but the chamber had a disused look.

"Now, surely I am in the Arabian nights," gasped Roland.

"Pooh! my dear fellow, I was going to be married once," said St. Maur, shrugging his shoulders, "and I wanted something bridal. This stuff is easy enough to get and make up, if you know how. That table over there with the swans, I made myself." And he gave it a gentle kick. "Pretty enough in a girl's room." He opened another door; it led into a narrow, stone cell, ending in an alcove.

The place struck chill, almost damp, the floor was of stone like the walls, and worn uneven, a common iron tressel bedstead stood in the corner, an oaken table, a press, and a couple of chairs formed the furniture. Above the bed, the wall looked of incredible age, considering the building in which it stood. Upon it was a rude fresco of the crucifixion, beneath this, in an irregular niche, was a broken earthen phial and fragment of dried sponge, and again below, the inscription "Fratri in pace," and the single word "Ora" in Greek characters, enclosed in a wreath of palm. Upon the table flickered a rude triple-wick lamp of brass, such as you buy to-day in Spain for a few pesetas.

St. Maur pointed to the wall. "Perhaps you know I once helped to get a concession for the Irish bishops, and when I went to Rome, the Pope, knowing my interest in these things, opened out a bit of catacomb for me, and gave me all that entire stone just as it was found. It is priceless," he said, looking at it with a kindling glance. "In that clay phial is the seed of Christianity, the dried life-blood of a martyr; its very memory is a prayer, and I have a fancy that my unknown brother remembers me sometimes, even in these far-off years. May be, as often as I remember him."

An omnibus lumbered heavily by a few yards off in the Lane, some one whistled for a cab, and the echoes rang strangely in the cell; the contrasts that met him, whichever way he turned, appealed with a strong pleasure to the younger man's imagination.

"And is this—is this a room you use then?" he asked, looking dubiously at the stone floor, the low bedstead, and its scanty coverings.

"Well, yes," replied his host with a light laugh; "there's a certain atmosphere about it, and I find I sleep better here than anywhere else. Besides, I have the conceit of facing my Fate, but you have not noticed my Fate."

Roland looked up, the wavering wicks burned so dimly that it was with difficulty he could pierce the gloom in the alcove, but he became aware of a set face in black marble, with sightless orbs, fixed stonily upon him. Involuntarily he shivered.

It was a bold, brazen-typed female mask that looked forth, one arm of the figure was outstretched, the finger slightly curved, as in invitation; aloft in the other hand she held a victor's wreath in gold.

"There is a story to the piece," said St. Maur, turning it an inch or two on its revolving pedestal. "It was discovered by the French when they were in Italy, in the ruins of a temple, dedicated, said tradition, to the fate of victories. Upon the base was a painted inscription, to the effect that her laurels were for conquerors. They carried the statue to

General Sherer, who was then commanding the army of Italy, but before it reached his quarters, he had been superseded by a young fellow unknown to fame, named Napoleon, in whose presence the case was opened.

"Now, curiously enough, although it was supposed to have been uninjured, except for that left arm which had been snapped off, it is said that as he stood before it, leaf after leaf detached itself from the wreath, and fell at his feet. Whether this be true or not, there is no doubt that he always regarded the piece with a perfectly fanatical veneration. He had the wreath carefully restored, and kept the statue in a locked closet with as much jealousy as if she had been flesh and blood. The savants were never able to get at it, and when the allied armies entered Paris, my grandfather, who was one of the royal aide-de-camps and a passionate antiquary, managed to get hold of—"

Ping! went something sharply upon the pavement.

"What's that? you've dropped something, Mr. Tudor, it sounded like half a sovereign."

"No, I think not," said Roland, feeling in his pockets and looking round, "I don't see anything."

"Well, I was saying he managed to get hold of one of the—"

Ping! ping! rang out with a clear, metallic intonation in the silence.

"What can that be?" said St. Maur in a startled voice. "Give me the lamp."

But, as Roland did so, a little shower of leaves fell upon him; tread as he would, he crushed them under foot, and the wingless Victory, with outstretched arm, held a barren circlet above his head, and stood looking out into the ages, with the same set serenity upon her awful features.

St. Maur fairly reeled to the wall. Roland stooped down and, brushing the leaves into his hand, picked them up.

"Ugh!" he exclaimed, suddenly throwing them down, "they are wet, or, no! why, I must have cut my hands with them; look! they are stained with blood."

"For heaven's sake, come away, man!" exclaimed St. Maur, catching his arm, "it's nothing, of course, a mere accident—the ah— the damp gets in here, you know, and one leaf falling would loosen the rest. On the top of the story it really was enough to upset one for the moment. I am quite superstitious about that statue. Come away now. I'll see about repairing it myself to-morrow. Good night. I'll look you up when you have let me know where you have fixed your diggings; good-bye, good-bye."

Roland went out into the sultry night, and turned into the park, where he paced to and fro through the deserted "Row" with a feverish energy. A profound disbeliever in "omens, dreams, and such-like fooleries," this strange incident, and the chance revelations of the past day, had set a light to his imagination, and his brain was in a whirl. In the first fervour of youth, and strength, and freedom, he felt as if the wide world had been created solely to provide a scope for his energies.

All the night long he walked the streets of London, in a sort of frenzy of exaltation, which, as the morning dawned, strengthened into purpose and resolution of a sterner hue. At sunrise he was upon the river bank; and the city lay away silent and dim in the trailing mantles of the mist, and as he retraced his steps, he watched the slow sun conquer pinnacle after pinnacle, until it had overcome the world. Wearied at length, the signboard of a venerable inn, posted upon a great elm, attracted him, and he turned into the house to rest.

A three hours' sleep in fairy land, a plunge into the river, which, under the New Thames River Act, ran darkling green and limpid even to the sea, and he walked into breakfast with the feelings of a god. A rustic table was laid out under a rough trellis-shed, looking into the inn garden, which was a tossed wilderness of luxuriant old-fashioned flowers.

The sun and shade were playing hide-and-seek among the leaves of the vine, which sheltered the arbour, and by the table sat a man, apparently the only other guest in the hostel, who had tilted his chair up against the sunny wall, and was whittling at a stick, with an energy that seemed to be quite superfluous. His long angular frame, his cavernous face, with its piercing eyes, and coarse goatee, his monstrous hands, and the abnormal amount of

wrist and ankle which he displayed, his long
Wellingtons, and broad-brimmed felt hat,
marked him as a Yankee of the purest breed :
his face, however, for all its singularity, was
a pleasant and a clever one, and his forehead
was out of all proportion to the rest of it.

Roland was in too good a humour with himself, not to feel friendly towards any companion whom chance might throw in his way, so,
taking his seat, he wished the stranger " good-
morning."

" Mornin'," said the thin man shortly, and
plunged into his stick until the chips shot off
in a regular little stream like a waterfall.

" You seem to have reached the top of the
profession," said Roland, rather amused than
otherwise, " I wish I could do as much."

" There's whittles and whittles," observed
the long man sententiously.

" Quite so ; suppose you drop your sort and
try mine," said Roland, attacking his breakfast.

" Well done ! that's very fair for nine o'clock
in the morning. Parse the salt, young man,"
said the stranger, throwing down the stick, and
falling to breakfast and conversation at once
with a will.

" Now yew Britishers—but there, I'm that
sick of discussin' national crickteristics, I won't
trouble you. But see here, I s'pose I'm a darned
rum clawed-out sort of a customer to your
optics perhaps ; ain't I jes ? "

Roland nodded, in polite acquiescence.

" Wall! I tell yew, sir, you're the exact same to mine no less, the whole boiling lot of you 'stockracy."

" I am quite as much astonished at ourselves as you can possibly be, for different reasons perhaps."

" Look at that, sir," said the American flourishing his fork at the distant city; " it's the grandest sight the world has to show, or ever had; it moves even the played-out buzzum of S. A. S., sir," and he beat his own. " Babylon was not a patch on it, Rome was a flea-bite, yet to walk through it is the saddest sight on airth, and who's responsible? yew air, sir, pairsonally."

A shade crossed Roland's face. " I know what you mean, I have had time to feel it."

" Yew British aristercrats hold in the holler of yer hand your own future, and that of millions, the happiness and well-being of half the human race, and yet you think of nothin' but pigeon-shooting, driving hosses, which any young fool can do, and dandlin' around yer wummin. Danged if ye'll see there's other things require doing almost as much, and if yew intend to do 'em, yer time's runnin' out mighty spry."

" I am no aristocrat," and Roland lifted his patched elbow.

" Jehosaphat! what 'cher take me for, youngster? I guess I'd place yew, if yew passed me on a dark night a mile away, and with no more on than Father Adam's dress suit. It's 'bout the healthiest trait yew hev, yew swells, that yew ain't made up of yer clothes, but you're D'generate all the same, there's not a dozen 'mong the whole ten thousand of yer, that's correct ideas 'bout himself and the place he ought ter take. Yer all for D'pendin' on your friends, on the pile your progenitors have made, on the set of your back hair and the curl of your front teeth. Wat yew deu, yew don't deu fairly and squarely, standin' on yer own bottom."

" What I may do, friend, I fancy will be done in that unequivocal position," said Roland drily ; " I've few friends, no interest, and a pile which is chiefly in perspective; but I've strength, and I've ambition, and I've an idea of combining the two."

" Say, stranger, air you in airnest ?" ejaculated the other, eyeing him with interest, and lighting a cigar a foot long, which he proceeded to annihilate together with his breakfast.

" A few," laughed Roland.

" Then Solomon A. Skump is your man," said the gentleman who presumably bore that name. " Yew may have haird, sir, of Solomon A. Skump ? "

Roland shook his head ; the man was rather a bore, and was driving clouds of highly powerful smoke horizontally to the right, left, and front of him, in a way that would have done credit to a factory chimney on a stormy day.

" No matter, sir," continued the stranger,

waiving the point with a fearful flourish of his
fork, while his piercing eyes gleamed like a
bonfire through the fog. " You'll sk'sly have
failed to obsairve the manner in which I take
my tobacco ;" here he poured the entire stream
point blank upon Roland, who, not to be beat
by a trifle, replied, with a convulsive effort not
to cough, that he really thought he had not.

" Then be good enough to remark it, sir, it's
typical," said the Yankee solemnly, " of the
way in which I take everything, my motter is
'through !' I'd a million once, I am through it
long since, and out at the other side. It's a
way with Solomon A., sir, he knows this world
as fur as it goes, which ain't too fur, and he's
pretty well tired of lookin' for novelty in it.
Say now, what's yer game, Canterbury, the
woolsack, or Westminster Abbey ? there ain't
many. No ? then cert'nly Parliament."

" I suppose so."

" A life time of grind, and if you're enough
of a lickspittle, a peerage at the end of it."

" That's not my idea."

" Wall ! there *air* bigger plums. What do
you say to prime minister ? "

" I haven't quite decided to run for that,"
said Roland with a slight yawn, " and my religion (I am a Roman Catholic) would no
doubt stop me on the threshold of Downing
Street."

" Bah ! your cussed blindness is enough to
rile a saint, there ain't more than two religions
in the future, belief and disbelief. If belief is

to stand, you Christians must join hands. Equality's the programme, the winning skiff down the stream o' time. Bigotry and progress ain't bed-fellows. But 'bout yer premier? there's no denying it's a big thing—while it lasts. Fifty years hence ('bout your time), it'll be bigger; but ain't yew tied up and bound down hand and foot; ain't yer very soul every one's but yer own; ain't most of yer leading, follerin' through places and at paces that don't suit ye? Bah! its a cherry that don't cut into two bites: there's fruit waitin' which it's pumpkins by comparison."

"There are no careers now-a-days worth talking of, or only two or three. To raise Ireland from the dust, to ' place' modern Catholicism, to save the Church of England, to direct the on-coming popular flood into a true groove. These are about all."

"Sir, yew air right, yew bet, yer civilization, sech as it is, is complete; yer social system 'stablished, that is for the present. Sir, if yew seek true greatness, reel power over yer race, genuine influence in the present, and a name imperishable in the futur, take the word of Solomon A Skump, spring yer rattle in a new world, and git for revolution. There's empires out west, that you might chop into countless kingdoms, and they're waitin' for the man; such empires as Alexander shed for, as Cæsar C. Julius would have been satisfied to own. 'Taint the chawed up, busted out, kerlapsed, turned kid-glove thing, that a renovated empire is in Europe. It's vargin soil, sir, in which lie treasures which put to shame those of my old name-sake, King Solomon, and which would buy out the old world body and soul, ten times told. That world is waitin' its master," he dashed his fist upon the table until the teapot reeled again.

There was silence.

"Wall!" he said rising, "adoo! adoo! proceed, young man, go yer own way, but if it leads yer into a blind alley, think on the words of S. A. S., make tracks right away and seek knowledge. I don't ask yer name, if ye're the grit I take yer for, the universe should be ringin' with it one fine mornin'."

"A large order," laughed Roland, "which way are you going?"

"Pekin *direct.*"

"I'm going that way myself for a mile or two. I'll see you as far as London Bridge."

"Thankee, my young hopeful, Solomon A. is sorter solitary skunk, he goes his own way alone, it's the final fate of all, farewell: to our next merry meeting." He drained his glass, and he was gone.

They were never to meet again, but his keen look, his uncouth accent, and the force of his meaning, stayed with his hearer. Upon this chance encounter with a stranger, one day hung the fortunes of his life.

He rose and sauntered to the garden gate, the American was already far away, his figure rapidly lessening as, with prodigious strides, he covered the dusty river-side road "makin' tracks straight for Pekin," until he was out of sight. "I wonder is this the regular thing in the world," thought Roland, as he turned into the inn; "if every twenty-four hours brings me as much as the first day of my emancipation, I shan't have to complain of the emptiness of life."

Ha! ha! doosed funny fellow that Yankee, something in him though, cracky, of course, with his countless kingdoms and barbaric empires. I suppose none of these fellows can really take in the ideas of an English gentleman of blood. No notion of "form;" and, with a self-satisfied smirk in a neighbouring glass, he twirled his nascent moustache, paid his bill, and set off, likewise in the direction of Pekin.

He walked as far as Piccadilly, it was a blazing July day, but his sole recognition of it lay in the tankards of ale which he consumed on the road. As he entered that street of palaces, two big fellows, who looked like soldiers, came out of a military club and hailed a couple of hansoms. One gave the address, Hyde Park Corner, the other Pall-Mall, and they drove off.

This trifling incident sunk fathoms deep into his mind; was this civilization? He had walked twenty, perhaps thirty or forty miles in the last twelve hours, he had been up nearly all night, and he would have backed himself with pleasure to start off at that moment, and do as much again before he went to bed.

He began to cast about critically, the youths
in glasses, the gay-gay " Crusher," as he hobbled
along the street, the number of bent forms and
hollow faces among the crowd of well-dressed
people, the false and ghastly look of many of
the women, gave him a positive feeling of pain
and indignation, not unmixed with shame.
There was mischief somewhere ; either the race,
the generation, or the individual must be at
fault.

As he stood at the top of St. James's Street,
undecided what to do next, he began to think
more charitably of his uncle, for in the course
of ten minutes, at least half-a-dozen men passed
him who might have been the old gentleman's
double, and it was this very personage who
was most on his mind at the moment.   It was
quite plain that some *modus vivendi* must be
arrived at, but he hesitated to return to the
Albany after his unceremonious flight of yesterday.   Finally, after wandering to and fro undecided, he compromised the matter by taking
rooms close by in Sackville Street.

They were pretty rooms, with large balconies
of flowers, and furnished in the purest Central
African style, which, as everyone knew, was
the only possible style in that particular year.
They were, besides, at the top of the house,
for he imagined that he might be able to
keep the muscles of his legs in order by ceaseless running up and down stairs on wet
days.

Thence he went to a tailor's, bought a coat

(a hero, alas! in a reach-me-down!), and ordered a couple of suits as a concession to the age. After lunch, he presented himself at his uncle's, a peace with honour to both sides was arranged, and so he settled comfortably enough into his place.

At twenty, one has time to look round, and this was what, for the present, he most desired to do. The life came pleasantly. Catholic young men of position were terribly scarce; but of girls there was no lack, owing perhaps to the mixed-marriage regulations, and one could not but be sorry for them. It was an unfortunate state of things, but to this, no doubt, he partly owed his easy popularity.

What town was to young Tudor, with its clubs, its dinners, its dances, let the man who has been thrown upon it at his age, and with a well-lined pocket, say. The streets were paved with gold, never were parks so verdant, or heavens so blue. How young and how pretty were his women friends, how frank and generous the men; and how totally unlike was it in all things to the dreary, slimy city of after-life.

By way of practice and pastime, he joined the militia, went through a training, and, as time still hung on his hands, threw himself with zest into a dozen pursuits. He tried painting with Lord St. Maur; buried himself in ancient history with the professor of it at the British Museum; studied tactics and fortification, art, politics, and anatomy; and during the winter put in regularly two days out of seven with the hounds.

His splendid health allowed him to sit up
for a week in succession; he admitted that if
it ran towards ten days, he felt it.   Questioned
as to how, he said modestly, that it made him
sleepy in church during the sermon! Meanwhile,
he flung himself into society with a boy's enjoyment, for he was of an age when talking to
young ladies furnishes the most delightful of
occupations, wherever he found the *entrée* he
went; his object was to learn.

A small Catholic university had been established in South Kensington, and here he met
and made acquaintance with some of the so-
called "leading men" of the party, and now
and again with a distinguished foreigner.   The
history of this foundation was so typical of the
stage reached by the civilization of the period,
that no apology need be offered for a few words
on the subject.

The edifice was a superb Romanesque building, adjacent to the well-known Oratory, by
far the loveliest Gothic church in London.
The magnificent fad of a magnificent convert,
neither money nor benedictions had been
spared to make it a perfect thing of its kind.
It stood in extensive gardens, shaded by great
elms, and speedily became a feature of the city
and the day.

The founder was no man for half measures.
He had brought over, at his own cost, the Arch
of Pudentianus, from Italy, and this he had put
up as a gateway; re-laying the foundation-
stone with enormous ceremony, and with his
own aristocratic hand setting a thimbleful of

mortar round the base of the Latin cross upon its summit. When the buildings were finished, he had the entire front stained with powerful acids, to give them the look of venerable age; and again, with his own hand, he had taken a workman's hammer, and knocked off a few odd mouldings and projections of sculpture to enhance the effect. Never was such an opening-day since the departure of the Ages of Faith; and the incense poured so thickly out of the windows on the occasion, that the police rushed in, and the fire brigade arrived in the midst of the ceremony.

But a crisis attended the birth of the institution, which well-nigh proved fatal.

A daily dole for the poor had been instituted; the noble founder saying he was not going to have any rot about it, he meant to show this stinking nineteenth century (I regret to have to quote his actual words), with its brutal infidelity, what was what. Every poor person who applied at a certain hour was to receive, without question, an alms, with bread and cheese and ale.

Now at this period, enormous efforts had been made by the city authorities, by charity organization societies, and private enterprise, to check the rise of London pauperism, and after many years these efforts were beginning to bear fruit, when this new essay almost defeated them.

The first day the dole was opened, twenty-seven people received it; the second day, 109; the third day, 534. At the end of the week, the number had risen to 4000; at the end of a fortnight, it was calculated that 15,000 applied during the day. It was impossible, in spite of all efforts, to assist one-half of these; and the most desperate street-fighting took place in consequence round the arch. Traffic became impracticable, people were half trampled to death; the military were called out, and the Riot Act was read.

Unfortunately, Parliament was not sitting; the Prime Minister was yachting, and the afflicted piece of ground lay in two parishes. The case was one of insurmountable difficulty.

On the Monday of the third week (there was no Sunday dole), the scene baffled description; it was calculated that at least 50,000 people were collected round and about the building, blocking every exit and entrance. The giver of these dire gifts was in the house, and a deputation of the authorities and of his private friends waited upon him, to beg him to withdraw the dole, at least for the present.

But a founder is a founder at the best of times, and this gentleman was no less. He dismissed the party very shortly. He regretted the circumstances, but having taken counsel with heaven only that morning upon this particular subject, his way had been made quite plain to him, to effect any alteration would be a shocking impiety; and he forthwith walked down to the gate, where he harangued the people.

He said the whole thing did his heart good, and was well worthy of the Isle of Saints, as he hoped to see England again become. He implored them, one and all, to lay their troubles on the bosom of Mother Church, there was room for all; and then he went in among the crowd, and began to distribute half-sovereigns instead of sixpences from his waistcoat pocket.

He barely lived to tell the tale. All went merrily until the pocket gave out, when a terrific rush was made upon the building. The mob wrenched down the railings, poured into the grounds, and assailed the archway, where the dole was distributed, in front and rear. A regular battle, long afterwards known as "the battle of Brompton," ensued.

The cavalry, who had been kept in readiness hard by in expectation of trouble, charged again and again with the flat of their sabres, and at length succeeded in breaking up the mob and driving it down adjacent streets, where it was more easily dealt with; but not before the archway and dole-house had been destroyed, the woodwork torn from the chapel piled around them and set on fire, and the remainder of the collegiate buildings gutted.

A list of 150 killed and wounded was the record of the day's doings, and everybody thought it very moderate, including the pious founder, who was discovered, more dead than alive, in a private shrine, which he had fortunately erected for his own use in a secluded part of the building. And he was perfectly unchanged. "If," he remarked, "a man couldn't take a little breeze of this sort when Providence decreed it, his religion was a farce." For himself, he had long prayed for the crown of martyrdom, and he announced his intention of continuing the dole on the morrow.

This, however, was a little too much. His confessor, who was a plain, sensible man, and one who understood his new broom very well, was called in, and threatened him with excommunication if he gave away another sixpence for six weeks to come. The impenitent penitent yielded on the spot like a child, and the end of the matter was that when Parliament met, shortly after, a bill was brought in, and hurriedly run through both Houses: the "Ecclesiastical Doles Act" was the first record of the session.

After this, the university flourished apace; there was no selecter coterie in London, hardly an old Catholic name, or that of any distinguished recruit, but figured upon its books, and the good bishop, who was president, hastened to secure an undergraduate so eligible as Roland.

Here then he passed a couple of years, finding it an agreeable lounge, where a Christian gentleman could pleasantly disport himself and make the best of both worlds. The atmosphere had been originally as mediæval as possible; shortly, however, the grotesque nudities of the late Italian school crept in, owing to modern Roman influences, and divided the honours with Fra Angelico, who had hitherto reigned supreme, in Oxford frames of unstained oak. The epidemic crossed the road, and half the South Kensington Museum was filled with bastard examples of third-rate Italian renaissance, to the exclusion of every higher and purer style; such curious folk were they of the day!

The educational standard of the new university was not high, even its friends admitted this, and if by chance you wanted a cosy talk upon the aberrations of a Greek particle, you were apt to wish yourself back at Oxford or Cambridge; yet a variety of subjects were taught, and you could learn there almost anything, except how to be useful. No thought of that; no idea of citizenship, no troublesome shadow of patriotic duty, ever darkened its threshold, nor did a soul seem to be aware of the great part which should await revived Catholicism in the England of the future.

Roland found his views scouted, but he gained no fresh ones; he ceased to trouble himself much either on this or other crucial points, and took refuge in society, which in the beginning, held an endless charm for him. After some time, however, he discovered that he was getting into the shallows of what had, at first, seemed to him the unfathomable depths of London life.

There were some eccentric points in the social system which did not fail to attract his attention; and it was remarkable, that the higher you went, the more this funniness became emphasized, until in the uppermost stratum it reached a pitch of extreme comicality.

Anything more ludicrous than the jest or earnest of these circles it would be impossible to conceive—the people they took up, and the people they took down. Oh, it was delicious! If you were content to associate with people

generally speaking in a modest way, and mere
professional men, you met with almost invariable consideration and politeness; if they asked
you to their houses, it was obvious the poor devils
did their best for you according to their lights.

The contrast between this and the great
houses was very marked. If you were fortunate enough to be asked to them, that was
enough, you were deliberately and ostentatiously bored, your miserable personality was
ignored. No one took the slightest pains or
trouble about you, and the flunkeys were
pointedly impertinent if you arrived in anything less than a carriage and pair. And the
manners of these "privileged classes!" At
length one began to have some idea to what
the meaning of the word "privilege" might
extend. Nor could more be said for their
morals. It was a singular feature of the generation, that people of title were not as a rule
either ladies or gentlemen, or indeed anything
approaching to those standards. There were
of course many and noble exceptions, but a
mere introduction was often sufficient to make
apparent the cloven foot. There was a topsy-
turveying of the value of things, which in itself
was highly ludicrous. If, for instance, you, a
stranger, dowered with every grace of mind and
body, had dropped upon the world from another
planet, you would not have made much way.
If, on the other hand, you had been wanting in
these graces, but had been able to claim close
kinship with a marquis, who after running

a-muck, had had to fly the country in consequence of crimes for which there is no name, assuredly the first nobleman you meet would have asked you to dinner; certainly his wife would have weighed you for her daughters.

As time went on, Roland, through his friend, Lord St. Maur, had introductions to several eminent men. He found the same law regulating all, and that it applied to every condition of life. The statesman, the preacher, the painter—each led him, gently, and by devious ways, to the foot of his own altar.

"Oh! friend, you are young, and generous, and have understanding, burn then at least one little grain of incense to my honour."

In time he sickened, and he found himself standing aloof from the show, in an attitude of curious criticism for a youth of his age. At least, he surmised the oddity of it from the fact that he was almost alone in his views. The various "sets" provided him with entertainment for a long time. For instance, there was a set of "smart" people, distinguished chiefly for being so uncertain of their own position that they dared not make a friend out of their set—hardly an acquaintance; and as the scale descended, the sets became terribly intricate and particular, until, in the lowest grade, the lines of demarcation were like the laws of the Medes and Persians. Real geniality of intercourse was almost out of the question under these conditions. Men belonging to the same club hardly dared so much as pretend to know of each other's existence; while the average middle-class Englishwoman was even less genial than her male kind, and always conveyed the impression that her own *status* was so uncertain that she had to be careful to whom she talked, and how. It was amusing to note the air of positive comfort and relief exhibited by these females if they could turn from their own equals, Mrs. A. or Mrs. B., to talk to Lady C., or some one their undoubted superior in rank. No matter if the talk was a mere snubbing, so long as the greater lady chose to condescend to administer it, so long did the lesser purr with cat-like complacency. In a society so composed, chivalry and courtliness were wellnigh dead, there was no room for them. The would-be man about town, who was not about quite so much as he desired, was almost as great an offender in this particular.

Few things struck the casual observer more strongly at social gatherings, than the quality of the men. The best were not represented, hardly the second best; on the other hand, there was an extraordinary prevalence of the ugly little snob, with an eye-glass, a lisp, a glib list of big names on his tongue, and on his uncouth hands dirty, wrinkled gloves, showing abnormal wrist. No matter where you went, he was there, be sure of it; and though girls complained that they could not get partners fit to dance with; in the absence of anything better, he went down. The difficulty of getting entirely well-looking, well-mannered people to your house (were you a host) was immense; if

you were limited, or if you limited yourself to
the upper classes, it was absolutely insuperable.
Fashion was in truth the most retrograde and
reactionary force of the period.

Another phase altogether remarkable in the
life of the time was the public—I had almost
written Protestant—estimate of "virtue" in
the case of man and in the case of woman.
Unmindful apparently of the law, that as you
sow, so shall you reap, the most pious old ladies
would calmly smile approval on the wildest
extravagances of their young men relations on
the ground that the latter were merely sowing
their wild oats, and that this was necessary
and essential to manhood. The sauce for the
gander was by no means the same as that
served up with the goose. If the code for a
man was lenient to foolishness, that for his
sister erred as much in the other direction.
It was impossible to reason with people on the
point. Either the thing was right, or it was
wrong; if right, why such anathema upon it in
Bible and prayer-book? Was this merely for
form's sake? If wrong, why was not even-
handed justice dealt out to all offenders alike,
irrespective of sex? Had you, a man, braver
than your fellows, pretended to "virtue,"
had you advanced such a claim for any other
man, you would have seen your hearer's face
relax (even had it been that of a religious old
lady). Indeed, it was evidently impossible to
keep the facial muscles in order, upon so facetious a matter. An "Oh, come, come now,"
and a titter hardly repressed, laid the claim low,

and you were ever after regarded as a wag of quite singular whimsicality. Yet there were people who found themselves out of place in such a world, and stigmatized half the existing social laws as despicable cant.

During this period Roland saw little or nothing of his friend Warburton Brabant, who had warned him at starting, "I have my own way to make, so don't look for me in the haunts of men. I shall take a plunge into deep waters, and in a year or two I trust you will see my head above the surface, and in a place where it will be likely to remain so." This had actually happened. It is wonderful what a man may do if he has a natural affinity for the particles floating in the social atmosphere, and through the medium of his brain is able to precipitate them in print. He becomes a power almost without a struggle. Brabant had, too, a further gift over and above his pen and his lute—it was for diagram. The article illustrated by the diagram was becoming (partly thanks to himself) a necessity of the age; in a few strokes he could place before the eye of the public anything, from a protozoon to a Lord Mayor's show. "I mean to have the *Times* a penny illustrated yet," he would say laughing. "See if I'm not a true prophet."

He was a man unhappy in his family his-history—of which more later. He belonged to a class which, although a comparative novelty, the age had already produced in truly unfortunate numbers; that of the gentleman with only his old name at his back. Men of his

type, less favoured, were swarming in the pur-
lieus of all the great cities, hopeless failures.
Not only had the time come when the best
blood in the kingdom was forced into the professions, and was found among doctors, lawyers,
architects, engineers; but it had been pushed
beyond these limits into trade, and often to
actual manual labour. *Facilis descensus.* These
unfortunates, without capital, without interest,
usually without business connection of any
sort, were expected by their more favoured
relations, and by the ladies and gentlemen who
had been so good as to bring them into the
world, to make their own way to fame and fortune, or at least competence, and much surprise
was expressed at their frequent and repeated
failures to accomplish that feat.

A man with an unusually long head, or an unusually brawny arm, possibly took a place with
no extraordinary difficulty; but either was by no
means an invariable attribute of gentle blood, and
he who was without them, usually went under,
and was never heard of again. It was instructive to count over the names of such persons in
one's own comparatively limited circle of friends,
for one thus gathered some idea of the real bulk
of these cases. One good result was traceable
to the circumstance—a more generous conception of social intercourse, and a decided height-
ening of the tone of the labour market. Men
of Brabant's type shook off the slough of social
ordinance, except such as was based upon reason
and good taste, and often succeeded in achieving
independence of thought and action, and in living

a life of higher calibre than was possible under the old conditions. To such a one the general acquiescence in these conditions seemed a sufficiently contemptible standpoint: no life worth the living could be led until a complete emancipation from all foregone conclusions that failed to reconcile themselves with his own sense of logic and right had been achieved. Here the two young men found common ground, and it proved the basis of a lasting friendship.

It was at this period that an event occurred which caused a tremendous sensation through the country and the world. A prince of the blood royal became a convert! It would be impossible to describe the mingled storm of triumph and execration that swept the face of the land, and indeed of half Europe.

The *Katholikon*, a leading publication of the Church in England, hinted that there were times when the goodness of God really exceeded belief, and the Catholic press, with two or three marked exceptions, followed in the same strain. Then it was that Roland first took his side definitely—with the minority; and as he expressed his opinion with incisive freedom, he found his place growing warm for him, and he decided upon leaving town until the affair had blown over.

He was not yet of age—twenty-four in his case—and he had never visited his estate. His uncle, for his own good reasons, had always thrown cold water on the idea, and had given him to understand that it was a mere fag end, and that it was greatly owing to his own advice and supervision, and that of a co-trustee, that it had proved so productive.

Roland may have had his doubts upon this matter, for he knew that his father had been well off, and that the fortune he was about to step into ought to be considerable. But the co-trustee was dead. No satisfactory explanation of his position was to be got from the lawyers into whose hands the management had lapsed, and he decided that he must go down and see for himself.

He knew that his inheritance lay apart on the sea-coast, in a wild western shire—a land where no man came. The old manor had long since fallen to ruin, and he had heard that it was a spot solitary in a wilderness, that great trees overshadowed the desecrated hearth, and a sluggish moat still rolled round, falling into a dismal pool, the more dismal legend of which still survived; that a mausoleum, a gateway, gardens, and farm buildings alone were left; lastly that the latter were inhabited, and that the place was managed by a steward.

Beyond this he knew nothing; a sudden and poignant curiosity to look upon the old home of his race rose in his heart.

" How will you go? " asked his uncle, who reluctantly approved when he could not prevent.

" Oh! I think I shall send on my portmanteau, take my saddle-bags, and ride down."

And so it comes that when next we meet Roland, he is cantering over the wind-swept moors and the great chalk ridges, which circle the melancholy demesne of Sombrewood.

CHAPTER VI.

It was at Pentecost, the feast of gladness;
horse and rider had idled through the leafy
lanes of June the livelong day, and with nightfall they came upon an ancient city, unchanged,
with the changing centuries.   It stood in a
hollow of the sand hills; a cathedral's massive
tower, the long ruined arcade of a palace, a
few dozen dwellings clustered round and on
the slope, far from railway and highway, without so much as a cockle-shell of its own upon
the waters, but living within a stone's-throw
of the murmurous ocean—such was this city.
A legend-haunted spot, and one unless seen
impossible to be believed in between the four
seas.   And when the horseman had eaten and
rested, and should have gone to his bed, he
looked out on a sky so heavenly fair that he
would have none of it. Only one more stage lay
before him, and if he would he might reach his
home ere midday.

The clock is striking two as he sallies out
into the fragrant purple night, and for many
miles a hedgeless road trends before him over
monotonous swelling crests of moor, a very race-

course of the storms lying breathless now under the star-besprinkled heaven. A heavy dew is falling soft upon all the new creation of the spring, vivifying it in the darkness for the light. As he rides, the solemn shadows of the mountain and the hill file past him in slow procession, and this strange youth breaks involuntarily into some chant from the offices of the Church, some pæan from the psalms of David, which comes to him straight out of his boyhood and the old college chapel, until the lonely way re-echoes with the song. And he rides on, facing to where the night lies paling in the east. He surmounts the crest of a low hill, and before him the landscape rolls away in slow waves of verdure into the distance, where looms a block of building crowned with towers, upon a pallid thread of estuary. He rises in his stirrup to peer forward; that must be the great fortress raised by the men of his own name and blood in the days when they were supreme in this land, and Sombrewood, with the Isles, the last poor relic of it all, lies a dismembered fragment, a few miles away yonder in the mist. His pulse quickens, and his face flushes; the emotion that comes upon him brings a choking to his throat, but he spurs on the faster, his face more hardly set. The cold air that plays upon his forehead ruffles the young bracken across the slopes, like a field of wheat. It is the first breath of the dawn, and presently, as he gets down into the valley, the woods close in upon him, and the leafage thickens until it arches overhead.

Minute by minute pulsating, the light throbs stronger and more strong, and as he plunges under the trees it glints on the white wet beech-stems, upon the crisp red under-leaves, upon the feathered mosses into which his horse sinks fetlock deep, upon the quivering birches, full of grace, that weep upon the hill.

And here is an inlet of salt water, and the wheel-tracks turning show a ford. It looks shallow, easy, and direct; but no! his horse refuses the water, plunges, and stands still—no coaxing will drive him through, and perforce the rider keeps along the beach, until he turns a bluff and emerges without warning into a wondrous scene.

At once the stupendous mass of the castle stands revealed on the farther shore, towering in its colossal bulk, like a fabled city, against the rosy gold of the daybreak, and, like a work of no human hands, it stands islanded in a lake of pale, cold, liquid fire. The tide is flowing up, running here in a stream of oil, and there, broken, swiftly over the stony shallows, where it hurries the clouds away, and under the limpid ripple lie the pebbles, cornelian, jasper, agate, to look at, every one of them. The spell of silence broods over all, the chance rustle of a leaf, the dropping of a twig, the ever-murmuring voices of the woods—these do but intensify the stillness; Nature waits with breath suspended—it is the fateful moment ere the dawn. "Cast thyself down, surely unawares we are come upon an hour of destiny." Some such thought he breathes,

and, strange to say, in all this beauty, it is
of death. A man should die certainly in such
a minute, but no—not yet—one more, and its
harmony will be complete. He is coming, the
God of all this world. "We are ready," cry
the river and the sea. "We are ready," echo
land and sky; the fair face of earth is like a
bride's awaiting, and she is tingling with expectation down into the lowest depths of her
being. Now the eastern heaven is heaped with
banks of dun-coloured cloud, but they are
melting away before His Face, they tremble at
His footstep. Lo! the veil of the Temple is
rent from top to bottom, and draws asunder like
the painted curtains of a stage.

Ha! didst thou see that? A shaft of fire
has gone out straight into the skies, pierced
the clouding nebulæ, and has sunk, quivering,
millions of miles away, right in the heart of the
zenith; another has shot out, and another, right
and left, and through all the eternal vaults
the Far-darter driveth his arrows. The distant
mountain is struck into flame and so also is the
near tower, and He has let loose a whole sheaf
upon the sea.

This is the fairy kiss of the prince, the bride
shakes off her slumbers, and turns her lips to
her beloved. Instant the sleeping world awakes;
the merry birds, calling to each other, wheel
and circle and chatter; myriad sea-fowl rise and
drift to and fro over the haven in a dazzling
cloud of snow. In the trees and in the flowers
there is a movement, the wood anemone and the

blue-bell are shaken with laughter, and every grass-blade quivers with the divine rapture of life.

Amidst those great rocks and yawning caves opposite, upon which the castle is piled, the sea birds find their home; there flits the scarlet-eyed sea-pyot, there the black snake-necked diver plunges and revels, and from the crannies come the red-legged chough, and the raven, amphibious both by circumstance. On the long ledges, perpetual sentinels, from imme-morial time, sit the elligugs, bowing always to the air; so thick they sit, that as they move in rhythm, yonder huge pinnacle seems to breathe in slow cadence. On that side all is stern and frowning in the shadow, on this the world is smiling in the sun. There the hoar rocks shoot up sheer; here the overladen branches dip themselves in the tide, and a virgin beach of silver sand stretches in long windings away. So pure is this tiny bay, that one pearly shell lying alone in its midst, catches the eye, and fascinates it.

Away up the slopes, spreads a hyacinth carpet of an azure robbed from heaven, and where the sward is green, nod single blossoms set like gems of great price, not in gold, but in a crust of diamond lace. Roland stands motion-less, half-expectant, but of what he knows not; his heart flooded with the beauty unrolled before him; as in a dream he looks abroad and around. Far up the hill the woods hang soft and tremulous, in a fairy mirage; the white mists are crawling from off the islands

of giant woodland, which rise from the broad
sweeps of meadow and of moor. Over a barren
cliff, from which the woods break away, spurts
a tiny crescent of intensest white, so steadily
shoots the fall that it appears quite motionless, but a little drift of spray clouds its
base, and even thus early Iris has fled her
dwelling in the skies and gone thither to
play.

He essays to break the spell and move away,
but he and his horse are caught half entangled
in a thicket; a cruel thorned briar encircles
them; a wild white rose is dashed in his face,
bedews it with her tears, kisses his lips, and
as he would remove it, rends them with a thorn,
leaving an after-taste of blood. But she herself
is the sacrifice, her petals fall fluttering to
the earth, the pale half-opened blossom is
trampled under his horse's hoofs, he is free and
away.

But who and what is this? Wisdom sprung
full armed from the head of Zeus! Who is this
that bounds forth out of the heart of Phœbus,
out of the red core of the sunrise, her dark eyes
shot with his lightnings? She has come out
of the sea like Venus, like her she walks the
waters, her zone is of gold, her hair filleted, her
mantle tipped with Miniver, and her feet are
bare. Before her bound two great fawn-
coloured creatures—*O dea certe*, with her atten-
dant panthers held in leash. As she flies, she
seems to skim the surface like a swallow, and
Roland, falling at one shock from the heavens to

the earth, finds in her the fairest vision he has ever beheld in life.

The dazzle in his eyes was too fierce to let him see distinctly, but for her the glory of the sunrise was full upon him, and this maiden, sooth to say, had an eye for beauty as keen, as was Roland's own. His horse, affrighted, swerved and dashed into the stream. The dogs, enjoying the fun, tore away from her and plunged in upon them, goading the beast half wild. Up rose a drench of spray; but the sand was firm, the current shallow, and the man sat like a centaur, laughing. The lady flew into the water, and at a word the dogs crouched silent, watching her with great eyes. She raised a bare white arm from under her mantle, and touched, or almost touched, the horse's blood-shot nostril. In a second he was down and sober, but with a shake that would have rattled a less firm rider than his master from his seat. The crystal waters rippled with musical murmur over her feet, she shook her wet skirts, gathered them up, and turned away without a word, but not without a smile.

Slender and active as a child, yet there was about her the budding dignity of womanhood; she might count perhaps nineteen summers, as the old novels used to say, and in truth she suggested the word. Summer must have had most to do with the ripening of that brilliant brunette complexion, and the matchless sun-bloom upon her cheek; summer was in her voice, in her eyes, and in her hair, and needs be that it was in her heart. Roland's first glance of criticism fell upon her feet, which shone wet like some pale-tinted sea-shell just cast upon the strand. "They are perfect," he observed mentally, with amazement; for will it be believed, owing to their barbarous foot-gear, our alternative selves hardly knew what an unspoiled foot was; and their unfortunate women were worse off in this respect than their men. Then his eyes went upwards to her figure and her face. "There is no fault in her," he decided. She had already gone a pace or two, when she cried, half turn-ing,—

"Roland—Tudor—come—come."

My hero sat rooted in his saddle, thunder-struck, and then he saw that she but called her dogs. Instantly he dismounted, and followed her, leading his horse.

"Pardon me, I am afraid I am trespass-ing."

"I am rather afraid you are," she replied, with an elaborate gravity and blushing, as be-comes a young lady caught barefoot, "but (carelessly) I am doing as much myself. I hope your horse was not frightened. I was bathing—that is—the dogs."

"Lucky dogs," thought Roland.

Now this "Jesuitical" young person was her-self going a-bathing, and under that long fur-trimmed mantle, which opened so cunningly at the waist, to show her zone, was a pretty garment, highly suitable for that purpose, but not for presentation before male eyes. He may have guessed as much, for he smiled.

"Perhaps," he said, "you can kindly put me into the right road, I fancy I have come too far. I tried a ford a mile or two back, which seemed by the wheel-marks to be well used, but I could not get my horse to face it. I confess, the tide was flowing heavily."

"Ah! Deadman's Ferry," she said, "it's most fortunate you didn't try it," and she looked at him with a half-frightened air. "It's only safe two hours before and after low tide, and it's a perfect trap to a stranger. The state of things down here is shameful," she continued, stamping her foot, "and so are the carelessness and ignorance of the people. There's hardly a sign-post within twenty miles. Everything goes to rack and ruin, and the very landlords are gone with the rest."

"It is scandalous," said Roland, delighted to have drawn her into conversation, "but who is responsible for it? You mentioned, just now, a name I think I know."

"Oh! my dogs. Yes, it's one of our names. The prettiest, I think, so I've divided it between them. But, I believe, there is a rightful heir, an infant—he should be a big one by this time—who owns this stretch of coast, with its superb scenery; but," and she grew more animated, seeing the kindred interest and amusement in Roland's eyes, "have you noticed the state that it's in? Was there a piece of fence the whole way as you came along, was there a gate on its hinges, or a stick or a stone where it should have been? It is beautiful, that is all one can say; and as for the way people trespass, why—"

"It is shocking," he put in, "but is there not a place called Sombrewood about here?"

"This is it; it is a large district, Sombrewood and the Isles, as it is called." And she pointed to the forms of three low islands away in the offing, like monsters sunning themselves in the blaze of the haven mouth, and stemming the wild surges of the open sea.

"The great house is up there, that's to say, it's down. All the houses are down about here. There are three on the estate, which do you want, the ruin, the dower house, or the manor?" and she looked at him very curiously.

"I have some—ah—business at the manor."

"Then that is your way."

"Is there a bridge?"

The maiden laughed. "There are but a couple in the county, none certainly in this part of it; but a quarter of a mile up the beach you will find a ford, you can pass at anything but a neap tide."

And so perforce he had to go, for she waved her hand. If she had erred in the conventionalities, she at least knew when to end the interview.

He went lingeringly, walking his horse. At intervals the deep bay of the hounds fell upon his ear, even after he had crossed, and turned his back upon the vale and the haven. He felt like an Adam expelled from paradise, but one who had left behind him his Eve; yet there was an inspiritment which communicated itself even to his horse's hoofs, and which then made him spur forward more eagerly to the site of the cradle of his race. And now he was coming in upon the place, and his mind was thronged with other thoughts, gay, fantastic, hopeful, for the most part, for what healthy youth can ever long look backwards on the past? The sun was creeping high and struck hotly upon the dusty road, on a cottage tumbled in woodbine, on a piece of red Elizabethan wall surmounted at intervals by stone balls.

The wall is lichen-stained and nods with flowers, and the high-road winds to a gate. All is still and solitary. A little child has run into the road, out of the cottage, to look after the horseman; inspired by heaven knows what instinct, the urchin gives him a lusty crow. And this is the home-coming for the last scion of that stock, which has held the place from before the day when that neer-do-weel younger son, Owen Tudor of the Guards, married his Royal and widowed mistress, and so founded a Kingly line.

Picture the scene. An inclosure rigidly kept and walled, like the garden of a good country house, nestling immediately beneath the precipitous brow of a chalk-down, where it lies, a very focus of sunshine. Its ancient timber, gnarled walnuts, red-stemmed pines, great hollies, thorns, and yews, bending their hoary heads together, clustering always in secret consultation, and sheltering what?—a heap of grass-grown mounds, out of which here and there crops a fragment of grey stone. Round about the verdant slopes of a moat, only partially visible; and below, again, a lakelet or pool shut in by dense overgrowth, so black, so stagnant, and so weird that even at broad noontide, on this hot summer's day, it is impossible to look upon it without feeling that therein is hid the story of a dozen crimes. The whole place cries aloud of many things, breathing both a blessing and a curse.

The entrance gateway still stands leading proudly up to the mounds. Upon either of the great stone pillars is the family crest wound with the motto, " Tu dors Rolande ! " which poignancy of mediæval wit no doubt expressed with proper force how intensely wide-awake the members of the family were generally considered to be. Now Roland was quite as much a family name as was Tudor; father and son had borne it unto this unbrokenly from the first, and it had caused trouble, for oh ! they were a truculent folk. So long as the Norman-French prevailed, the distinction between *Rolande père et Rolande fils* was simple enough. *Rolande père* had a chronic capacity for throat-cutting, marauding, and cattle-harrying; his son, out of the mere tenderness of his years, was a mere tyro at these manly sports. Only one of the warriors of this age had attained the limit of forty-five years, and he died of grief in that he was so crippled that he could no longer go forth to fight until the evening. The father once removed, *Rolande fils* stepped very prettily into his shoes, and led the way after the same fashion for his own boy. But degenerate days came. Fathers began to live to unconscionable ages; one of the Tudors reached fifty, and the individual who happened to be *fils* on the occasion felt that Heaven had indeed dealt hardly with him. Being a good son, however, he did nothing to hurry his father beyond dropping an occasional hint about doing as he would be done by, and so forth, which the old man, who was a true chip, took so much to heart that he set to work and succeeded in dying a natural death almost immediately after. Things went from bad to worse, as they usually do when they make the start; fathers continued to live up to ridiculous dates; three and even four generations of Rolands were in the world together at one time; the old social theories fell into discredit, and the confusion that ensued baffles description.

The family meanwhile had long subsided into the squirearchy; an event which took place after the wars of the Roses, when the Tudors were allowed to sit down again at Sombrewood, under the express condition that it should be nothing beyond a " pleasaunce."

" ' Pleasaunce ' forsooth," swore the then master, " so it should be." He had his ideas of what was pleasant, and if they differed from

other people's, he was sorry for it. The fine
old honours won by the cleaver and the
bludgeon—pardon! we should say the sword
and the lance—had been forfeited over and
again, the family had been attainted, and now,
when they would have set to work to carve out
their fortunes afresh, there was no one left to
carve them from. Their new neighbours were
a beggarly lot and took their pleasure otherwise. The then " warden " had caused to be
inscribed upon a pillar of the gate the word
" WEL COM " as a bait, which was intended to
convey shortly " step in and have it out," and
was put there as a hint to any good fellow
or friendly passer-by, lest wanting the rest
and refreshment of a fight, he should pass on
his way unrelieved. But it failed to draw, and
after a weary waiting the master had inscribed
upon the opposite post " BETT^R GON," and
had followed the word by going himself.

This worthy's history is characteristic of the
blood, and even after he was gone, he gave some
trouble, for, following the eccentric fashion of
the day, he had caused himself to be divided
into a number of small pieces, and as these fragments were widely distributed by will, the
funeral arrangements were necessarily complicated. No record tells where he all went to,
but he sent his heart to the Turks, swearing
that it had always been theirs in life; and so
generous was he to other friends, that when
it came to his own family he had nothing
left but the less honourable portions of his

person, which he bequeathed to his widow. The enormous responsibility of taking his heart to the Turks devolved on a trusty servitor, who went away with it and a large sum of money for his expenses; and who returned, after no doubt faithfully accomplishing the behest, in very fair time, considering the days and the distance; in fact, in about three weeks. In this time grief and the fatigues of travel had so told upon him, that he had been transformed from a spruce and worthy serving-man into a drunken sot, with hardly a rag to his back. But enough of these quaint legends, reverentially though one parts from them.

The family occupation was gone; even Churchmen counselled quietness and submission. In disgust the Tudors turned Protestant with the Deformation, and as they gained nothing by that, sulked in silence for at least six generations, keeping all the while family traditions, good and evil, right and wrong. Radicals where other people were concerned, of their own they were intensely Conservative, despite all inconvenience, and the Rolandic cognomen was an instance of this. The system had been adhered to until to-day, but the last and sole representative had all the honour and none of the inconvenience, and he had often thanked Heaven that he had his own name to himself, if it were only to be hanged in, should that mischance befall him.

But to return to the gate-posts. The legend that the truculent lord had caused to be scored

upon them so deeply was still visible, and
Roland's curious eye plainly traced the characters in the mouldered stone, WEL COM, on
the left, BETT^R GON on the right, and secretly
he wondered if it were well that he should lay
the unction of it to his own soul. The rusted
gate was unlocked and groaned on its hinges
like a living thing, as he swung it and rode
through in the bright sunlit silence. Nothing
stirred ; he went on and up to the mounds, and
stood upon the highest of them in their centre ;
there he stopped and looked round upon the
abomination of desolation.

To him the place was a grave, the grave of
things man learns to look upon as good, of
family, of honour, and inheritance. Yet how
prettily was the tomb decked with posies of wild
flowers : it was sheltered from rain and storm, and
countless motes of the sunbeams danced thick,
as though the place were their chosen home.
He stood long, turning to every point of the
compass, and questioning of the trees and the
grass and the stones. But they had told him
all their story at a first glance, and hereafter
they were dumb. His horse, used to his moods
and tolerant of them when they did not last too
long, grew impatient, pawed up the short grass
to see what it was worth, striking at once upon
the stone beneath. Thereupon he gave a snort
of disgust, shook himself, and finally espying a
lady very like one of his acquaintance in a field
beyond, uttered a prolonged whinny of invitation, which was promptly responded to. Roland

flicked his ears in reproof, and cantered him gently down to where a line of long, dilapidated out-buildings with a tower showed signs of human habitation. His brain was whirling with the many thoughts that came thronging in upon him, but his foremost was to find out the bailiff—Tyrrel by name—and his second was of breakfast.

Now this Tyrrel was an old man, long past his work, as was already proved, and this sultry noon, after his wont, he sat basking and smoking an early pipe in the porch. He was good for little beyond this and telling long-winded stories of the old place and its former inhabitants. For him it was peopled with ghosts, with ladies and cavaliers, and their serving-men and suites, so that when he casually looked up and beheld a bare-headed stripling come waving his hat and riding a white charger adown the mounds towards him, the sun and the breeze playing in his hair, and making a brave picture of him as he came, the old man merely crossed himself, looking upon the vision with a friendly smile, and said,—

"Ah, well—ah, well now, which of them, I wonder, will be that?"

But when the horseman did not vanish into thin air, when he pricked on with gallant show, filling the place with his presence and his voice, and descending, his horse's hoofs struck fire upon the flints in the shadow of the stable-yard, then, indeed, the bailiff rubbed his eyes and stumbled to his feet.

No doubt crossed him, none other would have so come.

" 'Tis he," he muttered. " He is come home, the young master himself. Now, oh, Lord! dost Thou dismiss Thy servant, according to Thy word, in peace."

And as Roland dismounted, the old man seized him by the hands and gripped and kissed them; but his tongue was too great for his mouth, for the moment he was speechless. And soon there was a commotion in this forgotten old-world nook, which had drowsed so peacefully a quarter of a century past. Mrs. Tyrrel came out, and, proud of her youth and activity—for she was five years younger than her husband, and by so much the more carried away by her feelings—she flung herself on her knees before Roland and embraced him, crying as though he was the saddest sight her old eyes had ever beheld. Then dropped in the labourers, an odd half-dozen, silent and deferential, with doffed caps, who stood round stupidly, until one brighter than the rest ran off to the village church, a mile away at least, and presently there came a merry chiming down the vale. So the church bells rang at intervals all through the summer's day, as though they were intoxicated, as certainly their ringers eventually became, out of the bounteous largess that fell to them at last.

Breakfast was procured, and lodgings were found for the unexpected guest. None so bad either of them, considering—the latter in the stable gatehouse, which had long been appropriated as the bailiff's quarters. This building was, like the rest of the fragments, of red brick, stone-dressed, and of the ordinary square Tudor type, battlemented, with a turret at the corner and an oriel over the arch; and the oriel-room, as it was called, was hurriedly set in order for Roland's entertainment. It was a cheery room and boasted of some panelling, a stone chimney-piece, and a private stairway down the turret, which led on to the oldest portions of the walls belonging to the period when the manor had been a fortress. These now formed part of the terrace-walk. The ivy had pushed round the oriel, and some fresh young shoots had spurted through the imperfect lattice into the room, and there was a rose looking in at the window, so that Roland, as he sat down to one of those breakfasts which only the country can give in perfection, was inclined to think he had fallen upon his feet.

As he sat, he pondered. The question was, what next? He seemed to have come to a dead stop in his life; a fanciful barrier appeared to be blocking him, turn which way he would. Of course there was a great deal that might be done here, if he would only come and set to work at it. A great deal, for instance, in cutting, trimming, and re-planting those woods which he had seen, and then there were those mysterious rights of his over the foreshore that he did not understand, but about which

Tyrrel had spoken to him certainly within the first five minutes. He could do very well in this room, which was evidently a spare one and kept for guests, and the old man needed help, for, as he admitted, things were going to rack and ruin for want of it.

Then his thoughts turned to his uncle. It was owing to him that he had been kept in the dark so long—for that gentleman's own good purposes, without doubt. He and the lawyers had manipulated the place among them so long as it was possible, and this was the result. His own first step on coming of age must be to gather the reins into his hands, but one of his trustees was dead, affairs were not arranged, and he could obtain only the meagre details which had first determined him to run down and judge for himself. Year by year the returns had dwindled—into hundreds latterly, and Tyrrel had already said that with a master there to do the work, they ought to be doubled.

It ought to be done, of course it ought; every other fellow who had a place of this kind looked after it, worked it up, and got all he could out of it; but, after all, what did he want with the money? If by exiling himself for life and working out his days down here he could put so many hundreds a year more in his pocket, what would he be the better? He had enough for his own wants, and could hardly feel called upon to shed the sweat of his brow in increasing his uncle's allowance, which was probably what it would come to if the estate

were made to yield more than it did at
present.

But why not, on the other hand, work hard,
rebuild the old house and the old family afresh
on a firmer basis? He might, no doubt, if he
tried. Why not marry (and his thoughts in-
tuitively flew back to a certain hour of the morning) and settle down? Why not subscribe to the
hunt, re-stock the woods with game, keep a
pack of otter hounds and a stable of horses, an
open house, have all his friends down, and play
the old English gentleman? It was all in his
grasp if he cared for it—at least, on a moderate
scale. Other fellows did these things and said
it answered, and that they got through their
time pleasantly enough. And all the while that
he was proposing these things to himself, he
knew very well that they would never do. The
conviction that there was a great career before
him, though he could make no guess at its
shape, never left him for an instant; as it never
does leave the man once inspired with it. After
trifling for a while, he dismissed these musings,
laughing at their self-deception.

Now the worthy couple below had no intention of leaving him long with his own company;
and he, as he had certain questions on his
mind which presented themselves as burning,
and were bound to be elucidated before he came
to any decision as to the future, was glad to
see the old man's face in the doorway.

" Now, sir, I'd just like wi'out the wastin'
of good time, which is always short, to be ex-

plaining to ye something about this flotsam and jetsam," he said, as he hobbled in.

"Very good, Tyrrel, very good; but isn't it a bit lonesome here?" said Roland, with a dash at a change of topic, for he was rather afraid of this, and wished to bring up another, though he shirked a direct question.

"Ou ay, sir, it be a bit lonesome for young folk, we old never think o't. But I was reminding ye—"

"Oh! yes, yes. Now I suppose there *is* society in the neighbourhood?"

"Ou ay, muster, there's a deal of it, such as it is. There's Muster Tomlinson, o' Tilbury. Now there's an instance. Ye'll not believe, afore that man had been six months in the place, what will he do but lay claim to the beach for thirty yards, wantin' for to build of a pier! Ay, but we had him there!"

"Oh! confound it—him I mean. Yes, of course. Do you say he's near here?"

"He's about the nighest; if you get the tide low, and direct across the haven, t'aint more than ten mile. Bought Strathmere's place, you'll recollect, sir. Bless me! What am I thinking of? Pardon, sir, and you never here before, so of course you can't. Then there's Robinson's; he bought t'old castle below, that you'll mind—the Avondales that was. Oh, Lord! 'tis sad, sir. But there, he's built a fine new place at t'other end o' the property, and he has put a lot o' money into it—God knows, not before it was wanted! Then there's

Griddles', up i' the north; a good fellow after his sort, while he lived. It's Mrs. Griddles' now. They've got all the Carew property. Ah! it's a sad, sad story. Thank God, sir, there's one of us still left to come back to his own."

Roland whistled.

"Let's see, then we have "— and he checked the names on his fingers—"Tomlinson *versus* Strathmere, Robinson *versus* Avondale, Griddles *versus* Carew. So that's what I've to expect, is it? And is there no one else?"

"Ay! but there's Trelawney, o' course," answered the bailiff, with a shade of reluctance. "'Tis he's master of Sombrewood, saving your presence. He's bought the place, bit by bit, as it went, you'll mind, sir, and he's took the dower house for his babby."

"D—n the baby!" exclaimed Roland, with irritation. "I suppose it'll come to the same thing with me as it has with the rest of the old lot—starvation in the slums."

"God forbid, sir; ye'll no starve here."

"And are these people all, and have they any families?" asked Roland, his heart sinking.

"Ou ay, sir, 'tis about the lot, and they're pretty thick with olive branches. There's Tomlinson and Robinson have both got the house full o' young kids, and Mrs. Griddles—"

"Well?"

"She's a daughter."

"Bah!" said Roland, getting up. The blow

had fallen, he had better go before he fell entangled in meshes of this sort. " I'll send a line to my lawyer, Tyrrel. I think I shall hardly be able to stay perhaps more than a week or so, just to set things going." And he dashed off—

" Sombrewood and the Isles (how strange it was to write !), June 4th.

" DEAR SIR,—In consequence of the total want of anything like accommodation here, I shall—"

" Eh, man," persisted the bailiff, astonished at this spasmodic movement, " but I was telling ye of the daughter."

" Yes, yes, I know," said Roland, writing on hurriedly.

" And I was going to say," pursued his companion deliberately, " that ye'll not be finding much society there, if ye were thinking o't, for the lady "—here his voice quavered—" has been married twice, and she fifty-five if she's a day. Now about the foreshore, if ye'll listen."

" Oh! bother," said Roland, pitching his pen across the room and breathing again with vast relief. " Look here, Mr. Tyrrel. I'll listen fast enough when I come back. I'll just go over now and see those fellows who are ringing the bells."

CHAPTER VII.

IT was a quaint, rambling building, with a wooden, shingled spire, lying on a sylvan slope, about a mile distant, to which Roland bent his steps. Its age was stated at various fabulous figures by the villagers, and even the sternest antiquary would usually concede it some 700 years, and allow that its site had probably been occupied by an earlier edifice.

Scalp remnants that once formed covering to some unhappy Dane were nailed upon the west door. With your own thumbnail of to-day you had only to explore a little under the rusty ironwork (date *circa* fifteenth century), and bits of thick dry skin, of the consistency of saddle-leather, out of which protruded distinct black hairs, would at once reward the search. If that did not satisfy you, then you were indeed an impossible creature.

The tower had been built by the devil in a single night, which may have accounted for its rough-and-ready appearance; this had been a penance given him by the saintly Saxon, patron of the edifice, in punishment for some rude remark the former had made during the building. The saint, who was certainly a 'Romanist' if he was anything, had, of course, washed his hands of the place at the Deformation, though they still had the impertinence to call it by his name: but to-day—in honour, no doubt, of the return of a patron after his own way of thinking (the living was in the Tudor gift)—he was pleased to step in and work a prodigy. As the heir set foot in the porch, the ringers burst into a peal of such fury that one of the bells turned completely over on its pivot. The rope whirled the lad who held it up the first story of the tower, and dropped him neatly in the organ-loft, which looked into it, twenty feet above, frightened out of his seven senses, but unhurt.

Now, as has been said, the devil had a vested interest in the tower, but the organ-loft was part of the church; clearly, therefore, the saint had interfered and outwitted him, as a good saint should. Clearly, also, Roland's footfall had set the magic going, and the fame of the incident was noised abroad afterwards, until he came to be looked upon in the light of a saint or demi-god himself; for the peasant labourer of England is hazy on such subjects, and to the heir with such a history at his back, ready to concede anything—in reason. The noisy crew were dismissed at last to their dinner, and Roland stayed to wander through the church alone.

The mausoleum was on his mind. "I will take counsel," he said to himself, "with the bones of the dead." Against one aisle lay the

Tudor chantry, through a blocked stone screen in which was a door: it took him ten minutes to turn the key. When at length he accomplished this, his steps were stayed a moment on the threshold; the dust everywhere lay thick, and rose in a cloud from his footfall. The chapel was literally choked with tombs, and they were one and all those of his own dead. He walked in alone, with his head bared and bowed, himself the last bright spark that burned amid the ashes of so many sires.

Few things can affect a man more powerfully than to visit for the first time some forsaken shrine lying remote, and there to see the name he bears cut in the mouldering brass or stone, the self-same arms upon the shield, and the self-same motto twined about it that is graven on the signet ring round his finger at this hour. To read there the curt records of the perished lives, the date of birth and death, or to note, perchance, yet older stones wanting even this brief chronicle, but telling mutely of all else gone utterly; lives which, in hidden ways, have moulded him to what he is, and but for which he who stands there would never have been : this is a stern lesson.

There was a small altar at one end of the chapel, for whenever one of the family reverted to the old faith, as had several times occurred, the old instincts had fallen strong upon him, and he had continued the masses for the dead. It was illegal, of course, punishable with death for near a couple of centuries; but the living was in the family hands, and at the worst of times they had managed to secure the right kind of man to fill the place. This chapel was, besides, their private property, quite apart from the Church, and they were not people to stop at a trifle when they meant a thing. The last heir of the blood, standing there in the midst of them, felt strangely at home. As stone after stone appealed to him and spoke, he went slowly from one to another, striving to shape a history from the incongruous mass, but without success.

The earliest appeared to be a plain, dark slab of purbeck, uninscribed, upon which was a sword with a cross hilt, as if laid down, upon this again was the monogram, " I. H. S.," and adjacent was a block with a rude lettering :—

" Hic jacet Guillielmus Tudor, miser et indignus Sacerdos, expectans resurrectionem mortuorum sub sigma T."

He passed on. Hard by lay prone a magnificent effigy, colossal in size, of a knight in chain mail ; around this figure was a mutilated inscription, beginning " *Orate viator*—" and ending " *Miserere mei Deus.*" In the pavement, near the altar, lay the brass image of a knight in plate armour, with the legend in English. It ran :—

" Here is ye buried under this grave
Rolande Tudor, may God hym save—
Longe tyme Lorde of Sombrewood hight.
Hav mercie, Chryst, Thou full of mighte."

Then came the last of the Gothic age ; it was
an altar tomb bearing a great brass with two
figures under canopies and the date 1515.   It
read :—

> "Here lyeth the body of Roland Tudor, Squire,
> Son and heire of Sir Roland Tudor, Knighte.
> Praye for their soules with heartie desire,
> That both may be sure of eternal lyte ;
> Calling to remembrance that every wighte
> Must needes dye, and therefor let us praye,
> As others for us may doe another daye."

These five appeared to be all five centuries
had to show.   Five centuries of living and
dying, of being born, married, and buried—
think of it.

Now came a change.   The blessed light of
the glorious " Reformation " had been poured by
their royal kinsman, the gentle Henry, over
the country, even to its remotest parts ; and
what the improvement of the people was, might
be judged by contrasting the next tomb with
that of the wretched Popish priestling in the
corner ; the man who, dying obviously in blank
despair, had pronounced his own epitaph,
" Miser et indignus."   The tomb in question
was what the stone-mason is apt to call " a
downright 'andsom' thing."   It stood out on
the pavement quite three feet, and it rose right
into the roof.   Upon it was a gentleman in a
night-gown, which, for reasons best known to
himself, he wore over a suit of classic armour.
In spite of this dual garmenture, he showed

a great deal of his person, and by him lay a lady in an equally anomalous dress, who showed a great deal of hers. They were evidently in bed, for they lay on a kind of mattrass, which was rolled to form a pillow at the end, and there was a sheet hanging down on them from an ordinary breakfast urn ; (this in a moment of erratic flight had alighted above,) and another, which they had presumably kicked off when it was too hot (a thing they must have been sorry for afterwards, for the place was usually cold as the grave), hanging untidily over the foot of the sarcophagus on which the mattrass was laid. That they should both have got in with their clothes on seemed inexplicable. There had been a quarrel perhaps on this very account, for the lady lay stolidly staring at the roof, while her husband, who had turned his back upon her, had raised himself on the pillow with his elbow, and was doing his best to explain that though appearances were against him, they were soon set right, for with his forefinger he drew attention to the following tablet :—

" Here lyeth, in Sublyme Confidence of a Glorious Resurrection, Roland Tudor of Sombrewood, in the County of ———, Esquire. . . . He was a lovinge Husbande, a model Father, a complete Friend, a generous Benefactor. He was universallie loved, and throughout reverenced ; in his single Person were all good Qualities vnited, until Death, jealouse of so perfect an Ensample, alreadie too longe delayed below, wrapped him suddenlie to Heavenlie Spheres, as the onlie ones fitted for such Excellence. His Wyfe hath raised this loftie Stone, a type of his aspiring Soule, in Gratitude. . . ."

An elderly and jovial gentleman, in white marble and a bag wig, next claimed his descendant's attention. He lay holding out to the visitor the right hand of good fellowship; comfort appeared to have been his first thought. He had had a good sensible sofa, also in white marble, wheeled in, whereon he might take his eternal rest, and he lay sprawling across it at his ease. His ostentatiously French paper-bound novel tossed down on the floor beside him, he was stonily contemplating the left buckle of his great square-toed shoe, which he had raised slightly for the purpose; and beneath him was graven a list of virtues, which would have done credit to an angel from heaven. This was sufficiently demonstrated by the celestial being who hung wistfully over him, plainly preferring his company to that of her fellows, and about to transfer the diadem from her own brow to the sausage curls of the bag wig.

But after all these were vulgarisms. There stood in the centre of the pavement, throned in solitary magnificence, a sepulchral stone which might well have made the traveller long for an awful bereavement, so that he might mourn it with such chaste elegance of sorrow. It was a melancholy urn of sable marble, veinless, glittering, and inscribed with a single word, " FUERUNT."

Here came a gap in the chronological order. The brilliant economic discovery of covering a multitude past, present, and to come, by the mere use of the plural and the perfect tense, seemed to have sufficed for several generations; probably the next who died despaired of beating it, and the family funds by this time were getting into the dregs.

It is not easy to divide and subdivide a limited property into a dozen portions for several generations, as the Tudors had taken to doing. That is a game which plays itself rapidly out, especially if none stoop to bring fresh grist to the mill. And the Tudors would never soil their hands with that sort of thing. Oh, no ! their younger sons would go into the army and the navy, and die off at five-and-twenty in debt and beggary, or they would turn Protestant and scrape into a curacy, or get hold of the family living, or cozen a rich widow, and the girls would run away, or fly to a convent; but as for learning a trade, or earning an honest livelihood in a profession, it is but just to say, the idea of such dirty work had never occurred to any one of them. The consequent decay of the race, and the opportune falling in of certain leases, had set Roland's grandfather upon his legs, when the family had been at its lowest ebb; and that the last monument in the chapel was more than worthy of its predecessors, was accounted for by the fact that he had erected it to himself in his own life-time.

He had been, as a young man, a lesser light of the Young-England movement, and it was his whim to have inserted in the pavement close to the doorway, where all the world might trample on it, a splendid brass, prodigiously emblazoned and enamelled in colour. The intense mediævalism of this monument put the Gothic tombs to the blush; there was not a saint nor an angel upon it, but his or her limbs were visibly distorted all through. He himself was represented in plate armour, and his spouse in a horned headdress of the same date. The inscription was the most cramped and illegible of them all, and his son with difficulty deciphered the characters: "eke z ye Dame Jemima hys wyfe " . . . a style of reference to his own grandmother which tickled him exceedingly. He walked round again, but these, with a few chaste stone " blisters," which had come out upon the wall to mere wives, daughters, or younger sons, were all.

This was the epitome of seven centuries, yet, except for the earlier ones, they served only to raise a smile of derision on the face of the heir. Half these men were certainly damned, if human action may be judged at all. Yet they leered at him pleasantly in marble, as who should say, "All is well." He was not superstitious, but he had half expected that the spot would be thick with ghosts; at such a time, and in such a place, how could so much testimony be silent, and to *him*? Again he looked round; there was no crowd of witnesses, the carved and painted effigies, mockeries of life, eyed him in a silence that grew into ghastliness.

" Nay, my master, but 'tis a fool's portion to be set thus for all time, conning an hundred

lyes concerning virtues I did never possess,"
mutely protested the man in bed.

"Prithee, my good sir, couldst look, as I
have done, unmoved, on thy right shoe-buckle
through two centuries?" appealed his neighbour.

And from far out of the years came yet
another voice, "Miserable and unworthy, I
await the resurrection of the dead, under the
sign of the cross."

The tattered bannerets hung motionless upon
the wall, the rusty helmets grinned and gaped
from the rafters, but the helpless fluttering of
a bright butterfly, wrecking its beauty in the
cobwebs of ages on the diamond panes, was all
the life and motion of the place. Taking the
poor prisoner in the hollow of his hand, Roland
went out, slamming the iron-bound door; and
in the echo it was as if peals of ugly laughter
rang through the vault behind him. With a
strong feeling of discomfort he hurried out into
the sunshine, and through the rank grass of
the neglected churchyard. The record of the
past, which he had read, was only such as
scores of families had to show, a vast heirloom
of vacuous inanity, and as he went away, he
breathed a sigh of relief, that he stood a man
free of these things and independent, with
his head above water. At the same time
he was bitterly aware that if poverty and hard
times had not killed off all the rest of his
kindred, neither health nor fortune would have
been his.

But what was to be his course? As he

walked back, sad and solitary through the meadows, visions came to him.

It was a day or two later, and the scene was not a hundred miles away. In a corner of one of the great parks or forests that stretched over all this western side of the country, in a glade where the trees had been felled to make a hollow, and by the side of a slow-flowing stream, which here widened to a lake, stood a little dower house, a modest edifice, but the picture of an English cottage home.

A flight of steps leads down from the French windows under the broad verandah, and the waters lave them with mimic wavelets. Under this verandah are rugs and rocking-chairs, you may sit in the latter where they are, and drop a line into the waters, and you may pull out, if you are lucky, jack, and tench, and minnow, and fresh-water pearl oysters, with real pearls in them; but you must not go a-fishing for these with rod and line; they are hidden in the roots of the reeds on the bank where it winds away to the river. Wonderful things the lake hides in its black breast; the lady of the lake had once caught with her bare hands a trout which lay asleep basking in the shallows, having gone to explore where the stream fell in; but that reminds one that she is on the steps now, and she is far more wonderful than the rest, a pearl such as no oyster will yield you.

There she stands, with a cloud of cle-

matis hanging from the eaves about her,
and roses and honeysuckle, which make it all
shockingly untidy, as they litter their tinted
petals on the white steps and the black, black
water. Here and there, the sun comes in
through the foliage and strikes the jetty surface
of the pool and turns it milky in the depths,
great blossoms of white and yellow water-lilies
float before her, and the swans rustle between
the young cockled leaves which lift, too strong
to float.

Is it possible to paint so pretty a picture in
words? Can one summon at all upon the
retina the faintest vision of the fresh delicacy
of the woman, of the bloom upon her cheek, of
the overflow of light that is spilled everywhere
from out the liquid depths of those great, grave-
gay eyes? How make this ink-stained page
exude the sweet incense of the flowers? how
bring to the nostrils the odorous fragrance of
the morning air, which plays upon her face
fair to tears?

We have seen her before; this time she has
condescended to the use of a pair of shoes,
with the superadded effeminacy of stockings,
and she is feeding her swans with biscuits and
rose-leaves, but chiefly with the latter, for she
is in deep thought. She is slim and supple to
a marvel, is this beauty, but then she is not yet
nineteen. And is she a little scornful with her
pouting lip? I cannot say, the servants do
not think so—nor the dogs, nor the swans:
but the few visitors that chance brings this

way are apt to say so sometimes. Now she is twirling something white above her head, as though she would toss it to the swans. Ah! to lop off that satin hand and forearm—say, just where the lace falls upon it, and, yes, with just that turn of the wrist, to run away with it, to put it into a glass case, and there preserve it as a thing of beauty and a joy for ever.

Alas! the flower withers in the plucking, your only chance is to take the plant entire with all its bloom, and this child is a perfect nosegay, which will wither certainly if the sun strike too hot or the wind too cold—then, with most tender nursing, she may last through the glory of the day. That must be the bargain of the man who takes her, and let us see at least what will be the outside of the transaction.

She is an orphan, living alone, under the nominal protection of a guardian, who is invisible for months together, sometimes for years. The little dower house has been settled upon her, and a few hundreds of income—riches, unfathomable riches she has ever found them. With her are several old and responsible servants, who, in some way that she knows nothing of, have been attached to and employed by her family since long before she can remember. She has her own horse, her pony-carriage, seventeen dogs, a pet canary, a pet hedgehog, a pet—but it would be difficult to say where the livestock ends. She is her own mistress now, and is understood to be an heiress in the future, but to what, she hardly knows.

Her guardian is one of the new men who have bought up the county among them. More than half the wild stretch of sea-girt, inlet-cloven coast, with its jumble of rock and forest and meadow, known since before the Conquest as Sombreweald, is his. This, with "The Isles" off the coast, formed the district of which the Tudors were hereditary wardens. Now, the manor farm, and a stretch of forest, with its foreshore, and the barren, storm-beat rocks which guarded the entrance of the haven, unproductive of anything beyond sea-birds and rabbits, are the sole relics of the property that Time has spared their representative. Bit by bit, century by century, the great estate has gone from them. Once they had owned the county, and the huge fortress at the top of the haven had been built to dominate it.

After the wars of the Roses the position was no longer tenable, the castle was dismantled; the manor became their head-quarters, and great portions of the forest lands about were sold—still the estate remained "Sombrewood and the Isles." But by-and-by a great mansion having been built on the alienated land, and the manor having fallen below count, a new "Sombrewood" arose, destined to no happier fortune. It had long since fallen to decay, and Mr. Trelawney, the last purchaser, had found it quite beyond repair. Built in Queen Anne's time, on a princely scale, it had proved a veritable white elephant to two or three families. In the grounds, how-

ever, stocd the dower house, and here the late
unhappy possessors had only just managed to
exist until the crash came that swept them
away for ever. So then the great mansion
stood in ruin, beautiful and desolate to behold.
It was built of a fine stone which was bleached
snowy by the weather, and a colonnade of
monoliths ran along the front, but it was roofless and open to the sky. As any bright day
you paced there and trod the weed-grown
marble pavements, and looked out at the blue
sky over your head, then adown the great
green glades half a mile wide, and upon the
giant timber which loomed monstrous and
seeming out of all proportion upon the upland,
and watched the swift sea-lights sweeping the
feathered surges below, the slow beam as it crept
across the herd of browsing deer, illusion fell
upon you. You were treading a nameless
temple of the ancient world, and you breathed
a prayer to its forgotten gods. And the great
charm of all was, that there had been no
plan nor deceit; nature, art, and chance had
whimsically combined to fashion this gem and
to make it unique. A ruin of a hundred years
in England gathers upon itself all the age of
a thousand years in Greece.

Mr. Trelawney, who was a bachelor, had
had the dower house set in order for his
ward; and that done, prettily and well, he
betook himself again to his old courses of
German baths and French watering-places,
while he left her with a responsible governess,

to be happy as best she might, and for long spaces at a time. When she grew older, he sent them abroad, giving her the best of masters on every subject to which she showed an inclination, and sparing no expense on her education. The girl responded with extraordinary alacrity, but although she learned many things, she never learned exactly her own circumstances or position, and this troubled her. They told her no more than that her name was Sybil Grey. While still a child, she had spent half her time in speculating as to her place in creation, and in building up superb edifices of fiction, which now and then some chance discovery would bring down with a crash. Once pulling over a shelf of books (for she had free access to the library), she had opened an odd volume of poems, a dirty, dusty little book, and her wondering eyes had fallen upon the lines,—

> " Drink, weary pilgrim, drink, and pray
> For the kind soul of Sybil Grey,
> Who built this cross and well."

And then and there she had sat down and read the whole poem from beginning to end.

The incident was a small one, but it gave a bent to all her after-life. The chance allusion to a former Sybil Grey, whose kindly fountain had quenched the thirst of a dying knight, formed in her mind a sort of parable, in which she found a mystical significance. She took to reading romantic poetry wherever she could lay hands upon it, to learning it by heart in thousands of lines, and even to writing it; but this she soon gave up, wise enough to recognize that power of thought and language is not a girl's gift. Still her mind and soul were flooded with unwritten poetry, field after field of enchanted meadow had been thrown open to her, everywhere were soft beds of asphodel, and thither she wandered and reposed without stint, happy, but with a nameless longing, for what she knew not, and with a necessary vagueness of purpose, for she had been brought up without religion of any kind. Undoubtedly Mr. Trelawney had had his own reasons for what he did, and for the way in which he did it—probably they were bad ones, but that does not concern us. To the little world round, as well as to herself, the girl was something of a mystery from first to last.

It may seem strange that Tyrrel had not spoken of her to Roland when discussing the neighbours, but as a fact he had. This was the baby whose importation he had alluded to, and there were other reasons why his information was not exact. In the first place the loss of the greater portion of the Sombrewood demesne, though it had occurred before he was born, was a sore point with the old man; he ignored that piece of the county altogether, or referred to it unhandsomely as the scrag end. In the second, Mr. Trelawney was an absentee, as has been said, and often took his ward away for months together in the summer-time. And

in the third—well, of course Tyrrel remembered,
when he came to think of it, that he had seen
the child, when was it? A month or so since,
ah! well—it might have been a year or two,
and she was running with her hoop, or was it
trying her pony over a broken fence? And he
remembered, too, that she looked quite a big
girl in her habit; but what was the pretty chit
to him, one also who had the ineffaceable slur
of new blood in her veins?

But all this while the lady has been left
twirling her letter to and fro.

" Shall I go, shall I not?" she repeats to
herself for the hundredth time. " The creature
is too dreadful. There is only one word for
her, and that, I suppose, I mustn't use. To
write to me like this, when I have only seen her
twice! but then it's deadly dull here, and I've
not met a soul since we left Vienna last
August, and this sort of thing comes but
once a year—not always that," she sighed.
" Let me see," and she re-read the note,
which was scrawled in the hand of a kitchen-
maid :—

" The Rookery, Friday.

" DEAR OLD SILLY,—Will she come and take
her midday feed with us on the 14th, 1.30
sharp? Some of the boys will be over, and I
must have a she or two to meet them. She is
the femalest I know; come to its ever affec^te,
" VICTORIA NAGE."

" It's monstrous!" ejaculated the girl, click-
o 2

ing her satin heel on the step; "but, after all, she's a kind woman, if she *is* a woman. She did get my poor dog out of the trap that day, and did bandage his broken leg, and was awfully good to him, wasn't she, Roly?"

The big dog sauntered up, and sitting on his haunches, thrust out his great paw; she took it, examined and felt it, with the air of a connoisseur.

"Yes, old man, we must go, if it's only out of gratitude; your leg and my heart restored, after most serious fracture; we owe her that, and we must pay our debts."

So Miss Grey turned to her pretty ebony and ivory *secrétaire* in the bay window, and wrote the following :—

> "The Dower House, Sombrewood,
> "Saturday.

"DEAR LADY VICTORIA NAGE,—I shall be pleased to join your luncheon party on the 14th, which I gather from your note is what you wish.

> "I am,
> "Sincerely yours,
> "SYBIL GREY."

"I suppose she'll think I don't know how to address her," mused the writer, her lip curling slightly; "well, it's time she had a lesson in manners. Whatever I may be to her— Victoria, she shall *not* be to me," and with that she despatched the note.

The Nages were merely visitors, it should be explained, who had come down into the wild country for sake of the sport, and had taken a lodge for the fishing. There was considerable evidence as to the actual existence of a Sir Something Nage, but hardly anything was seen or known of him, and what little fame was attached to his name, arose solely from his being the husband of the celebrated Lady Victoria. She it was who set their establishment on foot, laid out the sport according to the season, bred the horses, broke the dogs, managed the farm, rated the maids, and paid the men. She had back enough for all, while the individual supposed to be her lord—good, easy man—loafed through life, and took his pipe and his glass when and where he listed, which was pretty often, and in many places, thanking Heaven for the good gift of a wife who saved a fellow such a lot of trouble.

It may seem a pity to spoil sport, but it is best to be honest at the outset and tell the plain truth, which was, that Lady Victoria Nage was hopelessly insane, a lunatic at large —very much at large. There was not a single member of her family who did not count a loose screw. This was not necessarily of a mischievous description ; very often, on the contrary, of a rather benevolent turn was the screw, but it was loose. The most serious feature of the case was, that weak-headed young women, with the subtle instinct for which there is no word when it pertains to a lady, were led to follow, if only distantly, this odd creature with a handle to her name, under the curious impression that she represented in some mysterious way the right thing. Worse still, weak-headed young men were led to aid and abet her in all her " fun," from " pitch and toss " to manslaughter downwards.

This may seem to cover a large field, but " pitch and toss " was the mildest form of play indulged in at " The Rookery," or, as it was facetiously termed, " The Nursery." And for the manslaughter, as all the world knew, Lady Victoria was a traveller, and, as her first work (which had such a prodigious run), " Nigger Potting on the Pongo," amply proved, not a person to be lightly trifled with. In our own highly civilized day, the above will read like a romance, but the curious social development which was in process at the time of the shock to the world's system, which was explained early in the book, was, undoubtedly, leading up to such eccentricities.

In the end, then, Miss Grey resolved to go, and whether there were any after-thought, in her mind of a strange cavalier like a prince, come out of olden days, whom her own eyes had seen, it is impossible to say ; if there were, it never shaped itself into words, and hence the present historian has no right whatever to intrude, with the idea of shaping it for her.

One morning about this time, Roland was wandering through his woods, divided between admiration of the wilderness and despair at its devastation, when an extraordinary apparition confronted him. He had been pondering many things, and his thoughts had reverted often to the morning of his arrival. When and where should he see *her* again? It ought to be in just such a place as this. And this tract of forest was surely haunted. Could there be such a land of dead memories, groves and thickets inviolate as these, and not peopled with fancies? To-day, as he walked along under the giant walls of crumbling sandstone, all festooned with the drooping foliage of hanging woods that were glittering with dew, he had stopped, and as through a frame of star leaves he had caught a vision of the great castle painted like a film upon the far distance, he had waited a little, saying aloud to himself,—

"A minute, and King Arthur, with his knights, will come riding down through the trees, or perhaps it will be the ladies of his Court, or perhaps the Queen herself."

Then he went on, but he often stopped again and listened, with a laugh at the conceit, for the jangling of their armour and the crash of their horses' feet as they should come cantering down from the heights, and now—lo! it was no fancy—behind the screen of leaves the dry twigs were crunching under a horse's hoof.

It was a woman—and she came alone through the echoing wood.

Pah! what was this? A stench of tobacco? And was this a woman?

Roland rubbed his eyes, for the figure sat astride a raking chestnut, and wore leather over-alls, with spurs like a trooper's, under a short skirt, which did little more than cover the knee, and was the hollowest pretence at drapery ever beheld. "It" was habited further in a loose monkey jacket, a waistcoat, and peaked cap; in one hand was a hunting-crop, and in the other a big cigar. That it had perceived him was evident, for in the twinkling of an eye its right knee was flung back from across the saddle, its skirts were pulled down, and it had resumed the semblance of a woman— sufficiently, at least, to be credited with the feminine pronoun. Roland stood rooted to the spot, and as she passed him she raised her whip in salutation, hemmed deeply, and spoke,—

"Can you, aw—" the intonation of the gilded youth, or shall we say, the golden calf, was irresistible—"give me any idea of the way out of this? Fact is—aw—I have lost my bearings."

By this time Roland's adventurous spirit had resettled in its socket, the incident promised a fillip to his morning walk, and with a smile he turned on his heel and begged this strange Guinevere to follow him. He had fancied, with the innocence of his age, that he knew something of the world, but the last few weeks had taught him that there might be a good deal yet left to learn. This was plainly a case to be treated *en camarade*, but he was at a loss how to begin.

" I'm a stranger here myself," he said at
last, " but I think I can show you a short cut
out; that is, if you care to take it," and as he
cast his eye critically over the apparition, there
was mischief in it. So saying, he led the way
back to a green lane, at the end of which he
had noticed a locked gate of five bars. Now,
if this attire meant anything, it should be business, a point he determined to ascertain.

" Oh, I'll take it," said the lady carelessly,
and she flung away her cigar. " I should
apologize for smoking, but my doctor recom-
mends it."

Surely he doesn't recommend you to throw
your cigars away half-smoked, thought Roland,
but he said, " Pray don't mind on my account.
I *am* rather sensitive, but I can stand it in the
open air. I don't think any man should be
afraid of it there."

" Oh," laughed the lady uneasily, " the
wretched thing didn't draw; but if you will
allow me to offer you one, I—"

" Thanks; I'm afraid they're rather too
strong. I noticed it as I came up, and thought
they were burning weeds. One cigarette on Sundays is my usual allowance; no, thank you."

This little fiction filled up the space pleasantly
until they came to the gate.

" There," said the proprietor, stopping as he
pointed to it, " that's a way that will take
you straight on to the highroad. I'm sorry
it's locked, it's the only gate I've found about
here that is."

The lady's face changed just a trifle as she looked up, but the blood of twenty generations of noble lunatics boiled in her veins.

"It's a bad take off," she said, "but we'll try it, Bob and I," and she patted the chestnut's neck.

Roland was unprepared for what followed, and thought she was joking. Suddenly driving her spur into the poor brute's flanks, and cutting him a sounding lash over the quarter, she rose at the gate from a stand; fortunately for her it was rotten, her nag lifted himself gallantly to a thing no living horse could have taken in such a way—his forelegs well over, with his hind he crashed through the two topmost bars, and staggered sprawling to his feet at the other side.

"No take off, you see," observed the lady calmly, turning when she arrived there, "but I thought we could manage it."

"My poor gate!" groaned Roland, relieved at the same time that he had not to deal with a couple of corpses.

The horsewoman pricked up her ears. "May I ask—aw—to whom I am indebted for this courtesy?"

"I am Tudor of Sombrewood," he replied, wondering if she came with some travelling circus, for which she wanted his patronage.

"O—h—o" (whistling), "*indeed*, and I am Lady Victoria Nage; so now we know who's who; and I hope, as we are neighbours, I may have the pleasure of meeting you again. You

must look us up at ' The Rookery,' Mr. Tudor,"
and raising her whip she made away—the
chestnut with a peculiarly wooden expression
in his hindlegs, which seemed to indicate that
he at least had not forgotten the gate.

That life fell a little flat with Roland after
the above episode is not surprising, but he
busied himself with his affairs, of which he
found more than enough to his hand.

It should be here mentioned that, on attain-
ing his majority, he had stepped, *ipso facto*, into a
quaint dignity which had long lain vacant, waiting the time ; an empty, loud-sounding title, still
hereditary with the Tudors ; an odd survival
of a feudal office, but one such as may still be
found in certain remote nooks of the kingdom.
By right of birth he was Tudor of Sombrewood,
and Lord High Warden of the Isles. Formerly,
this had meant a great deal ; originally the
Lords Warden had held supreme authority over
all the haven and the coast defences, of which
the castle at the head was the chief. The
islands were military outposts, fiefs in fact, and
the various lands of the district had been
granted the family in charge merely. Gradually, however, after the easy fashion of that
day, the great family assumed proprietorial
rights over the land, the true owners thereby
becoming mere tenants at will—a change they
were powerless to prevent. The story is not
uncommon with the old landed gentry of
certain districts.

Round the entrance to the haven lay a dozen

or so of islands, several of respectable size, and capable of maintaining a garrison ; while others were mere rocks, scarcely big enough to admit of a stockade. So hard had been the fighting in those old times to get possession of these sentinel crags, that the name of the Bloody Mouth had attached itself to the place, and it was weird to look upon to this day. But now only the slow wash of the long Atlantic surges could be heard as they fell, breaking their crests upon the giant walls of natural masonry, where the grim face of the iron-bound coast was set eternally against the sea.

Happily for the young lord, there existed a miniature yacht, which lay off the stone jetty that abutted from his grounds into the haven. In this Tyrrel, transformed into a water-bailiff, was accustomed to go his rounds, collecting all the drift and wreckage, and keeping the eye of vigilance over the foreshore. Instantly on the master's arrival she had been docked, scraped, cleaned, polished, until she glittered like old mahogany, and looked almost bridal; and one of the happiest of the new warden's hours was when, having launched her at five o'clock in the morning, he sped down the haven in her for the first time, and flitting like a wraith through the frowning mouth, with its crumbling fortifications, felt beneath him the gentle cadence and the sweet rise and fall of the open sea, the breath of the breeze upon his forehead, and the salt taste of the brine upon his lips.

As the little vessel bent deeper and deeper to the gale, and dipped and rose, and plunged again into the blue waters, and shook herself from the sparkling spray in her flight, he uttered the single word " Eureka;" and the romance of it was spiced with danger as they neared the foam-fringed hills, standing so bravely in the ocean-bed. There, the tides swirled heavily between, in bright green hollows and bubbling whirlpools, and the waters raced through the narrows, and drew apart, yawning, to show below, rocks, stark, and bare, horrible ridges of black fangs that gasped and gurgled for a prey. Now surely they would be swallowed up on this fresh gay morning. The thought was not formed when a rush of transparent azure bore them into mid-air, twenty feet above, and the cockle-shell flew merrily away like a bird, flapping and lifting her wet white wings from the cerulean sea.

And at last they came to an island, where there were rock-hewn steps in the black cliff, and a four-squared boulder served as a landing-stage. There was a waiting for the wave that should make a spring to land possible, and an imminent ducking ere the yacht was cast off to leeward, where she might roll in safety, out of reach of the great blue monsters that raced each other past, a few yards away, tumbling shorewards one over the other, like living things at play.

Then came the " breather " up the cliff; of course the warden ran, who would walk upstairs when running was just as cheap, and when, at the summit, was a tiny desert, whereon the short brown grass waved crisply, and shone crystallized with salt in the sunlight? How the rabbits and the sea-fowl were fighting among themselves for the burrows!—but they made common cause and fled, and from the warm rocks below, the seals, at the sight of him, plunged like minute-guns into the sea. Of human habitation, there was nothing but a trace of low wall, grown about with sea-plant, a loopholed bastion, a broken arch giving upon a weed-grown dungeon—all thrown open to the air—safe and speechless guardians these, telling no tales of ugly secrets in the past.

To walk these barren steppes as lord and master through the title of a score of generations, here was food enough for a man's imagination: yet all the while he longed for some living human interest which should complete his story, and all the while his undefined ambitions lay gnawing at his heart. It was well to be Tudor of Sombrewood, a shadow though it were, and Lord High Warden of the Isles, no less so, but as means only to an end, and to what end? To what goal of human progress, of benefit to the race, and advancement to the things of God and man? This he pondered often, but not the faintest inkling came to him of his future way.

The same day, as he strode back to his tower, like a young sea-king flecked with yellow foam, and wringing the brine from his clothes, a card was put into his hand :—

LADY VICTORIA NAGE.
" At home."
Tuesday, the 14th. *Lunch* 1.30.
" The Rookery."

Certainly he would go.

CHAPTER VIII.

THOSE who live in remote districts, where houses
of entertainment, both public and private, are
from ten to twenty miles apart, know what
importance a mere luncheon party may assume.

The 14th of June dawned like a true summer
day, and the young warden, saddling his horse
(an old hunter) himself, rode out early, with
the intention of making a long round of it to
" The Rookery," and exploring right and left
by the way ; for he was resolved that no stick or
stone of his own country should be unknown to
him.   He had already ridden many miles, map-
ping the lie of the land mechanically—soldier
fashion—when he came upon a long chain of
breezy hill-slope, where he encountered a man
trying a thoroughbred over the grass.   Many
a dark horse had sprung to light, trained in
these solitudes, which were safe from prying
eyes.   And horsemen being rare products of
the soil, each greeted the other with a prolonged
stare, but they passed on, and Roland thought
no more about it.   The turf was magnificent,
and he pricked into a canter, which soon be-

came a gallop; the air was superb, so was the view, and below him the country lay unrolled like a panorama.

As he crested the down, and continued along the ridge, suddenly the rapid beat of hoofs behind struck his ear. "Ha!" thought he, "my friend again. Well, I don't mind trying it, though we're not exactly thoroughbreds, my nag and I," and the old grey tossed his head, laid back his ears, and bounded forward as the thud came faster.

"Well done, my man," laughed Roland, as after a minute or two the hoofs behind seemed rather to distance. "All the same, that fellow has a strain in him I shouldn't care about backing you against for much," and he spurred him on. But the rider over his stern had also apparently taken heart; this meant racing. Roland settled down into his saddle, and shook his rein free for business.

The turfy down stretched onward for miles ahead, so firm and smooth that it might have been a racecourse. Here there was a slight descent, and as they whistled through the air, his opponent now stretching close on the grey's quarter, the pace made was really excellent. So they thundered along for a space unchanged, Roland leading, and never casting a glance backward, when a low cry of distress rang through the air; and as he reined in sharply, a bright bay passed him in a raking stride, carrying a swaying burden. There was a glimpse of white face and dark green habit—of a woman—who that moment flung up her arms and slid from her saddle to the earth.

In an instant he was off and at her side. Confounded, he looked about him, but no other soul was visible. Horseman there was none, nor servant, nor jockey, on the whole expanse; and as his eyes fell upon the prostrate figure, for the first time in his life he knew the meaning of a shock of emotion.

The dream-maiden of his thoughts was stretched before him, white and helpless, in a dead faint. Her face turned and half-hid upon her outstretched arm, she lay there like the St. Cæcilia of the Roman catacombs—a conception which he had often thought the model of all womanly grace and modesty. And as he realized that they two were here alone on the wild hill, away from help, he was fairly bewildered. He bent over her, and his hand trembled as he touched her, for she looked a morsel for angels rather than men. And where was her guardian that he had let this frail child, with the burnished halo of dark hair round her saint face, be dashed there against a stone? Roland muttered an Ave as he lifted her, and resting her gently against his knee, as if she were a piece of porcelain, he loosened her collar from the slim, white column of her throat.

Luckily his presence of mind came back, and recollecting that after all the girl was mortal, he put his flask to her lips. Her eyes opened, wandered awhile upon the sky, and deep down in them he saw the glories of the blue heaven. Instantly the white forehead was flooded with a pale rose, which spread downwards to her neck, and one slight hand drew her habit together where it was opened.

"You would go on," she gasped faintly, "and I—I couldn't pull him in—and I couldn't speak, and I—" but she was off again.

Never had the man in his life before felt such a culprit. Never could anything weigh upon his conscience as did this.

"Are you hurt?" he blurted out. "For God's sake! say you're not hurt," and she again opened her eyes.

"No, I'm not hurt—I've been asleep; but where am I? Oh! I remember," blushing afresh. "Oh! what shall I do? I have no servant."

Hard was this on him, who would have been servant to her servant, had there been need of it.

"My dear, dear—madam," he stammered, "I think I can be as useful to you as at least ten servants, if you'll only let me try, and not be afraid."

She was lying against his knee still, and she weakly moved one hand upon his.

"No, I'm not afraid, and you need not be; in five minutes I shall be all right," and after this honourable surrender, she lay quite still, with her eyes closed a little time.

"What a goose I am!" she cried suddenly, springing into a sitting posture, and the life came back in waves of lovely colour to her

cheek, and flashed out afresh from her eyes.
" Upon my word, I never heard of such a thing
in my life!—I declare I haven't," and she lashed
her skirt angrily with her whip ; " but I daresay," facing Roland, " that you know what a
woman is, and what you may expect."

The tone of heart-felt despondency over the
short-comings of her sex was so genuine that,
all taken aback as he was, my hero laughed.

" I know that human nature is much the same,
whatever shape or sex it takes. I know—"

" What on earth made you go on like that ?"
she interrupted, with rising fury. " Look what
you've brought me to," and now she jumped
up hatless, for he dared not keep her, and the
wind was taking gentle liberties with her hair
as she stood twisting and twirling, to discover
the damages.

" I—I thought it was a man," said Roland,
hanging his head.

" A *man!*" she retorted scornfully. " Do
you think a *man* would have been run away
with for five miles " (alas ! for the verities, it
was barely one), " and then have screamed and
tumbled off in a fit at your feet without a word?
Bah ! it's ridiculous—but we're all alike."

" I don't think you are. I wish you were.
If they all—"

" Come," said the lady, drawing herself up
imperiously. " I can't waste time. (Bothera-
tion ! both strings of my habit gone.) Perhaps
you will kindly help me into my saddle."

He did so, and she vaulted into it, and caracoled to and fro, as she pinned afresh her hat and veil.

" I trust you'll allow me to see you safely home. I shall be so glad if you will make use of me ; and, after such a shaking, I fear it would hardly be safe for you to ride on by yourself."

Now the dastardly hypocrisy of the latter part of this speech was so palpable that she merely withered him with a glance, and said drily, " Thank you for all your help, I shall do excellently well, and," with a bow as she went, " I prefer to be alone."

But under this calm outside, her heart was aflutter as if it were bewitched ; quiet it, she could not ; it beat like a mad little wild bird imprisoned, it choked her, and she could hardly see distinctly. She was sore with him, and desperately sore with herself, for with all her sophistry, there was no denying that a sharp pang of pleasure had come to her out of her mishap. Her whole soul roused itself in revolt at this ; yet it was so, and it made her the more angry. She would go away at once, and she cantered off determinedly, to bury her hot forehead in the cool flow of the wind.

He, too, flung himself into his saddle, and, rather downcast, followed at a slower pace ; he could not force his society upon her, but it was something to have her there, in *quasi*-charge, even half a mile off. Lady Victoria and her lunch he flung to the winds, he would follow unobtrusively, and perhaps discover a clue which would some day reward his patience. It was very well for the lady to vow she would be alone, but when two people, equally well-mounted, are travelling the same road for miles, and that road is a long ridge of chalk-down, with a prospect stretching from end to end, it is difficult to secure complete isolation. When she had gone a mile she looked back, to see whether her habit sat aright, and noted the solitary figure following at a fretted walk; thereupon she pronounced him a gentleman. At two miles she looked round again; the distance between them had increased, and now he was cantering slowly. She knew the country, every inch of it; he had passed the one road that ran across the down, so it was tolerably evident that he was going the whole length. Then she slackened into a walk, and glancing back a minute later, found that he had done the same. "That *is* good of him," she said to herself, and relenting on the spot, she turned her horse about and walked to meet him. He could scarcely believe his eyes or his fortune when he saw her, but he hurried forward, thinking something must be amiss.

"We are going the same road, I see, and if so, it seems absurd to go it in this fashion: if you will really escort me, I shall be glad."

"So shall I," he said simply; "where am I to take you, let me do anything I can."

A glance passed between them, and in it, without a word, but through that inexplicable freemasonry which exists between true gentleman and gentlewoman, a mutual vote of confidence was ratified.

"I am going on to a place called 'The Rookery,' at the foot of the downs," she volunteered.

"And *I* am going on to a place called 'The Rookery,' at the foot of the downs," he made reply, with a ring of gladness in his voice. Here, then, was the end of his suspense.

"Are you? No? Are you really?"

"Indeed I am, and hadn't we better ask each other's names before we get there? I am Roland Tudor, of Sombrewood, and you?"

But the girl's heart leapt to her mouth and stopped her answer. She had dreamed of this, and here was actually in the flesh the descendant of a score of kings, the Warden of her mystic isles, and the rightful lord of all the enchanted country of her girlhood, and he was no less, but a hero, undoubtedly. Who but a hero would have been riding through the lone forests of her fairyland at sunrise?—the prince come back from exile, seeking his own. Who but a hero would have raised a fallen and fainting maiden, and so prettily brought her back to her senses? It will be seen that the current of this young lady's ideas was apt to veer very rapidly, but this was not uncommon with young ladies of this epoch.

"I am Miss Grey of the dower house—at least, I suppose I may so describe myself," with a deprecatory sigh, "and I—I—that is—but never mind;" then plunging despairingly and striking out afresh, " And are you just from town ? I hear it's going to be a good season ; is that true? I wonder what they mean to do about this colonial bishop's relief bill ? I think a prelate *in partibus infidelium* so usually—"

" Really, Miss Grey, I fear I have not studied the question," he interrupted, confounded by this unprovoked attack. " I—well, really it's a large subject."

" Oh! well, never mind, I only thought we might talk about something sensible."

" There's Lady Victoria," suggested he.

" That's unhappy ! " she replied, laughing; " do you know her well ? "

" Not at all. Do you ? "

" Certainly not."

" I have only seen her once, and then she splashed me with much unnecessary mud."

" Quite like her. She scatters plenty—not always on purpose—but some sticks, of course. Oh ! dear, now my hair's coming down, and I've hardly a hairpin left."

" How would this do as a make-shift ? " and the boy pulled out his breast-pin, a naked sword in miniature—this was the Tudor crest.

" Well, thank you, it is better than nothing," she said, running it through the great twisted coil at the back. " I shall look like a Swiss waitress."

The way was long, but there was plenty to talk about, what with colonial bishops and so forth, the two grew very earnest as they walked their horses neck and neck; and as they went, Miss Grey pointed out one historic spot after another, where they lay in the distance, solitary, sun and wind swept, and often without so much as a trace of human habitation near them.

"There," and a tan gauntlet that would have done credit to the modelling of a Praxiteles swept the horizon, "there, on that cliff, the Romans landed."

"I see—very pretty indeed," he answered absently, wondering where she bought her gloves; a thought he presently expressed in words.

"I have them made to measure," she answered; "ready-made gloves are a barbarism for a woman—don't you think so? And there," this time she used her whip, "was where the seventh Roland was driven into the sea by the rebels in 1398; and there is the battlefield of the four tribes, where half a Roman cohort was annihilated. Can you not fancy," and her eyes sparkled, "that you see them, these trampling legions, with their standards and their helms glittering on such a day as this, the savage hordes pouring on them from the ridge, and the final struggle in that bend of the river there? The place is all unchanged; there is no cultivation, as you see; the troops must have cut their way through these very woods. What often amazes me is that such records and such a story, for instance, as that of your family, should be allowed to die out of the land. Nobody in the world but two or three smoke-dried antiquaries and myself know anything about it." She laughed merrily, and for very pleasure to hear her, words failed him.

They had reached the end of the down, and there below were the wet white roofs of "The Rookery" glistening through the trees, and although they had talked for an hour, they seemed to have said just nothing at all. The girl stopped.

"Mr. Tudor, we must go in separately; we only met by chance; we are strangers, remember, and have to be introduced in the regular way."

"It's not quite honest, is it?"

"No, nor is the woman we have to deal with. I dislike the sort of thing extremely, but I know her."

"Well, I'll go by your advice, Miss Grey, and if it doesn't answer, you must go by mine next time."

Away she sped, and Roland watched her from the hill-top, jealous already, as though she were the apple of his eye, and only then remembering that there was no knowing at all who this Miss Grey might be.

Oh! the tender grace of the woman, the fresh fair face of the young summer, the music of the breeze, the clang of the hoofs, the rolling of the white clouds over the bright sky, the sun over all, and the pulses of young life throbbing in the veins. What in the mud-blackened after-world is ever again like unto it?

Half an hour later, Roland stood taking off his gloves in the hall.

"What d—d rot!" a female voice was heard to ejaculate meditatively, from some hidden recess, and the lady of the house emerged.

"Oh! Mr. Tudor, so glad to see you," she said, and she looked him over sharp as a needle, or he guiltily imagined it.

"You've had a long ride, awfully jolly lonely in these wilds, isn't it? Well, now I've got you, I shall introduce you to some of your neighbours, and perhaps you'll find something to chum with even amongst the aborigines."

Here she eyed him, as though she would have eaten him, but there was little to be gathered from his face.

Lady Victoria was to-day dressed in the ordinary garb of womanhood, if a leathern skirt and hobnailed boots may be included under that term, and as she stood talking, a door opened, and the master of the house came out. He was a gentleman of six feet, with a hazy manner and a tendency to uncertain curves as he walked, and he was wearing a velvet coat and embroidered slippers. She was accustomed to refer to him as "the scrap," he to her as "my diddy," when they addressed each other before the public. He shook hands, and observed, with a concentrated effort, that it was a fine day. Roland, with stoical composure, remarked that it was, but that the glass was not high enough to ensure its lasting, which the "scrap" cordially endorsed in a manner implying that it was the best piece of news he had heard for a long time.

The trio then adjourned to the drawing-room, where a near and noble relative of her ladyship, Lord Joseph Backstair, a pimply youth, with tufts of ill-grown hair about his face, was languishing upon a sofa, humming the air which had had such enormous success in " the best " circles that year :—

> " I'm a stoopy didiot, ho ! ha ! hi !
> I'm a stoopy didiot, ho ! ha ! hi !
> If you only knew me, I'm sure that you would cry,
> There's no one in this world is such a hass as I."

He finished his verse (which he was in the middle of), and then rose to greet Roland with all the ancient courtesy of his race.

" S—e—ı gla—ad," he murmured, extending a friendly paw, " s—e—r gla—ad."

Lord Joseph was a rather embryonic sporting character, but none the less remarkable for that; and this early stage made itself evident in his wearing his clothes so tight that it was wonderful how he ever got into them, and verging on the uncanny how he was ever extricated. This made his hands and feet appear to be preternaturally developed, and the utter curliness achieved in his hat-brim made him the admiration of all really sporting men. Both he and Lady Victoria combined literature with " life:" her taste inclining to romance—his, revelling in the cabalistic mysteries of the turf, as practised among the uppermost ups, and intelligible only to the initiated.

Lady Victoria flung herself into a low arm-chair, spread her legs out, and straightened them. She was a plain, undersized woman, thick-set, and strong as a badger.

"Upon my soul," she said, "these big feeds are a big nuisance: give me bread and cheese and beer, and I'm about satisfied any day, ain't you, Mr. Tudor?"

Roland replied absently that he was quite satisfied, which he was not, for he was fidgeting at Miss Grey's non-appearance; but as he spoke, the door opened noiselessly, and she swept in. "Was she really so fair, and really so unconscious of it?" he asked of himself as he rose.

"You two know each other," said Lady Victoria without stirring, indicating Lord Joseph with a jerk of her boot. Lord Joseph jumped up, took both Miss Grey's hands at once.

"S—e—r gla—ad, s—e—r vewy gla—ad; thit here, Miss Gwey, do now; such a cothy corner, and I've warmed it well," and he laughed the cheery laugh of a well-educated hyena.

"Thank you," said the girl, withdrawing her hands. "I'll take this chair by the window," and her eyes wandered to Roland. The hostess, however, made no move towards further introduction, but sat with her single eyeglass screwed into her pug-dog face, and stared stonily. "Rot," she muttered to herself, "d—d rot, but I shan't help 'em out of it."

Miss Grey looked flushed, but as there was nothing else for it, plunged into a lively conversation with Lord Joseph, for whom Roland

instantly conceived such a hatred as he had
never felt for any one but the unhappy baron
at St. Augustine's.

Now what had occurred on Miss Grey's first
appearance was this. Lady Victoria had insisted on taking her upstairs, and the very first
thing she noticed was the dagger in her visitor's
hair, which the latter had forgotten; and this
particular dagger, it happened, was carved on the
mantelpieces, the church doorways, and the
keystones, on half the old buildings in the
county—wherever, in fact, the name and power
of the wardens had extended. Over and above,
this one was palpably a man's breast-pin; and
if another link were wanting, she had seen it in
Roland's tie the morning she met him in the
woods—two and two usually make four.

"That's a pretty thing you've got in your
wig," she said, twisting Miss Grey round by the
shoulders. "I s'pose *he* gave it you; you're
a sharp 'un. No time lost there!"

Miss Grey's flush of vexation, as she put
up her hand to her hair, did not escape
notice.

"Oh! yes. I quite forgot I put that in;
it's Swiss, I think, but it doesn't answer—
I shan't try it again. Do give me some hair-
pins."

"You look as if you'd had a spill," went
on her persecutor mercilessly. "How do you
manage without a servant, do you always find
some one to pick you up? Look at your
elbow!"

" I must have grazed it," returned Miss Grey imperturbably, arranging her hair.

" Really, child, when your arms are up like that, you've a very neat figure ; how much is real, eh ? "

" Oh ! to flay this insufferable woman," thought Sybil, her fingers tingling, but she refrained, and quoted,—

> "Tell me now, before you go,
> Are you all made up or no ? "

" Now, Lady Victoria—well, Victoria, if you like it better,—I won't keep you to ask you any-thing else ;" and so she was rid of her.

It took a good deal of cold water and sponging to restore Miss Grey's face and temper, but at length she ventured down, as has been told.

The lunch was a success in its way. Lady Victoria's great idea was " life," after her own interpretation of that much-abused word, and even in these far regions she managed to see something of it. She had always various oddities by her, whom she had collected on her travels, and you were as likely to meet at her table the king of the Cannibal Islands as any-body else. Men were scarce, and such as she had contrived to gather to-day were of her own particular set, and approached an almost ideal type. Their coats and waistcoats were of identically the same pattern, evolved no doubt from a single pair of shears ; their collars were equally cut-throat, their trousers were equally

distended through sheer tightness, their feet
equally splay and pointed. A terrible gravity sat
upon them all; their conversation consisted of
broken sentences in an unknown tongue; signs,
nods, and unutterable meanings, hung upon the
faintest of clues, formed the staple of it; and
the awed bystander heard the first personages
of the realm fantastically alluded to as " Old
G "—" Q "—" Daddles," and so forth—it was a
glimpse of the empyrean. On Roland's right sat
a youth of his own age, on his left a lady; but
he began with the man, for he foresaw the lady
would be a serious undertaking.

" Glorious weather this."

The incipient individual addressed turned
his head slowly round in his four-inch collar,
without moving his body, elevated his eyebrows,
and jerked out " Ya-as;" then his head returned
to its first position with a sort of click.

" Perhaps he's clockwork," mused Roland.
I'll try him again. " Done any fishing
here ?"

The head started afresh on its journey round.
but something caught, and it stood still half-
way, jerking out the " Ya-as," as before.

This was discouraging, but at that moment
Lord Joseph, who was opposite, happening
to have an argument with a neighbour on
the subject of puppy-dogs' tails, which he endeavoured to close by causing that neighbour
to swallow a bumper of claret the wrong way,
and so choke; the automaton was suddenly
seized with convulsions and reeled in his chair,

declaring faintly, he had never hoped to see so fine a thing, alive.

"Are you better now, little one?" asked Roland kindly, as the former slowly recovered.

"Ya-as," he vouchsafed, resettling into immobility; and pivoting round, so as to turn his back, he began a vigorous assault on the innermost recesses of his jaw, with a toothpick.

This gentleman was the son of the Tomlinson erewhile spoken of, now for nearly seven years head of a county family. The old man had raised himself from a dung-hill, for which all credit to him, and his money had been evolved out of cheap liquor, which some averred was nasty to boot, but which was probably good enough for the people who drank it. He had obtained a commission in the Blues for his son out of an old customer, in lieu of a bad debt (through such tortuous ways did the world wag in this generation), and he now declared that he could finish up and die perfectly happy, in that he had made his son a gentleman!

The ill-success of this first venture, induced Mr. Tudor to turn his attention to the lady on his left. She was fearfully and wonderfully made; her dress was an arrangement in yellow satin, looped about with claret marabout feathers; it was portentously strained, not only where Nature had made it possible, but equally where Nature had made it impossible, and altogether it was as charmingly unsuitable a costume as could have been devised for a picnic and lounging on the grass. The creature's hands were blotched and puffy, as was her face; every now and again she gave a deep sigh, and once she essayed to lean back in her chair, but this proving a failure, she resumed a rigidly upright position on the front edge of it. All the while she smiled before her into the air at nothing particular, and then would come an odd corkscrew curl in the left corner of her mouth. She wore coil upon coil of yellow hair, impossible in its amount, and there was plenty of colour laid on her face, but it was not done well, and was visible without strain to the naked eye; her heels were wondrous, and this fairly completes her. To guess her nationality was so difficult that it would be presumption to try and do so; suffice it to say, she was a distinguished foreigner. Roland noticed that she only took two spoonfuls of soup, and one of fish, and that she sent away the entrée untasted.

"You're not eating; I'm afraid you've no appetite," he remarked compassionately, for he was making an excellent luncheon himself.

"Young man," she said, the agonized smile rising to greet him, "I don't mind if I tell you a secret."

"Too flattered I'm sure," he said, inclining his ear.

"I'm," hoarsely, "that bulged I can't." A whirlwind of sigh followed this.

"Dear me! how very distressing."

"I confide to you solemnly, sir," she went on, "it ain't a good day with me. I'm awful flobbity most times, but this day I'm stodged.

It's just luck, it's most unfortunit; six months I haven't wore this dress: for the last time I swooned six times, and I guess I was turned just wrong side out," here she fanned herself like a windmill.

" But why on earth do you do that sort of thing?"

" Young man, I'll tell you the sole reason. Selina M. Hobbs, sort-er friend o' mine and rival, don't cher know, dared me to it, and I warn't going to let her beat me. Well! she doubled up into a cocked hat very soon, and you see I've got kinder reputation for the thing, and you can't go back on your reputation. No, sir, and—" sending away a dish, " you can't eat apple pudding with suet, if it's incompatible with that reputation."

" I'm sorry for you," he said, with genuine feeling; " for mercy's sake try a fresh reputation in another line, I'm sure you must have plenty in you—"

" I guess I'd like to have something rather less at this moment," she gasped ; " but," as the ladies rose, " don't you fret for me, young man, I shall be quite O K, when I walk about and get into the fresh air a bit; farewell, adoo!" She kissed her hand to him and vanished, creaking and fluttering like a three-decker in a gale of wind.

" I call it perfectly loathsome and disgusting, perfectly humiliating to one's sex, to see a fellow-creature make such a fool of herself," said Miss Grey, stamping her foot, as the yellow figure with the golden hair passed in the distance.

The afternoon was waning, the play well-nigh done, and she and Roland at length found themselves together on the lawn, not, however, without considerable manœuvring.

"As if woman's dress were not essentially ludicrous and ridiculous at best," she said; "but man has been wise, he has so contrived that she shall love her shackles."

"You're rather hard upon yourselves," he answered, pleased with her satirical way, "and when you see the nobler sex, as typified in the present company—Lord Joseph and young Tomlinson, for instance—no wonder you blush for your own! I daresay—"

"Now I should just like to know who introduced you two," broke in Lady Victoria, dropping upon them apparently out of the skies, and cracking a dog-whip.

Miss Grey darted a glance at Roland, whose eyes shone with unspeakable ferocity.

"I believe we're not exactly introduced," she said with a placid smile, presenting an unchanging front to the impertinence.

"If you consider it necessary, perhaps you'll be kind enough to do it for us now," he said haughtily, raising his hat, for Miss Grey had confided to him the story of her persecution. But if he thought to abash Lady Victoria, he reckoned without his hostess.

"Bless you, my children, bless you!" she cried, catching hold of a hand of each and squeezing them into each other, " may you be happy," and this sportive little kitten of thirty odd summers darted away ere either of the aggrieved could speak a word.

" She's not altogether bad," began Sybil.

" Will you talk of yourself," said he with an effort of self-restraint, turning his back on their retreating foe.

" Well!" said the girl with determined good-humour, " what can I tell you ? Shall I begin like the story-books, ' I was born of poor but respectable parents in—.' Come!" as she saw a shade of strong vexation cross his face (how stupid and tiresome is a boy in love), " what do you really want to know ?"

"About your belongings," he replied, striving hard to be generous and amiable.

" Which ? I've plenty of them—dogs, pigeons, ponies."

" Inside the walls, I mean."

" Well ! I've my Narcissus, my Madonna, and the rest of my household gods."

Roland's brows lifted almost imperceptibly,—
" Humanity is not represented then ?"

" Oh ! yes it is, there's old Joe and old Joan, and Emma Betts and Mary Trigg."

" But your own family ?"

" I have none."

" None ? None at all ? But your aunt, guardian, or whatever *it* is ?"

" *It* is a vanishing, or vanished point. I have not seen my guardian, Mr. Trelawney, for six months."

"You live absolutely alone?"

"Absolutely."

"Have *no one* to take care of you, no companion even?"

"No one."

"You can go where you like, do what you like?"

"Yes—practically."

"That is very unfortunate."

Yet it was satisfactory, too, in a way; but what struck him seriously was that this pearl of great price, this ownerless Kohinoor, which he had chanced upon by the roadside, should be left utterly unguarded. This should not be; he would see to it. Already he was assuming proprietorial rights; and lo! the property, had he but known it, was in chancery—there was One awaiting to claim it in the future, before whom even Tudor, of Sombrewood, must give way.

But was this a gem of the first water that had come into his hands? As she stood he scanned her fiercely; she felt it was an appraisement, and with the full knowledge of herself she met him fearlessly and without art. A hundred girl faces passed before him, a phantasmagoria of his female-friendhood in London. Many of these were well bred and highly trained, were charming, gentle ladies, dowered with every grace of Christian womanhood; but they wanted the to him nameless, all-sufficing charm of this rare exotic; but then—he was in love, or something akin to it.

"I find no fault in her," he muttered at last, half aloud, dropping his eyes; but the girl caught the words, and flushed scarlet.

"Foolish boy," she said, "what do you know of me? Learn before you judge," and for the moment she was the grown woman and he the youth, so instantly does the woman follow on the child.

"I beg your pardon," he said humbly, "I was thinking aloud. But what a difficult position it is. Are you able to manage quite for yourself? you can know so little of the world."

"Indeed—indeed I know too much," and her dark eyes filled with sadness. "You forget, or I have not told you, that I have been forced in every way—cruelly forced, I call it, for a girl who was naturally quick. My guardian meant it for the best, but he did not spare me. I cannot tell why. I have a voice; at one time I think he must have meant me for the boards."

"The boards!" he ejaculated under his breath. "Never!"

"Oh! that is a thing of the past. He is too fond of me, and he has begun to discover I am useful to him. I still read a great deal, and learn what I can from all sorts of books; more than I should care to know if things were different, but necessary to me as I am. Women are fond of thinking their cases exceptional, but I really think mine must be so. Do you know of any quite like it?"

She took him into her confidence with

a quiet seriousness which was very pleasing to her hearer.

They were left alone, but they sat under a big cedar, in full view of the house, scorning the more secure retreats whither, by this time, every nymph had carried her swain. Lady Victoria did not do things by halves, and certainly, the privacy of the nooks she provided for her guests, was unimpeachable. The highest art had been expended on making them "safe;" they were arranged on semi-inaccessible points, commanding a view far and wide, but set round densely with shrubs. So cosy were these arbours, that stray couples were apt to forget the flight of time, and "The Rookery" being Liberty Hall, to sit out in them far into the night, until an agonized ringing of the dinner-bell from the house, or the springing of a watchman's rattle down the paths, brought them back again to earth. There was a certain look, a flushed, touzled air about those who came and went in these shrubberies. Roland resolved that he would put his companion to test. A couple passed by them into the shades, some matter of profound laughter shook them both consumedly: the lady carried a champagne bottle tucked under her arm.

Miss Grey turned her head away.

"Don't you think it would be better if you did not come here again?" said Roland sternly.

"You are right. I have had my doubts

all along; I wish I could find an excuse to go."

"We will slip away, presently; just now, you could not be better than here on the lawn."

Down by the house in front of them, they had organized a party of leap-frog, and Lady Victoria was giving her first-born son and heir, lessons over Mr. Tomlinson's back. The first-born was cheeky, and declared that his mother kicked up her heels over much, for which she boxed his ears, and the air was filled with a melancholy howling.

Meanwhile the twain were left undisturbed under the cedar, and Roland grew still more inquisitorial in his questioning; but, cynic as he was, with the depth of the cynicism of his age—he could not find that she failed him at any point. He passed from subject to subject, others than those to which he usually treated young ladies; on many she held her own, to many she confessed frankly, "I know nothing of it, it's a thing I have not come across." They had advanced as far into metaphysics as a Venus and Adonis, in whom young life pours fast through white and rose flesh are likely to do, and were lost in some bewilderment of each other, when there was a crash through the branches, and the son and heir, in the shape of a dishevelled imp, grimacing hideously, rushed in, followed by his enraged parent.

"Yo! yah! yee! I'm 'ike a baboon, ain't I,

Miss Grey?" he yelled, with a futile effort to stand on his head.

"No, sir, you're not" (a slap) "like a baboon," was the reply of the prompt personage in rear" (slap, slap), "no respectable baboon would behave to his mother in the way you do, he'd be ashamed of himself" (slap, slap, slap).

"Yah!" screamed the child, flinging himself into Miss Grey's petticoats, "that's" (sob) "the sevefth hiding ma's given me to-day, and I only said *I* was 'ike a baboon, I didn't" (looking up tearful, but defiant, from his place of refuge) "say *she* was."

The profound feeling and studied implication involved in this speech, were too much for the trio, who burst into laughter.

"Oh! Lady Victoria, let him off this time," said Sybil, "I'm sure he is going to be good."

The urchin's arms were round her neck, and he whispered confidentially, "I'm *not;* I 'tend to be a baboon, and baboons is bad."

"Very well," said the hostess, "you shall lick him into shape for me, and when you've done, you'd better come and have some tea, both of you," and, throwing her whip into Miss Grey's lap, with an injunction to use it well, she departed to play "Aunt Sally" with some choice spirits in the stable yard.

"Miss Grey, is ma a lady?" said the heir, clambering into Sybil's lap.

"Yes, dear, she's Lady Victoria," was the rather embarrassed answer.

" I didn't mean that kind," contemptuously.
" Are you a lady, Miss Grey ? "

" I'm a woman; I'm only Miss Grey," she
replied, sticking bravely to her flag.

" Well, then, I 'ike women best," said the
boy, kissing her prettily and politely enough.

Roland hardly refrained from applause, although he was pacing to and fro, chafing at
the interruption. The golden minutes were
passing, and he had yet much to say. A week
would be too short for it all ; for he had fallen
in love at sight long, long ago—half a lifetime
it seemed—and since then had never looked
back. At this moment he was plotting to escort
his mistress home ; nor was she altogether
averse, but it was idle. Had they been on the
square with her, to use her pure vernacular,
Lady Victoria would have sped them on their
way ; but they had not, and she resolved that
they should pay the penalty. She was so singular a woman that she liked to show her
power ; and when they went in to tea, she
quietly told Sybil that she had arranged that
Mr. Tomlinson and his sister should see her
home.

Lucky it was that Roland had trained himself into stoicism. Women do these things
better, and call up that hollow smile which
means, " Oh ! — you, I'll be even with you
yet," with quite no trouble at all. Thus did
Miss Grey, and asked for " a leetle—yes, just a
leetle drop more sugar," at the same time, with
a confusion of metaphor ; but before she went,

she slipped her hand into her knight's, and said, " Come and see, and judge."

" When ?   To-morrow ? " he whispered, hoarse with baffled hope.

" Certainly not," laughed she ; " next week."

He groaned.

" Well, say Monday, and come early for lunch."

So he rode home, as satisfied as a man may hope to be in love.

CHAPTER IX.

Miss Grey had had her own very good reasons
for deferring Roland's visit for a day or two.
Briefly, she was not prepared.

She had few guests, none at all of the opposite sex except her guardian, if he might be so
termed, and him rarely, but she had great
notions as to the fitness of things, and as to
how they should be done. Already she had
dubbed this last scion of the great family,
"king," and if it pleased his majesty to make
a royal progress through his dominions, then
at least he should be received as became him.
Of course he was the king, his ancestor's had
held kingly power out of times when the other
county families simply were not; beyond this
she did not dream of yielding him the title, but
was she wholly honest with her own heart?

As for him, the few days until the Monday
seemed endless, perhaps because he made no
resolute effort to emancipate himself from his
thoughts. Poor old Tyrrel and his wife were
dismayed at the sudden and alarming change
in him. He would hear nothing of the fore-

shore, and said that the flotsam and jetsam might
go to the deuce.   He had already begun to lay
the plans for new buildings, but now he would
attend to no business whatever, and sent away
an unlucky architect who had come twenty
miles across country one morning, refusing to
see him because, he said, he had a cold in his
head.

Cold or no cold, he spent all his time out of
doors, though it happened to be a spell of wild
weather.   He would ride maniacally over the
storm-beat downs, or would scud about the
haven in his yacht, with the lee-scuppers well
under, and the treble-reefed mainsail dipping
into the rollers as they passed; or, beating-up,
would launch into the rushing seas, that burst
themselves in thunder at the mouth.   Never
had the man and the boy, who formed the crew,
had such a time, and the worse it was, the
more he seemed to like it.   Never was pirate
skipper like him.   He would take them out
when and where he listed, would stand silent
at the tiller for hours together, giving his orders
by signs, and when he spoke, it was perhaps
only to tell them to haul off his boots and sou'-
wester, and to do as much for themselves, as
he didn't think they would weather the next
point.

After that there was a mutiny, which was
arranged quietly and without any fuss.   When,
at last, the yacht put in to the landing-stage,
the crew, by collusion, failed to "down-sail"
at the right moment, and as they had been

running-in with all set and a square sail superadded, and as the captain's experience scarcely
extended to three weeks, it is not surprising
that she went ashore, and walked up hill
some considerable distance, before she stopped.
The jerk well-nigh unstepped the mast and
snapped her bowsprit, she further stove herself
on the port bow. Now the "crew" were prepared for an outburst, and were ready to strike.
But, behold! their eccentric master sprang
out, just glanced at the damage, told the boy
to go for help, then walked away, as if it was
no further concern of his; and he spent the
rest of the day, which was wet, in inebriating
the cocks and hens in the farmyard with bran
soaked in rum.

These vagaries, which set Tyrrel and his
wife well-nigh distracted, lasted in some shape
up till Sunday night; but on the Monday, when
they were fearing what the day might bring forth,
curiously enough, the man seemed quite himself again, talked about the foreshore for at
least two minutes, gave the bailiff his orders
as usual, wrote a letter of apology to the unfortunate architect, and otherwise comported
himself to everybody's satisfaction. About
half-past eleven, he said he thought it was such
a lovely morning, that he would have his horse
round; and so, again, he rode out and straight
away into fairy-land.

Were ever such woods and hills and waters
as on that day? Yes, there were such for some
of us once, but never again, never again, until

perchance the Elysian plains open upon our spirit-vision in the islands of the blest !

When, after traversing the long domain, he at length reached the dower house, which lay sunk in foliage and the long lush midsummer grass, like a nest; the door was opened to him by a pretty girl in a sort of dark livery dress, and he handed over his horse to a small boy with grave eyes, who led him solemnly away.

His lady was sitting writing at her desk in the open window, when she heard boot and spur upon the stair. She half rose, and then as resolutely sat down to her pen, and when he entered, nothing was visible of the trepidation that hammered at her heart. Well as Roland thought he had learned her, his face altered with surprise as he looked. She was dressed in a gauzy black material, which by some art was made to outline the figure, but fell ruffling loose over the skirt, and, lest this should seem too sad a colour for the gay summer day, she had taken a long Eastern scarf of the palest yellow and made like a silken gossamer, and this she had draped round her, pinning it on her left breast with an old jewel, a heart of carbuncle, on which was dropped a pearl-like tear, the device in a border of rose-diamond lace. To balance, on the right side, a single rose blushing to scarlet nestled in her neck. Her sleeve was short, but over the arm to the wrist, not beyond, she wore a mit of silk lace, and in the woven coils of her dark hair was threaded a beaded fillet of yellow gold. Where had the child learned all this? It was studied, of course. Yet of all studies it was most natural to her; and so entirely was she the woman and the hostess, that the Lord High Warden of Sombrewood and the Isles felt both young and awkward as he stood before her.

" Welcome, friend," she said, as she rose and took him by the hand, and as it were led him to a chair. The salutation was an odd one, a little un-English, but it was prettily done. He took the chair, and she stood facing him. Then her height and bearing impressed him more strongly than ever. His vanity recovered itself, and whispered you are well matched. Conscious of a vast resource of power within himself, he did not fail to discern it in her, and something of a doubt crossed him lest perhaps their wills should run counter; and as he looked into the gentle face, he saw, by heaven knows what introspect, the revelation of indomitable will: here could be no easy victory.

" Are you glad I am come?" he asked hungrily.

" Very," bending over him and giving him her hand again. " Very, very, very. Is that honest enough for you?" she asked, withdrawing it. " You see," she laughed, " I hardly know how to treat you, in spite of my book experience. I must entertain you, but how? You are not my guardian, nor my doctor— though he would puzzle me almost as much now. You're not the clergyman's wife, you're not an old woman with a bad leg, you're not a rheumatic old stone-breaker, you're not quite a horse, not quite a dog. If you were any of these, I think I could make you happy."

"We're already on the road to that, I fancy; what do you say to treating me as a tame cat without claws?"

"Well!" she said, with a sigh of relief, as if that difficulty were settled, "Now you see me in my own shell, at last." ("At last," i.e. after almost a week's acquaintanceship! this looks as if time had been dawdling at the dower house.)

"It is a very pretty shell."

"Have you ever wondered whether the shell affords the same clue to the idiosyncrasy of the oyster as the habitation of man does to that of its occupant? Did you ever notice the scope that oystershells afford for—"

"Aren't these metaphysics?" pleaded Roland modestly, as one might reprove one's angel guardian, for too high a flight of tone.

"Are they? Well, isn't this a cheerful time and place for discussing them? It is good to be alive. You must make the tour of my den. This is my true sanctum, where visitors are *never* admitted, as you see. The other rooms are downstairs. I don't think they're so bad. The drawing-room is not chintz and electro-gilding, like Lady Victoria's; nor are lines of mahogany chairs standing sentry in unutterable gloom round the dining-table. But this is my shrine, my oratory, myself almost; and there are my Penates. You see, of course, I am a woman, and my surroundings show it, but you must make allowances."

This proud humility, half real, half affected, pleased him more than anything else. Taught by St. Maur and the society of artists which he had frequented in town, Roland was apt to be desperately severe on women's rooms, compounded as the majority of them were in this curious age, of the catchpenny upholsterers, the curiosity shop, and another institution not usually mentioned to ears polite. The girl eyed him anxiously, not for nothing had nature placed those two hillocks on his brow; she saw and recognized his criticism in the type of the outward man.

" You are very comfortable," he said.

" Am I? I hardly know. It's dreadfully difficult to make oneself *quite* comfortable in this world."

" So much so that it's never occurred to me to try and do it."

" I'm not sure that it's not a duty. Morality, as far as I can make out, was founded entirely on sanitation. The highest health and comfort and well-being are consequently to be aimed at."

" Ahem! May I ask what your friends say to your theories. Do they understand them?"

" My friends! I have none. I can't make any. But I have had some clever governesses of several nations with whom I got on very well. I had to send the last away, she was too clever."

" But your girl friends ? "

" I tell you I have none. Do you wonder ?
Fancy choosing one from the Rookery, for instance. Most girls are such frauds, you can't
conceive. They really have not three ideas in
sequence. You must treat them as simple
children ; and yet,—and yet, they seem to get
on, and to answer their purpose."

Roland laughed outright.

" It is the reaction of the male on the female," she continued gravely, " that has raised
nature to her present heights, that has given
song to the birds and colour to the flowers. I
take it you have to thank us for your development even into philosophers. Tell me, why
has not man bettered woman more than he
has done ? "

" Please don't look at me as if I were individually guilty," said Roland. " I'm sure I
don't know. Do you regard her place as so
unsatisfactory then ? "

" Eminently," she said, tapping her foot :
" the strongest proof to me of a future world
for her is the nullity and incompleteness of her
life in this. What is the life-work of the young
unmarried woman in the highest grades ? To
dress herself four times a day, to (perhaps)
arrange the flowers for the table, to (possibly)
get ready the gentlemen's buttonholes for the
evening. Ah ! we have fallen on evil days,
and our dress—which is all-sufficing for so many
of us—what is it but a gilded prison, within
the bars of which is caged a human soul that

beats cruelly against them. No, you have
cribbed and confined these poor souls so long,
they cannot fly, they cannot soar. Men are
not caged ; they are different, judging by their
books, not that I have tried them much personally."

"Am I to understand that I am on my
trial?" asked he, half amused.

"Well, I suppose you are to some extent.
Presently I will take you to the library, and
confront you with some giants. I want you to
help me in evolving a scheme of life ; perhaps
you can explain some of my difficulties. There
are 5000 volumes, all the standard works on
metaphysics, all the—"

"Good gracious, Miss Grey, I beg that you
won't do anything of the kind ! You are far more
likely to teach me. Indeed, before I could give
you a hint at all in any direction, I must know
more of the ground I have to build on," and
he looked very intently upon her face.

"Well," she answered carelessly, "I've
nothing but the vaguest theories. You know
I am inclined to believe all life works upwards.
Look at my dog for instance. Here, Roly,"
and the great hound lifted himself to her. She
took his head into her lap, and breaking a bit
of biscuit that lay on the table, held it before
him.

"Look at him," she said, as he eyed her
with lustrous dark eyes. "Did you ever see
such an expression ? Such tenderness, such
nobility, such grave thought, and all about a

scrap of biscuit." She patted his head, and slipped her hand into the beast's great mouth. " What is it all but the embryo soul in his dear old body. Depend upon it, the human soul is worked up to like the human body, through a tremendous pedigree. Poor old fellows ! I do all I can for them. I teach them to be obedient, and gentle, and generous, and I know that I am doing good, that I have helped them on their way. Isolated life is perfectly inexplicable for man or beast; we are linked in long chains."

"I think your theories are fairly definite," said her visitor, " and I am not prepared to dispute them at once."

" On the other hand," she continued, not noticing his remark, " the existence of animal suffering would seem to point to something purgatorial. What do you say to that ? "

" Well, if you seriously ask me, I say that as we have historic evidence that the brutes were created ages before man, it is not very likely that human souls were punished in their forms, before they had existed at all for good or evil ! "

" Ah ! " said the girl rising, her eyes flashing some greeting to him, " that is an answer. I like to be answered in that fashion."

"And what have you in this locket?" he asked rather indiscreetly, seeing one hung prominently in a velvet frame upon her writing-table.

" A dear friend's hair."

"Oh!" I thought it might be a miniature."
Neither the answer nor its tone pleased
him exactly. She went up and touched the
spring, it flew open; the friend's hair was snow-
white!

"Ah!" he said more genially, "a memorial,
perhaps?"

"Yes, of a poor little mad dog."

Her visitor could not but smile, even though
there stole a huskiness into the bell-like tones
of her voice. He looked at her inquiringly.

"I had the locket ten years, and never
found a human being whose hair I should have
cared to place in it; but this poor dog had been
my friend, my companion night and day through
several lonely years. He had become—well, a
great deal to me—and I—I was his god. You
won't understand me, I daresay." She laughed
a little uneasily lest he should; she need not
have feared. "But his feeling for me was a
sort of religion. Dogs are different; some are
never more, some grow half human from companionship. One day he was bitten, and he
sickened; he came to me as usual to be cured.
I know something of dogs, I have had so many.
I saw the look in his eyes, and that his jaw was
paralyzed; then I knew what was to come.
Still I nursed him against hope a day or two,
until to see the struggle between the dear dog-
nature and the demon that had gone into him
was too painful (you have seen a dog mad?)
and his poor god was stricken powerless. Only
one thing was left; I did it. I called him, and

he staggered to me. I think he understood.
I spoke a word, and he took the poison from
my hand, and stretched himself dead at my feet,
looking up to me. The poor distorted limbs,
the agonized face relaxed; he was himself
again, and wherever he is gone, I know that in
those happy hunting-grounds he waits his
mistress. Ah! there should be a frisking in
that world when I go thither." Her eyes were
full of tears. "But I have still higher beliefs
of dogs. Do you know his death half chris-
tianized me? I remembered a passage in
your sacred writings, in your Bible, you
know—"

What could she mean? Roland was at a loss,
but he nodded.

"Where it says that not even a sparrow
falls to the ground, and as I saw him fall
under my hand this came to me. He was
of more value than many sparrows, if it were
only that the happiness of a human being
was wrapped up in him. Ah! that is a beautiful thought, that of the Great Father ordering
all things for good. I declare something like
what you religionists call faith rushed into my
heart. Perhaps the dog was advanced, perhaps
even I was advanced by this dreadful stroke.
When I say perhaps, I mean I don't doubt it
a moment."

This set Roland thinking for a long time
after; the incident gave him a sudden insight
into her character, such as none other had as
yet done.

"We have been out of our depth, let us struggle back to the shallows," she said, interrupting his reverie. "Let us make a tour of my den. This," and she touched an old brass clock, "is the quaintest character in the house. It feels it a grievance, I think, to be set to regular work in its old age. It does not often condescend to use its voice, and when it does so, it is with a writhe of internal preparation; then it strikes in a hoarse, angry tone of indignant protest, and usually maintains a haughty silence for hours after. If very much put out, it will strike all the hours together on end, but then it is so upset it won't be itself for a week—liver I imagine. Still it likes to be noticed. Do you see how it holds itself up, and how regularly it ticks now? that is because we are both looking at it." How prettily she talks nonsense, thought Roland as he laughed aloud. "Now," she went on, "here is a contrast. See what you think of this; it will please you."

She led him to where a film of pale primrose silk, like her scarf, was draped against the wall; she drew aside the curtain and disclosed a coved and fluted niche, in which stood a statuette of Narcissus in marble, slightly tinted to a flesh shade. The composition was one of the most charming imaginable, the illusion lifelike. The rock against which the figure reclined was a block of veined quartz, and the whole was placed upon a mirror, not a clear mirror, but one in which the glass had been

ruffled and stained into the semblance of a
streamlet pool.

"Narcissus was an idiot," said Roland slowly,
as he scanned it. "All the same it's one of the
cleverest things I ever saw."

Miss Grey's face brightened. "Ah! I daresay you wouldn't care much about him. This
would be more to your taste," and she pointed
to a like niche opposite. Within stood a Venus,
nude, and equally beautiful.

"Do you know," she said, "I don't think
it was half a bad plan to deify an attribute and
worship it."

The goddess was carved in some pallid
translucent stone, which gave her a cold,
spiritualized look, as if she were not of earth
nor suited to it. Recollection, chastity, and
refinement were all expressed in the modest
pose of her graceful limbs, and the great, rosy
sea-shell in which she stood, added to the
etherealized effect of the figure. As one
watched, one looked for her to rise on those
slender feet of hers, and take wing into the
skies.

"To my mind, poor Narcissus is so very
natural, so human, one must love him; but
this expresses something else," said Miss
Grey.

"It is hardly my ideal of womanhood," said
Roland, feeling repelled, he knew not why.

"It is mine," she answered rather sadly;
"at least I think so, or she disputes it with my
Amazon."

Hard by on a bracket was a small bust of an amazon in bronze. It was evidently an antique, and a choice one. It had this further peculiarity—her strong, stern features bent unchanging over her right breast, from which the womanhood had been reft away.

" What do you think of her ? "

" She is an imperfect thing—no true woman," he said, recoiling.

" Ah, we are different. I think a true woman may go further—may tear the heart from her bosom in a great cause, could she find such a one." The light of her eyes flashed, and sank again.

" Come," she said, " let us burn a grain of incense to the embodiment of a noble thought, if nothing else.

Before the statue stood a bronze burner, with a perforated lid; into this she thrust a lighted cedar spill, and in a minute blue wreaths were curling snakily out into the moted sunbeam where it struck across the room, spreading their fragrance everywhere. Then she gathered a beautiful waxen blossom from the creeper that hung upon the window trellis. That morning, for the first time, it had opened to the sun. A coronet of dewdrops was upon its petals, and in its calyx lay a single diamond of purest honey. She placed it upon the burning incense; slowly the flower darkened, and writhed, and withered; but its odour went out with the incense more sweetly upon the air. Intensely watchful of every phase of human life, Roland looked on in astonishment.

"Is that your notion of worship?" he asked, half in jest.

"Yes; something like this. Natural worship should surely be simple; it's when you come to dogma you get into a mess. God is for all. Now, my idea of natural worship would be an altar upon a lone hill-top or cliff overhanging the deep; thither, before dawn, a spotless youth or a virgin (you would say the latter, but the male is the nobler) should bring, on a salver of gold, the first and most perfect fruits of the earth. Adoring thousands stand clustered and waiting silent on the hill-side, and as the first ray is shot over the waters, the sacrifice is laid upon the altar, to be consumed by fire. The winds of heaven themselves bear away its essence, mingled with the prayers of the multitudes, to the throne of the Most High. A sacrifice should be worthy of the name, and I would not be averse even from the shedding of blood —a dove, as the emblem of purity; I—but you are laughing at me, and you shall not laugh. You are a Christian I suppose, and I think I have heard you are a Catholic. Come here."

"What next?" thought he.

In a recess of the bay-window, looking on the garden, was a third statuette, one of the Madonna and child. As a work of art it was far inferior to either of the others; but it, too, was a pretty thing of its kind, simple, girlish, full of grace. Before it was a vase of white lilies, and beneath stood an old organ carven and gilt, with battered pipes rising aslant.

"This was done for me by a German artist," explained Miss Grey; "such a dear, good man, like an old patriarch. He quite believed in the whole thing, you know; and when I paid him, told me I had a protector for life for my money. The others came from Italy; my guardian had them done for me. The idea was taken partly from my own head, partly from a French novel. One of the first men in Rome did them, and, as you see, carried out a notion of mine to have the base of distinct material from the figure."

She stooped to the little organ, tenderly trying a stray chord or two. She was silent a minute, as if lost in reverie, but her lips moved; then, casting her eyes upward to the mother and child, she broke into a stanza,—

"Hail, Queen of Heaven, the ocean's star,
　Guide of the wanderer here below,
Thrown on life's surge, we claim thy care,
　Save us from peril and from woe.
Mother of Christ, star of the sea,
Pray for the wanderer, pray for me,
Pray for thy children, pray for me."

Her hand sank upon the keys, and the melody died lingering, but she did not move; her eyes glittered, and her thoughts were far away. With that fervour in her face she looked like a prophetess inspired—a true Sybil again in life.

Roland was inexpressibly touched; a legend of the early Church flitted through his brain, and he laid his hand upon her shoulder. "You are another St. Cæcilia," he said.

"And pray, who was St. Cæcilia?" she asked, coming back with a bound to her usual look and manner.

"Don't you know" he said tenderly, "the story of St. Cæcilia, the young Roman lady who sang so beautifully that the angels came down from heaven to listen to her?"

"The saints and I are strangers," said the girl, turning away with a half-sigh.

"Strangers? What, you who talk to me like this, with all your searchings, you have never come upon the lives of the saints; never heard of the virgin St. Agnes, of St. Catherine broken on her wheel, of Sebastian shot with arrows, or the legend of the forty martyrs, and their heavenly crowns?"

She shook her head. "Never."

"Then, thank God, you have something to live for."

"Do the men about town usually talk of the saints in that way?" she asked, with a cynical inflexion in her voice.

He rose above the taunt. "You will understand me if you will read these stories. They are some of the finest in all the Church Liturgy."

"The Church? What Church?"

"*The* Church, dear, of course," he said, imprisoning both her hands. She did not resist.

"There is no church for me," answered the girl, looking away from him out into the day, and upon the blazing flower-beds of the lawn.

"Are you not Church of England?"

"Indeed" (vehemently) "I am not."

"What, you are a dissenter?"

"Very much so; and from every sect and creed and church. I never enter such a building. The God I worship is under heaven as He is above it. He is in the sun and sky, the earth and sea, in man himself."

Roland dropped her hands. Here was some explanation why Miss Grey was not better known and better thought of in the neighbourhood. Tolerant as he was, for man or woman to have no religion was beyond him.

"I am not baptized," she said, determined that her exact position should be plain.

"But what? what do people say?" he asked, stupidly and weakly, for he did not care what they said, but the gravity of the thing oppressed him.

"I am my own mistress, and my own judge," she said coolly, and with a gesture of some disdain. "I have, perhaps, more education than many of the people about here. Now, there's the clergyman's wife, dear good woman, who comes and cries over me once a month as a duty; but if she wants help or advice, she'll come once a week."

"After all," said Roland, recovering his balance as he saw the need for it, "it's your own affair; but you and I have many things to talk of yet."

Here came a fumbling at the door-handle, which usually turned glibly enough. "Please, miss, it's luncheon," said the pretty maid, and shut the door in a hurry.

There were plenty of flowers for lunch, and even a few viands, enough, at least, for their appetites; the wine was good, for Mr. Trelawney had laid it down for his own use, the fruit superb, and the ale was handed foaming to Roland in a silver tankard. The guest was satisfied, which was saying a good deal for him, and after it was over they passed out through the low-beamed eighteenth-century drawing-room into the verandah, and betook themselves to the lounging-chairs and rugs. From the verandah, as has been explained, a circular flight of stone steps descended into the lake, which surrounded this side of the house like a moat.

"I never saw anything so enchanting in my life," exclaimed Roland, with conviction, as he stepped out.

The lake lay at their feet, with its lilies and its swans swaying on the dark, inverted heavens. Beyond, the great elms stood asleep in the sunshine, casting their tremulous shadows into the depths where the lustrous bronze was ruffled a moment by a silver zephyr. Opposite floated, as though it would pass away, an islet of flowers, which shot long brilliances, as from a prism, into the mirror. Away out of reach in a tangled corner the ducks were chasing each other into the pool, and screaming with the fun of it. Here by the house the bees went booming, and the butterflies ran riot in the clouds of clematis and red honeysuckle that hung from the roof, and where the pale-fronded wisteria, with its purpling spiral blossoms, twined its stems like great snakes round the pillars, and always the light of the ripple danced reflected upon the ceiling.

" It is perfect; that old boat pulled up under the willow, those swans darting about with one eye open (they always remind me of waiters expecting a tip), those two great dogs snapping at the flies; and I will add, you, as you just poise yourself with one foot in that grass hammock, and wave that painted fan, with those ridiculous lords and ladies on it. And oh, really, those fish ! "

" What are they doing ? "

" Well, just at this moment if they're not advancing in double column of companies from the right—left wheel—capital ! I declare I never saw the thing done better; but then I'm only a militiaman. Ah ! and do I spy a fishing-tackle in that corner ? " and he sank back into a chair, with a sigh of satisfaction. " Then, indeed, the picture is complete. This is a life to live."

" It should be," said the girl, with a trace of weariness in her tone. " Why isn't it, I wonder ? " Her face changed: " What are you talking of ? " she went on, sharply. " Complete? Rubbish! I don't know much about men, but this I do know, that no picture is complete to any man without a paper and a cigar."

"A cigar? Well, perhaps," said her visitor, meditatively, feeling in his pockets, "if I may —but a paper—have you really such a thing?"

"The day's," she said, tossing it to him, "that is yesterday's; we're a day late down here, you see, and very awkward it is for the stock lists and so forth; and I'm always so vexed when there's a division in the House."

Roland smiled rather satirically, and lit his cigar. For the first time, perhaps, in his restless boyhood his mind was lulled into complete repose, and he turned over the crackling pages lazily, until he was half asleep, when as he idly glanced over the columns, his eye was drawn and rivetted to a certain spot, whereon stood out in black and white his own name. He sat up and looked again—yes, there was no mistake; it was in the *Gazette*, and the announcement ran: "The Blankshire Regiment of Foot—Roland Tudor of Sombrewood, gent., to be sub-lieutenant, *vice* Chawbridge promoted."

"By Jove!" he said, bounding from his chair, "I'm gazetted. Congratulate me, Miss Grey, I didn't expect it for another six months —that must be St. Maur's doing."

"You forget," answered she, half startled, "that I don't know in the least what you are talking about. I suppose," and here some mischief crept into her eyes, "you are a bankrupt, and now you are 'whitewashed,' don't they call it? Well, it's a good thing over, isn't it? Now you must start afresh, and be more careful."

Roland laughed again. "Not quite so bad, nothing worse than the Blankshire Regiment. I daresay I seem like a lunatic to you, but when a man's been waiting ever so long—most join at twenty, but I dawdled about until this Frontier business cropped up; and I am glad, too, the news comes to-day, and here—though—" he hesitated, "it'll alter all my plans. I shall have to go back to town at once."

She made him no answer; but after this speech constraint fell upon them both; the girl made an attempt to shake it off,—

"Well, you'll have time for a cup of tea, and a stroll through the domain, as they call it; every inch of it should be dear to you for its history, and there really is something to see: there are the ruins, and the rose-garden, and, oh! lots of things—but, by the way, why don't you go into the Guards or the cavalry?"

"Alas!" he said, mocking, "is woman identical over the whole earth? I thought I had left that sort of thing in town. All the young ladies there want you to go into the Guards or the cavalry—but I'll tell you my reason, madam, if you wish, because I mean business."

Truly he looked it, and a fresh interest fired the girl's heart as she looked at him: she was

unspeakably glad that the news had come to
him then and there. Yes, he should be a
credit to his cloth. Next to Nature, a uniform,
she said to herself, but he made an old tweed
suit look well.

"Gent. and sub-lieutenant," repeated Roland.
"It doesn't sound much, does it? but bigger
men have begun with less."

"I'll tell you what, I've just remembered
there's an Army List in the library, do let us
go and look at it."

Miss Grey was not one of those young
ladies who know the Army List by heart,
as was made apparent when it was unearthed; it looked very thin and faded and
grimy, and was discovered to be two years
older than its owner. There was great fun
over this, the more so when turning to the
regiment, they found Major Lickpenny set
down as an ensign in that gallant corps.

"I hope we come up to time in other subjects better than this," said the hostess, surveying the crammed but disordered shelves with
conscious pride. Ah! you must look at my
books some other day. Now let us get out as
quickly as we can. I will read you a chapter
from something else," and together they
walked out upon the lawns; while the great
tawny hounds swung leisurely behind them.

"This was my idea," said Miss Grey, stopping him at the gate of an enclosure; "see
what you think of it. It's an old walled garden open to the south, and the elms shelter it

on the other side. My notion was thickets of roses."

She turned the key, and there before their eyes, were, as she had said, thickets of roses: red and white and yellow and burning crimson massed together, and the huge tangled bushes were weighed to the earth, heavy and bowed with the bloom. In the centre, the trees had been trained over a hidden structure, and rose in a fragrant pyramid of colour fifty feet high, down which the great flowers were tumbling in cascades. What a rose-gardener would have said I know not, for they were let go almost wild, and only those trained round the trellised arches of the walks were trimmed to reasonable dimensions."

" This is the spring time, and it is June," said Sybil, almost as with apology, in answer to Roland's look, and they paced the sweet paths and drank the sweet air for some minutes in silence, so strongly did the heart of each speak in dumb feeling with the other's. Then, with no word, they left the garden, and by slow steps mounted the wide sweep of upland until they came in full view of the ruins of the great house. Over them a snowy flock of sea-birds was hovering in a cloud.

The building stood, solitary, dismantled, silent, with so much of humanity in it as a sightless marble mask, appealing speechlessly to Heaven against its doom of desolation—now only the birds of the air dwelt under its marble eaves, it was the last resting-place of the swallows when they fled south, their first foothold when they returned again. But to the sea-birds, the countless wild denizens of that savage coast, this superb monument to human vanity was a breeding-place and a home. No gun was ever fired on the estate, and not a stranger intruded on them from year's end to year's end; with Miss Grey they were as tame as pigeons.

"Now, this must be the garden of Eden," said Roland, as he and she walked on to the terrace, and the beautiful wild creatures, with their bejewelled eyes, swept noiselessly above their heads, or settling on the balustrade, stared at them with head aside inquiringly. Then a grand to-do and confabulation took place, but the citizens were soon satisfied; a vote of confidence was evidently passed with acclaim, and each one went on about his business as before.

"What a splendid contrast, those urns aflame with that intense scarlet against the snow of their wings!"

"Yes, it was a fancy of mine to plant them with geranium. Stand here, and you catch that great vase in the courtyard; it is in the shadow; but look where the sun strikes fire into the flowers."

"Wonderful! Whether I look at you or your landscape, I can't help rubbing my eyes. Every minute I expect to see the curtain fall and the lights turned down, and you have wickedly gone and played up to all the illusions of the spot. Dear me! what an absurd world we live in. Fancy this sweep of country, with its house and coast and ruin, being unlet so long as it was, my bailiff tells me, at 300*l*. a year, while people are paying from 700*l*. to 1000*l*. for smoky dens in the side streets off Park Lane."

" I can understand it," sighed the girl. " You can hardly imagine what the world is to me who have heard so much of it and know so little. I have never been in London."

" We must manage to remedy that," said Roland, half muttering; " but how extraordinary ! "

" Oh ! I know Paris, Florence, and Rome well enough."

" London is the microcosm of the world. It is so great that every man and woman has his or her own London, and each is different. Eighty houses, and God knows how many human souls, are added to it every day ! "

" How awful ! "

" That is right, that is the word. But, oh, this is a place where one may speak of the awful problems of great cities."

They had found a little grove of ilex-trees and a sunny bench that looked upon the blue Campagna and the hill and mist and sea, and there they sat and talked; not much perhaps, but more quietly and more thoughtfully than before.

Suddenly, Roland sprang up,—

" Now, Miss Grey, really you're too bad, to see a man's face grinning over one's shoulder through the leaves in such a place. Wretched old satyr, I never dreamed of a statue, and you certainly have a knack of magnetizing your stone and bronze to life."

There, in the bushes, with the pedestal hid, was the brown weather-beaten head of a faun peering down on them.

"He has the look of a devil, and he is the sort of colour."

Miss Grey laughed merrily, "My dear darling old Pan. I never thought he'd frighten anybody. I often come up here and clean his face for him and blow the dust out of his eyes. Then I tell him all my secrets, and he helps me, you know, in his own quiet way."

She pushed aside the boughs and laid a tender, slender hand on the rough-hewn stone. The fearful grin on the creature's face surely broadened under the flickering leaves; he might well have passed for flesh and blood.

"I owe him a grudge," said Roland, as she stroked the stony locks. "Do leave him alone."

"Good-bye, dear old man," and she pinched the satyr's ugly ear. "I can see by your face you approve of it all; now we're going home."

Tea had been set out for them in the verandah, and when they returned, the mellowing rays were striking, almost level, upon the white cloth and darkling silver of the urn, and through the frail egg-shell of the cups. Neither spoke, for the good-bye lay heavy at the heart of each. They sat awhile playing with the things, and the shadows lengthened and deepened. At last Roland said,—

" I think you might come over one afternoon,
Miss Grey, if you will, and see my tower, and
my ridiculous ancestors, and my boat, and the
rest of me. My old housekeeper, Mrs. Tyrrel,
will be there to play chaperon in the background. It is a rough place, but, oh, my dear,
if you will come, we will make it as smooth as
we can for you."

There was no affectation in her.

" Do you think I might ? " she said straightly
and plainly, looking down, and the long black
lashes spread ray-wise over her cheek. " It's
beyond me, and I leave myself in your hands."

A thrill passed through him at these words,
but he answered quietly, " Very well. You will
bring your maid. I think I can arrange it
with Mrs. Tyrrel, and I will write." And so,
with no more than a handshake, he went away,
though he knew it not, out of the most perfect
hour of his life.

Youth never realizes this ; it says, " Surely
to-morrow shall be as to-day, and as many to-
morrows as we will." But it is never so ;
something is gone.

Even as he left her, the sinking sun was
kissing with slow lingering the far hills, like a
lover quitting his betrothed, " he setteth and he
hasteth to whence he rose." " Oh, my beloved, adieu ! a little while, and I return to you
afresh, anew, bringing with me all joy and
light and good things." So spake he with the
rider on his homeward way.

* * * * *

It was late ere he reached his tower, and he

smiled as he looked at his watch, for the legend of the monk and the bird from paradise came into his head. He had been three hours doing the seven miles.

The following morning brought letters—a long blue envelope, O.H.M.S.—the contents of which informed him in curt language that he had been gazetted to the Blankshire Regiment, and that he would shortly be required to proceed to Ireland to join head-quarters. Somehow or other the long-expected missive was uninteresting. The next was from his uncle, and in a very shaky hand. It may be given *verbatim et literatim.*

"The Albany, June.

"MY DEAREST NEPHEW,—I am surprized—I could find it in me to say pained—at not hearing from you, for as you well know the care and interest I have always taken in your afairs has increesed rather than lesened as my hairs grow grey." (This was mere romance, the Major's hairs did not grow grey, as he took very good care.) "Jack Arcy has told me all about you, and being gazzetted to the dear old corpse, he was the adjutant, and your magnificent reception. And I am glad you have got so many new friends, but you mussent forget the old. Is it true you are going to build the concern up again exactly like it was? He tells me it's a real good thing, worth, at least, 2500 p. anne., and that 10,000 has been lumped up by the lawyers. My dear, dear Roly, you may guess what this good news has been to your old uncle and guardian, with whom time has all along dealt very diferently. Dear boy, the old fellow is even more *pinched* (he doesn't exajerate the word, he does assure you) than usual. He won't name figures to you, but your own kind heart will interpret his hopes, and know that he is

" Your ever loving uncle,
" ALGERNON LICKPENNY.

" P.S.—Even 5 would not be amis, if *at once.*
" P.S.—I do hope they took your messure in Savile Row before you went down to that *infer* "—(scratched out, but not obliterated) " dear old Sombrewood."

" Now Arcy must be a cleverish fellow, for I never heard of him before," was Roland's sole comment, as he tossed the letter into the empty grate. The next was equally characteristic of the writer.

" The heart of the pale face and singer of songs yearneth towards his mighty brother, who since one moon has been absent afar, and who since the setting of a single sun is become a great warrior. Pardon me, my dear Roland, I have been studying the noble savage as the purest fount of human expression; but perhaps I shall make myself more clear if I say that I have missed you much in the month you have have been away, and that you were in the *Gazette* last night. In my humble opinion, as a man of peace, you are a born soldier, and so long as I am here, your memory shall not perish for want of a poet to hymn your deeds, but I have my doubts whether you will find space for the swing of your right arm in the British service.

"Rumour has been busy with you; there was a telling bit, anent a certain Lord of the Isles, running in the shilling society papers last week. I suppose it's in the penny ones this. A young lady of our acquaintance composed some vile verses on the occasion, and came to me as a literary man, to get them into print. Happy fellow! you have only to strike an attitude and the world will applaud.

"For myself, I have at last brought out my first serious child under the title of 'Ever So,' a volume of poems, and now I am at war with the publishers over a novel. Blind they are to their own interests, for they actually fail to see what it must mean to them in cash. I wonder whether any previous author has ever found this. Then, too, I have lit upon a magician (scientific) in a shanty in the Erith marshes, of all the world. My name will go down to posterity as the discoverer of a discoverer. You never heard of the retroscope, I daresay. Nevertheless, it's a name to conjure by; I place it, and I trust it will place me at the very least two thousand years in advance of the age. It is the dawn of an era of absolute truth; no more historic doubts. What do you say to seeing every public event of the past, and most of the private ones, with your own eyes, in the actual course of consummation? Last night, for instance, I watched the battle of Hastings from end to end, and it has

made me uncommonly sleepy to-day. I can
almost swear to it, that Harold was not killed.
A small body of men, about a dozen, got away
by a lane that ran obliquely to the coast behind
some hedges, about twenty minutes before the
last *mêlée*. Three horses (one a grey) had
been kept waiting all the afternoon in a hollow
behind a gorse thicket at the second bend of
the lane; three of the fugitives mounted these
and galloped inland like the wind. I am sure,
from the manner of the other two, that one of
them was the king."

At this point the reader's features relaxed into
a smile, but he went on, " The simplicity of the
thing is its great charm. You are aware, I suppose, of two everyday facts, i.e. that nothing is
lost in nature, and that every object is perpetually throwing off rays, which continue plunging
into eternal time and space. You know, of course,
that there are stars which see us not as we are
now, but as we were a thousand, ten thousand,
a million years since, according to their distance.
To refract and focus these rays is the germ of the
discovery. This once done, by successive en-
largements of infinitesimal points, in a sort of
constant photography, the picture is achieved.
Do I make myself plain? The only sight at
present obtainable is strictly bird's eye, but this
is not disadvantageous. The inventor's idea
is to lay hold also of the errant vibrations of
sound, to combine them with their luminous
belongings—and there you have the entire past
at your beck and call for ever! Mind your
ways, friend, lest some centuries hence your

descendants turn the retroscope upon you down at Sombrewood, and have cause to blush for their ancestor!

       " Affectionately yours,

          " WARBURTON BRABANT.

" P.S.—They brought out a new religion last week—somewhere in the Strand, I think—but it doesn't seem a particularly good one, so I shall stick to the old for the present. By the way, another 'important conversion,' Miss Connie Lightleg, of the Varieties, who was received into the bosom, &c., &c. What *are* we to do with our converts—nay, with our editors? No more just now."

Enough at one time, thought Roland, opening a third letter, which was from St. Maur. It was not a cheerful one; the writer was too deep a thinker to be ever very gay for long together.

" Affairs in town," he said, " have a curious look, as you will see by the papers I forward. There is a socialism stalking abroad that is both illogical and detestable, and means no less than moral and social ruin. It is gaining ground—and solid ground, if I may so express myself—like wildfire. The prodigious growth of population favours it strongly, but the country is careless and forgets that if London is swamped, half the empire will be submerged. The Church—I should say the Churches—are asleep, and yet religion is the only possible bulwark against this particular foe. Education without moral training is worse than useless, and can lead to nothing short of social suicide. I am sorry, but not surprised, to see the old-fashioned Toryism has come to life again in its most virulent form among many of the better classes. Well, the Liberals, or some of them, would insist on patting the Radicals on the back; the Radicals, in turn, have patted the Socialists (the party most easily recruited), and here we are. Depend upon it the day is not so far distant when every throat will be cut in Park Lane—my own assuredly included—unless they give a few of us who have worked our best for them, the choice of a comfortable tree to hang on. Even so, it is time to select your tree.

"I have been below the surface for some years now, and know what I am talking about. You are even more of an anachronism and species of feudal oddity than I feel myself to be, which is saying a good deal. You ought to be getting back to town, we want men of your cut sadly. I have much to tell you that I will not write. What on earth induced you, with your head, to join the service ? I met a friend of yours the other day, an author. He seems a clever fellow, but too much in the Greek or chivalric type. What can he be doing in this century of ours, which at heart rejoices in brutal ugliness, both moral and physical ? How else was London ever built, which is the type of us ? Some of his poems are as taking as himself. I forget his name —bring him to see me.

"Always sincerely yours,

"St. Maure."

CHAPTER X.

THE advent of the mediæval functionary to his high office did not happen without a corresponding flutter in the dove-cots of the county-side. The womenkind at Griddles' and Tomlinson's were desperately exercised with the romance of it. And when it leaked out that Robinson actually held the castle precincts of him, on an annual heriot of three horseshoes with nails complete—a debt which had been curiously allowed to lapse for some years, their enthusiasm rose to the highest pitch, for Robinson was one of themselves, and they did all want to be as feudal as they possibly could! Their menkind found their way to the tower, and the usual civilities were exchanged. These, however, did not ripen—then people heard little more, until all at once they heard too much, indeed more than there was to hear.

Although it must be admitted that the young warden was desperately in love, and no wiser than other men in a similar position, he was not so lost to the dignity of his race and his manhood as to forget what was due to them, or to wish to take shelter from the rough-and-tumble of life behind the screen of a petticoat. The last batch of letters had shaken his contentment somewhat rudely.

"Bedad, there's a foight, and oime out av it!" as the Irishman said bitterly, when he watched a scrimmage from his prison window. This very accurately explains Roland's feelings, nor were they rendered less acute by finding in the paper an account of a meeting in Trafalgar Square, two days before, when St. Maur, on his attempting to address the people, had been howled down and pelted. He must return at once; there was a place waiting for him, if it were only by the side of his friend. But he had work to do here, county work as well as private, and Sombrewood was not a place he could run up and down from once a week. It was twenty miles to the nearest station, and the few trains that came as far as the terminus, crawled rather than ran for the last hundred miles. Altogether, the journey was a fearfully tedious one. It would be a week at the shortest before he could leave; that would give him time to arrange affairs, and allow him a day on which he could entertain Miss Grey.

Now, concerning this, there was some trouble Very gently indeed he broke the possibility of such a visitor to Mrs. Tyrrel, mentioning "a guest" merely, but with no hint as to either age or sex. This "put about" Mrs. Tyrrel so considerably, that she even threw out a reminder (having fallen again to her normal levels) that he was but a guest himself. He was very humble, servile almost: he had not forgotten this, he said.

Well, of course, there was his room, and he must take his friend there.

Here was the crucial point, and the delicate matter devolved upon him of explaining that Mrs. Tyrrel's own room or her niece's, would have to be devoted to the reception of this friend, for she was a lady, and was young. Further, she would bring her maid with her. For the moment Mrs. Tyrrel was struck dumb, but she had lived seventy years in the world, and the case was not unprecedented, even in her limited experience. Her age and respectability entitled her to a high standpoint, which she took relentlessly, and succeeded in making the lord high warden feel very unlordly, very low, and very unwardenish generally. She said little, except that it should be as he wished, and ostentatiously reserved her verdict until after the occasion. None the less did the old lady resolve that the uttermost should be done. Great, be sure, was the confabulation among the authorities, and when the day came round, the oriel room was metamorphosed. The old panellings shone like ebony, the old black table groaned with flowers, the coats-of-arms in the upper lights of the oriel gleamed like fresh-set jewels, and the sun struck out of them that splendour of colour which only the centuries can achieve in glass. The master could hardly believe his

eyes, but when he attempted to express his
thanks he was relegated to his place, quietly
and effectually; not yet would Mrs. Tyrrel
commit herself.

Eleven o'clock—heavens! would the morning never pass? Poor master, even as he
counted the minutes, the hand of Fate was
raised aloft to strike him a blow that should
lay him low, as it would any one of us in his
time and place. Already the hour grew late,
he went out into the air and paced to and fro
upon the walls, like Sister Anne; then under
the twining thorns to the gate, where the
stony mottoes stared at him derisively "Wel-
com." "Bettʳ-gon." It was a blazing summer
noon. What could be keeping her? A new
dress to be tried perhaps—no! Somehow the
idea did not fit her, he dismissed it; in his
pocket lay a note that she had written, saying,
"I will be with you at twelve," and now it was
half-past.

There was no long view from the manor, it
lay too much buried by tree and down, and as he
stood between the bald stone posts of the gateway that led so pompously to nothing, he could
see barely fifty yards adown the dusty highway. How silent it was, how glaring; the
dark-green needles of the pine-trees opposite,
were powdered like the hair of the miller's men.
A lizard scuttled from one side to the other,
and vanished in the hot nettles under the wall,
leaving its trail, a little groove in the thick
white dust across the road. At last a horse!

but no carriage. A man jogged up quietly enough, and recognizing the master at the gate, handed him a note. The writing was *hers*, and he read while the letters played leap-frog, and other curious antics under his eyes.

" I cannot, *cannot* come. Guardian arrived unexpectedly last night, but to-morrow at same hour I *will* come. I have arranged.—SYBIL GREY."

" Very well. My compliments to Miss Grey, and it's *all right*," he said coldly, giving the man a shilling, and watching him away; then he turned into the gate and groaned. The sun went in, and it grew dark; or was it all his fancy as he went back towards the tower? His sight swam, and his breath came short; never had he felt the like of it before.

Mrs. Tyrrel was shocked out of her senses. She saw him " dazing along," as she expressed it, bareheaded through the sun, and ran out to drag him in, but he could hardly put his words together coherently. " Eh! my man; but I was frighted of him," as she told her husband afterwards; " and 'twas all because the lady's no' comin' till the morrow ! " Here she laughed; but for that, the gravity of the state of things impressed her monstrously. If this were the meaning of it, Miss Grey's visit must assume a very different importance. Such is first love; an "impossible" thing looked at from all points, and not less impossible when youth is overpassed and gone.

The reader will not be surprised to hear that

Roland recovered. In the course of two or three hours he could see straight again, and even get through a short sentence correctly. By evening he was almost in good spirits, and counting the hours until to-morrow's noon— but he could not rest—sleep he felt would not come to him; in fact he thought it would be a pity to go to bed on such a fine night; and when all was closed, he went down the private stairway which has been spoken of, and let himself out upon the walls by the postern gate. His nerves were still overstrung, and in sharp bodily exercise he found considerable relief. He walked briskly up and down for a while, but the space was too narrow for him, and he went down on to the green mounds that covered the hearth of his ancestors, and out of the grounds on to the hill-side where it stretched weird and black above. There appeared to be no life whatever; the stars were hidden, and the moon, and he could only feel his way.

"If ever ghost should show itself, it should be to me here to-night," he thought; "positively I should like it, but how to call one up? Crime and outrage have surely appealed to heaven long enough from this memory-soaken earth. What a scoundrel I should be if heredity is to count! There below, my great grandfather drowned himself, and there his steward, who found him, drove his horse into the water to make believe it was an accident. So the place has never thriven since, and holds a curse for

us all they say. Well! I will try it. I feel
like revoking a few of these old wives' tales."
He lit a cigar, and turned down the hill to the
pool at its foot.

In not a few country neighbourhoods is to be
found an ugly pond, which seems to exercise a
peculiar and fatal fascination for the wayfarer;
without special reason that one can trace, it has
been the haunt and playground of suicide.
Such was the Black Pool, as it was known
through all the country-side. Deep and dark
in shadow in broadest daylight, it was now
black as Hades, and as Roland groped his way
down to it, he could see absolutely nothing,
save now and again a pale tinge of phosphores-
cent light on the ripple of the water. The air
was oppressive and mal-odorous, as if laden
with decaying matter, and the turf spongy,
rising after the foot had passed, telling no
tales. It has been said Tudor had no nerves,
and the gruesome spot enchained him. He
sat down among the wide roots of a beech-
tree, and rested against its stem, for he was
tired.

"There is peace here," he mused, "but it
is the peace of the charnel-house." It was
very still. An owlet hooted from the tower—
from very far away came the melancholy howling of a dog—an acorn fell, breaking the stillness, then coiling at his feet, something slimy
glided past him into the pool, and the circles
showed, then fainted out of the water. The
air was close and heavy as with an opiate,

he grew dreamy, gradually the skein of his thoughts was loosened, unwittingly he slept.

And by-and-by a feeling of strange, unreasoning happiness crept over him, such as with surcease of pain comes to the sick man in his bed. All the floating anxiety of the day was lifted from him, and he looked about. Ah! he might have known as much; nought, and no one else but she could have poured that wild delight into his breast. She was at his side. They were back again, and walking in the garden of roses, and they drank of their perfume, and trod the fragrant paths as they had done before, in a silence too happy to break. All the while he looked at her in questioning and answer, his whole soul going out to meet hers in love and tenderness, and she led him on among the flowers, saying, " Dear love, come and gather with me, for it is the spring-time, and it is June." She herself was red and white like the roses; and he went in and gathered a garland of them, and twined them in her hair. Then she gave herself to him, saying, " You shall take me home," and they went out together.

But what was come upon the world? It was different surely—there was no garden here, and no flower, and the wind struck chill; he would have stopped and gone back with her, but it was vain—an unseen power hurried them on. He looked upon the changing landscape; the bare boughs were waving overhead with the winter wind upon her—and he saw that while her eyes looked unflinching into his, they were agonized with tears, and her face was white like a drooped lily; the roses in her hair had withered and fallen, and in their place was left only a crown of thorns, which had pierced her to the blood. He touched her hand, and it was like a dead woman's, but in her face was no fear, rather an inspired hope, and the very whiteness of it spread faint rays into the black night around, and then he knew all at once that they were standing together upon the brink of the hideous pool.

His tongue clove to the roof of his mouth, he could not speak, but he essayed to gather her in safety to his arms, and she, turning her worn, wan face upon him, flung herself into them like one bidding adieu.

"Dear love," she said, "I thank you always that you have cared for me, and have brought me to my true home." She disengaged herself and sank away from him, and as again he would have clasped her, "Nay love," she said, and she pointed to where the stars were fading in the eastern heaven, "until the daybreak and the shadows flee away," and she was lost to him.

He awoke like a madman. The scene of the dream being identical with the one in which he lay, he could not divest himself of the hallucination, or realize that he was the sport of nightmare. Stumbling forward, drunken with sleep, he plunged into the reed thickets and the sedge, calling aloud her name. The echoes of hill and wood rose mocking as if in laughter, and were still—but in his ears yet rang the voice of her farewell, and the perspiration rolled from his brow in heavy drops, while his limbs were cramped and paralyzed with slumber.

He looked upwards to the sky—it was daybreak, the shadows were fled away, the birds were twittering on every tree, every leaf and flower was turning to the light. Gone were the dreadful shades, the foul, black waters gone—at his feet lay all the golden glories of the morning heavens, unrolled as in a mirror darkly, and the sweet breezes blew. No phantom could live in such a scene.

"I have gone stark mad," he said to himself. "I prayed for bewitchment, and I have had my fill. Serve me right, serve me right!" Slowly he turned homewards, with the dream clinging round his spirit like a pall. Were the sins of his fathers in truth upon his head? It was as though he had aged years in that single night; and the resolve formed itself and grew fixed in his heart, that on that day he would cast the die, and seal, so far as lay with him, the fate of his own life and Sybil Grey's. He had not meant it yet. All had been so sudden. They were young, she was almost a child, but the vividness and horror of the dream was such, that realities paled before it, and it had given him some dim notion of what the loss of her would mean. It was not that he had doubts of her, but he would bind her to him by every tie that should be sacred in the eyes of God and man.

He let himself in by the postern, and crept shamefaced to his bed. He was not down early, but he saw Tyrrel in his room, and before midday the bailiff and his men were dragging the pool. Needless to say, that as he valued his reputation for sanity, Roland gave no hint as to his night's adventure, or any reason for the order.

"Ye'll no get to the bottom of it," was Tyrrel's curt remark when he received it, but he said no more.

Now they had nearly finished, and on one bank were piled hillocks of black, ill-odorous slime, but they had found nothing. The master sauntered up casually, smoking his morning cigar. To look at him fresh from bath and toilet, no one would imagine that he had been afield all night.

"Found anything?" he asked.

"Ye'll find nothing here, sir; there's no bottom to the thing, I'm telling ye, and I'll prove it," answered Tyrrel. "Look here." He took up a long piece of bent iron railing and tossed it in. "Now boys, drag away," he shouted. It was just the thing that should have caught the nets, but they drew them backwards and forwards, and to and fro, and nothing came ashore save the matted dead leaves and rotting twigs, befouled and sticking in the ooze.

There was a clatter and a cloud upon the white highway, and a brougham came dashing up a good ten minutes before its time.

" I shall get out here," cried a girl's voice, and as Roland sprang forward the carriage stopped. The door opened, a slender arched foot glanced upon the step, and a figure that matched it followed out into the bright sunshine, and was crossing the radiant gold-and-silver-sprinkled turf towards him. Each time her beauty had dazzled him afresh, and now again he had lost his tongue.

We will allow once for all that Miss Grey's theory was to make the best of herself at all times and places, and in every way. Self-improvement and progress had been the main-springs of her life, since she could understand the meaning of the words. In dress no less than other things she travelled in the same groove. A born artist, she had trained her eye with the utmost severity that was possible to her; the study of form and curve had become little short of a passion. Here she found herself alone. Many of her friends had a pretty taste for colours, but she had not yet encountered the female mind to which form was anything but a closed book. Latterly her dresses had been made from her own designs, and she had had professionals down from town for the making and fitting. So perhaps Roland may be pardoned, boy as he was, for his fresh admiration of her looks.

" What are you doing here?" she asked

gaily, as in glad but speechless welcome he took her hand. Irresistibly impelled, he led her to the pool. "It will clear my brain of its horrors," he thought, "as nothing else can," and they stood in reality, as they had stood in phantasy, upon its brink.

"Oh! what a dreadful place," she said, shuddering. "And in the midst of all this beauty, too, it's enough to give one a nightmare."

"It is," he assented grimly, but his heart was bounding with joy to see her there as she was. "One of my ancestors drowned himself in it, and several other people have followed his example."

"Oh! how *charming*," said the girl with a light laugh, running to and fro like a child escaped from school. "I am sure there must be a story to every tree in the place," and she leaned against the flecked white beech-stem where Roland had slept. "You must tell me them all," and she danced out into the fierce sunlight. The men had stopped their work and doffed their caps, and there in the long, lush grass she, all unconscious, made for them the prettiest picture their eyes had ever looked at upon earth.

"Now, I'm really surprised that you've not asked after Mr. Trelawney," she chattered, as Roland walked with her towards the tower; "and I want to know if I'm forgiven for yesterday."

"It looks very much as if you had *carte*

blanche from us all, and I'm afraid we must take what we can get—your guardian and I—but oh! yesterday. It was a cruel blow. But you will not understand." His brow knit slightly as he looked into her gay face.

But Miss Grey understood very well, though she did not choose to say so. She went an even better way to brighten him. "The dear, dear old fellow," she said. "You know he would have come with me" (a smothered exclamation from Roland), "but he's got the gout" ("Thank God," *sotto-voce*), "and he's going back to town" ("Heaven be praised"), "and," here her voice trembled with glee, "he's going to take me with him, and oh! you'll be there too, won't you?"

With difficulty the master of Sombrewood refrained from embracing his guest on the spot. He could have kissed Mr. Trelawney himself, and his inquiries after that gentleman's welfare became simply idiotic.

The carriage had gone on with the maid, and under the archway, Mrs. Tyrrel, in oh! such a marvellous cap, sternly awaited the mistress; but no sooner had she caught sight of Miss Grey, no sooner had she seen the gleam of her cheek and the flash of her eye, the turn of her neck, and the stately sway of her figure as she came; no sooner had the soft, dark eyes fallen upon her, and she had heard the low, sweet ring of her voice and laugh, than Mrs. Tyrrel was conquered utterly, and abased into the dust; for to her too the lady came as a vision of brightness, and beauty, and grace, all undreamed of before. Henceforth, until death, she was her slave, and the stern old woman's knees were trembling under her, as she led the way into the oriel room.

At last, at last! the coachman and the maid were settled, and the duenna was gone. The twain were a minute to themselves alone. Then Roland could resist no longer, neither did she.

"Welcome, welcome, dearest," he said, drawing her to himself, and tenderly lifting the silken scarf from off her shoulders. In the act and almost without intention, his arms closed about her. Half uncertain, she came, heaving a deep sigh, and hid her burning face averted in the rough folds of his coat. Then he kissed the thick coils of her hair and let her go; but she would not face him, and stood silent, looking from the window, and the new-born joy of a perfect understanding was added to them both. At this moment Tyrrel came into the room with the wine, and so broke the spell. "Do you mean to say," she asked, laughing, as he left again, "that that superb piece of antique furniture is really your very own? Why, he must be worth at least three hundred a year to you, with his florid face and long white hair; to own such a being is to be a feudal chieftain on the spot. I suppose he's real, not made up, waxwork, or anything of that sort, eh? Now I mean to rifle and turn over all your nick-nacks."

" I have very few down here; no statues,
no draperies. That pretty miniature is my
grandmother, whom I have been in love with
all my life; and there, in that brand-new oil-
skin, is my spotless sword, just fresh from the
makers. I ordered it at least six months ago;
they saw my name in the *Gazette*, I suppose,
and sent it down here, where it will be uncommonly useful!"

She untied the case and drew the weapon
curiously from its scabbard; as she did so,
the eye of love caught the lambent, scarce-
quenched light in his.

" We are rivals," she said, half sadly, " this
and I—I know it; but I will be generous, and
you shall have it afresh at my hands." She
kissed the shining blade, and the brightness of
it was dimmed a moment with the film.

" Put it away," said Roland, touched in
spite of himself; "it gets no chance nowadays,
the man grows old while his sword rusts."

" But if the chance should come, nothing
should stand in the way," said the girl, with
an odd tightening of her lips.

" Bah! the fault I find with civilization is,
that there is nothing left worth fighting for,
that is, as a soldier."

" You are right to limit it to that, there is
plenty left for other men—and women. Well!
and what else have you?"

" There is my inkstand, and in that corner
is an old guitar, which I found here, and
have tuned up to amuse myself; and there,

hanging up, are my saddle and spurs. Finis to catalogue."

"Perfect," cried the girl, enthusiastically, "you have all a great man needs to begin life with. Now I will give you a song."

She took the guitar, and tightening the strings to her liking, she sat down in the open window and carolled.

"That's a pretty thing," said Roland, his face, which had been clouded, clearing; "I am no judge, and hardly know a note, but you have a wonderful magnetism in your voice, positively you have gathered together every living thing on the premises. Look!"

It was true. She glanced downwards. In the yard below was a motley assembly; there was the bailiff, his wife, and his niece, two or three of the labourers, her own coachman and maid, the postman, and an errant butcher-boy on horseback, and round these all the dogs, fowls, and pigeons of the establishment seemed to be collected.

"A select circle," she cried, in a fit of laughter. "Stay a minute," for they were breaking up in confusion; and out of the window she sang to them a pathetic little native air, so prettily and plaintively, that long before it was finished, Mrs. Tyrrel was in tears, and the butcher-boy was flourishing a red bandanna, but perhaps this was to show he had one.

"Come, come," said Roland, fearful for his own susceptibilities if this went on, "now we must really have lunch."

When this was over, they strolled through the grounds out into the fields, until they reached the church. The mausoleum was unlocked with due ceremony, and Miss Grey ushered in. If she was at first somewhat impressed and overawed by such a display of moribund magnificence, her spirits were too high and joyous to be so for long. She almost danced among the grim effigies as she passed from one to another.

" I declare," she said, stopping before a life-size angel in marble, who was weeping in stony desolation over an urn, " I've often thought I should like to be an angel. I don't see why I shouldn't make as good a one as that melancholy lady—or gentleman, is it? It's provokingly sexless, for all its classic features, and impossibly perfect toes. What do you say now? I suppose my cream cashmere is not strictly angelic, but still "—and she posed herself in a like attitude on the other side of the urn, lifting a beauteous rounded arm from which the drapery fell away, and clasping the figure's marble hand and wreath,—" I *can't* weep, you know," she said, laughing.

Through the cobwebby yellow panes the sun of June—the sun of love—was pouring fiercely, flashing a jewelled light in an odd spot or two, where a remnant of the old stained glass was left in the traceries. The dust rose thick in the warm bright air, and through it the stone effigies looked dim, mere shadows of the past—

a ghostly array—and in the midst of them stood out in radiant reality, the bright girl-figure, telling of all life and health and happiness. The marble angel might have wept at its own discomfiture!

For Roland, he could only stammer some incoherent words, his heart was over-full. He led her tenderly away, and they walked slowly down to the shores of the haven, which lay not many hundred yards distant, where a flight of broken steps and a landing-place was still dignified by the name of the "Water Gate," though it was long since every trace of such grandeur had vanished.

A steady breeze had got up since the morning, and was blowing from the westward down the haven; just outside, the little yacht rode proudly at anchor, spick and span, all her damage repaired, and all her Sunday canvas furled. Had not the master himself helped to scour and scrape and clean and paint throughout the live-long week? And now she rose and fell—a fairy boat upon a fairy ocean—and the ripples traced a flickered marbling on her gleaming copper and the shining cedar of her sides. Half the crew were already aboard— that is, the smaller half—the boy, who secretly arrogated to himself the title of pilot, but who was, strictly speaking, not so much even a boy as an imp, as his unchanging grin and fiendish delight in storm and tempest sufficiently proved. He took intense pride in himself, in his clothes, in his yacht, and, since that week of

the gales, in his master, though he had mutinied
—but that was more for the name of the thing,
and to say he had done it.

" *Foam*, ahoy ! " shouted the captain. " Do
you think you can steer, Miss Grey ? 'Pon my
soul it seems a shame to take any one with us
on a day like this. I can manage the sails
well enough, and we'll hoist that young devil
ashore."

Miss Grey confessed to a slight knowledge
of the tiller, and knew port from starboard,
but she thought the *y. d.* in question had
better be allowed to come and play the part of
the sweet little cherub.

" Ah ! well, perhaps so ; he knows the reefs,
and he'll look after the boat while we land."

A definite purpose was in the captain's head ;
there was a certain stretch of beach on one of
those islands in the offing, lying open to the
wide sea and the westering sun, whither he
would take his mistress. So they went aboard,
and spread their snow-white wings, and beat
up into the " Bloody Mouth ;" and the sturdy
pilot stood forrard, whistling softly for the
wind, with his hands deep in the pockets of
his jacket, and looking out to seaward, the iron
grin upon his face. Can a man grin and
whistle too ? I know not ; but this boy could.
Then as they dipped into the green sea
swell, and hissed onwards through the swirling
rapids, he swayed to and fro with mathematical
precision, firm as on a pivot, and kept his
weather eye upon the nearing island, as steady

as a compass. Suddenly he stopped his whistling, but only once did he speak to the two who were so busy aft with the difficult task of the tiller, and that was to say,—

"Ye'll not have that trouble wi' it, captain, going home."

Was this satire, or weather wisdom?

Roland took no trouble to inquire, nor, as they landed at the rock-hewn stairway (not without difficulty, in spite of Miss Grey's nimbleness), did he heed at all the boy's speech, "Ye'll keep yer eye to windward, sir."

"All right!" he answered; "you just hang about here for an hour or two. Run her round Castle Island, if you like, and see how long it takes you."

Ah! but it was a gay scramble up the cliff, even though dress and shoes were not quite fitted for the sort of thing. What of that, when lungs and heart and muscles are? Only the wear and tear of a few shillings to the pocket.

"Now!" panted the girl, breathless with the enjoyment of it as they gained the summit, "I feel as I have often wished to feel, but have never quite felt before. Here we are on a real desert island; could anything be more delicious? We are a sea-king and queen! And look at our countless subjects," she pointed round to the birds that came and went to and fro, thickening the air, for it was still the breeding season. "And look here," pointing to the ruins, "this must be our palace. I think there are no roofs, but there is this bright blue dome over-

head; and if the walls are slightly out of repair,
just see, they are all gilt in the light, and
much, much prettier than if they were straight
and new and nasty. But what I like best of
all is," and she drew herself up with a little
conscious gesture, "that we are clean and
warm and well fed, and our clothes fit us, and
our yacht is dancing down below, ready to
take us back to dinner and civilization in half
an hour. This is precisely what I've wanted
all my life; this is a real ideal."

"Come I will show you the sea-king's shrine,"
said the boy in answer, and led the way across
the tufted sand-hills, with their new, strange-
tinted vegetation, their long blue and silver
grasses, pale pink flowers, dwarfed sweet briar
and bristling thistle, until they came upon the
other side, and looked down upon a sandy
beach, which lay stretched below, spotless,
to the setting sun. Shut in by walls of natural masonry, wrapped in dim silences, it was
guarded by great crags and pinnacles, like
mammoths turned to stone, their rugged faces
lit, and keeping eternal watch out over the
changing sea.

"Ah! what splendour!" cried the girl,
clasping her hands; "it is like looking on the
world of a past age or a future one. Man hath
not been here, it is not fitted for him, or, he
hath been, and his footfall is passed for ever
from the earth. Say something, or I shall break
into epic verse."

"Oh! I think it all; and you express it
capitally."

"Ah! and do look!" she said, as her eye ranged from point to point. "There is a pathway of burnished gold which leads from the beach across the sea through that bright break in the heavy clouds—there, there; straight into Heaven itself. See, the gates are standing open wide. Oh! come! come quickly with me! give me your hand; let us travel that path together."

Hand in hand they descended the broken steep.

"I feel as if I were doing something irreparable," she said, as they reached the foot; nevertheless, she skipped gaily from him, and ran to the sand, so that her light footprints lay deep on its pure surface.

"Ah! we shan't get to Heaven this way, I see."

"We will go as near as we can, Sybil," he called to her, and there was something in his voice that made her stop. "Sweetheart, I have brought you here to tell you one little serious thing. This place seems to me like a temple, where Nature prostrate worships her God. No human eyes look upon it, no human feet tread here. To us, to the men of my name, as you know, this and all the coast has been cradle and grave. On these crags generations of us have spilled their blood, and our bones are buried in the sand, and lie fathoms deep in these tumbling seas. Sybil, I have brought you here, because I have learned your mind—and it seemed to me a place where, of all others, I

might tell you of my love. Last night I had
a dreadful dream, my darling," his face was
very stern, and his voice grew husky. " I
dreamed—I dreamed—we were apart."

Mutterings of low thunder broke across the
sea—neither noticed it. On the girl the full
meaning of his words seemed to strike like a
bolt shot home. She stood like a statue, but
breathing hard breaths, her scarlet lips asunder
—then she burst into tears.

" You are happy to find words," she said,
putting her hands into his in complete surrender, " for I have none. Dear love, I can
only thank you that you have brought me
here," and she nestled to his breast ; but the
words struck dizzily upon his ears, for so he
had dreamed she spoke.

" I will not press you to anything," he said
tenderly. " I only wish to tell you, and to ask
you, when I am away, to keep me as a memory
to yourself quietly in your own heart ; and if
any one should come that you like better—"
she was resting tearfully in his arms, and looking up at his face and the drifting clouds
above, but at this a spasm of pain crossed her
features. It was but for a moment. She
wrenched herself free of his arms and leaned
against the cliff, with one hand tightened upon
her heart.

The sun was gone, the sky had become overcast with driving squalls, and the wind whistled
shrill through the boulders, but they heeded
not. At that minute was nothing anywhere

but themselves. Her eyes were blinded with tears, but they shone dauntlessly as she faced him.

" Roland "—it was the first time she had called him by his name,—" Roland, I swear solemnly that, for my part, nothing shall ever come between us ; that shall be for God alone, if God there is, and as He sees best." She raised her hand.

A flash of intensest lightning shot out from the heavens, and buried itself hissing in the angry sea. Crash heaped upon crash, followed instantly, and the storm closed in upon them black as ink. Fortunately, the rock shelved overhead, and for the present gave them a fair shelter. The girl's face grew deadly white ; she sank upon her knees, but Roland caught her again to himself.

" It is an omen," she said, shivering, and clinging closer to him. "I invoked Him, and He has heard me."

" A happy one," whispered Roland in her ear, "for it has brought us nearer than ever," and a long while locked in each other's arms they stayed untiring in the sounding sea-cave, but the gale did not abate. The waters rose and lashed the strand with many-thonged, white lashes, and the crawling foam swept up frothing about their feet.

" It's getting late," said Roland, looking out at last, " and the rain's not quite so heavy. My dearest child, we must run for it. It will be smooth at the other side of the island

by the landing, and we shall get back easily
enough. You mustn't judge of a sea by a
'weather' shore."

As they went, she turned and stopped, and
looked upon the white lightnings playing in
the vault, and the black billows mounting
into snow, and listened to the screaming of
the wind. "I thought it was the way to
Heaven," she murmured, "but it is Hell broke
loose."

Roland was fairly frightened, but it was not
for himself, he held his tongue with his fears,
and together they crossed the roaring upland,
staggering upon their feet.

"Look!" he said gaily, as they neared the
opposite cliff, "there's the *Foam* right and
tight below ; that young imp is worth his weight
in gold; and look, it's *smooth* all the way
to the haven mouth ;" but his heart sank as
he watched the white horses in the dim distance
chasing each other landwards in a mad gallop.
From the cliff, it is true, they looked down on
a triangle of comparatively smooth water, which
stretched its point narrowing away, but all
outside, on either hand, was one yeasty mingling
of tumble and pother.

Although the yacht hugged the lee of the
shore as close as she dare, her nose was dipping
heavily in the seas, and to get her in to the
landing-rock was a difficult matter, almost, it
seemed, an impossible one for the boy unaided.
The great waves lifted and flung her rocking
to and fro, and more than once, but for his

superhuman activity, she would have been stove.
At length, however, the painter fetched ashore,
and Roland knotted it on the rusted stanchion
that stood out from the rock. A drenching
rain was coming down again, and it was growing dark before its time. How on earth was
he to get Miss Grey on board? For himself
he could manage it. As the boat ranged up to
the rock he could spring to the deck by the
stay, but he could not venture it with her, and
he looked at her, cursing his own folly.

"My dearest boy," she said, answering his
look, "my nerves are as good as yours, and if
I'm not as strong, I'm almost as quick, as you
saw when you raced me up the cliff. Now I
know exactly what I will do, for it's no use
wasting time; if you'll take my waterproof, I'll
take myself. I'll just pin myself up and jump.
I know the lift of these seas better than you do,
and I shall get in as clear as you. You forget
I've a dingy of my own on my own private
puddle. Take that."

With a coolness that was almost provoking
she stripped off her cloak and tossed it to him.
The pitiless rain came down, beating, and soak-
ing her slight figure to the skin, as she stooped
and deliberately fastened up her skirt with
safety-pins. The water streamed down her
face, but her eyes were laughing.

"What a bore it is to be a woman," she said.
"Now—unless you wish to go first and leave
me to undo the rope." She stood on the outer
edge of the rock, and the surf below boiled like

a boiling pot. Roland was in terror; but what else was there to do?

"There, you see my head's pretty good!" The yacht yawed close, but sank in a hollow as it came; where the girl stood, was more than halfway up the mast. She did not stir, but with a lynx eye watched the waves. A big fellow came rolling sullenly by, and lifted the deck almost to her level. Exactly as it came she flew into the air, and landed clean and clear on one springing instep by the mast, her hand locked in the shrouds. The cockle-shell reeled and lay over with her weight, but righted in a second, and there she was, with a merry laugh on her face, beckoning to him. So entirely prettily and easily was it done, that the fuss about it seemed ridiculous.

He ran to the painter, but a three weeks' sailor is poor at his ropes. The imp shouted to him to come, they must cut it aboard, and he still hesitated, when a furious squall broke out of the west and burst overhead. The wind had veered a point or two to south, and the swollen rollers were driving obliquely on the landing. As he stood aghast, the rope drew taut and parted in the middle; the fringing strands, untwirling, struck him in the face.

Instantly the yacht was lifted away on the crest of a flying monster straight into the air. A dull, lurid red, like the Aurora in the darkness, was poured out over land and sky, and the whole atmosphere was filled with it. The terrible face of the waters was transfigured; it was as if those streaming hill-sides rolled in great billows of frothing blood. The boat stood still and quivered a breathing-space on the very summit of the wave, and he saw Sybil bareheaded, and with hands outstretched towards him. The yacht gave a reel, a plunge, and stern in air went down—so it seemed to him—like lead on the other side, and the rushing hill was dissolved away. What he did in that moment he hardly knew. Raving incoherent prayers he rushed madly up the hill-side, straining his eyes into the gloom; but the mist was like a wall, and only the light and roar of the sweeping seas came to him as he looked. His dream rushed back upon his memory; it was as though some one had stabbed him to the heart, and yet went on stabbing deeper and again. He had at least been warned—fool, murderer that he was! The awful moments lengthened to hours of blank bitter despair.

He flung himself upon the ground and crawled to the cliff-edge; hardly shaping his intent that he would not live through this, when, straight over where the yacht had vanished, a speck of brilliant colour gathered in the murky mingling, and in a minute had climbed the skies, arching its wondrous bow high over earth and sea, serene and calm, though its foundations were laid in the raging waters. Lo! the wall of mist was fleeing away landwards, and as it was hurried from off the face of the deep, there, cast to and fro, lifting and plunging, with her head to the roll, her ensign in tatters and her bowsprit gone, but sound and safe, lay the *Foam.* She had crept round somewhat more to leeward, and young sailor that Roland was, he could see that the danger was past. Then he went quite mad with joy, and he threw up his cap, and it was blown half-way to the yacht before he knew it; but what did he care? The storm was spent like a bursten bubble, there was bright pale sky behind, and even yet the sun was not set. In a few minutes they would be able to reach him again.

CHAPTER XI.

Now what had happened on board the yacht
was precisely this :—

Fortunately, before the rope snapped, Miss
Grey had stepped into the well; to this she
probably owed her life, for had she been on
deck, it is inconceivable that she would have
escaped being washed away by the first rush of
the billows that swept it. Luckily, too, the
boy had run up the after-hatch, so that the
craft was fairly water-tight, and only her
shoulders were exposed as she sat at the
tiller. He had stripped off the new jacket of
which he was so proud, and thrown it round
them, in spite of her protestations; he would be
freer in his jersey, he said.

Then came the accident, and as they were
shot into mid-air, she lost her head in terror,
and let go the tiller. This was such a moment
as the boy had dreamed of half his life; now it
was here, and he had no idea of letting it slip
—in sooth, never did boy do better. He would
show his stuff; casting himself flat on his face,
he caught the tiller as it was flung out of its

socket and dashed on the combing, restored it to its place, and clasped it tightly into her hand.

" Now, miss," he shouted, " hold like winkin'. If yer'll sit still and do as yer told, I'll answer for yer—if yer won't, I won't answer for nothink."

Then he crawled forrard on all fours, to get hold of the sheets, and hung by his teeth or his eyelashes—Heaven knows how !—keeping a look-out over the bows and flinging back his orders without doubt or hesitancy, in a tone which plainly meant obedience or death.

There were two dangers, only two—or there were three, if Miss Grey were included as one, which she certainly was—but the two external ones were these :—

Round the island stretched row after row of sunken ridges ; at low tide these were barely sunken, at high they were deep enough to be safe ; the tide was about midway, he knew. The other danger was the irregular broken seas into which they might drift, where the currents made by the channels met the long rollers from the open sea. He was well aware that there was no depending on the way of these waves ; at such times he had seen them rise in air all of a piece, and come down in a " lump," like a hundredweight of bricks, dealing a dreadful blow, such as might smash them utterly to bits.

For Miss Grey, the moment she realized that there was hope—and the lad had impressed it on her after his fashion—she sat like a rock, with a grip of steel on the tiller. She could see nothing distinctly, for a blackness like a pall had fallen; often she thought that her companion was gone, and that she was left to the battle alone ; more than once they seemed completely submerged. The decks were under, the icy inky torrent encompassed her, rolling over her head—all her breath was going—gone surely ! Still she held on, despite the dreadful dragging and tearing of the sucking floods which sought to clasp and devour her, filling her ears and soul with a hellish gabble of inarticulate sound ; and the next moment, choked and gasping, she looked down as from a hilltop on the swirling valleys around. Her hat was lost, and her wet hair streamed in her eyes.

She had strength yet, but the thundering of the blast, and the awful " scoop," " scoop," as they sank into the hollows, the writhing, flying black things that gleamed red in the lightning like devils, as they hung above and shot by in their witches' dance, and flung the yacht hither and thither and to and fro, up into the air and down into the deep, with screams, as it seemed to her, of fiendish delight—all this made her sick and dizzy, but she clung on with both hands, mechanically obeying the orders as they came to her.

" Down ! hard down ! " yelled the boy.

The tiller was nearly torn from her hand and her arms from their sockets, and as they swung, there was a crash.

There was no land anywhere, yet there rose,

' like an exhalation ' from the sea, a black and monstrous mass of streaming wall from out the cataracts of foam, they were on it—and now nothing could save them.

There was a snap, and the bowsprit flew up loose, then she gave herself up for lost, and involuntarily she called upon her lover in fare-well; but the next moment they were lifted and shot sideways, clean over the spot without touching, for it lay fathom deep below.

"Close," muttered the boy, as, still lying flat on his face, he cut away the wreckage with his clasp-knife.

Although in her way Miss Grey was fond of praying to Nature when it smiled upon her, yet never had she so besought her un-known God as now. But it was her lover's pangs that were at her heart; for her, she had schooled herself for so long that she would meet death as it came—now the hour was almost certainly here which she had collected herself to face. All her life flitted before her. After-wards she wondered that in so short a space could be compressed so many memories; but the physical fatigue, the sensation of being dashed to and fro in space, like a shuttlecock, soon overpowered everything else, and con-fused her impressions to incoherency.

While they hung thus between two worlds, suddenly she was aware of a thinning of the darkness; it was not the red glare out of clouds, but a steady growing light that was breaking in from above. What was she to think? Hope barely smouldered, but it re-lit like the smoke from a fresh-extinguished taper ; the light increased and grew brighter.

The waves rose sullen, and if their roar was still tremendous, as they discharged their furious artillery along the cliff, it was less frequent. The wind on the waters was in a minute fallen and spent, though high overhead there were clouds driving madly on a transparent sky, the burgee drooped upon the mast. She was able to release her aching hands a moment, but so numbed and stiff were they, that she could not gather the hair from her eyes. Then, too, she saw the great prismatic bow that shone aloft and was set in the sea—and once more she was a girl of nineteen.

" That's done," said the pilot, rising from his flat posture, and shaking himself like a dog as he went aft. " Keep her head full, miss," this was all he vouchsafed.

" Done ! "

Well, it had been a bad quarter of an hour, and poor Roland ! yes, there he was all the time : that solitary figure against the light on that looming headland. Poor, poor boy ! and he was throwing his arms about as if he were mad.

It was terribly rough still, and quite half an hour before they could make the landing-stage ; by that time the pale green sky was fading into a serene twilight. But before this, Miss Grey had been so deadened, that the boy went hunting in the locker out of sheer compassion, and he had brought out half a bottle of brandy, insisting that she should take a thimbleful. It

was almost as nasty as the salt water, but
life seemed to be ebbing away through her
fingers. She felt it was the only thing to do,
and took it, and she even urged a glass on her
protector, but he disdained the effeminacy, and
was content to see the improvement it wrought
in her. But withal, when at length Roland
jumped aboard, and came to her in the well,
she could hardly speak to him; she was half
frozen in her clinging, cold clothes, and her
strength was gone; yet, now it was past, she
would not have had it otherwise, for had they
lived together a lifetime, it could scarcely have
awakened in their breasts such sympathy between them, as this last hour had done. Such an
experience as it brought, lays bare one human
soul to another, but it does not fructify in
words.

"My poor little woman!" was all he said, as
he stroked her dripping shoulders, and gathered
the long, wet hair tenderly from her face.
"How cold you are, and how drenched!—but
it's all over now, and with the wind where it is,
we shall run back in no time. I tell you what
we will do, dear heart; we will land at the very
nearest point and take a sharp walk to the
manor across country. It's only a mile, and
it will bring the life into you again," for the
pallor of her cheek frightened him, and even
to her lips was she white. "But you might
have had a tarpaulin, if Bob had been sharp
enough. I see, he did give you his jacket."
He laughed cheerily.

The boat was now plunging free, away from

the island; it was still very rough, and they swung along gloriously through the hissing seas which raced and bowled beside them towards the mainland; and as they ran, the pace was terrific, but danger there was none.

"Well, you brought her through it, Bob?"

The imp was busy with his sheets; indeed, he never trusted those sheets alone for a moment together, but kept hand and eye ever watchful for their pranks. He did not answer all at once, but the iron grin softened into a smile, by no means a foolish one.

"Obedience is better nor sacrifice," he observed profoundly, with a glance at Miss Grey.

This was certainly intended as a compliment. She smiled a faint smile. "The boy is a hero," she whispered to Roland. "You must look after him well," and she pressed his hand significantly.

The tarpaulin had been got out; it proved big enough for two, and the well of the little craft was such, that the captain was able to stand at his steering with one hand, and keep his guest close and warm with the other under its stiff folds. If this had no other advantage, the physical sensation of returning warmth was inexpressibly grateful to her, for the life had ebbed low in her veins with chill. Gradually, her strength came back, and they were able to improvise a landing, once inside the haven mouth, leaving the boy to take the yacht to her moorings, and the captain fulfilled his true love's behest thus :—

"Look here, you young devil, you did very

well, and there'll be a five-pound note for you;
but you hold your tongue about it, and all
the rest of it, or you'll come in for a worse
bit of squall than you did to-day. Now mind
that ! ''

With this gentle hint he ran off to join
Sybil, who, much to her own surprise, was
already trying her paces up the path. At first
it was poor going, but by the time they reached
the tower, they were almost dry and warm
again, hardly to be recognized as the stiff,
spectral forms that had climbed painfully from
the yacht an hour before. Historic truth
must be respected, they were an hour, a very
good hour, doing the mile—perhaps they did
more.

When they gained the manor gardens, sheltered as these were, on all sides were visible
traces of the storm. The green foliage lay
thick upon the lawns as dead leaves in the
autumn, and the young boughs were strewed
about the sward with their torn white gashes,
and in the air was the fragrance of bruised
flowers and crushed greenery, for here on land
it was a summer's eve again.

The bailiff and his wife and niece, with the
coachman and the maid, had been cozily seated
at one of the unnumbered cups of tea which
was fashionable with the domestics of the
country-side in hours and out of hours, when
the hurricane burst upon the window-pane.
And although the party were rather comfortably dismayed, it was not likely that Providence had brought the young master back to

his own after so many weary years, to drown him like a dog in the first summer squall, more particularly since his chosen lady was with him. This was the feeling universally expressed and agreed upon, and as all parties had a great deal to say to each other, chiefly on the magnitude of their individual importance in the local scheme of creation, anxiety was happily dismissed. It was known of course that the two were in the yacht, but that they were outside the haven, in the open, no one dreamed.

After all, it was nobody's affair but the young people's, and they, when they returned in due time, as expected, made light of their wetting, and went into no details. Luckily, there was a sealskin jacket which had been left behind, and between them, the maid and niece contrived to find some dry things for Miss Grey, who refused to stay for more than a cup of tea.

In truth, she was worn out, and able for no further delay. She was restless and completely overstrung with all she had gone through, and Roland, on his part, was on thorns lest she should have taken cold. He piled the brougham with bear and other skins, as if it had been winter, and he had wine-bottles filled with boiling water put for her feet. Then he bethought him, there would be no great harm if he went a little way with her himself, and walked back; and she, if she could not quite approve, was too tired to resist. So he went in with her, and heaped the furs round about until she was buried in them, and they drove away.

Her mind was charged with the events of the day. Of her own free-will she was bound and fettered for life to the man at her side, the stranger of a fortnight since; her heart, as when first she had discovered herself, still beat like a bird caged in her breast, and she was terrified as she recalled it all, for she believed that in a special way they had been the sport of Fate.

" Roland," she said, after a long silence, and she threw herself into his arms, " I don't doubt you, still less myself, you must not think it, for I cannot conceive ourselves coming to that; but, Roland, dear," and here she stroked his face, and looked into it with a look he never forgot, " the Gods are against us, the omens are adverse. Nay, dear love, you laugh, but I know it; and, oh! it is heavy upon me. Think how it has been. There was your dream last night; we have had warning. I don't know what it was, or how, but by your face even now, I can see that it was terrible, and you did not laugh at that. And did you notice," she went on excitedly, " that though all was bright before, when you spoke of love, the skies broke over us and the lightning, and we were hardly pledged together before Heaven, when we were torn asunder by that devilish sea, and I know that you were near to death as I was myself. Oh, God! it was frightful!" she covered her face and sobbed.

His own was set and stern, but he kissed her lips and comforted her very tenderly.

Then he laughed, but it was a pretence, which failed to deceive even himself, and he stroked back the matted hair from the marble forehead, turning her face to his, and saying, "Dearest, you are overwrought, and not without cause. There is no fate, except sickness and death, that man's will cannot control, and we are alive and well, and young. As for the thunderstorm, my dear little girl, whatever we may be to each other, you surely don't imagine that we are of cosmic importance? What next? and next? Are we to have comets whirling about our heads if our love prospers, and blazing planets perambulating space if it runs uneven?"

He would not be serious, and the tones of his voice did her heart good, although his anxious eyes belied them.

She twined her arms round his neck, and said, still with tears, "Good-bye, for now I know that you must leave me. We shall meet again soon, soon; and although I hope it will be often first, and there is happiness waiting yet for us, I know too—ah! how well—that at last it will be at Philippi."

She broke into passionate weeping, nor could he console her.

Remembering what the shock had been to her nerves, he desisted, and saying, "God keep you, darling," he stopped the carriage and called down the maid to take his place.

Then, very sadly, he turned his steps towards home.

*   *   *   *   *

RIOTS IN THE WEST END.
LOSS OF LIFE.
WRECKING OF PRIVATE HOUSES.
BUCKINGHAM PALACE THREATENED.
LORD ST. MAUR AGAIN.
MILITARY CALLED OUT.

Such was the poster that met Roland's eye at one of the first stations on the line as he was returning to town next morning. So great was the run on the papers that not a single copy was to be had, and even those of the day before, which merely hinted at the possibility of these awful events, were selling at from 450 to 600 per cent. premium, or, more exactly, from fourpence-halfpenny to sixpence.

For all his impatience, the train dragged on like a wounded snake through the first part of the day. At one place the guard had a friend, and this friend had another, who in his turn had a little boy, who again had a something in his eye. There was a consultation over the case. All were agreed, apparently, that the guard was the man for the delicate operation required, and that the train and Providence combined, had brought him to the spot just in the nick of time. It was satisfactorily accomplished in the end, although no hurry was manifested about it, and the applause of the whole train, which was filled with the leisurely natives of the district, was universally conceded to the operator.

Finally they resumed their way at the old rate, but it was five in the evening before Roland succeeded in obtaining a halfpenny paper for the modest outlay of a shilling, which clearly proved that he had re-entered the precincts of civilization. When, however, the accounts came to be analyzed, the facts appeared to be rather less terrible than at first sight.

There had been riotous proceedings. The boys had been very bad, and the girls hardly less so. An old woman had been picked up in the streets and had died comfortably in hospital next day, but she was nearly ninety, and it was the doctor's opinion that the causes of this proceeding might be set down as old age, fatigue, and the heat of the weather. So far the loss of life.

Then a gentleman who lived in a back street, gaining his modest livelihood as a lender of small sums, and avuncular relative to any who might require one, had in some way made himself obnoxious to the mob, who had hooted and howled under his windows and had broken two in the area—so far the wrecking of private houses.

With regard to the fourth item, a drunken Irishman had been arrested in St. James's Park. He had shaken his fist in a policeman's face, and as he was handcuffed and marched off, he had hurled an imprecation at Buckingham Palace. In this rather restricted sense it was perfectly true the palace had been threatened.

As to Lord St. Maur, the main thing the paper had to say of him was, that it had been generally expected that he would have made his appearance and addressed one of the meetings, but he did not; so that his friend was inclined to quarrel with the manner of this announcement.

The last item was the calling out of the military. It happened to be the drill season, and the volunteers' weekly field-day took place as usual. The troops had marched through the streets "there and back again without encountering opposition beyond a few hisses."

Roland laid down the sheet, not without relief. He had pictured the inhabitants of London flying from their homes and encamped in laager in Hyde Park, and he fervidly wished that a little of his money had been invested in the Press, where it was possible to turn an honest penny with such simple facility.

It was dark before he reached town, and it had turned bitterly cold, the streets were black and dismal as he drove through them, and there was a suspicion of snow in the air, while a fall of recent sleet lay unmelted in the gutter. So eccentric was the weather endured by our unfortunate contemporaries, that if one stood in a street where no tree was visible, it was usually impossible to tell by mere sensation, what season of the year it was, or was not.

This was July, and all the world was hurrying by with red noses and chattering teeth, cut in twain by the east wind as it disported with their gossamer clothes, for had it not been 80° in the shade the day before yesterday?

Now if you had happened perchance to be in town in the preceding January, you would have seen the shrubs upon your leads pushing into bud, and a hundred and one silly green things forcing their feelers through the steaming soil and revelling in the soft air, only to perish prematurely after a short life, that must have been one of remorse, in the bitter blasts of May. On most days in that balmy January you would have met perspiring multitudes fanning their foreheads with their handkerchiefs, as they staggered along under their huge coats and fur capes, for the Britisher hated this sort of thing and set his face against it *ab oro*. He said, "This is January, and I must wear my great-coat and muffler or I shall die," and he did it, though he very nearly died all the same.

So now he went on repeating, "Confound it, you know, this is July, and, properly speaking, we ought to eat and sleep in the open air, and go as near to nothing at all in clothing, as we can with decency." And this he did accordingly, paying the miserable penalty with a heroism which had in it an element of actual grandeur.

When Roland reached his rooms, he found, as a matter of course, that his servant was out, and that the worthy man had decorated his fireplace with a paper pattern in red and gold, intended for a permanency.

His historic dog lay on the rug before it, vainly endeavouring to bask in its hollow splendour, and shivering miserably. The Skye had at this period attained to a green old age, he had grown deaf, his temper had become uncertain, his sight no less so, and he suffered from the hallucination that a perpetual fly sat at the end of his nose to buffet him. He had no teeth left, and his bark was consequently worse than his bite. Still, his bark was bad enough, especially if one's nerves happened to be overstrung. Further, if he suffered from—well, from internal pain—he immediately laid it at the door of the person who was nearest to him, and took his measures accordingly.

He was sleeping a broken slumber of discomfort when his master entered and called him. The dog sat up in his chair very leisurely, yawned and stretched, then he made a furious grab at the mythic fly, and expressed his sense of failure in a howl, whereupon he turned violently to the right-about and assaulted a something in his flank, which no doubt paid the penalty of the supposed fly's celerity. But at this moment one of his many twinges seized him, and tardily discovering that it was horribly cold, and that it was a miserable world, he put all these things together, and recognizing the cause in this unwarrantable intruder, made for him like a fury.

The paroxysm was severe while it lasted, but there was a something in the touch of that master's hand and the sound of his voice, that suddenly convinced the dog that he must have been altogether wrong; happily he was impotent for mischief, and therefore had no occasion for remorse, and he changed his manifesto into a mad dance of frantic joy. And when the red and gold vine-leaves were cleared away with a summary kick, and the master himself tossed him a biscuit, and put a match to the fire, which burned up cheerily, he gave a groan of utter contentment, and settling down in his basket, he started off for a sleep of fifteen hours straight away.

The man lit a cigar and fell to musing.

How frightfully dull it was, how black, how dingy, how cold, how ugly, how vilely uninteresting was London after all, and what a ghastly din the cabs made! He envied his old dog his fit of rage; if he could only have found an excuse for it, it would have been a relief to have had one himself.

He took his solitary supper, and lit another cigar; the fire blazed comfortably, and he grew dozy.

This ugly civilization was perhaps a necessity. After all it was only skin-deep. A few determined men and a few bottles of chemicals could turn the city into as picturesque a wilderness as the one which he had just left; no doubt it would be done some day, and these first threatenings of disturbance were the first downward readings of the social barometer.

" The sacking of London."

The mere phrase was enough to make the mouth of any man water, who had nothing to lose by it. Small blame to the foreigner and the Trafalgar Square patriot.

He was startled from his reverie by the loud pealing of the door-bell.

Without rhyme or reason the bell reminded him of *her*.

It was odd how, all through the day, as he came along, it had been the same; although his eyes and thoughts had wandered to innumerable subjects, they had all in some remote and mysterious way connected themselves with Sombrewood and Sybil Grey. The flaring posters, the roadside stations, the wild roses in the hedges, the velvet cushions of the carriage, and even his own door,—these actualities had merely served as a background on which he visualized her face. Sometimes the impression was so strong that he could have believed she was by his side, when, as he turned to her, it faded away.

In pursuit of such fancies he had already forgotten the bell, and was among his ancestors again. When presto! was this one of them in the flesh? It was a moment before he recognized his friend Brabant.

Always more or less remarkable, his appearance this evening was little short of extraordinary; he had entered with so little noise that even the dog had not turned his head, and he had come up to Roland's chair, where he stood looking at him with eyes that burned like lamps, his fine features were white as marble, and his short curls hung damp on his forehead. He wore a long, flowing overcoat of fur, which was open.

"Good Heavens! My dear Brabant," said Roland, jumping up to greet him, "is that you? I thought you were Sir Walter Raleigh.

at least, walked straight out of the sixteenth century. Why, you look like a ghost."

" I rather think I am one," said Brabant spectrally ; " I am engaged to be married."

Roland was accustomed to his friend's eccentricities, while he had a decided respect for his cleverness ; he had rather pitied him for his physical graces, as being likely to lead him into entanglement, and now here was the worst he had feared. For a minute he sat silent, while the visitor's face and hand twitched nervously.

The man and his hand are worth a glance ; the modelling of the latter was unusual for one belonging to that matter-of-fact epoch, the tapering of the fingers was so extreme, and the backward bend of the tips so marked, that it was almost a hand caricatured, while the arching of the nails was in itself a phenomenon of beauty.

That the owner was proud of it was possible, how else should a man be whose sense of perfection was such that ugliness gave him a species of physical pang ? But latterly he had come to regard it very much in the light of a nuisance, and he persistently hid it in rough gloves, where, if possible, it looked better than ever. As you looked at him, you could not help but feel that his appearance was absolutely unfortunate among the people of that age, to whom beauty, moral or physical, was a thing ridiculous.

If the Messiah had come among them, the lofty type of His culture would have ensured Him a certain toleration from the critics, but a small following. If Apollo had descended from the skies, his best friends would have hoped that the young fellow would " grow out of it."

Brabant had not the excuse of the god for his looks, no superhuman strength lurked in his biceps, and it was difficult to see what place he could fill with credit in the nineteenth century.

The Greeks would have placed him on a pedestal in the centre of a school, would have set their students to model from him. And on his showing the least signs of decadence, would have affectionately poisoned him, having taken one last cast of his limbs ere they consumed them to ashes, and apotheosized his memory as the god of elegance.

But to snatch the Apollo Soroctonos from his tree and his lizard, to dress him in the stove-pipe, the pea-jacket, and the straight funnel continuations of the day, to set him down here and now —this was indeed the irony of Fate.

The man had done perhaps the best thing possible under the circumstances by way of finding a niche. He had wooed literature as a mistress, and had, among other things, declared himself a poet, but with reservations. It was his ambition to inaugurate a new era in poets, and when it is recorded that he got his clothes in Saville Row, had his hair cut once a fortnight, rode a cob, and made his Muse keep his horse, if not quite himself, it must be admitted that he had gone a long way towards success.

The people of that relentless age were accustomed, not without reasons of their own, to look upon " poet " as synonymous with "idiot,' particularly where he happened to be young. But Brabant was by no means a fool, and, speaking broadly, the strength of his mind was in inverse ratio to the strength of his body, though, like the rest of the world, he had travelled some few of the roads that lead to folly. His pen was already beginning to work wonders.

It happened to be an epoch of high-class mediocrity in the literary world, a happy one for the advent of a young and original writer, and this one had a peculiar gift over words; he played them like a conjuror, and with the same dexterity and ease. When he took up the cudgels on a question, it was a pretty thing; as one read, one cried again and again, "Ha! a hit"—"a palpable hit," "a home-thrust," "well played," "well done!"

On the recent publication of his first volume, it had been his fortune to slay a celebrated critic, as effectually to all intents and purposes as if he had literally run him through the body. A new poet so very well able to take care of himself, had not been since Byron, and few cared afterwards to encounter the scathing torrent of his wit. Removed from the atmosphere of wholesome criticism, he found himself in a singularly unwholesome one of mingled adulation and abuse.

Coming of a good but impoverished stock, he had shaken himself free of his family, and flung himself into work with the fury of desperation; an unlucky luck attended him. He was one of those with whom it seems as if every circumstance of life conspired to spoil a good man, and this last announcement of his engagement, at so critical a time for himself, appeared to Roland to bring matters to a climax, although why he should have been surprised is not very plain, seeing that he also had been nearing the same goal for a month past.

He looked incredulously at his friend, and blurted out, " Going to be married, and at your age! Why, man, what have you done with your career?"

Since they had been in the lower school, "career" had been the word oftenest in the mouths of each.

"Hang it!" he went on, half angrily, "I thought we were to have gone on and done " (vaguely) " a world of things together, and we haven't even begun."

"My dear fellow," said Brabant, laying his hand on Roland's shoulder, "I'm older than you, remember—several years—and think what my experience is. What sort of a career do you suppose is open to a man of my type? My pen is as much as I can manage, and I am being dragged into a course of *tableaux vivants*, of drawing-rooms and their inhabitants, of upholstery and the designing of stage dresses, of love lyrics and 'at homes.' I am sick of it! We used to talk of Parliament. I might possibly get a seat across the Channel, but I don't think I'm very likely to knock the old state of things on the head in this country, or to lead an Irish mob to victory. No, something literary and artistic, given out from the safe shell of my domestic hearth, is the best I can hope for. Really," he looked rather shame-faced, "I've been awfully tried this season, you can't imagine what I've had to go through. Now, marriage is a great safeguard, and I feel deuced lonely—at night."

It cost Roland a slight struggle to keep his face. "It's a common complaint with un-married people," he answered drily. "I find good spirits are the best company one can have for my own part."

The remark was unlucky, his friend looked uncomfortable.

"That is where the shoe pinches; my com-pany are evil ones," he said with deliberation, and his eyes shone with a light which was almost alarming.

"Nonsense, man," said Roland, laying a friendly hand on his arm; "your digestion's out of order, I know what that is."

"You look like it," said Brabant with a hollow smile, as he surveyed his friend's power-ful figure. "Come, come! talk sense, and I'll listen to you, but don't talk of things that you can't form an idea of. I'll admit, if it will satisfy you, that my digestion is wrong; body and soul are awry, so much the more reason for taking care of oneself, or for being taken care of, which is easier."

The speaker, like most delicate people, was subject to fits of elation, to be followed by corresponding depression; to-night he was totally unlike himself, his particular abjectness struck Roland more than painfully. If the man wanted to marry, he had his own ideas for him, as some of us have for our friends, ten or fifteen years hence, and a woman such as he would choose him.

"Well!" he said, suppressing a sigh, "all joy to you, dear friend. I trust it will answer your highest hopes. You know your own case best. By the way, I haven't asked the lady's name."

"A-hem—Squeed—Lushington Squeed, I should say—she's—a widow, and—" catching the involuntary lengthening of Roland's face, "she's a niece by marriage of Lady Jane Squeed, you know."

"Oh! ah! of course, pretty and charming and all that, I am sure, if she's your choice."

"She's a fine woman—no one, I think, could deny that—and I've every reason to think she's a virtuous one."

"Good gracious, I should hope so," replied Roland, aghast at his manner, and hardly recognizing him for the same man.

In sooth, he had been burning for weeks past to unbosom himself to this very friend on his own affairs, but the idea of such a thing seemed out of place, in the face of a communication so made as this.

Just now there was nothing more to be said, and he was immensely relieved when Brabant sat down, and with a brighter face (oh! evil augury) turned the subject to something else.

"You had my letter, of course," he went on.

" You see, I'm in the thick of it. I wish you'd come with me to the publisher's to-morrow. The poems are a success; not out three months and we are in the third edition. And yet—will you believe me?—they hum and haw about the novel! 'Pon my honour, they're as bad as the women!"

Then he explained his grievance at length. A month since he had called at his publisher's, where he was received with all the *éclat* that befitted a gentleman so public-spirited, that he had consented to issue a volume entirely at his own risk in the case of failure, but with the proviso of half profits to the firm in the case of success; and whose effort had already proved that it did not mean the former.

The head of the house he described as an elderly gentleman, who combined an impassive appearance with the high-bred manners of a court. He had taken him into his sanctum, pulled two arm-chairs into close proximity, and then inclined his ear with his hand to it, for he was a little deaf, saying, " Now, my dear sir, what can I do for you ?"

It was very like an interview with his father confessor, and with difficulty the visitor refrained from wording his answer, " Well, father, since the last offence of the poems, which I hope has been partially condoned by their success, I have been guilty of perpetrating—a novel. *Mea culpa, mea culpa, mea maxima culpa.*" However, he said much the same, but in other words.

The old man was evidently startled; such a

revelation must have been new to him, and he was proportionately grieved. " Success in one thing," he hinted, " by no means implied success in another. It did not follow, because a man could jump over a gate that he could run a race, or *vice versâ*, and if he (Mr. Brabant) would take his word for it, never since the dawn of the Christian era, had there been so bad a time for the publication of a novel as the last six months had proved, unless, indeed, the six months succeeding should outstrip them, as seemed likely to be the case. Still—and Mr. Brabant must be aware what time was to him—he might just listen to a brief outline, a mere sketch of the plot ; and if Mr. Brabant had been satisfied with the former arrangement, why, perhaps, something of the same sort might be arrived at. Though, really, if he were to talk of profits, he might be accused of discussing a point of which he knew nothing—a vanishing-point, in fact ; so infinitesimal were these things nowadays," and here he laughed very facetiously, and jingled something in his pocket.

So the author began—for he knew something of telling a story—and his hearer sank back in his chair and closed his eyes. " The name, by the way ? " he asked.

" On the Spot."

" Ah ! that will do." His lips gave the faintest possible smack. " Very good ! " and his eyes closed again.

He clasped his fingers in the air before him,

pressing the tips of his thumbs together; but, as the narration went on, his hands began to twitch, then he sat up. "Good," he said, "capital in fact;" and he rubbed them.

Step by step the plot unfolded itself, and Brabant sank his voice, hesitating now and then to give a finer effect. Presently the old man twined his hand in the scanty hair of his temples. "Yes, yes," he exclaimed, "go on, go on!"

The teller proceeded steadily, and approached the climax, pausing with a depth of meaning, and from time to time mixing his syntax with the emotion of the moment. Then he commenced to quote:—

"The heart-sickness that seized me at these words (remember, I was scarcely more than a boy) was so great that I rose and left her. The spirits of the party jarred painfully upon me, and I wandered out alone. The site of our picnic had been happily chosen; one of the perished Etruscan cities, within easy drive of Rome. It was the stern embodiment of solitude; here and there the great blocks of ruin protruded from the woods of ilex, of myrtle, and of chestnut, marking where had once stood a vast necropolis. I climbed to one of these fragments, which stood remote from the path, and sat down upon a shattered marble step, under the shade of the solemn columns of the cypress that were set round about it. The silence was intense, and quickened only by the chirp of the grasshoppers. In the distance rose the blue Soracte, faint and tremulous in the heat-haze.

"Presently, to distract myself from my thoughts, which had grown unbearable, I cast about and began to examine the building against which I rested. It was a square block, shaped from a protruding ledge of rock, and more than half buried in the climbing underwood. It stood a little apart from others more ruinous, which were around. In most of these the roofs had fallen in, disclosing empty vaults. This one, however, appeared intact. My curiosity was aroused. Looking closer, I found a slab of stone set in above the step, the mortar round which appeared to be loosened. I pressed this and more mortar fell. Encouraged, I broke off a short, strong bough, and inserted it as a wedge into the opened cranny. To my surprise, the stone yielded to my renewed effort, tottered a moment, then of its own weight fell inwards with an appalling crash below.

"A sudden ray of sunlight in an instant flooded the blackness of the vault within, which appeared to be a square, roomy chamber or tomb, hewn out of the living rock. But what riveted my gaze was the single object placed in the centre of the floor.[1]

"There, upon a bier or couch of painted wood, adorned with bosses of ivory and amber, lay outstretched a warrior—perhaps a king, for in his helm were jewels — in bronze armour, his head slightly turned upon the

[1] An actual occurrence is here told.

pillow towards the entrance where I stood.
The sun streaming in upon him, the sparkling
dust-motes raining about his head, I could distinguish every detail of his robes, every hair
upon his face.   It was a fine, massive face, un-
altered apparently from life ; and the eyes,
with their hollow shadows, looked out into
mine wondrously.   What I did I hardly know ;
I must have uttered some exclamation.   I could
not look enough at this marvellous apparition.
Well that I did so, for, as I stepped forward
to descend, a shade passed over the features.
They were gone—utterly gone !

"I passed my hand over my eyes and looked
again ; when, like a vision which has been conjured for a moment and fades to nothingness,
the entire figure passed away—vanished—crumbled in and sank, the armour with the rest, as
though it were the merest simulacrum of unyielding bronze.   The stones fell from their
settings ; upon the bier, where but a moment
before the pomp of a forgotten age had confronted me, was an uneven heap of dust ? So
noiseless, so instantaneous was this transformation that I stood transfixed, petrified. '*Memento
homo quia pulvis es, et in pulverem reverteris*'
rang in my ears.   The emotion that fell upon
me was extraordinary.   I would have wished
all the world at my elbow, to have been witness
of the scene, to have heard the voice that cried
aloud to me.   In a sense my wish was granted.
I turned, and there stood by me the one fair
woman who to me was the world.   She had
followed me, and was a witness.   The tre-

mendous lesson had appealed to her soul no
less than to my own. Our eyes met; hers, I
know, brimmed over. She—she"—the nar-
rator's memory faltered and failed,—"well, of
course, she—"

"For mercy's sake go on!" gasped his
listener, who had jumped up, and was facing
him with staring eyes and lips apart. "She?
Oh, heavens! what did she do then?"

With tantalizing deliberation Mr. Brabant
went on to tell what her course of procedure
had been under these circumstances. By the
time he had finished, the publisher was dancing
about the room, clapping his hands and slapping his thigh. "Capital! capital indeed!
My dear, dear sir, *this* must be *the* novel of the
season. Good-morning, good-bye."

A month had elapsed, and the author had
heard no more, when one day he found the
MS. intact upon his breakfast-table, with a
printed note, in which his kind offer was declined. Such was the story from first to last. He
fancied the MS. must have fallen into the wrong
hands, as no explanation was given; but there
were reasons for his not leaving the house
which had already published one of his works,
and he determined on another interview.

He was afraid his impulses might lead
him beyond the traditional etiquette between
writer and publisher. Would Roland support
him?

He was the more urgent because, not only
did he intend to make them take the work, but
to make them pay handsomely for it as well.

Otherwise it should go to those who would.
Intercourse of this sort was very much like that
of a pair of lovers, and if the other side were
coy—no matter were it a maiden of sixteen
or a man of business of sixty—he should understand the game.

Certainly Mr. Tudor would support with all
the weight of his name and place, and so it was
arranged before they said good night.

END OF VOL. 1.

GILBERT AND RIVINGTON, LIMITED, ST. JOHN'S SQUARE, LONDON.

MOSTLY FOOLS.

A Romance of Civilization.

BY

MR. RANDOLPH,

AUTHOR OF "ONE OF US."

" . . . We arrive at the undeniable, but unexpected conclusion, that eminently
gifted men are raised as much above mediocrity as idiots are depressed below it."
FRANCIS GALTON.

IN THREE VOLUMES.

VOL. II.

London :

SAMPSON LOW, MARSTON, SEARLE, & RIVINGTON,

CROWN BUILDINGS, 188, FLEET STREET.

1886.

LONDON:
PRINTED BY GILBERT AND RIVINGTON, LIMITED
ST. JOHN'S SQUARE.

TO MY ADVERSARIES.

MOSTLY FOOLS.

CHAPTER I.

THE next morning Roland drove his friend into the city, and such serious things are life and love, that he had already passed the second bad night of his existence in pondering over the situation.

As they went down, he questioned Brabant closely as to the turn public feeling had taken, but he found him practically in the dark; for the moment the latter's attention had lapsed entirely to private matters, his poems, his love affair, his secret researches, these had sufficed to fill up his time completely.

" There had been meetings ? "

" Oh ! yes ; of course there had been; there always were."

" And there had been rows ? "

" Weren't there always rows—about nothing?"

He had been spending a good deal of his time in the Erith marshes, studying the retroscope; and his friend, Professor Vandam, had made further astonishing discoveries, of a nature that must revolutionize most of the known, so-called sciences.

Roland had for some time past suspected certain of his friend's tendencies; his suspicions

were now confirmed. Brabant admitted to dabbling in "psychics, or whatever you chose to
call it," and it was already easy to see the traces
of what had been accomplished in the tense ner-
vousness of his manner. The blade was fretting
the sheath from the very keenness of it.

"My dear fellow," said Roland, as he neatly
flicked the left ear of a barking cur in the street,
"better leave that alone, we shall be spirits all
of us, before we've time to look round. Do stick
to the world in which you find yourself. I know
there are a hundred thousand others, but you
happen to be in this one; make the best of it
while you have the chance. I can see the
thing's doing you no good."

"Bodily, no; but morally the gain must be
something enormous."

"I doubt it. If the teaching and weight
of the Church are not enough for you, you
are not likely to get anything better, out of
what Vandam and his set are able to supple-
ment it with. Besides which—and it's no use
mincing matters—you're not the sort of man
to meddle with things that take more out of
you than they put in. You look ill already.
Now confess you've had some unpleasant
experiences."

"I have had some curious impressions certainly, how far they may be vouched for as facts
is another thing however. I have ceased
to be surprised; an unnatural wonder, after
all, is no more remarkable than a natural one.
Things in the room don't stay as they are put.
Sometimes they will fall down or change their
place without the slightest noise. Candles go

out and re-light themselves. The shadows fall in wrong places. The dark of the looking-glass is peopled with some sort of busy life, and the walls will breathe in regular cadence through the night. But these are trifles. What has forced itself most strongly upon me, is the inexplicability of 'natural' events by natural causes, and the necessity of looking deeper than mere externals, for the ordering of things.

" It has opened out not a new world simply, but the hundred thousand new worlds you speak of, and their possibilities, to my bewildered sight. I believe that the law of the universe is 'progress,' not only for to-day and to-morrow, but beyond all the to-morrows into infinity; that gives one hope through present failure. It is quite plain to me that if there were no progress after death, the heavenly host would be bored to distraction with yawning. Remember, in the highest conception of a God, there is room for this."

" Well, I confess," said Roland, "that I'm for tangible progress in this world; it's the best guarantee of any future development we may hope for; transcendentalism is out of my line. I see enough work waiting to be done here and now, and I have no wish to tear aside the veil that has been drawn over the future."

" You mistake me. The study I have taken up is merely the extension of what we call the natural laws; not only is it legitimate, but it is essential to the higher life; in some form it is essential to all greatness. When you have read human life more deeply, you will see this—mark my words."

Roland did not forget them, but by this time they had now gotten into the land of pen-and-ink, and had pulled up before a large and splendid building in the prevailing fashion. This curious generation had, after jumbling through every conceivable craziness, pure and impure, settled down to a mixture of double Dutch and high Chinese, with a dash of the Renaissance flung in, and now half London was being rebuilt in this style, which they had facetiously named after a sovereign who, it was well known, had been dead some time.

Painful as the task must necessarily be, to expose the absurdities of the people who supplanted ourselves, it will not be without a certain satisfaction that we shall contemplate the vagaries of these phantoms, by the side of our own solid consistencies, and rejoice in our immunity from their follies.

This edifice was the outward shell and simulacrum of the great publishers and their business. There were other simulacra to be found elsewhere. Country houses, yachts, pair horse phaetons—but with these we have nothing to do.

The two friends had come on business, and after waiting some little time, were ushered into a sanctum, where the bland gentleman of previous history sat smiling more blandly than before.

Only that morning he had found it desirable to order a few more loose copies of " Ever So " to be struck off, just in case they might be wanted ; it was not worth while mentioning them as an edition. Yet, when the author modestly said he hoped things were going well with it, the publisher, who was apparently of a very sensitive nature, fell into a great despondency, and presently said, he was afraid the sale had stopped altogether.

Now, as the author had passed through the office, he had quite casually heard the work asked for, and he begged that the books might be consulted ; when it was found that nine copies had been sold that morning to five different orders, and it was not yet mid-day, whereupon he plucked up heart again.

But "The Firm," as the gentleman gave it to be understood he wished to be considered, was not abashed. He hinted very cordially that Mr. Brabant was to be congratulated on his business capacity as well as his good luck. A compliment which some of those present thought might be returned.

"And now as to this novel," said the Firm, placing the tips of It's fingers together, for It was aware of their business, "let me see; 'On the Spot,' I think. Permit me to remark, my dear sir, that on this occasion we were a little 'off the spot,' I fear; he! he!"

"As you are aware, I thought very highly of the general conception of the book, and the disappointment to myself has been a grievous one. I imagined that there must have been some mistake, and to prove to you that trouble is a thing of which we take no consideration whatever, I need only say that, on the first report proving unfavourable, I at once sent it off to two other individuals, who are luminaries, my dear sir, perfect luminaries in the literary world, who for years past have not stooped to read any other works but their own.

"One of them—a lady by the way; we don't usually divulge these particulars, but you will understand my object—remarks very aptly in a letter (a private one), that none but the most brilliant writing succeeds nowadays, she—"

"I should like monstrously to see the reports," interrupted Mr. Brabant, on whom a point was seldom thrown away; "that is, if it's not asking too much."

The Firm appeared embarrassed. "Too much! Nothing that you could ask, Mr. Brabant, is too much; but it's most unusual," It stammered; "most. Still between—"

"Gentlemen," suggested his client.

"Ah! yes, certainly, exactly," the Firm broke up into smiles; "that was just what I was about to observe."

"There can be no objection whatever?"

"None whatever. I have them here. It is most unusual," It repeated, "but as they are anonymous, I shall be happy to show them to you, in the strictest confidence."

Here he took up a portfolio upon the table, from which he extracted three separate reports, pinned together. One of them he laid before his visitors.

"Would you perhaps kindly read it aloud? I feel that the points will so strike me more forcibly," and Brabant flung himself into an attitude of studied attention.

The Firm was delighted, and, with some sonorousness of expression, read as follows:—

"'On the Spot.' This is a work of some pretence. It attempts to describe scenes from college, club, and male life generally. As the author is palpably a lady neophyte, it may be imagined with what result. She can have no possible experience of what she endeavours to depict. It has neither wit nor merit."

The Firm was so gentle, oh! so gentle, as It concluded this; just like a kind doctor performing a painful operation. It paused with a little pitiful smile.

" There really is a great deal in that," said Brabant, with conviction. " A maiden aunt of mine copied out most of the manuscript for me—I cannot deny this. Now you speak of it, she did *not* seem to know much of the scenes described, or to care about them; but here am I to answer in person for every one of them."

The Firm hastily took up the next report, and Roland blew his nose.

" No. 2. ' On the Spot.' This is an unpretending story, but in parts remarkably witty and meritorious. It is evidently the work of an old hand, and his aim is plain. Too much space is, however, devoted to love-making, and the author's tone is far too serious to admit of its being an attractive fiction. It is, besides, loose in structure, and much wants tightening up."

This was passed by in silence, and the reader took up

" No. 3. ' On the Spot.' This work is worthless. In the first place, it is far too condensed, and it is difficult to see what the writer's intent can have been, though it appears not impossible that it is an attempt to trifle with the feelings of the public. He laughs or weeps exactly as suits his caprice, and without the slightest consideration for his reader. What besides can be expected of an author, who makes his hero fall in love in half an hour ?"

"Heaven above, sir !" said Brabant, springing to his feet, and loosing the last shreds of his patience, "do you really put this forward as a serious criticism to me, who have fallen in love, and often out of it again, in a single half-hour, at least a score of times ?" He turned indignantly to Roland, who interposed in his support.

"My dear sir, I can assure you that I know a man *well*, who once fell in love in *five minutes*—and remained there,"—he might have added, that he stood there to prove it, but he did not. "As for my friend," he continued, " I'll answer for it, for he has seldom had a free half-hour since he left school."

The Firm was taken aback at this undaunted front.

"Really !" It said, "It had no idea that such things were, or indeed were possible, It led so idyllic a life of It's own, was implied ; but of course, if this were a guaranteed fact, together with the matter of the aunt, it would put a different complexion on the affair.

" Altogether—well, yes—there were certain discrepancies, it must be allowed, when the critiques came to be closely compared, and, on the whole, It was of opinion, that perhaps, with some slight alterations, It might venture to recommend publication on similarly cautious conditions with the former work. But," It went on to say, " you are young—you will for-

give me—you will do well to take a hint from
US. Now, We should have preferred a Christmas
Annual or a Manual of Society. No, no,"
It simpered, placing the tips of Its fingers
together as It caught sight of the author's
face, " not at all; I do *not* mean the work that
explains how you are to eat asparagus—not
that. No, I mean a sort of biographical dic-
tionary—a few smart lines on the smart people,
and those whom you would naturally suppose
to constitute society—under a thin disguise,
perhaps, no harm in that. The public are delighted with it, and will pore for hours trying
to lift the little veils you assiduously throw over
your characters—such little veils, you know,
merely " (and he placed his finger-tips lightly on
the table), "a tiny, witty transposition of letters
—quite sufficient. Thus, you want to describe
say, Captain Porter, you publish him under the
amusing synonym of Paptain Corter—so simple—so *effective;* Annuals in this form, talking
of synonyms, mean thousands. Then a little
résumé of what society is, and what it ought
to be, and how difficult it is to get into it,
and how many people think they are in, and
really are out in the cold, and how inscrutable are its unwritten laws, how incomprehensible to the generality, and how important;
how lovely is the life really led in the mystic
regions, how enjoyable, glorious, and refined,
and how exceedingly difficult it is to get at the
real right thing."

" But," interposed Mr. Brabant, " I know so
little of it—at least from that point of view."

" No matter, my dear sir ; you will, perhaps,

hardly believe me, that the people who, as
a rule, paint these enchanting pictures, are
clerks on eighty pounds a year, half-pay cap-
tains, or broken-down aristocrats themselves,
to whom the turning of three-and-sixpence is a
serious business."

But Mr. Brabant did not warm to the suggestion. He had written his book, and, curiously
enough, felt a predilection towards publishing
that, rather than writing another.

" Well, well," said the Firm after a fresh spell
of consideration, " what you really require is a
close study of the leading novelists of the day—
we publish no other, and a few additions—a few
carefully-considered sentences inserted here and
there, after the magic type of the fashion, would
have an immense effect on the fortunes of the
book. Now here," It turned to a pile of
gorgeously-bound volumes, " are three or four
of the very tip-top writers, whom the public
would read if they wrote in Chaldee. You have
merely to open any one of them at hazard, to
see how characteristic is every sentence of the
spirit that breathes through the whole. The
air of realism, of refinement, of *je ne sais quoi*,
is so, ahem! ahem! that really nothing can
possibly equal its—its—ahem! ahem!

" Here, for instance, is Lady Victoria Nage's
last—strictly speaking, it is not a romance,
though in parts it reads like one. Listen to
this." The Firm waved a white, bejewelled
hand,—

" ' To be surrounded by five hundred naked,
howling niggers, each brandishing his revolver,
while he carefully took aim through his long

spear at my unprotected person, was a situation which many of my Belgravian lady friends might have found unpleasing. To me, I confess, it simply added zest to the delightful air of the morning, and made the prospect of our comfortable camp-breakfast seem even more enticing. Why should I feel afraid? This was nothing—nothing to what had happened yesterday, and would happen again to-morrow. My Gatling gun was handy, but I disdained to use other than my woman's weapons. Seizing the three foremost ruffians with my teeth, I scratched their eyes out, and flung them to the earth, while their assegais exploded harmlessly in rear. The six next that came on I floored with a back-hander, which slightly sprained my left wrist.

"'My dear little toy-terrier, Fido, seeing me thus engaged, rushed madly into the *mêlée*, barking furiously, and driving the dusky demons before him like a flock of sheep. Those he tore down he ate up on the spot; and so fearful was the panic that he occasioned, that in less time than it takes to write it, the remnant of the stricken fugitives had disappeared—vanished utterly—so that when I looked up again, I rubbed my eyes in wild astonishment. Not so much as even one single corpse remained to tell the tale.

"'Where but a few moments before the yelling crowd had rent the air as they pressed on, was nothing now save the waving grasses, where the lark played, and the lizard warbled his peaceful ditty undisturbed.

"'Calling to my little Fido, whose savage

breakfast had painfully distended him, and whose pace was therefore slow, I turned on my heel and made the best of my way back,' &c., &c."

The reader slapped-to the book. "Now that's a mere casual page from her last work, 'The Hermaphrodite Abroad.' Delightful, isn't it? *risqué* too, slightly, perhaps; but what zest, what *verve*, what splendour of local colour! 'The lizard warbling in the grass,' exquisite! brings the thing before one's very eyes. There's nothing like a lady-writer nowadays. It's a pity you're not a lady, sir.

" 'The rules that bind, In slavish fetters half mankind,' do not bind the better half. Fact, logic, wit, grammar, sense, bow their faces before 'em, and the public does likewise. You see, sir, a woman can unsex herself so delightfully, but the operation has not the same charm when performed by a man.

"Now here's another," It continued enthusiastically, "you really can't have too many examples. Miss Masher's very last, hot from the press; the style is different, but the level is as high. Let me read you a sentence or two, and you'll see what I mean.

" 'We are at family prayers, our man-servant and our maid-servant, our ox and our ass (more than one of these latter), and Jack, and Jill, and I.

" 'This is *the* hour of the day when we three imps and sworn associates really enjoy ourselves to the uttermost. We have each brought with us a treasure casket. Jack's contains dried peas, Jill's cockchafers, and mine—snuff. How to combine these varied elements, and to employ them to the best advantage, now becomes a question. Peas have already been carefully sown in the passage outside, where it is dark, as a commencement, and the cook and our revered and reverend governor both slithered into the room as if they were drunk.

"'Look at old Martha's face,' whispers Jack to me. 'I know her corns is bad, for she told me so.'

"'A suppressed hush and a congratulatory pinch from myself are his reward; and under cover of the coal-scuttle, Jill gracefully offers to each of us a pinch of snuff (from my box, by the way, which is mean). We take a huge one. I pile up the beastly brown stuff on my little white thumb, so does Jack, so does Jill —drilled veterans we—we toss back our three heads, and we sniff together.

"'The result is prodigious. Our reverend governor sits at his desk, with one ragged wisp of hair waggling on his forehead, droning through his disreputable old nose. "I believe in God the Father Almighty, Maker of heaven and earth," when the united crash of our three sneezes rends the air; but happily he is deaf, and his bleary old eyes are dim—he neither sees nor hears, or we should rue it to this day.

"'Not deaf and not blind, however, is our only guest, who kneels but a pace behind us, Sir Ivor de Cressingham, grim, gallant, gaunt, graceful Sir Ivor, with his tawny moustache, and head shorn of its golden coronet of curls by many a stern campaign, who with great, grave eyes, has watched our proceedings from the beginning.

"'Why, I know not, but the devil has entered into me to disgust him. I have climbed up into a high chair, under pretext of kneeling there, and am now dangling my long legs, in their dirty white stockings, just under his nose.

"'Three facts further bring unhallowed joy to my spirit; they are, that my strings are out, that my shoe is well down at heel, and that I have a hole in my left stocking, through which a red, red chilblain cheerily pokes its little head. He will hardly love me thus, I murmur, but the infatuated old fool does.

"'Resurrection of the body,'" snorts the reverend one from the desk.

"'Ladies and gentlemen," whispers Jill, "this is merely typical of that interesting fact." She opens the lid of her box. Instantly spin forth the cockchafers, whirring and booming through the air, and with excellent good taste selecting Sir Ivor's bald pate, and dear papa's inflated nostril, as special points to whack upon.

"'We scream—in our sleeves, that is—it is too too exquisite.'

"It is, indeed," concluded the Firm, shutting the book. "Comment is needless. You can imagine how the high-class public jumps at this species of production. No man can do this sort of thing, and if he did, it would be a failure. But you might take a hint; we are always pleased to give a hint to a clever young writer," and the Firm bowed.

"And there's another thing; if I might recommend it, when you next try your hand, though this of late years has fallen to the ladies—the ladies, sir, are taking the wind out of our sails all along the line, he! he! I refer to the sporting novel, which has a distinct style of its own. The style of the stable and the pot-boy, sir, seems to take, when that of the nursery, and the not—ahem ! ahem !—too respectable— ahem ! ahem !—female—ahem !—seems to fail.

"Now here,"—he touched another volume, "is something like a hero—a guardsman who shoots grouse with his rifle, and enters his horse in a race for mares, with a heroine to match, who has two hundred thousand a year, &c., &c. Most life-like ! Ah ! life would be dreary if it were not for such realism.

"Here, again, is the thing attempted by a man, but a man who is in the position to attempt it, Lord Joseph Backstair. No doubt you know his lordship. An aristocrat to the backbone, and quite a veteran sportsman, seven-and-twenty at least. An aristocrat describing aristocrats,—that is very powerful, and to show you how the level is maintained, gentlemen, I will open it at random, quite at random.

"There, I told you so. Here are two wicked Marquises talking to the loveliest Duchess on earth. Listen to what one is able to say by himself, without so much as stopping to take breath.

" 'My dear little Duch. I know your game, but it's no use your trying your paces with those two clipping fillies, that carry the cherry ribbons round the paddock. You ain't in it, Duch, either of them could give you five pounds and beat you by a head over the open. Why, they're the most spanking little pair of tits in London, and two to one bar one, I'll back either of them, if not pulled.

" ' When your Grace does enter, you'll run to win on your own legs.

" ' If the sartorial potentate, whose divine art had clothed the Marquis's superb personality, could have observed him at this moment, with what conscious pride would he have noted the noble swell of his breast, the high-bred fall of his trouser.'

" But, gentlemen, no more ; in its way it is perfect ; read and mark for yourselves. ' Sartorial potentate ' ! " and the Firm raised the whites of It's eyes to the ceiling, and lifted both It's hands with a pretty little gesture, " Why, after all, it's only a tailor, you know ; but how exquisitely clothed ! and to the average reader, the idea of a real Marquis telling a real Duchess something about her own legs—I didn't quite follow it—but it's unique, and uniquity, if I may permit myself the expression, is what we must aim at. Gentlemen," It concluded solemnly, " I have little doubt that that incident occurred in real life."

There was silence for a minute ; no one appeared to doubt this, so the speaker continued, " You see, sir, you are not a lady, and—ahem ! I suppose, without offence, I may dare to say—not exactly an aristocrat ? "

Roland's eyes met Brabant's across the table ; the latter glanced casually at his face and figure in the glass opposite. " Well, no," he said ; " I suppose I'm not exactly."

And here the two visitors were rude enough to laugh, which seemed to put the Firm a little out of countenance.

" Perhaps," It interposed, " by delicately introducing something of the sort I have ventured to recommend, you may be able to make something of the work yet; I do not tie you down to one style; take your choice. There are certain things in literature, as there are in sport, which are absolute certainties. A repulsive Jesuit now, is safe—very safe. What is a repulsive Jesuit, sir? He's money—money in a lump—that's what he is—that's what we want. With such improvements, we might be led to reconsider it."

Brabant had already taken his hat from the table. "Thank you," he said, "thank you very much; but my style, I am afraid, will hardly adapt itself to yours. Perhaps it will be as well to try at once elsewhere."

The Firm cleared It's throat. "That would be a pity; let Us look at it again."

But the author and his supporter had bowed themselves out.

"'So much for Buckingham!'" exclaimed the former as they went; "but, mark me! that man will make an offer by the next post. I've foreseen what we've been coming to in fiction for some time past."

"I have noticed it myself," said Roland, "and I have seriously thought of starting (as a mere speculation), a Male Novelist's Alliance and Protection Company, Unlimited. It would have for its object, to provide readers for male writers suffering from the undue pressure of female competition, and to counteract generally the disabilities of their sex."

Brabant crossed himself. "Reserve a few shares for me," he said piously. "And now I think of it, you've stood by me staunchly in this, you've given me the inch, refuse not the ell—help me through a worse. I do dislike a family party, and I have to lunch at Harrow to-day. Come with me."

" Why on earth at Harrow ? "

" With the Squeeds, I mean."

" The Squeeds ? " exclaimed Roland temporizing, " my dear fellow—why, I don't even know them."

This was weak.

" I'll introduce you," said Brabant, laying the objection at a stroke.

" But,—ah ! your friend is a widow, living alone, isn't she ? Two are company, and—"

" Oh, no, she lives with her people ; she married her cousin, they were all Squeeds ; and her aunt, Lady Jane, you know—"

" Yes, yes, I know ; but they may not care to see me ; and women hate having you in to anything when they're not prepared."

As there were five unmarried sisters, Brabant thought they were not likely to be unprepared, and he said so.

" But I've really a great deal to do. Look here, my tailor's estimate came this morning," and he pulled out of his pocket a paper a yard long ; " 198l. 17s. 0½d., and very moderate too, just for a man's necessaries at joining. I don't always sympathize with paterfamilias, but, 'pon my honour, if I had one, I should be sorry for him. I'll look in on the fellow as we go back, and give him my ideas on the subject. I daresay I shan't stay beyond my drill. I think I've an idea what British soldiering means nowadays. I was talking to a big fellow the other day—one they'd shelved for life at forty —and he said the army means this :—

" ' A certain number of fools are selected (men with brains don't trouble the service), these are figged out like mountebanks, and either set to dance attendance on a lot of women at home, about the Court and so forth, or sent out to heaven knows what God-forsaken spot, to rot in pink and gold. As long as they fancy themselves and the girls fancy them, all is well; but after a score or so of years, that goes, and the man is usually obliged to follow suit, with the pleasant conviction that he has spent the best part of his life in pure fooling.' That's what he said; and, by Jove ! I more than half believe him."

" If that's the case, the more chance for a man with brains."

" We shall see," said Roland, appropriating the idea with no painful qualms of modesty.

" Where do you say these people of yours live ? "

" Harrow-on-the-Hill," answered Brabant, wincing, as if the name were distasteful to him.

" That's a far cry, but if you're quite certain I shan't be in the way, I'll drive you there. I had meant to go to St. Maur's. The Endowment Concessions Bill will be going up to the Lords, or I mistake greatly, and I fancy he'll wish to speak on it. I must see him. Then the *Katholicon* announces a meeting of ourselves at Regent's Hall, St. James's Street, this week. I've a word to say, and haven't thought about it yet. But here we are at the ' sartorial potentate's!' Come in, and let's have a look at the manner of the man."

He flung the reins to his groom, and they entered together.

"I wish to see the chief potentate," he said.

"I am he," replied a dignified personage, coming forward to meet them with a smile of the utmost affability. Gentlemen who came to order their uniforms were often pleased to be extremely amusing, but they usually paid for their whistle in the end.

"What can I do for you, sir?" asked the S. P.

"I've come here to get my outfit."

A spasm of unholy joy, which he could not altogether repress, crossed the tailor's face. It was so acute, that a little of it oozed out of one corner of his eye in the shape of a tear.

"Guards, of course, sir?"

"Of course not, sir."

"Perhaps the Blues?"

"Perhaps not," thundered Roland.

"Well, after all, the Cavalry were—"

"Look here!" roared Roland, "it's Infantry of the Line, if you know what that is, and I suppose you do, as you sent me an estimate this morning," and he pulled it out; "but really I don't like to rob you to this tune. By the way, have you any tooth-brushes?"

The tailor's smile was hollowing, his customer looked ugly, but he answered that certainly they had tooth-brushes, best walrus-tusk, some even as low as three-and-sixpence.

"Dirt cheap," said Roland. "Put me up one, or say two. Well, that'll be about all I shall want, I think," and he turned as if to leave the shop.

" But the outfit, sir ! " gasped the ninth fraction of a man, while the crowd of assistants went sniggering into the corners of the shop.

" Outfit ? Didn't I tell you to put it up for me ? Two tooth-brushes, that's my idea of a soldier's kit.   Ah ! I forgot, it's a little different from yours," and he looked at the estimate again.

" Why, I see you don't even include a toothbrush in the 198*l*."

The tailor was feeling better. This sort of joking was execrable, but still—and he actually laughed heartily.

" Pardon, sir," he said, recovering, and deftly unfolding a garment for inspection. " By a special patent process of our own, we are able to work in the gold lace an extra quarter of·an inch in width, in a way that defies detection. It's very handsome, sir—very, *very* lovely—and if you would only look at it—just one little glance, sir.   Then as to cut, my Lord—"

A spasmodic movement on the part of his customer caused him to stumble back.

" Pardon, sir.   So like young Lord Leatherhead.   Dear me ! dear me ! But I was saying, we are enabled to give quite a cavalry cut, to an ordinary infantry jack—"

" Look here," said Roland, repressing the real rage that bubbled in his veins.   " You may make me just the necessary coat, jacket, and trousers, if you can do it for five-and-twenty pounds.   Not a half-penny more will I pay. Good morning."   And he strode to the door, followed by the murmur of many voices.

" That sort of thing is all very well," was Brabant's comment as they drove away," and I see you've the wit of your type, but it requires a man of your physique to carry it off."

Mr. Tudor muttered a curse on all playing up to such rascally swindling, and declared his intention of calling for his letters, as he might have business. But alas! for human nature, there might have been a hundred business missives lying in wait, he would have let them lie ; all his thought was of an ordinary square envelope with the monogram " S. G." entwined upon it, and bearing as postmark the far-sounding name of a little town in the west countree. This was even now upon his table awaiting him. When he reached his door, he sprang down himself, no servant should bring it were it there, even the postman was a desecration. Such a note should have been borne through the air by a suite of carrier pigeons.

" My dearest boy," it began, " I am all right and well, and I begin my letter so, because I am sure that is what you most want to know. We are going to town next week, and—"

He read no more. Why should he ? The world, the wide heavens could give him nothing beyond. He put the letter in his pocket, was down two flights of stairs in two strides, and two more landed him on the box-seat. To Brabant's uncertain nerves such unexpected vivacity was oppressive. Was this the casual effect of business letters? It was not his experience of them.

"What a gorgeous day," said Roland as he settled into his place, whipping the mare into a hand gallop as he turned into Regent Street.

"It was—now it looks like rain; I felt a spot just then. May I ask, do you usually take Regent Street at this pace? There! they are calling after you—you'll get into trouble; and look here! I wish you wouldn't bow to people when you're driving at full speed, we nearly lurched into that cab."

"It was old Mrs. Smith—wonderful old lady! Did you see how well she looked?"

"She looked uncommonly relieved that you didn't run over her," said Brabant sulkily.

"There's Jones," exclaimed Roland, waving his hand to a passer-by; "good fellow, Jones. I always say Jones—"

"Confound Jones; do mind your whip, you nearly flicked my eye out."

As the spirits of the one rose, the spirits of the other fell, but neither stopped to analyze the augury.

The day was keen and bright, almost frosty, but the Londoner was not going to be done out of his July, and all through the parks he lay on his back in the grass, steadily catching lumbago; and he and his sweetheart sat on every bench, making the warmth of their affection supply the absent caloric of the sun. Beneficent local authorities had placed public seats throughout the entire suburbs, and most of these were occupied.

"I don't know why," said Roland as they neared their destination, and he pointed to one of these couples whose backs were turned to them,

" but that man with the curly hat rather reminds me of my uncle. Guilty conscience, I suppose. I had clean forgotten him. He's very attentive. Look ! by Jove ! I believe we've come in for a declaration ; he wants to go down on his knees, and she's begging him to stop it. How flattered the uncle would be, to be thought capable of going on his knees. 'Pon my honour, it's very like the hat. The devil ! " he nearly dropped his whip. " It is the old gentleman himself, and that's a deuced fine girl with him. I admire his taste. My poor five pounds ! " he groaned. " How she ever got him there, and how the dickens she'll ever get him back, she knows best."

He laughed boisterously, but Brabant did not join ; on the contrary, his face had fallen to zero.

" That is—my—that happens to be—ah—that is—Mrs. Lushington Squeed," he said icily.

How thankful was Roland in that moment that he had called her, " a deuced fine girl."

Perhaps the recollection of it softened his friend, for he went on in a more natural voice. " They don't see us—I—I—really didn't know, I wasn't aware, that she was acquainted with Major Lickpenny, and I should hardly think it desirable that—but here's the gate—and— they're coming on after us ; she's got him up, and given him her arm. I think he wants to take both her arms ; really it's very imprudent of her."

They turned into the grounds of a villa which, with a fine effrontery, announced itself in black and white on the gate-post as " Old Hall." It was neither better nor worse than its neighbours, nor particularly distinguished from them. Built in the stucco-front, brick-back, brass-bell, and venetian-blind style, it stood in its own grounds, which were almost as large as a small field, and laid out charmingly in the suburban fashion—if you cared for that sort of thing. A carriage-drive of immense length, half a mile at least you would say, and fearfully intricate in its convolutions, led up to the mansion, which Mrs. Squeed was wont to refer to in moments of expansion, as " The Hold 'all at Harrow-on-the-'Ill;" whence, and from the number of its inmates, it was commonly known as the " Hold-all." Some of her friends even, hinted that the elder Mrs. Squeed was a vulgar, cringing old woman, who clung to her rich relations like a leech, while she ignored her poor ones altogether.

The fair-minded reader will certainly allow, that up to this point we have been careful and considerate for him ; if we have had to talk of stupid common people, it has been done as briefly as possible.

There has always been someone with a handle to his name within actual stone's throw, or if he has been called away for a minute, some gracious figure of high-born lineage and romantic antecedents has invariably filled his place. Let him, then, be assured, no other society for us or for him; even here is Lady Jane. But, looked at from his own point of view, it will, doubtless, be a surprise to him to see the people who then moved, in what was pleased to call itself " society."

As to this family in particular, the head of it

had long since forsaken Harrow for Heaven, in which one will not blame him. The children were all girls. Maria, the eldest, with whom we are mostly concerned, had married her cousin Lushington, and had now returned to the parent nest as a widow, with a small jointure, which caused Mrs. Squeed usually to refer to her as, " our little *h*eiress." But as Maria was five feet eight, and otherwise generously proportioned, ill-natured people used to laugh at this.

Next to her came Rosilla (commonly called " Bud ") Vanilla de Mowbray Lushington Squeed; after her Horatia de Courcy Vyvyan Lushington Squeed, usually known as " Horror." The peerage had been depopulated to denominate the remainder, who, however, condescended to answer in real life to the simpler prefixes of " Sue," and " E." " E.," or " Eve," as she really was, was only fourteen, but already a power in herself. It was to her push and energy, and to the sharpness of her wit, that Brabant first owed his place in the family. Little though he thought it; she had recruited him through a friend. Her precocity was something superhuman. Her sisters all shone in the borrowed light of the heiress, but she boasted her own lights as pertinaciously, as did another little girl " her own shadow."

When Brabant had first set foot in the house she recognized him at once, as something very much better than usually fell in their way, and coolly recommended that now they had laid hold of a gentleman, they should take care not to let him go in a hurry. For herself, of course she was out of the running by circumstances, but she threw out the hint to those whom it might concern. It was not every day that Mrs. Squeed's "cycle," as she insisted on calling it, was enlarged by the addition of a real gentleman. Nowadays, when real gentlemen of breeding and birth grow on every blackberry-bush, this may seem strange, but it was true ; and while Miss Eve was properly taken to task for her impertinence, her advice was cordially acted upon. There was no doubt that here was the real thing. Although there was little money actually attached to it, there appeared to be a certain potentiality in the future, a hoard which young Mrs. Lushington Squeed, by no means so innocent as she pretended to be, gauged with unerring accuracy.

The Brabants were people of good position, although impoverished in consequence of mere numbers ; they had a small place in the country, and could show genuine sixteenth century brasses of genuine ancestors, which may, perhaps, be considered as equal to-day, to a nineteenth century patent of nobility. This a paragraph in the county history duly told.

" I thought you said you were originally Ayrshire, Mr. Brabant ? " the old lady had remarked, very sweetly, on his second visit; " we can't quite make out from the Red Book."

" Indeed ! perhaps you have not one old enough ? "

" Oh ! yes; we've a shelf of old ones, and we've hunted regularly through them from first to last," she answered, with the most perfect frankness.

" Well ! if you will look in the edition for the

year 1186, if you happen to have it, you may find particulars. We came out of Ayr in the beginning of April that year."

This was taken in all seriousness, and produced a profound impression.

County Histories and Red Books were almost the only literature patronized by the family; they were the Bible and Prayer Book of week-day life; and for Sunday reading, a penny Society paper, that culled the choicest morsels from its more pretentious contemporaries a week late, supplied all that the Squeed *ménage* could possibly desire. Hence it was, that without being exactly in it, or, in plain words, being entirely out of it, there was hardly a charming or beautiful incident taking place in that lofty ethical state, vulgarly known as "high life," of which they could not boast an intimate knowledge within a week or ten days after it had, or had not, occurred.

The Brabants were in reality, as their name suggested, of Huguenot origin, driven from France for their beliefs, with consistent irony they had been among the first of those English families that Rome had numbered among her recruits.

It now remains to be told how matters had reached their present stage, how it was that Warburton Brabant, writer, art—critic, and poet, who already bid fair to be the most distinguished member of his family, could claim proprietorship in the person of Maria Elizabeth de Sawnay Lushington Squeed, the flower and the crown of hers.

CHAPTER II.

WHEN the family of Squeed first emerged from the mists of history (some twenty or thirty years before), they appeared as Belgravians. Their growth seemed to have been contemporaneous with that of the locality—one natural to the soil, but one that never spread beyond the more remote riverside streets of that charmed district.

It was understood that there were " good " connections in the case, but these connections moved in another " sphere," and might as well have been in another planet for all the good that came of them. The family of Squeed was really of some age, and could trace at least to an honest merchant clothier of the City of London in the middle of the seventeenth century, if not to a cross-legged Crusader in the middle of the twelfth, as the head of the family professed to do. He had noted as a purely business matter, that the various Crusaders in the Temple Church lay there, neglected and unclaimed, and there seemed no harm in, as it were, appropriating one of them—on whose monument something faintly resembling an S could be deciphered.

This legend then prospered, as did its modern representative, who had made a little money in a perfectly respectable business, and who in the course of time, married a Miss Dumple, who also had a little money, and ambitions quite disproportionate. The Dumples, too, had moved among the gentry, and were very high and haughty people in all matters of lineage; but truth compels the admission that this Miss Dumple, who became Mrs. Squeed, was not a refined person, that she shortly grew red and stout, and that her memory failed her early with regard to the use of the letter H. From this union resulted a large family of girls, who inherited the yearnings of both parents in an intensified degree. The girls were at this time almost all "introduced," as they were wont to put it, and were young ladies who appeared to have been endowed with more than an ordinary share of the qualities likely to advance them in life. They it was who made the discovery that under their then conditions—i.e. of residence in a back street—it was not of the slightest use having " Belgravia " stamped in letters of green and gold half an inch high, on every sheet of note and every envelope, sent out by the household —not of the slightest—they tried it for years, and their experience should be a warning. New acquaintances, who occasionally jumped at them on first seeing their cards, on a nearer view dropped off one and all, and it only led to disparaging remarks and unpleasantness with regard to Belgravia generally, and the

bye-ways and alleys which arrogated such a
title. The more they clung to it, the more
angry did the absurd world become, until it
was plain that nothing was to be made out of
Belgravia, proper or improper.

But the family were prospering in other
ways and mounting gradually (such never
fail, in the long run, in English society). One
of the uncles (a nonentity who lived in the
house) became the third husband of an elderly,
ugly, vulgar widow, who was, nathless, the
daughter of an earl. With the advent of Lady
Jane, the family star may be said to have first
risen above the horizon. This worthy person
threw herself into the business. Within a
week after she had linked her fortunes with
theirs, she had looked up their "swell"
connections to a man. She was not a
woman to tolerate shirking on the part of
these individuals. She had the family formally
acknowledged, and found them a new fifth
cousin, who was a marquis. It did no harm to
this gentleman, for he never knew of it, but the
benefit that accrued to the family was incalculable. But more than this, she found them a
large "acquaintance"—such as it was, ready-
made—people who, on the understanding that a
quid should be forthcoming for the *quo*, were
prepared to talk about the Marquis before
strangers and visitors, as if he were a private
historic fact, and were expected to drop in to
tea.

Belgravia had been a failure. By her advice,
they shook the dust of it from their shoes and

blossomed anon before the world as a county family. Much discretion was necessary. To be within easy reach of town was a first consideration. On the other hand, the near localities were open to the reproach of being suburban. Eventually Harrow was fixed upon as combining the requirements to a nicety. A field was bought there, a " mansion " erected and christened, at Mrs. Squeed's suggestion, " Old Hall."

Mr. Squeed would have liked something more classic, but was over-ruled. The residential estate became a fact. Certain negotiations took place with certain compilers of family records, certain monies changed hands, certain hospitalities were dispensed, and the deed was done. Henceforth the Squeeds stood forth ' fast rooted in the fruitful soil.' As so being, they had to be met and faced. People on promotion are not always of the pleasantest sort, but they appear to be a condition of our fallen nature. At the time this history opens, Lady Jane was again a widow unattached, but not disinclined towards a fourth husband, should such a one present himself.

It had been a great day when Maria returned to the maternal nest as widow and heiress. It was not long since she had left it, and there were many good reasons, of which perhaps economy was the first, why she should come back, though this was never whispered. Poor Lushington's career had been brief and inglorious, he had been finished off within two years, and his own generous habits had possibly hastened the end. His relict seldom referred to him, although she sometimes deplored the quantity of old clothes he had left behind him which were lying idle, and she feared spoiling and going out of fashion. That she said was a pity, and so it was. At this period, and before the cold-blooded executors had put down everything in black and white, she was inclined to speak a good deal of her money. The amount, she was apt to say, mattered little; money was money, and to have it was to have it.

Her talk, especially at home, ran into vagueness and splendour. It was a pity that there was no river at Harrow. The Thames would have looked so well winding up the hill. After all money could do it—what could not money do? To fill up valleys and change the course of rivers, was one of its avocations. And here she would rattle the keys against the scent-bottle in her pocket, and in their mind's eye her sisters already saw the Thames climbing the hill. It was a shame that no one had yet decorated the interior of St. Paul's. That sort of thing should be done by a single mind so as to secure uniformity. But then there was the park for Paddington, and Hainault Forest waiting to be given to the public, and really the responsibility of deciding was too much, things must remain as they were for the present.

It will be seen that Mrs. Lushington Squeed plunged into great depths, and almost everything that certain royal ladies were described as patronizing in the penny society paper which was the family oracle, she said

that she really must take up. But when the
end of the first half-year had come, she found
to her astonishment, that she had run in debt
for gloves and ribbons; this fact she was wise
enough to conceal, and the following half she
spent more in talk and less in cash. After all,
her solicitor, her agent, and her banker were
solid facts which nobody could deny, and which
gave her a *locus standi* of themselves.

How did Brabant first get to Harrow? That
has never been fully explained. The story runs
that a friend, a native, took him for a walk
which led through the gates of " Old Hall."
Upon the lawn was an extempore party, and it
was a pleasant scene of sunshine and flowers
and girls. The young widow was presiding, and
at her best; the old lady remembered her h's,
the friend was confidential and spoke of ' our
local heiress,' and the other sisters loyally
played up. Mrs. Lushington Squeed, or Mrs.
Lushington, as she was called for shortness,
talked of throwing in the four adjoining pro-
perties and levelling the hill, to make " a
really good tennis-ground," a suggestion which
so staggered the new visitor, that he implored
her to think twice before she attempted it;
this she very readily promised to do.

She gave him a cup of excellent tea, and so
grateful was he for this unusual and unlooked-
for rarity, that for the rest of the time he singled
her out with marked attention. When at
last he left, promising weakly to come again
on another Thursday, and bring a man or two,
the flutter was considerable, for it was obvious

that he meant it, and in spite of a few rather
dusty old ladies this, and old ladies that, who
were *habituées* of the house, young men of a
like position did not attend, with the frequency
that might be desired by a mother with five
daughters.

It was curious how much more difficult it
was to get hold of young Mr. Brown, than of
old Mrs. Brown, his mother; and even dear
Lady Tomkins was quite common if you compared her with that slippery young man, the
Honourable Jack, her nephew. Every one knew
how tiresome he was, and how he had to
be asked for three years continually, before he
dropped in for three minutes at last.

When the guests were gone, Maria thought
it worth while to fling herself into an
attitude on the sofa, while the rest stood
about her in solemn conclave; all except
Eve, who, usually contemptuous of conventionalities, bore mute witness by her clean
collar and cuffs to the importance of the occasion. She, ah me! sat astride on the window-
sill, kicking her heels. There was a general
feeling in the air that this embryonic affair
must go on. Nothing so promising had loomed
above the horizon since poor Lushington's
time, and the belief in Maria deepened and
solidified.

"Well, girls, I congratulate you," said Mrs.
Squeed, *mère*, coming in upon them like a huge
hot walking jelly, and plumping herself down
in their midst; "a real celebrity, and so civil
too; three paragraphs about him in four weeks,

in our paper. I particularly noticed 'em, 'cos you know, I knew all about his people, they were great friends of Aunt Jane's—must have been, I'm sure, from where they moved, and they say he's just coining money. I asked him all I could about one thing and another, but I 'spect he's a little deaf, for he didn't seem to hear and didn't say much. I thought he'd been at Oxford, but he said it was Kensington—it's a nasty Romish place that Kensington; but there, it isn't the young man's fault. I remember when his grand-father was seduced, poor dear man, and the people hooted him in the streets, a lot of cardinals came down from Rome and got hold of him, and it was all up with him, for he was always weak in his head, and he went over and never came back. Oh, Shin-bone! it does make me wild when I think of those Jesuits."

Here she stopped and fanned herself vigor-ously with her handkerchief.

The girls took her talk very coolly. Popery was a well known red-rag with their mamma, and if she encountered a Papist she was like the dog with the pain in his inside— she made a personal thing of it, and, after a sanguinary encounter, invariably left the field, muttering under her breath "Shin-bone! Shin-bone!" which was supposed to be intended as an opprobious epithet, referring generally to the relics of the saints. But times were so bad, alas! that she could not now afford to sneeze even at a Popish young man.

" One has to look at it all round," she said, quieting down, " and he must have heaps of friends he'll be sure to bring in time. We can do a great deal before Thursday week. As he writes poetry he's sure to be æsthetic. I *will* get the new curtains, and we can stick Japanese fans and peacocks' feathers all round the dado. The fans are only a penny; we can do it for three and six."

" That's not art, mummy," observed Eve, with some sarcasm. " You had better let me and Bud drape the grate *à la* Florentine, and pin it up with live sunflowers—there are lots in the cabbage-bed—and then you'll have the real thing."

Maria heaved a sign; she was very elaborate herself, but her surroundings depressed her. " I have often thought," she said slowly, " that if I ran the verandah right round the house, and built a long terrace between the wall and the kitchen-garden, the place would look quite decent; but what can I do by Thursday week? No, it's impossible, even if I put a hundred men on it."

" You've only one thing to do, the lot of you," said Eve, digging the wainscot with her heel, " and that is—to feed 'em well; and "— slipping off her perch—" Maria, you may as well remember that we all look to you to bring a good name into the family at last, that will really belong to us."

The phalanx of elder sisters rose up to crush her, but she went from them like a streak of lightning, and was shortly lost in the cabbage-

beds. It was obvious that if it was to be anybody it must be Maria, for she had the wherewithal to make the thing possible, or was supposed to have ; and that astute young woman
fell into deep calculation, which she finally
concluded, by resolving that the stake would be
worth playing for. The man she had gauged
with accuracy ; a deep hoard of the capital
of labour lay undelved for, in his brain. He
was a social favourite, just spreading his
wings for flight, and if his people were poor,
they had a good connection. This would suit
the Squeed family admirably. Catholic society
was good ; better in proportion to its numbers,
perhaps, than any other. Then, to tell a secret,
Maria was not so young as she had been ten
years before—it would be a shame to say
fifteen—and in spite of the rumour of the
money, the men who might have been expected
to flock round her, had unaccountably fought
shy.

The world had grown so pitifully narrow that
even Mrs. Squeed had one friend who was Romish
(an adjective she pronounced with infinite
gusto, as having a pleasant smack of curse
and insult about it), a certain elderly Miss
Wigway, herself a recent convert—we should
say pervert—and this lady, though she had
never been quite forgiven, was admitted as a
sort of toothless wolf inside the " Old Hall "
fold. Miss Wigway was wont to refer cheerfully to the sacrifices she had made for the
Faith ; but there were people who thought
she had gained almost as much as she had

lost even in this world. When her advice
was asked it was given all in favour of the
scheme.

"Mr. Brabant? oh! certainly; in the very
flower and cream of Catholic society. Why,
only the week before last, her dear Duchess had
called the young man Willie, before her very
eyes, at her own table."

"But," objected in a breath the two Mrs.
Squeeds, to whom this information was tendered, "the young man's name is not Willie."

Miss Wigway hated hair-splitting. "What
does it matter what his name is?" she said
sharply; "she called him by it at any rate,
and Lord de Sawnay was standing at the
other side of the table at the very time."

Here was logic with a vengeance: the ques-
tioners were silenced, and the doubting hearts
were still.

What sort of house the "Hold-'all" was,
in which Brabant had now made good his
footing, was by no means apparent at first
sight, to the casual observer. The sisters, with
the exception of the eldest and youngest, were
comparatively characterless and insignificant—
all that showed on the outside was, that they
were four ungainly, red-handed, red-faced girls,
plain of feature and downright of speech.
Their home-life was not an idyllic one—the
four had not three intelligent ideas among
them; such as they had, they were in the habit
of expressing to one another with incisive direct-
ness, leaving little margin for mistake. Indeed, if you had by chance heard these young

ladies conversing, you might have imagined that
you were listening to a party of navvies, until a
certain shrill acidity of accent betrayed the sex
of the disputants; for among themselves, conversation simply meant snarling in a greater
degree or a less.

It was not a pleasant house to stay in; there
was no authority worth the name, "the mummy,"
as she was generally called, being held of little
more account than if she had been a genuine
one.   Whatever had to be done was done by
ceaseless nagging and hammering, until the
nagged and hammered one gave in at last, but
only after a gallant tussle, from sheer exhaustion.   From the top to the bottom of the
house, every one screamed at every one
else, until after a few days' residence, if one
happened to want anything, one yelled for it,
as a matter of course, and broke into strong
language if it were not produced forthwith.
But it was remarkable how this rabidity could
be calmed down when there was occasion for it.

If you met one of the Miss Squeeds in
society, you simply saw a shapeless, uncouth
female creature, too masculine to be at the
pains of cultivating a taste, or making herself
agreeable as a woman; too feminine to be at
the trouble of stringing three coherent ideas
together.   You caught a fidget and a twist, a
rucking up of the stocking, and perhaps a
smothered yawn at the tediousness of having
to behave with outward decency for an hour
at a time.   You received a blunt "yes" or
"no," to your courteous attempts at conversa-

tion, and then if you were wise, you fled to milder climes.

Absolutely devoid of accomplishment, speaking no language but their own (and a very funny language that was), these damsels were at times in such difficulties with their letters, that they had been known to get their maids to read and write them for them, and infinitely better did those sprightly young ladies do it than their mistresses. The only instinct that made itself at all discernible in the simple characters of the four Miss Squeeds, consisted in an animal leaning towards members of the opposite sex, the "sporting-crusher" preferred. It may seem incredible that such beings should have "gone down," but the eccentricities of the time made it possible in one way—in only one —and in this way they did it, by clinging like grim death to that microcosm of earthly greatness or earthly littleness, their aunt, Lady Jane.

Had you known Lady Jane, the riddle was no easier to read; she was as one of themselves grown old, and consequently no better. It would have been difficult to pick out a single good point in her; she was vulgar, toothless, repulsive—needless to go on. In spite of it all, she was able to walk into a thousand houses where really clever and charming people were accustomed to congregate; and what is more, she was able to take her h-less sister-in-law, with her string of ugly daughters in her wake. What were the clever and charming people thinking about? It is hard to say.

One thing else was necessary, I had nearly forgotten it, to make the position a complete success ; there were relatives on the other side that were bound to be " non est." There was the maternal uncle, Mrs. Squeed's own brother, a mere country doctor, who had broken down after years of honourable work, and whose family were now supposed to be—for she took good care not to know exactly—starving. There was the other brother, the solicitor, paying his way at least, and now with the first brother's children on his hands—but how should the Old Hall people learn this ? His name had been forgot, and this sort of thing went up, and went down, in the days of which it is here written. The family are interesting only as a type which bulked large in the social system.

For a guest it was understood that if it were desirable, all disagreeables should be hushed. A smile of harmless vacancy settled on the six wide mouths, and the tones of all were low and dulcet. Every member of the family, in fact, led a complete double life, one for public, one for private, which was a very charming and genteel thing to do.

Hence it came that Brabant walked through it all with his eyes shut. He was not always an observant man, and was usually more or less in the clouds. He pitied the girls for their want of good looks, and rather liked them for it. Maria indeed was not plain, she was at least a well-grown woman, and Eve's plainness was redeemed by her prodigious precocity. He had plenty of beauty elsewhere—beauty was enjoying a wonderful innings that season—brains were nowhere—among men and women alike. It was a relief to him to avoid the bustle of the London drawing-rooms, hot, ill-savoured, and ghastly in decoration as they mostly were, and to escape from the favours that overtaxed his strength. The reaction of his successes led him in a diametrically opposite direction.

It was pleasant to come down here to the green leaves and the country, among these plain, simple country folk, whose blunt, transparent honesty pleased and amused him, who did not bore him, but made him thoroughly at home. He could get a quiet talk and a cup of tea under the trees of the lawn, and they never asked him to sing and play; one Thursday followed after another, and he was soon the " enfant gâté " of the house. So far, he had no intentions whatever, and would have laughed had any such idea crossed him, but by degrees, unknown to himself, Mrs. Lushington managed to make herself indispensable to him. She listened to his troubles, poured balm into his wounds, laughed with him, wept with him. Brabant's wailings were on a large scale, over the shortcomings of the human race in general. On this the widow would be very expansive, for she too had suffered. She rose with him to the heights, sank with him to the depths, comforted him in his ghostly troubles. It was impossible to imagine anything ghostly or uncomfortable in connection with Mrs.

Lushington. She it was who was always at home, and who made him so, the thing most desired of men. It was wonderful how pleasant she could be when she took the trouble, and the superhuman cleverness of it all was, that it was completely invisible. He took to staying late, until after supper, where so self-restrained were all the young ladies, that none of them, on any one occasion, ate or drank more than twice as much as would have sufficed for a six-foot guardsman. So the moth hovered round the generous flames until it tumbled in.

The catastrophe fell thus. 'Twas upon a Sunday—the better the day, the better the deed. He had lunched with one of his " grand dams," as Mrs. Squeed, *mère*, always emphatically pronounced them, in company with some great literary lights, who had made a fuss about him, and treated him as one of themselves, with that kindly courtesy, which great lights were wont invariably to show lesser ones in those days.

He was still young enough to feel pleased with himself and the world, and afterwards his friend had driven him to vespers at Farm Street; and though it was only in a hansom, for she would not have her horses out on Sundays, and though her companion had been with her, and he had sat bodkin, he had found it not unpleasant, for the two were charming gentlewomen. At the church he heard—from the lips of a facile preacher, it need not be said—a sermon on chivalry, and when it was over he took another hansom, and drove through the summer evening towards Harrow, and as he went he pondered.

Yes, chivalry should be the touchstone of a man's life. The preacher (a man of great experience) had enlarged upon the coarse strength and general brutishness of man, the weakness, refinement, and dependency of woman. He did not hint that the monstrous perversions of modern womanhood had mockingly trampled this thing into the mud, to let it lie there for ever. Possibly, as he was a priest, he took a different view of the subject.

Chivalry in the atmosphere of the " Hold-all " —a vase of Sèvres for the feeding of swine! Nor had Brabant the faintest idea that he himself was the more fragile and the weaker vessel; and that they, the mother and her cubs, were strong, wary, unscrupulous females, harpies by blood, whose highest instinct was a vague one of self-preservation. They wore petticoats; that was enough for him. Through his very successes it had come about, that he had few women friends who could help him in such a crisis. He was at home here, and the temptation to lean, and be leaned upon, was strong.

The widow was sitting alone and pensive in the summer-house. He was concerned to see that she looked as if she had been crying; he pressed her to tell him the cause, but she could not or would not, nor was she comforted. Then the lesson of the day fell strong upon him, and in the ill-fated moment in which it is permitted man to mar a lifetime, he sat down and took her hand in his.

He spoke of life, perhaps, rather in the way
that a poet does, on the duties of men to the
dependent sex, on the claim of women to their
generosity. To this she signified a melancholy
assent, and all the while she drooped insen-
sibly towards him. How it was he never quite
knew, but he fancied it must have been that
she leaned her weight upon him (and she was
heavy), that he found his arm supporting and
half-encircling her; this was something new to
him, for the support had always been the other
way. She was very foolish, she said, and as
she still cried over her foolishness, he felt bound
to dry her eyes in the most chivalrous way which
presented itself. He was not unaccustomed
to the task—indeed, in every house where
there was a woman at all under fifty years of
age, he was sure of a scene if he went often
enough. But there was a difference here.
Henceforth was retribution !

Mrs. Lushington's cleverness and self-
restraint carried the day; she made no scene,
but rather let him make one. He was grateful
for the kindness he had had from her, and
he was sorry for the young widow so early
left forlorn. Both were really affected in their
way, and both apparently tried to speak dis-
passionately of their position, and when two
eligible people start to do this, the effect of
their theorizing is not far off. The woman
was not wholly bad, according to the lights of
what she was pleased to term her education;
she was doing a perfectly legitimate thing.
Does the cat fail to sleep soundly because she

has played and slain her mouse? She contrived to keep him at her side in the dusk of the arbour until nine o'clock. When the supper-bell rang she walked back to the house, clinging heavily to his arm.

"Poor brute!" said Eve to the company with genuine compassion, as she watched them from the windows, "it's U P. Now, I hope, the lot of you'll be satisfied."

But this was only first blood, and Bud, Horror, and Co. were far from satisfied; it was an omen of better to come, what they looked for was blood of their own. Eve's prophecy proved true. It was the sermon that had really done the work, and though Mr. Brabant had spoken no definite words, Mrs. Lushington let him see that she considered herself committed to him, gradually, gradually this. They had kissed—the creature's lips had been on those of every male who had given her the chance since she had been fourteen. But of this he was not aware, or it might have made a difference.

He did not take the final step without deliberation. He did not pretend even to himself that he was in love; his experience had given him a deep-rooted distrust of the passion that flames out fiercely and, in a moment, sinks extinguished into the ashes of its vehemence. He based his feelings, he said to himself, on something higher and more enduring, on respect, affection, and community of feeling. For the rest, other things were reasonably fair, something of money, something of connection, and so forth; and one day not long after, he

came, bringing in his pocket a betrothal ring—
a fragment of mediæval faith and workmanship,
which he had picked up after a long search
and found suited to his mind. He set special
store by this ring, and was at some pains to
explain its emblematic origin and meaning to
her, with what result may be judged from
an observation she made to Horror the same
evening.

"It's a rummy concern," she said, twisting
it to and fro on her finger. "I wish he'd
given me one of those gold pigs or frogs, or
something showy and fashionable; but, heigho!
after all, this must have cost him a pot—that's
something, anyhow."

A curious race, where ladies spoke in this
way.

To him she said, "There is to me a something
in those old-world symbols inexpressibly touching in their faith," for she had gathered and
garnered for use the jargon of the Kensington
schools, and could repeat a column by heart,
like a parrot. Brabant, in his clouds, was
satisfied.

* * * *

Mrs. Squeed and her progeny were in the
drawing-room when Roland and Brabant drove
up together. They were not unexpected, it was
Brabant's usual day for a visit, and, he had latterly played the decoy with some one or other
of his friends, until it had become a habit.

The old lady was short and stout, unremark-
able in every way, save that on her capacious
bosom rose and fell with a regularity varying

with the emotions of the moment, an immense landscape in bog-oak, which represented a fox-hunt, fifty in field at least. On her wrist was a bracelet to match, which depicted an historic scene, Windsor Castle by moonlight, if I remember right; and as the generous arm beneath had long since pushed beyond the bounds of its capacity, it was fastened together very neatly with some pieces of parti-coloured string and moulting black elastic. She wore a great many rings, but this was a family failing, an epidemic of rings and cheap lockets appeared to have broken out among the party. She waddled (the word, though regretable, is necessary) forward to meet her visitors, and taking one of Roland's hands between both her own, said, "Now, this is too charming; uncle and nephew together, quite a little family party. I am sure you must be the gentleman who knows my sister—sister-in-law I should say, but we are like sisters—dear Lady Jane, so well."

No? dear, dear, how very odd. She had made quite sure of it, for Lady Jane knew everybody, and certainly, to judge by his looks, Mr. Tudor must know everybody too. She had heard that he was Lord St. Maur's *great* friend; and she, well she didn't exactly know him; no, he didn't belong to her generation, but she remembered his grandmother perfectly well; and as for his dear sainted mother, she knew her well—by sight—she had often seen her in the distance, and she used always to say that if she could once meet her, she felt that she would have been the dearest friend she had ever had. And she knew his cousin—knew of him, that was—the Popish pervert, Canon what was his name? and remembered, ah me! when the Pope had gone and canonized him, and there, well it was a pity, but they must all make allowances, and—" but at this point the peculiar petrifaction in Roland's eye seeming to strike her, she playfully changed the subject, and set about introducing each of her five daughters.

"This is Rosilla, our Bud as we call her, my second, Mr. Tudor, but second if a mother may say so to none of her sisters. It's a joke against Buddy, that she'll soon be in full bloom!"

Rosilla blushed, as well she might, for she was thirty well told; then, as if there were no help for it, she gave a lunge at Roland which was intended for a hand-shake.

"And this is our little Horror" (the old lady said 'Orror, but retracted it with a violent spasm, and flung it from her on the spot).

"Now, you are laughing at our pet names, Mr. Tudor, but you know that the family bosom's a sacred thing, and it's only there we indulge in them," and here she laid her fat hand on Horror's red hair and stroked it relentlessly from her forehead.

The victim underwent this with speechless resentment, for it displayed her freckles and pale muddy eyes with their light lashes cruelly; but it was an axiom in the house that feelings were for private circulation only, and by no means for the public, so she merely kicked her mother sharply with her brass-tipped heel on the off-side as a gentle hint, and smiled, as she too lunged somewhere in the direction of Roland's ribs.

" Ah ! I often tell her," said Mrs. Squeed, wagging her head, and—good mother—ignoring her wounded shin, " that there's worse Horrors to be met with, though I say it that shouldn't " —and so on, through the rest of the flock down to Eve.

As Eve was not "out," she was always supposed to be in, to be nobody and nowhere, and her mamma slurred her over with a mere wave of the hand, but that young lady did not mean to be ignored. All this time she had been silently taking Roland's measure, and as she watched she had caught something of his thought. " My suspicions are confirmed," she said to herself, stamping ; " I can see exactly what he thinks of us, exactly what any real gentleman would think, but I'm not afraid of him, and I'll show him so ; I intend to be as good as him, every bit, when I know how." She went up, extending a stiff and scornful arm.

" How do you do, Mr. Tudor ? " she said. " Perhaps you are not aware that we have heard a good deal of you : now I hope we shall have the opportunity of judging for ourselves."

On this there was a prodigious onslaught of elder sisters ; one could not but be sorry for any one so seized and whirled about ; she was pitched into the background and lost among the skirts.

"And I do declare there's that dear, delightful, darling old Major," cried Mrs. Squeed, clapping her hands to create a diversion. "Mariar" (Mrs. S. always uttered the name so very distinctly in this fashion, that it would be mere trifling to write it otherwise), "Mariar has got him to the front door. That's our Mariar, Mr. Tudor, she's the one to get anybody anywhere," she turned significantly to Brabant, who quailed; "Ah! I often tell my girls there are worse things than a Major in the world, and worse Majors than your dear uncle, Major Lickpenny."

Roland was too much confounded to answer, and Brabant fled away.

It would be difficult to do justice to the meeting of uncle and nephew. The former was so affected, that he made as if he would have embraced Roland; as it was, he caught hold of, and hung upon his collar and one of his buttons, where he stayed for some time balancing himself, while erratic moisture oozed from the corner of his eye. He was plainly quite at home, but he had not recovered the shock by the time they went into luncheon, and as soon as he sat down in his chair, he doubled up, until the young ladies straightened him out again; and even then his hand was so shaky, that Mrs. Lushington was fain to help him through his soup with a spoon. He took kindly to feeding in this fashion, and as the plump, well-turned wrist steadily plied him, he leaned back, half closed his eyes, and murmured, "Pretty thing, pretty thing."

Presently some of the fluid went a little wrong inside, and there was anxiety, and suffocation, and trouble, which ended happily, however, and then some of it got wrong outside, and there was more trouble and more anxiety to remove the traces.

" Dear old man," chorused the ladies, " isn't he ? How proud you must be of him, Mr. Tudor—we all are."

Roland's looks showed his bewilderment. What did it mean ?

Information was at hand.

"He met Buddy last week at a flower-show, and his carriage never turned up ; he has had to discharge his coachman, he says ; so Buddy got him a lift back in a friend's, and next day he sent her that big locket. But now he's here he's fastened on to Maria, and that's a pity, isn't it ? That's how it is, you know. Ah ! you don't know us."

By some jugglery, Eve had flitted in at the last moment and inserted herself next to Roland, to whom she conveyed this information confidentially. It was too late to oust her without a public scandal, of which she was well aware, so she felt perfectly safe.

" I don't care very much for him myself," she went on in the family whisper, which was singularly distinct, " but of course they're civil to him—one never knows what may turn up, and "—with tip-tilted nose—" of course you're bound to be, or he might cut you off with a shilling."

But this view of the case was altogether be-

yond Roland's powers of gravity, and he went
into such a fit of laughter, as was seldom indulged in by young men belonging to Mrs.
Squeed's cycles.

The repast was on a considerable scale, and
was served by three male beings in livery.
Could a family of such distinction sit down
with less ?   One was—well, the knife-man (that
is right, Mr. Printer, your very smallest
type, please.   Quasi-sacred secrets of this sort
must not go about at large where any one
may lay hold of them).   This person then was
there when he was wanted, to give prestige to
an occasion.   The second was the gardener and
factotum, whose *ensemble* when on duty inside
the house, was really of a very high class type,
and included a pair of bushy whiskers, which
he found unmanageable, and unnecessary, when
at his usual avocations, and therefore discarded.
He belonged consequently to that happy order
of things that defy detection, such as false
eyes, false teeth, false bosoms—and he gloried
in the belief that recognition was impossible.
The third menial was the page-boy, he at least
was genuine and beyond cavil.

Meanwhile anecdotes of the aristocracy flew
about and enlivened the too fleeting hour.   On
one occasion Mrs. Squeed remembered that
it had been so dark, that the Duchess declared
that she couldn't see 'er 'and before her
face, at which the sarcastic Eve opined that
she must have been more in the dark than
usual.   And all the time the volatile Mrs.
Lushington played the saddest of pranks with

her old man, and kept her young one ever so far away. She was, as she frankly admitted, in spirits; she talked incessantly, and managed in time to silence the entire company and absorb the talk to herself; the sisters only yielding after a hard fight, and the guests being simply powerless to slip in a word edgewise. Then she laughed gaily, and, oh! with such a keen enjoyment at her own little jokes. In truth she usually laughed in places where no joke at all was apparent to the casual observer, as,

" How cold we have had it lately, ah! ha! ha! ha! ha!" which helped to make the conversation very amusing indeed. And all the while she banged and jingled with her chains and her bracelets and her lockets—these elegancies she wore in great numbers—and she threw down a spoon or two, upset a glass, and laid down the law, that this was so vulgar, that such a peculiar style, and something else was only found with very funny people, so peremptorily, that had you been there, you must have sworn that it was so, if only in self-defence; and declared with the Major that she was the most fascinating creature on earth.

She was plainly a child of impulse, this gay young thing, as yet untainted by the world. One could fancy that brow clouding over in a sudden burst of tears with all the charming caprice of an April day. There was the infantile heart worn upon the sleeve, that would cry for the moon and be desolated because it had it not, the mind to which as yet no hard facts of logic had been able to force their way, the intellect which complacently expressed itself by gibbering at random and without doubt on every subject under heaven, fearlessly grappling with it, no matter how. What should such a woman be, but petted and spoiled and made much of? what other could she expect than to have true hearts like pretty toys laid at her feet, while denying all responsibility for her whims?

The type of her mind was deserving of study: its most notable characteristic was an animal ignorance, which precluded the possibility of surprise. If you took your favourite dog for a stroll down Piccadilly, and preferred to walk on your head rather than on your heels, it is quite certain that it would make no difference to him, and that he would follow in the same matter-of-fact style as usual, speaking with all his little friends by the way, but without special reference to yourself. So if you, reader of the masculine gender, had gone to call on young Mrs. Squeed, wearing your wife's bonnet inside out and hind-side before, she would hardly have noticed it; but if she had, she would merely have said probably, that there was something odd about you, she could hardly say what, but it was not the style she had been accustomed to in her set. For all she knew, in that exterior darkness where Lady Janes were unknown, there might be whole races of articulate-speaking men whose custom it was to wear the bonnets of their wives, inside out and hind-side before. Now even in these curious times it was rare to find this type

of character extended beyond three or four
years of age (its natural limit), well into middle
life, and this no doubt gave it its great charm.
The artless ingenuousness of it, its wayward
impulses, and obvious forgetfulness of self
in more senses than one, together with the
presumed money-bags, were irresistible—no
wonder if victims lay thick on her war-path,
no wonder the poor Major had succumbed at
sight. Brabant had often found her variable
in small things, but to-day's phase came to
him as something new, as a revelation and a
singularly unpleasant one.

For the first time during the meal he came
down from his clouds, and questioned himself
seriously, almost with alarm, as to his friend's
verdict. He wished that he could have given
her a hint to be a little quieter; and if she had
not been quite so facetious, as she scraped up
the soup from the Major's padded breast with
her spoon, he would have been better pleased.
He wished those precious bracelets wouldn't
jangle quite so much, and that she would leave
the forks alone, so that he could hear what
Eve and Roland were talking about. He
wished she would not speak of her little
slippers, and her this, that, and the other;
wished she would not contort her face, and
laugh, with her head on one side, at her own
jokes; wished she would hold her tongue; and
finally, wished himself and Roland far away.
But it had to be endured to the bitter end,
which was not until the whole table sat
glowering at each other, silenced in despair.

Although Roland made an excellent luncheon, he was none the less, more concerned for his friend than he cared to own. The people were intolerable; he had made it a rule never to go among such, and his first thought was how to get away. After coffee he speedily put it into execution.

With a look in his face that spoke more plainly than words, Brabant saw him as far as the gate. It was half in his mind to make some apology—a bad beginning. Odd that he should never have felt like that before, but then there never had been anybody before to bring her out as the Major had done. He forced a bad laugh; "you must know her better, my dear fellow!" he stammered, as they stood watching the nag being put into harness.

Roland was not ready for this, and he affected to believe it was the mare.

"Ah!" he said, carelessly, "I know her well enough, and I've got her so well in hand that she's not likely to play me tricks."

With which ominous farewell he went, but as he drove back, one only thought filled his head, and that was how he should save his friend from this match—it would be fatal—of that he felt sure. There was the unimpeachable authority of history to the fact that poets, artists, and all true geniuses generally make poor husbands, and he knew his friend's high-strung, difficult nature far better than the owner knew it himself. As for the woman, he would not be hard on her, she was perhaps no worse than many of her neighbours. Blunt speech, random chatter, and uncouth manners were no rarity in society of any pretence. It was only in grades where people were born and bred mere ladies and gentlemen and nothing more, that it was thought necessary to take the trouble to be invariably civil and courteous—all the same she would not do.

He had plenty of time for reflection, it was the height of the season, and when he re-entered London, block succeeded block, but he was lucky, for he managed to get out of the worst within half an hour after getting in, and it was not later than five o'clock when he turned into Park Lane.

CHAPTER III.

THERE is but one Park Lane, and there is hardly
likely to be another. Its long, unwritten
history is, for the most part, irrevocably lost;
but it was certainly a highway to the river
when the Romans first struck the Edgeware
Road, through the dense forest that sheltered
the northern side of their camp on the Thames.
Looking to the future equally with the past, it
is some of the most classic ground of modern
London. The nature of a town landscape is
fleeting at all periods. Great as the Lane is,
its capabilities are as yet but dimly recognized.

To Roland, on this bright summer day, it
presented a scene which was one to soothe
ruffled nerves; the streams of carriages and
people were in themselves a living wonder.
Where on earth could all these well-dressed,
well-to-do people come from, and how much in
hard cash would they and their carriages, their
wives, daughters, breast-pins, country-houses,
and other possessions, represent?

It had so happened that one day early in
that season, a private beauty had gone forth,
and sat herself down on the grass below the
Grosvenor Gate. She had been discovered by
another explorer, the spot had been carefully

marked, and from that moment became a nucleus of the world. In the afternoons the old Row was now a desert, the eastern side had taken its place, and Fashion had further decreed, without condescending to give her reasons for so doing, that on Thursdays should be the chief gathering. This was a Thursday, and so it came that the crowd was prodigious. It was like a monster garden-party without the hostess, and the painful obligation of un-wavering civility. The pretty faces, the par-terres of bright flowers, the waving plane-trees, and the rustling palms that threw a broken shadow over the sunlit lawns; all contributed to make a picture that might set a man think-ing, or almost a woman. It was the heyday of society, and the people who had threatened only last week, and the print of whose iron heel still dinted the grass, were nowhere to be seen.

Overlooking the very centre of the assem-blage stood St. Maur's "villa," its virgin marble glittering like driven snow in the slant-ing sun. The translucent colonnades of the ambulacrum, the frieze fronting the Lane, with its festoons of glowing agate that sparkled like jewels, the banks of exotic flower and leaf which rose on either side, and the fountains plashing over their brims in the shaded court-yard, gave it the appearance of an Aladdin's palace. By the side of this fairy-like erection, Dorchester House, which stood lower down, was a huge smoke-begrimed prison, fit only for the northern barbarians and their inky sky.

A little crowd was gathered on the pavement, looking in between the clouded shafts of pale Mexican onyx,[1] which formed the outer balustrade, with a keen delight on the marvels within.

" That is Lord St. Maur," whispered some one, as Roland drew up, and the people parted respectfully on either side to let him through.

" No, 'tain't, his 'air ain't cut so curly," said the well-informed man who is always there or thereabouts, and there was a push to look at the crest on the cart, which appeared to bear out the last speaker.

St. Maur was not in, but was expected at any moment, and Roland betook himself to one of the balconies, a retreat called by some long Latin name which he had forgotten; a fact which would not prevent him from smoking a weed in peace. It was an ideal nook in a London house, a place shut in by marble walls, artificially tinted from white and palest salmon down to a crimson black. Into it the afternoon sun struck fierce, but tempered by great bushes, overladen with fair blossom, and a striped awning was stretched above outside. Through the balcony came a sight of the surging crowds below, and beyond lay the blue, misty glades of the Park, running into illusive and, as it seemed, illimitable distance, like those of a noble forest. Faint, again, through the tremulous haze, as if in mid-air, hung the

---

[1] " Idiotic ! " exclaims the reader. So it is,—that we don't see such things, when the cost would be scarcely that of a ball supper.

westernmost towers and spires of the great city.
There was a comfortable couch in the corner, an
easy-chair or two of humble cane, and in the
centre a little bronze Victory, ostentatiously
holding forth a trophy of arms, supported a
small table of crocidolite with a vein of molten
gold, shot with gleams of fire, meandering under
its liquid, jetty surface.

On the tesselations of the pavement lay a
few rose-petals, curled by the heat, which the
evening breeze had littered down, and on the
table was an open box of cigars.

"St. Maur is a great man," said the visitor to
himself, as he leaned back and the slow wreaths
ascended; "he touches the ideal of earthly
happiness. He is always busy with great or
good work, and when he rests from it, it is
in surroundings such as these, which his own
brain has robbed from the treasure-houses
of Nature. What a bed of Asphodel for the
mind!"

Oh! that woman's voice! if he could but
get it out of his ears. Then he thought of
another woman; but there was desecration in
bracketing the two in the same hour, and he
turned his dear love away, until he could feel
that his soul was purified for her. He
smoked his cigar, and all the while the little
figure of Victory mesmerized him with her wide
eyes, and the lustrous dusk of her limbs, as she
held out to him untiringly her trophy of arms.
He laughed at St. Maur's fondness for Victories, and wondered whether the statue below
had had her wreath mended yet. This led him

back again naturally to his own first conquest
over a woman; there lay the letter in his
pocket, and he took it out to read. It was
short, but it told enough, for it named the day
when Miss Grey and her guardian would be in
town, and their hotel; one that looked upon
the Park and the Row.

"I know," the writer said, "that you always
call Hyde Park Corner the centre of the whole
world, and if I am in the world at all I would
be at its centre; and so, good-bye, for I will
trust no more words to paper, and you shall
read on this blank sheet more, than if I had
crossed it five times over."

At length St. Maur came, but, even before
they had shaken hands, Roland read failure
writ large over the whole man. He appeared
tired and dispirited, glad as he was to see his
friend, for whom, apart from his liking, he had
entertained an almost superstitious feeling since
the first day of their meeting, when the laurel
crown had shed itself at Roland's feet.

He flung himself down on the ebony tri-
clinium in the arch of the balcony. "Look
at those pretty children," he said, pointing to
the crowd, "they are playing over their own
graves."

"Well, my dear boy," he went on, "you
come in time, bad though the time be. The
east of London is upon the west, and it now
remains to be seen how the ten thousand will
cope with the million. It's all in the natural
order of things—hard winter, trade depression,
increase of the pauper population, education

without religion—and here we are. The train has been well laid, and only waits the match. The Endowment Concessions Bill, if it fails to pass, will probably do it for us. We have been going too fast. I have tried to put the drag on in vain. Progress is all very well, if you can make good each step as you go ; latterly we have been too hurried for this. Who would have thought five years ago that such a Bill were possible for a generation to come ? There is this hope, that the country means well, and that the true democrat, as distinguished from the communist, has his *raison-d'être*, but it is communism we have to face. There is one alternative, a tremendous Conservative reaction ; that may save us to our undoing as a party, but the revolution comes just as surely at the end of it."

"We must learn to fight."

St. Maur shrugged his shoulders. " Yes, my dear friend, you'll have to do that, and so perhaps shall I ; but our war must be a civil one, which is what I've not much stomach for. By the way, you've been gazetted, I hear. I suppose we shall see you a second Lord —— ;" he mentioned a great military peer.

" Thank you, the taming and training of the noble savage is no more to my taste than civil war is to yours."

" No, the British soldier of to-day is not to be envied. It isn't his fault after all, and it's hardly worth while getting up a Continental fuss, on the chance of evolving the real thing."

"I don't see how else it's to be done," said Roland, "unless you try Ireland. It's my belief that any man who draws a naked sword there, and makes for the Castle, is sure of a highly respectable following at any hour of the day or night. There lies a reputation! But seriously—what do you mean by civil war?"

"I mean," said St. Maur, his fine face darkening, "that is what is coming upon us. If the ebullitions of the last week have been ridiculous, nevertheless they are straws pointing the way of the wind; the people have got to the helm, and are just waking to the fact. Things will go wrong—are going wrong. At the first sign of disturbance, at the first symptom of weakness, there are, God knows how many tens of thousands of Irishmen throughout the world waiting to fly at the country's throat, who will make common cause with the mob. In view of these things I cannot be hopeful. The Churches fail us. What is yours doing? Nothing to stem the rising tides, and yet no more splendid opening ever lay before any body of men, than that which has dawned upon Catholicism in England, at this hour. I do not mean of benefit to itself only, but to the nation, civilization, and the human race. And why? Because she has a large following among the poor and those very Irish, and because, in the face of the impending flood, she alone of the so-called Christian Churches is likely to preserve her cohesion and coherency. The Church of England is the

Church of the upper classes; in spite of the good work that it has done, it is weakened and disintegrated. Now its endowments are trembling in the balance; if these go—what then? The Sects will certainly unite against it and against you ; that will be their notion of propagating religion.

"For myself, I believe that if religion is to be propagated in the future, it must be greatly, if not chiefly, through the Catholic Church, a Church which in all climes has proved itself understanded of the people, for it is the people that we have to deal with. But you have no laity in this country that can take its proper place, and, for want of it, stand a fair chance of shipwreck. The priests and the women appear to do all your work (excellent work it has been, so far as in them lay), but when it comes to a question of dealing with secular questions, or more particularly with secular mobs, these two factors are hopelessly handicapped. Now, what is your public outlook, judged from the inside? I should really like to hear your views at length; they tell me that you made a ferocious onslaught on sociology at the University."

"My dear St. Maur, you are a rash man to ask an English Catholic, born and bred, such a question—a question so far outside and beyond vestment, plain chant, or the ballet," answered Roland, with a smile of peculiar meaning. "What am I to tell you? We have, as you know, a compact aristocracy; that, every Englishman must admit, is a great thing, to begin with, but what do they do? We will hope they save their souls, for I can tell you of little else. There are exceptions of course, but I am so desperate a Radical that I consider first of all the man as he is, wholly apart from his rank."

" I know it," said St. Maur, " and frankly, if a man is born to my position, and is not an actual idiot with his tongue hanging out, it is secretly held a matter of congratulation, and even then his tutors and governors do their best to atone for this freak of Nature in a fashion which undoubtedly helps to perpetuate the peculiarities of the race."

" Yes, I don't know that we are worse than our neighbours outside the pale, but you may have observed that we live in an atmosphere of mild intrigue, of countesses and prelates in purple. You must have seen how we hold aloof from the national life, until it is taken for granted that if a man professes our creed he is a dilettante, an impossible fellow not to be reckoned with. You must have noticed the grooves in which the Catholic laity expends itself; the paralysis of utter fatuity appears to hang over any public expression on our part. We are absolutely without a single man to give an impulse in any direction that can be considered seriously.

" There was much said and written years ago on the Oxford movement; its importance was exaggerated. True, from the point of *appearances*, it changed the face of the English-speaking world. The advent of a dozen thinkers was no doubt very gratifying, but it was to be expected, that when thinking men were fairly confronted with the Church, a certain percentage would give in their adherence; the masses, however, were untouched by the move. And mark the weak point; most of these men were clerics, some of them became so under the new order. Many became laymen who were never lay, and never will be. For the most part they are totally unfitted, by taste and training, for grappling with the hour. The result (to ourselves) was a certain social *éclat*, which, to my mind, we should have been as well without."

" No doubt," said St. Maur, " no doubt, and in consequence of these various things you are still ' outsiders,' the people do not understand you. You want representative men, a real aristocracy."

" No man is a stancher champion of aristocracy in the true sense than myself," said Roland, " but in cases where it means mere pretence, every effort of my life will be to smash, pulverize, and demolish it. Had it not been for the Life, and Colonial Peerages, I think we may assume that the House of Lords would hardly have survived until now. By this concession to a logical age, it is plain that the highest types of intellect in the empire have been secured to the order. But this does not affect us, for so far, Time has not bestowed any single distinguished name upon us. We ourselves are hardly wild enough to dream of such an entity as a Catholic statesman, and yet if he is possible anywhere, he should be here, and to-day. Catholic countries, strictly speaking, have ceased to exist over the whole world. The causes of this, I take it, are far more internal than external. If in a progressive era you stand still, you do not retard the age, you are simply left behind. Catholic peoples, headed by Catholic aristocracies, have, out of sheer inertia, blocked the way; they have been ridden over roughshod, or quietly left in the lurch.

" This is precisely what is doing in England at this moment. For want of a strong and active middle class; a class that I may perhaps term the business class, an inert and somnolent aristocracy is paralyzing the entire vitality of the body. Their attitude may be compared to that of Buddha, wrapped in complacent contemplation of his own navel.

There is work to be done outside the Church and the school—worldly work—in spite of some of our friends, who, I believe, take up the position that matters mundane are not for the children of light. I do not stand alone in my ideas, as perhaps you know. There is a small set of us, unknown to fame, who feel, that if our faith and our profession are anything but an idle boast, we should be moving, and moving in the van. In a small way we have been able to effect something. We have started coffee-houses, we have supplied lay-workers in the temperance movement, we have initiated cheap and good literature, devoid of cant, for the very poor. We have organized elections to Boards of Guardians and municipal offices, and we have found the candidates. We put a man into Parliament for a Home constituency the other day, a thing that all the world said was impossible. In this way we have opened out the lower public life, which, after all, is the foundation of public usefulness."

" Upon my honour," laughed St. Maur, " you are taking my bread out of my very mouth. I shall be jealous if you go any further. I wish to Heaven we had a few more like you and your friends. I assure you, you are not the only people who hang back from work that it is a sacred duty to perform. Now here, in Mayfair and Belgravia, the entire number of men—gentlemen—who take up these questions is not a couple of dozen. You can't get ' gentlemen ' to take them up. The other day I had occasion, in a Poor Law matter, to ask the vote and interest of the proprietor of half Piccadilly. The answer I received through his agent was, that the gentleman in question " took no interest in local affairs " —beyond drawing between fifty and a hundred thousand a year in rents, that is to say. It was one of many answers of the sort, though none was more gross. You are doing a good work if you can educate your upper classes to their position, and your creed will benefit."

" Well, yes, and I trust something has been gained in the breaking down of bigotry by the magic effect of personal contact; but I am by no means saying that the day is past when the raking up of filth and the flinging it to and fro is to be considered religion. I am convinced that is the one thing that brings its own Nemesis certainly with it. 'God is not mocked.' We ourselves with all our lights, have excelled in bigotry any of the so-called Christian Churches, and we have paid for it rightly, we are paying for it, nor need we expect Heaven to avert the consequences. Just now you hold the palm; it is still impossible, for instance, in spite of the number of our poor, to get one of our own people elected a guardian in this the first parish in London.[1] Nay, I have lately heard of a city where the inhabitants enjoy a great cathedral, filched of course from the old faith, and yet object to ground being bought for the erection of a Catholic church!"

"The impudence of the British cad, whether he or she belongs to the upper or lower classes, is beyond belief," said St. Maur; "still I should have thought it could hardly have gone so far as that. The fact is, the reform of Mrs. Grundy on points of this nature is a matter in which every intelligent man must be interested. So long as he is not a free agent in the choice of his beliefs and unbeliefs, so long as his religion is decided for him by his mother-in-law or his maiden aunt (deuced well-informed old ladies of course), so long will civilization and all religion suffer."

It had grown dim. The suffused light was dying out of the western sky; the great blossoms of the oleanders, under which the speakers sat had closed over them, petal by

[1] What a contrast to our own enlightened times—1886!

petal, and now hung heavy with sleep; the evening breeze struck chill, and a fragrant mist had gathered in the park.

"Well, well, we were born in a veritable dark age, I always say," exclaimed St. Maur, jumping up, "but at any rate we've electricity, and they won't beat that in a hurry for light and warmth."

He touched an amber button in the wall. Round the cornice of the little room ran an inlay, with festoons of fruit and flowers modelled in jasper and chalcedony, in sardonyx, beryl, chrysophrase, in cornelian, and lapis-lazuli, in topaz and amethyst, which instantly sprang to light. The wreaths were of autumn leaves, yellow, brown, old gold, and crimson, and the effect was more charming than can be described.

"I have just finished putting the light into the house myself," said the master, "and I do feel inclined to swagger a little about it; it's the first treatment of the kind in London, and I have turned it to a thousand uses, as you shall see."

"My dear St. Maur," said Roland, "it's a sad thing you hadn't to make your own fortune, or you should have been divided, since you might have carved a dozen out of your own right hand."

"By the way, you haven't seen the ambulacrum lit; it's been done since you were here, and I'm now trying a little religious allegory—always a dangerous thing. Heaven forgive me! If there's one thing I hate as a rule, it's religious allegory, or its embodiment in picture or statue. Still I am fairly satisfied with this."

They passed through the corridors, and turned into a room which the master designated as his workshop; the walls were—*mirabile dictu*—of plain whitewash, and there was all about a genuine litter, in the midst of which lay —hardly discernible—here and there a choice fragment, a moulded torso, yet damp, a metal railing of scroll-work unfinished. All about lay the tools of half-a-dozen crafts, and propped on the bench was a bas-relief approaching completion. So dark had it become that it was difficult to distinguish it clearly, when, as Roland looked, the pallid marble grew gradually luminous, disclosing a sculptured head of the Christ, from which emanated faint rays of light. Whether strictly legitimate or not, it would have been difficult to conceive anything of a beauty more refined and unearthly; in itself, it was like a prayer embodied.

Whatever Roland thought of it, he said little. Perhaps he was considering rather jealously, the kindred spirit his friend would find in Miss Grey. Religious statuary he regarded as helpful to the very ignorant and the poor in general. For " holy pictures," plaster Madonnas, and stained-glass saints, he had few feelings beyond dislike—they were objectionable, however necessary for the aid of weaker brethren. The materializing of so lofty an ideal as this to the cultured mind, he considered a mistake.

" You have gone as high as any man is likely to do," he said rather coldly, and they passed on ; St. Maur was plainly chilled.

" Come, then," he said, changing the subject.
" You must see my den, that's been finished
since you were here last." He led the way on
to another room, through a deeply panelled
door, set round with bosses of bronze.

" I dislike being disturbed when busy; these
thick walls and that heavy door with the por-
tière, make this retreat as solitary as the
Sahara. When I have work in the evening, I
have a cold dinner laid here, to which I can
help myself; if you will help me with it to-night,
I will drive you down to the House afterwards:
you must hear this debate."

" To be honest, I was hoping you would ask
me," said Roland, " and it will give us an
opportunity of finishing our discussion."

" Very good, but tell me how you like my
sanctum."

" I think I could hardly improve upon it
myself; will that satisfy you? What is your
frieze, and where is your dado?"

" Hold!" said St. Maur, " lest I fell thee; no
dados here; you will talk ' high art' next, and
then you should never leave this alive. The
frieze is of tile, a facsimile of tortoise-shell, and
I defy you to tell it from the original. In cold
weather the room is warmed by electricity, and
those whirling ivory fans in the ceiling are also
worked by it; they are ventilators."

" Then they are a revelation in that article."

" Those figures on the wall I sketched in myself, almost white on scarlet, how do you like
them? As to the lighting of the room; you see
these blocks of rock crystal, how mellow the

light is that comes through them, and how they splash faint prismatic tints over the wall and ceiling—that is another dodge of mine. Simplest thing in the world; the crystal is bored, the electric wire introduced, the cavity exhausted of its air and sealed, and there you are. I have even carried the principle further for my table in the dog-days. Look here."

He drew aside a curtain and displayed a round table laid with a cold dinner, which looked none the less tempting for so being. It was all very simple, a few plates of a bright self-colour, a couple of flagons of fluted glass, into which gold had been run streakily, such as we call Venetian, but which was Roman a thousand years before it appeared in Venice, and a few narrow tumblers to match, in one of which flamed a crimson flower and frond of palest great-leaved maiden-hair. In the centre, upon a salver was a block of ice. It was this that attracted Roland's attention, for it was an iceberg lamp, shedding a brilliant suffused light.

"Same principle," said St. Maur carelessly; "only here you have to use a glass for your vacuum; no perceptible heat, you know, and even in summer the block will last a day or two; a whitish ice, what we used to call 'cat ice' at school, is the best—gives that frosted look."

"My dear fellow," he went on as they sat down, "take my word for it, ugliness and sin are as closely connected as cleanliness and god-liness—a people can never be really happy, until they have learned to love beauty for its own sake. If beauty were not an essential, why were the heavens and the earth and the flowers given to us? Man and his work only can be ugly and vile, and it is because he alone is capable of sin. Form, good form, and bad form, must be facts to all ages; no cycles can change the nature of the sphere and the triangle by one jot or tittle. The human form, we have it on the authority of Scripture, is to be one of the joys of heaven, and I fancy that must be the reason why it is to us mortals a source of ever fresh and unfailing delight. Colour, probably, is an eternal reality, and the harmonies of music are echoes from the celestial harmonies of the spheres.

"But how are you to impress these facts on a generation that besmothers its walls in cracked plates, and gluts itself with idiotic cards by the gross at Christmas and the New Year? And if you have a mind to be a statesman, my friend, I will tell you a secret that you will not learn in the House of Commons as at present constituted. In the æsthetic advance of a people lies a real moral advance, a tangible thing for governed and governing, political economy notwithstanding; out of the jumble of contradictory ideas we shall yet see light.

"Now, there has been enough rubbish talked lately, and by men who should know better, about the workman. It is urged that, as he does all the work of building and beautifying, and of production generally, he should enjoy the fruits of it (which he does, by the way, in his wages). Men have had the goodness to come here, and talk like this of my villa, to me, whose brain has designed it from the beginning, for whose requirements the house was built, and whose hand actually directed the chief part of the work.

Perhaps my case is exceptional, but the principle holds good, in all that is done by the artisan for his employer, without whose wants and taste it would be simply *non est.* The British workman is often enough a simple dunder-head; his ideas of luxury and refinement are unlimited 'grub,' and, too often, unlimited liquor to match. To the man of this class everything in the shape of property is a matter of jealousy, and he is blind to the logic of the facts that stare him in the face. He cannot carry out any decent work, still less conceive it, and although professedly a constructive force, is in reality a destructive one. Remember, I am not speaking of the trained and intelligent artisan; he is one of my best friends, but of a class infinitely below him in the social scale, and one which unfortunately outbulks his in alarming proportions.

" To approach social problems at all, you must clear your mind of cant. Every man, even the best, has something of the cant of his class attaching to him. I will give you an instance. I had one of your ecclesiastics here the other day, Father ———, you know him, of course, he is a small celebrity; he threw up his hands at what he was pleased to call the awful luxury of the house.

" 'My dear sir,' I said, 'you forget, or perhaps you are not aware, that all this has been done in the sweat of my brow, and in conjunction with severe mental work. These tinted marbles and rare bronzes to you, no doubt, represent only pride and pomp, though it is hard to see why, for you must have some idea at least, of the difficulty of production. To me, they mean so much brain-strain, so much disintegration of mental and bodily tissue, so much toil and travail, so much achievement, if you will, in the face of difficulty. As I have done this in order to help, in cultivating the mind and refining the taste, of thousands who otherwise have little beyond the education of the gin-palace; and as I hope eventually to leave it to the nation, to prove in perpetuity what Nature and art—or may I say, God and man—can together accomplish towards the beautifying of life, I can hardly think that I have done wrong.

"He might as well have taken me into the Garden of Eden, and because I gathered of the flowers, and gave thanks for the sunshine and the beauty of it, declared that I had sinned. But your Church certainly educates her poor in beauty, in which she has my warmest sympathy. Your lower education appears to be altogether excellent, and the teaching orders do their work well."

"Fairly so," answered Roland. "The system tends occasionally to the advancement or damning of a man, according as he has made himself agreeable or the reverse to his old masters, and I need not go further for an example than the priest you have named, who found such iniquity in your sticks and stones. He is, as you say, a celebrity. He makes the women cry when he preaches a sermon (when he does not cry himself), yet he refused to help, by even so much as a good word, a poor fellow educated under him, who with his wife and family was literally starving. Not only that, if not actually in words, by his manner, he endeavoured to dissuade me from helping him.

" ' The man is in rags,' he said, ' and his wife and children are in rags.' "

I failed to see that this was any reason against him.

" ' He has quarrelled with his family,' he went on.

" ' Yes, and although he has been working hard for many years to support himself, he is now starving and almost broken down. A word from you, sir, would be of immense assistance ; I could then perhaps get him a place.'

" The priest walked away with a remark I need not repeat."

" He must have had something against the man," said St. Maur.

" If he had had every crime in the Decalogue, I don't see that it would have excused such a course of action. It is plain that in this way a power which is singularly undesirable may come into the hands of the religious orders. To gibbet this sort of thing where found, in the fiercest publicity, is the only safeguard against the like abuses which creep into every human society. The more openly things can be done, the better.

I have always said that if, in the beginning, we had, not only submitted to, but courted, the inspection of our convents, in six months the Public would have been satisfied once and for all, and would have understood them in a way they are never likely to do, without. I do not speak without experience. I was 'the chiel among them takin' notes' for several years. I lived among ecclesiastical students, and was as one of them. I know the priest, secular and religious, from the embryo upwards. I know his good points, which I admit are priceless, and his bad, which happily are few, but of which he is no more devoid than any other mortal. One of the weak points is, that few of these men are gentlemen by birth, which, after all, is of minor importance; but, what is more serious, few of them get the chance of becoming gentlemen by education. Hence a smallness and touchiness on matters of criticism, which the true gentleman scorns to show, but if there is cause for it, sets to work to amend.

" The future of our Church in this country depends entirely on its powers of co-operation and amalgamation. At present, in spite of all that has been done, Catholicism exists on sufferance. Our position is due rather to the tact of a few leading ecclesiastics than to any claim of our own as citizens. Until the strong light of publicity illumines every phase of the Church in England, we shall never stand well with the British public, or in a really secure position. Such is my opinion, take it for what it is worth. I think, however, we may safely leave the churchmen to their own affairs, it is the conduct of matters virtually lay, and by laymen, that calls for criticism. I ventured the other day to attend a meeting, with the avowed purpose of proposing an inquiry into a small matter, which several of us thought desirable. At the door I was met by a high official, who took me aside, and implored me to give up my intention. He did not deny that I was quite right, for a moment, but he trusted for my own sake I should desist; and why, I ventured to ask ? Because I should make a personal enemy of the Duke of X. ! !

" The thing was worthy of the comic papers. I hardly know the Duke by sight, and I give him credit for better things, but the incident is a superb example of our system."

St. Maur shone his glass thoughtfully against the iceberg.

" We are in the same plight," he said. " The anomalies of the Church of England are unspeakable. I doubt if she will ever be popularized, and she is in a worse position, for she holds the spoil. For us, as for you, a new departure is necessary, or we shall have all our churches about our ears, if indeed we keep our ears to have them about. It may be fifty years hence, it may be six months. Our civilization has had a reflex action, and in proportion as it has advanced, so too has the number, the power, and the desperation of the mob. When our day of reckoning comes, as every thinking man admits it must, the French revolution will be child's play beside it. The best, it seems to me, that we can hope to do, is, to postpone it indefinitely, and this, the proper use of our opportunities may enable us to do. If the creeds, instead of flying at each others' throats, were to unite where they may, i. e. on first principles, look what an immeasurable step this would be, and surely you and we, as the most intellectual, might set the example."

" One would think so, but I am afraid there is little hope of any such robust religion. So far as we are concerned, there is no means of arriving at an intelligent public opinion on this or any other subject. We have no salons, which, by the way, are a great want, no organization, not even a club. I believe there once was such a thing. *Fuit Troja*. This influential and aristocratic body could not support a third-rate club in a second-rate street, which proves how public spirit is understood among us. It is an extraordinary position that the body is in. We are so old, that by our side every other church and creed is an upstart of yesterday ; so young, in our present place, that we may be said to have hardly learned to articulate."

" But you have a representative body of some sort ? "

" Very much so. It calls itself ' The Catholic Centre.' I see they've advertized a meeting for next week, and have hired the great Regent's Hall, St. James' Street, for the purpose. I daresay there will be two or three dozen people present, at least, including the reporters."

" That is hardly representative, is it ? "

" Yes, exactly of Us as we are. If it is

all bread and butter, chiefly the latter, as it ordinarily is, you will have column after column in the *Katholikon*. If criticism finds a voice, the whole thing will be relegated to a foot-note. It's a pity. What an engine a really representative Centre might be made! I don't mean a political engine, but a social one. I think every man who has investigated the subject, is agreed, that the formation of a Catholic political party would be the greatest misfortune that could befall us. Our business is to be everywhere and in all parties, lending a hand wherever there is good work to be done. If Roman Catholics shall one day be found among the best in every groove—the straightest politicians, the justest magistrates, the bravest soldiers, the finest of cooks, if you like—as with their pretensions to higher lights they should be—that will be something far finer. At present, it is plain that, in all these things, we fall below our neighbours, yet a perverse world will maintain that the proof of the pudding is in the eating!

"But come with me to the meeting next week. I intend to say something to the point, if I can. We shan't have anything about the Endowment Concessions; they never talk about matters of politics, or present concern—it's too dangerous, and it's forbidden. I will have a slap at generalities. On these occasions, St. Maur, I confess I envy you; had I but a handle to my name, they would list to me like an oracle. My, in that case, valuable utterances might possibly be wafted to the See of Peter. I might even be placed on the committee, think of that!"

St. Maur laughed. "I shall be delighted," he said.

Their talk rambled on to the more immediate subjects of the hour, as, leaving the table, they dashed, fast as a pair of thoroughbreds could take them, down to Westminster.

In order fully to understand what has gone before, and what will follow, it may be well to take a bird's-eye view of the "situation" at this particular moment. It must be remembered that the race portrayed are our brothers and sisters; that they have come from precisely the same antecedents, and have marched *pari passu* with ourselves. Such being the case, there is room for no little astonishment at the course taken by events; not that the events themselves are to be wondered at —cause and effect had worked in their usual way—but because of the unexampled rapidity with which questions, once mooted, ripened to a head. Many matters had long been floating in the air, as it were, in a state of solution, which became solid facts to be dealt with, when some accidental circumstance suddenly precipitated them. The close of the century was marked by a number of things, any one of which almost, might have been considered epoch-making in itself. Of these, were the spread of a general feeling for religion, broadly speaking, and a vast accession to the strength both of Dissent and Catholicism.

To balance this, however, there had been a great increase of Agnosticism, and general unbelief. On all hands a certain tolerance had necessarily been the upshot. The spread of education and knowledge had likewise been very great. Science was flourishing as it had never flourished before; the old withered tree of Art had of a sudden put out fresh leaves and blossoms, and bid fair to renew its youth. One of the most alarming of the new facts was the increase of the population, and the rapid rise of a democracy without tradition or experience. This, again, gave popularity to certain views upon the tenure of land and property, which, if not quite original, were certainly fresh to the generation that was now forced to listen to them for the first time.

Among the not sufficiently recognized causes of the astonishing out-put of the age, was the vast advance that had taken place in the art of war. European struggles had been begun and finished satisfactorily—at least to the conqueror—within the space of six weeks, and this in itself had allowed a progress at a rate hitherto undreamed of. The fact that the issues of peace and war lay more directly in the hands of a few great financiers, than in those of earthly kings and princes, tended marvellously to produce commercial confidence and prosperity. Nations were now for the most part virtually in contact, not through and by means of, a few more or less empty-headed diplomatists, but through considerable bulks of the people; but, while wealth, and comeliness, and well-being had increased and intensified, so had their opposites, in the shape of poverty, ugliness, and squalor. It was an age of extremes.

The masses had been educated, and, for the first time in all history, the government and upper classes stood face to face with an instructed populace; one that virtually held the reins of power, and one that was doubling and trebling itself with all the speed that Nature and Art would permit, and so ever tending to reduce the ci-devant governing classes to a smaller and smaller minority. The people had eaten for the first time of the fruit of the tree of knowledge, and were now fermenting under it, a state of things which brought within the range of practical politics, many airy notions which for centuries had lain *in nubibus*. Already the spurt that this widespread schooling had given made itself evident in a thousand different ways; every shopwindow bore witness to it. The cheap and excellent periodical literature that crammed the book-stalls, the latest trifle in knick-nacks, the last working-man's speech at his club, the superior organization of all bodies and parties,—whose name was become legion—all these were the evidence of it.

The universal searching of spirit had further had one excellent effect. It had led to a merciless verification of historical record, and history was no longer a tissue of deliberate lying and malice aforethought, worked in with a few main facts, and written with the set purpose of backing up at all costs the party to which the historian belonged. Queen Mary and Queen Bess had almost settled into their normal places, which in itself was little short of a miracle ; but such were the miracles that education was able to achieve.

This Protestant people, as they still were, nominally, had come to admit something of the debt which they and the rest of the world, owed to the Roman Pontiffs and their subordinates; to the monasteries, with their monks and nuns, at one time the sole guardians of light and learning, the links between the older civilizations and the new ; and withal, the tillers of the soil, the teachers of the people, the protectors of the poor, and the handmaidens of the sick. This system Englishmen saw growing up again around them with little jealousy ; nay more, with actual cordiality, as affording the best practical solution to certain questions such as the employment of the always-increasing number of unmarried women. The old debt was at length acknowledged, and a generous, if tardy, repayment had begun. The Public attitude had become practically this—" Anything you ask in reason you shall have ; but let the reason be such as the average mind outside your pale may grasp."

Catholicism had consequently made great strides, so great that a few fanatics beheld in it the imminent conversion of England ; too blind to see that the nature of the age would no more allow of the wholesale adoption of any one creed or belief, than it would of any one style of government, or architecture, or other feature

of the middle ages. It might have been thought
that recognizing the power for good, the bulwark against revolution, infidelity, and social
chaos, which the Catholic Church represented
in England as elsewhere, every member of
it would realize this; and so far as in him
lay, put forward the most strenuous efforts to
strengthen its position, not by weakening that
of his neighbours, but by looking more closely
to his own goings. How it actually stood the
following pages will disclose.

CHAPTER IV.

THE Roman Church in England presented a sufficiently interesting problem, to those without as well as those within, for hardly was a hearth, however well defended, but showed the vacant chair of a " deserter."

At this time, it may be said to have consisted of four sections, or, if the ecclesiastical element, which was the most influential of all, be classed separately as one, of five. Its great numerical strength lay in the poor, who were chiefly of Irish extraction, and so unhappily divided, as by a brick wall, from the upper classes. Then we may reckon the old Catholics, after these the converts, and lastly, the children of converts, all of whom we will consider in order.

The old Catholic families possessed, and deservedly so, a great name. There must have been considerable grit in any stock, which had had the vitality to survive the three centuries of disembowellings, rackings, finings, imprisonments, and social outlawry, which had swept over their heads. But it was not in the nature of things that this stock should flourish in undiminished strength, and if in these latter days the social prestige had been regained a hundredfold much had been lost by repeated intermarriage within a limited circle, much by the ceaseless grinding of the penal laws, the tradition of which, upwards of half a century of emancipation had not been able to obliterate. There were exceptions, but as a rule, if the name of an old Catholic were spoken of in connection with any undertaking, the hearer shrugged his shoulders, knowing that it was " vox et preterea nihil."

It was seldom that their names were mentioned at all, in relation to every-day life; the owners of them, in many cases, sat apart in their country seats, or in their big town houses, in lofty seclusion, occasionally entertaining a Cardinal or a Bishop, and not always understanding exactly how to do it. A convert Cardinal was very small fry to their ideas, which were grounded on a generous conception of their own dignity.

So far as public position was concerned, the Catholic peerage stood very much in the same line with the old families. Instead of taking that lead to which their position entitled them, they stood aloof from public affairs, or nullified each other's votes in the House with a scrupulous exactness ; and they seldom essayed the lower flight of opening their doors to science and art. It was a significant fact that their records, like those of the old untitled families, could show no single name of distinguished eminence in the present, through the past three centuries of persecution, or even since emancipation, when all possible careers had been thrown open to them, except the culminating offices of Prime Minister and Lord Chancellor. This was equally the case with the whole body, the public knew no Catholic name as such, and there was a general and perfectly natural belief in consequence, that there was something in this creed which, *ipso facto*, unfitted its members for the actualities of life; and this at a time when a tried and patriotic statesman professing it, had there been any, would probably have secured no inconsiderable following among thinking men.

Realize the position. It was a time of peace and prosperity, but out of these very things had come an upheaval; quasi-religious, quasi-social questions, were the questions of the day. Protestantism, in all its forms, stood painfully disintegrated. You had here, side by side, a religious organization, a Church—the great Church of history, the one human society which shrinks from the solution of no human problem as too difficult, which holds in its laboratory a remedy for every evil to which the social flesh is heir; and yet at this crucial moment it came forward with none. Its followers, instead of leading by the extra light in which they were so fortunate as to bask, groped blindly at the tail of events; no matter of state reform, no single item of the national progress had ever owed its initiative to them. With every good intention, which we will allow them, they had fallen under the ban of a fatal transcendentalism, and such labour as they did contribute, lent nothing to the advance, and eased in no faintest jot the friction of the social machine.

This has reference solely to the lay element; the priesthood was undoubtedly doing its part, and perhaps more than its part, for this had been forced upon it by the inaction of the laity. No doubt existed as to the good the former had achieved, were it only in the education of thousands of children in the elements of Christian morality in the schools, but this is outside our text. There appeared to be something in the system which forbade determinate lay action, and threatened the prevalence of a sacerdotalism, which, whether looked at from the inside or the out, in times such as these, could only be fraught with extreme danger, and must mean shipwreck at no distant period.

Now, to take another great section of the Catholic body—that of the converts, among whom were some distinguished men, certainly the most distinguished of the whole body: men of high intellectual capacity and resolute will, who, in the days when it was difficult, had fought their way into the Church through obstacles which, to such a class of mind, must have seemed well-nigh insuperable. As a rule, the friends they left behind, were filled with rejoicing, for henceforth, no matter how promising their previous career, they were nowhere. The snuffing-out process had been begun with them forthwith. These men presented salient peculiarities, according to the sources whence they had been drawn, and no doubt they were a very difficult class for the authorities to deal with—the more so, as a large proportion of them, as has been said, came out of the ministry of the Church of England. Distinguished almost invariably for their piety and learning, the awful mental process gone through in the struggle, too often left an enduring sensitiveness which unfitted them for work. Theirs were lives thrown out of gear with this world, at least. Many of them, dismayed by the manifold unpleasantness of their position, retired into their shells once and for all, and took to their families, their fruit-trees, or the minor prophets. Others waited to be sought out, and waited long.

In marked contrast to these were the lady converts, who were not thin-skinned, and not as a rule retiring—they smiled comfortably, sometimes, perhaps, a little sarcastically, at any allusion to their change of opinion. Such, from time immemorial, had been woman's undoubted privilege, and the outside world was wise enough not to get itself into trouble, by arguing the point with them. They were usually energetic, independent people, very genuine and with more push and go about them than the men—a little too fond of a dubious relic or a pious fiction, but active often, if it were only in gaining over their friends to their own ideas. The day had gone by when any lady or gentleman, who came forward and made profession of the Faith, was patted on the back by the Faithful, as though he or she had done the Almighty a considerable favour. There were still, however, recruits who had in no wise lost by the change,

as in the case of Miss Wigway. She, poor
lady, in spite of her strong affinity for the
great good things of this life, had gone down
and down in the world, until she had little
indeed to look to. By some chance she had
found her way into the fold. Instantly a
kind-hearted Countess had taken her up, and
gathered her under her wing.

She had made much of her, for the woman
had been truly an object of compassion; and
had introduced her to other Countesses,
until these great names had become common
household words, and their kind owners had
brightened, as with a ray of light divine, the
dingy respectability of her dreary lodging. So,
presently, Miss Wigway became aware that her
lines were falling in pleasant places. She, who
was old, and plain, and desolate, had made
many friends, such friends as she had looked
for all her life with unspeakable longing, and
lo ! now it was accomplished, together with the
virtual certainty of salvation !

Altogether the converts, male and female,
experienced such variety of treatment from
without and within, as often to disconcert
them and their new co-religionists. If, for
instance, an elderly nobleman joined the ranks,
three weeks after, the civilized world would hear
with astonishment this gentleman's dicta quoted
on some point of Catholic discipline. A month
later and he would probably occupy half-a-
dozen more or less responsible places, as chairman at various religious meetings, where his
speeches would be reported at length to the

world, as if his opinion were worth considerably more than two straws. It was made sufficiently plain how things were going when the Royal Duke, who was in his dotage, or almost so, had come over. In six weeks this man was at the head of everything, while the frivolous world held its sides with laughter.

The lady converts then, it will be seen, were the best off, and fell naturally into natural grooves. If there was nothing else to do, there was always woman's work, and certainly it could not be urged that they did this worse than their neighbours. Indeed numbers, now that they were the wives of ex-clergymen who had lost their preferments, behaved very generously both to their husbands and the state. And this brings us in a perfectly natural sequence to our third section—the children of converts.

It was evident that this must be the class that would eventually preponderate; but at present, owing to the date at which the chief influx of "conversions" had taken place, the younger generation had hardly made its way into the world, nor was it yet reckoned with. The thinker would note that here were men who would enter life under conditions wholly apart either from the old Catholics or their own fathers. They would be strangers equally to the penal laws, as to those of controversy, and would probably care as little for the one as for the other. For them there would be no ugly tradition of disabilities, no painful record of a blasphemous family war kept up under the pretext of religion. They would stand exactly on the levels with their countrymen, Protestant or Nonconformist, so far as this world went; and it was plain, finally, that if any class could set the Church in England upon a satisfactory footing, it was this, and no other.

There could be little cohesion between the sets of a body so constituted, and anything like united action was consequently unknown. The great Universities, although open to all, were at present under the ban, more or less direct, of the authorities. This alone was a drawback of the first class, for it effectually prevented anything like a *rapprochement* among the rising generation, at the very time when it was likely to prove of most importance, to their own interest and those of their party. It led to a further exceedingly unsatisfactory aspect, by setting a certain portion of the laity, in what appeared to be antagonism with their bishops, for the latter were unable actually to close the doors; there were parents who would send their sons, and sons who would go. As young men who went into the army or navy had precisely the same ordeal to pass through, save that it was a much fiercer one, and experienced at an age considerably earlier, the objection to the old Universties, where Catholic tradition yet lingered in a most unmistakable way, was not altogether patent to the observer.

With this brief explanation of the lay of the land, we may venture to accompany St. Maur and Roland to the meeting of the "Catholic

Centre" at the Regent's Hall, St. James's Street.

The " Catholic Centre " was a society which had sprung into existence one fine morning with a flourish of trumpets. No one had ever yet precisely mastered its *raison-d'être*, and it was, perhaps consequently, regarded as an inspiration. It was felt that to form a lay nucleus which should be non-political, and should bring all shades of opinion under one roof, where they might act harmoniously in concert, for the furtherance of Catholic interests, was precisely what was wanted. The venture, however, had not proved a happy one, and it had been found impossible to galvanize it into real life. One man after another had taken a leading part in endeavouring to push it to the point of achievement, and one after another had failed. Authority, perhaps, had not looked very warmly on it, and its name was quite unknown to the outside public, for it had never done anything to mark its existence, beyond blocking the way towards organizations of a really practical nature. At one time it had a mere ordinary every-day Duke for its president, but when blood royal came upon the scene, naturally the first good man, who had been born and bred a Catholic, with his fathers before him for a score of generations, modestly dropped into the background, and handed over the reins to H.R.H. For was it not evident that a special Providence had designated him for the position from all eternity?

The great annual meeting of this society was

now about to take place, and if we lay a slight
sketch of it before the reader, it is not without
apology, as it has no intrinsic importance whatever. At the same time, it will serve to show
better than anything else, to those who may be
interested, certain aspects of the lay Catholicism
of the period from the inside.

Roland and St. Maur were among the first
arrivals; indeed, there were only two people
in the hall when they entered it, one of whom
was the courteous Secretary, who brightened
visibly at the sight of a new face, as being
possibly that of a recruit, and as also contributing to swell the importance of the
assembly. Presently a member or two dropped
in; there came a Bishop, as an honorary one, and
species of spiritual policeman, and after him
several shabby-looking men in seedy overcoats,
which, however, nobody considered much, for
these were Peers of the realm. One of the
latter, a particularly scrubby little man, came
up, welcoming St. Maur with honest effusion,
and began a lively conversation with him, for
St. Maur was a standing problem. Reared in
the thick of the religious caddle of the century,
he could hardly be termed a heretic, for did
he not contribute to Catholic churches, worshipping in them often, and support certain of
their schools? *Why* did he not see his way?
What was keeping him back? Why, oh! why?
What, oh! what?

Then there entered one or two young men,
oiled and curled, and with very pretty boots;
these had evidently taken great pains with

themselves, and represented the world, the
flesh, and the Devil, as far as was to be expected
in such an august but unworldly assembly.
A few sympathizers and followers congregated
round Roland, whose views were beginning to
be known, and who had ventured to give expression to them on previous occasions; and
many of the Opposition, as they came in, gave
him a friendly nod.

"Well, old man, trying it again?" said
one.

"Wish you success!" laughed another, for
Roland had given notice of a motion gently
criticizing the executive.

"I shall vote against you," said a third;
"must have law and order, you know."

But evidently his views were not altogether
unpopular, and it was dimly felt there might
be something in them. Lastly, came the great
man himself, and if no little boy swinging a
censer of incense preceded him, it must have
been because, with true greatness of soul,
H.R.H. had discarded that ordinary appendage
of royalty where semi-religious state ceremony
is concerned. He was, however, surrounded
by some very important people, and so many
of them, that by the time the gathering was
complete, there must have been three or
four dozen people in the room, including the
reporters.

"This is a big thing," said the Deputy Sub-
secretary, rubbing his hands with glee as he
passed Roland. And another instance of the
faculty of taking a large view and rising to

the occasion, presented itself in the fact that
the whole meeting was gathered upon the platform.   The body of the hall loomed vast,
silent, and deserted, but that had its advantages, for it enabled the papers to say
that the platform was crowded to suffocation,
and that upon it might be noticed So-and-so,
and So-and-so, giving an imposing list of the
whole assembly.

The proceedings were opened by the President, who, poor old gentleman, was rather
husky and incoherent, and apt to fly off at a
tangent on no perceptible provocation ; but he
was understood to say something to the following effect, and the four reporters set to work,
as if their lives depended on it :—

" He had no intention to break the first rule
of the society by discussing a matter of practical moment, but as the Endowment Concessions Bill had been read for the second time
last night, he thought he might just venture
on one word, as that word would represent the
feeling of all the most distinguished members
of the Catholic aristocracy—in fact, of all
whose opinion was worth consideration.   They
had probably, most of them, heard of this
Bill ; still, as many of them very likely had not,
it being a mere matter of worldly import, he
would explain, that the Government had brought
in, and might even carry, a Bill for inquiry into,
and redistribution of some of the old endowments of the country.   Now, most of these
were the endowments of which they, the
Catholic body, had been robbed more than three

centuries ago. These had doubled, quadrupled, and in some cases increased to a hundredfold on their original values. Every penny of that money, and to this he thought there could be no dissentient voice, was theirs—theirs by right, human and divine, and there could be no question of division between them and the rest of the English people.

"But now there were further endowments, post-Deformation endowments. What should be their attitude as to these? These, too, had increased in value almost at the same pace. They had not been left by Catholics for Catholic purposes, it was true, but what of that? If every penny of this also were restored to them, it would hardly represent a tithe of the interest of which, during three centuries and a half, they had been robbed. Therefore, he said unhesitatingly, all this too was theirs, and theirs by right." (Prolonged cheering.) "There were some who had the impiety to pretend that these endowments had been left to the people, and should be divided in equal proportions among the various creeds; that it was their right. But what right, he should like to know, could belong to heresy, what right had the very negation of right? Only one, and he said it in all charity, the right of perdition." (Enthusiastic applause, amidst which a prelate was observed surreptitiously to pull his Royal Highness's coat-tails.)

"Very well, he need say no more. This was a burning question, but it was not likely to burn their fingers, as it was a rule of the

Society not to meddle with such, and he must beg that the subject should not be alluded to by any other speaker. The object of the Society, as they well knew, was to keep the Pope in his place; and this, he thought, had been done very satisfactorily during the past year. The Pope was at home, and likely to remain so; the funds of the Society had been pretty evenly divided between prayers and postage stamps, of which he was glad to say the former were now nearly as cheap as the latter. He thought they should always remember that they were the salt of the earth. He was surprised to hear last time that there had been something like adverse criticism in the wind. Some, he was afraid, hot-headed young men objected that Catholics did not sufficiently come to the front; but he would remind them that in the child's picture-book and fan-painting line, they had names of world-wide reputation, and that a very distinguished member of that Society had actually started a comic paper. The gentlemen he saw around him were sufficient guarantee that everything was carried out as successfully as possible. Adverse criticism and comment were to be deprecated in every way. Nothing could be more un-Catholic. There was a little proverb about the evil bird that fouled its own nest, and he could not but think that this exactly applied to the case. Catholicity in every phase was beyond criticism, above it—especially in this Society, where you got its quintessence." (A voice: "Question?" supposed to be an official's, and spoken with a view to giving vivacity and sparkle to the proceedings.)

" Yes, of course there was a question to be considered, and always would be; there was the question of poor missions, which, it had been urged, this Society should take up. Many of them, he admitted, had been driven to give up the ghost for want of funds ; but, on the other hand, several enormous churches had been built, and if these were often in places where there were no congregations, what an admirable faith it showed as to the certainty of creating them ! Then, again, he was proud to say that in many places where the church had originally been built in bad style " (here he shivered slightly), " where it was rococo or old-fashioned, it had been pulled down, and as a rule something noble and gorgeous in the very latest style, with reredoses, and rood-screens, and clerestories, and finials, and all that sort of thing, had been erected." (Applause.) " There were people —but he thought it could only be these hot-headed young men, who would live to learn better—who said there was other work to be done. If there was, God would do it ; and he wished to know if these gentlemen thought they could do it better themselves. What was the way to set about work ? While candles could be lighted and Hail Mary's said, was a man expected to do more ? Was he to strip off his coat, and buckle-to himself ? Surely not. There were many ways in which work might be done. The Association gave a dinner now and then ; he thought if their critics knew

the labour of getting up a dinner, of selecting
the *menu*, and despatching something like five
hundred circulars, they would not speak so
lightly of the work undertaken by the society.
Then there were pilgrimages; Mr. Snook, the
eminent conductor, was even now organizing
one to the shrine of a quite new saint,
whom he had discovered somewhere at the
Antipodes. Let these unquiet spirits take this
pilgrimage, and he would answer for it, the
Church in England at least, would be more
benefited, than by any other course they could
propose.

"For himself, and he spoke as representing
many distinguished persons, he felt perfectly
sure that no man who approached any question
in a judicial or critical spirit, or who had the
hardihood to suggest that improvements were
possible in their *modus operandi*, or in fact in
anything else, could ever enjoy the confidence
of the party; such an one should be discredited
in every possible way, and rightly. In conclusion,
he would say, that he hoped he might be allowed
to move a vote of general admiration to all his
distinguished colleagues, which he could not
but feel was eminently well deserved," and amid
ringing cheers, the royal gentleman here resumed
his seat.

The cheers perhaps were for Royalty and
loyalty, rather than anything else, and the
speech would probably have passed without
other than complimentary notice, had it not
been for Roland, who, after waiting patiently
through a second, a third, and a fourth eulogium

from other enthusiasts, rose to his feet. Roland
at this early period might have been called the
enfant gâté of his party; he had not yet raised
the whirlwind which afterwards swept over
his head. His taking manners made him generally popular, and his brains made him valuable—alack! almost unique in his particular
position. He had been stricken with amazement
and dismay at the sudden promotion of his
Royal Highness, and, confident in his own good
intention, he ventured to offer a few remarks
on the speeches just delivered.

He said that, " to be brief, he would assume,
for the sake of argument, that they, the English
Catholics, more particularly as represented in
that hall, actually were the salt of the earth,
but the question further occurred to him as to
what might happen if the salt were to lose its
savour." (Murmurs.) " Well, he was not going
to say that this was altogether the case, but it
was clearly a possible contingency." ("No, no,"
the energetic official again.) " He had no wish
to be unduly critical, as he was painfully aware
of the weak spots in his own armour, of his
youth and inexperience. It was, besides, an
ungracious task to question the collective action
of men, who individually expended thousands of
pounds on every species of charity and good
work, even to the extent of impoverishing
themselves; and such men were happily not
rare among them, and some such—it would be
needless to name names—sat at the table before
him. He was not so ill-advised as to attempt
to speak to them on the Endowment Conces-

sions Bill, as this, being a matter of immediate and urgent import, he was well aware that it was by no means a fit subject for discussion; but if he might venture on a general survey of the position, he would put it in this way :—

"That enormous concessions had been made at various times latterly, to themselves—only in justice, perhaps—but they had been made ungrudgingly, by the English people as a matter of justice, and in spite—this was to be remarked—in spite of a very imperfect and, in fact, distorted notion of what the Catholic religion signified, and while the majority of them, owing to their education, believed it to be an aggressive and dangerous creed, and one which they would be morally justified in keeping under in every possible way that lay open to them. In his opinion, the generosity which their countrymen had shown them, in times and circumstances of peculiar trial, constituted a heavy debt, which it was the business of Catholics to repay; he would say nothing as to their own claims, as requested; but might there not be counter claims?" ("Oh! oh!") "Well, if, for the sake of argument, there were, they could not be better repaid than by taking part in all the good work which they saw going on around them, in bearing their share of the public burden.

"And," he went on to say, "I am the advocate of lay action among ourselves, because it is plainly impossible for the ecclesiastic, with the numerous special duties of his calling, to co-operate with the outer world in the duties

of civil life in the way in which it is possible
for the layman.

"Even the most prejudiced will hardly deny,
that enormous good is being achieved outside
the pale; good that I can only regret we have
no hand in. I have not that strong opinion as
to touching pitch (if pitch it be) which prevails
in some quarters, and I own to a sneaking
admiration for what has been done in this way
by creeds, whose aids to a higher life are far
less than those we ourselves enjoy. Let us be
just, gentlemen. Putting aside what has been
accomplished with our native heathen, Protestantism and Nonconformity have almost
equally with ourselves carried the rudiments of
Christian belief—of the Catholic faith, if you
prefer it so—over the whole world. Wherever
the arms and commerce of the nation have
gone, there too has gone its religion, and not
as an empty name merely. We cannot but
admit that the Church of England has done
a great work towards both evangelization and
civilization, not only among the heathen, but
among all classes at home, who stood hardly
less in need of it." (The silence over the
little assembly was ominous in its intensity.)

"Gentlemen, are we really better than our
neighbours, as you yourselves will allow that,
according to our knowledge, we should be?
Do we see the Catholic leading the way in this
or in other countries? and if not, why not?
Is this 'Centre' a nucleus of enlightened
action? Have we made our impress on the
National legislation? In alien sects are to be

found, and in no niggardly number, men and women of all ranks, organized in societies, devoted to practical good works—people who would do credit to the Ages of Faith; indeed, their hard-working, simple goodness often puts to shame the aggressive didactic attitude, which is pleased to christen itself religion, in many more orthodox quarters. Are we not, perhaps, defective in some of the qualities that make up the Englishman?"

Here an excited and excitable gentleman rose to his feet. "Your Royal Highness will, I trust, excuse me; but I rise to order, I am forced to stand up, for I am quite unable to sit down. Gentlemen," he cried, "you will not have forgotten, I am sure, the remark that Julian, the apostate, made when—"

But his Royal Highness intimated that Mr. Tudor was in possession, and begged that these observations might be reserved until later; and with a withering glance at everybody in particular, the Confessor in embryo collapsed.

The speaker smiled an irritating smile, as if this little incident had rather strengthened his case than otherwise, and he went on, "A gauge of the nation's moral altitude, is to be found in the enormous sum annually forthcoming in voluntary religious offerings by the various sects, a sum calculated at eight millions sterling, almost a tithe of the revenue. This, too, is apart from what is subscribed in alms to undenominational works, such as hospitals, relief of the poor generally, accidental disaster funds, and the like. To these, again, the sums subscribed are simply enormous, and have never been matched in any other nation or time. This is the outcome of no particular creed, but of a profound Christianity, and I cannot but think it one of the noblest records " (" hear ! hear ! ") " that ever nation had to show. England—"

Here the Confessor (by which we do not mean that he held priestly orders, for he was a layman—very lay—but that he was ready to shed the last drop of his blood) sprang up again ; he was foaming at the mouth.

" Your Royal Highness ! " he gasped, " must excuse me ; I should like to move a revolution —I mean a resolution—this instant. No true Catholic can listen to this ; England, we all know, is a Sink of Iniquity. One of our greatest Divines has happily described it as ' a moral stink-pot held under the nose of the Almighty.' (Cheers and counter cheers, amidst which his Royal Highness rose and said, " that, while the meeting evidently sympathized with both the speakers—as he did himself—he thought it desirable that Mr. Tudor should be allowed to finish his remarks without further interruption.") That gentleman then continued,—

" I really have to thank my opponent, if I may so call him, for affording us practical illustration of the spirit which animates a certain section of our body. I cannot but look upon it as ill-advised and superfluous, to say the least of it. I would submit, with all deference to the opinions of those present, whose experience goes so far beyond my own, that the age is one when every form of Christian belief should unite, to co-operate to the uttermost—and why? Because we are confronted by a worse enemy than any Christian creed, however imperfect and mutilated, and that is, Unbelief. If not exactly proven, there is good reason to think that this mere negation of light, this darkness, is the great enemy that threatens the race, and which may even yet lead to its total relapse. Not that the teachers of Agnosticism excel their fellows in badness; on the contrary, we know that they are; for the most part, men versed in the science of humanity. But their beliefs or unbeliefs are totally inapplicable to the masses, the logical sequence of whose acceptance of such tenets, must be the denial of almost all existing rights, whether of the individual, or his property; and, if human society is to continue to be, must involve its reconstruction, if that be possible, on a totally different basis. I need not remind your Royal Highness, nor you, my lords and gentlemen, how it is sought to combat this materialism in many ways; how learned societies—or at least societies of learned men—have come together with the object of undertaking the serious investigation of the phenomena, which we are accustomed to designate as the supernatural, with the hope of discovering an, as it were, tangible basis for morality, and building thereon. But it is obvious, however far their researches may carry them, that the founding of a rational and categorical belief, wherein a man may hope to save his soul, is beyond their reach.

Whatever phase of modern thought we examine, it is impossible not to feel how strong is the position of the Catholic Church with regard to it. I would submit, we hardly know our own strength, or how to put it forth best, for the general utility." (A voice: "We don't care about the general utility.") " The Church is strong because modern investigation leads up everywhere to her tenets. So with this last; cordially admitting the supernatural, as a possibility of all times and places, one of her leading dogmas is the inter-communion of the living and the dead.

Putting theologians aside—who must, I suppose, be credited with the honesty of their opinions—there are few men of education outside the Church who pretend any longer to a belief in Hell, though few rational beings probably, have discarded the idea of future states of reward and punishment. The belief in Hell has literally perished for want of a Purgatory; and in this particular, again, modern intelligence and research has approximated to the standpoint of the Church. The scope, too, of the Church is wider by far than any of her rivals in this country. She alone, of what may be called the high-class creeds, has succeeded throughout the world in reaching the great mass of the people—the lowest of the poor; but she has not succeeded in this in England, and it seems to me we may fairly ask ourselves why not? Have we made any serious effort to popularize the faith? Will a Mozart mass at eleven with an hour's sermon, advance matters?

Will long Latin vespers and compline in the evening? I doubt it."

Here the "Confessor" before alluded to, who had founded a church with the sole object of controlling a choir in a lovely lace surplice, and getting his fill of plain chaunt, was seized with hysterics, and carried out, where he was undone, and presently grew calmer. For a moment Mr. Tudor faltered—it was hard to be serious—but he went on.

"Of old, I believe, the lay Friars preachers, themselves of the people, went among them, telling them in their own tongue the wonderful works of God. *In their own tongue;* therein, gentlemen, if I am not presumptuous, lies the secret—i.e., in language such as will carry meaning and conviction to the simplest. This secret has so far been discovered only by some of the non-conforming sects; sects which, by their composition, merely represent various forms of intellectual ignorance. Yet they have contrived to hit the nail on the head, and the feelings they evoke are a witness of it. The very elevation of the Church Liturgy is an insuperable bar where the mind is scarcely capable of realizing the plainest elementary truth. Yet these plain truths must be grasped before any superstructure is built upon them. So I say, gentlemen—and I must again apologize for drawing upon my own short experience among the people—that these sects have done, and are doing, an admirable work"— ("Oh! Oh!")—"and I would that we had more share in it ourselves. When I look on

the diet served up for the ignorant, on the way
in which we are in the habit of dishing up the
Eternal truths for him, upon my honour, I must
make haste to laugh lest I weep. It is unintelligible and un-English; need I say more to
point its failure? The people are the great
problem of this and the future age. The re-
straints implied by the refinements of civilization do not affect the masses, and it must be
the temporal, no less than it should be the
eternal, concern of every true citizen, to provide
them with the more efficient substitute of moral
enlightenment. I would that we appealed more
to the many and less to the few—more to the
poor and less to the rich; for here is danger.
Thirty-five years ago we were cursed and spit
upon; the pendulum has swung back; at this
moment, the Church runs the risk of becoming
the fashion. The world has often delighted to
play at religion, and signs are not wanting that
it is ready to play with our own. If it is to be
represented chiefly by an aristocratic clique, if
it is to be the stronghold of the boudoir and
the drawing-room—farewell, then, to nine-
tenths of its influence for good, farewell to
our best hopes for the future. This would
indeed be a finale to our glorious history of
martyrdom and struggle. Better a hundred
times that the penal laws were back upon us
than this. In conclusion, gentlemen, as I must
be brief, although much more might be said,
there is one thing which seems to me of
primary importance. One thing we lack;
a leader, or rather many leaders—laymen

who, while respecting due authority, will go forward fearlessly in the path of public duty, who will be unsparing of criticism, and unresting in their efforts to set right what may be wrong among ourselves; who will form for us as a body something like a truly representative constitution, and so gain not only our confidence, but that of the outside public; and who, putting forward no irrational claims, will maintain the Church in England in her public place, as a fountain-head of light and leading, of honour and example, a main-spring of the health and happiness of the nation itself."

Amid considerable half-suppressed applause, Roland re-seated himself. It had been observed that the Royal Duke in the chair had not only given a tacit approval to the sentiments uttered, which were certainly much averse from his own, but had put down interruption with a firm hand, and insisted on their being heard out to the end. Twenty-two members were accordingly prepared to spring to their feet and prove that, in a Pickwickian sense at least, they were ready to support the venturous upstart in his views, when a most untoward thing occurred, which the Devil himself must surely have been at the bottom of. In the momentary pause that ensued, a terrible sneeze shook the hall, and there was no mistaking that it issued from the Chair. Now, that worthy gentleman, who for some minutes had been peacefully dozing, had just taken from one of the prelate's boxes a pinch of snuff of unusual strength and amplitude, with the object of rousing himself for the next emergency. Further, a little zephyr had for some time past been mischievionsly at play upon his head, which was bald and susceptible. To be more scientific, a slight chill had induced a reflex action of the nerve centres. In the circles, however, in which Royalty travels with its satellites, such a trifle may carry a great and peculiar significance. It sufficed, at once, to extinguish the hopes of the active spirits. His Royal Highness had sneezed—that was enough. The two and twenty members sank back into their seats, not without a sigh of relief, for after all, anything new, or of the nature of a change implied trouble.

Lord de Sawnay then rose, and, in a few well-chosen words, said how delighted they all must be to hear every side of every question, especially when those sides were so ably expressed as they had been that day, and he felt no doubt whatever, that the usual vote of mutual confidence and admiration would now be passed without a single dissentient voice.

Upon this being carried with acclaim, the proceedings wound up, and H.R.H., with that urbanity which distinguishes Princes, sent an emissary to Mr. Tudor in the shape of a private Monsignore, who, to judge by his face, had enjoyed the discussion amazingly. He brought an invitation to tea, which had been laid out in the adjoining room, and thither the two friends went, Roland with an expression of comic dismay. The Prince received them, was affability itself, and with the humility of the saints, he handed them each a cup of tea.

" Capital speech," he said, " cap'tal! All do something some day, you know," and he laughed. " Must—really must, don't you know—but you want some sugar," and,with his own hand, he indicated the basin, promising Roland at the same time, a great career, but upon what grounds was hard to say. The prelates and great people chatted amicably on the mighty topics of the weather and the crops, or the terrible example made of the last controversialist who had crossed their war path, and all went merry as a marriage bell.

It is a strange sensation for a youth, who feels within himself the assurance of a surpassing strength, and the moral certainty of a career before him, to mix with a crowd of the quasi-celebrities of the hour. His self-confidence, without which no man ever achieved great things, is inborn. However much he may question, he cannot tell whence it comes, or whether he will owe his place to Fortune or to his own exertions—all he knows is, that this assurance is there, and his business is to justify it. He is unknown, unthought of, a kindly glance, a friendly smile, a nod of condescension is the best that he has to expect. Nobody pays much attention to him or his ideas, and yet—he laughs in his sleeve at the thought,—twenty years hence, some of these men may be ready to give their right hands, merely to be able to say they have conversed with him for five minutes at this time. He knows, so far as any man can know of the future, that when their little casual greatnesses have been forgotten, his present littleness will be remembered, that it will be his name, his individuality, that will be stamped upon the scene. Meanwhile, if he is strong, he can wait, it is only weakness that frets and is impatient.

A glimmering of this sort, which certainly did not make its way into words, passed through Roland's brain as they left the building. He slipped his arm into his friend's, and they strolled away together.

" They don't appear to fetter freedom of speech," observed St. Maur, drily; " that's something."

Henceforth, the position of the two friends was to undergo a change—the Disciple was to become the Master. In the strong face which St. Maur looked upon, he recognized a leader.

" Force will ever be your 'ultima ratio,' my dear Roland, I can see that, but force is of no avail here—the horse and the water. And I will warn you of one thing at the start. The world is ruled not by force, nor by money, but by sentiment alone."

CHAPTER V.

THEY walked down Piccadilly almost in silence, it had become close and sultry. Away over the city hung a storm menacing, but still, as it seemed, far away. St. Maur was immersed in thought, and Roland strode on, relieving his irritation by consuming a cigar at a furious pace.

" My dear friend," said the former at length, " I am sorry for you, I am sorry for everybody concerned, for ourselves as much as anybody. You know my ideas. I am emphatically a Protestant, not that I adhere very closely to the Church of England, but that I protest against any religious conception that is not grounded on common sense. In company with many others who are really working among the people, I have looked to the great religious organizations (foremost among which I place your Church, even in this country) to do their parts, and I have never understood till to-day why you have failed, where all others have had their share of success. You need, indeed, an infallible church to stand caricature to this tune. I don't mean to be ill-natured, man, but you must see that the thing is shaping to sheer foolishness."

"The truth can stand anything," said Roland, dejectedly. "We have centuries before us, but at this moment we are going back, not a doubt of it. I don't want quantity, I want quality. However, you must not take this hole-and-corner meeting as in any way representative of us. The Catholics of England have yet to find their mouthpiece."

"Yet I see this Society, speaking in their name, memorializes the Prime Minister, or petitions Parliament, on the slightest excuse."

Whereupon, Mr. Tudor fell to laughing so immoderately that he could not answer, and St. Maur went on.

"It is a pity a few more of you have not your keen sense of the ridiculous ; it often strikes me that nothing is more likely to help a man to his salvation in this world, if not the next. But why is not this sort of thing exposed ? I can conceive few duties more sacred. even for an English Roman Catholic. Who is to blame ? "

"Not individuals so much as you might imagine," answered Roland, grave again. "We are entangled in a network of circumstance. One man cannot speak because he is tied in this way, another in that; bread and butter, you know, very often. Then there is the fear of scandal outside, and this is the only serious part of the whole affair.

"What scandal can be worse than a hushed one ? "

"I agree with you, and after all, we are in no worse plight than other societies of men, it is a mere matter of discipline. It is partly that we have no experience of collective action, we laymen. Take these people we have met to-day, and you will find them one and all (almost) worthy Christian gentlemen, but they are not the men to drive such an engine as modern Catholicism. Authority mistrusts any public proceeding on our part, and, 'pon my honour, I entirely side with Authority, at present. Still, leading strings are for babes; we must train, organize, educate ourselves towards virility. As an outsider, you will hardly understand our peculiar difficulties. The last has been your fault," and he laughed, "you are killing us with kindness. Protestantism has opened wide its friendly doors, so long closed against us, and the rush (on our parts) has been terrific. Perhaps you are not aware that the last new thing with us, is not to know too much of each other, but to move in exclusively Protestant spheres; it is exceedingly funny."

"I can conceive the women falling into that," laughed St. Maur, "but I should never forgive a man."

"Nor I," assented Roland, frowning. "No man will ever be leader or spokesman with us who has failed to identify himself with us, faults and all, from first to last, there is enough virility in us for that, at any rate. If one of us pushes up outside, well and good for himself, but he will never represent *us*. We do

not want men who are secretly half ashamed
of us, but we do want sadly public men who
will drill us into something like a practicable
form.

"True, in the revolution of the wheel, the
Roman Church comes up as a problem of the
first importance for the country. How is it to
be solved ? Will it lapse, as it has for the most
part on the Continent; or will it play the great
part undoubtedly open to it, in sustaining the
public burden ?

"We shall see. There are many who hope,
with me, but they have hardly found the
courage of their convictions as yet. I suppose
effort is never wholly fruitless, but, my dear
fellow, let's drop the subject, and get a
mouthful of air in the Park."

"By all means. I will show you something;
come with me."

It was now between six and seven o'clock,
and at the corner the people were pouring into
the Row—a human torrent. That year a
back-waggle of an eccentric but fascinating
character, had come into vogue with the
women, and it was not uninstructive to take
one's stand by the posts, and to watch the
complete satisfaction of the pretty things as
they pushed through, and went swinging on
all adown the line. But even this attraction
failed to keep the two men at this minute,
although it had arrested a crowd of their
fellows, and they passed across into the open
spaces of the glade beyond, where the company was scant, and a few out-siders stood

watching the scene from a distance. Through the foliage, the walls of the Roman villa glittered afar with the sheen of a pearl shell. Here and there on the yet green grass lay a waif and stray of the people, ragged and tanned, looking into the changeful sky; and in the air was the buzz and hum of the greatest city of the earth, greater at this moment than it was yesterday, and in ever-increasing multiple to be greater to-morrow than it was to-day, and so to be apparently through to-morrows unnumbered. Wonderful fact to realize.

They halted under a shattered oak.

"The Park has seen curious things," said St. Maur, "since the days when Edward the Confessor granted it first to the Monks of Westminster. Here, where we stand in this spot, a little desert in the heart of a population of five millions, was 'the Ring' (which, by the way, I believe, was a square—of oak-trees) where all the world went with his wife through two centuries—the Row of the day. And yonder, to the left of the Serpentine Bridge, where that ugly stone now stands sentinel, was the old conduit-house which supplied Westminster with water, and the 'Bloody Bridge,' which, when gentility was invented, was discreetly turned into Knightsbridge. South, at Hyde Park Corner, and midway between Stanhope and Grosvenor Gates, you may almost trace still where the earthworks were levelled, which formed two of the chief forts that defended London on this side at the time of the Rebellion. The lines ran past the top of Berkeley

Square, where the fort, ' Oliver's ' Mount, gave
its name to Mount Street.   London is unlike
other modern cities, it has been more jealously
conservative ; and every odd corner, every rise
and fall of a few inches, every awkward angle
has its story for those who can read it.   But
London is not really modern, she is only six
centuries younger than Rome herself, and is so
far unchanged that the heart of Roman London
is the heart of the city of to-day.   Somewhere
there, near my house, far underground, rot great
hecatombs of bones, the bones of those who
filled the charnel-pits of the plague.   All along
that eastern side, where the rows of the plane-
trees now are, stretched an avenue of fine
walnuts, which were cut down to make gun-
stocks in the French war.   Up yonder was
a green lane, that once ran by the side of a
stream where Green Street runs by Brook Street
at this day ; and under the Marble Arch is
buried ' the stone where soldiers are shot,' as
an old map has it.   These things do not
particularly concern you and me, but there is
something beyond that does."

He led the way to the northern boundary of
the park.   They passed out and reached the
iron pedestal which marked the site of Tyburn
Gate, and looked again into the turmoil of the
street.

The heavy omnibuses, laden with outgoers,
were charging ponderously by ; the cabs dashed
past to and fro.   Opposite, the portals of the
Parks railway station were disgorging a rowdy
gang of holiday-makers, who were in the best

of spirits. One man was wearing his sweetheart's hat, with a broken feather dangling
over his face. She, with a bottle in newspaper
tucked under her arm, was hanging upon his,
and his hat, which she was wearing, came so
far over her eyes that she depended upon him
entirely for guidance—a bruised if not broken
reed—and they were chanting merrily as they
staggered on, " I'm a stoopy didiot. Ho! Ha!
Hi!" &c.

Here too came the city tourist, and in his
tourist suit of grey shoddy, a flabby cap, a long
monkey-jacket, knickerbockers on his bandy
legs, and blue-topped gum-shoes upon his splay
feet, a foul black briar-root set amid the ill-
grown red hair of his redder face. Was ever
the image and likeness of man so prostituted?
Yet for all, the man and his class were probably
good citizens, if only they had not made of
ugliness their God. These and a thousand
kindred sights and sounds presented themselves
to the two as they stood, but for St. Maur he
saw and heard none of them, his thoughts were
far away, even though they were chained to the
spot where his feet trod; he was wholly absorbed,
and his lips moved almost as if he prayed.
He turned to Roland,—

" The spot whereon thou standest is holy
ground."

Faintly came the chorus from the distant
revellers, and tipsily.

" I will tell you," he continued, " why
Catholicism appeals so strongly to outsiders
like myself who are searchers after principle.

I have not your beliefs. Many of them I reject utterly. You will never get over the fact that the frequency of 'miracles' in former days was due, not to their being the ages of faith, but the ages of ignorance and credulity. Still, there is much in your faith that is priceless, but your people ignore their strongest points; they know Hurlingham well, but the very name of Tyburn is forgot.

"This," and he pointed down Oxford Street, "is the *'Via Sacra'* of England, a sacred way which no spawn of modern days can ever wholly pollute. Do you see nothing among the cabs and the carriages and this ugly crowd? For my part, I never look upon it but the long file of generations flits backward, until my eyes rest on grim processions, that move out from the city gates, and slowly onwards towards this spot. I see many such. Now it is a criminal who is to be hanged on Tyburn tree, and the people are cheering him and giving him to drink all along the road. He will die game, and he will die drunk.

" And I see others, these too, are criminals before the law, but they are different, and there are many, many like these. Strapped upon hurdles, with their arms outstretched as upon a cross, or two and three bound together and heavily ironed, their faces pinched with long imprisonment, their limbs nerveless from the wrack and the torture, powerless often almost to the lifting of a finger, but in their hearts a dauntless exaltation, I see another set of men dragged up the long rough road from London town. These are the good shepherds who have ventured their lives for their flocks. This, no less, is the goal of their hopes, and they are come hither, that little company, that now at last on those long careers of toil and privation, may be laid the crown of martyrdom. If you have read history as I have done, they must come before your eyes as realities yet living. They are many, cleric and lay. Monks of St. Benedict, and St. Dominic, and St. Francis, black friars and white friars, and they carry often some insignia of the priestly office that the yelling mob may yell the louder. Some are brought to the stake, for there have been fires here as there were at Smithfield, and some are for the gallows, but not as we understand it. This means a disembowelling while yet alive, so that a man should look upon his own entrails; quartering and dishonour after death.

" Through a century and a half, until the faith has been stamped out of the land, they come this way, the bands of soldiers with their drums and fifes, the hooting mobs, and the condemned felons; the tableau is imperishable. So these brave men laid down their lives, in truth or error matters not so much; these are the principles of immortality. Their blood it is that flows in your veins; such is the stock from which you of to-day have sprung. What say you to your ancestry ?"

He crossed the road, and Roland followed him in silence. They came into a dingy little square of mean, smoke-begrimed houses, where semi-genteel respectability was writ large over every portal.

"Here," said St. Maur, taking off his hat, "is the chief spot of execution, a few yards from the junction of the cross roads.[1] Here thieves, murderers, and highwaymen un-numbered, have met their doom. Here, Cromwell was swung in air, long after his death, and with the dust of these, with this," he scattered a wheel-mark in the road, "mingles the honoured dust of more than half the martyrs of the Reformation. What is to be the harvest of such a sowing? One might have thought that Nature herself would have had tears for the scene of such tragedies, that her noblest sons could not be nought to her—but it is so. She is heartless; so far as we know, she ignores the best that she has made, equally with the worst, and man has stamped the spot as wholly vile. So at least it is accursed. Look, how vulgarity has set upon it for its own."

Beyond, in the Edgeware Road, the shops for cheap jewellery and servants' underclothing were flaunting their bravest. Overhead the rosy gold of the summer sunset was rolled in great masses, but it seemed that no ray from it could brighten the stunted trees or the dirty brick face of the hideous square.

"Come," said St. Maur, "let us get away. Some day, I mean to offer them a memorial of marble and gold and precious stones for the

[1] "Tyburn tree" came westward as the city pushed out, but here it stayed.

centre of their garden. What do you think
will be the answer of men who are content to
live their lives in such dens of dismal respectability as these? I know beforehand they will.
refuse it. Yet it is one of the things in life that
I should like to do."

Roland said not a word—this was his way when
he was much preoccupied. St. Maur's earnestness impressed him profoundly; the lesson
came as a happy corollary to the meeting of the
afternoon. For the first time he vividly realized
the splendid pedigree of English Catholicism,
not that part of it which ran back into the
almost pre-historic times of the country's first
conversion, which too was from Rome : not
the part pertaining to the days when she had
been mistress in the land, and had covered
it from sea to sea with her sanctuaries;
but the part of it which spoke of those
latter days, hardly yet out of the memory
of very old men, when she had been trampled
in the mire and extinguished utterly out of
sight. In the struggle of humanity towards
the higher life, could be few records more
glorious. The blood of the martyrs is the seed
of the Church : even now the new growth was
shooting healthily; it was for the training of
it that men of his type were thoughtful, that
its root should strike where the soil was fittest,
that it should have space and freedom, sun and
light; that it should be pruned of dead wood,
and, neither cramping other good growth,
nor cramped itself, should become a goodly
tree. Why should they have troubled their

heads about it at all? Was not this a matter
for councils and synods, and ecclesiastical
authorities generally? Possibly in the first
instance; but side by side with the activity of
the priesthood had grown the apathy of the
layman, until the Church resembled an army
composed entirely of officers, from which the
rank and file were absent. What work could
there be in such a corps? Woe to Catholicism,
if in this country, as in some others, it should
come to mean clericalism, pure and simple.
There was the danger already,—that its sole
public exponent would be the priest.

＊　　　＊　　　＊　　　＊　　　＊

"That's the prettiest woman I've seen this
season," exclaimed St. Maur, rather abruptly.
"She's so fair, that I make no doubt she's a
fool."

A carriage piled with luggage, evidently
coming from the Great Western, rolled past
them: in it was an elderly gentleman, much
muffled, and a lady.

Roland looked up, but was too late to see.
What did he care? there was only one pretty
woman in the world for him. So he answered
readily, " I daresay." Yet, if there be such
a thing as the communion of soul with
soul, he should have felt something; for she
who was being hurried away from him, and
lost to sight in the crowd and the fast-gather-
ing darkness, was none other than Sybil Grey.
The explanation of this was simple. Mr.
Trelawney's doctor had ordered him up to
town a day earlier, that was all.

But perhaps there *was* something in the air, for on the morrow, Roland ordered his horse at half-past seven, and cantered into the Park to achieve an appetite for breakfast. The morning was divine. Summer had returned with a rush, and all things were giving her glad welcome. The unwearied ripples of the water, the drooping leaves of the Row, which seemed to be always whispering low, with a half languorous enjoyment, " Look how tired we are; but the season is nearly over, and it has been very pleasant here in the shade." After a few turns Roland stayed his horse under the statue of Achilles, where many adventures have happened, and doubtless many more will take place. He was wondering whether the waiters at his club would give him breakfast or merely the cold shoulder, if he went in so early, when he noticed a lady riding slowly and alone, as she came up the avenue from the water-side. There were very few ladies out; he thought he had met them all; they appeared to be horse-breakers of a semi-professional type for the most part, but this lady was not one of these.

" That's a neat habit, it reminds me of Sombrewood," he thought, and he was base enough to go forward to see more. But as he went the vision grew upon him, and he could not restrain a cry; for the moment he doubted his senses. " Sybil! Sybil!" was all he could stammer.

But if he was disconcerted, she was not, and she cantered up, her hand outstretched, and laid it in his. " Yes, here I am in the flesh. This is not my astral body, as you might suppose, though I think from what I can see, I shall often send it here when I go back. But poor boy, you look bewildered; what do you know about Buddhism? Not even that Christianity was founded upon it, I daresay. Ha! Well, never mind, it is a positive relief to find any one ignorant of the subject. Now you'll like to know how we came here, and should you ever pass this way again, and look up at that big hotel, remember that on the third story, the fourth window on the left from the end, is me: do you understand? I think you are struck dumb."

But he was not; he was only listening hungrily for her laugh, which he knew would come.

It is not usual, perhaps, for a young lady, and a stranger, to turn out before breakfast on the first morning of her arrival in town, and to canter about the Park alone.

But Miss Grey would seize Time by the forelock, and look at the lay of the land, so that when she first walked in the [Row, it should be as an *habituée* of the place. Hence it will be gathered that with her guardian she was a spoiled child, and so far as she could be spoiled, she was; this was the truth.

It might wring the heart of an old man or woman—say of three or four and thirty—to think how impossible it were, even given the identical circumstances, to reproduce in themselves the enjoyment of that morning ride, enjoyment for which even they twain for a long time, could find no tongue, and which it is hopeless to describe in words. The Park was theirs, almost theirs alone, and that morning they lorded it where they listed, for Miss Grey hinted that the like of this could hardly happen again. What the future might bring forth she knew not, but she fancied that certain female hands were waiting to mould her into shape, and she laughed very proudly and very prettily as she said this. There were, too, certain female wings under whose sweep she was to move, and she thought this might imply a clipping of her own.

Although Roland glowered sullenly in his soul, he could not but admit that the arrangement was desirable. For all his democratic notions there had been anxiety at heart that everything should be done as it ought to be. No girl could afford to disregard the usual routine of a *débutante*, under penalty of losing a something by it her whole life long. In the course of his social theorizing he had been unable to invent any particular improvement in the matter, only he would have chaperons chosen for qualities beyond rank or wealth. Here he was as powerless as Sybil herself; all depended on Mr. Trelawney, of whom he knew nothing.

It was arranged between the two that Roland should see this redoubtable gentleman—rendered now doubly redoubtable by the gout—on the morrow, for to-day was to be the Doctor's own; until then they could not well meet again. Sybil reluctantly admitted, as it were, a piece of her sex's humiliation, that certain "things" were necessary if she was to spend a month in town; and a day, or at least a few hours, must be devoted to getting them.

"Not that I want very much," she said, rather disdainfully, "but one must cover oneself with something, if it's only sackcloth and ashes." It is pleasant enough for a woman to say this when it is no more than the truth. As Roland glanced at the coils of dark hair, shot with purple gleams, that overburdened her shapely head, he thought of Lady Godiva, and answered,—

"I suppose so, but the less the better; nearly all the people one sees are overdone."

The lithe outline and almost stern simplicity of her form had been to him from the first a source of inexpressible delight. He found it absolutely free from that inelegance to which even the best female figures are liable—the want of length, which unduly emphasizes bust and hip, exaggerating the line of beauty into fault. There was, too, especially about her arm and shoulder, that suave flow of muscle beneath the surface, which in a healthy young man or woman, is perhaps the most beautiful thing on earth.

"When you have been here a little while," he went on, "you will be aware, as I soon became, that there are zones of dress—dress-circles in fact. There is the Mayfair zone, or, more properly, it is the centre of the circle. There most of the women are tall, or, if they are not, they manage to look so. Their dress is simple and well fitting, but not exactly so inexpensive as it pretends to be. Belgravia comes next, with a certain added gorgeousness, splendid, but hardly so tasteful. Of course, I am speaking of Belgravia proper."

Our eccentric cousins, it should be explained, were in the habit of settling on a fashionable point, and then running it to death through a descending scale, and over heaven knows how many miles of country, so that its inhabitants might still keep the coveted heading on their note-paper. The Park gates were such centres; you might be wandering through some desert wilderness of bricks and mortar miles away from everywhere, when, on asking your whereabouts, you would be confounded by hearing that you were in Queen's Gate.

"Well, then, there are Kensington and Bayswater, which are zones. Merrily jangle the bangles there, and the ribbons flip and whisk in your eyes if you go near enough, and there are mangled humming-birds and puffed sleeves, and monstrous hats with nodding feathers. It is quite a style of its own, that of the Westbourne young lady, who I conclude must fill a vacuum for the Westbourne young gentleman, or she would hardly exist: and, lastly, there is the suburban zone; and there, I believe, they dress like old pictures without waists, and wear touzled hair and heelless shoes of brown leather, a little down-trodden for choice. Then I ought to warn you about South Kensington and Brompton. Has any one warned you? No? Because it is serious, and don't

let us be overheard. To tell you the truth,
they are one and the same." He spoke in a
hoarse whisper. "Oh! you have much yet to
learn, but you must never, never hint that it
is so, or that you know of any connection
between the two. Indeed it is better to ignore
South Kensington altogether. Its very name
carries an indescribable unpleasantness, and
although they *are* one and the same, remember that Brompton is all that is best
and brightest, and most beautiful; South Kensington nothing of this. I cannot say why;
there seems no particular reason, and it might
even have been the other way about. I can
only warn you of facts as they are. Now,
you're laughing; what can you find to laugh
at in that?

"I daresay you don't think much of my
ideas on dress; but, I have tried training.
I have looked for the finest pictures and
the finest statues—yes, and by Jove, for
the finest men and women, ever since I can
remember, and something must have been
hammered into me. I give it to you for what
it is worth."

"Soon I think you will not be uneasy," she
laughed; " all my training has only been a preparation for what I have reached to-day; and
the things you tell me, though I was never here
before, I seem to have known half my life before you speak, and I follow mentally at your
heels. I declare you have bewitched me."

Although they had been jesting in every-
day talk, she seemed to feel his influence gain-

ing upon her moment by moment, and she
grew afraid, looking with wide eyes upon him
almost wistfully, as though to beg his forbear-
ance. They had been traversing the lonely
bit of road by the powder-magazine, with its
charming garden and gables gay with creepers,
and as he had last spoken he had laid his hand
upon her wrist. The unspoken thought she
had answered was his own, and the next words
she took out of his mouth.

"There may be difficulties with Guardy.
Yet I hardly think there will. Come as you
are, and be yourself: that is the best advice
I can give you."

Now this very matter was in his mind,
and her discovery of it astonished him. Since
boyhood he had known that he could of
occasion read his comrades, and even bend
their wishes to his own with a certain facility;
but the idea of putting his own thought into
another person's brain, and of that person
bringing it forth as his or her own, was
new to him. The mind he had now to deal
with was, without doubt, especially susceptible
to his influence. He was not satisfied; if this
were possible there was more beyond; the
idea seized him that there might be tangible
proof. With a powerful effort he concentrated
his thoughts and visualized in his mind a cross.
After a minute Miss Grey laughed.

"Really, I am afraid these morning rides
can't be as good for the constitution as I thought,
or I am tired from yesterday and want breakfast.
I could declare I see a cross there in the air

among the trees in front. How very odd. I
hope it's not a bad omen, and that I'm not
going to be ill. Oh! no, it can't be, for now
it's changing to a horse-shoe, and that's good
luck. Oh dear! I'm afraid I've invented a
liver. How horrible! Now it's gone."

Roland desisted. When she had spoken of
ill-luck he had changed the cross to a horse-
shoe; it was all perfectly satisfactory, but,
strong as he was, the effort made his head
swim. So, then, he could at will sway her
imagination by his own; for at will the conception of his brain had been shot into hers.
His eyes were lit with a secret pleasure; this
was union such as he had dreamed and despaired of. He and she, then, were to tread
a higher path than other men and women,
though not higher than others might aspire to;
and it was but natural, for with him as with
her, aspiration had been the motive power of
young life.

The wide application of this new-found faculty
he never guessed, nor would he then have
cared if he had, but as a matter of fact, the
hour was an era in his history. There was a
man who woke up to the discovery that he
had been talking prose all his life, and had
never known it. In the same way, there
have probably been men who have awakened
to the fact, that they have exercised an unconscious power over their fellows from the
first; a direct, although hardly recognized influence, according to laws which, if unknown,
are as immutable as those which regulate the

action of gases, fluids, or any other of the
elements in Nature's laboratory. It was the
consciousness of this power as a purely
natural one, which throughout his career, held
Roland Tudor aloof from the fatal arcana of
superstition to which he might otherwise have
yielded. In this lay the fount and origin of
the prodigious influence over his fellows which
he was afterwards to wield, even though he
remained ignorant of its precise mode of action
to the end.

He did not now betray himself, but he could
hardly let her go for the joy in his heart; and
she, although unconscious of special reason,
sighed as though her own had been wrenched
from her bosom.

When at length he was gone, she fled upstairs
to her room, her whole frame throbbing with
an emotion that shamed her. She stood before
her glass, and the sun streamed in upon her,
making her to her own eyes, half unwilling, a
bright vision of happiness.

At the open window the young leaves shook in
rain of sunshine, and on the pavement below,
a ragged artist, a cripple, stood propped painfully against the railing, soliciting alms. A
moment she looked at the scene, then upon
herself again. Turning away, she clasped her
hands as with a spasm on her heart. "Oh!
God," she cried, "Thou hast given me over
much," and the memory of the morning never
faded away.

Roland saw her again in the afternoon, and
it was on the self-same spot, whither he had

gone, like any other foolish love-sick boy, to conjure back the hour. She drove past with another lady, whose face he knew, but not her name. His true love's eyes were far away—she was dreaming; but as he looked upon her as though he would bury his glance in her being, she slowly turned her head, her face suffused, her lips trembled, and her eyes caught away all the fire and flash out of his. She waved her hand gaily, and was gone, the brightest of the thousand bright girl-faces that flitted past.

Roland accepted the situation with philosophy. and perhaps a little amusement. Such powers he had imagined were monopolized by boa-constrictors, Indian jugglers, and the like. Though he had occasionally encountered a terrible individual, in a historical novel, and a cloak, who could scowl from behind a pillar and wither a heroine, with quite no trouble at all. His own influence was hardly of that sort, but the natural outcome of his heart, which had beat fiercely about the barriers that bound it, until it had burst them and gone out whole and entire to its better, higher self.

Any anxiety which he had felt on another subject was removed when, the next afternoon, having been shot to the fourth story of the big hotel in the pneumatic lift, he happened to see on the table in Mr. Trelawney's ante-room, three cards, " Duchess of Ancaster," " Marquis of Thomond," " Lady Glendore."

These names were good for anything, he was aware, and with the exception of the last, better than he could have hoped for. He was absurdly pleased, as the reader versed in the science of aristocracy (and it is sincerely to be hoped that none other will ever scan these pages) will allow he had every reason to be.

If he had never before known fear, he knew it now, and for a very uncomfortable sensation, as he was ushered into Mr. Trelawney's room, and found him there alone. At first sight, however, he was struck favourably, and the impression was mutual. Dogmatic, and perhaps a trifle dictatorial, Miss Grey's guardian was still a fair sample of that type of fine old English gentlemen, whose gradual extinction is everywhere deplored, but which will probably last, and more or less in its pristine form, as long as the nation itself. He belonged, and this Roland had not been aware of, to a great London family. A Trelawney, and not by any means a remote one, for he had lived into the time of George the Second, had had the good sense to buy up some of the brick-fields and cabbage-gardens on the outskirts of the Green Park, and again, north of my Lord Burlington's, a ragged scrap that adjoined the Conduit Mead. And now, presto! a dozen of the palaces of Piccadilly stood upon the cabbage-beds; and great red-brick double-Dutch buildings, hardly less splendid, towered high into the sky all along the Mead. These things had quickly made of that ancestor's prolific stock, not only a great London family, but a great county one as well, and in several counties. Although this particular Trelawney was but a stray member of it, he had enjoyed all the advantages of the connection, and some share of the more substantial benefits that had accrued to his clan.

"How do, how do, my dear sir; now I know all about it," were the first words he said rather testily, but greatly to Roland's relief, as the latter sat down. "It's all wrong, of course—at least I suppose so," and he scratched his head with some vigour. "O—h, my leg! Tut—tut— if there's been any fault, man, I suppose it's been my own. Mind you, I'm not saying exactly that there *has* been yet; we shall see. You're a Roman Catholic, I believe; that's a pity, fine young fellow like you. Well, it can't be helped. We didn't have religions in my day, 'cept the poor devils who had to take to the Church. Roman Catholics are not what they were in my time—danged shady lot, sir, then; poor, sir, mean—very, socially speaking. But, don't ye see, a lot of good people take it up nowadays! No doubt it's a much better thing than it was, no doubt; what I mean, don't you see, the right sort of people have taken it in hand —Court lot, and all that, and I daresay they'll make a very decent thing of it before they've done, as a religion. The ladies'll manage it all, if you'll just let 'em alone; they're fitted for it. Must have religion, sir. Never manage the women nor the lower classes without it. Ha! ha! Don't care about it m'self—such a damned uninteresting subject. After all, I often say yours is as good—now it's got into good hands

—as the precious old parsons' with his infernal tithes."

Mr. Trelawney had mounted his hobby, and was happy. "Oh, ho! my leg. Bless him!"

"Well then, as to Miss Grey, my ward; you understand—it's rather sudden, isn't it? We must think about it, talk about it. No, you needn't tell me about yourself. It's some time since I learned English history, but I haven't forgotten where Tudor of Sombrewood comes in; Regent, Warden of the Marches, Lord of the Isles, and all the rest of it.

"Religion's the rub! Of course I shouldn't like my ward influenced. Not that I am prejudiced, oh! not at all. As she's a woman, sir, I don't suppose a little religion'll hurt her, if you can get it in. I've never got it in myself, and I've never troubled about it for her. Let the girl use her common sense, I say. She's plenty—all girls have when they like, but they think they get more by shamming foolishness. It depends a great deal *who* she gets it through. Now there's Lady Thomond; you know her?" Roland bowed. "She's one of you; not one of your cranky pervert women, but fine old A 1 stock. Now, I shouldn't mind much if she took it there—oh, ho! my leg—she's promised to look after the girl; but I mean to give her every chance in every way that I can.

"Then there's the old Duchess of Ancaster; known her since I was a boy, sir; knew her mother, sir—monstrous fine woman she was, too. Ah! well, she'll take her out a bit, and present her, and so forth. She's a sort of Puritan, hates Papists like poison—hates 'em, sir—regular danged good old sort; but she knows the inns and outs of the business, and she'll do Syb justice, at any rate in this world.

"Well then, there's Lady Glendore. Oh, yes! young fellow, you needn't look like that. No, sir, the worst young woman in the world, isn't likely to do my ward half the harm that the best young man may. I know what you're thinking of. Her ladyship did get rather merry at that ball—well, that's a year ago, and she's not twenty yet—and she chucked her bracelet at some fellow's head, and marked him. Well, so she did, but the fellow was a cad, sir, a cad, and deserved it. She always was a jolly little girl, and now she's a swell. I've borne her on my knee as a child, and, by Jove, I wish I'd never had anything worse to bear—oh, ho! my leg. I daresay you think me an old sinner, but I can see you're not a prig; and 'pon my honour, if I was a girl perhaps I'd marry you myself. You might be one of the good old lot I belonged to, by the look of you, and *we* never had any trouble with the women.

"I'll trust you, boy. What I want is this. I'm helpless here, can't do anything but swear —don't mean to,—can't help it. I want everything done properly, and I mean to have it so; you'll do your part, I'm sure." Mr. Trelawney put out a shrivelled hand, which Roland took.

"My dear sir, for her sake, for yours, and I may say for my own, I will do all I can. I won't say what she has become to me, because

I can't, and because, if I could, you wouldn't listen."

" No, no, shouldn't listen," assented the old man, repeating it after him and shaking his head; " never stand that sort of thing, never could. I don't wish to keep y' off; a girl's always glad of a run in the park, does 'em good."

" Well, I couldn't wish her in better hands than Lady Thomond's," said Roland, not discussing the point; "and I've other women-friends as nice, she must meet them."

" Very good, very good, that's right," said the old gentleman, raising himself in his chair, and as he did so, scanning his guest's features with an almost painful anxiety. " You'll be cautious, won't you? I daresay you're better than I was, hey—young fellows weren't always cautious in my day. She's a dear girl, but a girl's always a misfortune."

A mist gathered over his dim eyes, and he let Roland's hand go. " It'll come right, I daresay; I'm sure I hope it may, and if it does, why you know you needn't be afraid—there's enough," and he tapped his pocket. " Yes, certainly enough. You've only one thing to be afraid of, and that's the priests; they'll get the soft side of any woman."

Roland was rude enough to laugh. " Come, sir, I've seen something of priests and women, and I think I know better; the—"

" No, no, I don't mean any harm. Hang it, no, give the devil his due. What I mean, sir," he said in a fierce whisper, and he drew

Roland down, " is putting into their heads *some confounded rot about saving their souls.* Well, good-bye, my boy, thought you'd like to see me alone, and hope we shall have more to say to each other some day. Take care of her now. Remember I'm a cripple. No more storms at sea, please; no, nor quiet rides before breakfast. Ha! ha! I know all about it, can't be too careful, can't. Good-bye, my boy, and why—damn it all—God bless you! Come whenever you like."

The drooped eyelid fell on the shrunken cheek. I doubt that he saw very plainly. With a slightly heightened colour, Roland left the room.

CHAPTER VI.

IT may be here remarked, as the subject has been touched upon before, that the Endowments Concessions Bill was thrown out in the Lords, and there was nothing more to be said about it, this Session at least. Contrary to expectation, there were no disturbances, merely a few squibs and crackers, which were promptly put out. Owing to its reformed character, the position of the Lords now was so strong, that there was no manner of doubt that they presented, in the aggregate, the highest rational and intellectual opinion in the kingdom. Even the educated barbarians of the slums were aware of this, as they were, thanks to State training, of many other things which they did not choose to admit; so with the growling of an unspent thunderstorm, the verdict was accepted,—for the present.

It was felt, and by no one certainly more keenly than the Lords themselves, that the delay was an ephemeral one. "Last my time, perhaps," was the generally expressed feeling, and there the matter rested.

But at this time Roland had other things on his mind than politics. He had been pleased, and even touched by his interview with Mr. Trelawney; but when he came to think it over at leisure, he had not got so far as he had hoped to do. He had gone in with the intention of learning something of Sybil's family, their history and position; but the subject had not been so much as mentioned, and how it was he had come away and never found the means to ask, he hardly knew.

Meantime, six weeks lay before them, an eternity, so long, so important, so crowded with epoch-making events, as we consider them at this time of life, such as balls, water-parties, pigeon-matches, and coaching-meets, that each week as it flew by, seemed to contain the concentrated essence of an existence.

It came about that Lady Thomond was mistress of the revels. Ill-natured people were apt to say that this lady had solved the difficult problem of combining the worship of God and Mammon. True it was, that although she was out every night until two or three or four, as the case might be; every morning she was to be seen thickly veiled, and in her black serge, somewhere near the bottom of the church at early mass. And while her name was on half the charitable committees of the West End, it was seldom absent from the list of patronesses, whenever a new entertainment went a-courting the public favour. But as she was still a young and vigorous matron, filling an important social post, and as she had always a girl or two under her charge, whom she took up and piloted through, in lack of girls of her own, it may be doubted if there were any desperate wickedness in this. The young ladies usually "went off" quickly and well, and a sporting gentleman of nineteen, who once remarked "that you could always depend upon a filly, if she came out of the Thomond stables," merely expressed in his own beautiful language what was assuredly the general feeling. In spite of her manifest good works, rumours had more than once reached her ladyship's ears of indirect ecclesiastical censure on her worldliness and extravagance, and she was wroth at the suspicion of it.

"Fiddlesticks!" she was wont to say, "now I should just like to take those worthy old gentlemen by the ears, yes, and that young Father Snippet with them, who only left college last Christmas, and who has his Heaven, and Hell, and Purgatory cut and dried quite to his taste, and the whole scheme of creation, and tells us all about them on the slightest excuse—of course he's infallible on these points, but what does he know about house accounts?" "What the dickens" (a Marchioness was allowed this term at this period) "do they know about giving dinners? They hardly know how to eat them. What do they know about table-linen, and dusters, and servants' aprons, and coals, and stable necessaries, and one's own wardrobe, and one's man's wardrobe? What do they know of the toils of the lady of the house —a house like this, and of paying its bills? Pooh! All their bills are paid for them.

Housekeeper first, Catholic afterwards," she would laugh.

" Necessity first, and luxury later, for religion is a luxury, my dear, if you live in the world at all, say what you will. I've a big Protestant man to look after, and I mean to do it well."

It will be seen from the foregoing that the lady was "thorough" if she was anything, and indeed her director averred that whenever they met, he stood much in awe of " direction " himself. It was to Miss Grey that she thus unbosomed her ideas, for by natural selection Sybil had come to be her chief companion this year. It was chance; is not everything chance? In commercial phrase, girls were "lively" that season, the demand was brisk, the competition fierce, and the particular one whom she had started with had already gone off, much to her own surprise and delight, much to her friends', " wooed, married, and a"—and honeymooning away in the far Pyrenees—and all by the second week in June.

The hands of " the wicked Marchioness," as her friends used to call her, were empty, or as empty as such hands could ever be, when Sybil came upon the scene; and though other great ladies were interesting themselves in her, it soon came to be understood that Lady Thomond was sponsor-in-chief. The bright, active, gentlewoman of forty, left the impress of her sensitive and sensible mind on everything she touched, and did·showman to the world's raree-show, in a way that her *protegée* might have looked for in vain anywhere else.

It was equally fortunate for Roland Tudor;
so far as he went he was approved of, although
Lady Thomond thought him over young; but
when she had talked with him a little and
learnt to know him, her mind was divided as
to whether such a young man should be thrown
away—these were the words she used to
herself—in marriage. Anything in the shape
of a presentable male, provided always the
wherewithal were there, would do for mere
marriage. It was all her marrying girls looked
for as a rule, and she herself thought that they
were fairly in the right, but there were higher
things in the world and scarcer; there were
careers, and careers of a sort that nothing
should be allowed to thwart. Of such a sort,
she never doubted, was the one that lay before
Roland Tudor. She was a woman of deep
penetration, and she had come away so impressed by her first serious conversation with
him, that for days afterwards, busy as she was,
she could not get it out of her head.

She felt hardly less strongly with regard
to Sybil, that she was by no means to be
thrown away in mere marriage; the two
might, in fact, be very well, or rather very
ill thrown away upon each other, if they
married. There were careers for women, too,
not that they were usually very satisfactory
things; but in this age, when all was opening
out, better and better might be hoped for.
She could never look at Sybil and fancy her
falling into the eternal groove of womanhood,
the house-mother and the nurse of children;
her gifts pointed to something exceptional,

but here was the little goose already engaged,
and to the detriment of an equally exception-
able young man. Having once discovered each
other, Lady Thomond was not surprised at their
pertinacity in the idea, but she would not hear
of any public avowal of the engagement.

"No, my dearest," she had said in the
beginning, "keep it quiet, deep down in your
own heart if you like, but you will both be
freer and happier for not letting the world
into your confidence—if it must be so," and
she sighed.

A secret understanding is a most delightful
thing to most lovers, and there was little
difficulty in persuading the two to acquiesce in
it. The Marchioness had seen too much of the
world to be easily upset, but she was a little
taken aback on hearing that her new charge
possessed no religion whatever.

"Dear Lady Thomond," Sybil had said on
one of their first drives, when the subject
happened to come up, and she was being
interrogated on the point, "I really have no
particular religion ; my thoughts are a sort of
religion in themselves, that is, since I have
been so happy, for in everything, I seem to
see the reflection of a Divinity. But if you
ask me precisely what I am," and she said
this coldly, as if she would not have her heart
probed, "I cannot say ; I am many things ; a
Buddhist perhaps in some, an epicurean in
others ; an altruistic pagan philosopher I hope
in most. My mind refuses Christianity ; it is
too lofty a conception ; if it were the truth, its

professors would be angels, and fly away,
whereas they are oftener in the dust."

With any other of her girls, Lady Thomond
would have said, "Oh! nonsense," would
have given her the choice of two or three
respectable creeds, and insisted on her adherence to one of them, but she merely slipped
her warm, white hand into the girl's glove.
She was shocked, but would not show it.

"Brave, big words—so big, I scarcely understand them; but I think you were cut out for
a heroine, or a saint, my dear," she said.

"Why not both?" laughed Miss Grey, her
old humour returning. "Yes; in my heart, I
would have it both, and at all costs."

Lady Thomond had not been slow to discover the gifts of her *protegée;* she had had
considerable experience with girls—had been a
girl herself, and thought she was acquainted
with most varieties, but this one fairly astonished her as something fresh. Indeed as
Sybil's face and personality became known,
it was apparent that a new light had arisen in
the firmament, and the jaded season rejoiced.

The first public evidence of this was a vile
coloured engraving, entitled "A Star in the
East," in a society paper, which might have
been expected to know better. Miss Grey had
been taken by her friend to distribute school
prizes somewhere in Whitechapel; the enterprising social had then and there seen its way
to a discovery, that of a fresh and unquestionable beauty, and in a sphere where beauty
is perhaps not quite so common as other

good gifts. So Lady Thomond, who was really the head and front of the affair, was merely laid in (in flat wash) as a background, while Miss Grey, in purple and gold, and an attitude she had never assumed in her life, stood in front, clustered about with smug little boys and girls in all their Sunday best.

There was some indignation, and more amusement, when this reached home, but it was only the beginning of what became a perfect persecution. These extraordinary English people of the period forthwith went as mad about her as if she had been a new wild beast, a white elephant, or a mermaid; one would have thought that there was for a whole month no other single pretty woman in London. It was not flattering, for the Public were accustomed to do this spasmodically, and really over anybody or nobody at all, if the whim took them; and it had grown to be an admitted thing that there could only be one at a time—one General, one beauty, one æsthete, &c. The individual who was happy enough to secure this place, was sure of his or her due meed of appreciation, perhaps a little more. There was one grand exception to the general rule, and that lay in the number of fools.

How the photographers obtained her lineaments it is impossible to say. She had never sat for any portrait since she was a child, yet presently there were a dozen of her perhaps in one shop window, and in a dozen different poses —romping in a swing, smelling a dead bird (presumably to see if it had gone bad), play-

ing bo-peep behind the curtains, or heaped
about with roses and lilies, palpably of the very
best that paint, calico and silver paper could
grow. And hardly less artificial was she herself. Of the face she made no particular complaint—in some way they had procured her
features, and the victim could only laugh at the
ingenuity that had done it—but the figure, the
hands, and the dress struck her dumb with
amazement when she first saw them. None of
these were hers, of that there was proof positive;
but they were so like, that at first glance, they
seemed to be the same. The trimmings were
almost exact, yet not quite—the lace, for
instance, would be of the same date and make,
and arranged in the same way as her own, yet
the pattern was different; but here and there
the artist, whose fault was certainly not timidity,
had boldly launched out, and draped her or
undraped her entirely after his own fancy.

The figure usually was almost too lofty in its
conception for real life, and there was in it a
suspicious smack of the superb lines of a hair-
dresser's dummy; still it was hers in caricature.
How it was arrived at was, like the rest, a
mystery, and never to be revealed.

Miss Grey was more indignant than ever in
her life before; but intolerable and insulting
as it was, it had to be borne, and she found
the best way to bear it was in silence. No
name appeared on the cards, which were sown
broadcast over town and country.

To portray Roland's disgust would be impossible. Everywhere he heard of nothing but

"that new woman!" and his friends, in all ignorance, would openly proceed to canvass her
charms before him. At the first discovery of
her face in a window he had gone raging to
Lady Thomond, who had managed to send
him away slightly ashamed of himself and his
vehemence, which was the best frame of mind
for him if it could have lasted. Still his wrath
was deep, and Sybil, who saw it in his face,
trembled when she met him, however, by tacit
consent on both sides, the subject was avoided;
but a little incident at this time added fuel to
the flames.

It was on the occasion of the opening of the
north transept of the new cathedral, in Westminster, that cathedral which was at length
being raised, chiefly by public subscription,
and had so become in some sort a national
reparation, for the ten thousand churches filched
away by the Deformation. Its scaffoldings had
for some years past dominated all the roofs
of the City, saving those of "The Abbey,"
and "The House." One transept was now
completed, and, pending the erection of the
remainder, was to serve as the "Pro."

An immense concourse of people had come
together, and in the train of the Royal
Highness, who was the figure-head of the
occasion, walked other Royal Highnesses of
alien faith, and so many distinguished guests
of all creeds and no creed, that mere Roman
Bishops and Cardinals were nowhere; the
affair outside being looked upon (and there may
have been something in the idea) as a step

in the general advance, and almost as important as the opening of an aquarium or cookery exhibition. The local authorities had always warmed to it after the usual preliminary battles. A neighbourhood of slums had been abolished by the new building. House-rents had quadrupled and were still going up, and rates—ah! this was very sweet—were mounting with them; the " blackguard low Irish " of the district would be kept in check. Altogether it was highly satisfactory.

So great was the sympathy with the movement, that it was whispered that an Anglican prelate, with I don't know how many " priests " in his wake, had offered, as a branch of the Universal Church, his and their services for the opening. Will it be believed this offer was declined with thanks? Sad to find Rome, in spite of all that is done for her by her well-wishers, maintaining ever the same absurd and impracticable position—at least so said the Bishop. He was disappointed, for he had always been a man of large heart, a man who loved a rowdy street procession, a band, and a free fight, and saw much holiness in it, and who encouraged the people who went to heaven this way; and did not see why he should not extend the same leniency to other people who went another way, and preferred orderly processions and good music.

There was sweet reasonableness in this; but what would you have? It is certainly not the logical who succeed in this world.

One of the finest choirs ever assembled in a

London church had been brought together for the High Mass; but at the *Credo*, the Italian *prima-donna* who was to sing the offertory piece, fainted, amidst universal consternation. It so happened that the leader of the choir had that week been at one of Lady Thomond's "at-homes," where Miss Grey had sung the identical solo ; he too was an Italian, and she had put down his profuse and excited compliment to foreign politeness.

But the *maestro* had been perfectly sincere, and when the catastrophe occurred, instantly bethought himself of the lady who might—ah ! heaven—possibly be there. The blow was bewildering, but he managed to crawl down from the organ-loft and pass the word for Lady Thomond. She was fortunately found directly, and with her, Miss Grey, to whom he well nigh went down on his kness. His frantic gestures explained the situation ; would she have pity on him, on the Church, on the world ? Would she ?

She laughed a little and coloured, it seemed so absurd ; there must be plenty better able ; but if none happened to be there—why of course she would—why not ? And without more ado she quietly slipped from her place and went up into the loft, the congregation all unknowing.

The long amens of the *Credo* had died away in a thunderous burst of the entire choir, and the great organ began to trumpet forth the prelude to the song, when a silvery trill was heard which rose and swelled liked a bird's note, and instantly the vast crowd became alert, and were aware of something new and unlooked for. It grew stronger and louder, until it burst into melody which flooded the whole of the great building, and drowned the senses of the listeners in a sea of sweetness.

Then a wondrous thing happened. So intense had been the first shock of surprise, that it had held the people motionless, and spell-bound in a breathless silence ; but in a moment, with one accord, three-fourths of them fell on their knees, as if they fain must join in spirit. And yet it was but a little every-day prayer that had so awakened the first echoes of the arching vaults,—

> Ave Maria gratia plena Dominus tecum,
> Benedicta tu in mulieribus, et benedictus
> fructus ventris tui Jesus.
> Sancta Maria mater Dei, ora-pro nobis
> peccatoribus, nunc et in hora mortis nostræ.

How could singer here on earth throw such beseechment into these simple words ? As the last notes died away, there ensued a dead stillness for half a minute at least, succeeded by the low sussurus of many tongues. For there was hardly man or woman in the building who did not turn to his or her neighbour and speak. Many of the latter were crying, and there were two men present, and as likely two hundred, who were more affected than they cared to own. The two were St. Maur and Brabant. Roland had not happened to be there ; these two, when the service was over, met at the door.

Now, it was only to his superiors in rank

that St. Maur was a thorn of grief; a man need only be below him in the scale, and he would go half a mile out of his way to serve him, or merely to be civil. He and Brabant had met more than once lately, and there was much sympathy in their natures, so now he slipped his arm into the latter's, and said,—

" Well ! if you've still time for verse, you've had a fine subject for it this morning; who on earth could she have been ? I must find her out before I venture to show myself abroad; if ever the voice of poor humanity reached to heaven, that voice should."

" I can't conceive," answered Brabant; "I keep my eye pretty steadily on the horizon for the new stars too. But, talking of verse, did you notice as she sang, the sun came out and struck the gilt figures of the angelic choir round the chancel, luminous with rainbow light from the windows ? I had hardly noticed them before, but for the moment they were living things in mute worship, and hovering motionless with poised wings to listen. When the sun went in a minute after, they faded back to stone. I have had Saint Cæcilia in my head ever since."

" Beautiful, beautiful,—a divine voice. I don't know now whether it was the music of it or its pathos. That a human creature should pray aloud, and that such a congregation as this, should spontaneously fall on their knees to pray with her, is a thing past my experience. There is an old-world beauty in the thought of it. Who can she be ? "

"Ah! St. Maur; how'do? Fine tone that. So you're in for the Liverpool this year, pot of money, I s'pose? Thought you'd given up the Turf." This acquaintance made way for another, his co-director in a railway, who was in his turn succeeded by an M.P. Brabant did not get another word. But this was always the way with the many-sided St. Maur. He was like a multi-faceted stone, and whichever side was uppermost, at the moment, seemed to flash the brightest.

Ere an hour was out, so was the secret, and it spread like wildfire. From that day Miss Grey became as marked a social feature in the country as the House of Commons, or the Lord Mayor of London himself. In proportion, however, as she was sought, she withdrew into her shell. If Lady Thomond hardly appeared to notice this new departure, it was because she thought much, and would have much to say if she did speak.

So the young gentlemen, whose moral being derived its chief sustenance from the legs of girls and of horses, and who had been growing inconsolable, for there was nothing particular about in either line, and it was "such a beast of a time till Goodwood," took heart of grace, and mobbed Miss Grey. Whithersoever she went, they went too, in a body, and were noisy in their encomiums, until it eked out that she had looked coldly on a certain great personage, whom they regarded as their chief—snubbed him, rumour said, ye gods!—a personage so great that the mind, aghast, refused

to place the two ideas in juxtaposition at all.
Then some of the bolder spirits hinted that
they had always noticed a sort of under-current,
sort of want of form—" doosed hard to explain,
don't-che-know, y'know, and all that—but—
aw—palpable, quite palpable, mons'ous pity,
ya-a-s;" and in less than a week, at least two
or three hundred of the nobility and gentry
had seceded, and carried away their hearts in
safety to lay at the feet of some new idol,
one who should be more pitiful for the sufferings of royal humanity. In a short time it
was only the quite vulgar, the people up from
the country, and the people who didn't know
what was what, that mobbed Miss Grey at all,
and this made a vast difference. Happily
relieved by this state of things, she was
able to resume her former freedom, and to
enjoy herself with all the zest of youth. Fortunate the girl who, in her first season, falls
into the hands of the social wire-pullers! She
was an integral part of every fête, a necessary
figure "everywhere," she knew " everybody," in
the idiotic jargon of the period, meaning the
few hundred people whom the speaker honoured
by considering as desirable acquaintances.

If Roland had been annoyed about the
photographs, the incident at the opening of
the church was not one which was calculated
to pacify him, and when he heard of it, he
decided that he must speak with Sybil.
Here a piece of his own most private property
had been brought to town, and lo! the whole
town had gone crazy, or he had. The very

firmament seemed changed; he had thought it
entirely his own concern, this coming up to
town, and behold, it was a thing of public
rejoicing for all London, and Great Britain
and Ireland were ringing with it. Only to-
day one of the papers had suggested, in
apparent sanity and gravity, that her path
should be strewn with wild flowers whenever
she walked abroad; another had talked about
draping the balconies of the Senior Gaby's
Club with black, in mourning for the failure
of its members. Was this the language
of compliment? He, himself, could only see
her occasionally, and sometimes for but a few
minutes together. He grew moody and savage,
and when, at the end of a fortnight, he reckoned
up, he found that he had quarrelled with half
his best friends, and had insulted, in more or
less serious fashion, a dozen or more of his
mere acquaintance.

St. Maur had taken him to task; had found
him out in fact, for St. Maur had a clear
vision. All he had said was, "My dear
Roland, why didn't you tell us of your
beautiful neighbour in ——shire, and of her
gifts?" But he had only pressed his friend's
hand a little the more warmly, when he saw
the look that came into his face; for he meant
something pleasanter than a rebuke, and Roland
had turned away his rough answer, saying
nothing, feeling much.

Then Brabant had met him, and harped
upon the affair of the opening. He said that
he had seen the singer and made her acquaint-

ance; it was a most interesting and almost unique case, and some day, when he had time, he would tell him all about her. He did not add that he had been seriously wounded by her charms, which was perhaps as well.

But so it was, and he had dragged himself back, with slow and lagging steps, to the suburb, whose name, as enunciated by Mrs. Squeed, " Harrow-on-the-'ill," rang in his ears with a miserable and mystical significance. Maria and her money had seemed as dross, and Lady Jane as naught. He appeared slightly dispirited, but he merely observed that he was working up the incident into a *chansonnette*, which he thought must be pretty. Whereupon Roland had turned upon him, without warning, and said with the utmost ferocity, that he couldn't conceive how any man could make himself such an idiot. And, as he did not vouchsafe any explanation of this view, Brabant went angrily away, and there was war.

Although he little guessed it himself, Roland was jealous, and it *was* rather hard, that here in his own world, he should come and go like any other nobody, while Sybil, at three weeks of age in that world, should be all things to all men. He would have her a queen of society by all means, but only when he had fashioned her to it in his own way ; besides, nobody could rule properly until they had thoroughly learnt to obey, this was an axiom with him.

But when at last he came face to face with her, and would have put his thoughts into shape, the words died on his lips. It had been all nightmare and chimera, and he inwardly cursed himself for a fool—almost a knave.

On this particular morning they were left alone in the little sitting-room, high above the tree-tops that looked upon the Row; Sybil, cool and fresh as the lily, that unfurls and looks for the first time upon the face of her sun-god. So she looked upon her lover's, and as the fragrance of her hair and of her breath surrounded him, and the light of her eyes glowed with the morning; as the fruit of her red-ripe lips was pressed to his, and her bosom strove heaving upon his own, he realized that he was still no less than all in all to her, even as she to him. The whole environment of his existence again changed, phantom Happiness herself had fled for refuge to his arms.

At that moment he could not but feel a divine compassion for all the human race unblest as he. He pitied St. Maur, and, from his heart, Brabant, to whom he felt a sudden inclination to go on his knees, as to all his injured friends.

"I guess what you have to tell me, dearest," said Sybil, laying her gentle hand upon his mouth, "and if you will close your lips, I will shut mine, or open them solely at your bidding. I will be the celebrated automaton singer, and you only shall keep the key. Will that do, my tyrant?"

The tyrant thought it might do for the present, and after they had sat together in the window talking for a long time, they bethought them that they would go down and join the crowd below for a stroll before lunch, which was to be, by special invitation, at the Roman Villa. The Row was already crowded, but the instant Miss Grey was discovered, there was a sudden surge, and the two were hemmed in where they sat, in the centre of a block that was desperation to contemplate. Any facetious individual who was so minded, might have walked on the heads of the people, from the posts at the Corner to the Park gate, and what a soft paving he would have had, for all its density! It was difficult to look absolutely unconscious, but Sybil was growing inured to her trials; and Roland, feeling the necessity of the case, let his glazed eye fix on vacancy, dropped his jaw that he might tap his teeth the better, and essayed to personate as infinite a gaby as could be found on a long summer day within the area of Hyde Park, which was attempting a good deal.

"Roland, Roland! for Heaven's sake don't look like that, or I can never, never speak to you again," came an agonized whisper in his ear.

But he knew when the right thing was in the right place, and that the wisest man is he who best knows how to play the fool; he persevered stolidly, but all the time he was secretly enjoying the panorama before his eyes. A crowd even of well-dressed and comparatively well-odorous people, was never without its meaning to him. It was pleasant to note how far good breeding and good taste could go. Their comments on Miss Grey were so plain, and direct, and unstudied, especially those of the women, and there was no difficulty in catching what was said, for they stood upon her train or her toes to deliver them, adding injury to insult.

Individuals, too, were interesting. There were some would-be public beauties about, whose introductions had not been sufficiently good for complete success, and their treatment of the subject was scornful in the extreme. One there was who opined that a girl who had so behaved to the great personage, should be shut out in the exterior darkness, and never have another chance. But against this one, was pitted a lady who said, for her part, she thought it the most awfully swell thing Miss Grey could have done to have smashed him up so, and wondered what the first speaker would have given for such a chance herself. The perfect harmony of the two friends was jeopardized, but the fight was taken out of them by the struggle for existence that raged round Miss Grey's chair, and for want of breath they could not go on with it.

Meanwhile a hundred types, many of whom were careless or ignorant of the great attraction, came and went. There was the man whom accident had made a celebrity, and after whom a head or two was turned, as he passed even in this crowd, but whose own head—poor devil—was turned considerably more than that of anybody else.

And there was the man, born to be a celebrity, but who by some confounded ill-luck had not been recognized for one, though he was past thirty, and he moped through the medley as if he were waiting about to be hanged. Neither of these had any eyes for the beauty. Then there was the upright-white-waistcoat-curled-whisker-Baronet-might-be-a-Peer-man, who was a good deal about, and very happy, constantly button-holing one of his duplicates, and telling him State secrets as to the Government's intentions, and Miss Grey's intentions, and his own intentions, of all of which he knew almost as much as you do. And here, in great force, was the young man of few seasons, who was utterly miserable, and who groaned as he said to his friend,—

"Pretty jolly sickening this, 'ole man, isn't it? but 'flah must do his turn."

As in every social tableau, the women were the strong point of the scene, for in sharp contrast with our own time, there was not one under forty, and very few above it, always, of course, excepting Miss Grey, who had the faintest perception of the ridiculous. This ensured a steady and admirable variety in the fashions. There were the women who had plainly just jumped out of bed, and huddled on a dressing-gown, and although it is to be hoped they had washed, they certainly had not brushed their hair. Some were tied up in ornamental pillow-cases, and could only stir three inches at a time, and there were others who were bunched out, mostly behind, but sometimes before, and it must have been very unpleasant to sit down unless you were fond of sitting on steel ribs which often broke up sharp. And

there was a youthful bride, who had taken
a silk night-gown out of her trousseau, and
had draped it over her dress as a thingumy
(there appears to be some uncertainty as to the
scientific name of the ornament); it made up
very prettily, and she gloried greatly in so wild
and wicked an exploit. And by her came another
who wore something outside that she should
have worn in, and she too "fancied" herself,
and that she had done a really fine thing.

There was also a marked variety who had
had their hair cut short, and wore stern
matter-of-fact coats, and high collars that made
a red rim round their foolish throats, and
"pot" hats that imprinted deep purple rims
on their foreheads, and who strutted up and
down, imagining that they looked like men, but
who really resembled squinny (the school word
describes it best) school-boys, whose schooling
had been a failure. With these were patronizers
of a certain bi-lateral garmenture, to wear
which must have been in itself a source of unfailing delight and a joy for ever !

And the multifold aims and objects of the
crowd were not unapparent. Hither came the
stout old lady from the country, who would
insist on making her way into the very centre
to get sight of the new beauty, and who having
done so, promptly fainted away, and was
trampled to death, or should have been if she had
had her deserts. Here came the *habituées* who
tried to look like neophytes, and the neophytes
who, without trouble, passed for *habituées !*
Here was the business-like young person, who

never went anywhere, even to dine with a
friend, without having raffle tickets in her
pocket for a pet case, but whose ideas of charity,
it had been ascertained, began (and ended) at
home; and she was steadily pursuing her
mission.

Nor must the riders be forgotten—the man
who did not come often—just three times in
the season, say, for the name of the thing, and
who was really to be pitied, for he did not
" run " to more, though he probably had his
money's worth, as did the public, for when he
did come, he was a thing of beauty. And
the man who rode the wild horse of the Andes,
or that animal's twin brother, and who charged
everybody, but old ladies for preference, on
the crossings, until, to his surprise and indignation, he was given in charge himself. And there
was a lady who was thinking as much of herself
as of any other subject, perhaps, and who held
her arms woodenly at right angles to show
what she called her figure, but which was not
hers at all, but Madame —, the great *artiste's*,
very creditable to that lady too, and none the
less so, that it had not been paid for. It was
an unusually brisk day. The fun grew fast
and furious. Lower down, a merry earl and a
baronet were " having it out " in the fashion of
the period, and heavy odds were being taken and
offered ; but it was impossible to see all. Now
the mob, looking more jostled and harassed
than ever, appeared to be breaking in one direction, and as it gave way, disclosed a compact
phalanx of marching, muscular females, who

resolved themselves into Mrs. Lushington Squeed and her three sisters.

Where there was pushing to be done, where there was anything to be gained, where there were neighbours to be elbowed, trust them, no nonsense there, they made straight to the core. And although Mr. Tudor crushed his hat down upon his eyes, and turned up his coat collar to his ears, they bonneted him, and put his hat straight to make sure—Mrs. Lushington explaining that the crowd had jogged her arm. She was dead beat, she said, and he was forced to give up his chair, and what grieved him more, to exchange his pet expression for one of deferential pleasure at the occasion.

That the picture might not want a moral, at this moment came a buzz of voices; a low truck was rapidly pushed through the shrinking crowd by a bevy of police, and passed, almost before the horrified spectators had realized that the upturned varnished boots, the huddled figure under the sheet, from which ran a little dark drip on to the path—meant a suicide. The dead man had been one of the merry company, and he had chosen thus to set a seal on the proceedings. The line of faces on either side was a study. Many nervous women actually looked shocked and sorry, but every woman is not nervous; the Squeeds eyed the apparition with a stare of astonishment, and as it vanished, Horror remarked with a hoarse laugh, " Well, that fellow's no trouble about his cab-fare home at any rate." And

after they had forced an introduction and had
shaken hands emphatically, every one of them,
with the new beauty, and had told her of Lady
Jane, and asked her to Harrow, Mrs. Lushington
said she really must have a word in private
with Mr. Tudor.   This word proved to be very
difficult of delivery, for there was much flutter
of her fan, and some deep-drawn sighs, before
it would come out at all.

It appeared that Major Lickpenny, on the
day he had lunched at Harrow, had, after his
nephew's departure, become first very hilarious,
and then, as she cautiously expressed it, not
very wise, and this was related in a tone of
generous and kindly compassion.   From being
not very wise, the step downwards to being
excessively foolish, had apparently been a short
one, for he had then and there gone down on
his knees and made her an offer of marriage.
There was little enough in this, the sort of
thing she implied by her manner, that might
happen at any day or at any hour to any man.
But when she refused him, being engaged
already, as the Major must have known, to
Mr. Brabant, and refused him as nicely as
she had ever done anybody, he went straight
away, without even saying good-bye or giving
a hint of his intention, and threw himself into
the pond in the garden.   The pond was not a
deep one, well, perhaps not more than two
feet deep at this time of year; it was where
they got water for the cabbages and things,
and the moment he was in, he had screamed
to be taken out, for he said it was dreadfully

cold, and as they were all on the lawn at
tennis close by, they had fished him out in a
trice, though the dear old man repeatedly
declared he would much rather die, then and
there if they could manage it. They had taken
him into the house instead, given him hot
bottles and brandy and put him to bed, but
the shock to their nerves had been something frightful. He was still at "Old Hall,"
and the speaker was nursing him. It had
been a very painful case, but the most painful
part of it was yet to come. It was that he, the
Major, declared solemnly that should he ever
get well, which he hoped was not likely, he felt
morally certain that he should do exactly the
same thing again, with the object either of dying
or ensuring an indefinite prolongation of his
treatment. " ' The bub-bominable water was so
beastly cold,' you know his funny, odd expressions, she laughed, crashing her fan—I repeat
the poor old dear's exact words—but this was
the only thing he objected to." Mr. Tudor must
go himself and see what he could do with him.
Not a very hopeful prospect, for the old "dog"
valued his reputation, as such, as a thing beyond
price ; it was all that was left to him now, and
any chance of enhancing it was inexpressibly
dear to him.

Mrs. Lushington told her story while the
sisters catechised Miss Grey, and at the end of
it they changed about. The three young ladies
undertook Mr. Tudor, the widow, Miss Grey.
(" Three paragraphs, a guinea at least," mused
Mrs. Lushington, as she opened the conversation.)

" What queer people one does meet here, Miss Grey, doesn't one ?"

" I was just thinking they were rather odd."

" I always say that's the worst of town now-a days, there's such a mixture, one hardly knows how to talk to the sort of people one meets."

" It *is* very difficult."

" Oh ! there's *dear* Lady Glendore."

" So it is ; do you know her ?"

" I—ah—no—that is, not exactly ; I know a friend of hers, and she was in the next house but one to us at Folkestone last autumn, so I feel almost intimate : I always say she's *quite* the lady ; what do you think of her ?"

" Well—I—I may safely say I think, that she's the fastest friend I have," answered Miss Grey with gravity.

" Indeed!" The speaker scanned the celebrity closely. Although she was very well dressed (which inspired respect), she was very young, and there was a great simplicity in her manner. Mrs. Lushington was wondering if a little romance and patronage would come amiss. It might be as well to try.

" You didn't know her poor brother, Sir John, I suppose ?"

Miss Grey shook her head.

" Poor, poor Sir John," sighed the widow.

" What was amiss with him ?" asked Miss Grey, a little bored.

" Oh !" and Mrs. Lushington's forehead contracted into a pitiful frown, " didn't you know ?" She shook her head, drew a long

sigh, and contemplated Horror's broad back
with intense meaning.

"It was a very, *very* sad case," she said at
last with slow deliberation.

Miss Grey began to apprehend.

"He hung about her for weeks, months,
years, I may say. I saw it all, though he said
nothing."

"But surely, surely," hazarded Miss Grey,
"if a word would have set things right, he
might have said it?"

"Ah! no, no. You see—" the painful expression in Mrs. Lushington's face rose almost
into agony; "the poor fellow was so much in
love—so desperately struck—he *really could
not speak*. I have seen that sort of thing *so*
often in our family."

"Indeed! how very, very sad; and what
became of him, then?"

"Oh! he's dead; went abroad and died
soon—very soon after. It usually happens so,
doesn't it?"

"I don't know," answered Miss Grey, feeling
that her own experiences had hardly gone so
far as this—"and she?"

"Well! you know she's so dreadfully accustomed to these things, perhaps it did not make
the impression on her that it should have
done."

Such was the sad story of the lost Sir John,
and from it may be judged something of the
loyal way in which these sisters clung to one
another. There were many Sir Johns in
history—that was, in their history, as re-

counted by themselves. This subject was thrashed out; still, Mrs. Lushington did not stay her hand.

"You are quite new to our London, I believe?" she said, overlooking the beauty casually. "You have an *immensity* to see."

"Yes; I was never here before; I must confess to the country cousin."

"Ah! you'll like it better as you get into it all, and learn our ways."

"Oh! it's delicious," exclaimed Miss Grey, with well-dissembled enthusiasm, clasping her hands, "to come here and see them, and to get hints for one's self—for one's dress, you know," and she looked from the three Miss Squeeds' round, wrinkled backs, prominent in the sun, to Mrs. Lushington's over-loaded splendours; "and what it must be to live in the heart of it all, at Hampstead, I think you said—oh! Harrow, was it? I can only imagine."

Then Mrs. Lushington was smitten with a sudden fear, and rose, saying they really must be going on to look for Lady Jane and Mr. Brabant, who had promised to meet them, and whose carelessness and stupidity in failing to do so, explained their being there without a gentleman.

As Roland had observed his friend a few minutes before, making his way due east, he conscientiously despatched them after him due west, for, in his remorse, he felt that no good turn he could do him was too great. Then after allowing time for the coast to clear, as to-day they were to have no escort, he and Sybil struck into the solitudes among the azaleas and rhododendrons, and through a shady by-path strolled slowly up towards the Lane and the palace of Lord St. Maur.

CHAPTER VII.

THE luncheon was not altogether extempore, although some of the party were. Miss Grey had long been anxious to see the inside of the villa, and to make acquaintance with its celebrated owner. He, on his part, was equally anxious to make hers; but he would have Roland bring her himself, as a guarantee of good faith that no attempt should be made on his claims. He had too, as usual, a whimsical idea in his mind of bringing together a few odds and ends, his new friends with his old, by way of fresh combinations, in the study of which he found unfailing delight.

He must have a married lady to do the honours, and having left it to the last, he had run out into the Park a few minutes before, and, as luck would have it, met Lady Jane Squeed, who had joined her four nieces on their way to a pastrycook's.

One of the greatest penalties of rank at this peculiar period was, that everybody who enjoyed it was forced to know, in a way, everybody else in the same fortunate position. When therefore he unwarily ran into

Lady Jane, there was no getting out of
her, or of her four nieces, who were introduced circumstantially then and there. But
St. Maur was not a man to quail at difficulty;
time was running short, and he suddenly remembered to have heard Roland speak of Mrs.
Lushington's engagement to Mr. Brabant, who
was to be of the party. The very thing! He
plunged into the Rubicon and invited the
whole cohort. Here were two widow ladies,
chaperons enough for five-and-twenty unmarried ones if required.

There was not the slightest feint at hesitation as to accepting the invitation, for St.
Maur did not ask everybody to his house.
" Not the sort of people you would have expected at all." This was a marked tribute to
their intellectual, if not to their social status,
and besides, here were five luncheons for nothing. The ladies then went on their way
rejoicing, leaving their host to pursue his quest
among the highways and hedges.

Roland and Sybil had loitered, and the
consequence was that when they were shown
into the great hall, as the heavy curtains parted
asunder, they were courteously received on the
other side by Lady Jane Squeed, Mrs. Lushington Squeed, Miss Horatia, Miss Rosilla, and
Miss Susan Squeed, who held their chins
three inches higher, every one of them, than
they had done in the Park, and whose mood
had changed from one of dubious humility, to
one of hauteur and condescension. Roland
turned stony, and even Sybil felt that to be so

received at the top of those jasper stairs was a spoiling of it all. Mr. Brabant was shortly announced, and impressively received in the same way, and he, although tolerably well seasoned, could hardly control his amazement; but Mrs. Lushington condescended to no explanation; on the contrary, she demanded one for his failure in meeting them. Then she introduced him in a cruel and casual way to Miss Grey (an unnecessary formality, had she been aware of it), and instantly called him off to look after herself.

Meantime, St. Maur had button-holed a youthful ex-minister of not more than fifty-five, who pretended that he had not two minutes to spare, which, indeed, was his normal state, but who managed to spare exactly two hours, a fact which possibly gave the Opposition that temporary shakiness which was observable about this time. Two or three other strays had been found, among them Miss Wigway, with her erst director, a clergyman of the Church of England, who was doing his best to lure back his lost sheep. She had bowed so low, and they both looked so dreadfully hungry, that St. Maur could not resist asking them, and he sent them in to join the rest of the party. The assembled guests had some time to wait for lunch, for the sudden incursus of so many had caused a hitch in the kitchen, a hitch which it required the presence of the master himself to smooth away.

Suddenly a well-looking personage in a cook's cap and apron, and with a decided twinkle in his eye, appeared in the midst of the company, and, apologizing for the delay, vanished as quickly, in a fit of laughter at the circle of astonished faces. From his heart the master loved a joke, and he was never tired of watching its effect upon his visitors.

"So dear, so delightful, so unique!" the Squeed party agreed, and Lady Jane hinted that it "reminded her of the old Romans," but in what particular she did not go on to explain. Mrs. Lushington said, rather irrelevantly, that personally she rather liked Romanists and their ways, they were so picturesque; at which Roland cast a side glance at Brabant, who affecting not to notice it, sulked apart, superciliously biting the ends of his moustache.

When St. Maur reappeared he was in his ordinary loose velvet coat, and he led the way into the dining-room with the formidable name, where a sociable round table was laid. All one side was thrown open to the air, with only the glowing shafts of the ambulacrum for enclosure; and through these one gazed as from a daïs on the court of fountains, the lane of lanes, and upon the trees of the park, tremulous in the heat haze beyond. The day was one of those that remind one of the tropics, and for a few hours transform this country into a very land of the sun. Screens of transparent mother-o'-pearl, rosing indescribably in the light, were drawn across where it struck, and together with the loaded orange and oleander trees, whereon was far more of bloom than of leaf, tempered its radiance to an enchanting gloom.

The numbers were not evenly divided, as there were, if one may use such an expression, too many ladies, a not unusual feature of the day; but the gentleman in the cassock and Roman collar made himself so agreeable and attentive, that he was equal to half a dozen at least. He gave out a Latin grace for the table, and was altogether so very priestly, that had it not been that in the course of the meal he refused mustard, on the score of its being a saint's day—"one little act of self-denial in honour of our dear patron," —he would never have been looked upon with suspicion.

But to begin at the beginning. Mrs. Lushington, who was growing so rapidly at her ease that one trembled, set the conversation on its legs by lackadaisically remarking as she furled her fan,—

"Now I call those screens a really capital idea; is it your own, dear Lord St. Maur? To my mind they are more truly decorative than the cane window-blinds, or the muslin ones with the bows. Banner-screens are very nice, but they have got *rather* common. But you ought to have some flower-boxes, they are selling lovely ones, oh! quite lovely ones, in the Edgeware Road. Dear old early English subjects. 'Little Bo-peep,' and 'Miss Muffit,' and 'Jack Horner,' you know. I think it such a great thing if you can be amusing as well as ornamental, isn't it?" This she said so coyly, and with such meaning, that the gallant host could do nothing but admit it, with tender reciprocity. "And why, oh! why did you select this peculiar period for your house?" she asked, riveting him with languorous eyes and head aside.

"Because, my dear madam, civilization, beauty, and refinement reach the highest point in the Græco-Roman." Then, seeing by her eyes that he was flying too high for her, he changed his tone. "Perhaps you were not aware, he laughed, that in many things the Greeks would look upon us as ignorant barbarians. Think to begin with, in what superb condition they kept themselves with their baths and ointment, their games and their open-air lives. Do you know, that by the mere use of ointments and the strigel, the flesh of even an old person may be brought to look like waxen opal."

"Indeed! Really?" she gave a languid flirt of her fan. She was lost in thought, which fructified a week later in the ordering of an actual strigel, copied from the antique, for she never let anything escape her which was likely to prove of use.

To finish the episode, now we are upon it; she, either through incapacity or inexperience, happening to try it on her neck for the first time in the secrecy of her chamber, almost cut her head off, and when sufficiently recovered she ordered it to be buried by her maid. This was one of her failures, but that young person, profiting by the lesson, reserved the strigel for herself, and in time became very adroit in the use of it.

This, however, was still in the womb of time.

Mrs. Lushington changed the conversation. "And you've no chair-backs, now do let me work you some."

"Thank you so very much, but—I—ah—to tell the truth, that's a point I haven't cleared up; but I don't think the—ah—Romans—used them, and so, perhaps, I hardly could, at least in this room."

"And you've no china. I miss the china. I couldn't *live* without it. One can't fix one's *real* affections on these things as one can on china. Now, I've a teapot at home. I can't tell you what it is to me. Do you know, I have learned to *love* that teapot with all its quiet little ways."

St. Maur turned to Lady Jane with some haste. "Let me see, I think all your family are great in taste, Lady Jane?"

"It's 'eaven on earth," replied Lady Jane promptly. She was very deaf, and did not look up, for she was at that moment engaged in making the uttermost out of the final drop of soup, with a fragment of bread, a fork, a spoon, and several fingers. The host quailed for the pattern on his plate, but he did not answer—modesty forbade him.

"It's 'eaven on earth, that's what I call it," repeated Lady Jane decidedly, dropping her implements with a crash and a sigh, "and I was brought up at Court, ye know." She seized St. Maur by the sleeve, and dragged him down, whispering confidentially, "If such as

you and me don't know what's what, I wonder
who does; y' see, you and I were born in—the
purple."

"Quite so, quite so; and have you taken a
house in town this season?" asked St. Maur,
changing the subject.

"No, I'm still in my own little place at
Putney. I always say, no place like Putney.
I've never ceased thanking my doctor for
ordering me there. The people of Putney
look down on Londoners, y' know," and she
primly straightened her knife and fork, "and
I've so many friends there, y' see everybody's
very glad to know me."

"Naturally, naturally."

Why has not Lady Jane been described?
To be honest, because it goes against the grain,
and because, to the present reader, such a person
must be ludicrously unimaginable. What? a
lady of rank—by her own showing brought up
at Court, ugly, vulgar, cringing, disgusting in
her habits, and dropping her h's—preposterous! The public would never stand it, a
public of costermongers would not stand it, and
you are asked to believe that an aristocracy
would! Alas! it is so, but these were funny
times. She shall be left a good deal to the
imagination.

Mrs. Lushington had been chilly to her *fiancé*,
as has been said. That he should have failed to
find her among the five or ten thousand people
in the Row that morning secretly aggrieved her,
and the introduction to Miss Grey was in itself a
parable which he should take to heart. But St.

Maur so particularly addressed him and so often, even asking his advice about some matter of drapery, that she quickly veered round. And Lady Jane remarked that "the young man, though hardly what her niece might have looked for,"—and the old crossed eyes waxed very soft upon St. Maur, for there was yet time if a better arrangement offered—" was still a nice young man, but too pretty, much too pretty, and they said he wore silk dressing-gowns, which didn't soot young men."

The dear, crumpled old lady, with her wizened, parchment skin and blear eyes, was wearing a primrose satin bonnet, which had strings of maroon velvet, and her doubled-up little atomy of a figure was clothed throughout to match.

" My ideas may be peculiar," replied St. Maur, " but to my mind he should never be out of fancy dress, he should be set to gladden the world in satin and lace."

" Oh, shocking! immoral!" came a shrill squeak, and Lady Jane threw up the joints of her claws; " I'm surprised at you."

" Now," laughed the host, " if you suggested that some of your sex would look better in broadcloth, I might be disposed to agree with you; but for him certainly I should say a doublet of crimson satin, a plumed hat, and a scarf of old point, and I should put a jewelled rapier in his hand—and then—why then, I think I should set him up in a cabinet."

" I think it would be 'ighly improper," croaked his listener, bending over her plate, and uncertain as to how much of this might be serious. "It's *wicked* to dress a man in satin, it's so "—sniff—" unmanly, quite unsuitable to any but the fair sex." And she glanced complacently at the sheeny wrinkles that spread over her shrivelled bust, straightened her crooked spine as far as it was possible, and pulled her " body " down.

" Well, well, the garb of male humanity is, after all, a secondary matter from the æsthetic point ; but it is rather melancholy to foresee that we, stamped as we are by our clothes with the hall-mark of a counter-jumping age, shall be the laughing-stock of posterity. It is very bad, but not quite so bad as it was ; we no longer wear black cloth coats and open shirt-fronts by day, or fly-away silk bows as people did in 1850, or one-button gloves —pretty, graceful thing a one-button glove. It is an awful thing to be told, wear so and so, or forfeit all the privileges of society among your fellows ; but what I chiefly object to in all this, and what I should still object to, even if the fashion were the most perfect ever invented, is the surrendering of that individuality which is priceless to character, and essential to manhood. I have a good many friends who have been kind enough to listen to my notions, and to each in turn I have said, For Heaven's sake, my dear fellow, cut your hair long, or cut it short, or curl your hat-brim, or straighten it, which ever you like, try something a little different from everybody else. It is annoying to talk to Brown for ten minutes before you find it's Robinson. Our present standards are

eccentric. I am inclined to think beauty and
bravery, chivalry and comeliness, most of which
things we have knocked out of the qualifications of
the modern gentleman, went very well together."

But Lady Jane shook her head, and closed
the subject with a snap, the more viciously
because it had caused her to miss a favourite
entrée, which was now banished past recall.
Miss Grey, who sat on the other side, here took
up the thread; for some minutes her eyebrows
had been lifting perceptibly, as she realized
Lady Jane.

" I have always imagined that it was Puri-
tanism which is responsible for our national
ugliness."

" Undoubtedly," replied Lord St. Maur turning to her, delighted to get back to his ordinary
tone, for a discussion at the top of one's voice
is exhausting, and he perforce had to talk to
the table as well as to Lady Jane. " There's a
great deal to be said for the dark ages for all
their darkness; undoubtedly it was the Reformation and its offspring that converted the old
England, the England of beauty and romance,
into the howling wilderness of moral and physical debasement which it afterwards became.
The poor-house, the mad-house, the slums and
Little Bethel, these were the first-fruits of the
Reformation. The gilt ginger-bread of the
gin palace, the smoke-begrimed brick boxes in
which Londoners live and die, these, also, are
its lineal descendants. There was good, too,
through all the evil, great good; but it was
bought at a heavy price, beauty faded away with

the old religion. Beauty was first of all stigmatized as sinful, and then somehow it came to be vulgar, which it is even now to some extent, but not to the extent of being common. Ha! ha!"

"Yes, the penalty was heavy, but I suppose we deserved it," said Miss Grey thoughtfully.

"I fancy so: we are a nation of perverts and apostates, or were in the sixteenth century; a nation that at the mere word of a brutal tyrant changed our beliefs as we would have changed our coats. Society was so constituted that it was possible, it glorified the deed and made it the fashion; and from that society our own is descended—a pretty pedigree. That is one of the objections I have to society."

Here Mrs. Lushington, who had caught the last words, put in, "*I* always say that the people one meets in society are *the* great objection to it."

A veiled flash shot from under Miss Grey's long lashes, and was not lost upon St. Maur, who replied, "I have thought so myself sometimes."

"And how sad it is one sees so few of the old families nowadays," continued Mrs. Lushington, airily. A remark of this nature should be made airily, or not at all.

"I'm inclined to think there's a little misconception about families; we are all much of an age. It's really a matter of keeping a diary. Hodge is as old as Howard, but Hodge has not been as careful with his records."

As Mrs. Lushington was driving four or five-in-hand as usual, and keeping all her side of the table in talk, she did not hear this; indeed, she was one of those people who look upon an answer as a superfluous interruption to the current of their own ideas. St. Maur turned to Miss Grey again.

"I remember the time, and it's not altogether past and gone yet, when in many families a young girl might not look in the glass without being thought vain; when if she put a ribbon into her hair, or a rose into her belt, to please her lover, she was set upon by her female relatives as if she were one of the lost. Or if she cut her hair to a fringe, she was considered by these peculiar people—half of whom were secretly dying to follow her example all the time—a social pariah. The things women have to suffer from women have often seemed to me intolerable."

"Ah! my dear Lord St. Maur," rushed in Mrs. Lushington, "I hear the dreadful things you are saying; but what are these things in comparison to those which a refined and delicate woman suffers at the hand of man?" The table, for some reason or other, chose to laugh at this remark, and the speaker joined in—why not? There was evidently a joke somewhere; not that she was at the trouble of discerning it, for she rambled off afresh into incoherent chatter.

"Happily," went on Miss Grey, ignoring the interruption, "I only know of these terrible things by hearsay; but how inhuman to blight the poor little spring-tide of a woman's life. It is, as you say, I believe, a part of these people's religion to do it; but nothing can alter the terrible conditions of a woman's existence—conditions that men never realize. Before we are well started in the race we begin to go off, and the world is able to say, 'Ah! she's not so young as she was.' How can a woman ever be as young as she was when she is *passée* before she has had time to look round—say at three and twenty? Then we go on burdening the earth, older and plainer, and more dependent day by day, until we are eighty, perhaps ninety," she glanced at Lady Jane, "or it may be a hundred. Oh! it's all a horrible mistake from beginning to end. A man's gifts are for life—a woman's but for a year or two; and before she is trained to use them they are gone. She is over-weighted in all her conditions, even her clothes are a slavery to her."

"In one thing I differ from you; people need not be as ugly as they often are. If a woman's mind is beautiful with her body, she will keep a beauty and a fascination of her own to the last—even for men. We all know dear old ladies who have done so, and in the religious orders, I have sometimes seen nuns who have lived to a great age, with smooth, white complexions, perfectly unwrinkled, and with the merry light of an eternal youth in their eyes. Depend upon it, this ugly world is at the bottom of all our wrinkles."

Miss Grey sighed. "You are a believer."

"Yes, in the sex," he said, more lightly. "By degrees they are lifting themselves, but it is in their own hands. I doubt whether we men can do much to help them."

" When I think of what their influence is, and what they might do with their few hours of power, and what they do do, I am hopeless for them. As a rule, a girl's influence is out out of all proportion to her sense if she is pretty.

" When she is just out of the schoolroom, and her ears are still tingling from the governess, she has a wonderful power put into her hands; the wisest men listen to her, and she can sometimes thoroughly infect them with her ideas. One morning she wakes up to find all this gone. It is too late to weep, it is gone for ever; and henceforth she may lead the life of a cabbage; indeed that is the life most fitted for her."

" Oh! there are a few things left; she may take up Female Suffrage, charity, sensible clothing."

" She won't at heart; secretly, she sighs for woman's empire," answered Miss Grey, " and to go back to clothes, as a woman always does. The other day, I was at a dress-reform meeting. It was an affair of the mildest. Some rather odd-looking women, peeresses I think, but very badly dressed, read and spoke some very poor speeches from a platform; a heavy, benevolent gentleman, who was with them, said he attributed all his success in life to his having abstained from lacing and high heels. He recommended the colour of ashes as the most wholesome, but he said nothing of the sackcloth, and—and—I think that was nearly all. Then there were peculiar pictures and model dummies about. The improved things, which I admit were repulsive, were deserted, and every woman in the room, and every man too, gathered round the 'frightful examples,' and thought how charming they looked in comparison, and all the girls, I am sure, went away determined to dress up to them as nearly as possible. The reformers go the wrong way, they eschew beauty; and real needs, such as sensible pockets for purse and watch, or protective skirts against London mud, are ignored."

"I must allow," said St. Maur, "that at the bottom of half your troubles in this way and in every other way, is the persistent unfairness of men, and that is the best word I can find for the relations between the two sexes."

"True, they are either extremely over-civil or contemptuously indifferent. I don't know which I dislike the more."

"But things will right themselves, we are on the road; one fault is that we are in too great a hurry. I believe it's a profound truth, that progress is not to be measured by anything under a geologic period. We are apt to forget, I think, that we are a fallen race, working upward—perhaps even to its pristine conditions of perfection."

"And what, I wonder, may those be?"

"Well, there is the idea that perfect man includes woman in his own proper personality, and *vice versá*. It is common sense, the human is single, not dual : woman is merely man under certain additional disabilities."

"I think I must object to that," laughed Miss Grey, "I shall draw the line at the achievement of perfect womanhood."

"You may do worse. The progress of the woman is in reality the progress of the race. I have long been convinced of that. But you never have had fair treatment, and according to the received rate of evolution, hardly will, under ten thousand years, which appears to be about the time it has taken, to transform the man-eating devil-worshipper, into the philosophic philanthropist."

"Talking of that sort of thing," said Brabant, as the speaker stopped in a general pause of the conversation, "reminds me of my friend Professor Van Dam, whom, by the way, I live in hopes of introducing to the civilized world. He was telling me the other day, how he had often murdered children, whom he had previously stolen, and eaten them for breakfast." (Sensation.) "I ought to add, perhaps, that it was in a prior state of existence. He assures me that we all have done the same."

Here a young gentleman, whose part had hitherto been purely ornamental, lisped, "How very, very interesting! The discoveries made every day now, are astonishing, one really wonders where we shall get to at the pace we're going. You see," he said, modestly, finding he had the ear of the company, "I really may claim to know a little on these matters, having been one of the original founders of the Ghost-propagation Society." The public evinced their interest in rapt attention. " I was indeed able to announce to the Society two *great* discoveries, based entirely on my personal observation, only last week. Do you know, but of course you cannot, that ghosts *wear out?* The average duration of a ghost I have found, by actual experience, to be from one to two hundred years. Now, I think I can make this evident. Who, in these days, ever heard of a Norman ghost, for instance? The thing's absolutely unknown, even a mediæval one is rare, most rare, perhaps unique. Now, mark the change when we come to the Stuart and Jacobean periods. We find them comparatively common. From an exceedingly accurate and intelligent series of observations, taken by my grandmother, I have discovered that most of the ghosts of her day were dressed in the clothes of the seventeenth century, whereas it is notorious, quite notorious, that the ghost of to-day is Georgian in date, and makes itself visible in Georgian garments. Ghosts, then, it is plain, do not appear until after a lapse of years, they have their day, grow out of date and die off. Arguing from these premises, it seems quite certain that our immediate posterity will behold these strange visitants in chimney-pot hats and trousers, of which, up to the present time, there has been no single authenticated instance.

" The second discovery is even more important. I have had the good fortune to focus one of these fragile beings through my—ah—eye-glass, thereby setting at rest the question of their objective reality, once and for ever—I ah—"

At this moment the ivory fans of the ceiling became agitated, and as they whirled, diffusing a delightful breeze, down through the silver tracery of the panelling were wafted clouds of rose petals in a miniature snowstorm, until they were littered thick on the table and the pavement, and as the attendants trod them under foot, their inmost fragrance smote the nostril, and filled it with delight.

"Charming! charming!" echoed the whole table, and the host laughed.

"I'm glad you like it. I flatter myself we've improved on Nero: he used to have bouquets thrown, which affords too great a scope for practical joking. Now, this is so simple, I should like to explain it to you. An axle, a crank, and a fly-wheel, which is moved by the ventilation of the kitchen chimney—these are all—"

"It *is* a good idea," interposed Mrs. Lushington, "when I set up house again, I must try something of the sort."

Mr. Brabant looked at her sternly, but she furled her fan very casually, and sipped her wine; and one of the sisters, Bud, leaned across the table, and said in an audible whisper to Horror, that it was exactly what she had always expected Maria would do.

Here the little modest woman, whose name was Wigway, and whose voice had not been heard before, said, "I should like to know on what terms you stand with your housemaids, Lord St. Maur ? "

" My dear madam," he replied, " tell it not in Gath ! I have at my beck a trusty body-guard of charwomen, and my handmaids, for the most part, are carpenters and polishers, hewers of stone and drawers of water."

Meantime Roland, who was seated by the great man of the occasion, had had a little conversation with him. The ex-Minister, who was good-natured enough in private life, and generally speaking, when off his stilts, happened to be a particular friend of the host, and as such had heard of his neighbour. Now it so happened that this gentleman—Mr. Smith by name—had been considerably exercised in mind for years past, by this eternal Catholic question. Not that he was inclined Romewards himself, he was too good a " protestant " to have any religion whatever. His ideas on the subject may be briefly summed up thus :—

" This is a religious country, and one of entire religious freedom and equality ; here in our midst is a great religious organization of the highest class, though of a foreign character, and numbering about two millions. Socially speaking, it is excellent in every way, so far as one can judge, it is on the side of law and order, on the side of government in fact, yet it may be said to be wholly unrepresented, and without a voice in any public department, for Irish members don't represent it here. If it be a question of Roman Catholic pauper lunatics, instead of finding an accredited spokesman of their own on the board, we have to go round and unearth a cardinal or a peer, and the peer certainly won't know too much about it. This is awkward for us, if it isn't for them. It is their own concern if they don't care to have that voice in the government to which their numbers and social status entitle them. But it appears to me to be a question whether this really is the case among them, whether there may not be men whose abilities and position would not naturally force them to the front, if the cold chill of ecclesiastical censure did not fall on any attempt at a forward movement. How is it that never a man among them has taken a place before the country? They have men who should be leaders, but they are without followers, they represent no authority, and the Church of Rome wants authority, and doesn't much care where it comes from. Hence individual action is always discredited, until it reaches that pitch of success which means authority, when it is accepted blindly. Certainly the man who first succeeds in amalgamating the Catholic vote in this country, becomes a power of the first order."

Of course, being an "outsider," Mr. Smith had long ago decided that the fount and origin of this paralysis was to be sought in the sanctuary. How far he was right, it is equally, of course, impossible to tell. He himself was a Conservative, but not to the lengths to which that party was pushing in the struggle for existence, and he was wont to say that when Catholicism did take its place, it must be side by side with that party, because of all the Churches she was the most essentially conservative—a feat of logic in which it was not given to every one to follow him, as there were many who thought that religious, was somewhat wide apart from political conservancy.

After he had talked for some time with Roland on the subject of Ancient British pottery (which he maintained was equal to the Greek fictile ware of all but the very best period), and when he found that, although the latter was not versed in the subject, he talked on it rather better than a man usually talks, on one of which he knows nothing, Mr. Smith bethought him that here might be a recruit to be educated, and forthwith sounded him as to his views.

" What are you going to do with your life? You ought to be one of us," he said.

" A leader of the Opposition? " laughed Roland.

" Why not? How old are you? "

" Twenty-four."

" Well ! when you are still ten years younger than I am at this moment—you should be that comfortably. You've the physique, which is half the battle ; and if you can talk politics as well as you talk pottery (I see you're not up in it, but you talk common sense), you must succeed. We want you—want you sadly, and the need of you grows greater and greater. We can't have two millions of the best citizens in the country unrepresented, and we must have representative men who have worked their way

up. Your social standing as a body is first-
rate, quite first-rate. But we want men for
the Commons, and we must have 'em somehow.
You see you're such a splendid Conservative
force—I mean even non-politically—and the
more the Radical element spreads, the more
you'll be wanted on both sides of the House.
Oh! we've seen this a long time; but you're
like a parcel of eels, somehow we can't lay hold
of you. The few spokesmen you have are
peers. Well! the peers mean a good deal
more than they used to do, but they're not
enough by themselves, however clever they
may be; and yours, happening to be all hereditary ones, are not remarkable for brains. I
can't make you people out—none of us can.
You're such an impracticable lot. You hang
back everywhere, as if there was something to
be ashamed of; and yet, when one comes to
make inquiries, one can find nothing very bad
about you, barred this damning point. If a
good man does go over to you he's snuffed
out; we never hear of him again. Now, you
young fellows with fortune and leisure, it's
your business to change all this. Tell your
Cardinals, as they can't speak from the Treasury bench, that there must be some one there
to speak for them. Work your way up in the
natural order of things, get yourself well
laughed at to begin with; nothing like it—
impresses your individuality on the public.
Admit and repudiate your mistakes, happily for
most of us, 'the House' has a d—d bad memory,
they like to see a man come up smiling after

failure. Hammer, hammer, hammer, it's the
only way. It's not outside prejudices you have
to combat, but your own internal ones. Surely
there is a party among you opposed to the
questionable manipulation of every subject by
means of a few paid tools. You're aware, I
suppose, that under present conditions, any
expression of opinion professing to emanate
from your body is a laughing-stock to every
honest-minded man. And look at the way
your peers voted the other day on the Concessions Bill, twelve on the one side, twelve on
the other, and there was one pair. Pretty
typical, I think."

So far the statesman's views had coincided
singularly with Roland's own, but his conclud-
ing sentence proved where they were to part.
It was delivered in an undertone, and was this.
" Now I'll tell you the best thing you can do.
Get on to some big man of your own lot, and
stick to him. Stick to him like—like a leech,
until you're able to strike out for yourself."

Roland laughed aloud.

" Hardly my line, I'm afraid, sir ; but up to
this point I've followed you very closely."

" Ah ! you won't laugh some day, when you
know the world as I do," said Mr. Smith good-
naturedly, sipping some wonderful champagne.
" You see, you Romans have no connection; that's
what you want to establish, a governing connection ; and the only way you can work it, is
through your aristocracy. There's His Royal
Highness now. Begin as his deputy-assistant
secretary."

" He certainly wouldn't have me, for I'm a species of radical. My idea of a true basis for our representation is Ireland, the only Catholic country left."

" Then you are probably a revolutionist as well," said Mr. Smith; " but, dear friend, a man at your age has no politics—can't have— why, at twenty-four, I was a *sans-culotte* myself, and a little blood-letting on a Continental barricade did me no harm. But Catholic Englishmen should not go to Ireland for their seats."

" I am not sure of that. The debt we owe to Ireland can never be repaid. She it was that kept the faith alive through three centuries of persecution, and finally won us our liberties : in what have we shown our gratitude ? Some years hence we may get an English representation ; but we must sow before we can reap ; at present our real vantage-ground is Ireland."

" And that is a house divided against itself."

" There you've probed our difficulty to the core, sir ; but if the right man arises he may do wonders ; for my part, I believe that the man makes the age, not the age the man, and the tendency of this Democratic age is to strengthen the hands of the individual, contrary to all expectation. It is something to find a work to one's hand which is worth the doing ; this I take it is the grand difficulty of a beginning, so little *is* worth doing. The next step for a man is, surely, to give a satisfactory answer to the question, ' Who is he ? ' "

" And if he fails, as an English Catholic going

to Ireland in these days is pretty certain to do, what then?"

" Oh! then, why he had better dive and come up again the other side."

His new friend looked him over with marked interest, but shook his head. It will be gathered from their conversation that the political phase of the day was not altogether unlike our own. The same problem to be worked out, it matters little whether it is done by arithmetic or algebra, the data given in each case being equal. Mr. Smith said no more, but mentally resolved that he would keep an eye on the young man for the future, as on a possible recruit, when a titter made its way round the table.

Religion, it appeared, had been on the *tapis* elsewhere, and Miss Rosilla Squeed, who up to this time had hardly ventured on the expression of an opinion, through awe of her surroundings, had so far overcome it as to give out that her great objection to Catholicity, would be the going out to vespers at seven o'clock in the morning. The gentleman in the long black coat and Roman collar, was fairly convulsed at this, and said something about the Rubric; but Miss Squeed, having once taken up her position, clung to it. Nothing would ever induce her to this, she said, especially on a cold morning; she couldn't see anything to laugh at in it; nor in the fact of Protestants—and here she looked very angrily at the reverend gentleman—introducing all that sort of stuff. This rather wild shot told;

the clergyman who had refused the mustard, had not disdained the dry champagne, and this had put him in a pleasant humour; but he quailed before the awful word.

" My dear young lady," he said in an altered voice, " when you say ' Protestant,' I really don't know what you mean one little bit, I—I give you my word I don't; it's a term I "—here, as the table was generally listening, he raised his voice—" a term I have never really been able to comprehend. There are various branches of the great Catholic Church, the sound " (a voice—" yes, and the rotten "). There was another titter, but nobody looked the least like the voice; all were apparently listening with intense interest to the speaker, who, waving aside the obnoxious inuendo, went on.

" I was about to say, when I was perhaps a little rudely interrupted, that the sound of the word ' Protestant' is obnoxious in itself. Now I never go up to the pulpit—"

" What does he say about going down to the pit?" croaked Lady Jane, with her hand to her ear. This misconception was set right, but it put the speaker out.

" What I mean is, that at my own little place, I flatter myself that even members of the older, and perhaps more venerable branch of the Christian Church, will find the marks of the—" (" beast," came a ventriloquial whisper). " The marks of the Church are four," he continued, raising his voice to drown interruption. " We are one," and he laid a well-shaped hand on the breast of his cassock. "It is tolerably well known, and indeed I will not pretend to deny, that my Bishop takes a slightly different view from myself, but he knows better than to interfere; this is mere detail; consequently, however, we are one, virtually one. We are holy—wholly holy, I may hope," and he beat his breast with his clenched hand. "We are Catholic; to deny that would be absurd, that is *the* great point. We are apostolic, yes; I think we may venture to assert that, too; we are thoroughly apostolic." With a last blow, the white fingers waved gracefully and emphatically out of sight.

"I tell you what," he said, leaning over confidentially to the other side of the table, "you should see our processions of the Holy Ghost. There's nothing like 'em in all London."

The table, however, did not rise to this, the speaker did.

"I shall not be breaking up your delightful party, my dear Lord, I trust; now pray, *pray* don't get up, but I have some lady penitents at half-past three, and I have to go to Turnham Green. If I might just retire—one moment—your charming oratory—so grateful—five minutes' recollection can do me no harm. And, by the way, if any of your friends," and he looked round, "could get me the pattern of those two sweet little maniples from Farm Street, I should be *so* much obliged. Good-bye, good-bye, so many, many thanks."

And he was gone, like some very strange vision.

"He's a good fellow," said St. Maur, in tones of semi-apology, "but he hardly does himself justice."

"I didn't think he failed on that score," blurted out Mr. Smith, who seemed rather cross, as indeed did all the Church of England contingent. Lady Jane was in a quiescent stage, and her plumes were nodding, but she muttered something about "foolery" and her "young days."

"It's too bad of you, St. Maur," whispered Roland. "I believe you collect people here as if they were wild beasts, to study their habits, but," (aloud) "is he really gone to say his prayers?"

"I can't understand a man really believing in the efficacy of prayer," exclaimed Mr. Smith, aggressively; "it's such a palpable imposture. What I mean is," for he saw a peculiar expression in the faces of his audience, "it may have its ultimate effects and all that, but so far as anything visible and tangible goes, why you can prove it." Silence.

Far in the background, to speak metaphorically, sat Miss Wigway, as usual watching for her opportunity—it had come. It was her *rôle* to pose, wherever possible, as Defender of the Faith (in capitals). Here was a chance not only of playing this part, but actually of having a discussion with the great Mr. Smith; certainly the opportunity of her life, and one which would enable her ever after to begin a sentence with, "I was the other day discussing with a member of the late Cabinet the, &c., &c." To Miss Wigway, as to Father Snippet, heaven was no strange place, and the manners and customs of its inhabitants were no secret to her. She knew all about any saint you liked to name, and what this one or that was doing (for had she not herself often set them tasks for that very day)? Further, she had very definite data as to purgatory, and as to who was there, and who was not, and she would tell you without hesitation. Or, if you happened to go to her for advice, you might be stunned by the information that "Our Lady wouldn't like this, or St. Peter wouldn't care for that." She had now been in the fold for nearly six months, so must be looked upon as an authority. Her heart throbbed and her head swam, as with all eyes turned upon her, she took up the gauntlet, but she went bravely on.

"I suppose it's impossible for those outside the pale," she said with cold and deliberate sarcasm, "really to appreciate prayer, and the luxury of the communion of saints; but I can assure the gentleman who has just spoken, that I have myself, daily and hourly, the most substantial answers to prayer. For instance, if I'm in any difficulty, I speak to St. Joseph. I did this morning, and the answer I received was *most* satisfactory. He's so used to my ways now, and he once told me—"

But Mr. Smith couldn't stand this, and some of the faithful were feeling rather hot at the sweeping style of the new broom, when he interrupted,—

"I can't say anything about the saints, my dear madam; I don't know the saints, and they don't know me. I mean prayer, as it's generally understood. Pray for anything you like, and see if you'll get it, if you don't set about it in other ways. Pray for one sick man, and send another to the hospital, and see which will get well first. I'll give you a positive proof of what I mean. You will probably admit that the Sovereign is the best prayed-for person in the kingdom. In every church and chapel on every Sunday, and in most well-ordered private families, there is the special prayer said for him or her. Are you aware, my dear madam," he asked, impressively planting his thumb far into the midst of the table, "that statistics prove the Sovereigns to be the shortest-lived class in the realm?"

Miss Wigway gathered her skirts, and waited a moment; a supercilious smile curled her lip.

"Indeed," she said, "no, I was not aware of it, but I'm not the least surprised, not the least; and I will venture to say you have answered yourself with your own mouth. The prayer for the Sovereign—may I ask, have you ever noticed the attitude of the congregation during that prayer? In heretical places of worship it naturally counts for little, and in our own it comes at the end of the service, when people are buttoning their gloves, pinning their veils, brushing their hats, or hunting for their umbrellas. Prayer so said, would infallibly not only *not* be heard, but would *most certainly* have a negative effect, if it had any at all. Hence the proportionately short life of your kings and queens."

Again there was silence, followed by a subdued buzz of applause and laughter. Miss Wigway sat stock-still, her hands nervously plucking at her dress; she could see and hear nothing distinctly, but what did that matter?— her thunderbolt had fetched home. Mr. Smith threw up the sponge.

"Had you there, had you there fairly!" laughed St. Maur, delighted. "Give in gracefully, Smith. Now, if you are ready, shall we go and take our coffee in the aviary?" and he gave his arm to Lady Jane.

The scene had been perfect, and to think that it was hardly six months since Miss Wigway (an enthusiastic Ritualist) had been wont to say reprovingly to her "Roman friends," if they spoke of going to the Catholic church, "No, my dear, *we*"—mincing her words severely —"we are *Catholics*, you are *Romanists;* we go to *church*, you to *chapel*." And if the building in question happened to be a cathedral, with towers and a dome, and the one Miss Wigway frequented did not possess so much as a belfry —this made no difference; and now she was so perfect a pattern of ladylike Catholicism, that she went to confession once a week, and scrupled not to keep priest and fellow-penitents waiting three-quarters of an hour at a time. Indeed, so protracted was her penitence, that ill-natured people said she told her friends' faults as well as her own.

From such small matters as have been here

related, some idea may be gathered of the religious "thought" of the day from a social point of view. The gross bigotry, the monstrous flippancy, the cheerful, unaffected dishonesty with which the topic was everywhere handled, were its chief characteristics. It was the one subject which it seemed impossible for the Englishman to meet, and look in the face fairly and squarely. With the bulk of the upper classes religion was a mere matter of respectability, and a man adhered to it, without reasoning, because it was his father's, or out of deference to the memory of his aunts. The pulpit was too often a mere platform for the airing of the niceties (or nastinesses) of the particular preacher's theologic (or theo-illogic) crotchets, and for abuse of those who differed therefrom. All creeds were offenders in this, and an honest man could only turn away in shame and indignation. With such teaching, it is not to be wondered at if many faltered, and if the half-educated, semi-savage denizens of the drawing-room, of the Squeed type (who formed a great part of the congregations), did not make any remarkable progress on the pathway of perfection. With these, church-going in a figging-out was the Alpha and the Omega.

The first principles of religion were misunderstood. If a man lost wife or child through a bad drain, he fancied he proved piety by affirming that it was the will of God. The nemesis of Nature upon ignorance had yet to be made plain.

CHAPTER VIII.

T HE party filed out through the long suite of ante-rooms, but their progress was slow, for there were a hundred miracles of grace and ingenuity to be admired by the way. Mr. Brabant found himself fortunate in having secured the beauty to himself for the moment; and she, too, was interested, for she knew his name well, and had read his poems, and she found in him a notion of wit which was altogether a novelty in London society. Then also he was like one of her cherished *penates;* but critical was Miss Grey at all times, and she found fault with him on this score. Only the latent strength of a god, she said to herself, should be so clothed—in a man such a delicacy must needs be weak. To do Brabant justice, he had long since discarded the "beauty man," and was never so happy as when, in an old dressing-gown and spectacles, he pursued his congenial work of flaying his fellow-creatures at home. But, being a poet, as was explained before, he thought it necessary, in the interests of his race, to dress for the public.

She laughed with him, and said, as they passed from room to room, that " never had she breathed so freely in any show place before. Usually they had given her fits of melancholia, with their gems of antiquity side by side with modern advertisement groups in plaster; but here was a house without a particle of plush, without a square inch of stained glass, a red engraving, a Chippendale chair, or even a plate upon the wall. Here the sunflower was not, neither was sage-green known at all." And her companion replied, with some little scorn, that "such things were good for the æsthetic grocer and his crew, but this was a temple of art fit for the immortals, or for an English gentleman." From this it will be assumed that his ideal of an English gentleman was a high one, and was founded rather upon the possibilities of the future than on the actualities of the past.

"This would have been impossible a few years back," he went on, "but modern discovery, invention, and facilities of travel and transport, have brought most of it within the reach of every well-to-do citizen. Now we have to make the people discontented and fretful with the hideousness of their surroundings, to show them that it is all their own fault, and their own making, and that even beauty is possible for them. Once you implant the germ of the feeling for art and beauty, in the mind of the lowest savage that prowls the street, he becomes a conservative force, he is no longer a mere wild beast ravening for destruction."

"I cannot tell you," said Sybil, "how that

theory appeals to me; will the country take it seriously to heart in time ? "

" I hope so; we are working towards it, many of us hard enough, Heaven knows ! " and a wearied enthusiasm lit his face. " We have opened all the museums and galleries free, at last, on Sundays, after a bitter struggle, and many private owners are very generous. The ' Villa,' as you perhaps know, is thrown open to the people when Lord St. Maur is away, and he has made it over to the nation at his death. He gives concerts in the great room we have just left every week, free of charge, and I am told he does not remove a single ornament. It is a magnificent faith, but I believe he has never lost a farthing by it. No man can do more than he."

While they chatted thus, more taken up with each other than is usually the case with new acquaintances, an ominously threatening eye was upon them both, although they were happily ignorant of it. Brabant went on to tell an amusing story about a lady neighbour of their host's in Park Lane, who had followed the fashion, and let in the many-headed beast every Sunday.

" There was not much to be seen, but there was the soap in the soap-dish in her bedroom, and the bath, and the lace on the curtains, and the blue bows and the rest, which was very interesting in its way. St. Maur did not go quite so far—he kept his tooth-brush to himself."

At the end of the suite of ante-rooms lay the

great staircase under the dome, which the party
were beginning to ascend, St. Maur still leading the way with Lady Jane, when an accident
of a sufficiently startling and inexplicable nature
occurred. Without warning, a shower of icy-
cold water descended from above, pouring in-
discriminately down the necks of half the
company. With a scream Lady Jane shook
herself free, and the party scattered on all
sides. On looking up a pair of hands might
have been observed squeezing out a sponge of
not particularly clean water, through the onyx
balustrade at the top; but this was all. St.
Maur sprang up the staircase in three leaps,
but was only in time to see a pair of heels
vanishing in the distance behind a heavy *por-
tière*, and to catch a burst of faint laughter.
The heels were gentlemanly-looking, and
there was no trace of petticoat above them.
All the same his suspicions amounted to a certainty, and he muttered, " Cousin Vic for a
fiver ! " But pursuit was hopeless.

He glanced round the landing. On the white
and gold tesselations of the pavement, where a
shaft of sunlight shot through a cluster of
purple and yellow roses, stood a tin basin of
water with a block of ice in it and a sponge, and
he had only just time to slip all this beside a
marble nymph, where he trusted the greenery
would conceal it, when his guests were
upon him. The attentions of the party were
still directed to the renovation of Lady Jane,
who was more frightened than hurt, although
soap-suds are not the best thing in the world

for primrose satin. She and Mrs. Lushington, who had also the benefit of the *douche*, were secretly indignant, and the smile with which they both declared that it was excessively funny, and that the damage was really nothing at all, was pitiful to see.

Meanwhile two other visitors had joined the rest from below, as they came up, and they were infinitely distressed at the occurrence, and most assiduous in their efforts to repair the wreck of Lady Jane. These were Lady Glendore, and Lady Victoria Nage, and the latter was especially severe on the stupidity of the thing, on the strength of being a cousin of the house.

" How'do, Villiers ? " she said to St. Maur as she reached the top ; " too hot for anything, ain't it ? Thought we'd come and cool ourselves in your marble halls. You're always pretty cool here."

" Yes, we're pretty cool, some of us at least, I admit," laughed St. Maur, for he had noted the patent shoe and had no longer any painful doubts.

" But I say, is this the latest thing out of the Greek ? I thought you only chucked down flower petals and rose-water on the nobs of your guests ; soap-suds are something new, and to my mind they make a beastly mess, worse than your rose leaves and rubbish. Dear, dear Lady Jane, I am so sorry to see you such a figure. Here, let's try and take the creases out of you, and straighten you up a bit ;" and she pulled that unfortunate old lady here and there, slapped her, rubbed her, and shook her, and finally declared she looked a world the better

for it, when the poor woman had been
" knocked " almost silly—comparatively speaking, that is—for it was no great distance to
knock her.

Then Lady Glendore took up the cue. " St.
Maur," she said stamping, " how often have I
told you that your charwomen would bring you
to grief ? Charwomen and swagger combined,
the two things don't go together. But, Vicky
dear, what *are* you looking at ? "

" Why, I declare," ejaculated Lady Victoria,
" if I haven't found out all about it. Look
here! it's so hot, that I'm blessed if this improper young woman has not been washing
herself in iced water over the banisters! " And
she pushed back a rose-bush. " There ! "

At the foot of the nymph, who had plainly
been bathing, and who now was busy with her
towel, stood the tin basin and the sponge.
This was irresistible, and not the least delightful
part of it was the utterly unconcerned look
of the marble maid, as she sat facing the
company sublimely undismayed by the discovery.

" Vic," said St. Maur under his breath,
" wait till I catch you alone."

It was no matter of surprise to him that
evening, on going to his room, to find in
succession, his bed in apple-pie order, the
sleeves of his dressing-gown sewn up, a spur
rowel outwards in each of his slippers, and
a boot-last in one of his gloves, which was
strained to bursting point. Such was the very
crême de la crême of the high-bred wit of the

day, as understood by the smartest set and their humble imitators. It was apt to pall after a time; after you were five-and-forty, for instance —but this by the way.

" You're going for a smoke, ain't you?" said Lady Glendore, " we'll join you, please;" and Lady Victoria flicked their host over the shoulders with her dog-whip. " Now gee-up, old man!" whereat everybody was vastly entertained, with perhaps one or two exceptions.

The Squeeds looked on with unspeakable envy. " Oh! Bud," said one to the other, " wouldn't you like to do that sort of thing, and everybody admire it! Oh law! what a baw! we're not countesses."

" Things *are* divided unevenly in this world, to be sure," sighed Horror; " it's beastly." The acme of the Squeed ambition, it should be told, was to be invited down to one of certain " good houses," and there to take their share in the Saturnalia which it was the extraordinary custom of the day to license on these occasions. Lady Victoria and Lady Glendore were presiding deities at most of the gatherings; but so far these golden and glorious opportunities had not come nigh unto the Squeeds; and the hope deferred was very heart-sickening.

They had one and all realized profoundly that the eleventh hour was upon them, and that if something were not done now, which once for all should put them " in their proper place," it would be too late. In consequence the most desperate efforts were being made. The mother, as being utterly unpresentable, was kept out of sight; while Lady Jane was put through such a course as would have killed any one less toughened by worldly wickedness.

Their absurd " At homes " were regularly sent to the papers, week after week, and—Mrs. Lushington being a secret but professional paragraphist—were usually inserted. Her own name, "Lushington Squeed," as having a certain ring about it, was always used,—if a man cultivated this species of literature, he could not fail to know it. That was something. Push and impudence would go a long way; an impression was certainly being made. The majority of the society of the day were not only profoundly uninteresting themselves, but had no rational outside interests; and among these the mere repetition of a name, week after week, was found sufficient to awaken an interest, but the work was slow.

The aviary, a sort of summer smoking-room, was in a courtyard, round whose walls, within a zone of glass, flitted a colony of humming-birds, amid a luxuriant growth of their native foliage. The inner walls, which were of masonry, were hidden inches deep in moss and lichen, and many-hued undergrowth; and the atmosphere was kept humid by tiny waterfalls, which welled out at intervals through the moss. There was heat and shelter, light and air, so that the vegetation sprouted, and the flowers blossomed to semi-miraculous perfection. Here, dew-besprinkled, trembled along the marge, an infinite variety of maiden-hair, in rolling beds, interspersed with feathery fronds of other species that rivalled it in delicacy,—a very couch for fairies, and the miniature tree-ferns over-arched it, shooting into the roof; and these, again, were in great gala, twined and hung all about with festoons of radiant blossom, and always, like gems flashed in the sun, the marvellous inhabitants flitted hither and thither, with crest gold-gleaming, and iridescent breast. It was as if you had delved a bit out of some inviolate tropic woodland, brought it home, and set it there, with all its living things entire, in a glass case.

"A paradise without the serpent!" observed Brabant to his betrothed, as he lit a cigar: "did you ever conceive anything so charming?" He spoke good-humouredly, in his ordinary pleasant voice. Miss Grey had drifted off, and he was preparing to enjoy his cheroot. What was his surprise, when the lady addressed turned upon him with a heightened colour, and said fiercely,—

"Oh! of course you think so, why not? Ha! ha!" with an inflection of terrible sarcasm. Her face was inflamed and purple; the veins stood out on her forehead, and her voice was such that Lady Victoria's strident accents sounded sweet and womanly by comparison. It was so loud that half the people turned round, and Bud whispered to Horror,—

"M.'s turned snuffy; I thought she would if he went on spooning with that new woman."

Had she struck Brabant a blow he could scarcely have been more staggered, but he

answered quietly, " Very well, my dear," and
walked away. A man so sensitive that the
smallest thing seldom escaped him, he was
at a loss as to the reason of this outburst.
What vexed him most was that the world
should have heard it. Roland had turned
round and looked him full in the face. It
might have been supposed that it would have
led him to seriously reconsider his position ;
but, no, the *rationale* of engagement and marriage were so imperfectly understood by this
eccentric race, that reason was the last factor
in the composition. Men married every day,
with their eyes open, knowing perfectly well the
effects would be disastrous ; and women no
less. He relit his cigar with outward equanimity, and sauntered round, looking at the
birds ; and Mrs. Lushington, as she gazed after
him, thought that she had never known what
it was to hate a man, or for that matter, a
woman, before. Her breast heaved as from
a shock, she could scarcely keep back her
tears ; yet, if she had been paid for it (and she
would do a great deal for money), she could
not have put her thoughts into words. A
brute instinct raged within her ; and such
social training as she had received was not
calculated to assuage it.

The party were now dispersing—the great
man, Mr. Smith, was gone ; there was no
one else of whom Lady Victoria was afraid.
From her point of view the rest were nobodies, and she had no hesitation in mono-
polizing her cousin, and playing any pranks

that occurred to her. "Well," she said, pinching his arm, "you are a rum lot, Villiers, and what a rum lot you do get round you. You've got my professional beauty here. I discovered her ages before any of you cockney duffers. Yes, and I started that affair." The lovers had wandered apart, under pretext of the birds, and her eyes followed them with interest.

"I began that for them at my place," she said, with a certain pride, which proved there was something of the woman left in her. "They hate me all the same. I'm sure of it; but she's good form, I admit."

Here a sigh—was it for her own womanhood?

"Yes, you selfish fellow, you may give me a cigar, if you've got a good one."

"My dear Vic, I can't have a wolf in my fold. You'll play the mischief with my ewe lambs, and I've several of them here. Go and inoculate Lady Jane with your views; or some of her nieces; you won't do them so much harm."

"What! are those three lumps Squeeds? I could have told it with my eyes shut," she said, with profound conviction.

Meanwhile Brabant had smoked his cigar, and equalized his mind. It was absurd, there must have been some mistake; now he thought of it, of course—he must have been blind—she had been splashed, and the grievance was the best bonnet, enough to upset any woman. To smooth matters, he made up his mind to the sacrifice of the rest of the day—no slight one for so busy a man. Mrs. Lushington also had sobered, feeling there had been a mistake;

and when he came up and asked her, with a semblance of kindly enthusiasm, if she would not like to do a little shopping or calling, in which case he was at her service, she received him graciously as of yore, and looked as sweet as possible. She pursed her mouth, put her head a little on one side, smiled in a way that signified a mechanical amiability, plumed herself a little up and down, gave him her vinaigrette and her fan to hold while she set herself in order, and wondered if there were the slightest chance of finding the Gorehamptons if they called. She had promised Mrs. Gorehampton so often, that she was quite, quite ashamed of herself, &c., &c.

The idea of time having a specific value to anybody was not one likely to occur to her; and eventually, after a good deal of talk, the Squeed party departed, carrying off Mr. Brabant, as a useful piece of personal property, for another couple of hours on the treadmill. The two arch-conspirators went away, and St. Maur, Roland, and Sybil were left alone.

Then positive orders were given that nobody else should be admitted under penalty of death, and the three wandered together through the glittering dusk of the chambers, through hall, and alcove, and terrace, and they lingered over the bronzes, the marbles, and the flowers. In this company, St. Maur was a different man —grave, gentle, kingly, and Sybil's admiration for him grew apace. It was a pleasure only to listen to his voice, or, as she had often said to herself of Roland, to hear English spoken by a

gentleman. There was fascination in its mere
accent, for, extraordinary to relate, even this
had come to be a rarity. Roland, too, had
returned to the full possession of his senses;
the trio found an inexpressible pleasure in
each other's society, and the last hour when
they were left alone, made it one of the red-
letter days of life. Something of a gentle cynic
was Miss Grey, and she was amused to have
witnessed, at a distance, the befooling of the
morning. Her education, she felt, would have
been incomplete, if she had not seen the
things that were going on in the charmed
circles, and she did not regret the time as
wasted.

When the sun grew cooler they went up on
to the roof, which St. Maur was laying out
in a terrace with hanging-gardens, draping the
dappled marble of the cornice with festoons of
flowers and leafage. Sybil clasped her hands
with a child's delight at the sight.

" You see," he said in explanation, " ten years
ago this wouldn't have been possible. There
were fifty chimneys on this one roof, and now
there is only one—the kitchen—and that con-
sumes its own smoke. Now that electric heat-
ing has been perfected there ought hardly to
be a coal fire in the district; in fact, most of
my neighbours have given them up, but they
keep their chimney-pots, I suppose, by way of
ornament, for if there is one thing the true
Briton loves, and dreams of, and lives for,
that thing is 'the beautiful.' You two can't
remember what London was a few years ago,

and its inconceivable filth. Look into the distance now, at the absolute transparency of it. This has been the greatest step ever achieved."

Here a footman appeared with tea, which was served in shells that had been mounted as cups; and these, as they stood in the sunshine, were lit up with an opalescent lustre, which put to shame the finest china. Again Miss Grey exclaimed,—

"I declare I thought I had the prettiest service on all the earth, just as yesterday I thought I'd the loveliest bonnet, and this morning I saw one lovelier far; and now this tea-service. I yield you the palm, but it is bitter."

"Ah!" laughed St. Maur, "their great charm is that they cost half-a-crown apiece—within reach of all the world. I imported a quantity, for I do think it's a great thing to prove to the people how cheap sheer beauty may be, but they tell me nobody's bought them. I confess I don't care for china; the best is unsatisfactory. You seldom get exactitude of form. The colouring is usually barbarous; it is crude without the glaze, and vulgar with it. The pleasantest side of the idiotic china mania is, that it has kept down other things that were really good at comparatively cheap prices. Look at the superb water-gilt metalwork of the empire, the finest the world has ever seen. For years past they have been busily breaking it up wherever they found a piece, for the sake of the gold upon it. A few years hence, when fashion comes round to it, as it is sure to do, it will be priceless. I don't know if you noticed the 'mountings' of the dining-hall. I collected them all over Europe, and if you look into them you will see that they have the colour of pure gold, and are finished more highly than the work in the jewellers' windows in Bond Street, to say nothing of the designs."

" I can believe it," said Miss Grey. " I never saw anything to equal the delicate tracery of gold over the veining of the marbles, and the clouding of that crimson-black wood. My poor, dear little dower house ! its nose will be quite out of joint."

" This pitiless refinement is all very well for Cæsar Augustus," said Roland, waving towards his friend, " but it wouldn't suit everybody."

" Oh ! " said St. Maur, " you may treat these same forms as simply as you will. Why should a simple thing be ugly ? Take a hyacinth-glass ; I can't admit the flower to my house, for the plain reason that when I see it, I see with it in imagination the ghastly tall blue glass of my youth. I may set it in an onyx vase, but it is of no use. I ' visualize ' that horrible object, and the flower is irretrievably spoiled.

" From peer to peasant, all the world grew hyacinths in these glasses for years ; and sometimes they increased their loveliness by setting the glass on a stand of bright-green wood, and supporting the flower by long iron wires."

Miss Grey's carriage was announced. She

laughed and rose. "We break out in a new line to-night," she said, "I must be going. The Wyndhams have promised to call for me, and take me to a woman's suffrage meeting. It'll be a terrible change from this, I'm afraid," and she looked round.

"Ah!" laughed St. Maur, "my principles apply there. Knock off the superfluous ugliness; there really can't be any reason why the women who want the suffrage should *all* be old and ugly, dowdy and ill-dressed, and not very well-mannered into the bargain. Put out the strength of womanhood, not its weakness; and if you can educate pretty women to be sensible, the way to success is short enough. But without this, mind!" and he shook his finger in mock menace, "it will take that ten thousand years we were talking about."

Roland stayed on a little when she was gone, and paced the terrace arm-in-arm with his host.

"Let it be soon," said the latter, answering his thoughts, "if you take to yourself the flower of such a woman's life; there is so much the more ground for gratitude and affection ever after. She will help you on your way, whatever it be."

"It will not be my fault if it is not all arranged very shortly," answered Roland with some hesitation, and the subject was changed; he could not discuss it, even with St. Maur.

"I've been very much amused with your party, I confess," he said; "but you seem to have a special faculty for exposing the seamy side of human nature."

"It is the fault of my position. I am amused like yourself; but really sometimes I am so disgusted that I vow I'll forswear my kind for ever. I declare I rather like Lady Jane, simply for disagreeing with me. The grovelling of most of these dreadful old ladies with daughters and nieces, is humiliating to human nature. One of my amusements is to ask them here to meet their poor relations. You see, I sometimes know more about these stray relatives than they do themselves. Ah me! I have strange experiences in my social experiments; the humour of the thing is often—is usually priceless; but the pathos of it!—not that people always wish to go wrong; but they are over-ballasted by the weight of our fallen nature. Sometimes I am tempted to turn upon my way, to go back, to despair, with the conviction that man is working in a vicious circle. If the ages have but evolved an upper class such as we know, what hope is there ever for the masses?

"Yet sometimes I see signs in the heavens and the earth of a new departure—this hyper-sensitiveness which has come upon the world, or at least on the leading races of it, this conscious consciousness of the nations is a new thing, and points to a future very different from the brute past, which was one of simple consciousness. Ah! my dear friend, what might one not do for the world, if the power that has been in some hands came into ours at this stage?" and he looked gravely and sadly, leaning over the balustrade, on to the

countless roofs of the great city wherein was
all his heart, and the love and labours of it.

There was a silence.

" I have thought," said Roland, " that the
social problem will first be solved in a new
field where the old limitations do not exist ; and
if I could suggest a way, it would be under a
beneficent despotism. The masses are children,
and will remain so for ages yet."

" Perhaps," said St. Maur, waking up as
from a reverie, " perhaps so ; but I was telling
you of my social perplexities and the amusing
side of them. Do you know De la Rue ? "
Roland nodded. " Then you know the sort
of fellow he is—regular bore—always putting
his foot in it and pestering one ; he is intolerable : I had made up my mind to cut him. I
must tell you that he scraped an acquaintance
with me by the merest accident. Well, one
day I saw him coming the other side of the
street, and in pursuit of my intention walked
on, when I happened to catch the fellow's eye
—he had, I think, divined my intention—there
was a haggard, hang-dog wistfulness in it I
shall never forget. My resolution broke down
utterly at the sight of it, I could not go on. If
I could do so much for a fellow-creature by
merely recognizing him, surely it was my duty
to do it. I ran across the street, I shook hands
with him, I asked after his wife ; the man was
transfigured, and now "—St. Maur groaned—
" when we meet he rushes at me, he wrings my
hands, holds me by the coat, tells me half-a-
dozen Government secrets, and how many of

his children have had the chicken-pox—these are the rewards of virtue."

Roland laughed. " Good. I can cap your story with an instance of humiliation in a lower grade which happened to me the other day. I was slanging my dog for some misbehaviour in the street. ' Come here ! ' I shouted. ' Don't you hear me, sir ? What the devil do you mean by it, you brute ? ' Up runs a cabman. ' Beg pardon, sir,' touching his cap, ' didn't know you was in such a hurry. Sorry to keep you waitin', sir ! '

" I believe there's nothing humanity will not swallow in the interest of self."

" Yes, the progress of the new evangel is so slow that it has grown old before we can mark perceptible advance. There is this comfort, that the leading lights of thought have certainly reached a pitch never approached before. I wonder, by the way, if it has ever struck you that there are portions of the Bible which are a perfect mine of scientific truth, and expressed in scientific language ? I don't think that is generally realized. The growth of the Christian, for example, is described in the actual terms of biology."

" That may be, but you want some authority for the proper interpretation of Scripture," said Roland drily.

" You have it in modern science."

" Possibly. I don't despair of seeing your authority and mine march hand-in-hand yet. But I must be going," and with some words of sympathy on the subject of Brabant, they parted.

On the morrow of the day just described Roland awoke from an uneasy slumber with a feeling of vague discomfort; unhappily he could not attribute it to indigestion, as he was ignorant of the meaning of the word; the cause, if cause there were, lay deeper. He breakfasted in bed—a thing he had hardly done before in his life—smoked a cigar, had his dog in to talk to, and read the paper; but all to no purpose, the feeling remained. The ash of his cigar fell and burned a hole in the bed-clothes; his dog, after enduring for a long time patiently every species of outrage to his feelings, gave him an ugly snap, as a reminder that it was time to finish. The paper was dull, for it was a notable peculiarity of the period that the silly season came into full force considerably earlier than with us, and was at its height during May, June, and July.

The day's programme read like a microcosm of human inanity. Four-and-twenty choice spirits were to meet in the Park, and drive four-and-twenty empty coaches four-and-twenty empty miles or so, till their four-and-twenty empty heads were satisfied with the honour and glory so achieved. Fond as Roland was of horse-flesh, there was a mild magnificence in this which moved his derision mightily. He would not go. What was next? A great bazaar to be held, where a hundred chartered idiots in costume, were to keep shop in burlesque, and sell rubbish at fabulous prices to ten thousand unchartered idiots, who were good enough to go and gape and be gulled!

No! he had no taste for seeing ladies of birth emulating the manners of their sisters of the pavement, even in the sweet name of charity.

Next, was a concert in the slums, given by some noble ladies of not very noble antecedents, out of pure philanthropy. Philanthropy had been a strong point (in its restricted sense) with most of them; but evolution by invariable law, moving from the homogeneous to the heterogeneous, what had once been the love of one man had expanded into love of several, and was now distributed over the million.

The next item was the public reception of a dusky potentate, whom it had taken England twenty thousand men to thrash a year or two since. He was to drive in triumph through London, to lunch at Windsor, and to dine with the Lord Mayor. There was a lecture at the British Museum on " Sexual Threads of the Gynecemenæ." There was—but why go on with a list which to the reader of to-day must appear nothing short of absurd caricature?

Roland would have none of it. At twelve o'clock he walked down to Hyde Park Corner. He was still eaten up with the groundless fears of a true lover, and could not rest until he had seen Sybil, and told her of his trouble. But what trouble had he? When he tried to put it into words, he was forced to laugh at himself, and he longed for the first glimpse of her face, which alone could cure him; but when this came, he felt as though he had been struck, and knew that his heart had told him true. The clear eyes of darkling onyx, lit with fictitious brilliance, told him, ere her lips, of grave mischance. In the first moment the disaster seemed overwhelming to both of them.

It was briefly this. For the last day or two Mr. Trelawney had been prostrated by the extreme heat; he had grown worse, and his doctor had ordered him back at once to Kissengen. By Lady Thomond's recommendation a Sister of Charity had been engaged as nurse, but he wanted Sybil with him to look after his affairs, and to act as his secretary and superintendent, and they were to start as soon as might be. All her plans must be thrown up. She would have to go, and, of course, this meant separation for the present.

The twain talked a long time very desperately and tragically; and Sybil shed tears as she clung to her lover, and looked into his face, trying to comfort him. But this was worse than Tantalus; the fruit of all his desire lay in his arms, making the prettiest apologies for snatching itself away. For a long time he would not hear of it; and he even insisted in forcing his way to her guardian's bedside; but the sight of the drawn face disarmed him, and the more so that the old man held out to him a thin, trembling hand, and said,—

"My boy, I am sorry for this, but you must leave her with me a little while—it won't be long; it cannot, and you shall not repent it. I'll see to that." Even as he spoke a spasm of pain crossed his face, and the nerveless hand fell and crumpled up on the counterpane. "It's

one of my bad days, boy," he exclaimed; and
he settled back with bowed head and dim eye,
looking into vacancy. It is not always that
the young get as much consideration from the
old. Roland, shocked by the change in him,
was touched to the heart and silenced, and soon
after he went away. He spoke of letters and
so forth, and then he kissed Sybil; but he
would not say good-bye to her, out of some
superstition. Yet a dismal vista stretched
before him, for he could hardly see her again
before the winter-leave season, January next
year, and this was July. Horrible!

He went out into the hot sun, and struck at
random down, deep into the unknown heart of
some low and mal-odorous district. It was
so hot that few people were about; the dirty
back-streets were silent and deserted; a whiff
of sirocco ever and anon raised a little cloud
of dust and cabbage-stalks and nameless nastinesses, and swept about him; but he walked
on unheeding. After a time he came to a
region where some dreadful children were
playing with some dreadful toys in a dreadful
enclosure, compounded of a railway-arch, a
graveyard, and a rubbish-heap; while a dead
cat, dragged from the latter, formed the *pièce
de résistance* of their game. Presently an organ-
grinder came up, and the imps took it in turn
to dance, with the poor cat as partner. Here
was a medley of social, economic, and sanitary
problems which arrested Roland, and which he
set himself to try and solve. He offered a
penny to the cat's partner, if she would cast it

from her, and twopence if she could find means
of decent burial; but on the discovery that the
cat was a property, the entire circle claimed a
vested interest in it, and the solution became
more complicated than ever. The rumour of
money in the neighbourhood brought out a
second organ-grinder, who made life doubly
hideous, and Roland swiftly sped away. But
in the next street came a fellow bawling, with
a packet of papers tucked under his arm—a
ruffian with a stentorian voice,—

" 'Orrabal massaker! More expected confidently! Tragikal berludshed! Startling nooz!
Defeat of the rebels! 'Art-rending hincidents!
Revelation in Iberia! 'Orrabal massaker!" *da
capo.*

The words fell on Roland's ear as the grinding
of the music-hall ditties, for such cries, coming
from north, south, east, and west, were unfortunately no rarity, but by degrees, one by one, they
realized themselves. "'Revolution in Iberia!
Horrible massacre! Bloodshed; more expected!'
By Heaven, that's the very thing for me!" for
he was sore and savage at heart. "Here! Hi!"

He bought the paper, glanced hastily at the
telegrams, and made up his mind.

A month still lay before him, a gaping
month of empty time before his leave expired; he could be on the theatre of war, he
calculated, in a few days. The insurrection
had broken out in a corner of the Continent, and the two opposing parties had taken
the field. Secretly he had burned from his
earliest recollection to see the war-game played

with his own eyes. He had already delayed joining the army for some years, in the hope that the call for soldiers in one of the nation's little wars, might give him an opening. But none had come, and he had now reached the extreme limit of age permitted by the regulations. The opportunity of seeing a few blows struck, with a foreign service before he settled to the routine of barrack life at home, was irresistible. He had literally no preparation to make; what served him in his riding tours would serve him now.

It was four o'clock when he heard the news, and eight saw him start by the night-mail from Charing Cross, his sole luggage a small valise. The familiar streets wore a strange look to him as he drove down. He told no one of his plans, and simply left word at his rooms that he was gone into the country for a fortnight. And as he went, a profound conviction fell upon him that this was his first flight as a man full-fledged; this was the moment he had waited for so long, and with such stern eagerness of impatience. This, the outcome of the merest chance, was his true start in the battle of life. He got away without observation, but in crossing the Channel a curious thing occurred.

He was lying back upon a bench by the paddles. There was a crush on board, for the London exodus had already begun, and the trampling crowds passed and repassed; but he heeded them not, for his thoughts were elsewhere, when among the many, in the dusk of the distance, he fancied he singled out

the face and figure of Sybil Grey. She was
dressed as for travelling in her furs, and the sea
air was striking chill. As she came, the dim
light of a swinging oil-lamp fell upon her face,
and the pallid moon illumined it; beyond, the
stars were twinkling in the black canopy of
heaven. For the moment she seemed like the
one reality in the world of shadows, as they
flitted to and fro. She stopped before him, and
looked with a great sad sweetness into his face.

"And now you go without me, dear love,"
she said, and the words seemed uttered within
him rather than without; "and it is right that
you go your way as I go mine, for so it must
be until the end; but still I am with you
always, we have not said good-bye." He had
not thought that he had closed his eyes, yet his
limbs were spell-bound as with sleep, and it was
a minute before he cast off the shackles and
sprang to his feet. So vivid was the impression that he did not stay to reason; but
feeling sure that he had actually seen her,
he plunged hither and thither through the
crowd, to no purpose. He sat and waited, but
the fair aura came no more through the long
watches of the night, nor any that was like
her. Convinced after a time that he had been
deceived, he desisted; and if her words and
look smote him, he laughed at them as the
conceit of his own brain. To dream of her at
all was an omen of success, and the spirit of
despondency passed from him as a summer
cloud.

It was on the fourth morning after this that

a solitary rider might have been seen crossing one of the tumbled deserts of northern Iberia. He wore a loose jacket—in its belt was the leathern case of a revolver—breeches, and long riding-boots; a couple of saddle-bags hung to his crupper, and upon it was his waterproof, strapped in a roll. A sturdy little grey Arab carried him jauntily over the pitiless, barren track of country, where hill overlapped hill, towards where the blue Sierras cut the pale sky of the morning with a monstrous outline of jagged teeth. Often, as he had come along, had Roland stopped and listened; there was nothing in the air but the gentle voices of the morning. And now a pleasure danced in his veins, distinct from any that he had ever felt before, for there fell upon his ear a sound, unfamiliar indeed, but one that he felt he had been born in some sense to love from the bottom of his heart, and with it came a quickening of the pulse. As yet he could see nothing; only the endless hills confronted him, always with new crests, where the burnt grass was shaking itself free of the night dews to the music of the wind.

A not unusual event had occurred in the country. Half-a-dozen Governments had been overturned successively, and half-a-dozen parties were now fighting at intervals, and when it suited them, and when it was not too hot, and not too cold, and not a saint's day, for — whatever it might prove to be — the Empire, the Crown, the Dictatorship, or the Presidential Chair. This thing, whatever it

were, had gone a-begging for some time, for
nobody would have it at a gift; and the only
possible outcome appeared to be, that he who
was strongest should seize it and hold it for
his own. "So they want a king," mused the
rider, as he pricked over the hills, and the
morning sun unrolled at his feet the fairy
panorama of hill and dale, of bosky wood and
blue mountain, set in a girdle of summer sea.
"'Pon my honour, I'm more than half inclined
to make a bid for the place myself; if only I
were not a sub-lieutenant of the Blanks, I
believe I might do something here."

This particular soil was the paradise of ad-
venturers; nowhere would a hard head, and
a little hard cash to back it, go farther. The
nature of the country and the people made
careers possible here, of a sort that could be
nowhere else under heaven; and had Roland
realized this at the time, he might probably have
thrown up everything else, and cast his fortunes
with one party or the other. But he was over-
young to detect these facts, and where he
might have written a page of history, he did
but learn his alphabet.

Ha! surely that was the ring of field artillery.
In effect the falling away of the hillside revealed a low, drifting line of white smoke, and
he pressed on with redoubled speed. In that
country is neither hedge nor ditch nor other
impediment to man or beast, save where a few
giant aloes stand in a clump, or a little grove
of sunny, wind-shaken trees form a landmark
for miles round; or where the rugged track of

a stream meanders from the hills, deep down
in the rocky bed it has taken so many centuries
to carve.

A very pretty little fight was in progress
below. It was not a decisive battle—nothing
is ever decisive in this land—but some three or
four thousand men were engaged on either side.
To the eye of the casual observer, there appeared
to be far less; so sparse, so scattered, and so
thin were the lines, that it seemed absurd that
either side should offer serious resistance to a
concentrated attack. If there is one thing
more objectionable than a fox-hunt on paper,
it is the account of a battle—it takes as much
skill to tell it well, as to fight it. The arrangement of this particular struggle, which it was
Roland's fortune to witness, was, however, so
simple and pretty—if the term may be again
employed—that it is impossible to refrain from
a page or two. The man or woman who has
witnessed from some breezy upland the progress of autumn manœuvres, may picture the
contest very accurately, scenically if not tacti-
cally. The country round about was a desert;
there were no spectators. The two armies had
it all to themselves, and were fighting it out
unheeded, on a plan of action which had the
merit of being obvious to the merest tyro.

One party held a long, double-crested hill,
which they had furrowed with trenches, while
the other was attempting to dislodge them by
an attack from the valley; and it was in the
right rear of these latter that Roland found
himself. He rode down rapidly, until certain

unfailing indications informed him that he was within range; and with the *sangfroid* of ignorance, he halted upon an exposed spur of the hillside, and watched the battle as it toiled a few hundred yards below. Which side was he on, he wondered? He hardly knew so much as the names of the contending parties; and as he had no particular reasons for special interest in either, his sympathies naturally went out to that on which fortune had cast him; the more so, when after some time it appeared evident that it was destined to failure. Meanwhile he sat and smoked placidly.

Presently dismounting, he tethered his horse to a stump, and took out his field-glasses. From where he stood, no detail of the field escaped him; and he became so absorbed in the spectacle that he forgot everything else. Now and then something in the shape of a reminder came singing by, or buried itself in his hillside, throwing up a cloud of dust, but he heeded it not. His entire attention was taken up with a plan of his own for turning the enemy's flank; and as, one after another, the rushes made from the front failed, and the troops fell back foiled, under the hot fire of the trenches, the idea took stronger hold on him.

CHAPTER IX.

HE left his post of observation to scrutinize more closely the lie of the land around. Riding from point to point, and keeping as far as possible out of sight, he rapidly mapped the leading features into a pocket-book.

It was several hours before he had made the survey to his satisfaction; but when he had done so, he snapped the clasp of his book with the pleasant feeling that he could fight the battle, on whichever side might be required of him, with equal comfort. He had by this time gained one of the more distant spurs of the range. It was now late in the afternoon, and the total cessation of the firing warned him that it would be idle to return to the field with the hope of seeing more that day. He was besides half-starving, and he stood for a long time divided in mind as to whether he should go into camp and throw himself on the generosity of the authorities, or make his way back to the village from which he had started in the morning. The reflection that the contents of his pocket-book might not impossibly secure his execution as a spy determined him; and he was retracing his way, when he perceived high on the slope a little farm or homestead. Solitary and forlorn, it was the only sign of human life within eyesight, and it appeared wholly undisturbed by the unusual events taking place in its vicinity. He turned aside to this with the hope of procuring food, if not rest; and when he reached it, found its sole tenants were two elderly women, who, although infinitely alarmed at his appearance, on discovering what he stood in need of, busied themselves to do all they could for him. He managed to gather from them that the men of the establishment were away at the war; and as they appeared friendly, and put a stable with a loft at his disposal, which would serve him and his horse for the night, he decided to remain there. The house was poor, but clean, as houses mostly are in those parts, and almost void of everything in the shape of furniture. Nevertheless, he procured an excellent supper. Unfortunately, his ignorance of the language prevented his learning any of the particulars he was most anxious to learn. The two crones, who were kindly beldames, gave him an early breakfast at daylight, and he again set off in quest of the armies.

The landscape lay smiling before him in the low, bright sun-rays, all innocent it seemed even of human presence or living thing; but as he neared the scene of action, he came on a knot of stragglers, and here and there a man wounded or worn out, prone in the deep heather of the glens. None of these took the slightest notice of him. He went on, finding now and then some trace in the form of arms or bag-

gage which had been dropped or cast aside and
left. Presently, as he gained the ridge on
which he had stood the day before, he noted
a train of covered waggons, yoked with oxen,
making their slow way across the plains
from the field, and as the whole of the two
camps opened out to his view, he perceived that they remained in precisely the
identical positions, and that both were on the
alert, in a state of preparation for a renewal of
the attack. He had not long to wait.

About nine o'clock, the force holding the
opposite hill opened fire from their advanced trenches, and the side on which he
stood were not slow to respond, taking the
offensive at once, but with the same result as
before. More than an hour he sat in his saddle
watching, and growing more and more impatient, as the failure of the attack became
more conspicuous. He dismounted, and went
down somewhat nearer, in order the better to
see ; and the same idea that had come to him
before, impressed itself more forcibly upon
him, as he considered the disposition of the
field and the troops.

He could see something from his point of
vantage which was not visible from below.
Through the valley ran one of the deep, rocky
watercourses that seam all this country,
spreading wider through the lowlands, but
narrowing up the hill, which it wound round
like a deep furrow cleft in it; he could trace
it upwards through the actual position held by
the enemy. Indeed, they were using it as an

improvised trench, and here was a secret way
into their very heart.   He made a rapid drawing on his cuffs—on the left a map, on the
right a free-hand ; and then, as another thin
line was sent reeling back, he made up his
mind.

He shut up his glasses and rose to his feet, when
he was struck a violent blow full on the chest,
which caused him to stagger and fall backwards,
where he lay gasping for breath, as he had been
flung, staring wildly at the sky.   His first feeling
was one of mad impotent rage ; his next was,
" I shall be hit again. Heavens ! how shall I get
out of this ? "   Slowly his breath returned to
him ; he sat up and put his hand to his chest,
panting heavily, his impression being that he
should find nothing less than a grape-shot
lodged there, but, to his infinite surprise, there
was not a trace of blood.   He opened his vest ;
a great black bruise had risen upon the breast-
bone, but this was all.

" I'm a fool and a coward," he laughed, half
ashamed of himself, springing up a second time
and jumping into his saddle.   The ball had been
a spent one ; but for all that, the blow had been
severe, and was sufficient to drive the breath
out of his body for the moment.   However,
its ultimate effect was a stimulus.

He left his post and rode rapidly down the
hill to a spot, where two or three regiments lay
in reserve under some sort of shelter.   The
happy-go-lucky style of this guerilla warfare
had something of the comic about it to his
eyes, and as he had studied half the European

battle-fields since the days of Marlborough for
his own amusement, and under one of the best
tacticians of the day, he seized the salient
points without difficulty, and he laughed as he
went.

" I needn't waste words, as I don't happen to
know any; but I think I can show them the
way."

Coming down from the rear, it was not until
within a few yards of the Reserves that he was
discovered, when he was set upon and instantly
made prisoner.

It is trite to note the chapter of chances in
life ; but it is not improbable that he would
then and there have been shot as a spy, had
not the officer in command been able to speak
French. It was very evident that his capture
was considered one of no little importance,
and for a few minutes the whole Reserve was
disorganized, as ten men hanging on to his
bridle and claiming him, each for his own particular prize, dragged him before their chief.

" Who are you, and what are you doing
here, sir ? " asked the officer in command in
excellent French. He was a soldierlike-looking
man, with remarkably little nonsense in his eye.

" I'm an English officer," returned Roland in
the same tongue, bowing, and lifting his cigar
from his lips, " and I am here for—*le sport!*
But if I may speak a word with you in private,
I will tell you something. *Ils s'amusent* on the
hill up yonder."

The officer was taken by surprise. Certainly
in his experience there was nothing too mad to

believe of an Englishman, and this one had a peculiar air, though he looked like a gentleman. But the commander was too good a soldier not to be suspicious; he bowed sternly, ordered the horse to be taken to the rear, dismissed the men back into their ranks, all but the two who held the prisoner, and said coldly,—

"Well, sir, speak."

Roland had met his match. "Pinion my arms if you will," he said, "but for heaven's sake let me have a word with you in private and at once, and let us stop the waste of good fellows on that hill!"

Again the officer took the measure of his prize, apparently relenting; he consulted a moment with two or three of his juniors, who stood whispering together, and made a sign. Roland found himself free, and the two walked out together, a few yards in front.

This gentleman was a Colonel, and no less than a grandee of the country, and he looked keenly at the interloper, weighing him and his words, but he said little. Roland showed his sketch, and led him to where he could point out the course of the water-way.

"You are right!" exclaimed the officer at last. "Follow me!" and hastily leaving some directions with a subordinate, he mounted his horse, ordering Roland to attend him to the front.

"You will pardon me," said the latter, explaining as they went along, "it seems to me possible to mass a few companies in that little

copse at the bottom, where the stream runs
through it. Thence we can enter the bed
unperceived, and a crawl of three hundred
mètres will take us right into the enemies'
lines. Then if the feint is continued from the
front while we are on our way, once arrived,
we shall be in a position to enfilade their
trenches, and a continued attack from the
front must carry them."

" *C'est un brave garçon*," said the Commander
of the Reserve, smiling, as if to himself ; but he
made no further comment, beyond quickening
his pace.

The General-in-Chief, with a few of his staff,
stood watching the action from a comfortable
and fairly secure quarter, also considerably in
rear. He was an elderly man, with a white
moustache, the ends of which had been so
trained as to appear nearly a foot in length.
He spoke but broken French and two words
of English; these two were " All right," and
he at once made use of them on the prisoner's
appearance and introduction, after which some
discussion ensued, which did not reach the
newcomer, but was to the effect that—

It was really too early in the day for a
decisive movement; he had intended to fight
up to five or six in the afternoon—that was,
of course, with the exception of an hour or
two at mid-day for dinner and a slight *siesta*,
which both sides would require. Then, as the
sun drew off a little, they might perhaps see
what a spurt might do. This sort of business
was always tedious, and the enemy had un-

accountably taken advantage of the few days' delay which there had already been, to intrench themselves rather strongly.

Well, if the affair could be settled before dinner, by all means—he shrugged his shoulders —he was quite ready to see the young Englishman and hear what he had to say. Roland was beckoned forward, and the Colonel acting as interpreter, the great man listened courteously to his explanation, gravely enunciating "'Ole rye" at intervals; but when he was shown the pocket-book and the map drawn upon the cuff, the old man was completely won over. He declared it was the best field-sketch he had ever seen in his life, and ordering up a drum told his visitor to make a copy of it on the head; but the latter promptly ripped off his cuff and made him a present of it. He then took the drum, and in three minutes produced a rapid outline of the position from where they stood. The General was mightily delighted with this, and gesticulated more emphatically than before; a long and excited confabulation took place among the officers, of whom the Commander of the Reserves appeared the most impatient, and anxious to make trial if the scheme could be put into execution. The General was good-natured, but plainly inclined to put it off, at least till after dinner. " The idea of the watercourse," he said, " had frequently occurred to himself, and there could be no special hurry about the matter; it would be a venture the more, that was all." And while this pretty by-play went on, so did the attack in a half-hearted, desultory way, like a game of which the players on both sides were weary, and yet every minute men were falling, and at every advance up the slope the dark spots that were left, moving indeed, but neither forward nor back, increased in number. The Englishman looked on with silent indignation, and the General lit a fresh cigar.

" Very well," he said at last pettishly, " you can try it, Colonel. You will take four companies, I will put two regiments into the wood where you will enter the channel, and if you ever get up there—ouf !—I suppose we shall see you, and I will advance the front line. Now, look sharp "—he consulted his watch—" and, mind, you go on the condition that you lay dinner for us up yonder in the enemy's camp."

All that Roland understood was that his scheme was to be attempted, that he was to take part in it ; and the thought crossed him strangely how, only that day week, he had been sauntering in the Park, dreaming of the possibilities of life, and all unknowing that the hour of his desire was upon him.

Leaving their horses in the rear with an orderly, the Colonel and he forthwith descended into the spinny below, which was but a thin and meagre hiding-place of willows, on a sandbeach thrown up by the stream. The two regiments promised were told off, and immediately marched in, the two first companies of each selected, and they started, Roland borrowing the short sword of an under-officer. The enemy, however, had perceived the first part of the move; and as the wood was within easy range, commenced to shell it vigorously; and no sooner was the expedition on foot than the two regiments were forced to evacuate the place at a run. Perhaps their opponents took no count, or perhaps they attributed the diminished numbers that poured out of the wood to the terrific effects of the ten minutes' shelling; at any rate, the movement up the watercourse appears not to have been suspected for a moment.

It was a severe climb, often on all fours, through and over the wet boulders all the time; but fortune was kind, and it was accomplished without hap. In all the four companies were no better muscles than the Englishman's, and he proved it by forging ahead easily the whole way. Indeed, the brown-skinned pigmies that followed him were exhausted before they had gone half the distance; and, impatient as he was, Roland knew that it would be fatal if they so reached the top. More than once they halted, and their Commander gave them a long rest before the final rush.

Never was a more lucky chapter of accidents—and so it ever is, for one side or the other, in war. Towards the top the brushwood over-arched the stream, to such an extent as to render the assailants wholly invisible; and they were actually inside the enemy's lines before they were perceived, and able, as Roland had predicted, to enfilade the advanced trenches. Then, at a given signal, they swarmed out over the banks and took them in flank. Dire was

the confusion. Once hand to hand, the men
on both sides fought like devils; but there
was no more firing—it was too close an
affair for that. A wrestle, a blow, and the
hardest had it. Roland, one of the first,
sprang out of hiding, and into a two-foot
trench, where he literally fell upon the first
man he met, hurled his rifle from his hand,
breaking it in two. Then as they rolled over
clasped, and he could not raise his sword-arm
properly, he struck out straight, and with the
heavy hilt, catching his antagonist on the
temple, slew him. *C'est le premier pas qui
coûte!* All his life he never forgot the spurt
of blood and the look in the poor fellow's
mangled face as he fell—but this was no
moment for pity.

Oh! the rough and tumble of the hill, and
the flourish of legs and arms and knives.
Over the whole surface of it where he stood
seemed nothing else; and he was set upon by
two others right and left, one of whom he
felled senseless with his fist, shooting the
other through his revolver case as he tipped it
in his belt. The man was round him like
a cat, and he had no space to draw it; but he
shot upwards as he was able, and the next
instant was carrying a corpse, whose arms
were gripped about his neck, and whose teeth
were locked in his neckcloth. He tore it
loose, and the body fell with a dull thud to
earth. Then he stopped to breathe, to
straighten himself, and recall his reeling senses.
The space before him was cleared, but all

along the line they were hacking and hewing
and stabbing and rolling over in a death-
struggle. The havoc of these first few minutes
was terrible, and the trenches were blocked
with the dead, heaped one upon the other;
and upon these, again, the living still wrestled
in the throes of battle. He looked down;
the General had been as good as his word.
The assault was being delivered in force.
The front companies were taking the hill at
a double, and were even now closing on the foe.
The remarkable feature of the day at this
stage was, that a complete lull ensued in the
firing, the two sides being so mixed at the
point of contact that it had become impossible.
The white smoke still hung motionless, cleav-
ing to the hillside, and pierced only by the
shrieks, yells, and cries of the combatants.

Up above, there was confusion; and where
the drifting cloud parted, betwixt the rifts,
could be seen where they were massing in
force to repel the attack. In a few minutes,
however, the trenches had been carried, the
firing recommenced, and the entire of the two
little armies grappled with each other, in the
shock of a general action, which extended irre-
gularly all across the hill.

But if the one side was disconcerted at the
sudden turn of affairs, the other was equally
elated. There appeared to be a chance of
something decisive, and secretly this was what
both sides had longed for in their hearts, for
weeks past. Half an hour had changed all,
and although it was a punishing struggle up

that rocky slope, crest after crest was won, and at each, the attack gathered confidence for a fresh effort, until it seemed to the men themselves as if they had been dowered with superhuman force, and had come there on wings.

Three parts of the way the Englishman led—the Mad Captain, as they were already calling him. He, the first, reached one of the mountain guns, which lay unspiked, but on its side, overturned and abandoned by a ridge of cropping rock, over which, in the hurry of retreat, the enemy had been unable to drag it. A deuced awkward thing is a gun high up on a mountain, when it is time to go home.

Roland took out his penknife, and was in the act of scratching his initials upon it, when he was again hit. Achilles was wounded in the heel. It was not a bad wound or a dangerous one, but it tied him to the spot as effectually as if he had taken root there. He flung himself upon the ground in horrible chagrin, and disdained to bind up the place, until his friend the Colonel came upon him, wofully short of breath, and insisted on its being done. The work, however, was over. The enemy—as the latter was able to inform him—had quitted their old positions on the heights, and were in disorderly retreat across a distant spur, leaving arms, baggage, and a wreck of *impedimenta* by the way. This appeased him slightly, and he muttered to himself as he bound up his wound,—

" *Vixi!* Why a man should go to Melton to break his neck, I can't imagine, when he can get this sort of thing any day of the week, if he chooses to take the trouble."

And in this, it must be allowed, he did not differ from a number of young Englishmen of the day, who were wont to go out and take the most exceeding pains to get killed, in any or every quarrel which did not concern them.

The battle soon passed out of his ken as it swept upwards, and he found himself alone but for one or two who, like him, had dropped by the way. The gun happened to be the only one taken on this particular occasion, but it was a couple of hours or more before the General rode up to the spot to inspect it. He was accompanied by two or three of the Staff, all very hot, very dusty, and vociferating at the top of their voices, when they suddenly came upon Roland, who was lying where he fell. It was now an hour past mid-day, and the sun beat maddeningly upon him as he lay helpless. This, together with the loss of blood, made him sick and faint for the first time in his life; he tried vainly to rise to his feet.

" The Englishman!" they all cried simultaneously.

The General himself sprang from his saddle, and between them they helped him to the other side of the rock, where a stretch of purple shade fell on the heather. The relief was unspeakably great; his parched tongue moved again, and where they set him, propped against the hoary crag, he could still catch sight of the beaten force defiling into a valley on the other side; but the pursuit had ceased—the men were bivouacked for dinner.

And, behold! it was a beauteous summer day, and on that golden hillside the merry zephyrs played and the merry birds sang, all undisturbed. The stillness of the noontide had gathered swiftly upon it, and from the rocks the bright flowers nodded as in sleep. Still, a few passed to and fro upon the hill. The Staff had flung themselves upon the ground in the shade, for a moment's rest, and had pulled out flasks and sandwiches, talking incessantly the while and often giving Roland a significant glance, but he was unable to understand a word.

Presently three figures appeared on the near horizon of the hill. Two soldiers were supporting between them a wounded officer, who had been taken prisoner. He swayed heavily from side to side as he came, his face was deadly pale, and his lips drawn up over his teeth. Over his white trousers was a fearful stain, dark and dried most of it, but in the centre a wet welling spot of brightest red. When he found himself in the presence of the Staff, with a mighty effort he drew himself together, but there was a look in his eyes which told how terrible was the physical struggle—they were almost sightless; holding himself, with unshaken hand he drew his sword, and, inclining his head, offered it to the General. That officer, bowing deeply, drew back and made way, saying something that Roland did not understand, and the next moment the prisoner came forward a step and laid his sword in Roland's hand, saying in French, " Sir, I give you all I have," when instantly the donor staggered forwards and fell lifeless at his feet.

Only in that land does such a scene blossom out of the soil like a flower indigenous to it. It took Roland wholly unawares; perhaps, too, he was unnerved by his wound ; perhaps the realization of such an hour as he had dreamed of, unmanned him; but his eyes were moist as he took the precious gift of the giver who was dead.

*　　*　　*　　*

Now the fame of this day and a hundred distorted versions of its incidents were noised far and wide.

The war had dragged so long, that the correspondents had been gradually withdrawn ; but on the frontier still lingered one who found the climate suit him better than that of England. He had hung on the skirts of the army for months without seeing anything in particular. He had grown surly in consequence, and had exchanged the life of camps and their alarms for the security of a shady lodging, and a garden where he could write at his ease, and colour his local sketches, without being subject to the endless annoyances of the "infernal soldiering." The poor man had been desperately hard up for copy, to say nothing of cash : the billiard-table of the country was an abominable thing, and it was impossible to realize anything upon it. And this was the greater hardship, because billiard-marking had been one of his many professional duties of late years. There had been nothing to record for weeks, the last engagement having taken place in quite a different part; and by some means he had contrived to stand equally badly at headquarters, both in the field and in Fleet Street.

All this last week he had been employed in evolving and perfecting a nonsense verse, which he hoped would gain the guinea prize offered by a comic contemporary. When sent, it ran as follows :—

> " A person who lived at Santander
> Swore a goose was the same as a gander;
> And they had to produce and examine a goose
> Before he admitted the slander."

This may seem to be mere trifling, but however unheard of in our own day, such was one of the many phases of comic paper and war correspondent in that. And will it be believed, while we are upon the matter, that the above did not win the guinea?

The first news of the battle reached this gentleman late in the evening, when he was hardly in a fit state to receive it. The telegraph clerk, who was a crony of his, had gone to bed, and it was only on condition of their making a night of it, at his chum's expense, that he would consent to re-dress himself, and let the world outside know anything of the matter, for he was of his nation to the backbone. The original draft of the telegram, which was put together between them, is reported to have been somewhat as follows—needless to say, the telegrams from the seat of war were not subject to the same superviison as in our own army :—

" A decisive battle has taken place. The rebel forces have been defeated with great loss, and are retiring on ——. A romantic incident characterized the day. It appears that the well-known Captain Rollo, who has been with the army as the informal representative of the English War Office for three weeks past, was present as a spectator at the first attack, which failed disastrously. Thereupon he coolly walked up to the General commanding, and volunteered to carry the position single-handed if supported by a squadron of artillery. This was granted, and, proceeding cautiously, he scaled the outlying gabions at a gallop, destroying at one blow the counterscarps along the whole line. The panic that ensued among the enemy at this terrific stroke it is impossible to describe. The majority of them mounted the *chevaux de frise*, which were rapidly becoming ungovernable from fright, and fled for their bare lives. Five troops of infantry were then sent to support the intrepid Captain, which pouring in a withering fire of round shot, and shelling right and left as they went, fell upon the stricken remnant of the foe and drove them from the field. The success has been complete.

" I was slightly in rear during the progress of the action, but can vouch for the virtual accuracy of the above details. Shall hope to

send more to-morrow, for which I shall apply
to my old friend, the hero himself, whose war-
worn face and kindly eye are so well known to
the *habitués* of club-land. He is little changed
since we last met, although the hair on his
temples is grizzled; but it is the lot of few
men to carry years and experience so lightly.
It is rumoured that he is to be offered an
honorary Colonelcy. Indeed, it will be no
breach of confidence to say that I was consulted on the subject only last week by the
highest possible authority, when my advice was
given emphatically in favour of it."

This reached the London office, it so
happened, when the small hours were growing
big, and had it not been for a clever com-
positor who was a volunteer, a smart fellow,
and whose conscientious scruples were touched
on reaching the round shot, it might have gone
in entire. As it was, the paragraph in its modified form had a considerable effect, more
particularly in military circles.

Now there came to see that correspondent
to bed the next morning, a brother billiard-
marker, who had once held a commission, and
when he had read the rough copy of the telegram, he said that it would not do—unless,
indeed, it had been sent to the *Times* (for this
paper at that period had, by a natural development, resolved into a serio-comic), and
of this he appeared to entertain no doubt whatever. His forebodings were gloomy and
destined shortly to be realized; and being a
man of business-like habits, within forty-eight

hours he was able to stand himself in that war-correspondent's shoes, and, further, to "stand" his friend a handsome supper in celebration of the event. In consequence of this change, the next notice that traversed the London press was of a more cautious nature, and ran as follows :—

"There appears to be little doubt that the success of Thursday's operations, of which a slightly exaggerated account at first circulated in this country, was, in the first instance, greatly due to the skill and foresight of a Major Rylands, an Englishman, who holds a somewhat undefined position in the Government ranks. The happy ruse which appears to have been the turning-point of the day was actually conceived by him. He accompanied the storming party, when he performed prodigies of strength and valour worthy rather of a mythical hero than a man, and was twice wounded. The soldiery are enthusiastic, and the leading journals speak in the highest terms," &c., &c.

Bizarre figures of the sort were not unknown in the annals of recent wars—indeed, it was not an unusual feature of England's struggles with savage potentates, to find these individuals directed by some ex-soldier, some intense Frenchman or Irishman, who there discerned a fine field for his hereditary antipathies.

A game of cross-questions and crooked answers in the "House" was the result of these various matters. A gentleman whose thirst for information was the terror of all parties, and not least of his own, gave notice of the question,—

"Whether her Majesty's Government has despatched a well-known English officer to the theatre of war as the accredited representative of the War Office? Whether it is true that the success of Thursday's operation is greatly attributable to this officer, and, if so, whether this is in accordance with the position of this country, as defined in regard to the belligerents?"

A rather mixed query, to which the simple answer came promptly, "No, sir." (Ministerial cheers.)

"Am I to understand that Major Rollo or Rylands is *not* acting in the capacity of representative of the War Office?"

"There is no such officer in the 'Army List.'" (Loud cheers.)

It was curious to note that during the two or three days after the first announcement not a soul was to be met in Pall Mall but knew "old Dick What's-his-name—Rollo—Rylands; changed it for property, y'know," perfectly well; several had been at school with him, and one or two had dined with him the Sunday before he went out. After this, however, his acquaintance sensibly diminished. A certain doubt hung over his authenticity, and it is impossible to be too careful in such a case. At no previous period of the world's history had names the same knack of flashing into world-notoriety for a few hours, and of being with a like speed obliterated.

A week elapsed, a new actress, duly puffed from America, made her *début*, and the subject was half forgotten, when another telegram appeared, which whetted the public curiosity. Letters, it should be remarked, there were none, for the simple reason that there had happened to be no one on the spot to write them, active operations having been unexpected. The average Britisher took little interest in anything outside his own rather narrow limits. Still, he liked a battle for breakfast, just to explain it to his wife before he caught the 'bus City-wards. It gave a fillip to that commonplace event, and made her thankful that, with his extraordinary military talents, he had preferred going into the City to going into battle.

This was the latest :—

" The Yankee adventurer who goes by the designation of Captain Roland has been the hero of another escapade no less successful than the last. It will be remembered that this dashing swash-buckler was wounded in the foot on the last occasion, and has consequently been unable to march. This did not, however, prevent him from riding, and he joined an expedition which was undertaken at two o'clock yesterday morning under cover of a heavy mist. The virtual destruction of the rebel camp was the result. Two regiments only of cavalry were engaged, to which the Captain, who has made a survey of the country, went as guide, and he appears literally to have led the force in a mad dash right through the enemy's camp. Our fellows carried torches soaked in petroleum, by means of which they were able to set fire to the tents, and the wind blowing the smoke across to the spot where the horses were picketed, the whole body of them broke loose, and a wild stampede ensued, which, together with the flames, caused a perfect panic. Into the midst of this our cavalry made sudden swoops, causing confusion worse confounded. There is little doubt that, had they been supported, I should have been able to write to you of a victory which must have ended the war—in these parts at least. As it is, the foe have been forced to retire within the walled hill-town of ——, whence they will probably not be in a condition to operate for some time to come. When Roland found how things were going, he himself rode back the five miles at full speed, with a request for reinforcements; but it was the old story. The General had turned in, and could not be prevailed upon to prosecute the affair, urging that it would be some hours before a sufficient force could be got under arms, &c., &c. So the chance passed as usual, and with the first streak of dawn the cavalry returned triumphantly, the conflagration they left behind them, gloriously lighting up their road home. Roland was carried into camp on the shoulders of the troopers. His appearance was greeted with the wildest enthusiasm by all arms. The mock Captain has become a real one, and has been presented with a commission. His sobriquet with the men since his first appearance has been 'the Mad Captain.' He has managed to endear himself with all ranks, and as he is, or pretends to be, a devout Roman Catholic, he finds favour with the men.

" He is a taciturn youth, over middle height, and of prodigious strength of build, with which goes, rather oddly, eyes piercing as a hawk's, set in refined features of a classic type. He certainly speaks excellent English, and without any appreciable twang. He is courteous, but not communicative, and has proved himself no impostor—so far as the art of war is concerned. Field-maps are almost unknown in the service in this country, and there can be no doubt that his talent for surveying led in the first instance to both successes. Sketches of the two fields, which he is preparing, will shortly be published," &c., &c.

The next telegram a fortnight later was, simply, these two words, "Roland disappeared." No one who knows the customs of the period will be astonished to hear that it occupied half a column. What the mysterious process was, what subtleties were used to enlarge it to this, it is not easy to say, but the column began as follows :—

" The adventurer Roland has disappeared from the scene as mysteriously as he came upon it. Foul play is more than suspected, for it is well known that the renown he had achieved, and the favour he had earned, had already won him many enemies. The authorities are infinitely distressed, and will, no doubt, offer a large reward, although so far no trace has been found of him alive or dead.

If dead, he has very likely been made away with secretly, and his body carried to the mountains, where it is most unlikely that it should be found. On the other hand, it is assumed that, if alive, he may have fled across the frontier to avoid detection. Several British officers have joined the forces within the last few days, in consequence of the late display of activity; and the rumour now runs that he is a cashiered officer, formerly in the British service. If such is the case, he would, of course, be more than unwilling to encounter the risk of discovery, which would go far to blight the brilliancy of his prospects in his new career. The probability, after all, is that he is a mere lucky adventurer, coming from Heaven knows whence," &c., &c., *ad infinitum.*

It will be surmised that Sub-Lieutenant Tudor found himself in some difficulty as the expiration of his home-leave drew near. His fortune had been such in his three weeks of soldiering that he was sorely tempted to throw up his appointment, and cast in his lot with "the cause" in this foreign land; but being first and foremost a red-hot patriot in his nature, he could not make up his mind to the wrench. To escape was not easy; the opportunity, however, offered of carrying despatches to head-quarters. He undertook the delivery—not without some little enjoyment of the feeling, as he lingered on the plains, that he was keeping the great world waiting for its breakfast-budget. The despatches came safely to hand, but the bearer returned no more.

The next and final paragraph is from a letter

emanating from the same quarter. The paper bears the date of a fortnight later :—

"The inexplicable disappearance of Captain Roland, of which I telegraphed to you last week, has been by no means cleared up, but rather heightened by the arrival of another mysterious individual, who, however, pretends to be nothing further than the missing captain's confidential servant. If so, he is a smart fellow, and must, I should think from his appearance, be drawing a good salary.

"His manners are superior to his class; he speaks the language perfectly, and appears— for I have had some little conversation with him—to be a connoisseur in works of art. He has brought with him two magnificent presents from the erratic individual whom he calls his master. One is an antique diamond snuff-box, which he presented with due ceremony to General ——, the chief of the staff; and the other is a superb revolver, mounted in gold, silver, and ivory, for the Mad Captain's particular friend, Colonel ——, who, it will be remembered, first made his acquaintance by taking him prisoner six weeks ago. The snuff-box bears the initials T. R. entwined, which may, of course, stand for T. Roland; but it is now more than hinted that the missing gentleman is a member of a collateral branch of the R—sch—ld family, or young Lord R——, who is supposed to be travelling in Australia, but who has been lost sight of by his relatives for some months past. Certainly his distinguished bearing and mode of speech preclude the idea of anything like a mere adventurer, as I have always said, and would seem to warrant some such assumption as one of these latter. It is a matter for regret that he should have chosen from mere caprice, to nip in the bud, so promising an episode as that, of which he was the hero here. It is to be hoped that he may be induced to return; but the servant, to whom I expressed this wish, was singularly reserved—even more so than his master. I could get nothing out of him; nor, I believe, so far, can any one else. He has evidently plenty of loose cash, and he spoke very intelligently about the pattern and workmanship of the snuff-box. The General has taken a great fancy to him, and would, I believe, have treated him *en camarade*, so much regard has he for any one connected with his dear lost Captain. But the man is modest and retiring, and keeps to his place. He is leaving again at once. So the romance for the present finishes, unless you unravel it at home. I have seen many gallant young Englishmen in the field, but never one who showed better metal than our lost ' Captain Roland ! ' "

The same paper announced on another page that Sub-Lieutenants Jones and Tudor had proceeded to Ireland to join their regiment.

CHAPTER X.

"Now, sir, I weally must wequest to know the meaning of this. Here's a bad smell, sir"—sniff—"an infernally bad smell. And what I want to know, sir, is, why the doose this hasn't been weported to the Adjutant-Genewal?"

The speaker was a buttoned-up, purple-faced, elderly gentleman, in a cocked-hat, plumes, boots, and other splendours, who held one nostril gingerly inflated over an open grating, and with the other delicately inhaled an antidote from a scented handkerchief.

"It's, ah! the most unsoljahlike smell I ever came acwoss in my life."

"Really, sir," ejaculated a much-belaced and bepadded individual, with a ferocious moustache and further nodding plumes and boots, and the rest of it—the Aide-de-camp, in fact—"it is," with a pretence at a critical and discriminating sniff, "most unsoljahlike. But I am credibly informed by Mr. Grubble"—here the Quarter-Master stepped forward, shaking in his shoes, which, from old habit, he placed tight together at strict attention—"that ah, in fact, until, sir, you happened to come here, the—ah—the odah—was—ah—not such a one as could be considered offensive."

Mollified by this satisfactory explanation, the inspecting General clanked away, ringing his spurs and his brazen scabbard fiercely on the pavement.

"And now, ahem, Colonel Cheapsyde," he roared, "be good enough to let me see your young officers. It is a mattah which I wegard as of the first importance, that the young officer should be twained by the good example of his supewiors, into soljahlike habits fwom the—ah—vewy commencement."

"They are here, sir," said the terrible Colonel, mild as milk in the presence of the great man; and in effect, in the centre of the square, where a hundred windows looked down upon them, were to be seen two gentlemen balancing themselves alternately, and not without difficulty, first on one foot and then upon the other. The brilliant Staff converged into a circle, to consider this spectacle at leisure. There was an impressive silence as the two automatons continued their performance, and what their private feelings may have been it is impossible to say.

"Halt!" cried the General at last in a voice of thunder. "Mr. D'Arcy, call out the young gentleman on the wight, and ah! meashah that lace on his sleeve."

Roland stepped forward to the ordeal, and

the Aide-de-Camp pulled out a tape yard-measure.

"I regret to report, sir, that it's at least one-sixteenth below the regulation," stammered that worthy with bated breath.

"I thought so," snapped the General, and a dreadful silence fell on the assembly. "Colonel Cheapsyde," he said at length in freezing tones, "would you have the kindness to tell me what you expect to make of a young officer, who has the audacity to join his wegiment with the lace on his sleeve one-sixteenth below the wegulation? Or perhaps you will tell me what I, whc am eventually wesponsible, am to expect from a Commanding Officer who permits such a thing, and an Adjutant who fails to detect it? It's *most* unsoljahlike."

The Colonel could hardly have felt comfortable under the circumstances, but his face showed no sign; he was accustomed to take it out of his subordinates to the same tune, which proved that he had a high moral conception of discipline, and of the gentlemanly tone that should pervade all ranks. Had his General Officer ordered him to go home and insert his head in a bag, he would certainly have done it, and grumbled nothing.

"Discipline," he was wont to say, "*must* be maintained;" and if the reader is curious to know in what way it was maintained under such a chief, the following pages will disclose. With the older and married men we have little to do, but the mess, which gave the tone to the corps, was composed almost entirely of young fellows, and these their commander was able to mould after his own heart.

The scene was the Barrack Square in a certain town, an Orange stronghold in the north of Ireland, where the Blankshire regiment was in quarters, and the precise date was the day of the annual inspection. Sub-Lieutenants Jones and Tudor had only arrived in the preceding week. Jones was a good-looking, fool-faced lad, of easy temperament, who was pleased with his new feathers, profoundly elated at possessing a real man-servant of his own, at being allowed to sit up as late as he liked, and to order as many brandies-and-sodas as he chose. The poor boy looked upon the goose-step and its concomitant disagreeables, as a necessary set-off against a life of undoubted gentility and idleness, which it was his highest ambition to lead; whither or to what end he never considered for a moment. Ten years, twenty, thirty of this sort of thing, and the densest duffer will question something of its meaning at last; but in the beginning, all is "beer and skittles." The boy's public school-training had turned him out a fool. He had a smattering of Greek and Latin, which was likely to be as useful in the practical business of life, as the banjo and the bones. Hence, the army was the only thing open to him. Here it was supposed that a youth of his type could be comparatively happy, with his one accomplishment of Latin verse, and his present and future expectations from his father standing at a hundred a year. There were strange notions abroad on the education of a gentleman, when

this was the curriculum, and the Blankshires
and their like were regarded as a finishing
school!

To Roland, his new step in the world was
like going back to the beginning of things,
and he felt that he might as well have stepped
into his cradle and sent for his nurse to rock
him. It was certainly hard on a young man
who had gradually arrived at the conclusion
that in the whole wide world there was nothing
particularly good, only different degrees of badness, to have these new standards set up for
his imitation. So far, his enormous precocity
had always placed him ahead of his fellows,
but he now found himself in a sphere where
precocity availed him nothing. He was entered
for a species of donkey-race, where the first
must necessarily be last, and the last, first—the
laurels were for the most empty-headed. Happily, perhaps, he did not grasp all this at first
sight, and he turned out with Sub-Lieutenant
Jones to drill every morning, and listened to
that officer's interminable talk of himself, and to
his theories of existence in general, which might
very well have been those of a scullery-maid in
her first place, with all the patience in the
world. He did not dislike the boy with whom
he was thrown much, and he resolved to do
what he could for him.

The Blankshires were, in their own particular vernacular, a "Quack Corps;" the
title was sufficiently suggestive, but what it
precisely signified I am hardly soldier enough
to explain. I do not know that I should

have cared to belong to them: yet one was always informed mysteriously, of the fierce competition to which any candidate for that honour had to submit; indeed, it was hinted that nothing short of a personal friend of the P—ce of W—s stood any chance at all.

It may seem curious, that a set of gentlemen with so extremely high an opinion of their own position, should admit that anything could possibly be higher, yet so it was. The Household troops, for instance, were often mentioned, and in impressive tones; and one of their number, who had been sufficiently intimate with a captain in the Hot-water Guards to be kicked downstairs by him, was looked upon as a made man ever afterwards. The cavalry, too, were spoken of, and always as good fellows, and ones to be encouraged, even imitated to a certain extent, in the bow-legged walk, the peculiar planting of the elbows, and the aptitude for conversation of a character wholly unbefitting that of an officer and a gentleman, which, incredible to say, were the chief characteristics of some few cavalry regiments of the day. And there had been some who had declared they would as soon be in the Pinks, say, as in the Blankshire regiment itself; but the admission was generally held to be a mistake. It was fully understood in the regiment that no other ever had been equal to it, ever would be equal to it, or ever could be equal to it.

The truth was, though Roland was unaware of it, that the competition had been all to get him. When his name appeared in the lists, several Colonels who had antique editions of the landed gentry, and wives to keep them up to time, directed the aforesaid wives to "spot" Tudor of Sombrewood, and the result was in each case so satisfactory, that no less than five had applied for him by return of post. This secret was, of course, buried for ever in the national archives. But if it was essential for any corps that was looking up, to lay hold of this sort of young fellow, no less essential was it to impress him from the first, with the importance and social standing which accrued to him as a member of the corps.

Like many Commanding Officers, Colonel Cheapsyde had been unfortunate of late; he had had to take in youngsters who were the sons of men doing the dirty work of earning their own living—mere professional men. Disgusting as this was, the advanced Radicalism of the day necessitated it. By dint, however, of careful and systematic training under the regimental system, these promising lads had reduced the slur to a minimum, by acquiring the genuine touch and tone, the lisp, the elevation of the eyebrow, and the peculiar drop of the lower jaw, with the tongue thrust slightly between the teeth, which were the visible and outward characteristics of the regiment. Mentally too the advance had proceeded *pari passu*, leaving nothing to be desired. In an incredibly short space of time, such brains as they were blessed with, had become absolutely sodden and unreceptive, only flashing out into momentary brightness at rare intervals, when there was talk of a half crown ' sweep,' a new button, or an extra twiddle of lace. And if, after a year or two, the boys returned as finished gabies to the modest parental roof-tree, and the roof-tree disagreed with them, it was hardly surprising. Parents and guardians *did* occasionally own to some disappointment in the line of development taken by their darlings, which only proves what rusty old people the parents and guardians of the day must have been, and how little they could have appreciated what really was what.

Shortly before Roland joined them, the Blankshires had been happily delivered of a rascally Lord, who from first to last had smashed at least a dozen brother officers, before he happily went through the process himself, but to whom the regiment had clung throughout, with a desperate and affectionate tenacity worthy of a better cause. There were still left, however, two seedy Honourables, who were *ipso facto*, leaders in all the fun of the fair, and who were, if possible, more pimply, more dunder-headed, and more scatter-brained than any of their fellows, and this was saying a good deal. There was one fact that pressed sorely on the shoulders of the gallant Blanks, and that was the hard fact of poverty. With all their devotion to three-inch collars and acutely angular toes, to gold lace and trimmings; with all their refined tastes, and they had many, genuinely lofty cults, " none of your slummy *bric-a-brac* and pot business, but women and wine and racehorses, yachts, and the best of 'em all, you know;" these things were so far out of their reach, except in an infinitesimal degree, that it appeared no less than cruelty in Mother Nature, to have implanted instincts so impossible of attainment in their breasts.

Although he little guessed it, Roland was the richest man in the regiment, and might have bought up half of them out and out, had he felt inclined for so dubious a purchase; though truly, if he had bought them at his valuation and sold them at their own, the profits would have been very considerable. By some means a rumour of prodigious wealth, many hundreds a year of his own, came to be circulated. How incredible this rumour was with regard to a subaltern in the Blanks, it is impossible to convey to any outsider, and it led to his enjoying a toleration not often extended to a newly-joined subaltern. The Jews had latterly been having a terrible time of it with these gentlemen; one could not but be sorry for the poor Jew who had fallen into their clutches. One, it was said, had poisoned himself, and two of these *ci-devant* bloodsuckers had been drained empty as a pricked bladder, and had gone—oh Nemesis !—through the Bankruptcy Court.

One incident of this date is worth recording, as it will give a clue to the state of affairs.

A few days after his arrival, Roland noticed a subscription list in the ante-room — man drowned at sea; widow and six children left, and so forth—the case seemed a good one, and

without looking, or thinking more about it, he
wrote down his name for five pounds. Within
an hour of his doing so, the whole of the barracks was in commotion, and an unofficial
gathering had even been held in the Sergeants'
mess. It was a mistake, of course; the fellow
had meant five shillings, or perhaps five pence.
This was allowed on all hands; but even five
shillings was felt to be intolerable swagger,
when the senior Major's name was down just
above it for one. The result of the various
discussions was that the bugle sounded "the
officers' call" shortly after, and with the others
Roland made his appearance in the orderly-
room.

"Mr. Tudor," said Colonel Cheapsyde, sing-
ling him out of the circle, and fixing him with
a red eye, to which that of Mars was faint in
comparison, "oblige me by stepping forward a
moment. You are perhaps not aware, sir,
that your name stands in the subscription list
before me for the sum of 5*l*. It is fortunate,
sir, for you, that it has been thus early brought
to my notice, or the probabilities are that you
would have been taken at your word. Of course,
five shillings is what was intended, and this, I
wish to say, is considerably more than what we
consider it good taste on your part to put down.
The spirit of a true gentleman, sir, which I
never fail to inculcate on every young officer
joining this regiment, and which you will do
well to study in your brother officers, is one
which should have preserved you from such an
error. One shilling is regarded as a very good

sum, an excellent sum, for the generality of these appeals. You are possibly not aware, sir, that it is my duty as Commanding Officer to cut down ruthlessly anything like unnecessary expense."

Roland listened to this standing to attention, in his shell jacket (he was not yet advanced enough to be trusted with a sword), and at the end he said coldly,—

" I put down five pounds, as I thought that the case was a good one—but I will make it ten—or, if you prefer it, sir, withdraw it altogether." Sensation.

The orderly-room clerk fell back in his chair, gasping for breath, and knocked a pane out of the window behind him with the back of his head; a dozen scabbards clanked upon the floor; the Colonel, struck dumb, scratched himself vigorously. Here, on the one side, was rank insubordination, the grossest impertinence; but, on the other hand, what unknown possibilities might lie in such a subaltern. He—the Colonel—had a wife, he had daughters, a mess to keep up with respectability, and what not besides. The world conquered the flesh—that Commanding Officer flesh, sorely-averse from apology to a subaltern.

" Mr. Tudor," he said at last, strangling his emotions with an off-hand gruffness in his throat, " I am sure I shall not make a mistake if I ask permission to withdraw my—ah—remarks—made—ah—under a misapprehension. You have acted throughout with the utmost feeling and generosity, and I feel sure that in so doing I shall have the approval of your brother officers."

The sabres clanked vociferously, and the usually vapid faces brightened almost into animation. One or two jaws even that were habitually dropped, had been gathered up into their proper place, under the tension of the moment.

"But," continued the Colonel, his sternness returning somewhat, "I can hardly allow this to stand. You see, Mr. Tudor, that military etiquette is an exceedingly delicate thing, and unless indeed—" suddenly brightening—"the sum is lumped in altogether, as coming from the regiment, I don't see—I really don't see—but perhaps, Mr. Tudor, you would not be disinclined to this course?"

"Certainly not, sir," said Roland, "I should be extremely pleased with it."

"Excellent!" replied the Colonel. It was not the regimental form to talk much; but the scabbards made the deuce of a noise upon the floor. "Mr. Adjutant, ah—let me see—five other subscribers at a shilling—put down five guineas subscribed to this distressing case by Lieut.-Colonel Cheapsyde and officers of the Blankshire regiment, and, by the way, just send it in to the local papers. Good morning, gentlemen, that is all I have to say to you."

The badge of the regiment was a golden calf rampant. This was ostentatiously blazoned on uniform, plate, furniture, in fact, wherever there was space for it, and of course it had to be lived up to. Ah! they were sad dogs, and it would

neverhave been supposed by a listener to the conversation in the ante-room, that the wolf ever
came near the door, for the talk was on the
largest scale imaginable. Their entertainments,
when they did give them, which was not very
often, were gorgeous. If you dined with them
on an ordinary guest-night, you had a series of
endless courses (damnably cooked), in glittering
services of gilt plate, and not the meanest
subaltern there, but felt it his duty to take at
least three times as much "liquor" as was good
for him. But the particular point of these
guest-nights was to invite some of the natives,
whoever they might happen to be, and to insure that every one of them left the table
drunk. If a parson could be so caught
the fun was naturally doubled, and it was
obvious, that whoever the victim were, the
facilities which he offered in this state for light-
hearted amusement, were greatly intensified.
He could, perhaps, be induced to play the big
drum, or to stand on his head, in noble emulation of some gentle subaltern who led the way.
Or he would laugh, or he would weep, as the
case might be ; he was, at any rate, certain to
make a fool of himself, and this was the grand
thing.

Then there were balls occasionally, when a
neighbouring regiment had to be cut out, or
shown " how to do the trick," and so the merry
round went on, and man after man "smashed"
in the very best style, giving, as he left, a gold
snuff-box, or silver candlesticks, or a tankard,
with the regulation calf upon it (which, if

paid for at all, was by his creditors), as a parting gift to the mess, to prove that he had gone down gloriously in the fight, as a soldier should. It was the survival of the fittest in its sternest sense. How a man ever passed through the mill, and rose to be a field-officer, he himself could hardly say. Indeed it was seldom done, the strain was over-fierce, and the upper ranks were almost entirely recruited by exchange. In spite of its pretensions the unfortunate corps had little or no interest, and was a species of military rubbish-heap, upon which any man, who was not particularly wanted elsewhere, was tossed. Cheapsyde and his immediate predecessors, had been noisy and pushing enough to make themselves unpleasant at the War Office, and the consequence had been a selection of the worst stations in the British Empire, as the headquarters of the regiment during the last thirty years, a circumstance which had not contributed to improve it morally or physically. It is not, however, to be supposed that the foregoing descriptions apply to every officer individually; but they fairly characterize the majority, who had the upper hand, and originated the *esprit de corps*. There were exceptions; but they were in a hopeless minority.

A curious system prevailed in the army at the time, which, to our own higher lights, must raise a smile. No matter what a man's previous character and convictions, in other words, no matter how vast a nincompoop he might have proved himself during his career, if, by any

accident, the command fell to him, the past
was blotted out, his word was taken as gospel,
and his confidential report on the character
and qualifications of any officer under him, was
accepted without question.   Here was a magnificent chance, for a man who could bide his
time, of paying off old scores, and the opportunity so offered of turning the tables on a less
fortunate brother officer, was often irresistible.   But this system, which meant " rings "
and cliques, plotting and counter-plotting, was
by no means confined to the regiment, it prevailed throughout the army.   Its results were
chiefly evident in the periodical thrashings
which, once or twice in a decade, some naked,
half-armed band of savages was able to inflict
on a British force, fortified with all the latest
appliances and munitions of war.

Under Colonel Cheapsyde the hugest activity
prevailed in the Adjutant's department, for only
in this way could the regiment have been kept
together at all, and that gentleman had a keen
appreciation of the side on which his bread was
buttered.   He seldom cared to be off duty ; when
the Colonel gave a picnic, for instance, he would
go round afterwards, spurs, boots, and all complete, and collect the empty jam pots for Mrs.
Colonel, with every grace in the world.   So
there was perfect accord in this quarter, and
floods of little blue missives, under the terrible
title of " memorandums," were poured forth
upon the head of any ill-fated officer who failed
to fall in entirely with the views of the C. O.,
or who fancied that his individuality was worth

preserving. Almost the only remark vouchsafed to Roland, on the first night that he dined
at mess, was anent this very official, to whom,
it was hinted, he must look in fear and
trembling.

"Yaave not a—seen the Adjutant yet, I
s-a-pose?"

"No, not as yet."

"Ah! my l-a-d" (the speaker was certainly
a couple of years younger than Roland), "tha
smartest soljah in the sarvice! Dan't knaw if
ya'ave noticed the pipings on the—a—tails of ar
f'llahs pea-jackets? Naw? He—a—'ntraduced
'em, and—a—'n-vented the twiddle above,
don't-cher-knaw? Expense frightful—didn't
care a dam—Dook awfully pleased, y' knaw.
Shaw to give him a brevet, and I tell you what"
(lowering his voice), "it made the 5th Mump-
shires so de-vlish jealous they're reg'lar
hipped, and off *their* feed!"

The Blankshires were seldom in want of
society, for they carried their own about with
them, and the regimental ladies contributed
not a little to the *mise-en-scène* wherever it was.
It must be allowed, that at the mere mention
of their names, my pen dashes into its ink
with the joy and vitality of renewed youth.
There is so much that might be said of the
regimental ladies, of the sisters and the
friends who often came to live with them; but,
although it must be obvious to the unbiassed
reader that no approach to any character in
this book ever did, or ever could, breathe the
air of real life, I am appalled at the tempest

which the slightest misapprehension on this subject, might arouse. If, by the merest chance, any lady of any regiment, in any service, or clime, should take up the cap, and say it fitted her—like a bonnet. What then? No, the risk is disproportionate. Besides, even in the Blankshires there were real ladies, as well as real gentlemen, though it was made so unpleasant for them that they were—figuratively speaking—nowhere. Woe to the unfortunate lady, with the traditions of a gentlewoman, whom the chances of matrimony had brought into their ranks—*pace*.

For the rest, it must be admitted that from the wife of the Quarter Master, who, as lance corporal twenty years before, had married a black in the Bahamas, up to Mrs. Mash, who passed for a beauty, at any rate, in the colonies, and who had somewhat vague expectations of one day moving among the titled aristocracy as one of themselves, that they could all be exceedingly pleasant when they liked—which was not always. The pleasantness consisted chiefly in hacking about the subaltern's cobs, and the wearing of hats and gloves, or other tokens of good feeling supplied by the same gentlemen, in the betting of boots, or any small and useful articles, which, if lost, were never, of course, paid; and in playing such a desperate and complicated game (for the husband's position, as captain or major, was, of course, reckoned in) on the heart-strings of these poor young men, that—but I have said I wouldn't, and I won't. There is only one little fault which I feel bound to find with them, they possessed a really too accurate knowledge of regulation minutiæ. If, for instance, you were on your way to relieve a besieged garrison, or to serve the rations, as the case might be, and you were met upon your way by one of them, it ran thus :—

"How d'ye do, Mr. Blanky, and where are you going? I did not notice your name in Orders." "I am going—to Bath—to Jericho" (or wherever it were), "to relieve the garrison by assault"—or, perchance, the ration bugle having sounded, "I go to see the salt pork served out." "But where is—that is—isn't a sash de rigueur? I thought—and surely in Friday's order-book I saw that the cap-covers were to be discontinued, and—" But by this time you had fled upon your road, and only the words borne high upon the wind followed you. "Mind, Mr. Blanky, at nine o'clock tonight; remember, you promised to look in upon me," and your men, perhaps, smiled noisily in the ranks, and your Corporal guffawed, and you would have slain him, to say nothing of her.

One peculiarity of the elder ladies should be mentioned before the subject is dismissed. In some occult manner they had contrived to impress their husbands with a singular similarity of ideas, so that in time these officers came to be not altogether unlike old women themselves.

The Blankshires did not escape that criticism from the outer world to which the best of us are subject. Some people said there was a bad tone about them, not much principle or religion, and that sort of thing. But how could this be? for, besides church parade, every subaltern went to evening service on Sundays in mufti, and sang hymns in the most marked and impressive way, and threw winks and smiles and coughings, and flowers and gloves, and sometimes a hymn-book at the girl of his choice, and especially during the sermon, so that altogether no end of fun was got out of it by both parties. Then there were people who urged that they were a stupid regiment, but this is easily proven a calumny. The verandah and window of the mess looked out upon the street, and never a woman passed, in wet weather or dry, were she young or old, pretty or plain, but something was said. It was not always easy to catch, but it was something that always raised a laugh, and was always amusing. To treat one single, simple topic so as to be ever fresh, surely showed an infinite variety of wit.

The common occupation in hours of idleness (and there were many such), was to lounge across the verandah railing, staring at any woman whose calling unfortunately led her past the barracks, while the subalterns smoked, and at long intervals, closing one eye, spit upon the pavement below. If an unsuspecting wayfarer could be thus victimized, well, you would hardly deny them this. Then there was amusement to be got in the coal-heaving line, when the ration of coal was brought to the mess, and this afforded a noble opportunity of

stoving in a neighbour's hat that was ob-
noxiously new and pretentious, and had the advantage of being a high-bred and gentlemanly
sport at the same time. But certainly the
hardest work that was undertaken was in pipe-
colouring. There were men there of twenty or
thirty years' service, with whom it had been
the sole achievement of life. It was pleasant
to hear them descant upon it; and pleasant it
was, too, when evening came round, to see
these grey-beards link their arm in that of
some youngster, and go forth to enjoy themselves as gentlemen should in the slums, so
that the young innocent might be put up to it
all, and really understand life—the boy fresh
from home or from school. Yes, it was cheery!

They were not a talkative regiment. What
little conversation there was, was almost incomprehensible to the outsider, so clipt and cut
and cabalistic was the language in use. About
three months before the Derby, however, a
marked vivacity gradually spread itself, and this
became the one topic, so that the unsporting
mind was sometimes driven to wish for a
change, and grew to loathe the name of every
noble animal. But when the great day came,
and some one of the subalterns, more dashing
than his fellows, had a real telegram from a
real live bookmaker, saying that five pounds
had been actually won or lost by him, then
there was a flutter in the dove-cot, and the
pink missive was pinned up conspicuously in
the ante-room, that all the world might know.
But in ordinary times, when this elaborate

horsiness, or perhaps it would not be harsh to
say donkeyness, had worn off, the conversation
was always worth listening to, if it were only
for the comparative novelty of the social views
put forth, and the easy scorn with which any
approach, to what a misguided world styles
principle, was treated.   One could not help
wondering what human society would be like
were it reconstituted on the basis which approved itself to these young gentlemen.

Roland, finding himself in an argument one
evening, suggested by way of experiment rather
than anything else, that these views scarcely
seemed to him compatible with religion.

" Oh ! damn religion," came the prompt
answer.

" Well, with morality, then."

" Oh ! curse morality."

" But I mean," he persisted, " a man's own
intellect will tell him."

" Oh ! intellect be blasted," and there was
no doubt that it was completely, in the case in
question.

" Tell you what it is," continued the speaker
generously, " you come along with me to-night,
and I'll see you through ; it's an infernally
blackguard hole this place, but we do manage
to knock a little life out of it down town in
the small hours."

" Thank you.   I'm not driven to the slums
yet for the life I require."

The other twirled the scrappy end of his
moustache.

" Deah boy," he said, coming down to a

familiar manner, and putting his arm in Roland's, " shaw you'd like it if you only tried it. Do come, old man." A laugh was Roland's reply; this seemed rather to offend his new friend, for he said hastily,—

"Oh, very well; course you know best. By George! I wonder if you've half a crown about you. Hit infernally at Nap last night; lost seventeen and six, and had to pip up then and there; lags a fellow doosidly." It was not often that money hung in Roland's pockets when it was asked for, but this time it did. He hesitated, then turned his waistcoat pocket inside out, so that its contents—a few shillings —fell upon the floor, and without a word he walked away.

"Tha' f'llah's mad!" ejaculated the other, staring blankly after him, and then fell promptly on his hands and knees to gather in the harvest.

On another occasion, an embryonic sportsman lashed him to desperation by a disquisition on the pedigree of the horse. The new subaltern, able to bear it no longer, let fall an uncomplimentary expression.

"What the doose do you know about it?" said the lecturer, turning fiercely upon him.

"I know that his remote ancestor was a five-toed animal," replied Roland, with a superfluity of drouth. This was received by the assembly as a most facetious idea.

"Where did his hoofs come from then?" adventured the sportsman, not knowing how far this was to be taken seriously.

U

" Survival and development of nail of second toe. You weren't aware of that ? "

" 'Pon m' sawl cawnt say I was," returned the questioner, decimating what stood for his moustache.

" Then don't talk to me again about the pedigree of the horse," said Roland, lighting a cigarette and departing.

Unhappily the severity of this was much modified by the density of his hearers' ignorance. It was generally agreed among them that this was ill-timed funning, under the guise of superior knowledge, an altogether unforgivable offence.

Some time before Roland joined, one of these precocious youngsters, who had lost a pound or two over a race, thought it worth while to mark the occasion by blowing his brains out. He left a letter for his chum—a scrawled, misspelt document which, when deciphered, was understood to say—that he wished his friend better luck, and hoped to see the " good things " turn up more frequently in the next world than they did in this. " Tu nos *bona* fac videre in terra viventium," runs the verse of the old Latin hymn. This was his version. Poor lad—poor lad!

Almost every hour now brought Roland some fresh experience of what was expected from the Blankshire standard of an officer and a gentleman. As he walked down to the parade-ground, where he and Jones did their uttermost to represent battalions in the field— he met the Colonel's little boy, who, as one of

the keenest soldiers in the regiment, frequently
came down to inspect the manœuvres of
Messrs. Jones and Tudor, whereby he fancied
he gained an insight into the law of battles.
The child had been crying, and Roland asked
him what was amiss, to which the boy made
answer, " Oh ! they're all so cross at home, I
hate them ; and papa was naughty again yesterday, and so mamma cried all night, and I heard
Tom (that's our man and nurse's husband) tell
pa to go to H—ll, and that he'd a good mind to
shoot him through the head and send him
there ; and he won't let Nursey stay any more.
And what I want to know is, why pa doesn't
put Tom in the guard-room, and when I asked
him he boxed my ears ; and so, b-o-o-h, please—
I've come to see you and Mr. Jones turn into
battalions."

This transformation was speedily effected
by the aid of a few ropes, but for the life
of him, Roland could not take his eyes and
thoughts off the little, pale-faced, big-eyed
boy, who sat so patiently all the long while
upon the grass, diligently watching, and learning the first rudiments of the art of war.

There should be the makings of a fine soldier
—yet, alas ! the ordeal !—and he could not help
wondering whether a golden mean might not
be found for the youthful officer, between the
prig on the one hand, and the blackguard and
the dastard on the other.

CHAPTER XI.

ABOUT this time came a letter from Sybil, from which the following is an extract :—

"Oh! my beloved, what spell have you worked upon me, that I accept without questioning all you do? Where was my heart that it was filled with joy, when you went away from me as you did? and would not say good-bye. By that magic you broke the neck of the parting, and we cannot be apart. However fantastic this may sound (and it looks absurd enough in writing), I feel it to be true. But, oh! what a life you have led my spirit. You remember that hot morning when you left me, how hot it was! and I was so tired that night with packing, that I could not sleep, but lay in a kind of waking trance, often thinking that I saw and spoke with you. And the journey had so run in my head that I fancied you too were travelling, and I went with you a little way, but oh! dear love, not far, as I wished and wished again, for I was dragged back to my sleepless pillow. And since then my thoughts of you have been so wild and unreal, but I will hardly speak of them, for I

know you will laugh at me. Whether I have
suddenly become clairvoyant and have been
looking into your future, I do not know, but I
half suspect it, or my wish may be father to
my thought, for whatever you do with me, this
is the one thing you must do with yourself.
I have dreamed that I saw you leading the
charge over the hills in some strange country,
fighting shoulder to shoulder in the ranks, and
cheering on your comrades to victory. Yes,
it was victory, I am certain of that, as I am of
the scenes, and the men, and the uniforms, and
all the rest. And it has been so vivid, that my
heart has been stirred to its depths, and I
hardly knew if I dreamed or no. And all the
while, doubtless, you were snug in your rooms
in Piccadilly, for I see that you only joined
your regiment a week or two ago. Why have
you never written?

"I believe what has confirmed this folly in
my head, was a paragraph in a French paper
(we have seen no English latterly, for we are
up in the mountains), about the fabulous exploits of some guerilla chief, a man they
call Rollo, who they say is an Arab leader or
prophet from Morocco, though another paper
declares he is a Frenchman. The name suggested yours, but the exploits were rather those
of Claude Duval with the chill just taken off.
I suppose love shows itself in this sort of
mental vagary, but I confess it is new to my
experience, and a little alarming.

"We did not stay at Kissingen, but came
up here to the mountains and the woods.

Guardy is much better. The two dogs, Roland and Tudor, never were so happy as roaming through the beech-woods, where we go all together, the dogs and I and the little sister who came as nurse. There are many quaint wayside chapels and shrines, and the people are so good and so devout. It is quite beautiful to see human beings whose faith carries them through from cradle to grave, with never a stagger or a halt. I have made friends with the good Pfarrer of the parish, he speaks a little English, and always calls me 'My lady Grey!' Every time we meet he asks me if I am of the family of the Lady Jane Grey, and explanation being hopeless, I always reply, 'I don't know,' which always astonishes him afresh.

"And this reminds me of the real, true Lady Jane, *our* Lady Jane, whom we met last week at *table-d'hôte* at ——, whither we had driven in to hear the band. But I have more to tell you. With her were Mr. and Mrs. Brabant, and the trio were apparently honeymooning together. So then it is all over, but probably you know more about it than I do. We heard that they had eloped, that they were married privately, and that Lady Jane came after them by express to save appearances. I daresay this is scandal. Narcissus was drooping, but it was not over his own loveliness, I fancy, nor over his wife's. It was just as beautiful to see him walk into dinner as ever, which it could not be if he were conscious of it. I sat by him, and confess I was more than

ever impressed with his powers, but he is
Sampson shorn. He seems to me a man of
strong ambitions, chafing under lack of strength
to pursue them. It is his theory, he told me,
that mere brain work does more to mould the
age than the pulpit, the platform, or the sword,
and that the real wire-pullers of the world, are
those thinkers, who are clever enough to popularize their theories, and so bend its neck to
their yoke.

" As for his wife, I disagree with her as much
as I do with Lady Jane's bonnets. Her manner
is what I should call a bad one, incurably, for
it is in the grain. She was very red, very rustly,
very strainy in the seams, and very acidulated
—at least I thought so—and she had a way of
chewing her soup which contained the essence
of mad aggravation. Your poor friend shook
with unspoken feeling, and finally dropped his
spoon in despair. I noticed too that he did not
venture on any of his theories in her hearing.
She was full of her health, or the lack of it,
but said nothing of his, though he looked woefully pale, much as if his sole diet for weeks
past had been of white butterflies. She spoke
of some friends they had met in Paris, a
Marquis whom I did not know, and hardly
thought that she would. We also saw Lord
St. Maur, but only for a few minutes; he was
passing through from the south, he told
us. He is charming always, but don't you
think he is rather *odd?* He speaks of you
with a suppressed enthusiasm which I will not
quarrel with, but which strikes me as *unusual.*

"A fortnight hence we hope to be returning to Sombrewood, which has that one solitary remnant of my heart which is left when your claims are satisfied. I would not lose the gold of my autumn woods for all that is in Christendom. And you—you must come for a few hours, if it be only to look after your timber; and if you will send me a few lines, I will 'expand' them for myself, and make of them a volume, greater even than this threatens to be when it is sealed up." * * * *

And of the answer the following extract will suffice:—

* * * * "You cannot tell what your letter means to me, reaching me as it does, and bringing me glimpses of a paradise from which I have been cast out, the very sunshine of its pastures and the very breath of its flowers. But words at best are idle things between us two, and I cannot reply to you on paper as I would. Some of your news took me completely aback. I had not heard of Brabant's marriage. Poor dear fellow! I feel as if I had been wanting to him, and now it is too late. Of the Blankshires I can only tell you that I do not intend to remain with them a minute longer than I can help; but when I have learned my A B C, there is a garrison course, and this I must certainly go through. There is also a chance of manœuvres in the spring; I shall stay for these, and if I find it worth while until I can go up for the Staff examination. I am not given to brag, I hope, but I believe with six months' work I shall know more of soldiering than two-thirds of my brother officers rolled into one. Had I not seen the state of things, I could never have believed it. The regiment was last in action in 1796, when it ran away. Since then it has hardly had ten years home-service, and there appears to be no God-forsaken spot on the face of the globe, in which it has not rotted meantime. When a man comes to grief in his own corps, it appears that he is usually gazetted to us. I could possibly stand it a little longer were I a member of the serjeants' mess; these men, at least, have a few soldier-like instincts, are decent fellows, and comparative gentlemen. The regiment, take it as a whole, is quite worthy of my uncle, and my uncle of it. I can't say more.

"What are your ideas of Ireland? What mine were, I suppose. What those are of most untravelled Englishmen, that it is a barren island, inhabited by outer barbarians. The way in which my eyes have been opened on many subjects has been astonishing. Barren it certainly is, the greater part of it, such as England may have been, say in the reign of King John; but I have come to the conclusion that the barbarians are ourselves, who are doing our best to strangle a perfectly legitimate aspiration towards nationality. Though this principle is obscured by the most serious drawbacks, it is a sound one at bottom, my word upon it. Remember, that this wretched country lies cheek-by-jowl with the most prosperous one upon earth, and that for seven hundred years it has been governed by it. Were I

a Kelt. I would certainly shed my blood in the
cause. As an English Catholic, owing everything in the shape of social and religious
freedom to this nation which has won it for me,
I am deeply stirred on their behalf. I wonder
if anybody ever wrote a love-letter of this sort
before? But these things may deeply concern
us and our future. Brabant's theories on wire-
pulling are very good up to a certain point, but
the *ultima-ratio* always has been, and always
will be—force—the sword and the brain that
wields it.

"I must get a few hours at Sombrewood
some day,—I think I can manage it. Until then,
dear one, I commend you to your unknown God.

"Your true lover,

"ROLAND.

"P.S.—I was the man you read of in the
papers; this between ourselves."

For a span this postscript blotted out everything else. The feelings with which Sybil
read and re-read it may be imagined. Without
a word her lover had left her side and plunged
into a sea of peril; partly, perhaps, to console
himself for their enforced separation, but
equally as much to satisfy his restless craving
for action. Her breast was sore with heaving
for him, and a little for herself; for what place
had she in a life whose *ultima-ratio* was con-
fessedly the sword? Of the way in which the
matter had first reached her she questioned
hardly at all. At all times profoundly impressed with the mysteries underlying life, one

prodigy the more made little difference, and this was so very natural a prodigy; but she treasured the memory to her heart.

Roland, in her eyes, was plainly of that heroic band which, in all times since her foundation, England has sent conquering and to conquer to the uttermost ends of the earth, pioneers of civilization and empire. This was no unmeet beginning, and she bore it philosophically, thinking. a little sadly too and jealously, of all the career that is offered to woman, and this seemed to her infinitesimal at best.

Then she dismissed her dreams, and sent off for all the English papers she could think of, likely to contain a notice of the affair, and upon a card she wrote to him these two words, for she was at a loss for others :—

"Well done,"

which she signed with her initials. To which, in due time, came its answer in the monosyllable,

"Thanks! R. T."

So there the matter rested, for these two enjoyed a calm of soul in their mutual confidence, which is not very usual among lovers.

Here we must follow in pursuit of the bride and bridegroom, and although it may not be the customary thing to accompany a couple under the circumstances, still Lady Jane has led the way, and where she leads we may safely follow.

Those who, with ourselves, have watched Mrs. Lushington Squeed's career, will be aware that there was a deep, if somewhat irregular, vein of romance running all through it. She was to

marry a literary man of the most *recherché*
(this is her word, not ours) class; young,
well-looking, and a sweet singer of songs,
who was a man of family to boot, and the
great question had been with her secretly,
for a long time past, how best this might be
done with *éclat*. She had hunted up all her
literary acquaintance, and was sure of a good
notice when the affair did come off. Moreover, she had set upon a colonial Bishop, and
well-nigh engaged him for the occasion, but
difficulties cropped up, and a disheartening
feeling that all this was rather " mild," and
that the Public had half a dozen really good
things of the kind every week—bishops, brides-
maids, orange-blossoms, and the rest of it.

Besides, notwithstanding all Lady Jane's
loyal endeavours, it was not probable that the
list of marriage guests would bear close inspection, although four knights' ladies had
been sworn in for the purpose, and these may
be anything under a duchess—and look it—in
print.

Then an enormous difficulty came about,
that of being married within the walls of a
Catholic church only as required by the Rubric.
Mrs. Squeed, on hearing of this condition,
exploded in a torrent of something not very
unlike blasphemy, and prettily said that her
daughter might as well go on the streets at
once and pick up her man, that such trifling
with the Scarlet Lady of Babylon, whom she
described as a drunken ——, sitting on her
seven hills, implied a common cause with her,

and the like of her; with much more to the same effect. Then, with a final burst of genuine tears, she waddled from the room sobbing that all that was now left was to pray, because of her daughter's sin.

Consider, oh! Christian brother and sister, this little scene—it is imaginary, purely imaginary, ha! ha!—but surely if the great God above us could be moved to merriment, such bathos of His high worship would be the thing to do it.

As for Mrs. Lushington herself, she took a coldly circumstantial view. Social *éclat* was her aim, and she thought that possibly a kind of typical hard case might be made of it, which would find its way into the social papers; but after mature consideration she dismissed this idea, and finally decided that nothing short of an elopement would set the world agog at the end of August. If it could be in time for the Cowes week all would be well, for society would be gathered *en bloc*, and the papers would be on every table.

There was no great difficulty; her mother had refused to have anything to say to the ceremony, and had gone into the country for a visit; there only remained the sisters to be "squared," and they were not girls to hesitate when anything so promising was in the wind. Eve was not told, as it was generally felt that her trenchant spirit would cleave the scheme as a knife does an orange. There was only one drawback worth mentioning, and that was Mr. Brabant himself. Mrs. Lushington

knew him too well to suppose for an instant
that he would lend himself to such a notion,
for his dreamy spirit was a singularly practical
one.

Now a mere every-day elopement is held to
consist in a gentleman running away with a lady,
but here the original plan was devised of revers-
ing that order, although, of course, the former
was outwardly maintained; and this was the way
it was done.   The two had agreed beforehand
that they would dispense with all needless ceremony; Brabant was to get the necessary papers,
they were to be married quietly on a certain
day, and Devonshire was talked of for the
honeymoon.   The bridegroom to be, was as
anxious as most men of that eccentric epoch,
to avoid flutter and expense, and Mrs. Lushington's singular compliance with this desire of
his, might have made him suspicious, but did
not.   He was too busy to be much at Harrow,
and Mrs. Squeed's outburst had reached his
ears, though the news of her departure had not;
he therefore arranged the preliminaries with
his *fiancée* by letter.   The answers he received
seemed to him slightly incoherent, but great
point was made of as early an hour as possible.

In accordance with this, when the morning
came, Mr. Brabant, with a college friend who
was to tie the knot, and another as best man,
sauntered about ten o'clock into a shabby little
London church or chapel, a relic out of the evil
days of persecution, which stood three-parts
concealed in the " backs " of a great thorough-

fare. A very creditable carriage and pair was already prowling uneasily before the door. The blinds were down, but occasionally the peep-hole at the back gave a convulsive flap as the carriage passed to and fro. When the trio appeared, a young lady suddenly popped out of it, exactly attired in a neat travelling overcoat, and thickly veiled. She came straight to Brabant and caught his arm; she was deeply agitated, and it was some moments before he recognized Mrs. Lushington's maid.

"What—what on earth has happened?" he asked nervously.

"Oh! Mr. Brabant," exclaimed the young woman, "my poor, darling mistress! She has" (mysteriously) "fled away at the last moment. They have driven her to elope at eight o'clock this very morning."

"Gracious, mercy!" ejaculated Brabant, turning ashy pale. "Eloped? Good Heavens, with whom?"

"Why with you, sir, of course, and here she is."

"With *me?*" exclaimed the stricken man, his brain reeling; but comparatively relieved, he plunged into the carriage, and found himself in his bride's arms.

If he had hoped for an explanation he was disappointed; she was violently hysterical, and could only cling to him, sobbing,—

"Oh! Warby, Warby, you'll forgive me, won't you? I told them all it was eleven, but I fled secretly away at eight, and my mum—mum—mother knows it not. My poor sisters" (one of whom, by the way, had ordered the carriage), "oh! whither will they think me gone, for your sake."

"Mad!" whispered a mocking demon in his ear, but he knocked him down, and only said with the faintest shade of irritation,—

"But, hang it all, my dearest Maria, this was the day, and this was the church, and it's all arranged as you wished. I don't understand. I left it with you to settle things at home, and, d—— them! they can't pretend to interfere, or not to know. Really it's too bad of them to frighten you into this state, and I thought your sisters might be here, and a friend who would give you away."

"Oh! Warburton, there's no one to give me away. How cruel to remind me of it, but if you are there to take me, what does it matter?" (sob)—and then, growing calmer, she added solemnly, "Let it be consummated, and let us flee the country."

He looked at her curiously. "Flee the country? My dearest girl, why, what for? I've ordered breakfast at —— Hotel, and thought we'd run down to Devon by the—"

"Oh, Heavens, no! If we were pursued it would kill me. And the law, Warburton? Oh! Warburton, think of the law. No, dear friend," and she slipped her hand into his, "at the eleventh hour, my dear old schoolfellow, the Baroness Von Homburg, writes from Boulogne to offer us an asylum."

"A lunatic one?" again whispered the demon in Brabant's ear. But all the latter replied, resigning himself, was, " Very well, my dear; it is immaterial where, if you are pleased."

" Let it be Boulogne then, till the storm is spent."

Meanwhile the priest was waiting, and the best man, to whom all this was as Greek, had been holding a desperate flirtation in the porch with the pretty maid, who had almost persuaded him to elope too. Nor need it be concealed that this young lady was the life and soul of the affair, and that she it was who had first suggested it. It did seem tiresome that the best man was to be left behind.

The paragraph, therefore, which was the all-important part of the business, came off successfully; but then it was the end of August.

" Elopement in High Life ! " " Oh, here ! you know," said the Deputy-assistant Sub-editor, when it was handed in to him; " hardly high life, is it, Mr. Robinson ? "

Mr. Robinson, who was primed for the business, said that " high life " it certainly was, if he were any judge, and with a red pencil he underlined the name of Lady Jane.

" Yes, yes; I see," said the Pro-editor, " but one swallow, eh ? "

The writer then pointed out the name of the Baroness, but the D. A. S. E. would not recognize her as more than a sparrow. However, when he looked at the other " paras," he found that his Ladies-in-Waiting and Major-Generals had been quite below the average

that week, and, as Mr. Robinson still confronted him, he said testily, "Oh, well; stick
it in."

So the world became aware that "a romantic
affair took place last week, when the charming
and wealthy widow of the late Mr. Lushington
Squeed, of Squisby, and great-grandniece of
Jemima, half-sister of the late Sir Horatius
Cockles, eloped with the now well-known Mr.
Warburton Brabant. The marriage, which
appears to have been arranged beforehand,
took place privately in London, and it is hinted
that the union was blessed by the Cardinal-
Archbishop of Pimlico himself, after which the
devoted couple continued their flight as far as
Boulogne, where they found sanctuary with an
old friend of the bride's, the Baroness Von
Homburg. The matter, which originated in the
difference between the faiths of the contracting
parties, has, it is whispered, been arranged to
the satisfaction of all concerned; the ever-
active and youthful Lady Jane Squeed, the
bride's aunt, having undertaken the negotiations
and caught up the runaways at the Hôtel
B—— in Paris. Mr. Brabant will certainly
have made a stroke with the public by giving
his poetic notions the *actualité* of real life."

It must be admitted, that this paragraph made
the best of things, and was likely to achieve the
end calculated by the lady who had inspired it.
If the relationship to Sir Horatius, who had not
existed within the last fifty years, appeared to
be a little strained, how wily was the chance
reference to Lady Jane at the end, which implied

at least a score of titled aunts. "Of Squisby" was put in for pure effect—there was no Squisby—never had been; but on reading the notice most people remembered it, and some thought they had stayed there. In every way the insertion was a success. There were old gentlemen who had known of Sir Horatius, continental travellers of course recollected the Baroness, while most people at Cowes had experienced the difficulty of keeping Lady Jane at a reasonable distance, and sympathized profoundly with a niece who had been so pursued. Then, too, a semi-heretical elopement, which the Cardinal-Archbishop had gone out of his way to bless, must be something special. But this part of the report, too, was pure invention.

Luckily for the cause, moreover, a great religious organ, "The No Popery," took up this point in a leader, under the triple title (in gigantic capitals) of "More Pollution—Roman Rape—A Widow entrapped by Jesuitry," and it called upon the Parliament of this Protestant people to vindicate the glorious principles of the Reformation, and to take the matter up, and threatened it with fire from Heaven if it should fail. It was not until a score of letters and papers to boot, had been received at the office, pointing out that the Cardinal-Archbishop had been in Vienna on the date mentioned, that the Editor desisted from his call to arms, and remembered that it was just the time for his summer holiday. So Harrow and all who appertained to it were made happy, for anything is better than nonentity. To his latest day, the man chiefly concerned in all this, never understood the why and wherefore of it, and circumstances soon led him to desist from fruitless questioning.

But, to retrace the thread; the wedding well over, without let or hindrance, a series of fresh troubles, which began at the station, arose. Brabant had hurried on to take the tickets, which included a second class for the maid; but when his bride discovered this, she declared that she could not consent to be parted from her for a single instant, and the young lady, with the calmness of the most perfect breeding, assured him that she had never travelled second class in her life. It was not a time for sarcasm or jest, or he would have proposed to use the ticket himself, and the repression of the witticism upset him, the more so that, having so spoken, the maid turned away, as if it were no further concern of hers, and began to chat confidentially with her mistress, leaving the care of the baggage entirely to him. Mrs. Brabant, to give her her new title, had always said that she made a friend of her servants, and when it was not an enemy, this was perfectly true; too much so to her husband's thinking. Now, as he looked at them, he saw that the girl had discarded her waterproof, and was as well dressed as his wife, that her clothes fitted her better, and that, as she was decidedly the nicer-looking, the attentions of the guard and porters were entirely directed to her. By way of setting this right, he took up a roll of wraps and held it out for her to carry. She eyed him a moment, arching her fine eyebrows, pulled out a light shawl from the top, and said, " Thank you so very much ; I dare say we shall find it chilly crossing ; one doesn't bring one's furs in August."

Mrs. Brabant's composure had by this time completely returned ; in proportion as this was the case his own deserted him, and he did one of the rashest things ever recorded of a bridegroom. Taking her aside, he said, "My dearest, I should like to give that woman warning at once and her wages. Don't you think we can manage without her ? "

Mrs. Brabant transfixed her man sternly, " What, Altiora ? And pray who's to do me up, I should like to know, and all that ? "

" My dearest " (poor fellow, little did he think what he promised), " I'll do you up, and undo you too, if you like. I'll do, in fact, anything—"

" Thank you," freezingly, " I could get on,"— sob,—"without you, far better than I could without her. Little did I expect, Warburton, that the first thing you'd do would be to try and deprive me of the only friend that is left to me from my dear old home."

The husband was taken utterly aback at this unexpected speech ; his bride's whole demeanour was new and strange to him ; the woman he had courted seemed to have vanished suddenly away, leaving a different one in her place. Already, though he little guessed it, he was tasting the first fruits of marriage, and she was only reverting to her natural self as distinguished from her "society" self;—all he had known before.

Still, there was something to be said for her, and we hasten to say it. Everything in Mrs. Brabant's trousseau, from her boots upward, was a size too small for her, and this could hardly be conducive to pleasantness and good humour. She was a helpless, feckless creature, who thought it lady-like to do everything clumsily —or more properly, to be unable to do anything for herself at all; her maid was literally her right hand, and in all the secrets of the prison-house: it would have been impossible for her to have appeared in public without the girl's help. Brabant was a mere baby where the real woman was concerned, and he failed to see this. Probably he could not have conceived such a state of things, but he recognized that there was dire offence in what he had said, and went to work to make amends generously. He squeezed his wife's hand, rushed out and bought Altiora a shilling fashion journal, helped her, after his wife, into the same carriage, gave her the seat by the window, and half a glass of sherry from his own flask—in fact, treated her with all the attention of which he was capable, and to do her justice she did not fail to respond.

An ominous "lop" was curling the face of the grey sea when they reached Folkestone, and the bride declared her intention of going below to lie down at once. Brabant saw her comfortably settled and her numerous wants attended to, and as Altiora said she was a good sailor and would look after her, he left them and returned to the deck, which, for reasons of his own, he was sorry he had ever quitted. There he seated himself on a bench near the smoke-stack, and grimly set his face against some hours of misery, for the wind was dead a-head, and it had come over very thick. It proved to be a nasty passage, and as he grew worse and worse, he felt that everything depended on his remaining a fixture. Once he moved his little finger, and he was never quite the same man afterwards.

The sea dashed in and drenched him, but he stirred not, although half frozen, and he was gradually made aware that he was lying, one of a heap of most objectionable corpses, in a forgotten corner of the vessel. Then a sailor threw a tarpaulin over him, and for many years after, that unwitting sailor had a blessing on his head at a spare moment. There were people going about who stumped and stamped horribly, and there were dreadful noises, convulsive rushes of rattling chain, throbbings and heavings; for the vessel herself was very bad at times, and hardly seemed as if she would recover. The smoke-stack by which he found himself was approximately warm, hence the affinity of the cold corpses with it, one of whom projected an elbow into the centre of his spine. Six years he had been there, with that elbow growing into his back, he could have sworn it. It was horrible, but he was powerless. Then, by-and-by, when Hope had fled, came some one else, somebody who seemed to possess ordinary human life, and took out the elbow and removed it, perhaps threw it overboard, and put something warm about him, and propped him so that he could breathe, and put a pillow for him, so that he was able to doze off, and the inferno was changed for mere purgatory.

"You brazen-faced hussey, you; you artful minx. I'll teach you, and you shall go back to England without setting foot on shore. I'll pay you your wages, and I'll—"

There was shaking and tumult, and the speaker dissolved in hysterical weeping. What fresh phase of ugly nightmare was this? It sounded like his wife's new voice, for before they had left London she had developed one previously unheard. He opened his eyes, trusting that the dream would vanish; his bride's face, swollen and distorted with anger, glared above him. She was suffering acutely, but not from sea-sickness. What had he done, and what was amiss? It was getting dark and he could hardly see, but he realized that the fine brown eyes were close by, in dangerous proximity, and that the comfortable living human passenger to whom he owed so much, was none other than Altiora, who, in making him comfortable, had not forgotten herself. Mrs. Brabant, however, appeared to think otherwise, and the maid not disdaining the gauntlet, a slanging match ensued, putting to shame the storm that raged in upper air. Happily they were just at the pier, and the public were too busy to listen to it. Altiora sprang to her feet like a young war-horse sniffing battle.

" Lor, mum ! I should like to know what on earth do you mean to insinivate ? It's common humanity, and I'd a done it for my grandfather, or the Kahn of Crim Tartary, I would, and it's shameful," (sob) " of you, that's what it is, when I only covered the pore dear creature with a shawl."

" I'll pore dear creature you," screamed the bride, bursting with fury, " while I'm down in the cabin, dying for all you know or care, you two are up here, sitting on the paddle-box, with your arms round each other's neck."

" No, no ! " muttered Brabant faintly, " my dearest. I'd an elbow up my spine, that was all, and she—"

" Talk about dyin'," broke in Altiora, " look at him. Tain't my fault if you don't know how to take care of a man when you've got him. As for me, I wouldn't touch one of 'em, much less yours—not if he were the Pope of Rome—not with the end of a barge pole—not if I were paid for it, there now; and I wish I'd never been born to be slave to such a brute beast, I do—booooh ! "

The wretched cause of all was really too ill to take in the situation ; speechless annoyance, and the sentiment that he would not care to be married every day of his life, were uppermost, but as he was half dead with nausea, nothing mattered much, and he was presently conscious of a dismal jolting over roads of horrible stoniness, and of arrival at a dingy house in a dingy street.

Boulogne, at this particular time, was a place of which a good deal was thought. You could go into society there and get a real baronet, if you wanted one, say, at half a crown for the afternoon, and very cheap too, when you think at what some of these confounded fellows set themselves down, on English soil. And there were ladies of good family; you could get them, not quite so cheap, perhaps, but very reasonably, and who would object to be taxed for such smiles? If you had a sovereign in your pocket, you might swagger where you would, with some of the best blood in England hanging upon each arm, and so long as that lasted you were King of Boulogne, for you were not likely to meet, in society at least, a rival.

At the door of the dingy house up to which the sororcidal war had been continued in all its bitterness, the party were received by a showy and demonstrative person, into whose arms Mrs. Brabant cast herself, calling her, her "dear, dear Baroness," and so great was the joy of the meeting, that she instantly forgot all her grievances and looked at life through an entirely different lens. Brabant expected no less than to see Altiora dismissed by return; but it was not so, she was indispensable, and her mistress knew it. In three minutes the quarrel was forgotten, and his wife's dulcet tones and light ringing laughter were to be heard all over the house. Positively she was a playful thing, in the gayest mood, the most amusing humour; and you would not have thought a cloud had ruffled the surface for a week.

The new-comers were shown into a room where gorgeousness and squalor seemed to hold perpetual struggle. Brabant flung himself exhausted on the sofa, and the three ladies chatted together, with that easy familiarity which ladies use, when no male being worth mentioning is present.

The Baron was invisible, and so remained to the end of their stay, nothing being ever seen of him but his slippers outside his bedroom door. These, of course, may have been delusive, and no doubt a wedding-ring has been supported on less; but though, personally, I never liked the Baroness Von Homburg, I will not take her character away by hinting she had not a husband, the less so that I am credibly informed she had, at one time, two or three. On one point there was cordial sympathy between her and the ex-widow. Her idea of a man, and she often expressed it, was that he should be *kept in his place*, and this was one which obtained in the Squeed family. Poor Lushington, the only man they had possessed latterly, had too often found his place under the table, but when not there, and approximately sober, he had been absolutely at his wife's beck, and it never occurred to her that it could be otherwise with her second husband.

That individual's awakening impressions on his revival, were not of a pleasant nature. The Baroness was noisy and over-dressed; she glittered with shop-window jewellery and ribbons, and spoke English with a truly extraordinary concentration of foreign twangs.

Not without ceremony she invited her guests to inspect the suite of rooms placed at their disposal; and with a sinking heart Brabant followed the two ladies, or should we say three, to view them. It was a dingy array, remarkably like that of an ordinary lodging-house, and where the Baron and Baroness lived and 'kept up their style' it was impossible to say, unless it were in a sitting-room, which showed decided signs of habitation at the back. Still it was the gift horse, and Brabant decided to make the best of it, and of the dirty, little dark bedroom which the Baroness referred to, rather coarsely, as the "nuptual chamber."

A week passed away, a week of wondrous experience to one of the party. Never unhappy bridegroom had the veil more ruthlessly torn from his eyes. The bride, without more ado, simply descended from her stilts and was herself. Of woman at home, this sort of woman at least, he had been happily in densest ignorance, and he was so confounded by the knowledge when it came to him, that it reduced him to a state of stupor.

One day he wandered out alone on the breezy sunlit downs, where from well-nigh weeping, he was seized with irrepressible laughter; and yet, Heaven knows, the thing was serious enough for him. He remembered a man and woman who had married and separated within the week, and the thing had been inexplicable to him. Now he understood this, but he had married deliberately with his eyes open; it was his own fault and doing, and whatever came, he was bound in honour to go through, and make the best of it. His strong sense of humour would carry him some way, though he reflected sadly, that he would rather have exercised that quality elsewhere, than on his wife.

He sat long on the bright wind-swept hill, thinking how, perhaps, in time he might mould and model her, until they should see things from a like point of view; but thirty-five years of experience (she had that day confessed to thirty-five) are not easily moulded. Besides, his temperament and training unsuited him to the task; he who had scornfully turned his back, over and again, on this and upon that which the world cried up, because they were below his standard, forsooth! And here was the companion with whom he had hoped to live the life beautiful, alack! alack!

No man with many talents, but pays a terrible income-tax. In Brabant was a genius for the beautifying and raising of life, and for this thing, a cry has gone forth ceaselessly from refined womanhood in all ages; this had been his charm with the sex—this his spell. How many had scarcely kept their arms from his neck, when with no special thought he had talked with them, and grown earnest over what was good and right, just and glorifying in the world; and he had seen his listener moved to the core, and had never questioned the why of it. He might have chosen from many such women, and some were surely true, and would have been help-meets for him, treading his path, and pointing out his way; but now alack! alack!

The first blow had been a crushing one, he had been shocked to the heart. That a lady should raise her voice and use such words as his wife had done was terrible. It was also much else. The woman sank into something absolutely monkeyish and unhuman, in her self-abandon-ment at times, and a record of his pin-pricks may not be without its use, even to the super-refinement of our own age, in which such a type is of course ludicrously impossible.

There might be release, but religion, common-sense, and a perception of the ridiculous whispered—" Take up thy Cross!"

END OF VOL. II.

MOSTLY FOOLS.

A Romance of Civilization.

BY

MR. RANDOLPH,

AUTHOR OF "ONE OF US."

" . . . We arrive at the undeniable, but unexpected conclusion, that eminently gifted men are raised as much above mediocrity as idiots are depressed below it."

FRANCIS GALTON.

IN THREE VOLUMES.

VOL. III.

London:

SAMPSON LOW, MARSTON, SEARLE, & RIVINGTON,

CROWN BUILDINGS, 188, FLEET STREET.

1886.

LONDON:
PRINTED BY GILBERT AND RIVINGTON, LIMITED,
52, ST. JOHN'S SQUARE, E.C.

TO MY ADVERSARIES.

MOSTLY FOOLS.

CHAPTER I.

THE last thing of which the average woman should dream is to become the wife of a poet, as history has sufficiently shown. No good is likely to come of it, but, on the contrary, an infinity of harm. The man who is always worshipping an idealization of the sex which he has set upon a pedestal of his own making, is apt to have comparisons forced upon him when he displaces it and sets up an idol of flesh and blood, and these comparisons will not be to the advantage of the latter. But never a doubt had Mrs. Brabant as to her powers and charms; she felt equal to any amount of idealization; and, as from first to last she has received a good deal of sympathy from her sex, it is only fair to give some account of what, rightly or wrongly, her husband considered as grievances, and, without any idea of pronouncing a verdict, to allow the world to judge for itself.

First of all there were voice, tone, and style of language generally; but as Mr. Brabant had not had the advantage of moving in the smartest set of all, he was unaware that she only followed the prevailing style. When at a coffee-room dinner she silenced and absorbed the talk of a whole long table, rattling out a torrent of incoherent nonsense at which she laughed incessantly, while she showed the gold on her back teeth to the uttermost ends of the room, he thought it simply gross. But then he had kept ostentatiously aloof from all association with such people as Lady Victoria Nage and Lady Glendore, the unapproachable and irreproachable models and exemplars of the Squeeds and their set. All he saw in it was home-made vulgarity. The surroundings in this their first retreat were not agreeable to a man of Brabant's temperament. To begin with, the water supply was extremely scanty, and their ablutions consequently infrequent; but his wife said it saved a great deal of trouble, and this annoyed him. Shortly, too, he made the discovery that she had a dreadful habit of " chucking" her things here there and everywhere, and of dashing her boots on the floor like a schoolboy; this played more havoc with his nerves than perhaps anything else she could have devised.

Then there was the crucial question of dress. If there was a thing on which her husband prided himself, it was on the draping of the human figure. The nude and the manner of clothing it formed his particular hobby; he had paid much attention to it, and had that very winter "dressed" a favourite actress with an *éclat*

that had caused her toilet to become the talk of
the town. He had in consequence been selected
to design the dresses for a new piece, placed at
some outrageous period in the mists of history.
An artist by nature, he was exacting to a degree
in all that concerned form and colour; the
more so, that there had arisen (as in our own
day—the thing was inevitable in cosmic development) a sun-flower-cum-touzle-cum-humbug
business, which had to be put down at all costs.
But with all his cleverness he was ignorant as
to the foundation on which he built. A man
looks healthy, natural, and pleasing at any
stage of his dress, and until this time Mr.
Brabant had no idea of the idiotic figure of
fun that feminine humanity is pleased to make
of itself, all unblushing, at the various stages.
It proved to him, once and for ever, that
humour could not mean the same to woman
that it does to man. That a human being
should rise in the morning one shape, and by
dint of time and patience, or the reverse, by
squeezing here and " improving " there, should
through toil and travail assume a totally
different one, and as such present herself to the
world as the identical sentient Ego, struck
him as the most ludicrous thing on earth.

Mrs. Brabant was stout, and inclined to grow
stouter, and he now learned that a dinner-dress
might mean desperation and hysterics, a day-dress
mere spitefulness, but that only in a tea-gown
could he expect perfect amiability. His first
notion, on having a woman of his own to drape,
had been that it would be a mutual pleasure

to both. Before their marriage he had chosen
her colours, and had had the few poor stones
she possessed reset after designs prepared by
himself, and in her cumbersome way she
appeared to be grateful. Besides this he had
picked up one or two little pieces of antique
work, and given them to her; among others, the
Early-Christian engagement-ring, which in the
lady-like diction of the day she had pronounced "rummy." But it happened that the
ideas of Madame von Homburg on the subject
of colours and jewellery were as definite as, and
very different from, his own. This would not
have mattered, but that she speedily infected
his wife, and the two ladies made common
cause, and pooh-poohed his notions as an
unwarrantable interference with the liberty of
the subject.

Then the man had gone on when he had
his wife to himself—perhaps it was not wise
of him—and found fault with certain under-
garments, which were mis-shapen with a strange
and wilful ugliness, and loaded with cheap
trimming and tawdry lace by way of refinement. He objected that this was wholly unnecessary deformity. Discussion had ensued,
and he had said in his own defence that the
trained taste of a gentleman and an artist,
should be better in all things than that of a
shop-girl and a milliner. Mrs. Brabant wished
to know sarcastically how trained artistic taste
was to be defined. Her friends at Harrow, for
instance, had often used that very term with
regard to her own, and in Lady Jane's "circles"

her things had ever met with marked approval.
She had always been noted for being, if anything,
slightly ahead of the fashion; what more could
he want? Mr. Brabant remembered Lady Jane's
bonnets, and groaned.

"The fashion! oh, heavens! No, my dear
girl, set your own fashions, if you will, so long
as they are graceful and pretty. Let us find
the sort of style that suits you best, and stick
to it. My designs, I promise you, won't grow
old-fashioned in a hurry. I've some by me I
did as a boy, years ago, and I defy you to
date them. Why—because they are traced on
the natural lines of the body. But if all you
think of is to follow the fashion, why that's the
sole ambition of the British slavey, or of our
friend the Baroness here, and you put yourself
on their level at once."

He spoke, of course, foolishly, and with unjus-
tifiable warmth, for the subject touched him
very nearly. His wife raised her handkerchief
to her eyes and began to cry.

"No, Warburton, spare your sneers at my
friends at least, if you haven't the heart to
spare me." Then she heaved greatly, and waxed
excited. "Oh! how I wish now"—sob, sob—
"I had married that dear *darling* Major Lickpenny, when he asked me." And having duly
worked herself up to this pitch, she flung
from the room, and the interview terminated.

Had she been four years of age, instead
of nearly forty, he might have known how to
deal with her; as it was, he was wholly at a
loss. That she was without an atom of self-

command or restraint was made plain by her
face, which puckered and grew distorted into
a grimace with the slightest thing that went
wrong.   When he had married he had expected, perhaps not altogether unnaturally,
that his wife would keep herself in order;
he had not thought that that duty would
devolve upon himself, nor had he any fancy for
playing bear-leader to her across the continent, or
so long as they were in public together. " Is it
possible," he mused as he left the room, " that
a person can have come to such an age, and
have learned so little of what is due to themselves and their fellows ? "   Unfortunately, it
was not only possible, but a fact.

Then milder thoughts prevailed.   After all,
he had to deal with a woman, that woman
was his wife, and by the fact held a position
in his eyes which none other could, but of
which she herself had plainly no notion.
Something of his first tenderness returned to
him, and for a little while things went more
smoothly; but when he would attempt a little
love-making, as a thing that might not be
out of place, his · wife was at first dumb-
founded.   This was a thing of which she had
had no experience; finally she decided that he
meant to insult her, and flounced away in tears !

Here was a serious rebuff.   A man will forgive
a great deal; what will he not forgive if a
woman hold a heart for him ?   But how if it be
otherwise ?   A profound observer has remarked
that a man takes his wife for better, for worse;
but that although this is the historic formula,

in no single authenticated instance has there been found any bettering about it. This case, it will be allowed, showed a more than usually rapid deterioration. I am sorry for Brabant, and I hope it is not impertinent to say so. If this book belongs to you, as I trust it does, and not to the circulating library, I would suggest the shedding of the sympathetic tear upon this very page. His wife was as likely to understand him and his aims, as a cow the binomial theorem, and it was her nature to set down what she did not understand as conveying covert insult. With a good-natured Zulu she would probably have done admirably;—tastes, feelings, education, and aims would have been all in common, and fairly on a level.

What a pretty little responsibility rests with those who provide wares for the marriage-market! This was a very average specimen of the period, neither better nor worse than many others. Her family and friends had managed to implant the notion in her head, that if she were "firm" from the first with her husband, all would go excellently well. With this idea she struck a theatrical attitude of armed defiance, and this led to a peck of troubles.

Conversation simply meant discussion, and there was no avoiding it. If for instance, Mr. Brabant said, "My dear, you've dropped a hair-pin," a whirl of passionate declamation followed. She hadn't dropped it, and she couldn't drop it, and she wouldn't drop it if she could, and nothing pleased him, and she was the most miserable woman on earth, and

she would never wear a pretty thing again,—
from which the depths of her depression
might be gauged. From this profundity she
jumped to the wildest elation consequent on
the slightest change. The postman's knock, the
entrance of the maid with tea, the passing of a
pretty bonnet at the window, were quite sufficient to work the miracle; and an hour after,
perhaps, she met her old friend, Miss Smithly,
on the Pier. Then there was joy and laughter
and the crackle of wit; and the pretty things
came out again in scores, and all the colours of
the rainbow.

The days dragged on;—the afternoon was
usually killed by a drive in a hired carriage,
and the Baroness went for company's sake,
an arrangement that all parties found best.
To Brabant's annoyance, his wife always insisted on sitting with her back to the horses,
and this she did day after day, until one afternoon she suddenly burst into tears and declared
that her life was a purgatory to her in consequence, and that her husband's heartless cruelty
was bringing her to the tomb. What vexed
him most was that the Baroness evidently believed it. On these expeditions Mrs. Brabant
was always too hot or too cold, and woe to him
if he did not know which by intuition, for he
found he was always to blame. Then, also, he
made the discovery that he was not allowed to go
out, or to look at anything, or to have anything,
were it even so much as an ice, unless she
were there to share it. Had she been a child, a
dipsomaniac, or a certified lunatic, his course

would have been plain before him; as it was, he could not see his way at all. There are few men who would not be annoyed if—struggling themselves against odds of health or fortune, and having married a few annual hundreds— their bride in the first week of the honeymoon should turn upon them in the presence of others and say significantly, "Alas! my money has been my curse!" This she did, and her husband vowed mentally that it should not be his.

Again, a little difference arose over a bonnet —a mere trifle; but Mrs. Brabant improved the occasion, and having duly worked herself up to a pitch of fury, ended with,—

"Oh! Warburton; you took me away from my once happy home! I have been bitterly deceived! Nay, do not t-tut-touch me! Unhand me, wretch! Let me go back! Oh!" (crescendo), "Warburton, let us part!" and she fell back on the sofa, dissolved in tears.

This was slightly stagey, but she had achieved considerable success on the drawing-room boards in days gone by, and it was likely to be useful now. How far she was acting probably she herself did not know. Brabant got used to the formula, for it often came round, and they had not been married a week, before she found that her hair was growing grey and falling out, and that her rings would not stay upon her fingers, and told him so with a melancholy satisfaction. She was very sorry for herself in truth, and wept copiously and often.

She had been deceived; she who had always looked upon man as an inferior kind of woman, (this was the family tradition of the Squeeds,) had found something over and above in this one. She had fancied his gentle exterior meant a pliant spirit, and all the world knew he was a fool by profession. Such was Mrs. Brabant's interpretation of the literary calling when it embraced poetry, but now she felt the grip of steel under the velvet glove, and what more cruel aggravation could there be than the discovery that he was not such a fool as he looked !

He, too, was sorry enough for himself, but far more sorry for her, and pity is akin to love. There had been a mistake of course, it could not be remedied, and he was aware that no man's good name is safe if it gets into the keeping of a woman, and she is determined to drag it through the mire. He must reckon with this possibility, but he hoped for better things. However he determined to assume the reins of government. The Baroness pleased him not at all, her friends still less, and his first step was to give the order to move on. As the move was to be to Paris, to which his wife and Altiora both looked forward as an earthly paradise, there was little or no opposition; merely a suggestion thrown out that Madame von Homburg should make one of the party, which he promptly nipped in the bud.

But on the top of this came money troubles; he made the discovery for the first time that his wife's purse was confided entirely to the keeping

of Altiora. Mrs. Brabant declared that it was
impossible she could take it herself, she had no
pocket: in her set pockets were not considered
correct. "No lady ever thought of such a
thing." Whereupon he said that if she could
not, he must, for as a banker he looked upon
himself as Altiora's superior. This evil news
spread apace, and it was wonderful to see how
the three ladies collapsed under it, and went
about through the house looking thunder; but
he gave them the day to consider the matter,
and in the evening Altiora sullenly put the purse
into his hands. It felt woefully hollow in the
flanks, and upon being opened was found to
contain five shillings, a half-franc piece, a
glove-button-hook, a couple of pattern tickets,
and a postage stamp (much damaged owing
to its having been taken off a misdirected
letter).

As he happened to know that forty pounds in
notes had been there when they left England,
and as all his wife's expenses, so far as he was
aware, had been a few ices, he wished to
hear more. But Altiora pursed her mouth,
pirouetted deliberately on one of her lofty
heels, and observed that she only kept the
purse safe, and how her mistress spent her
money, she really couldn't imagine. Then
she asked prettily if she could do anything
more for him, and finding she could not, she
swung herself and her improver out of the
room.

The position of an inexperienced man who
finds himself for the first time unprotected

among a party of women who all look upon him
as a natural enemy is trying, and requires extreme caution.   It was obvious that Brabant
could only indirectly control his wife's expen-
diture ; but he knew something of dress, and
Altiora's he reckoned must represent almost
a hundred a year.   This he thought he might
well withstand.   Madame von Homburg, too,
since their arrival had blazed out into a fresh-
ness of splendour, which was very different
from the ancient gaudiness of the apparel in
which she had first received them ; and this
seemed to point to one channel by which
the money must have flowed away.   However,
on mature consideration, he decided to hold
his tongue, to let the bad money go, but
to take care that good did not follow it.
He therefore conjured up a bland good-bye
for the Baroness, coupling it with the fiction
of his kindest regards to the Baron.   She
was suspiciously grieved to part with them,
and the ladies kissed each other for ten
minutes before they got away ; she recommended them most emphatically to a hotel kept
by some people, who were, she said, " quite
friends " of hers in Paris, and to which she had
kindly directed all the luggage labels.   But on
arrival there, the master countermanded the
direction and drove to a hotel in the Rue de
Rivoli.

It so happened that the inevitable Lady
Jane was in Paris for her autumn bonnets,
which she found no less essential now than she
did sixty years back, and here it was she joined

them under circumstances which will be briefly
told.

On their arrival the two ladies looked
brighter than they had done for some time,
for Altiora was beginning to feel her restrictions
as much as did her mistress, and stood sadly
in need of a fillip. It may seem odd to put them
on the same level; but at this eccentric period,
maids, when they were not as good as their
mistresses, invariably considered themselves
so, and in this case there was so little to
choose between the two that there is no harm
in bracketing them together. Mrs. Brabant
carefully examined the visitors' book, and
even to her falcon eye it appeared satisfactory; she herself entered their names, and called
her husband's attention to the list.

" Oh! Warburton, darling, I am sure that we
have done well, and this is a first-rate hotel.
Look here! there are two dukes and a marquis,
and we come next but one to the last, and *do*
look, here is Lady William Sykes just opposite.
Oh! I *am* glad we came," and she looked up
with positive affection in his face. "Mind,
dear, you don't forget to take our places for the
table-d'hôte."

Brabant knew his wife had been abroad
but seldom, and wondered what was to
come of *table-d'hôte*, but he was too thankful
for the gleam of sunshine to inquire particularly
into its source. At dressing-time Altiora
came up highly excited; she had received
a great deal of attention from a great many
different people, and there had been cham-

pagne for tea in the hall, among those gay gallants the couriers. She had learned a great many interesting personal details, and was bubbling over with them; further, she had seen on the first-floor landing a pair of boots so exquisite, that no shadow of a doubt rested on her mind that they belonged to the Duke, if not indeed to the Duchess. Brabant, whose last visit to Paris had been in the festive character of a youthful Bohemian, silently voted the whole business a bore, and yawned through the gilded passages with undisguised *ennui*. His wife's dinner toilette seemed to him absurdly elaborate, but he had learned the wisdom of holding his tongue, and they reached the dinner-table in peace.

Whatever Mrs. Brabant's expectations may have been, they were not realized. The room was comparatively empty when they sat down, and though she scanned each new arrival as if she would have eaten them, this did not help to turn them into the right people. Her husband occupied the chair on one side of her; secretly she wished him at least one further off, if it were only to give the second duke a chance. In spite, however, of the embossed crimson velvet dress, the vacant chair next to her remained unoccupied for a long time, when it was suddenly pounced upon, by a certain species of British female which may be fairly described as malignant. She was elderly, she was grim, she wore a stern rusty black serge, and round her neck a red woollen shawl; on her hands were mittens, and upon her head was a high, immaculate muslin cap, unbending as cast-iron. This of course made her full dressed at once, and proved how eminent was her respectability. She gave one glare at her neighbour, a distinct sniff, which was not one of approval, and forthwith set herself squarely to her work, in aggressive silence.

The opposite seats were filled by a family whose attractions did not increase on closer acquaintance—they were a father, mother, and two girls;—at one moment the mother seemed the most objectionable, whereupon the father would out-distance her, tucking his napkin into his chin, and ladling in his food with a horrible adroitness. Then the girls would out-do both, in some dreadful knack of eating or drinking, until the appetite of the on-looker failed at the spectacle. They spoke hardly at all, and the only remark caught by their *vis-à-vis* was a loud one from the youngest girl, a child of seven or eight. It was to the effect, that she could not conceive what could induce a man to play a revoke at whist; she smacked her lips as she enunciated this, rubbed them on the back of her hand, and looked round the table for applause. There may have been fifty people at the table, but there were not three, whom you would have picked out as ordinary decent gentlefolk !

For some occult reason, Mrs. Brabant had grown highly indignant with her husband, and could hardly eat a morsel; her dress was a mere case of pearls before swine, and she half resolved to go upstairs and take it off. The malignant female at her side disappeared early, pushing ostentatiously against her plate some printed matter on the colour and components of hell-fire, which Mrs. Brabant, perhaps rightly this time, received as an insult. But when dinner was over she decided to stay as she was; the dress was too tremendous an affair to be lightly changed, so selecting a gilt ottoman in the centre of the "salon," and disposing the crimson velvet elaborately over it, she settled herself sirenwise for the evening, while Brabant strolled out to smoke a cigar. Altiora came and went to and fro at intervals, with fan, smelling-bottle, or gloves, which added greatly to the importance of the affair.

For an hour or two this bye-play was wasted on thin air, she was left quite alone; but about ten o'clock a dreadful-looking elderly man came, who sat down near her and took snuff, mumbled over the papers, and made disagreeable noises with his throat. All that woman could do to express her abhorrence, in silence, Mrs. Brabant did, but to no avail. She would have gone, but her dress was such that she did not care about moving, until she could go once for all, and she was waiting for her husband. Then the awful man, who had been leering askance at her for some time through his smeared spectacles, addressed her, and asked her what she thought of the weather. Mrs. Brabant looked at the ceiling and looked at the floor, shut her eyes and gulped down this new insult. The man chuckled, scratched himself offensively, then stooping down, with a grunt, he deliberately pulled off one of his boots. The boot was typic of the owner, its removal caused him evident relief; he leaned back with another grunt, this time of satisfaction, and swung his denuded foot slowly up and down in the cool air. It was cased in a wrinkled grey sock, much darned and discoloured, and if she could have managed it, Mrs. Brabant would certainly have fainted, for he again addressed her, and this time as " my dear."

Then with a mighty effort she rose to flee, when two fine-looking young fellows, in spotless livery, swung into the room and up to the sofa. One of them asked if his lordship was ready to go to bed, and leaned down and pulled on the old gentleman's boot. His lordship said he " sposed " he was, and casting a final leer at the crimson velvet, hobbled out between them, leaving it almost in a state of collapse at the discovery.

Brabant found his wife rooted to the spot when he came in.

" Oh ! B.," she exclaimed excitedly.

" Warburton is better, my dear," he suggested.

" Well, Warburton then. Do you know, I've met the Marquis after all. Such a dear, quaint old man, and *so* pleasant. We've been sitting here talking—that is, at least—he was—and—and—" There was not much more to be said, so she finished up with, " he was *so* friendly; we shall be sure to see him to-morrow."

Her husband's delight was of a mitigated character; he merely asked if the Marquis had said much, to which his wife truthfully replied, not much, but that he had looked a good deal. She retired, a prey to conflicting emotions. To think that she had snubbed him, HIM; she could find no words for her thoughts. But it was not irreparable, could not be, should not be; and as Altiora released her from her trammels, she unbosomed all the painful story, and that acute young lady carefully marked the details for her own future behoof.

Every day let poor Brabant a little further down the scale; every day he hoped he had touched the bottom of his troubles; but the climax was yet afar off. He grew moody and irritable; his wife's endearments, when they came, which was rarely and always in the wrong place, goaded him, and Altiora had taken to wearing a distracting smile which supplied the last straw. He was pining to get back into his groove. When he looked at the English papers they maddened him. Here was a fellow taking advantage of his absence, pretending to discuss his pet subject in his pet print; here was a dolt laying down the law on the Founts of Greek Form; here was another making a spectacle of himself on the subject of the Catholic party; and yet another who thought he knew the meaning of Compound Electoral Districts. Bah! he had guessed as much. Calling for

paper and pens *ad libitum*, he sat down then
and there, and desisted not until he had smashed
the three several gentlemen to his complete
satisfaction. There was a little too much of
the Admirable Crichton in all this, his friends
were apt to say. However, once done he felt
better—luckily the elopement paragraph escaped
him altogether—and went off to his wife's room;
not that he thought he was missed, but he had
this excuse, that it was his own as well, for they
had not taken a sitting-room.

It was a long time before he could gain
admittance, and when at last he did so, it
was like a milliner's shop turned topsy-turvy.
On the table were seven-and-twenty wigs, of
every shape and shade and colour, and as many
pairs of boots and shoes, intended apparently
for no sterner work than the ball-room. There
were some doll's parasols, or what looked
extremely like them; Lilliputian muffs, and
Brobdignagian hats in plush, which he hated.
Everything was littered with garniture, and in
the window sat a woman, picking or unpicking
as for her life.

The fact was, there had been a desperate
battle with the trousseau, and the trousseau had
conquered. Mrs. Brabant had, in an heroic
moment, had it made to a measure which
fifteen years before, as a girl, she had been perfectly able to compass; but fifteen years, with
their concomitant increase, are not to be trifled
with. Altiora declared that her fingers were cut
to the bone by the incessant struggle, and that
always just when she thought her goal was

happily attained, a strap, a screw, a bolt, or
a buckle would fly, and the work had to be
begun again from the beginning. She was
worn out, but still sympathetic, as with a
fellow-woman and sinner. Her advice was to
take the bull by the horns by means of internal
remedies; she knew of a case, where these
steadily persisted in for three months enabled
a perfectly fabulous waist-band to be worn.
Then there were the shoes: those of the trousseau had proved a simple impossibility and
others had been procured at Boulogne; but
again Mrs. Brabant had fallen victim to the
fascinations of outward appearance, and these
too she had been forced to renounce as hopeless,
although she laid the blame on the colour, on
the bows, on the lining, and in fact on everything but the size. The wretched man foresaw,
as he looked at the collection, that the same
thing was again inevitable, and said so, which
drew down upon his head wrath from all the
three women; the lady in the window observing
that the gentlemen were always so droll.
Altiora, for her own reasons, was especially
indignant, as she knew that eventually the
rejected things must needs come her way.
Indeed she had no objection to using them on
the sly as it was, since she was providentially
able to do so.

He then took up a tightly-curled golden
wig, and asked if it were necessary; his wife
gave him one look. Had he forgotten already
how her hair had turned grey, and come out
in the last ten days? Thereupon he went

away quickly; but the truth of it was that Lady William Sykes was wearing a superb wig after a design of her own, and Mrs. Brabant had spent a good deal of the previous evening in the study of it at a distance. Further discoveries were made by Mr. Brabant as time wore on, such as, that only one woman in Paris could make a dress, only one a bonnet, and so forth. The run on these distinguished individuals may be imagined, as also the price they set on themselves. But the difficulties and almost superhuman peculiarities of Mrs. Brabant's figure rendered them absolutely necessary, and Altiora declared her conviction that such was her similarity to her mistress, that nobody else could fit her; and she, to the great people's indignation, sent her orders with the rest, and was greatly surprised and hurt at their refusal to have anything to say to them.

There was one pitfall which might have been avoided by a little ordinary caution, but into which Brabant had tumbled head over heels. He fancied, like a few other men, that he knew a good-looking girl when he saw one, and had been rash enough to express his opinion freely and often. This was quickly put a stop to. If he said of a passing woman that she was tall, had a nice expression, or a pretty colour, he learned on the spot that she was rather short than otherwise; that her expression was the worst part of her, and that her complexion was tallowy. Through this discipline he soon acquired the habit of silence, even when his wife would select some terrible female from the *table-d'hôte* and say she might not be exactly beautiful, but she was stylish and quite the lady; and Altiora agreed with her, that the young person whom Brabant had had the ill-taste to admire yesterday, was coarse, snub-nosed, bilious, vulgar, and other things less suitable for publication.

While she thus somewhat emphatically asserted herself, Mrs. Brabant was pining, so she said, under the most infamous bondage, and dared hardly call her soul her own. A slave was no worse off than she, in the shackles of an unsympathetic union. Her husband was never pleased with anything that she said or did, and why it was she could not imagine.

Sunday came round; Altiora always had a head-ache on Sunday mornings, and never appeared out of a *peignoir* before lunch. After attending a late low mass himself, Brabant escorted his wife to the English church, a stucco tabernacle, which nearly converted her instantaneously to "Romanism," and as she had three new prayer-books she took them all, and he had the honour of carrying them. Telling him to wait about until it was over, she nodded and went in, while he wandered on along the quays by the river.

A serious matter was on his mind. His wife had at length handed over to him her bank-book, and he had made the discovery he had half anticipated. Not only was it overdrawn, but it had been constantly in that condition for several years past, and this had been met by as constant selling out, until the capital had dwindled to the scantiest proportions. There it was, in black and white before him, and it appeared that as a widow, living at home, with no calls or expenses to speak of, she had been piping to the tune of a couple of thousand a year. There was absolutely nothing to show for it, unless a heap of unpaid bills, a number of unwearable dresses, and a quantity of shop-window jewellery, in shop-window patterns, could be considered as a *quid pro quo*. He foresaw that nothing but hard work, and work that was successful, on his part, would justify them in setting up house at all. The torrent must be stopped, and for the present they must stay abroad and economize to the utmost. He would break it to her that day. This he resolved before he turned back to meet her.

Unfortunately he chose dinner-time for the purpose. They were sitting by themselves at a little table in the corner, and Mrs. Brabant was hysterically bright, for she had so contrived that Lady William Sykes should tread on her train as they came downstairs. Quite half a minute's conversation was the result of this manœuvre; she found that they had *so* many tastes in common, and this made her gay as a young fawn. Brabant was delighted with the opportunity, and cautiously began his operations; but it would not do, the moment he touched on money her face fell to zero. She had been brought up to think nothing of money, her money, she often said, and she sighed heavily, had been her curse. If it had brought her what she wanted, it had also brought her what she did not want.

"Oh, yes; I am well aware of that, Maria. You've said so once or twice, but hang it, you know" (the man's temper was beginning to oxydize under this constant acidity), "we *must* think about it. I really must insist upon your thinking about it. I was looking at your bank-book to-day."

Here the waiter, who was an Englishman, became entangled with the wine glasses on the table, and Brabant, changing his voice, said that he had noticed a few spots of rain. The waiter went hurriedly away, two yards at least, and turned his back, and the spokesman continued, "And I see, by Jove, that you've had two notices already this month that the account is over-drawn."

"Oh!" said Mrs. Brabant, repressing herself into freezing composure, but with an ominous heave that escaped her husband's eye, "ladies don't pretend to understand their horrid papers and business. In *my* family (toss) we are not brought up to that sort of thing."

"But, by Jove, Maria! it's no use mincing matters; you must attend to that sort of thing, or let me do it for you. By heavens! we shall be in the Bankruptcy Court next. I'd no idea of the state of the case. My good name I do value, if you don't. And here you are, going on with your confounded wigs and things."

Something in his wife's face stopped him dead. She was sitting rigid and motionless, staring before her with glassy eyes starting from her head. With one hand she had grasped the soup-ladle in the tureen, and was moving it with a melancholy expression, to and fro. Her look fairly frightened him.

"Ha! ha! ha! HA! HA! HA!" The busy bustling room silenced and sobered instantly. A fiendish shriek rang to the roof like the death-whoop of some savage chief. The soup-ladle flew through the air, striking Brabant upon the forehead and drenching his face and shirt-front. His bride rolled over in a heap to the floor. Happily they were by the door. In an instant the attentive waiter and one of his fellows carried her out and into an empty sitting-room, where they placed her on the sofa. A dozen elderly ladies poured in from the dining-room and took over charge of the case. Brabant, frightened and bewildered, shook himself together as best he might, and staggered in after them. In the mirror opposite he saw a huge bump on his forehead from which the blood was oozing, and his drenched shirt-front, but nobody took any notice of him, until the waiter espied him, and came up. He knew, or thought he knew, all about it.

"Never you mind, sir," he said, "'taint nothink. I'll get you some hot water. I saw it was comin' fast enough, and 'ud liked to have warned you. I've seen it" (lowering his voice) " scores of times with that class of female. 'Taint like a lady, sir; they ain't got the self-respex."

This he said confidentially, and the shaft quivered to the quick in his hearer, but there was no resenting it. The patient was coming to, and the ladies in attendance were asking how it happened, and what it was.

" Well, you see," stammered Brabant, " the a—soup was spilled, and a—I found it rather hot. And a—"

At this moment his wife re-opened her eyes, and as they fell upon him she set to shriek afresh.

" Oh ! that dreadful, dreadful, man ; take me from him. Ah ! Lady William " (clutching) " save me," for that lady, too, had come to look on. But when thus appealed to, she thought she had seen enough of her new acquaintance, and, with a glance at Brabant which was not devoid of humour, she slipped from the room. He, too, went out, not knowing well what to do, and she waited for him.

" Take care of that poor creature," she said, with a glance of compassion at his forehead, " and don't forget yourself." She said this for the sake of his good looks ; she was sorry for him, and being a woman of the world, thought, like the waiter, she knew all about it. His tongue thickened and grew clumsy in his mouth ; he could not answer her. He need not have been so infinitely distressed ; he was to have these little scenes once a week on the average, and usually in a public place, and though he little thought it, he would get used to them.

In the course of an hour Mrs. Brabant was

sitting up perfectly restored, laughing and talking in the most amusing way, rather glad, it seemed, than otherwise of the incident that had led to her making so many acquaintances.

When her husband returned from washing his wounds and redressing himself, she received him smilingly; she made no allusion to the late unpleasantness, but introduced him to a friend or two, and asked him if he would care about any tea. Having grappled with these astonishing facts, and declined the tea, he left her, and went out for the evening. "Merciful heavens!" he thought, as he walked hurriedly through the cool air, "is this what domestic life means? Has every man who marries to go through this with his women-kind? If so, I marvel at the density of the population." But if he fancied now that he was out of the wood for that evening, he was much mistaken.

A long time he wandered about aimlessly and despondently; down whichever vista he looked he saw life-long failure,—moral, social, intellectual ruin; for her certainly, for him probably. From the carriage-and-pair to the doorstep is no long distance, as he well knew, when a woman is resolved to travel that road. He was wretched as only a young man can be. Presently he came to a public garden, lit with Chinese lanterns, and he turned into it. He was in no humour for amusement himself, but it was some distraction to watch the crowds as they flitted by, and he began to note the people and their dresses. It was, as he soon

judged, a low, disreputable haunt; the women
were all of a certain class, and not of the
best in that,—their finery soiled, crumpled,
flaunting. But there was a dress which he
could not help remarking, for it reminded him
of one of his wife's,—one about which there
had been the usual affray,—he had called it
"flashy."

As it came by once more into the light, he
sprang to his feet; there could be no mistake,
it *was* her dress, her mantle, and even her
fan. The wearer was thickly veiled, and clinging to the arm of a short, mis-shapen, elderly
man, who walked lame, and in whom Brabant
had no difficulty in recognizing the Marquis
of P—. They had passed without noticing
him. A rush of blood almost suffocated his
heart as he looked after them—then came
the thought that if it was his wife, and she was
here alone at this hour, with that man, his
course would be clear, and he could be free of
her as soon as he would. He followed them
(surely he had the right), and with a sort of
stony indifference watched them go into a dim-
lit arbour, where the woman coolly seated
herself upon the man's knee, and put her arms
round his neck. Then Brabant strode in
upon them; the woman threw up her veil and
laughed, actually laughed.

"Lord have mercy on us, if here ain't
master!" It was Altiora, thank God for
that. Still, this was his business.

"I must apologize, my Lord, for intruding,"
he said, taking off his hat, "but it's just

possible my wife may be requiring her maid, and I shall be greatly obliged if you will allow her to go home. If you weren't old enough to be my grandfather, I'd knock you down. Pray accept the wish for the deed. Good evening."

But Altiora never went home; she and the "costume" and the fan, and much more beside, vanished utterly away. Next day's paper announced that the Marquis had changed his hotel, and in the same print Lady Jane Squeed's name figured by the merest accident among the arrivals. Her aunt! say rather an angel from heaven at this crisis. To her Brabant went in his despair, and, without entering into details, gave her to understand that desperate trouble was brewing, and threw himself upon her mercy. So it was that Lady Jane accompanied the happy couple to Kissingen; and so it is that this too brief outline of the first days of a honeymoon must conclude.

CHAPTER II.

A YEAR or more had passed—eventful times, during which a tremendous Constitutional struggle — long delayed — was in progress. Aristocracy and Democracy fell to, in a desperate effort for supremacy. Out of this contest, contrary to all expectation even on their own side, the Tory party, the Conservative principle, arose triumphant. Their adversaries were utterly worsted, routed along the whole line. The spirit of change had gone too far and too fast; it had taken to itself questionable allies; the people wavered and trembled; in their rebound their cause, for the time being, perished. The verdict was one which the nation was not likely to revoke in a hurry, and it only remained to be seen how the Tories would manipulate the wondrous power which had so unexpectedly dropped from the skies into their hands. But of these things later.

There were places and people that the rise and fall of Governments affected little. Such was the Blankshire regiment, although its members, being " aristocrats " to a man, rejoiced at the victory of "the good cause." Such was the solitary domain of Sombrewood, where it stood apart from the great world, with its hoar woods and its crags set in the rushing seas, and circled about by mists. Only twice in this space had the king visited his little kingdom, and, although there was joy among his subjects at his coming, on both occasions he had found change; neither places nor people come back quite the same, however short the time of absence.

He had begun to rebuild, only on a small scale as yet, but jealously laying stone upon stone, exactly on the old foundations, and the gradual accomplishment of this was a deep secret pride, of which he could not speak to any man—hardly to her for whom it was intended.

In Sybil the change was for the better. Like an opening flower that every morning unfurls a virgin petal afresh to the day, such seemed his true love in his eyes, a thing incomparably rare and beautiful and precious. She was graver, and there was an indefinable difference. Whether he was entirely pleased with it, even his own heart could not tell him.

He, too, was altered, and was growing old; he was in sight of thirty. Thought had sobered him; and there was ever in his mind to lay hold and grip the passing hour, and to lay it down as a stepping-stone to the next.

Mr. Trelawney meantime had become a confirmed invalid; and it was plain to Roland's eyes that the old man was breaking slowly.

This gave him grave cause for anxiety :—for one thing, Sybil, dismissing all professional aid, had constituted herself his nurse, which implied incessant care and anxiety. And now there was no getting away for change, and the fearful dreariness of this prolonged period might have broken the health of a girl far more robust than she. Her lover eyed her tenderly and anxiously, but she was bright and gay, and always laughed. Plainly she loved the yoke, and already he was beginning to have some dim vision of the flights of unselfishness to which she soared.

He was especially wishful to gather particulars of Sybil's birth and parentage. This was much discussed between the two, but all she herself knew was that she had been left an orphan at birth, and never on any single occasion had her guardian enlightened her any further; he had evaded the question, and had given her to understand that the subject must not be pursued. So now when Roland pressed him he again evaded it, but always with a promise that when he had time, at some future day, he would tell him all; and as the matter plainly upset him, Roland, though secretly aggrieved, gave way and took his departure, still unsatisfied.

He had returned to Ireland from his first leave, with a month of it unexpired, in order to join a particular course of military engineering which he was anxious not to miss. This unheard-of proceeding so astonished his regiment that they never recovered it, and it confirmed them in their suspicions of a lurking insanity about him. He had already passed an examination which marked him as a singular if not unique specimen of the British subaltern; his maps and military sketches, when they reached the district head-quarters, created a sensation which lasted quite a couple of minutes, for nothing so good had ever been sent in before. The General commanding set a mark against his name, which was meant to be one of honour and glory and future notice, but unfortunately he was a careless individual, and of undecided character (though extremely fierce). He had hieroglyphics against most of the names of one sort or another, and being a suspicious man, who liked to keep his own counsel, he was always changing his marks to make them unintelligible, and in this he perfectly succeeded, even to himself. The mark soon began to mean " below par," " idle," " careless at drill," " bad draughtsman," &c.; and that which he had set against Mr. Jones, who was all this and a little more, exactly the reverse. The consequence of this was, that for some considerable time Lieutenant Tudor groaned under serious official disabilities, which he was at a loss to understand, while he saw the fortunate Jones promoted into a higher grade and treated with special favour. This could not last. Poor Jones broke down hopelessly, and was soon relegated to his proper place.

It was not for some months that the General, after a night of anguish over his ciphers, which had plunged him into hot water in a quarter where subalterns are not, discovered an old key, and re-corrected his lists by it, with Roland's name among the rest.

Meantime the summer passed away, or in military parlance "the drill season," and Roland, having done all that was possible at this period, returned to head-quarters, where he was but coolly received.

It was felt that he was a young gentleman whom it would be exceeding difficult to keep in his place. "Here was a man who really was in the landed gentry, you know, and had been there since 1066," as was rather loosely said. The regiment would have taken an honest pride in him if he would only have let them. There had been, within the memory of man, but one other like him; he, however, had never possessed more than a flower-pot unmortgaged, and had only graced the regiment six months. But there was a terrible set off in the case of "this fellah Tudor, you know." He had given up half his leave to attend "shop," he knew the meaning of regular shop terms; he was not a gaby to be puzzled by a gabion; he could see further through a vedette than most men. It was rumoured, but this seemed incredible, that he knew all the bugle calls, and that the intricacies of a rear-guard had no terrors for him.

He might have been forgiven these eccentricities, perhaps, had he fallen in with the social and festive ideas of the regiment. If he had spent only one night a week with a few choice spirits in the slums, it would have been something. If he had hired a wretched hack, and tried to break its neck and his own, over the stone walls even once or twice in the season, this would have been better than nothing. If he had interlarded his speech with stable slang, and modelled his tone and his clothes after their sporting captain, the apple of the Blankshire's eye, a wretched, pimpled, under-sized imp, with bow-legs, whose special forte was a flat race, wherein, to do him justice, he succeeded to admiration; then there might have been hope for this tyro. If he had sat up now and then and pretended to get drunk, which he might easily have done, if his stomach would not stand the real thing; and made believe to be jolly and a good fellow, as many a man did who was not particularly so—if he had played till five o'clock in the morning, and lost more than he could possibly pay, how much he might have contributed, to break up the dead levels of the Blankshire existence. If he would only talk like a rational being, i.e. like a stable-boy and an omnibus-cad rolled into one, with a dash of the sporting Jew sharper thrown in; and if he would—(d—n him!)—see a good joke when there was one, i.e. when the inexhaustible subject of woman, lovely or otherwise, was treated with some infinite new humour—but he wouldn't—(bl—st him!)—he wouldn't do any of these fine things, and though he said little, and did less in the mess; that that little was offensive in its manner, was agreed by the majority, hence he came to be left very much to himself.

But a crisis was at hand. It has been told that the regiment had not been out since the year 1796, and that on that occasion they had not distinguished themselves. The excitement, then, may be imagined, when one night, after mess, without previous warning, orders were received for it to proceed immediately on active service. It should be remarked that at this period, Ireland was in a normal state of what English people were pleased to term "revolution." The news sobered even the most desperate of the rollickers, who, having given vent to their feelings by a short but heroic war-dance on the ante-room table, when most of the furniture was demolished, settled down grimly to their preparations. It was felt that here was a golden, if tardy, opportunity of wiping out the slur of 1796, and the grindstone in the barrack-yard, ground noisily on the sabres the live-long night.

The conflict was a civil one, and was likely to be a disagreeable job. Operations were to be undertaken against a certain body of "rebels" in the neighbourhood. There were, alas! usually rebels to be found somewhere, if one looked closely enough, in Ireland, and the case of these was not especially different from many who went before, and were to come after.

There had been several bad years—it had been a severe winter, terribly severe on the poor natives rotting in their bogs, yet human needs existed even in these wretches, and as the pinch grew fiercer cried aloud for a hearing.

The crop had been a failure—not the wheat crop, oh! no—I refer to the annual harvest of sea-weed. The people asked little of God or man. It seemed a trifle hard that human creatures, with the feelings of men and women, should be driven to sustain life upon this refuse of the melancholy ocean, which it cast grudgingly upon their barren shores, but it was harder when this, even this, was withdrawn; then, indeed, the struggle for existence rose to agony point.

There had been riots—not bread riots— certainly not—they might be more properly called sea-weed riots. Thereupon some wretched agitator got it into his head, that boats might be useful along the coast, and a landing-stage here and there. Practically speaking, there were no boats for miles and miles, the population were altogether too poor either to build or to keep them; but this ruffian had the hardihood to suggest that the Government should lend them a few, and advance a few pounds wherewith to start the enterprise. Then not only would the people be able to tide over the evil day, but they would be able to live, and live in the luxury of plenty, as they were now starving in the midst of it, and a permanent industry would be established.

The Government hummed and hawed, and the famishing multitude did not take it kindly. If you stopped to argue with a drowning man as to the many different ways of rescue, he would probably spend his last breath in a curse upon your head as he went under—the case was a parallel.

The English people, shortly before this date, fearful of an overwhelming wave of universal Radicalism, had, with a supreme effort, shaken off their shackles and returned a Tory Government to power, not one of moderate conservative, advance, opinions, which will condescend to be asked questions, and sometimes even to answer them—but one of good old crusted, high and dry Toryism, with no nonsense about it. King, Church, and State, and plenty of them, the lower classes relegated to their proper place, power entirely in the hands of an aristocracy owning responsibility to no man, but condescending to give God as an ultimate reference. There had been a struggle to get the neck of the Nation under the yoke, but the prophets had cried out that it was the one shibboleth that could hold weight against the Revolution, and now it was on its trial.

This Government then, decided that the suggestion was unheard of, that to treat with a body of rioters would be madness. Further clamour ensued, the clamourers consequently were forthwith proclaimed as rebels, and as many as possible of them were caught and flung into gaol, which, in the winter, is apt to be a cold and cheerless place. Some few, thinking they might as well be hanged for a sheep as a lamb, had laid hold of their pikes or pitchforks, or any old fire-arms they could unearth, and had fled with their wives and families to the hills, where they had formed an encampment and entrenched themselves. But here the unfortunate necessity of their stomachs still pursued them, and as the sea-weed did not grow upon the hill-tops, they were driven to raiding for provisions.

It was against this stronghold that the Blankshires were sent, with orders to reduce it at all costs, and to raze it to the ground.

The expedition was not fortunate at its commencement. The rain fell in torrents from the moment it quitted the barrack-yard. Even in the height of summer an Irish mountain is not the dryest spot on earth; the high road merely skirted the hills, and the ground over which the unlucky corps had thence to make its way, might be described as a series of precipitous quagmires. When the road was left the waggons had to be left likewise, and all necessaries were brought on by fatigue parties. Two days and a night of this—the night spent in a deserted village, where the regiment learned the meaning of eviction, for the cabins had been unroofed long since, by their Christian proprietor—reduced the corps to such a state, that anything like a serious attack upon them might have proved fatal.

The officers suffered most, lounging over a balcony all day, combined with spitting, even when it is followed by abnormal activity at night, is a bad preparation for this kind of work, and hardly one of them that was not half dead with cold and fatigue. It was not

until the middle of the third day's march that
they sighted the rebel stronghold, which consisted of more roofless huts, surrounded by
loose stone walls, which might have afforded
pretty sport enough, had they been really
manned by an armed force.

The Blankshires, at the best of times, entertained salient views on the Irish question; the
natives of the country were, in their eyes,
simply savages, the cry for food was rebellion.
Extermination was the sole possible remedy
for Ireland's woes. " Blow them into the sea
—or chain the brutes in gangs, and transport
the whole boiling of them, sir, to the Antipodes,
and if you could only manage to scuttle the
fleet on the way, why, by Jove, sir ! you'd be
doing humanity and religion a service." That
was the phrasing of it.

Not one of these fire-eaters had ever read a
line of the history of the Country, or wasted a
thought in ' what he called his head,' on the
subject, and in this particular the majority of
Englishmen at home, were not behind them.

If these were the feelings of the regiment
in the piping times of peace, they had been
considerably accentuated by the privations
of the last forty-eight hours, and had it not
been that half of them were incapacitated, a
merciless assault would probably have been
delivered at once. As it was, it seemed best
to begin mildly, and they sat down to think
about it.

The Colonel hid his perplexities under a
sphynx-like air which, however, he found

difficult to keep up for long together. He knew not quite so much of soldiering as his upper nurse, who, being a soldier's wife, had considerable knowledge of regulation minutiæ. His head was well nigh gone, and his sense of responsibility and importance, together with the rheumatism he was feeling in both knees, had reduced him to a perfectly drivelling condition. Luckily, there was a newspaper reporter present, which helped to preserve him from total breakdown. Such a man, as Cheapsyde, could not advise with his juniors, although he was absolutely at a loss how to proceed; yet it was obvious that something impressive must be done and at once.

A bright idea crossed him—this young fellow, Tudor, was supposed to know all about the infernal etiquette of the thing. There might be dirty work—but subalterns were designed by Providence for dirty work; besides he was almost the only one present who seemed fit for duty, and his Captain had gone on leave, to visit a sick grandmother three days before. This was fortunate as it gave Lieutenant Tudor the command of the company. The Colonel called him up, and in a ferocious but trembling voice, gave some incoherent orders about volunteering for a scouting party, telling him to take his company out to the front and look about; and as the correspondent happened to be present, he spoke of it as a " forlorn hope," for this sounded soldier-like and impressive. Delightful to find oneself in the field and under the command of

such an officer ! but this was what the British
soldier of that day had occasionally to go
through. The lay of the land was to be carefully
ascertained, and whether the enemy were likely
to be dislodged by a feint, for now he came to
think of it, the Colonel was averse from the
shedding of blood, more particularly of his own.

The excitement that reigned in the ranks
was tremendous, as Lieutenant Tudor, with
half a company, began his advance in skirmish-
ing order. The young soldier was of two
minds ; a stockade was a stockade, and as such
a joy to his heart, but he was sorely grieved
for the deluded wretches behind it, armed with
their pikes, their flint-locks, and their empty
bellies. He had his own ideas as to how the
thing should be done, and his orders being
completely incomprehensible—had the less
scruple as to carrying them out.

They had gone a couple of hundred yards
when a few puffs dropped from the low walls
before them, and one of his men, a weedy lad
of sixteen, fell screaming. At this spectacle,
the regiment lying in reserve below, were so
profoundly moved that they threatened to get
out of hand altogether.

"My lads," yelled the Colonel hoarsely,
galloping down in rear of the ranks, and
slashing the air with his revolver, under the
mistaken impression that he was waving his
sword, "steady, my lads. Remember Fonte-
noy and What's-its-name—no—I mean, my
lads—forget 'em—this day will remove the
slur."

Here he stopped abruptly, dropped his revolver, which went off (slightly grazing his bugler), and clutched the pommel of his saddle, for the ground was not good for galloping, and galloping at the best of times was not the gallant officer's forte. Meanwhile Roland strode up to his wounded man, who sat up, weeping bitterly.

" Where are you hit ?"

" In the harm, sir ; knocked me rifle out of me 'and ; 'urted me dreadful, sir ; drawed blood. Look 'ere, sir."

" Show it me."

The lad pulled back his sleeve, and displayed a long scratch, where the skin had been cut by a spent ball.

" Get up, you cur ! Take up your rifle ! "

The instant the man was on his feet, Roland collared him and administered a kick in his rear, which flung him several yards to the front.

" Now, sir, double up ; and if you drop again before you're dead, I'll blow every atom of brains out of your miserable skull ! " He whipped out his revolver significantly.

This incident took place in less time than it takes to tell, and the result was everything that could be desired. The men were, one and all, raw boys, fresh to service, and one and all shaking with honest " blue funk." Roland saw this, and calculated the effect. Done under fire, which sounded warm, although it was nothing of the sort, and in full sight of both sides, the trifle told marvellously.

" Now, my men," he shouted, " steady together. We've been sent out to look about us, and it's quite plain we shan't see anything this side of that wall. We'll try it at a rush. Fix bayonets!"

The intervening space was good dry turf. It was a short story. A cheer, a rush, a few irregular puffs from the defences, which crumbled under the onset, a few blows, and a little shouting—in three minutes the thing was over, and the entire rebel force—fifty or sixty men, women, and children, all told—were in full flight over the hillside, beyond the huts. Roland collected his men, blown but triumphant, and re-formed them, disdaining pursuit; but in a minute came a galloping behind.

"By G—, Mr. Tudor," yelled the Colonel's voice, "what the h—l are you doing? Will you fire, sir, or will you not? Are you going to sleep, and let the rebels escape, before I can bring up the regiment? By G— above, sir, will you fire a volley?"

"There are women and children, sir," was the answer.

"Will you obey orders, sir?" screamed the Colonel, almost in a fit.

"I decline to obey this particular order, sir. We have cleared the stockade. I can do no more. Here is my sword. But no"— He took it, snapped it across his knee, and flung the pieces to the ground.

By this time the Adjutant had come up, and with him the correspondent. The situation sobered the Chief, and the delay undoubtedly saved the rebels. Roland was marched to the rear, under arrest, by the Adjutant, and the regiment having come up, the stronghold was burned. While they were employed in levelling the defences, the senior Major, having caught the drift of what had happened, rode up to the Colonel. He was one of the few men in the regiment who had kept his head clear, and was not on good terms with his Chief. He knew something of the confounded civilian prejudices which exist in the outer world, and are apt to tie the hands of the most energetic commander.

"By G—, Cheapsyde," he said, coming up, "you'd better let that young fellow go. You've just about saved your commission by the skin of your teeth, thanks to him. But you always were a fool."

This was plain speaking, and not altogether according to Cocker[1]; but the Chief feared his junior, as a man does fear his inevitable successor, so he merely replied, mildly, "What the h—l do you mean, Hardy?"

It will be observed how pretty was the language of these gentlemen when under temporary excitement.

"I mean, sir, that there were women and children in the crowd—saw 'em with my own eyes. I s'pose I needn't say more."

"Well, but, Hardy," stammered the Chief, very red, "they're all rebels together, ain't they? And I've heard you say, yourself, you'd string up every man, woman, and child in the country, if you had the chance."

"But," and the Major smiled grimly, "you

[1] A great military authority of the day.

hadn't the chance; that's just where it is; the infernal public won't give it you; and, after all, it don't seem quite the right thing, does it, in cold blood, after you've thrashed 'em? We've been out two days, and it's just about decimated us with sick, and they've been here two months, and I don't s'pose they're the better for it. The men say a lot of 'em were carried away by the others up the hill and over those rocks. Nice place, that mountain, to cook your supper and sleep on, without our giving 'em extra sick to carry up. Why on earth didn't you take 'em prisoners, if you wanted to do anything?"

"They never gave us the chance," groaned the Chief. But," he continued, dropping this unpleasant subject, "young Tudor's exceeded his orders. I sent him to look at the place, and by G— he took it before I could stop him, as you saw. The thing was over in ten minutes. Then, when I got hold of him, he insulted me; and the cub had the impudence to snap his blade in my face, d—— him! I've sent him to the rear, in arrest; but by G— it's deuced awkward."

"Was it before the men, all this?" asked the Major, sharply.

"No," sulked the Colonel, "I got the cub in a corner."

"Got yourself in a hole," sneered his junior. "Precious lucky for you it was in a corner; that's your way out of it. Say there was a misunderstanding; you're blind as a bat, and couldn't see. Swear it, and lay it on that. He got the plum to-day, and he must have it."

This was where the shoe pinched. The plum was a very small one, a mere currant; but such as it was, Lieutenant Tudor had got it; and this gave dire offence in a regiment, where already he stood not too well. However, the upshot of this conversation was, that he came out of arrest within half an hour of going into it, and for the time being, no one was much the wiser, all this having taken place during the " action." A report certainly spread abroad of something wrong, but no details eked out at present.

Meanwhile the regiment had been busy looting the stronghold, and in a short space the walls had been thrown down, the huts set on fire, and all the valuable loot extracted. This consisted of two three-legged stools, a pig (a manifest felony), and a prisoner—the last an unhappy wretch, who had been too weak to crawl away at the time of the assault, and too friendless to be carried. When brought out, his hollow eyes shone like lamps in his sunken cheeks, and his rags hung about him as on a skeleton. But the value of this living corpse as a trophy, it was impossible to over-estimate. He was given half a bucket of brandy and beef-tea on the spot, and put into an ambulance, where the surgeons came and felt his pulse every ten minutes on the return march, to the disgust of the rest of the sick, who failed to see the delicacy of the situation.

The stronghold was then burned, and a despatch from the field of battle, conveyed post haste by a young and distinguished Staff-officer, who had been present on behalf of the world, told the expectant public, in brief, soldier-like language, just tinted with an occasional fine word, of the complete and unqualified success of the operations undertaken against the rebels.

The return march, and the regiment's triumphal entry into the garrison town, headed by three bands playing different war tunes, was one of the grandest things of the kind on record. By dint of constant feeding night and day, and a liberal supply of liquor, the prisoner had so far recovered, that at the outskirts he was set down from his ambulance, and made to march in handcuffs, in the centre of a square of fixed bayonets, through the main streets and up to the barrack gates; where with every circum-stance of pomp and pride, he was handed over to the representatives of the Civil authority. By this time not a button but had been wrenched from him by his captors, as mementoes of the event, and in the interests of decency he had to be completely sewn up from chin to toe, to keep his clothes on his back at all. He plainly had no idea of his own importance, and such an ignorant savage was he, that he seemed surprised at these several proceedings.

Then followed speeches and dinners galore, and fêtes and fireworks. Meanwhile the regi-ment was secretly divided on an important question—the returns of sick and wounded. There was a magnificent show of the former, but strictly speaking only one of the latter, and the knotty point was, as to whether the bugler winged by the Colonel should be included in the roll of honour. The boy contended that he had been hit in action, " and that was all he knowed about it," and as to allow his claim was to double the number of wounded at a stroke, it was eventually given in his favour.

The succeeding week some of the Service papers (not all) launched out on our young soldiers and their prowess, and a distinguished authority on this subject, made a capital speech after a capital dinner.

And the Britisher, who enjoyed nothing so much as his battle for breakfast, said it was a very fine thing, and that the complete absence of bloodshed made it finer still, and proved this to his wife, who said she was very glad, but being a woman could not, of course, quite understand it. And nearly every Englishman went to bed on the night of the great news, comforted at heart to think, how satisfactory it was, and how simple and easy and painless it was to keep Ireland in order, and what a fool he had been, ever to have had any doubt on the matter.

Yet, there were Continental critics who sniggered and were covertly rude, and even a few British officers who groaned in their sleeves, to see the papers taken up with so solemn a discussion of so solemn a farce; though certainly it was a change from the grievances of the canteen corporals, and the woes of the assistant gunners.

So then Lieutenant Tudor returned to the all-absorbing interests of garrison guards and

orderly officer.   He was a good deal discussed
among his brother officers, who had began to
feel his latent strength, but he was none the
more liked for having led the way up in the
hills, and he went his own road as before,
equally indifferent.

There was, however, one man besides the
Colonel and the Adjutant, who had seen the incident of the broken sword.   Coming up, he
had watched it at a respectful distance, as became a good correspondent, whose duty, as
every one knows, is the exact reverse of a good
little boy's, for he has to be heard but not seen.
This was Mr. McFaggarty, the representative
of the press, who was prodigiously struck by
it.   Secretly he was a red-hot patriot at heart,
but unfortunate necessity had obliged him for
the time to become a red-hot flunkey, in which
way he had at least the satisfaction of de-
spoiling the tyrant invader, of a certain
annual stipend in gold, for Mr. McFaggarty
was an excellent romancist and teller of
tales, and his services were well paid in Fleet
Street.

The story, nothing losing, was by this little
bird chirruped abroad over all the country
side, and the hero of it woke one morning to
find himself famous; and when he marched with
his men to the dirty little benchless chapel one
Sunday shortly after, the whole congregation
rose like one man, and began to pray aloud for
him.   " Holy Mother o' God protect him.   Bless
his sweet vargin sowl.   May the saints show
him the way to glory, and the Divil himself

niver git a hair av' 'is blessed head." And there
was crooning and crying, and dragging at his
hand and clasping of his knees, and the priest
flew out of the sacristy and laid about him
well, with his fist, before he could get his people
"straight" again. All very quaint and curious,
low and animal, no doubt, yet the receiver of
this homage was secretly touched to the heart
by it. After mass came a request from the
priest for an interview.

Father O'Leary, the priest of the parish, was
a sturdy, bull-necked individual, in whom moral
and physical strength were conjoined with no
small portion of humour. He had taken so
active a part in politics during the late stormy
times, that the Government had very nearly
made a confessor of him, by putting him in
gaol. Roland found him at breakfast when he
was shown in.

"By the pow'rs, sor, it's roight glad I am to
see ye!" exclaimed the good father, seizing his
visitor by both hands. "Me house is homely,
but oi'me aware of ye renown, sor, and ye
hoigh position in the hoighest of hoigh society,
and I trust to see it hoigher yet."

Roland, slightly embarrassed at this greeting,
thanked him and said he hoped it would be a
fine day.

"Indade, sor, but 'twill, if that big lump o'
rain up yonder don't come down upon us. But
now, sor, ye'll join me modest board, there's a
moighty foine fish there; at eight o'clock this
mornin' he was runnin' about, little thinkin' he'd
be here to meet ye at one."

But as he had already breakfasted, Roland declined.

"Ah! ye're a raal gentleman, and widout doubt ye prefer to do the swell when ye can do it chape, and ye can do it chape here, sor, for oi've the finest cigar in the West to offer ye."

So Mr. Tudor "did the swell," and took one of his host's cigars; the priest, when questioned as to their origin, giving a knowing wink, which I regret to have to record, but cannot admit *per se* as an argument against Catholicity.

"Well, sor," he went on, "oi've a proposition to lay before ye. Perhaps ye'd wish to be changing ye state."

Now Roland was aware that the bright eyes of many damsels had brightened at his approach since the affair on the hills, and he nervously apprehended that the reverend father was, like many others, an inveterate match-maker, ready perhaps to bestow upon him the very flower of his flock, and he rather hastily said that he thought not. The priest looked disconcerted.

"But bedad, sor," he said confidentially, catching his guest by the sleeve, "what I have to propound, will make ye twice the man ye are."

"Thank you, I am single, and prefer remaining so, to being doubled at present."

"Oh, ho!" chuckled the host; "sure there's toime enough for that. What I want to ask av' ye is, would ye take a sate in the Senate?"

"In the House of Commons?" stammered Lieutenant Tudor.

"Bedad, sor, ye've hit it. Ye're a foighting man, sor. Holy Moses, the foight there is in ye!" and he gazed at him with the unspeakable admiration of an athlete whose day is past, for one whose day is yet to come. "The thing is to get it out. Ye're an English Catholic; that's agin ye. It's not moighty fond of 'em we are over here, but afther that little business of yours in the mountains, och, bedad, 'twas the foinest man aloive ever heard of. The Saxon toirant found his match there!"

The worthy priest clapped his hands and rolled back in his chair, laughing till he wept. "Oh! 'tis the bhoys will be afther givin' ye a sword of honour, with doimonds and the loike stuck about it, for the one ye smashed over his head."

Lieutenant Tudor rose and paced the room frowning. "What is known of this, sir?" he asked.

But the priest was not abashed. "By the piper, me dear, isn't every mother's son in the country's soide talkin' av' it at this blessed hour? And sure, didn't Johnny McFaggarty, representative of the entoire London press, see it wid his own oyes? Moy! but 'twas splendid. Ah! sor! ye've grasped the National idea. That's all we want here. Ye'll do, sor!" and he clapped his guest heavily on the shoulder.

Annoyed as he was, and a trifle amused, the proposition had taken hold of Roland's imagination, and he was lost in thought. Here was an opening ready made, of which he had never dreamed, his sympathies were already engaged, and there would be hard fighting. What more could a man want? Making due allowance for the good father's enthusiasm, there was certainly a possible career in it, commendable for many reasons, but it was not a matter to be decided off hand.

"I'm full young," he said thoughtfully.

"Is it young, sor?" shouted the priest. "Didn't the electors of Ballinamucky jest set up young McBlathery when he was still an infant in the oye of the law, and wasn't it six months they had to wait before they could elect him to Parliament at all, at all? and wanst he was there, was it six wakes before he defied the Spaker, hounded down the Proime Minister himself, and sent the whole of the Treasury Bench (the traithors!) snaking away wid their tails among their legs, unable to say wan word in their own definse? Oh! 'tis a broth of a boy he is, and niver was the loiks av him seen before. But, bedad, sor, you're a cut above Mr. McBlathery."

Roland breathed a silent hope that he might be, but said nothing.

"Man," went on the priest, his eyes glistening, "take it or lave it. But oi'me tellin' ye a peerage isn't in the same breath wid it. Now will ye listen? Ye've seen the rise of Mr. —, oi suppose. He's the greatest man in the world, but he's wore out. 'Tis just miracles he's done, but he can't go on for iver, and the pace is killin'. We must have a man of his toype ready for his shoes, a betther wan if possible, though that 'ud be moighty hard. Now,

sor, this little chance has just put ye in wid
the runnin'. Ye can enther to-morrow, if ye
will, the best nag o' the year. If ye play yer
cards well, in foive years ye may be Dictator,
in ten, by God above who made ye for 't, we'll
have ye crowned King of ould Ireland if ye
wish it."

All this reads like the wildest romance,
but such was the state of the country at this
time. There were Nationalists, and Nationalists, but the Revolution was undoubtedly
looking for "a King," and if a man would
cast in his lot with it, if he were a gentleman
(this was essential), if he had a hard head, a long
pocket, and the courage of his convictions, as
such he might have been crowned, but it was
not difficult to foresee the end of it. The name
and fame of the incident, in the taking of the
mountain stronghold, whose hero was an
Englishman, of historic birth and a Catholic,
was sufficient to lift him half-way up the tree
at once. It was not because Lieutenant Tudor
had refrained from firing upon women and children, but because he had defied Authority, and
snapped his sword with impunity in It's face,
that he had become the hero of the hour.
Although the Blankshires were happily an exceptional regiment, and the odium into which
they had fallen was chiefly due to a succession
of bad commanding officers, parallel mistakes
had been recorded on the part of the English
garrison in Ireland.

Like half the young men of the day, Roland
had settled the Irish question a long time

since in his own mind, to his complete satisfaction. Power was what he wanted, he felt exactly what ought to be done, and no lack of confidence in himself to do it. He put behind him all notions of Revolution as pure bunkum. He was a loyal Englishman to begin with, and believed, that while fostering the aspiration of the people towards Nationality, as an essential factor in the Nation's well-being, even-handed justice might be meted out to all sides. He was averse from confiscation on the one side, as a breach of the moral law, as he was from starvation on the other; and he fancied that he saw his way through all difficulties to an era of happiness and prosperity. He appreciated the warmth and enthusiasm which binds together Irish hearts, as he reprobated the Socialism which, under various false externals, had crept in and made its place there. It should be a noble debt the Nation should owe him, if he ever laid a hand to their affairs, and he imagined that the open sesame of all difficulty, would be in a straightforward, unbending course of right.

"Well, Father," he said lightly, to disguise his real feeling, "you must give me time to think of this. But if there's a seat going, won't some of your own flock be looking for it?"

"Och, bedad, sor! I'd be sorry to hear any of moy lambs blatin' in public. They're a bit black, some of moy sheep," and he winked a second time. "Now, sor, oi'me thinkin' I'd droive ye up to the borricks in stoyle. Oi've the finest carr in the West at all, and sure the mare's a picture, let alone the carr."

"Oh, pray don't think of it," said Roland. "I—"

"Well, there *is* wan objection," said the priest; "the wheels is out av' it. But now here, sor," he went on, dismissing the point, "I'll spake wid his Grace, it's takin' his vocation he is—he'll be round here next wake. Manetoime, ye'll be loike Gideon perhaps, and askin' for a proof. Now what'll ye have as a token of what the bhoys 'll do for ye? Shall they break ivery windy in the borricks, barrin' yer own, this blessed night?"

Roland seemed to think this would be unnecessary, so the good father did not press it, and they shook hands.

"By the way," said the latter, hesitating, "now, I s'pose ye haven't any particular devotion to the sowls in purgatory?"

"In moderation," laughed Roland, and tossed a sovereign on the table.

"Faith aloive!" ejaculated his Reverence, amazed at the facilty of its production, "p'rhaps ye'd be preferrin' to make it two?"

"Indeed I shouldn't," laughed his visitor, again taking up the coin. "Now I think of it, a sovereign's too much. I'll make it half. Good-bye, Father, we'll have another talk shortly."

It has been said that the padre had a notion of humour, and though he was the loser by the joke, his whole heart went out to the man because of it. He rolled with laughter.

" Bedad ! " he said, slapping his thigh, as he watched the retreating form. "That bates creation for brass. He'll make the grandest patriot ould Ireland iver had ! "

Meantime Roland hurried through the streets, hoping to slip into barracks unnoticed, but the boys shouted after him, and the women flung ungainly blessings at his head as he passed. As for the little children, they knelt down in the mud all the way along, for his blessing, an embarrassing situation for a lieutenant in the line. The next week he sent in his papers.

CHAPTER III.

THE scene was the ante-room of the Blankshire regiment, and the *dramatis personæ* were the Colonel and a friend of equal rank belonging to the Staff.

" So poor old Skrimshank has applied for the Chiltern Hundreds. Well, he has not set foot in the House for the last three sessions, and quite right too. The place is a regular pot-house, sir. No gentleman's a chance now a days. I wonder what blackguard they'll put up in his place. What an infernal shame it is."

" You may say so," groaned the Colonel, " no gentleman would take an Irish seat now a days if he were paid for it. Look at the brutes they've got in now. Not one of them fit to black a gentleman's boots, sir, by Jove ! What d—d rot it is talking about the people and their rights; it's all come of this precious education. I knew it would come, I always said it would, when they began to educate. Why, when I was a boy, there weren't two schools to a county. Their rights ? God bless my soul ! Keep the beggars down in their proper place, that's what their rights are. If you lift them out of their place, they'll hoist you out of yours. I told 'em so twenty years ago, and look what it's come to. Why, sir, only last month, when I led the regiment into action—"

But there is no need to continue the Colonel's remarks on this subject. It was curious that whatever was started, he always drifted round to this; which, as the sole time when he had been under fire, served him for conversation throughout the remainder of his life.

This man was actually an Irishman by birth, although he belonged, and always had belonged, to the hostile camp. At one-and-twenty he had discarded his real name— O'Flaherty—taking that of some Cockney relatives—Cheapsyde—and he had turned his back upon his native soil, hating it and everything connected with it, with an intensity which, to the average Englishman, was simply inexplicable. There was no enemy of that unhappy land like the man who owed it his birth, but had found friends and fortune across the channel. Colonel Cheapsyde simply ignored the fact of his nationality, and privately looked upon it as the brand of Cain. He never referred in any way to his connection with the country, nor would he so much as tolerate an Irish paper in the mess; all of which circumstances being perfectly well known, did not tend to endear him with the natives. Things had been sufficiently unpleasant since the return of the regiment to headquarters, and now they were threatened with an election. This meant bloodshed more or less, and bloodshed he did not pretend to like. There was always the difficulty about confining it to one side.

Enter the Adjutant. "There's been fighting down the town, sir. No. 1267, Private Joseph Mullins, just brought in stabbed."

"Good God!"

"Seems he got hold of a girl, and the brutes set upon him. It's a regular riot, sir; they're howling out they'll burn the barracks down."

"I've another piece of news for you," said Major Hardy, coming into the room. "Lieutenant Roland Tudor, H.M. 1st Blankshire Regiment, is to be put up as the National candidate."

"By G— above!" exclaimed the trio, and a moment's silence fell on the group.

"It's a deuce of a business down in town," went on the Major. "It seems that idiot Mullins got hold of some fellow's wife, and they've half murdered him. I've just seen the Garrison Adjutant, and he's telegraphed for a hundred extra police. Of course, sir, you'll get the regiment under arms at once."

The Chief was not the man for an emergency. He sank back in his chair pallid, as if he had been struck. Great beads stood on his forehead; there was real danger, and the man was as sneaking a cur as ever donned a uniform.

"What'll I do?" he gasped piteously, reverting to his native tongue—as he often did when he lost his head. "The responsibility of it is killin' me."

The Staff officer looked at the Major, and the Major looked at the Adjutant; three pair of

shoulders were ominously shrugged. Empty-
headed, played out in mind and body as were
the majority of the Blankshires, there were
men among them, about whom the traditions of
the British soldier still hung. It would be
unjust to take their Chief as their type. Hardy,
for instance, though his brains were no bigger
than those of his brethren, would have confronted an army corps with pleasure, and
there were two or three like him, whose joy lay
in absolute idiocy of foolhardiness. You may
have worse qualities in a soldier; then, again, you
may have better. Without a word, but with
one significant look, the three men left the
Chief in his arm-chair, and hurried off to take
what precautions were possible.

Meanwhile the " row " down town became
very apparent. The savage howling and hooting of the mob grew louder and nearer. A
brilliant idea suddenly seized the Colonel. He
rose and staggered through the passages till he
reached Lieut. Tudor's quarters. He found his
subaltern at his desk, with some confounded
plans of fortification littered all about.

" Mr. Tudor," he began in a thick voice as he
sank into a chair, " I trust that you are too
honourable a man to bear malice. I am aware
that your position in this regiment has—ah—
at times not been as pleasant as it might have
been. That unfortunate—ah—error in the
field, due to my having left my—er—eye-glass in
barracks, I am sure, as a gentleman, you have
long ago forgotten. I have heard only this
instant, and with the greatest possible pleasure,

that you are to be our parliamentary candidate, and I need hardly say how the good wishes of myself and your brother-officers will accompany you on your new career" (here he shook his subaltern's hand unsteadily), "although our views are perhaps slightly divergent. But I regret to say, that there appears to be an election riot in progress outside, probably consequent on your nomination. I shall be very glad, Mr. Tudor, if you, who have influence here as the only Roman Catholic officer in the regiment, would take immediate steps to see what—ah—can be done.

"Anything like brute force would, I fear, merely result in irritating the people; indeed, I should be sorry that any officer or soldier should show himself outside. At the same time, I cannot but think that if you could say just one word to them from the balcony, perhaps ah—serious—ah—trouble might be avoided. Hark !"

There was an ugly sound in the air, and although the Colonel had so far recovered himself as to achieve his old manner, one glance at his face had served to convince Roland that something awkward was in the wind. Without a word he threw open the window and strode out into the balcony. A surging mob packed the narrow lane beneath; the appearance of the red patrol-jacket was the signal for a volley of stones and a stray pistol-shot. The window crashed behind him and fell in a thousand pieces; he himself was struck by one of the missiles in the forehead. The blood

streamed into his eyes, almost blinding him.
Nevertheless, he moved forward a pace, caught
the rail, and wiping his brow essayed to speak.
Suddenly a shout of recognition went up ; the
sight of their favourite, wounded and bleeding,
but standing alone and immoveable, face to face
with the angry hundreds, acted like magic on
the crowd. There was a groan of horror and
dismay, and in the place of threats and curses,
they called upon him with every wild expression
of endearment that affection could suggest.

" Come down wid us, masther dear," shouted
an armed Colossus in the crowd, stretching out
both his hands towards him, " and we'll protect ye out of this accursed sphot ;" and one
and all re-echoed the cry, " Ochhone, me dar-
lint ! come down wid ye ! "

Roland looked round—there was no time for
explanation. Hardy was rapidly mustering the
regiment in the barrack square ; indeed, had
he not been delayed by the idea of charging a
disused mortar which lay there, and bringing
it to bear on the rioters, that desperado would
probably have drawn his sword, and flung
himself at the head of the regiment in their
midst, 'ere this. The aspect of affairs decided
Roland. Knotting his head in a handkerchief,
he went down hatless into the mob, who
promptly lifted him on their shoulders, and with
the wildest whoops ever heard by mortal ear,
bore him in triumph to the dirty shed, which the
Borough dignified by the name of town-hall,
where he made his first public speech, amidst
such enthusiasm as is only to be met with on

such soil and under such circumstances. Thus the barrack windows, all save one, were spared, and a fortnight later, Roland Tudor, of Sombrewood, in the county of ——, Esq., was returned without opposition member of Parliament for Ballymoolee.

The change from the position of a subaltern to that of a legislator was great. The arena of Parliament is one which a man usually enters with high hopes and expectations, and in this he was no exception; they were doomed, as will be seen hereafter, to disappointment.

Roland's return to London gives us the chance of picking up again a few of those acquaintances whom, like the rest of the world, we have dropped when we did not particularly require them.

The meeting with our first friend Major Lickpenny, is a melancholy—in fact a final, one. True to himself to the last, the old man died screaming, after a night of debauch, in a locality for which there is no exact definition known to ears polite. By the same post that Roland received notice of his uncle's death, came a letter from the man himself, begging for the usual loan, with even more than usual urgency, and offering (as usual) by way of repayment, to initiate his nephew into a little life on his return to civilization. Well, well! the initiation had been of a different sort, and the grim comment of the one letter upon the other, did not escape his nephew, who by return issued the necessary orders for the Christian burial of his remains. So the Major's little farce was played out to the end, even when the directing spirit had fled; nothing now remained but to collect his debts and pay up the bills, which were chiefly for champagne suppers, and ladies' fancy underclothing from the Burlington Arcade. Well may we grave R. I. P. to his memory!

On his return to town, Roland found things greatly changed. St. Maur was away for months together in South America, where he had bought largely, and the sole addition to the villa was a rookery, the denizens of which fought for the monopoly with their sable brethren in Curzon Street hard by. The owner had retired into his shell. His work had dwindled to a minimum, for the high Tory Government in power allowed him but scant supply of elbow-room. Progress, as he understood it, was at a standstill; the retrograde movement which had set in was carrying all before it.

Perhaps there are few worse signs, than when a new Government proceeds immediately to reverse the policy of its predecessors. The slow advance of years was to be nullified in a few sessions. The Ministry had come in with a tremendous majority. Liberalism had had its trial, and had brought the country to the verge of revolution, said the property-holders, who, thanks in great measure to its having fought their battle, now constituted the bulk of the nation; and the understanding was that it was to be crushed out. Such reactions take place when least expected, and as if by magic. The tussle was a desperate one, but a Continental revolution occurring exactly in the nick of time, had given the required spurt in favour of the property-holders, and out of the ashes of the struggle, the high Tory party had risen like a Phœnix.

It was necessary, of course, to begin cautiously; but it was recognized that the fundamental error had lain entirely in the education of the people, in the attempt to raise them out of their proper sphere. The national scheme of education was therefore abrogated, nor was any measure ever more popular with the rate-payers, who had long groaned over an ever-mounting school-rate. The buildings were either closed or devoted to the teaching of light and fancy work, such as could harm nobody. The boys were taught painting on china, and the violin; the girls to make pin-cushions and trim their bonnets, attendance being entirely optional.

It is impossible to do more than indicate all the reforms which were initiated. The public-houses, as old English institutions, representing vested interests of a sacred character, received every encouragement. The museums, which had been opened on Sundays and holidays, were again closed. As several small wars cropped up, consequent on an increased sense of the national dignity and the need of asserting it, among black people at least, the army was increased and swelled to a size which it had never reached before. This was achieved by universal conscription—that is to say, conscription with a twenty-pound penalty, which made it universal with exactly the classes required; and as there was now no difficulty about proper coercion, there was no further anxiety about Ireland or the dangerous classes, which had been so troublesome to former administrations. The right of public meeting was prohibited, and in London the vestries were reconstituted, the local government being very properly vested in the local clergyman and a few of his subordinates.

Labour having become extremely dear, the question of slavery began to be mooted, and it was discovered to be a natural and beautiful institution, not only ordained by Providence, but sanctioned by Holy Writ. There was one overwhelming argument in its favour: it had been a feature of the golden age of Toryism, and social economists were not wanting who proved its actual necessity in the highest stages of cultivation. There was, unhappily, here and there a good deal of factious opposition to many of these far-reaching schemes, and it was not until a new Reform Bill had been passed extending the franchise to women and children over twelve years of age, that real progress was made. The Conservative and intellectual gain, consequent on this brilliant stroke, was prodigious, and thenceforth all went merrily. Protection came in again, and what the duty on wheat ran to, per quarter, it would be rash to say, for fear of upsetting the farmers' minds. Co-operative stores were closed. The bank holidays (detested of housekeepers) were abolished with acclamation. The railings were again set up round the London squares, and the dirty classes were shovelled entirely out of sight. There was no end to improvement, and as there was no doubt that they were on the right road at last, everybody was extremely happy—that is, everybody who was anybody; and only a few millions of nobodies complained, who, having watched their star slowly rise through long years, were utterly aghast at its sudden declension.

Meantime the Church of England flourished; never were the loaves and fishes more plentiful or more secure. The Church of Rome, too, flourished, for in a way, common cause had been made by the two. The figure-heads of the Roman Church in England were so highly aristocratic, and if the bulk of its members were not so—they wished to be with all their hearts, and it came to almost the same thing. A movement like the present towards feudalism and mediævalism brought back the days when the Church had been mistress on the earth, and naturally enlisted their sympathies. The "respectable" Dissenters were high Tories to a man, for to be so put them on the level of Church people at once. The lower class of Dissenters, the Irish, the atheists, and those sort of folk, who unfortunately bulked largely in the big towns, were placed as far as possible under police supervision; and it having been found that the atheists (who were a rapidly increasing body) dressed very badly, and wore shocking bad hats, the most rigid measures were taken to exclude them from Parliament and every place of emolument and distinction. Indeed, it was not until a young marquis, dressed from Savile Row, took the lead of this party that they made head at all; but after this their progress was like a house a-fire, and it was now beginning to be thought an exceedingly gentlemanlike form of unbelief.

Under these varying circumstances, of which it is only possible to give an outline, St. Maur's occupation was gone. None knew better than he, the elements that simmered beneath the surface, yet he was powerless. All he could do, was to turn the villa into a great school of art instruction, for the artisans of London; for it was a theory of his, that whatever a man's passions, once he understood the labour, value, and beauty implied in a work of art, his natural destructiveness would be reined.

Meantime he had kept an eye upon his former *protégé*. They had last met, on the latter's return from his military escapade abroad, when Roland had walked in upon him at ten o'clock at night, and had divulged the secret. They had had but half an hour's conversation in the cell which St. Maur called his bedroom, and the bronze Victory was their silent witness. St. Maur, who loved the fillip of an adventure, and was a soldier at heart himself, though the chief events of his military career had been the trooping of colours on the royal birthdays, hurried off a day or two after, with princely gifts in his pocket, as before told, for the benefit of his friend's companions-in-arms. He had gone *incognito*, and no one had been the wiser. The two had not met since, but had corresponded six lines a year or so, one for every two months, and it was by his advice that Roland had taken the proffered seat in Parliament.

So far as the outer world was concerned, the years that Roland had been with his regiment might as well have been passed in the cloister; almost the only events discussed at mess being those, technically so called, in the sporting world. But the time had not been lost; all he now wanted was 50,000 men, with which to test his skill. As, however, nothing much bigger than a subaltern's guard seemed likely to present itself, he left his old corps with the less regret.

He rapidly made the discovery that he had become a personage in the interim. The circumstances at Ballymoolee had leaked out, and the mere possession of a seat in Parliament opened many doors to him; not that his principles were approved of in society, but it was felt that he had the makings of an interesting and valuable convert. His old friends were assiduous in looking him up, and it was interesting to note the climbing that had been accomplished in various quarters.

The Squeeds were to be met everywhere. They had slowly but surely been creeping into those positions, which they were so well qualified to adorn. The tactics adopted by Bud and Horror, of bringing out impromptu remarks, carefully hatched at home, and of a character sufficiently risky and facetious, but not too much so, had succeeded to admiration; and they were fraternally pronounced by their men, " Howling good sort, you know! " Extreme caution had to be exercised at first, they being at the fag end of the scale, mere fifth cousins of a marquis, who had never heard their names, and having only one Lady Jane in their possession. But though they were not pretty, not young, and had no money, they had by this means reached such a point, that there was now hardly anything they were afraid to say or do; and they could laugh, swagger, smoke, kick up a row, or administer a slap, almost with Lady Victoria Nage herself.

The consequence of so much and such excellent spirit was, that half the heavy young men-about-town were in love with them; for there was nothing these gentlemen appreciated more than to be met nine-tenths of the way, and on their own level, without fatigue or boredom. The terrible mother in the background was against anything serious coming of all this; but could you have seen these young ladies mimicking and making fun of their mamma to their friends, you would have died of laughing; and on recovery of sufficient breath, had you been a man, would have proposed to one of them yourself.

Eve was married; her reply to a certain member of the Heavies, on being asked her name, " Squeed, I'm sorry to say," having so charmed him, that he felt he could do no less than change it for her at the first opportunity.

This year a most unexpected thing had happened—an immense thing, a thing of the first magnitude—their sister, Mrs. Brabant, and her husband were coming to town, to take a house for the season—in Grosvenor Square, they hinted, but it was not quite settled.

Roland found a letter waiting for him at the House of Commons from the latter, the first he had had from him for a length of time; for since his marriage Brabant had been singularly uncommunicative, and had even failed to answer the missive of congratulation which Roland had sent him on that occasion. After touching on various subjects—his health, his literary successes, which, he said, had astonished even himself—he went on to speak of their return to England.

"I hear," he wrote, "that there are excellent houses going for the traditional song all through Belgravia, which I don't object to in summer, but Mrs. Brabant gives me no choice between Grosvenor Square and Park Lane. There is a street, however, in that neighbourhood, 'Upper Snook Street,' which appears to have been especially built to meet the emergency, and I have heard of a house in it, No. 100A, which, perhaps, might do. The advertisement calls it a little jewel, and intimates that there is an annual struggle, among the crowned heads of Europe, for its temporary possession. As I suppose you do not intend to turn out the Ministry within the next week, perhaps, like a good fellow, you will go and look at it for me. I don't particularly affect a bijou residence, even when its rent for three months, is set down at that of a mansion and deer-park for the year; however, the profound insight into female character, which the critics declare has been the making of me, will help to tide me over even this. If your report is satisfactory, we shall hope to be in town in the beginning of April—that is, three weeks hence."

There is one point in this that requires explanation. Much of Belgravia had succumbed to the fate of our own Bloomsbury and Soho. A beauty-loving people, such as the leaders of the generation had become, and one with whom the preservation of health was a household science, refused to countenance any longer that hopeless stucco wilderness of pretence and miasma. Those endless rows in deadly monotony, the plaster fronts of which—cracked, seamed, and peeling, or patched up and glittering in hideous dirty whiteness—stretched through maddening distances, had fallen into deserved contempt. While it flourished in its plaster pride, it had been the type of all that was worst in the British character.

There was dignity in the grey stone fronts of Bloomsbury and its Georgian houses of red brick, in Belgravia was merely the ostentatious apeing of it. The worst of it was, that these dreadful structures were built to last their ninety-nine years, and though many were prematurely decrepit, there appeared to be no deliverance from them except by foreign invasion; but the rents had fallen to a third or a fourth, and the world had fled backwards to its old haunts, where leases were everywhere falling in, and it could build as it listed. In the last days of the late Government, a great enfranchisement of leaseholds had taken place; and the patriotic love of the Londoner for his unique city, for centuries repressed in every possible way, began to express itself in an architectural magnificence worthy of the site and the age. Bloomsbury was restored to fashion, and in the superb possibilities of Regent's Park was being slowly achieved an earthly Utopia.

Mayfair held her own; no turn in Fortune's wheel could ever depose her from her throne, short perhaps of a return of the glacial period. But there were in her bosom two very distinct classes of inhabitants. Gathered round the great ancestral houses, were their swarming collateral branches, but interspersed with these was a large percentage of people on promotion. These might be usually recognized by their double names, which had become a startling abuse. If their name were Bugby, they took a house in Grosvenor Street and called themselves Grosvenor-Bugby; or in Piccadilly, and called themselves Sutton-Bugby. There were few things in which morality was laxer, but the eminent obscurity of the individuals made it possible—made it answer. It went down. These people, however, paid their footing; they were useful, and, therefore, presumably happy.

Since the day of his marriage, Mr. Brabant had scarcely set foot in England. He had

sternly adhered to his first resolution to set
things right by the sweat of his brow, and
his wife, after many futile struggles, had condescended to acquiesce. They had finally
settled in an obscure foreign watering-place, the
quiet of which, if deadly to Mrs. Brabant, was
highly vivifying to her husband and his work.
Indeed, from this moment, in spite of domestic
drawbacks, it took a marked spurt; his gains,
no longer spasmodic, became constant and
assured. His first book issued from this retreat, and bearing the title, " Glimpses of the
Nineteenth Century, compiled from Contemporary Records," achieved a huge success. In
this, taking the day's papers, monuments, and
leading features, he twisted and misread them
with every possible ingenuity, the result being
a superb caricature, which the Century described, as it were, with its own lips.

If necessity had made the writer a literary
hack, instead of Prime Minister—as he had
originally intended—he was fast growing re-
conciled to the position. He could never be
made to see that honourable labour (even when
successful), implied loss of caste. Nor did he
sympathize with his wife's high-bred scorn of
anything outside amateur work, although she
was at much pains to impress it upon him.
And when, by degrees, instead of seven-and-
sixpences (for she still supplied genteel paragraphs to genteel papers) came rolling in hundred after hundred, the fruits of his labour,
Mrs. Brabant changed her note to that of a
turtle-dove. In public she was as heretofore.

There was no great public at "Fadaise-les-bains," but before it she would say, "Poor dear Warburton, he is *so* fond of his scribbling," (which was very far from the case), "I never can get him out, it's quite an *occupation* for him. I think it such a *great* thing when a man has resources, and is able to amuse himself out of harm's way. I'm sure I'm *too* thankful."

A day dawned at length when debts were wiped out, hundreds had mounted into thousands, and Mrs. Brabant saw herself within measurable distance of her old aims in life. It almost restored her husband to her heart; she forgave his shocking brutality in the early days of their marriage, and cautiously broached her point—the next London season. Rather to her surprise, she gained it without opposition; much, however, remained for discussion, even when this was settled.

There was the street. "Position is *everything*," she said.

"Everything," admitted her husband. He had fallen into a way of assenting to most of her propositions by this time; she never knew exactly what to think of his readiness in this respect.

"We ought to be able to get into any society we choose. I'm sure, when I think of my relations—!" she sighed, as if not quite certain on the point. "You *did* dine once with the Prince, didn't you, dear?"

"Yes. I was had in to amuse him—sort of monkey and barrel-organ business, you know," he answered with gravity, as he stood looking from the window and drumming his fingers on the pane.

"I suppose there's hardly a chance of the Royal set?" threw out his wife as a feeler.

"Hardly, I should say—but—I believe there's some very tolerable society to be had in London out of it."

"The best people, I've noticed, seem to keep to themselves a good deal,"—this regretfully.

"Well, my dear"—brightening—"why not keep to *our*selves? That's an excellent idea."

But it was not Mrs. Brabant's.

"I do, do think London is too delightful," she exclaimed, throwing herself back in her chair and clasping her hands with the childish enthusiasm of forty summers—"and oh! Warburton, the door-knocker."

"The door-knocker, Maria?"

"Yes, yes! to hear it going from morning till night," (yet Mrs. Brabant complained of her nerves). "Oh! and all the little notes flying in—it's my ideal—my ideal of true happiness."

Warburton gulped down an exclamation.

"Yes, and all the little social duties. Oh! I do love them, and to say you're so full of engagements you don't know which way to turn. It's heaven!"

"I have sometimes thought," observed her husband drily, "that I would draw up a little code of social duties for Londoners. Rule 1: 'For every desirable acquaintance you make, hunt up two to whom you yourself may be of help or use.'"

Mrs. Brabant flung herself back in fits of laughter. "Oh! Warburton, you dear, funny fellow," she gasped, "how clever and *witty* you can be when you like!"

It must not be supposed from the foregoing that her husband disliked society. On the contrary, he found in it an inexhaustible mine of instruction wherein he could delve and delve again. His powers were rusting for want of opportunity—he had been abroad too long. He saw with equanimity that his time was short, and resolved that his last effort should be made in his beloved London.

Mrs. Brabant's plans were not so much upon the surface as appeared at first sight—she had long resolved with herself that her present matrimonial venture was a failure, and must be improved upon with all possible speed. She had diagnosed her husband's case only too accurately. She could wreck his nervous system at pleasure—and very great pleasure it had given her to make the discovery,—and she felt positive that whenever the times were ripe and her plans ready, she could kill him off with ease in the space of six months. She had never exactly put this into words, but it was there, laid up in her head. If to record this detracts somewhat from the amusing side of her character, it is to be regretted. Her resolution, quietly taken, affected her externally in nowise, unless it were to make her a trifle more contented in a position which she knew was only a temporary one, terminable at will. For the rest, her husband's successes had fired her ambitions, and she was even now making the discovery that she might shine independently in a light of her own. A little novelette of hers, entitled " The Frivoller," was making its way, with *éclat*, through the pages of a penny society paper. It was time to be turning homeward and thinking of founding a *salon*.

It will be remembered that Mrs. Brabant's ideas had a certain vague grandeur. When Grosvenor Square was pronounced to be out of the question, she had had a fit of hysterics, had torn up her lace wrap, and broken some of the china on the chimney-piece. This did her good; in the course of an hour she was all smiles again, and her husband ventured back (for it was now his rule to retire to a place of safety during the storm), bringing with him a page out of the London directory, which the house agent had sent him, giving the list of Upper Snook Street. When she had looked at it and seen that there were two marquises in a row, one of them the nobleman whom they had met in Paris; and that one happy house was wedged in between them, the number of which on paper looked as important as theirs, and her husband told her that this vacant house had been offered him and might be her's, she fell about his neck and cried in a paroxysm of sheer affection.

It is wonderful under what conditions human life may be supported, and it shows how Nature seeks to accommodate herself to circumstances, that Brabant had actually been able to turn his troubles to account; for had he remained single, the world would have been the loser of the admirable domestic novels, with which he had enthralled it for months past.

A species of armed neutrality had long since been arrived at. It was not pleasant, but it was the best that could be hoped for. Mrs. Brabant had her own way as far as her husband could give it her, and a reasonable supply of cheap china was kept on the chimney-piece, in event of a crisis. For the rest, now that he had pulled her and himself by incessant work, out of the slough of debt, into the sunshine of comparative prosperity, he was nipped fatally, and he knew it; his health was steadily giving way. It was this feeling which drew him Londonwards to the scenes of his first successes. He would look on them again. Another year and it might be too late.

On receiving the letter then, in accordance with its instructions Roland proceeded to view the house in question. He found it the most curious and entertaining little place, a veritable *lusus naturæ*. Altogether differing from the natural growth of the soil, it seemed to have shot up accidentally in the elbow-space left by its two big neighbours. The explanation of this was, that an ancestor of the left-hand marquis had ordered a palatial lavatory outside his house, an order which he had afterwards rescinded. He had in place of it run up the strip he called No. 100a, and as such let for a fabulous rental. In London these trifles mean history !

The rooms were like a succession of cupboards
opening out of each other, but there was an
unlimited supply of Lilliputian ebonized furniture, and in every corner was a bracket with
useful little black balustrades, and velvet-
mounted picture-frames containing photographs
of the Royal Family and the reigning beauties,
all slightly idealized by the artists. There
were dolls' tea-cups, and mirrors, and china
ornaments in wondrous profusion. The tiny
grates in the sitting-rooms were draped with
chintz, pink satin sash bows, and cheap lace,
never was anything so sweet and suitable; and
as for stained glass, you might have fancied
yourself in a cathedral, for wherever there was
an objectionable look-out, and it seemed there
were many, it was hidden by the rare design of
a pointed-leaved plant, with red ball fruit
sprouting out of a sugar basin.

There were plush-legged tables, where many
generations of smuts nestled cozily, and there
were bright blue and yellow flower-boxes with
nursery scenes on them. There were dados,
two or three of them, all the way up all the
walls, and now and then trespassing auda-
ciously on the ceiling. And there was a show
of plates, like a kitchen dresser, some grave,
some gay, some sound, more cracked—the
head of a *ci-devant* beauty restored to her
pristine youth, her foot treated separately, and
glorified in a pink satin shoe and gold stocking,
cheek by jowl with the "Horrors of Peace and
the Blessings of War," the work of an uncertain
amateur, and interspersed with exquisite things

in sun-flowers, sage-green, and so forth. And there were chair-backs, ye gods! humorous ones, which of their sheer selves threw the beholder into fits of laughter; and there were artificial flowers, dusty rather, but so cunningly placed in corners and in real pots that at five hundred yards' distance, supposing that attainable, they might have passed at least for a very good imitation, which at five feet they certainly did not do.

There was certainly nothing like it in London, said the housekeeper, who further told her visitor of the prestige that attached to the house, and how all the connoisseurs of the age had been wont to assemble in the reception-rooms, as she facetiously designated the four large cupboards; and how the connoisseurs had approved and enjoyed themselves. Then she took him upstairs by a series of ladders that had been filled in, and were consequently hardly dangerous at all to a young and active person, and she led him to a single room. This she said had been the Lady Mildred's, and she had preferred it to all others because of its view of the park. If he would only stand on the dressing-table, open the top of the window, and lean well forward sideways, he would see what she meant, and Roland, who always caught the spirit of the hour, did so, and twisted himself further and further out under the persistent encouragement of the domestic.

"You can see the tops of the omblibuses in Park Lane of a fine day, for I've done it myself," she said emphatically; "and the view of 'Ide Park, sir, is a hitem of isself in the lease."

But the adventurous man, whose head was failing him, refused to go further. He came down and slowly ascended the next flight of ladders, pondering on the strange idiosyncrasies of the late Lady Mildred. He had a look at the closets where the servants slept, on separate shelves (luxurious creatures), and they went downstairs.

"I see, there is a garden laid out with ornamental paths and conservatories," he said, referring to the advertisement.

"Which there certinly his, sir," replied the elderly lady at his side, "this his the garding," and she opened a stained-glass window giving on a tiled space the size of a respectable chessboard, round which in various stages of misery rotted five stumpy remnants of the extinct flora of some long bygone period. "The gardings, sir, his slightly in arrear, but the colservatories does look very nice," and she pointed to two of the dreadful inclosures known as window-gardens, "has I waters hevery day myself."

The more-favoured plants in these were most of them artificial, and real ones had been put in here and there to enhance the illusion. But while these latter exhibited a stolid indifference to all earthly things, and to the care and kindness which had been lavished on them, the artificial ones marked their appreciation, by breaking out into fungus and bright green and yellow spots, to which the housekeeper pointed in triumph as signs of an abundant vitality.

"The moss do grow beautiful hall over 'em," she said tenderly. "Lady Mildred hallus said—"

"Who was Lady Mildred?" interrupted Roland sternly, "I thought this house was Mrs. Bottibol's."

"Which it were, sir," said the old lady, curtseying, "and Lady Mildred was 'er friend as 'ud stay for weeks together, so affable like."

And thus it was the mere miserable owner was ignored and forgot, and her very name only rescued from oblivion, by the fortunate chance of a friend with "a handle."

This concluded the inspection. There were other things sufficiently noticeable, which, however, were not to be seen. For instance, an aroma of its own hung about each separate division of the house.

"That is quite true, sir," said the agent unblushing, to whom Roland preferred this complaint, "but may I ask, sir, which is the one you object to? The one on the upper landing, the one on the left-hand side as you enter the front drawing-room, or the somewhat peculiar, but not altogether unpleasant atmosphere which pervades the butler's pantry? A friend of our late client's, a Lady Mildred, used to say she even preferred the—"

"Ah! thank you, I've heard something of it. Good morning." And Mr. Tudor hurried away to send his report in to his friend. He did not mince words.

"The house is a disgusting, ill-built pig-sty, trimmed with cheap velvet and soiled ribbon," he wrote; "the only spot where a mouthful of fresh air is to be had is on the leads at the back, and these are overlooked, overhung almost, by the houses on each side."

Little he guessed the effect of these simple words on Mrs. Brabant's imagination. To be overlooked by two marquises, each of whom would no doubt be hanging out of his top-story window half the day long, on the chance of a glimpse at her; earth had nothing to offer beyond this. The house was taken by return of post, without word or bargain as to price. It will be judged that poor Mrs. Brabant did, now and again, get her own way in mere trifles of this description.

. . . And lastly, of Sybil Grey? What of her? and whither had her doctrine of persistent progress carried her, landed her on what far shore in all this time?—and it was long to look back upon, for in a young life the years are epochs.

Mistress of her solitary domain on the wild coast and the sounding sea, she had not quitted it now for many months. Her guardian's health had become more and more broken, and although they had other help, she was now tied to his side always as secretary and nurse. The life was trying, the more so that she combined with it a good deal of reading, partly on his account, partly on her own; but the pulses of existence were slowed, and there was a shadow upon her heart, for the King of it was there so seldom, and written words are empty things. And through the dread winters, it would have gone ill with her, and surely she could not have borne it so long, if it had not been for the companionship of the tumbling seas, which were His of course, where they shot themselves upon the barrier precipices of His realm, and roared in noblest cadence through the long months, greatly filling with their hollow murmur the little dower house, night and day, and flinging their flakes of yellow foam, like tokens of conquest, over all the land and into the dank garden, where the bare network of the rose-stems trailed in tangled outlines on the winter sky.

And had it not been for the sawing and the swaying, the friendliness of those tremendous woods which were His, and in which she wandered through the dripping months, or when the snow fiends wrought their wrath upon the earth, her loneliness and isolation would have been terrible. But there was for her a ceaseless joy in the storm as it caught the trees ; and they writhed and groaned above her head, bending over her in kindly fashion, and speaking in tongues that went straight to her heart, while the deep bay of the hounds that bore His name rang through the leafless underwood. If it had not been for such companionship, those first winters—she reckoned them the first, as though she had known none other—would have been awful in their dreariness ; but there was the spirit of life itself in the fierce convulsions of the sea, in the yearnings and the strainings of the forest.

Now the spring-time was come, and a new-born

flush to her cheek, a new-born flash to her eye.
And why? Simply that there was no helping
it. In the equinox she had walked up to the
ruins of the great house; the wind-blown
shrubs were lying over, powdered with a
delicate green bronze, and now and again a
leafless bough shook, all beflowered with pale
pink blossom. The sea-girt lawns stretched
down to a glittering, yeasty whirl of snowy
foam, and pale-green hurrying waters, lit by a
fitful sun as the great rolling clouds swept
onwards, with broad shadows, over the bright
blue heaven, over the dark-blue sea. But
never was a sail on that wide offing. She
was alone—always alone—only the white birds
were crowding back in their tens of thousands,
and as they rose at her approach, they blotted
out the sun, and swooping in great sheets,
settled afresh, where the hoary colonnades of
stone looked out on the unresting ocean.
There, too, stood the grim stone satyr, laughing
at time. What was a year or so to him who had
known two thousand of them?

The scene recalled her lover, almost as
though he stood once more at her side. Such
happiness was now strange to her. That intimate mental communion between them, which
in early days had carried with it such wild joy,
had by slow degrees faded out. She had clung
to the phantom, but phantom-like it had glided
away; now she could hardly tell whether it
were ill or well with him—or if so much, no
more. Her spirit no longer followed his as a
dog its master, and all questionings of her own

heart were vain. The fault—if fault there were—could hardly be hers. She had watched him from a distance, step by step, with a confidence in his career which events were but just beginning to justify. It was woman's way. She might have been satisfied, few men at his age had done as much; but she had divined in him powers, which made her restless with impatience that he might find scope for their use. This seat in Parliament was very well, but it was a trifle, and would do perhaps till he reached some maturity. The cause was always a good one, and there were great possibilities in it; but to be fettered as a mere delegate, the mouthpiece of one man, which was the case with the Irish members of the day, was a thing which she well knew he would not long stand.

In her childhood's days she had been left so solitary, that it was no wonder she had fallen to egotism, and that her life had been entirely self-centred. Then had come the dawning of her beauty, and in pleased amaze she found it held up to the homage of all men, until in a sudden revulsion she sickened of herself. The remedy was at hand, and from the moment she realized the road she had been travelling, she turned her thoughts averse; there was not one now, but was for others—for one other, her guardian, over and above her lover. But oh! it was a weary time; it is not always that women think, but when a lone woman of deep capacities is led that way, through what an awful mill grind the slow years. First this

goes, and then that; this belief, then that
unbelief—more cherished still. This position
is no longer tenable, that must be given up,
alas! Yonder beauteous prospect melts into
illusion, that shadowy fear grows hard in a
grim reality—ageing experiences with no help
for them.

So the seasons had swept onward, summer
and winter with little to note. But with the
years came a change, slowly forced upon her
with an irresistible conviction—her spirit
always pressing onward had reached new
goals, she had tasted of living water in the
fountains of the desert, she had received
baptism. In Christianity had burst upon her
a splendour before which all other systems
paled. It was as though she had wandered
hitherto, under the moon and stars, marvelling
at their brilliance and taking it to be light—
when lo! the Sun arose, and it was day!

In her last letter to her lover she had been
able to write:—

"Thank God, I am at length a Christian.
I cannot tell you what this implies to me, or
how it has come about, and I am afraid to
speak of it even to you. Religion with my sex
is often, I know, a mere safety valve for silli-
ness. Mine at least shall not be this; it will
never mean pet curates, the setting up and
dethroning of private popes, or the vagaries of
æsthetic charity. What it will mean I cannot
at present tell, and almost dread to think. I
have learned nothing, as you know, in

churches; yet I know that my Redeemer liveth, and am struck mute at the realization of what I have hitherto looked upon as a fantastic but beautiful fable. Still I am adrift, though it is on a sea of light, and to pin this faith on any one creed will be perhaps impossible. Alas! for the battle of the churches. What of Christ is there in that? Besides, I think I should distrust the words of mortal man; the trees and the rocks and the ages have spoken to me, and taught me my faith, and there is a voice in my heart.

"I know this is almost the language of a fanatic, and that half the nursemaids in the kingdom fancy they hear such voices, and why not? Is any human creature so mean that the Creator shall not speak with it in its own tongue? There can be no better safeguard against delusion than prayer, and you will laugh at me for a new broom, but it has become my one solace, I may almost call it amusement, for day and night it comes to my lips involuntarily, without thought and without fatigue. And you, too, pray for everything in your church; nothing is too great, nothing too small—so pray for me."

There was more, but this extract will suffice, and Roland wrote in answer:—

". . . You have made a great step, dearest Sybil, but, as you admit, you are only half-way home, and you will never rest there. But do not expect me to influence you. Man's religion, I hold, is a thing between himself and his God, and if a woman's seldom rises quite to this, the nearer it gets to it the better; in nothing do you need more every iota of your independence. It is, of course, the one question for the individual, and he who pretends to ignore it, simply writes himself down a fool, for it must come home to him at last, and with a vengeance. But remember that faith is a matter of intellectual conception; you can never have mathematical proof of the truth—not the proof of Euclid, for instance—and to do your sex justice, they don't often require it, but you may have such proof that you shall feel bound to embrace it, and at any sacrifice.

" Whatever community you join, your first feeling will probably be one of sorrow and disappointment at the evils you find within it; but you will be too wise to be discouraged or distressed at this: the bad comes to the surface, the good hides itself away. It will take you some time to distinguish between religion and the mere cant of it. Every species of folly will be thrust upon you in its sacred name, and often—God knows—by the people who mean best. Beware! faith is a gift from heaven— credulity a curse from hell. Common sense is the best of Directors.

" Now, no more, for I am not fond of expressing an opinion on this subject, though I often wonder, to see how it holds its own as *the* topic, even in these most matter-of-fact days. The House adjourns on the ——, and I shall have the Easter holidays with you,

if you can take me in. The last few years
have been so full with me, that we never seem
to have had more than a few hours together.
Henceforth we will make a new arrangement,
that is with your consent."

CHAPTER IV.

NEITHER time nor space avail to speak at length of the days at Sombrewood. To be there and at leisure in the budding spring-time, it seemed to Roland as though the hands of the clock of time had been straight put back four or five years; but even as the two walked together through the glades, where the sun was firing with indescribable pale greens the tender shoots against the shadows, though the woods were as young, and the earth and the sky, both realized that years, few though they were, had come upon them. Duties and responsibilities had meantime grown up and fettered each; and though love had not waned, no longer as formerly might they be to each other the one and only thought.

Roland had gone down prepared to press his suit; it was time, he thought; to some extent, his position was made. His few years' nursing of the property had produced unhoped-for results. His uncle's death had freed the estate of a considerable charge; he had measured his thews and muscles with those of his competitors, and was satisfied as to the future, so far as man might be. They would take a house in

Town for the parliamentary season, and spend
the remainder of the year in travel, or between
the two domains of Sombrewood and the Isles,
for at this last spot the long-planned improvements were being slowly carried out.

On the velvet mounds of ruin had re-arisen
one wing of the old manor. It was a modest
restoration, but the red stone from the cliff,
and the oak from the forest, had not been
spared, and it stood like a fairy fortress
queening amid enchanted woods and waters,
and small though it was, would be more than
sufficient. And the little dower house, wrapped
in its summer cloud of eglantine, with its rose
bowers and the solemn elms standing sentinel
—why, it was but a stone's-throw to it, and
there Sybil's cozy nest should stay untouched, if
she so willed it. What more could they want?
Nothing, certainly, admitted she, the wealth
of it all was too plenteous, its extent made her
tremble, but yet—

They were standing by the lake's side on the
steps of the verandah. The lower rooms, as
will be remembered, opened with French windows upon this, and these had been appropriated to Mr. Trelawney. Leaning on her
lover's arm she drew him to the casement,
which stood wide. The old man lay asleep in
his chair buried in his furs, and the first warm
breath of the spring crept with a stray sunbeam
into the room. His face was white and worn,
he was plainly suffering in his sleep, when a
smile gathered on his lips and his eyes opened.

"I have had a dream," he said, looking at

them, " a dream, unlike most, that does not
vanish with waking, and will perhaps come
true. Ah ! children, years are long even to go
back on. Look at the many that spread before
you. You won't grudge an old man the few
odd grains of sand in his glass."

No other word was spoken, but Roland
pressed his hand, and drew his true love closer.
All was said, all understood.

But it was not without a sigh he noted how
her cheek had paled, and how a languor had
crept into her carriage, which, even though it
became her, told that the first vigour of her
youth had fled, hardly to return. Yet it did
almost at times ; for one day, to his delight,
when they had gone down to the manor to look
at the new buildings, she had run to the
water-side, had jumped into the dingy and
pushed out, pulling an oar merrily over the
dancing waves. And " the crew," now grown a
bronzed young man, said she was born to it, and
that it was a shame she was not there to do it
every day of her life and bring her colour back ;
and in this he echoed the sentiments of all
the country-side, who said it was most tiresome,
and that they had waited long enough. And
now the sea-king's tower had grown into a
castle, but no result followed, yet something
came of the visit.

On taking his seat, Roland had plunged with
the zest of his age into half the political
questions of the day. He had already begun
a course of pamphleteering, and was up to his

elbows in literary work. In this Sybil, well
broken to a secretaryship, volunteered to help
him, promising that it would bring her roses
back! And henceforth budgets of foolscap
were ever on the road 'twixt London and
Sombrewood, to the enormous edification of the
local postmistress and her friends, who knew
all about it, and who affirmed, with some show
of reason, that a lover who corresponded on
this scale must be worth his salt, and sapiently
predicted that this must be the beginning
of the end.

It was a step forward in good truth. With
the foolscap was usually a hurried scrawl, if
only of directions. This was work—real active
work in the world, such as Sybil had sighed for.
She was part and parcel of his every-day life,
and was satisfied.

Roland was at length among men who
owned to some public interest in life, but
the bulk of it was expended in talk, mere talk;
and one or two questions on military subjects,
which were asked him by aged and responsible
senators, fairly staggered him by the audacity of
ignorance they displayed, which would have
done credit to a colonel of the Blankshires
himself. When he had been six months in Parliament his conclusions might have been thus
summed up:—

"It's a pleasant, sociable place, but the men
are like a pack of children—there are not a
score among them who know anything of
sociology as a science, or who have any idea

whither the political momentum they aid or initiate is leading them. Each looks at the stone he himself places, ignorant of the structure he is helping to build. Hence, nine-tenths of all our legislation is farcical, and worse. Government is a science for experts, not a game between two or more parties. Party is the bane of the country."

Conceive the popularity of a new member daring to enunciate such ideas! The average schooling of the gentlemen of England, which had been better written fooling—in so far as it was a preparation for legislative work—went far towards explaining this state of things.

It was not long before Mr. Tudor drew attention to himself and his views, as an incident that occurred shortly after he entered the House served to show. One morning, as he sat at his letters, a written card was brought to him in an envelope—

" MR. GREEN,
SHOREDITCH."

Neither the name nor the address went far towards enlightening him as to his visitor's identity, but as it was not his way to refuse himself to any one, he ordered Mr. Green to be shown up. There entered a shambling, ill-kept individual in a rusty black frockcoat, trousers, and boots; in his hands were a pair of black gloves, almost as black inside as out, but still preserving their original flat crease, and plainly never worn; his nose was bluish, his eyes,

which looked weak and watery, were shaded by
spectacles, and above them rose a huge forehead, out of all proportion, as it seemed, to his
ill-developed physique. The visitor seated himself, deliberately wiped his big forehead, and
tucked his napless hat carefully under his chair
between his legs.

The young M.P., who expected a constituent,
was puzzled. "May I ask," he said, "whom
I have the pleasure of—"

"I am Mr. Green of—ah—Shoreditch—that
is, at least, I am to you—and I am—ah—
I—" and he looked round mysteriously, as if
to see they were not overheard, "I may call
myself a—manufacturer." He smiled, showing
an irregular row of uncleanly teeth, such as
sent a shudder through the beholder, while he
leaned forward and worked his talon-like fingers
in a dreadfully suggestive way up and down
his knees.

Mr. Tudor, who failed to see anything amusing in this, merely bowed and asked in what
line.

"In a *very* important line," replied the visitor,
leaning forward and speaking in a confidential
whisper—"that is, to a gentleman situated like
yourself. I am a framer, a builder, a manufacturer, in a word, of great reputations." Under
his bushy brows he shot a glance, which was
not wanting in keenness, at his hearer.

Mr. Tudor took out his watch significantly.
"If you have any business which you wish to—"

"Pardon me," interrupted the other, with a
not ungraceful gesture, and it struck Roland

H 2

that, in spite of appearances, he had the accent and something of the remains of a gentleman about him. "Pardon me, sir—I forgot myself. I forgot that it was improbable that you should at once understand me, and I am accustomed to be on such intimate terms with my chiefs, owing perhaps to my being—I may venture to say it—so indispensable to them," he straightened himself in his chair—"that I am accorded a certain amount of—ah—familiarity. But to business," here he drew his chair up close to the desk. "Sir," he said, "the man you see before you is a second wrangler, it might have been a senior," and a momentary cloud passed over his face, "some said it should have been— but no matter—that is a trifle and I merely allude to it *en passant* as such. Mathematics were never, properly speaking, my forte—though" and he shrugged his shoulders, "should you ever want a budget, a sensational budget, such as would overthrow half the old-fashioned notions of finance, we might put our heads together and make something of it, and it would not be the first time, sir, for one of us. But that, of course, is *in nubibus* at present. I have watched your short career, sir—permit me to say it has been admirable so far—but you want advice, sir, you want assistance, you want knowledge, experience—forgive me—and these, sir," he drew himself up once more with a semi-theatrical gesture, "are what I have to offer you—again, in a word, a great reputation."

It had helped Mr. Tudor much through life,

that he had never wanted time nor inclination to enjoy a joke. The present occasion tickled him, he leaned back in his chair and laughed. "And the terms?" he said.

The gentleman in black looked half offended. "That is the last thing I should have mentioned," he replied with gravity; "but I can only assure you that they are so small, so infinitesimal, that you yourself will be the first to cry out at them. All I ask of the world, as long as I inhabit it, is the wherewithal to keep my soul in my body, and such covering for the latter as this." He looked down at his threadbare knees, "surely that is not grasping?" It did not seem so.

"But if you have these gifts, you can make fame and fortune for yourself."

"Sir, personal ambition is *dead, dead*," and he struck his forehead; "it was not always so, there are reasons—no matter. You may have noticed, sir, on the envelope that contained my card, my family crest—crossed out—cancelled—"

For all the strangeness of his manner, there was the impress of something beyond pretence in all this. There was a pause.

"Now let me ask you," he went on, turning sharply upon Roland, "has it never struck you what a vast amount of work some of our public men get through? What a species of omniscience seems to hang about them, especially the younger ones who are on promotion?"

This query went home. Mr. Tudor had not

only noticed it, but watched, with a feeling akin
to despair, the labours of some of his colleagues.

"Look now, for instance, at young Lord
R—," said the other, pursuing his advantage;
" he's a clever fellow, no denying; a monstrous
memory, that's the chief thing—that I can give
you. But first count up his accredited work
through a month, about last election time.
Seven speeches in one day on one occasion; all
different, all to the point. Two or three on
most days; the pamphlet on the depreciation of
silver, the letters to the *Times* through five days
on the Women and Children Franchise Bill, the
political novelette issued just on the eve of the
election. I say nothing of the ordinary routine
business of his office, which he certainly did
not neglect, of the public dinners, foundation
stones, addresses, and even balls, for which he
found time."

" True! Five ordinary men would have
had their work cut out for them there,"
said Roland, recalling it with something like a
sigh.

" Well, sir, it did take five ordinary men to
get through it, *Quorum pars magna fui*. I
say it in all modesty—the rest were mere
scribes. This in "—and he shook his head—
" strictest confidence. But, after all, he is only
one of many. Look at our late leader, turning
out an amount of work at seventy-five that
would kill three men at thirty. Curious the
public don't see through it. We worked for

him too; but, for reasons of my own, I am free and open to an engagement, of course in the strictest honour on both sides. Name your wishes, you may depend on me. I should like to give you some proof of what I can do."

Mr. Tudor was in the habit of absorbing facts, without giving in return; he got up and paced the room. A man of this sort might do invaluable work for him—plain, above-board work.

"Give me a chance," appealed his visitor, abandoning his swagger and dropping his tone almost to a whine; "I will work steadily, by G— I will; you shall never repent it."

"I will try you," said the M.P., wheeling round. "Just now I happen to want a short magazine article on the decimal coinage; the opinions of the best authorities put together and comp—"

The thin man rose. "No more, sir; I understand exactly; only say when. I can give you something light and readable in forty-eight hours; but if you want it gone into scientifically, you must give me double. Promise me a week, and you shall have it in four modern languages—choose them."

"Very well," answered Roland impassively, "let it be a week, and in English, Russian, Dutch, and Spanish."

"Exactly," said the other, making a note in his pocket-book; "this day week you shall have the MSS., when I shall hope to hear from you again. I need expend no more words, and

will wish you good morning. Remember, if
you decide to employ me, I am yours, yours
only, and secret as the grave." With a bow
of some ceremony he left the room.

To make a rather long story short, the
manuscripts were duly delivered at the promised
time; and with them came a request that if
they proved satisfactory, the author might have
the further pleasure, of despatching them to
their destinations with Mr. Tudor's name attached. He also hinted that in this case, he
trusted remuneration at the rate of a guinea
a paper would not be thought exorbitant.

Before replying, Roland submitted the various
MSS. to experts, from one and all of whom he
received a like assurance of the really first-rate
quality of the work; he then wrote, asking Mr.
Green to call again.

When the latter appeared, it was evident that
he was but just recovering from a drinking
bout. He looked more broken down than before, his voice was tremulous, his words almost
incoherent; his story was written in his face.
Roland, who was profoundly moved by the
case, offered him fifteen guineas for the papers,
and to have them published in his own proper
name.

The suggestion was received almost with
scorn; he, humble as he was, could coin money
if he wished it. Money was dross to him—he
had not sunk to that. His own ambitions were
as an extinct volcano, but the power of building
up another man was still left to him; this was

his sole object, through such a channel he
might yet do great things in the world, which
had been his dream from the first. But he
would sink his identity in his patron's; the fame
should be for him, a bare subsistence was all
he asked for himself, and to be unknown. He
would take five guineas for the MSS., but only
on condition that they appeared in Mr. Tudor's
name.

This Mr. Tudor declined. The man got
up to go with grievous disappointment in
his face, went out taking his papers, and
Roland never saw nor heard of him afterwards. Perchance he found a less scrupulous
employer.

The life Roland now fell into was essentially
that of a club, and it pleased him little. Of all
the dreary aspects of civilized being at this
time, none were drearier than the club; domestic life might have its horrors, but they
paled before those of a club existence.

Here was the golden calf, with his eternal
billiards and brandy; here the keen young
buck of fifty or sixty, trim-whiskered and close-
buttoned, who, when he thought him of sufficient importance, would take him round the
corner, catch his button-hole, and tell him
the secrets of the Government, and what he had
privately advised them to do. Here the man
who knew what was what, and the man who
did not know what was what, and was perpetually asking that it might be explained to
him. Then there was the man who had grown

too old for these things, who hobbled in early
in the afternoon, day after day, with an awful
regularity, sat in his particular chair in his
particular corner, where he alternately mumbled
and slept over his paper till bedtime, with the
exception of the hour he devoted to mumbling
his dinner and pint of wine.   Until a day came
when the whole aspect of the room was changed,
his chair was empty " for good," and his successor in it mumbled about him, that he was
quite young and brisk when he started this rule
of life, and that he had lived by it for five-and-
forty years.

Such were some of the tritest figures in the
dismal list.   If anything could spur a man to
action, it might be this, that he should escape
the average fate of the average man in the
average club.   To one like Roland, whose eyes
were always fixed on the heights of human
achievement, nothing came more forcibly than
the fact of these cabbage lives, and the meanness
of the general aims.

One man would die happy if he could previously move to Lancaster Gate.   Another
at fifty, burned and thought and talked always
on the subject of a colonial governorship, 750*l*.,
house, coals, candles, and a pestilential climate,
which, to hear him talk, might have been a
nick out of Paradise.   With another a C.B., or
rather the want of it, had soured the last fifteen
years of his earthly sojourn.   Yet another made
no secret that he considered the *entrée* of certain drawing-rooms the grand point of existence.

Not as a means to an end, be it understood, but as the end itself. His cheeks were rouged ready for it when it came, as, it was to be hoped, it would soon, for it was getting late with him, and the night cometh when no man can work, still less play. Roland looked on the propounder of these views, much as he might have done on a monkey suddenly gifted with power of speech. What a prostitution of virile tissue was here! What a molehill was the highest of these heights—say, a peerage! He fell a-laughing whenever he considered it all, and seriously resolved to ask his confessor if a man could be justified in considering nine-tenths of his fellow-men as idiots; for to this he had arrived. Personal greatness may be out of a man's reach; the chance may never come, he reflected; but his friends, his companions, his models may be the greatest of the earth, and he scanned his well-filled book-shelves and their well-thumbed volumes with a certain complacency.

Even thus early he began to see the failure of his parliamentary work. The Government, having come in at the head of a huge majority, had run everything before it for a session or two. But its very success had carried the elements of disintegration. It had split into factions, divided and subdivided, as had the Opposition, until Heaven knows of how many parties the House was now composed. This result had been foreseen in the good old days, when there were only two parties or three at most; but there was no helping it, and endless, hopeless discussion was the result, to a complete congestion of public business. The deadlock had become insupportable in the last session, and thinking men asked themselves what next? As an Irish Nationalist, Roland found his hand against every man, and every man's against him. Ordinary argument on the merits of a question was simply thrown away. All that friends and enemies alike expected from him was a torrent of abuse whenever the name of England was so much as mentioned, and as it happened, notwithstanding his views on Irish coercion, that he was a patriotic Englishman, he was driven perforce to hold his tongue.

One evening, as he was leaving the House, a member, old and experienced, came up and took his arm. " Let me give you a piece of advice," he said kindly, " for I fancy you're the man to profit by it. All you want to succeed here," and he jerked his thumb backwards, " is impudence. Jump up in time and out of time; fascinate the Speaker as a snake does a squirrel; give 'em no rest; say everything about everything every day—it doesn't matter what—say it."

" Better be unknown," laughed Roland, " than have the finest fame as a fool."

" Not at all; there you're mistaken. Block —obstruct—defy—question—kick up a row— make yourself a perfect pest all round—fling your notions of a gentleman to the dogs, and if you only stick to it you're bound to succeed.

There's nothing you mayn't hope for. By Jove, sir, if a man's only a big enough nuisance—and it's essential he should be a thundering one—he's bound to be prime minister. That is the shibboleth of leadership. Mark my words, sir, it has come to this."

Now the gentleman who volunteered this advice was not an Irish Nationalist, but a member of that party which was accustomed to arrogate to itself the title of "Constitutional."

How true his remarks were, Roland shortly discovered. The dignity of debate was gone. At the approach of a crisis the utterances became more and more hysterical. "Vox, vox, et præterea nihil," and certainly the noisiest of these windbags produced the greatest impression abroad. There was a womanishness about all this mouthing, that struck the new member with dismay. It seemed to point to a stage of national degradation; for once the liberty of speech is so abused as to make legislation impossible, the reins pass from the many to the few, possibly to one, and he a dictator.

In consequence of this state of things Roland's attention was drawn to other quarters, in which more definite progress and vital interest were to be found. Of living men those who attracted him most, were men of science. The march of discovery had latterly been at such a pace, that there appeared no end to the vistas so opened out, and the standards of knowledge threatened to be revolutionized.

The need of a universal language for the mutual intercourse of peoples, had grown so pressing, that some time since a conference of the nations had been held in Paris, at which it had been eventually decided to adopt modern Greek. The change wrought by this was equally swift and surprising. Within the space of half a dozen years Greek had become an ordinary accomplishment, and the spurt and stimulus given to the world by this simple means was astonishing. The teaching of it, as of many other subjects, was much facilitated by a contrivance that came into vogue about the same time—a small clockwork affair called a talking machine, which could be carried in the crown of the hat. This, when wound up, repeated, at its owner's will and pleasure, the lessons, conversations, exercises, as the case might be, for which it was made. One of these little engines would contain the material of an entire grammar. A marked improvement in the eye-sight of the population was one of the first results of their introduction, and there was no limit of course to the application. It became the custom for a man to publish his works partly in books, partly in these cylinders. The novelette cylinder (one vol.) became at once a prime favourite at the circulating libraries.

The development of electricity, by which new miracles were worked every day ; the discoveries in explosives, whereby a man could carry in his waistcoat pocket that which would lay a wall in ruins; the invention of a gas so buoyant that he might be lifted into the air by a bag no larger than himself;—these and many other things pointed to extraordinary changes in the condition of life. It was not generally realized that the man or the nation having the wit to be first in combining and utilizing these in the next great war must achieve an irresistible superiority. If ambition were not wanting, it seemed likely that a man of determined type might play the part of all the conquerors the world had hitherto seen, rolled into his single self.

Extraordinary as it may appear, although at this period all Europe was armed to the teeth, the English War-office, in fact the virtual control of the whole British army had fallen into the hands of civilians, thoroughly well-meaning individuals for the most part, but as far away from the true soldier, on the one hand, as the gentlemen of the Blankshires were on the other. It would, indeed, be hard to over-estimate the admirable civil qualities of this body, their belief in peace, goodwill, and charity to all men, and their eagerness to repress that undue military enthusiasm and thirst for blood which, as everybody knows, is the weak point of the British soldier, from the drummer-boy to the field-marshal commanding in chief.

With the public, the good old dictum that the officer was a fool, and the soldier a knave, remained in force, and certainly there were not wanting officers and men to prove it.

When a little war was on hand, and a thousand men were sent off to thrash twenty thousand black fellows, this was conveniently forgotten, and they were one and all the gallantest fellows alive, except when, occasionally, the black fellows took the thrashing into their own hands, when a corresponding revulsion of feeling took place.

The result of this playful treatment from the public and the authorities, did not prove advantageous to the service; it became unpopular with all classes, it was found impossible to sustain the army by voluntary enlistment; the thing had dwindled to a skeleton. and not a good skeleton either, and conscription of a certain sort had at last been resorted to.

Naturally such a governing body would have nothing to say to the fantastic novelties that science was ready to lay at its feet. It had enough to do to supply a new hero or a new scape-goat, whenever the British public clamoured for one, which was once or twice in a decade. Any attempt to raise a serious debate in the House on army matters, was laughed to scorn by the swarming politicians on all sides, who were immersed in questions of so much more importance. If by chance the subject were mooted, it was in such a way as to raise a feeling akin to despair in the breast of a soldier. Although Roland had left the service, he did not neglect these matters, which must, sooner or later, affect it so vitally, but he was eventually driven to abandon his efforts as hopeless, and to turn his thoughts in other directions.

There happened to sprout, at this time, a budding shoot from an old stock, which was received with great derision by the learned ; it was weak at present in tangible results, and had need to be modest in its intercourse with an exacting world. This called itself " Psychology," and now claimed to be reckoned with the exact sciences. Its devotees averred that it was the one which lay at the root of all existence, and as such was worthy of fundamental study. In the charmed but bashful circles, where these matters were discussed, the name of a new man and shining light, Professor Van Dam, had been mentioned with honour, and Roland recollected that this was the man whom his friend, Brabant, had " discovered" some years since. The latter was now in town, and he wrote off to him suggesting that they should take an afternoon to go down, and hunt up this personage in the Erith marshes. The answer came, " By all means," and named a day.

The life of an active Member of Parliament at this time was so filled in, that he was often driven to receive his friends in the oddest times and places. In a cab, between four and five in the morning, for instance—or in bed at one o'clock in the day. But as there had been two extremely lively all-night sittings this week, anent a water bill for some small village in the

West of Ireland, Roland felt a peculiar longing for fresh air, and, tearing himself resolutely away, drove from his one o'clock breakfast straight to Upper Snook Street.

His visit was not happily timed. The troubles of setting up house had sorely tried Mr. and Mrs. Brabant, the former had found fault with every thing; from the fusty plush to the mouldy plants, nothing pleased him; and when the name of the Lady Mildred had been breathed in his ear, for the fourteenth time in support of it all, this unprincipled man had cursed the Lady Mildred, and gone on his way unrejoicing. Then an incident had just occurred relative to some clothes, which it would be a shame to suppress.

Since her widowhood, now nearly ten years, Mrs. Brabant had treasured several of her late husband's suits, which she declared she had not the heart to part with. They had been carefully warehoused meanwhile, and on her arrival in Town she had sent for the box, which she unpacked herself, and, without so much as unfolding them, despatched them upstairs to her husband's dressing-room, on a tea-tray, and with a message of hope that he might find them useful. It would be idle to deny that the life Mr. Brabant had led since his marriage had soured his temper. He could not see a joke as heretofore, even when it was not meant, and if he had an infirmity it was as to how he clothed himself. He said not a word, but eyed the pile, as the maid afterwards informed her mistress, like a "maniacle." Mrs. Brabant sighed, and said "it was just like him."

He had excuse for feeling aggrieved. He, himself, was slight and straight, and supple as a willow, so long as he had his health, a good deal of shape about him, too much, perhaps, for manly beauty—while the dead-and-gone Lushington, he knew by report, had been no particular shape at all, and as his hand, in its latter days, had been somewhat unsteady, most of the coats, and all the waistcoats, were much besprinkled down the front. But, as Mrs. Brabant very truly said, "what if the things were old-fashioned? Her husband had always said, haughtily, that he was above fashion, and as if it mattered how a married man's clothes fitted, nobody looked at a man or cared how a man dressed. If poor dear Lushington's clothes were too large, and she supposed they would be, now she thought of it, why not have them taken in? Eliza could do it—that accomplished female had already altered a petticoat-body for her mistress to her entire satisfaction—and look at the saving of expense it would be, and all this money could be spent in carriages and theatre tickets—and of course there were a few trifles she wanted herself, but then she was a woman."

This and more she hinted to the said Eliza, her last acquisition, who cordially agreed with her upon every point, down to not arguing the matter with the man, but letting him have his tantrums out to himself. This favourite word of Mrs. Brabant's was not ill-chosen for the occasion, for, as soon as the maid had left the room, Brabant flung open the window, and, without examination or remorse, kicked the tray and all upon it, into the right hand Marquis's back garden.

Now the right hand Marquis was a man not altogether without his peculiarities, as we know; his town house, what with rent and taxes, stood him in at fifteen hundred a year, but he never came near it by any chance, except when he happened to want his corns cut, and that operation he could not bring himself to face more than once a year. When, however, this mishap did befall him, he instantly came post haste to town, because in Snook Street (Lower) resided the practitioner whom he had befriended —to the extent of a couple of introductions—at starting, and who now, out of gratitude, doctored him for nothing, and the name of the thing. For a week past this Marquis had been suffering, his corns, or perhaps his conscience had upset him; it is unnecessary to go into detail—suffice it to say that he had suffered. When, by chance, going to the window, he noticed an extensive wardrobe draped all about the marble vases of his court, and, as suffering makes few men amiable, he rang the bell fiercely.

" Turtleberry, what the devil do you mean by hanging my clothes out to air, all over the

courtyàrd, exactly in front of the drawing-
room windows? You'd better take care, sir,
what you're doing, it's not the first time,"
&c., &c.

Mr. Turtleberry was indignant, he declared
it was the first time, and threatened that it
should be the last, for he thought his master's
complaint had reached his brain. But when,
with his own incredulous eyes, he actually beheld the garments, he dashed out into the open
and speedily knocked up Number 101, who
was just now represented, wholly and solely,
by an elderly drab and three elderly children,
who in a row regretfully disowned them. Then
Mr. Turtleberry cast a look upward on the slip
of lath and plaster which was pleased to designate itself Number 100A. Here he caught a
furious glance out of an upper window, and a
superb wave of a hand.

"Bring them in here, Turtleberry," said a
more modulated voice, and with that the valet
returned to his master, taking an armful.

"Nobody don't know nothink about 'em,
m' lord," he said, "but there's a gent next
door—'offle 'otty, as looks as if they weren't
his'n."

"Turtleberry," said the Marquis, meditatively, "I can't help thinking they must be
mine—you see they were on my leads. That's
a capital overcoat, Turtleberry, just let me try
it on. Ha! excellent," and his lordship smiled
at himself in a glass, in a better coat than he
had worn for the last twenty years—" of course

it's mine, you idiot! Don't you see how it fits? What the deuce are you screwing that ugly mug of yours for? Help me on with that dress-coat, sir. First rate! I don't know when I've seen one like it." Nor did Turtleberry—on his master's back.

"And the waistcoat? Ah! I remember it was a little spotty. It does seem a pity; but, ah! you may take that waistcoat for yourself, and those patent pumps. I don't know when I wore 'em last. Put them all back in my dressing-room. Mind, Sirrah, you don't let them get tossing about the leads any more."

The Marquis went back to his study and resumed his perch on the family tree, which, when not busy in his harem, was his solace, his aim, and his end. And Mr. Turtleberry, with a naïve expression of surprise, too rugged in its simple homeliness for these polished pages, disappears from them for ever.

Could Mrs. Brabant have learned this, there would have been balm in Gilead. To think that ten years ago her head had lain, as a good wife's should, on the bosom of a dress-coat, which was hereafter to soothe the declining years of an undoubted Marquis! To the casual observer, this expression may seem strong, but it does not overstate the case. The old man's declining years *were* soothed every time he put on the coat, by the thought that it had cost him nothing, and was he so very different from the rest of the world in this?

Could Mrs. Brabant have looked forward! could she but have known! And she stood in need of consolation, for she was on the point of making the discovery that to be in Upper Snook Street did not necessarily mean to be *of* it. There was up-hill work before her, to an extent she had little expected. The season was waxing, but no one had called, really no one—that is a few dozen " scrubs," as she was pleased to denominate them—old school-fellows—friends of the days .she had thought left behind, at Harrow-on-the-Hill—people who lived in the Suburbs, or north of the park, where she now declared it was impossible for her coachman to track his way, and so excused herself from return visits. This was hardly wise in a person still on the middle rungs of the ladder, for the Suburbs were annoyed and ventured to pronounce it bad form. What will not Suburbs do when their blood is .up ? Some few people of importance, whom she had met abroad and made very dear friends with, seemed in no hurry to come, and their pleasure at a chance meeting, in the park or elsewhere, was of a mitigated nature. Yet enormous pains had been taken ; the faithful band of scribblers, whom she still held in leash, had announced their arrival in every possible print; her husband had been referred to as a junior lion, likely to engage the attention of the world, etc., etc.

It may be thought, from certain portions of her history which have been given to the

public, that Mrs. Brabant was a foolish woman.
Nothing of the sort. She was extremely wise
in her generation, which she had studied profoundly; the hysterics, the extravagances, the
demeanour, public and private, were all calculated to a nicety, and with a purpose—that of
getting her own ends, what those ends were
she confided to no one. She had been clever
enough, at a time when her affairs were falling
into disorder, to entangle a rising man to set
them straight for her, and there was every
prospect of her mounting up as his reputation
mounted. Unfortunately, the clever young
man showed a disposition to mastery, which
was not consistent with her ideas, and it
was with the object of striking him down with
terror and dismay that she abandoned herself
to wild fits of hysteria and the ways of a lunatic
generally. Between ourselves, her nature was as
cold and calculating as a bank cashier's, and
once she had her own way the ebullition ceased.
Her husband marked it all in silence. If her
own way was what she wanted, she should have
it, as far as he could give it her, but anything
beyond, she herself had put it out of his power
to give.

The sisters flocked about her in the new
house, but they grew snappy for want of
company, and Lady Jane, alas! was no longer
available. That gallant old lady was past
ninety now and was breaking; for over three
quarters of a century the good woman had
conscientiously worked the season. At ten

years of age her mother had made a companion of her, and so, as child, girl, wife, mother, grandmother, and great-grandmother (though we have had no occasion to notice her in these capacities), she had pressed steadily on unfalteringly, and when her own flesh and blood had died out, she had turned to her nieces and played for them. But the fine old crone was failing at last. She had passed the stage of reason, yet the poor thing was far from unhappy. She spent most of her days in trimming a bonnet; sometimes it was with gold tissue and artificial pearls as big as plover's eggs; sometimes it was with streamers of many-coloured ribbon, such as would have supplied half the recruiting sergeants in the kingdom. Then this yellow, wrinkled atomy had a scrap of bridal veil, which she would throw over her bald head and sit under, smirking for hours together, with a bright contentment in her face, such as her reasoning existence had never known. No more wearisome plotting now; all was realization. She no longer appeared in public, but would sit in her finery and tell circumstantial narratives of the day or the night before; how delightful it had been at Buckingham Palace, how gracious Royalty had been, and how she had danced (last night) with a personage fifty years in his grave.

Pay her a morning call. You will find her maid (now mistress) reading to her from the last fashion paper, while the old lady, fumbling with some rubbish in her lap, listens intently.

"As an example of what millinery can do for loveliness, we may mention the superb robe worn on the occasion by the Princess G. This may verily be said to have presented an earthly embodiment of celestial poetry. The skirt was looped with creamy velvet shot with colour, from purest white to the blushing crimson of a sea shell. Over it wandered a rippling fall in rivulets of lace, interspersed with a perfect galaxy of diamonds. The shoaling lines · of light on the white moiré body proved an admirable foil to the dusky radiance of the train, while a petticoat, covered with cascades of lisse—"

The maid, seeing your entry, stops.

"Don't stop. Oh! Parker, go on," screams the beldame; "read that again—read that again, from 'what millinery can do for loveliness.' Go on."

"Shan't," says Parker, peremptorily, laying down the paper. "You've had enough."

"Enough! I declare, Parker," shrieks the old lady in tears, "I'll give you a month's warning from this very instant."

Parker gives a knowing look, almost a wink, and says, "Well, but here's a gentleman come to see you."

"A gentleman?" whimpers the crone. (She is all but blind). "Oh! Parker, Parker, see if my hair's all right, and my veil. Oh! of course, he's come to see the trousseau"—for life is all one bridal morn to Lady Jane now.

She totters to her feet, receives you with a profound curtsey, says a word of welcome, and then, with a little triumphant gesture, points to the antimacassar, the old coverlid, and the rug upon the sofa. One after another she turns these over for your inspection, handling them as though they were of gossamer. "Aren't they lovely?" she appeals to you. "Did you ever see such embroidery and such silk?"

And you, if you are human, must admit it, and praise them and her and all.

While the old hag's heart is filled with this fierce delight, and she mumbles and laughs and picks her ribbons, we will bid her farewell. What does she dread of a world to come? She will enter it one fine day, grimacing under her bridal veil, mincing her steps, and leaning on the arm of a Royal Duke!

To return to Mrs. Brabant, her first idea for taking society by storm was a day "at home" every week. It fell in with that economy which other expenses made so desirable; tea and tea-cake would go a long way, and could never mean bankruptcy. No great alacrity, however, was shown in response. The first week, though trumpeted in a penny print, brought nobody; the second, one who called on business; the third, three people who came together—a mother and two daughters; the fourth, nobody; the fifth, one; but at this point Mrs. Brabant broke down and sternly abolished it. It was not worth the discomfort of the best dress, and the sitting with her hands in her lap for four hours, to see a weekly average of one person. But this is anticipating.

This particular day was the second on the list, and Mr. Tudor was the individual who called on business, the business being to get her husband away. This was not easy; so delightful, so charming, so pleasant was Mrs. Brabant, you would never have guessed that a moment before, she had been plunged in utter despondency, at the thought of her wasted dress. It was tedious work, sitting in the solitary magnificence of the front cupboard, and watching through the sham stained-glass windows the carriages, as they dashed up to other people's doors. But the time had not been thrown away. She had learned the coats of arms on several, and as she happened to have a Peerage and Landed gentry in her lap, she had hunted them out and put names to them, which was very interesting and instructive. By dint of minute scrutiny, she had discovered exactly in what the establishments of the three houses opposite consisted, and already knew the sweethearts of two of the housemaids by sight. She had also discovered—a matter on which her brain had been clouded—exactly how many buttons were *de rigueur* on an under-footman's coat, and she had learned that No. 101 only had in a couple of tons of coal at a time. Ah! what may we not learn if we will but lay out the hours given us to profit? As moralists, we may be forgiven for pointing out, what an example an English lady of that period sets to her sister of this.

It was with some difficulty Roland and his friend escaped. He was shocked with his appearance, the languor of his manner, and the lack-lustre of his eye; and could not help speaking of it to Mrs. Brabant, who said she had not noticed anything, but that he fidgeted himself to death. Here she smiled to her back teeth, tucked her feet up on a foot-stool, and poured two pennyworth, certainly, out of the six of cream, into her tea. Presently, the two left and went out arm-in-arm, the man on the threshold of life, and the man on the threshold of death, as men ever do unknowing, though with each was some presentiment of it. There was, in spite, a species of gaiety in his friend's manner which struck a painful chord in Roland's heart.

"My dear Brabant, you look terribly pulled down," was the first thing he said. "I wish you'd let me take you to a doctor."

"My dear fellow," came the answer with a careless laugh; "when a man has heart disease, consumption, and a wife, you wouldn't have him look as he did before he possessed these blessings? As for a doctor—we are on our road to one now—a man who works miracles of many sorts. I've had it on my mind to take you for years past. Whatever he may or may not do for me, I know that he can do great things for you. You have had the common sense to see that—I am glad of it. To dabble ever so little in mysticism wants courage."

Roland laughed. " My courage keeps up with my convictions."

They drove on through the great city and all its long suburbs, street after street, mile after mile, almost in silence. Although the day was warm, Brabant sat, white and chilly, in a heavy fur cloak wrapped to his ears. Presently the air seemed to revive him. " You have brought back the days of my youth," he said at last, with a plain enjoyment; " but I'm marked, old friend, and must face it. We started even, and I thought we should have pushed on to the temple of Fame together. But it is not to be. ' Two women shall be grinding at a mill, the one shall be taken and the other left.' It will be the same with us. You will be at your work long after I am at rest. Even now the lightest is almost too much for me.

" However, the world usually treats a man rather better than he deserves, and it is his duty to slip away quietly without distressing it with his little grievances."

" What is your complaint?" asked Roland, with a brevity that hid what he felt.

" My wife," replied the other with a singularly unpleasant laugh; and then, in a sort of desperation, but still flinching and half-hearted, he laid his trouble bare to his friend. This was as though a surgeon should use his knife upon himself. Long before he had finished, his listener would fain have cried, "Hold! Enough!" But Brabant persisted, and seemed to find a melancholy pleasure in the self-torture.

To all intents and purposes, Roland had known but one woman. In the light of her perfections all womanhood had been illumined for him, and he had veritably believed that in the way of truth and honour, of gentleness and refinement, in point of civilization in fact, woman stood actually beyond man. It was his happy experience, and the chivalrous nature of the strong man had naturally responded to the thought. He had had small personal experience of the sex; their absence from the active business of life had put them out of his range. He had, of course, met many women of no very high type, and their pursuits, their joys and sorrows, were to him like those of children, and things of no more account to a man; but of social growth of this sort he had no knowledge whatever. Not to be amused was impossible; there was always something highly amusing in Mrs. Brabant and her transparencies, but indignation moved him most.

"What can you do with such a woman?" asked Brabant, with almost comic despair.

"It's very bad," said Roland, "very bad. I —I—think if I were you, almost, I should hit her—that is, if I were you."

"What! strike a woman, and that woman your wife? I should hardly have expected—"

" Well, my dear friend, I was trying to look
at the matter in the pure light of ethics.
She's behaved to you—at times—like a fiend
rather than a wife. She's as big as you,
five times as strong I should fancy, her arm
must be double yours, and you say yourself
that her health is magnificent, except when she
over-eats herself. Why, my poor dear fellow !
the creature must be a coward to bully you as
she does. It's not the way one usually talks
of women, but when I look at you the thing's
quite plain to me." And he groaned as he
cast his eye over the wan elegance of his friend,
which no thick gloves or rough overcoat could
disguise.

" Perhaps, after all, my liver has something
to do with it," said Brabant more lightly.
" There are days when, because of it, I am
an agnostic, I go to and fro swearing that
nothing has any existence under Heaven, that
nothing *is*, but I and my liver. But I won't
trouble you with it; these are the arcana of
the shrine of suffering; you are outside the
pale."

" Well, well! So much the less purgatory
for you."

" Purgatory ? I feel sometimes like the man
whose utmost hope was for a lessening of the
pangs of hell."

" My friend," said Roland, " I may know
little of the troubles you speak of, but that I
know, at any rate, is indigestion."

Brabant brightened visibly. " Well, please

God it is," he said. "I often think if the chances against us were what the pulpits would have us believe, it would be the sacred duty of every Christian parent to strangle his off-spring the instant after baptism!"

"There is logic in that."

"And yet, with broken health and broken hopes on one side of the grave, and all the awful possibilities of the other side staring a man in the face, I can still imagine his predominant feeling would be one of curiosity. I can fancy him—I can fancy myself, that is,—standing trembling, with one foot over the brink, peering into the darkness, forgetful of trouble and pain, absorbed wholly in a tremendous wonderment of what has come upon me, of what the next minute may reveal. This, it seems to me, might—*must* be the attitude of a man who has once dipped, be it ever so lightly, beneath the surface of the mysteries of Nature."

"Is that an orthodox position?"

"Why not? What are these mysteries? What is this science? Is it apart from religion—a part of it, or opposed to it? It is no essential of a creed, certainly, but it is all the same the unwritten law of the Creator. Truths are never antagonistic, neither does the Church, that I am aware, impose any finality on research.

"How about the bull against Galileo?"

"Ah, that's a bull the wise Catholic takes by the horns," laughed Brabant. "Existence is an 'unthinkable' thing; one doubts if it has reality outside the individual. One can conceive an Intelligence, otherwise constituted than ours, walking slap through our Cosmos from end to end, without the wink of a metaphorical eyelid. Man on this particular speck, but for the fact of the Redemption, would be a first-rate curio—no more. Viewed in this light, he becomes prodigious!

" Putting these loose ends together, I incline to the belief that the basis and foundation of our system is simply ethic law. The permanence of the ' Word ' over ' Heaven and Earth ' seems to point to this."

" I hardly follow you," answered Roland.

" Well, well ! My theory is that Man is safe, if he will. Cosmos was never begot of Chaos—Intellect of Vacuum ; the secret of Evil lies in its possible permutation into Good."

" I have rarely indulged in speculations of the sort."

" That is the weak joint in the splendid suit of armour you have been blessed with. You fail to grasp the sequential necessities of Being. This study has been one side of my life since I first tasted of metaphysics at college. There has been another side: I have been successful. 1000l. for my last book, 1500l. for the next. And a man who has the impudence to be a gentleman, almost an amateur, into the bargain ! Still, so far as this world is concerned, I am ready to go. I fancy it was given us to wreak our intelligence upon, and I would have done something for it before I went, just for ' auld lang syne.' I would have discovered the remains of the Ark on Ararat, or invented a flying machine—anything to give a spurt to the age. But now, I see, I shall do none of these things; I am resigned and ready to go behind the scenes."

They were rattling down a dirty river-side slum—a horde of children were building castles of dust and refuse in the kennel; so tattered and filthy were the unfortunate urchins, and so monkeyish, that they scarcely looked like children of the human race. Then among them staggered something in the semblance of womanhood, blowsy, fiery-faced, and reeking of gin, who reeled and fell upon the pavement; there she began to kick and bellow and to make day hideous with her ravings. A policeman came and lifted her up, not unkindly, considering that he was a man, and what he had to deal with, but he warned her to begone. She loaded him with shrieking abuse and clutched and tore at his whiskers, thereupon a brother officer came and took her arm on the other side. Then she flung herself, face downwards, on the earth, but, between them, they carried her off, and out of the little crowd that had gathered round, and so, kicking and screaming, yelling, cursing, and blaspheming like a mad, drunken beast as she was, she was hurried out of sight, and her cries rang till they died away in the distance.

"Unpleasant," ejaculated Roland, briefly, flicking his nag away from the scene.

A peculiar light flitted in Brabant's eyes.

" Deucedly," he said, lighting a cigarette, " particularly when it reminds one for all the world of the wife one has taken to one's bosom for life."

" Good God ! " exclaimed Roland, horrified, " does she drink ? "

" No, she hasn't that excuse," replied the husband.

Then Roland knew that his friend's grief was too deep for words.

CHAPTER V.

PRESENTLY they came upon a piece of open ground, where an intelligent, well-to-do man was preaching to a small crowd of grave-looking people, all more or less well dressed and well behaved.

"There's the modern Friar preacher," said Brabant, pointing; "certainly we English, with all our absurd vagaries, are a religious people. Look at the genuine devotion on those fellow's faces. I've often thought it a mistake, if I may so express myself, for a man to be born to a religion in this age. That must mean bias, and it is the duty of every thinking man to work out for himself, the reason for his belief or unbelief. That is why *I* own to a particular respect for that sometimes terrible personage, the convert. He, at least, has been honest with his own soul. But, in many ways, I think a man may reckon the accident of his birth as the first and greatest mistake of his life!"

"It has not been so with me," said Roland.

"No! And how bitterly I have envied you your freedom. Contrast your fate with mine.

Look at the way I was trained for a citizen," and he went on to give a history of the true British bringing up, which it had been his lot to endure.

His father, a man of sternly utilitarian views, and soured somewhat by the sacrifices he had made for his conscience, was utterly unprepared for the fine crop of men and women whom he had introduced to the world; and, although he lived to see his eldest son fifty, he never thoroughly realized that any one of them had passed out of childhood. He was a good man, and well intentioned beyond all others. With an invariable lecture on the moral benefit to be derived by the recipient, he had conscientiously thrashed his boys all the way up, so long as it was possible, handing over the girls to their mother for the same purpose: for he was too just a man, as he often said with pride, to make any difference between his children. This was for outward going astray. When they went wrong inwardly, their good mother again took up the cue, and administered black dose with a terrible impartiality.

They had been kept down, not exactly unkindly, but merely in their own infinitesimal places; this being, avowedly, the end and aim of their home life, and they had been made to wear short jackets and short petticoats till all the neighbourhood laughed at them, and revolution was with difficulty suppressed on the family hearth.

Fortunately for Warburton, he was a younger

son; he consequently escaped the first experiments, and his father's theory of education, necessarily modified as years went on, did not fall upon him in all its ruggedness, still it was hard enough. The boy was of the most delicate and fragile make, evidently what he wanted was a cold bath every morning of the year, a good sharp walk, and plenty of sago pudding. If he showed a disinclination for any of these —why the child must be ill—a black draught was the natural remedy. So the little, shivering wretch, was walked off his short legs, in vain pursuit of his father's long ones, a very labour of Sisyphus, for, no sooner attained, than they started pitilessly afresh. Meanwhile, he was regaled with stories of the champion walkers of England, and the great deeds of wonderful boys, and the lad, who had plenty of pluck in his weak little heart, would, in sheer bravado, walk out, by himself, miles and miles; and he would take no food, because the last hero he had made acquaintance with, had managed very well without it for a week. Until he would drop into the hedge, fainting, by the wayside, to be picked up, in pity, by some passing waggoner. He would be ill for days after, but proud beyond words.

He was a terrible fidget, for even thus early the germs of nervous disease had been laid in his system, and it was one of Mr. Brabant's peculiarities that, though extremely nervous as to his own health, he pooh-poohed the idea of anything in his children, incurable by the simple treatment of the domestic pharmacopeia. The usual remedies were applied, and supplemented, not ungenerously, with birchings, cold water, and early church, but even these drastic measures failed to cure the complaint, which Mr. Brabant decided must be obstinacy, and treated accordingly. Then the unlucky boy, whose cleverness ran out into a hundred grooves, developed a decided taste for art and letters, beauty and colour; he took to painting scrolls and little naked cupids on the panels of his cupboard doors, and to inditing heroic poetry and love lyrics, he grew careful as to his clothes, and particular in his neckties.

This new departure was spoken of in conclave by the authorities, as if it were but one remove from perdition. Whence should such notions come, except from the evil one? They were mercilessly scouted. The cupids were sent about their business. The lyrics were burned. He was dressed in the ugliest clothes possible, forbidden to buy any more pretty ties, and those he had were taken away.

Wise parents! who failed to see that all the boy wanted, was intelligent food for his all-devouring mind, a little brightness and a little interest in the colourless life of home. The family funds did not allow of the hunting, shooting, or boating, that fell to more fortunate lads. His fault had been that he tried to make the best of it. Poetry and art came to him as singing to the bird. Accursed these on that prosaic British hearth, where virtue, respectability, and ugliness sat enthroned as gods.

Mr. Brabant lived the life of a small squire, absolutely devoid of pursuit, thinking only, worthy man, of paying his bills. His wife had many admirable virtues, so many that it seemed unnecessary that she should live in the confessional, as she practically did. All this church-going made home a very uncomfortable place, and if there were a fault to find with her, it was that she would invariably back up her private opinion as being that of the Deity —were it only anent the eating of the sago pudding.

Children in this strange age had an ugly habit of growing up, a habit at which Mr. Brabant was never tired of expressing his surprise and annoyance. After all, the wind was tempered to the boys; as time went on they escaped and went their ways. With the girls it was different, there was no escape for them from the routine maddening to young life. Two of them died of it. It is no exaggeration to say died of it, died of dullness and tyranny. They were originally bright girls, as full of cleverness as their parents were of stupidity, but youth passed away slowly, it was true, but surely. Men were not encouraged at the house, for their father considered them dangerous creatures in the abstract, and the girls, realizing too clearly what lay before them, wisely and quietly faded out of life, unable to bear the constant taunt of their ingratitude for their many blessings. The rest of the white slaves lived on, and as the old people grew older, more exacting, and more querulous, the misery of it increased. " Either you or I must die," it was come to this, " for there is no other relief under Heaven." An unpleasant, but not uncommon alternative in a Christian household! It took Warburton a long time to forget and forgive the theories, which had been instilled as facts into his young brain, as though no shadow of a doubt had ever crossed human intelligence on the subjects. It was not wonderful that Agnosticism became a rampant feature of the age. If this was done in the green wood, consider the dry. Imagine the bringings up of the old orthodox Protestant household, where Calvinistic and Puritan principles still lingered.

The worst feature in these "religious" families (no matter the creed) was their resolute and absolute stultification of the gifts of reason and intelligence, their deliberate severance from inquiry and the highest and most honest thought of the day. Surely if fire ever descended from Heaven, it would be on such perversity as this! The sincerity of their ignorance probably saved them. The first thing an intelligent youth did on escaping from home, was to shake its dust from his feet and to unlearn as fast as he could nine-tenths of what he had gathered there. So home often became a training-school for every possible vice, and the few who held aloof from this, nourished a feeling of disgust for the ruthless chicanery

which had been practised upon them helpless.
Happy families were the result. It would hardly
have been worth while to go into this detail,
but that the Brabants were typical of the
time. When the family grew up, there were
a dozen ladies and gentlemen thrown on the
world with practically no resources whatever. The whole country was blocked with
genteel beggars, educated in the most complete
uselessness, in Greek and Latin, music and
drawing, for the gentry were highly conservative on these points, and the folly of the
fathers lay heavy on the children. If a man
did cut through the vicious circle that hemmed
in the poor gentleman, and pushed his way
into the real arena of life, the cost was heavy to
himself. He had neither money, connection,
nor friends who could help him. The idiotic,
idle lives of his foregangers were a hopeless
stumbling-block. For what he accomplished
he had himself alone to thank. Warburton
Brabant had cleft a way for himself, but he
had broken down under the strain, and not a
little of what he had done, he owed to the
guidance and advice of a chance acquaintance,
Professor Van Dam. . . . . . .

The travellers had emerged from the outskirts of Woolwich, and had come upon a
treeless waste, dreary and far-stretching, where,
here and there, the smoke of burning weeds
curled upward through the misty distance, and
the masts of great ships crept slowly across the
sunk horizon as though they sailed the meadows.

" Did you tell your friend, the professor, we were coming ? " asked Roland.

" No; that would have been a waste of good paper and stamps," laughed the other. " He will be there, sure enough; he would not have let us come for nothing."

" A convenient friend. I wish all my constituents were like him."

Then he remembered that such a thing had not been without parallel in his own experience, but he merely said carelessly, " I suppose he is a clairvoyant ? "

" Remarkably so," was the rather dry answer.

" Steady! steady! What are we dancing at ? " said Roland, whipping-up the mare which had swerved. " I wonder what that was ? Two or three times, since we got out into the open, I fancied I saw some one following us or coming up at the side. That's the worst of these hooded gigs; you never can tell. Did you notice ? I never saw a milestone so like a human being before. It must have been the milestone, there's nothing else, and on a road like this without hedges one can see any distance. Hi! steady, old lady! " for the mare had bolted again. " By Jove ! there *is* some one there. It must be a fellow on a monocycle ; I wish he'd pass or let us."

" Pull up," said Brabant, his face not changing a muscle. " You're mistaken. It's the Professor himself."

And, in effect, when the mare was pulled to a

walk, there was a gentleman, also walking quietly, actually alongside the gig, who did not seem to have hurried, for he was very cool. He was an elderly man, with a pleasant, keen-cut face of a high, remarkably high type, and he wore a frockcoat and tall hat, not a very suitable dress, certainly, for this windy high-way over the marsh, but then he was probably coming from Town, where appearances would have to be consulted, even by an angel dropped from the skies.

Brabant put out a thin white hand from under the bear-skin. "Ah! Professor, this is too good of you."

Meantime, that gentleman took off his hat and paid his greetings in a slightly foreign accent, fixing an eye, keen as a hawk's, but more kindly, upon Roland. "A fine stage pro-perty that eye," said the latter to himself; "I suppose he's like the rest" (for Roland had often been on the track of signs and wonders, which had melted away like snow in the sun, before investigation), "or is he the scientific necromancer at last? It looks just possible, his living here in this out-of-the-way place," and he returned the salutation with a certain cordiality.

"Let us give you a lift, my dear sir," he said, "there's just room for a third, and you must be still some way from home. We were on our way to you, as I daresay you guessed."

"Very glad, delighted to receive you, but exercise does me good. I must have my walk. Drive on, I shall be in as soon as you are. I happen to know a—in fact, a short cut. Ha! ha!" he waved his hand, "Au revoir," and turned back.

"Then we must be going the wrong way!" said Roland, pulling up sharply. "I thought you said this road led straight to the place."

"So it does."

"But," returned Roland, "he's gone straight the other way, and there is only this road; you can see it for miles." He stood up and gazed round, for the hood prevented their looking back otherwise.

"Why—where? God bless my soul! he's not there! Good Heavens! the man must have got on to the marsh, and gone under. I declare there's not a trace of him; or, perhaps, he's in the ditch. Here, hold the reins; if he is I'll have him out in no time."

"My friend," said Brabant, imperturbably, "don't make a fool of yourself. I know the man. Take my advice, and drive on as he told you. If he isn't as good as his word, never take his or mine again."

So rather savagely and in silence, for he disliked argument almost as much as he did mystification, Roland sat down and sent the mare on her road. Before they had gone far, they encountered another wayfarer, this time on horseback. They would hardly have remarked him, but that he seemed in a special hurry, and kept his face studiously turned away as he passed, as though the river barges had suddenly developed points of extraordinary interest.

"Do you know Hubert de B—?" asked Roland, when he had passed.

"What, the son of the Ambassador?"

"Yes."

"No, not at all, personally, but I am told he does most of his father's work."

"That was he," said Roland with conviction. "He's grown shy apparently. Odd his being out here."

"Do you think so? I once met his master, the Emperor himself, on this very road."

"Seriously?"

"Seriously."

"It speaks well for your friend" (with some sarcasm).

"Many people and things do that," answered Brabant, lightly; "but there's the place."

Before them a low, white-bricked cottage, with out-buildings, solitary as a pelican in the wilderness, stood by the road-side, unrelieved by bush or tree, as commonplace a piece of cheap builder's work as you could well see. Plainly the Professor did not strive to enhance his position by his surroundings; and at the door, in a loose velvet coat and slippers, who should be there but the owner himself.

"Welcome, gentlemen, welcome!" he said, as they drove up. "The moment I came in I ordered dinner to be laid for you. It will be ready by this time, and I trust you will be ready for it, and excuse an extempore affair."

The visitors were shown into a room, where there was a table with three places laid, and what proved to be a small but excellent dinner.

It was not a quarter of an hour since their host had left them on the road. Roland was stupified and angry, as a man is who sees with his own eyes a fact which he cannot explain. There must be trickery somewhere ; there were two men, brothers perhaps, and alike, and he looked at Brabant, who appeared wholly unconcerned as if nothing in particular had happened. Although the dinner was highly creditable to the cook, it passed off but indifferently. Roland was pre-occupied by his own thoughts. Brabant's appetite was that of an invalid, and the host, it was noticeable, merely played at eating, taking nothing but a few vegetables on his plate, and drinking only plain water.

If they had hoped to draw him out they were disappointed. He kept provokingly clear of every topic of special interest. However, he made himself pleasant, talked about the Play and the Park, in a way that proved him a man of the world, and about his pigs, his hen-roost, his laboratory, his new buildings, and so forth. He complained that he had more visitors than he always cared for—people who came out of mere curiosity and without introductions, and said he sighed for the halcyon days when Mr. Brabant had been his only friend and pupil in England—a chance one, too—for they had picked each other up, at hap-hazard, under an archway in a thunderstorm. He told how he had bought the eligible cottage *ornée* with the unrivalled prospect, which a speculator had raised in the midst of the wilderness, meaning to make it the germ of a new London. But it was not to be. The marsh had swamped the builder and his plans. The house remained a hermitage and a beacon, and no other of its kind grew up about it. Had he not been able to make it self-supporting, it was difficult to see how he could have existed.

All this did not help matters forward much. Brabant appeared nervous of touching on the subject of his own health, or on anything of particular interest.

" I had hoped," he stammered at last, as they rose from the table, "that you, perhaps, would let us have half an hour at the retroscope before we go."

" Bah ! it is in embryo," and the inventor shrugged his shoulders. " It is, besides, out of order; but still, you want something to amuse you while your horse is being put to, and I think,"—he looked at Roland,—" it may not be without use. We will begin modestly, say with a pack of cards."

" The man is a charlatan, after all," said Roland to himself.

The Doctor perhaps read his thoughts. " You're above and beyond this, no doubt, gentlemen—no doubt. Yet there is a great principle involved; a straw will show the way of the wind. Take a card, sir."

Roland took one, the two of spades.

The performer handed him the pack. " Take charge of it; I don't want it any more. Put your card back, shuffle it as you like, and then throw the pack where you will,—on the table, the floor, I don't care where."

Roland did so, and tossed it finally on a cane-bottomed chair.

"Now watch," said the Doctor. He commenced to make passes some two feet above. The cards immediately stirred, lifting themselves slightly from the centre. Roland passed one hand between the operator's and the cards, and the other to and fro under the cane seat. But the cards were absolutely isolated. When the passes stopped, the cards lay motionless. When again begun they stirred as before. On looking closer it became evident that one only was in actual movement, that it lay under the others, which it shook from it as it moved, now with a jerk, now almost with a hop like a frog's. By degrees it worked itself free, came out from the rest, and rearing itself with a last effort, fell over on its back.

" The devil! " said Roland.

" No, my dear sir, not at all; merely the deuce—of spades. Your card, I think," smiled the Professor, and the unbeliever modified his views.

" That is a pretty trick," he said ; " the man who can do that can do more."

It is probable they would have gone no deeper than this, but at that moment Brabant was seized with a faintness, and sank into a chair. The Doctor went up, seized his wrist as though feeling his pulse, and in less than a minute a bright colour came into the sick man's face, and a light equally bright to his eyes.

"Thanks, thanks," he said, as he sat up again. "It was nothing, the heat of the room; but I really feel as if you had poured life into me, like water into an empty glass," and he stood up.

"Ah! my dear friend," said the Doctor, who looked anxiously at him, "if you always lived with me, you would not be troubled with these fits. You should take care of him," and he turned to Roland.

"I wish I had the chance," answered he; "but now, I confess I am astonished at what you are able to do. May I·ask, was that natural or super-natural? Are you a spiritualist, pray?"

The Man of knowledge laughed, "Very much the contrary, but I flatter myself I can beat one on his own ground."

"Will you explain a little?"

"Certainly. The fact is, pretty well all that the world has dubbed psychics can be reduced to physics. I am speaking of phenomena. Without doubt the two are inalienably bound up, and there is really no hard and fast line between them. But you may plunge into the abyss of physics and carry the broad light of

L 2

science to its innermost depths, you may even
work miracles with your knowledge; yet at the
crucial point, the connection of the material
phenomena with the vital consciousness—that
is, with the spirit—you shall stand arrested.
Here is a blank wall which you cannot scale,
and through which there is no door, except
perhaps that of death. You must be content
with the scraps that are flung over to you from
the other side, miserable scraps they are,
though enough perhaps for miserable man, and
for these you must go to theology."

"Then are you a theologian?"

"I am not particularly concerned with that
side of the question; it is out of my reach.
For my purpose man is but a highly decorative
tube, the science of life, the science of juices; or
if you will, he is a piece of molecular architecture, brought about by action and inter-action
(there are many ways of putting it), while
the science of death is a knowledge of those
organisms which eventually undermine the
structure. The order of things has been arranged, once and for all to the mind of science,
which has at least this merit, that it makes
good its steps as it goes—that order has never
varied one iota," and he shook his finger, "the
appointed crown and reward of labour in
this direction, is an insight into the wondrous
forces of Nature and the power which that insight
brings. In this way Providence may place in
the hands of the basest materialist (I use the
word for want of a better), dominion over life

and death. You Catholics (pardon me for
saying so), may pray yourselves black in the
face over a pestilence, and it will not be stayed.
But your man of science comes, and to him it is
given to say absolutely to the scourge, ' Thus
far shalt thou go, and no farther.' Such is
the benediction of Heaven on research. If
your saints have worked these miracles, as undoubtedly they have, it has been by instilled
knowledge. The man who studies Nature, and
the man who studies Nature's Master, cannot be
far apart; and again without doubt, the latter
will have the advantage.

" I dare say you have heard ladies talk
about miracles in the drawing-room; it is a
favourite subject with them, and they treat it
very prettily, if not very wisely. It would be a
great thing for religion if an intelligent doctrine
of miracles were generally accepted. The
Saviour Himself could not work a miracle
contrary to Nature's laws. God in Heaven
could not make two sides of a triangle smaller
than the third. Could He do so, He would be
going back upon Himself. The materials for
' miracles ' lie all round, ready to the hand of
him who is fitted for them. The world is far
from fit for such knowledge : I mean simply
from an intellectual standard. But there have
been, and there are, men and women who have
fitted themselves, and have received it, who,
studying Nature and her works, have been
admitted to intimacy. Your saints went
straight to the fountain-head, hence they

stayed pestilence and laid storms.　There is the
strongest historic evidence of it; but was there
no *mechanical* explanation of their acts?　I
should insult your common sense to suggest it.
They merely controlled certain currents, just as
you might that of an electric wire, if you wished
to send a message, and it is obvious that if you
had possession of the battery, you might apply
its forces in a thousand different ways.

"But my friend," and he placed his hand on
Roland's shoulder, "it is unfair to tantalize you.
A nature like yours, from its very physical
strength, must be materialistic to the highest
degree.　So far as this protects you from deceit,
well and good; but don't let it carry you too
far.　A man with his head," and he pointed to
Brabant, "might, if he cared to undergo the
ordeal of training, achieve such a mastery that
he could crumble you and any scheme of yours
to dust."

Roland was silent.

"Give me your hand," said the host.　Roland
would fain have done so, but although only the
tips of his fingers rested on the table, he could
not withdraw them, and he speedily discovered
that all sensation had left his arm.

"Now," said the Doctor, "isn't that better
than laughing-gas or chloroform?　I could cut
off your arm, and you should feel it no more
than if I snipped off your sleeve.　All this may
seem child's play, but I can assure you that it is
just as easy to go on and impinge on your own
particular province, to deprive you of *free*

will and to impress my own upon you in its place."

The young M.P. roused himself at this, for he had fallen almost into a stupor. He faced his interlocutor with some sternness, but in the coldly circumstantial look of the other, he saw neither excitement nor jest.

"I feel it," he said huskily after a minute, and his eyes dropped. "I feel as I never thought to feel to living man." His own unspoken thought was, "I have wasted my life, and dangled all my days on the outermost fringe of things," and with the sense almost of shame that crept over him, there opened out a vista of possibilities, that made his head giddy and his eyes blind, in the rush of it. This— this—yes, this was what he had imagined dimly, and sought to grasp. He fairly staggered into a chair.

"My friend," said the Solitary, with some earnestness, "we begin to understand each other. I had not intended to go thus far with you, for I saw that your spirit was set against mine, and it would have been idle. But you were wise enough to bow, and you shall be no loser. I am not flattering you, but stating what to me at least, is a self-evident truth, when I say that you are a man fitted to do great' things. It is written upon you in unmistakable characters. But I warn you that while your mind is set on achievement, it is well—it is necessary, that you should know something of the mastery of matter, that lies within human range, but which is only found in the hands of a few. Against such forces, if you work in ignorance, you will struggle in vain; working with them in parallel grooves, you shall find such strength on your side as shall be unassailable. A man of your calibre can hardly imagine that the Cæsars, the Shakespeares, the Newtons of the world, were dowered on the same intellectual scale, as the Browns, Jones's, and Robinsons of the streets. Their achievements were the outcome of knowledge incalculable to the average brain. But this knowledge does not die with the individual. It is handed down, and so, ever increasing in bulk, grows more and more resistless, and there are living men who hold the keys of it. There have been many of them, in many places and under many names. They do not trouble the light of day much, for to them it is as darkness; but they come forward to help in the selection of fit instruments whenever there is a prospect of furthering the profit and advancement of the human race. They are as wirepullers out of sight. A storm does not gather without warnings for the weather-wise. It has been known in certain quarters for a long time past, that the world, as it begins a new cycle of knowledge; is approaching and is even now on the verge of a fresh cyclone of revolution, one more violent in its course and more radical in its results than any that history has known. Already the hand of Fate trembles on the curtain. Europe itself is too small for the next act. The men who will make and share and direct in this cataclysm are going their several ways, ripe men already and marked, though they know it not. There are certain antecedents which would seem to point to the actors in the future drama. There is no reason why I should refrain from telling you that such are your own. Your past cries it aloud."

As the Doctor made this assertion, he leaned over the table and directed a piercing glance at Roland.

"I cannot believe prophecy," said the latter, shaking his head. "Pharaoh's wise men could work miracles, but that was a test beyond them. Besides, how can you know this?" he went on, like a man who would find faith if he could. "How can you know this, I say? It is wild, visionary, most improbable. I have left the army; I am a mere private member of Parliament, and one whose hands are so tied that I think every day of resigning my seat. I am engaged to be married; I shall settle down, probably to farming; it's the best career I see open at present." He spoke lightly, but there was some bitterness in his soul.

"My friend," answered the other with some impatience, "man's career as truly lies within him as the statue within the block. The shaping of it is the work of himself and circumstance, and yours is already rough hewn, as you shall find by your past. You may take it to heart, to begin with, that there is no difficulty in finding out anything of anybody, as to their present or past condition, and that their future may be deduced from it with almost mathematical certainty. It is the working out of the problem, of which every human life consists, on data more or less ample, as the case may be, which the experience and observation of centuries, enable us to do with almost unerring accuracy. I have told you that there are men who have preserved and set down records out of immemorial years. We have hundreds of sources of knowledge quite unknown to the world at large."

" Here," and he flung open a cupboard; " do you see those rolls ? They are papyri from the archives of El Fayoum, a city destroyed in the tenth century ; they date from the first, and are in eleven different dialects. A man must be a specialist to decipher any one of them, but these are things of yesterday, and I am not talking of a thousand years or of ten thousand, for that matter," and he snapped his fingers, " but of such a period as your mind would refuse to conceive in connection with human history. That which to ordinary men in the first flounderings of civilization, is a mere chaos of accident, is to some few an orderly arrangement of sequential facts. In the far distant future, perhaps, even the people will be brought to understand that no effect is without its cause. The world moves on ; population and knowledge and the duration of human life ever on the increase ; its toils grow, and its throes, with its achievements. With grander scope it moves ever to grander incident, but history has been so falsified, that there is no true reading of its science for the multitude. There lies westward a great Continent, and you might cut many Europes out of it; it was born to mankind but yesterday. Within itself is centred everything of human possibility, but only out of travail are great births. That new world is as truly of the future, as our old world is of the past. Men are no different, nor are their passions less. Its story has yet to be told. I may speak to you in riddles, but it is written of men like yourself, that their fortunes and misfortunes shall change the face of the globe.

"Nay, you doubt me still?" and he caught Roland by the wrist. "Why, I read you like an open book. What more would you have me tell you? Of your thought that you will rebuild the fame of your race; of your other self, the very soul and life of your existence, who came upon you out of the sunrise? Of the dangers that tore her from your arms in the moment of your betrothal; of the phantasies that have troubled you from the beginning; of her fears and the secret ambitions of your heart—?"

"Hold, sir!" cried Roland, shaking him off somewhat roughly. "No more. You have bewitched and bewildered me. I don't know what to think—what to believe. I am confounded. As a boy—but I have forgotten that I ever had such dreams—"

"They are upon you, nevertheless; the world only waits the call-bell. I have brought you here to tell you so."

This remark, which half an hour before he would have resented as a monstrous assumption, Roland received in silence, and shortly the two friends went out together. As they drove rapidly back towards London across the treeless, silent expanse of the marsh, the April wind blew chill, but the earth, fresh soaken with rain, exhaled the odours of the spring, and the hurrying clouds were torn in flying wreaths against the clear blue-black of Heaven.

"You prepared me for nothing of this sort," said Roland, as they came again into the track of civilization, and saw the lights of scattered homesteads twinkle in the distance.

"I hardly knew what to prepare you for, the man is so entirely various. Sometimes he is the mere man of the world; sometimes he is the pedant; sometimes the scientist: not often the prophet and miracle-monger."

"Now that I am out of his presence I doubt my senses. What can be the meaning of it all? Does he actually do these things, or does he bewitch one's eyes and ears into believing them, by some phantasmagoria?"

Brabant shook his head. "I cannot tell you, but, for my part, I believe in him. I know by experience he is above deceit."

"But what, in the name of all that is inexplicable, is he?"

"I can tell you nothing. To some extent

he built up my fortune, for he pointed out, very exactly, the road which led to it at starting, warning me of its briefness. I am glad that you have met—glad to hear what he had to tell you, but not surprised. No; a man in my state is not easily surprised. I long since knew that if the chance came you would meet it half-way. For me I fight another battle!"

* * * * * *

From this time forward the star of Roland Tudor's life began slowly to mount upwards. There was no sudden or marked departure, but his ventures were happier in their results; the wheels ran with a lessened friction, and a species of modified success attended his efforts. He is a clever man who reads aright his own motives, and the knowledge greatly assists in divining those of others, and in the realization of that sub-conscious cerebration, which probably plays so important, if so unrecognized, a part in human history. If Roland had not traversed any distance, yet chance had led him into the right path; his rough see-and-believe theory had received a rude shock. He was removed from the specious idiocy of Belief limited by Under-standing, and henceforth he skimmed the surface more lightly, from a knowledge of the depths below.

The years rolled on, and he had become, 'by the comparatively simple process of exist-ence,' an accepted fact. The times were ripe for a statesman of his faith in England, but over the wide horizon no faintest trace of one had yet appeared, though he was anxiously looked for by many eyes. Indeed, the enormous number of Catholics in the British empire made him almost a necessity. There were men of that religion in both Houses, but they may be shortly dismissed by saying that "they knew not Joseph." They were too grand, or too clever, or too great, or too recent, or too something, to fill the place, and as for any ideas of bringing out modern Catholicism, and working it in unison with its surroundings, to the enormous benefit of all concerned, there was not a glimmering of such a notion among them. The highest light vouchsafed to most of these legislators seemed to be, to put forth to the world, as impracticable and impossible an aspect of their faith, as it was capable of assuming.

Roland Tudor was the first to insist that in such an age, it was essential that the principles of Catholicism should impress the national legislation. He it was who first struck the true path wherein the Catholic statesman, without in any way separating himself from the interests of the bulk of his countrymen, might rigidly maintain those peculiar to himself and his co-religionists. Straight, steadfast, moderate in his views, as even his opponents admitted, he came to be felt as a man of some strength of position, and he acquired a considerable following, both among priests and laity.

He began to be talked about as a man who had actually found it possible, to organize the Catholic vote. This had been done by the establishment, all over the country, of neutral registration societies, which led to the education of the poorer voters, by giving them an intelligent interest in the questions of the day. The good work, which he had been foremost in promoting, had an unforeseen result; out of it his personal popularity grew like wildfire. With the official world too, he began to stand equally well; it was no longer necessary to hunt up an Archbishop, on every puny question. Here was a man on the spot, who had evolved order out of chaos, with details at his fingers' ends, ready with the answer. He was consulted on all sides; his fairness on public questions was universally recognized; he seldom claimed or asked anything, that he was not ready to meet, with offers of such counter concession as was possible. Yet with his own people it was felt that their real interests were safe in his hands, for he had the rare art of drawing the line at the right point. The fact was, his place had long waited, and any layman of parts, who had the wit to step into it, was secure of a niche in history. He was the pioneer in the country of the future, by the mere accident of his time. His place and name must go down to posterity, magnified out of all focus. It must be remembered that the true *modus vivendi* for the British Catholic had not yet been found, in spite of the removal of his disabilities. This problem of how he was to take his right place, no more and no less, it was Roland's ambition to solve. In the beginning, various things occurred to assist him in his efforts. Authority, naturally distrustful of so new a departure, came round to encouraging the movement. A safe and capable man—that had been the desideratum. He appeared to have arrived. Again, a feature presented itself which strengthened his position.

It was found desirable, indeed necessary, by the great colonies to have spokesmen in the Imperial Parliament, and the only way in which it could be done was by courting a home constituency. The enormous mutual benefit to be derived in this way was soon perceived, and it rapidly grew to be the fashion. When Great Trumpington suddenly developed into meaning, the Australasian continent, and Little Pumpington, Canada West—those two modest localities rose to a dizzy height in the big world. In this way several leading colonists who were of the Roman Church, found their road into Parliament, and in this way was formed the first nucleus of an English Catholic parliamentary party. Of this knot of men Roland became the virtual leader. The prejudice which they had to encounter at starting was enormous, and it was not until they had lived it down, and it began to be perceived that their aims were neither selfish nor aggressive, that the public recognized that such a body might be an actual boon to society. But the preponderance of ultra-Toryism, or what might be called the boudoir phase of politics, was at this time a serious drawback. The lady league was an element Roland had already reckoned with, but it drove him hard, and there were certain prelates to be found in the drawing-rooms, who supplied the material for still greater difficulties.

The prominent position into which he was now pushed, presently brought him into straits, and complications arose requiring particular nicety in their treatment: rumours of these, perhaps over-coloured, went about.

One evening, as he left the House, he met, in Westminster Hall, St. Maur, who, when he was at home, which was but rarely, now that he and his party stood so far below par, seldom attended the debates. They smiled as they encountered each other, the smile of men in the sympathy of misfortune, and, linking their arms, walked out together along the riverside. St. Maur was the first to touch on the subject.

"You've done wonders, my dear Tudor, I consider, but I'm afraid the length of your tether is nearly reached. This rapping bishops over the knuckles, and putting peers and princes in their places, won't do—at any rate, under the present *régime*. Perhaps when we democrats come in again they will take it more kindly."

"My dear St. Maur," laughed Roland, "it is, of course impossible, to explain the actual state of the case, to a heretic so benighted as yourself; but I beg to state that I have never rapped episcopal knuckles, except with a feather, and in the utmost privacy; and I have then and there gone out into the street and turned my cheek to be smitten, as a punishment and proof of my high state of discipline. You don't seem to see, that it was absolutely necessary to demonstrate to the British public, that the Catholic layman was a man who could, and should, walk alone in lay matters, and this with the perfect trust, confidence, and approval of his ecclesiastical superiors; that it is his business to advise them in mundane things, as it is theirs to direct him in spiritual. Until this comes about, and I admit that it has *not* come about as fully as it should (chiefly owing to the dearth of capable laymen), the country will not believe in us as politicians, or, what is more important, as citizens.

"For your other charge, as to peers and princes, I have simply given expression to my ideas that the men who are to lead English Catholics are to be made—not born to the place. The contrary, as you know, is the popular idea. You know, too, of course, that I have never advocated the formation of a Catholic political party. I simply look that we should not hang back, as we have hitherto done, but should take our place as men ready to bear the heat and burden of the day in all parties, and in all spheres where good work is to be done. I want to see our people foremost in the large-hearted schemes of public improvement, which are characteristic of the age."

"Yes, I know you are an honest man, but

the drawing-rooms will be too strong for you. Every shady duchess, every lady of light and leading, whose brilliancy is somewhat tarnished, and whose followers have fallen away, drops into your fold as naturally as an over-ripe fruit. You can restore the bloom if any one can—I suppose that is the idea, eh ?—and these people unfortunately carry weight with their names. You see you have no intelligent public feeling among you as a body (pardon plain speaking). What are your newspapers ? Venom and the Syllabus, the unearthing of a Greek root, the different versions of a dog-Latin hymn of doubtful mediævalism, these, and the records of the movements of your aristocracy, are the subjects which week after week brings forth. Still I admit, from a literary point of view, your press is strong, and holds its own. It is its grotesque egotism that is its damning point. Why don't you take advantage of the Universities for your young men? Instead of founding huge cathedrals, in some out-of-the-way village, which are but monuments of folly, why don't your rich men put down 10,000*l.* and start a first-class review, wherein subjects of vital interest might be given the world, discussed from your particular point of view ? You, and a few like you, will never educate such a mass of incoherency as you present in the bulk. You have done much, you have tabulated the position, but you will never lead the English Catholics, unless you are prepared to spend twenty thousand a year on painted windows and gilt candlesticks."

"You speak my own thoughts. We are terribly behindhand. We must pray for better things."

"I am not sure," said St. Maur, rather cynically, "that prayer is meant for these exigencies. Do you remember a certain foreign Pretender, lately dead, who would spend three hours in his oratory, previous to issuing the most idiotic manifestos ever read by mortal man?"

"I do," laughed Roland, "and I confess I prefer a man who will get his praying done quickly and quietly, and come out and put his shoulder to the wheel. But I am not without hope yet, though I foresee that if things don't take a turn, our struggle for the integrity and independence of the Church in England must fail."

"Well! when it does, as I foresee it must and will, I shall expect to see you out West, where I have a biggish foothold now."

He hailed a passing omnibus, sprang to the knife-board, and was gone.

CHAPTER VI.

THIS particular year of grace, or disgrace, had been in every way phenomenal, and during it the conflict of ideas progressed rapidly towards that ultimatum, which was to turn it into conflict of a sterner nature.

There had been a general reaction against the spirit of Progress throughout Europe. Driven to bay, the element that called itself " aristocracy " *(lucus a non lucendo)* had by some wonderful luck and cleverness, contrived to hoodwink the people, and had persuaded them anew to rivet their own limbs in fetters. Not that the lower classes were particularly well off, or comfortable in them—everywhere the poor suffered and were mutinous, but armies of officials and police, everywhere kept them down, and, on the whole, maintained excellent discipline. This had the further advantage of supplying employment to vast numbers, for half the people were engaged in keeping the other half in order. In England, vested interests reigned supreme, all that had been previously done for the bettering of the working-man very easily went back, and the four whitewashed walls that belonged to some one else (often minus the whitewash), became his ideal home. Never had been known a better season in London, the Court was unusually gay, and a fictitious brilliancy was thrown over all, by the prosperity of the landed interest, which blazed with the final glitter of a firework before its extinction.

The clash of ideas, now temporarily stilled, had been between those of the old world and the new, and the flames of the burning question raged across the Atlantic. America had for some years begun to know a new thing, a class of men who were not only monied, but leisured. Until latterly, hands had been too busy on that favoured Continent, for Satan to be able to find them much of his particular work; but now that this class had become adult they raised the cry for a titled aristocracy, a privileged class, defined from the people, and it may be remarked, that in this cry, the feminine voice rose highest. It availed little to catch a Continental duke, or even an English peer, now and then. They could not keep him —and their dollars merely served to grease his chariot-wheels at home—at his home, that is, to say. It was urged, not without reason, that there could be founded in the States an hereditary nobility, which would hold its own for wealth, taste, and refinement with any in Europe; that there were possessions as princely, estates that would swamp a small kingdom, and that these had been often built up by a single brain, proving an aristocracy of intellect, which equalled or surpassed anything that

Europe could show. It was possible that these
notions originated, in the first instance, with
Europeans, several English and Continental
notabilities having bought large tracts of land
out westward, and the jealous emulation between State and State, added intensity to the
demand. Such an outcry, it was obvious to
the observer, meant history, history written
close, and with headings in capitals, and this
was what was actually to follow.

Among the most successful buyers of land in
the West, was Lord St. Maur, who, after a
vain struggle against the tide at home, had
quitted England in disgust, and had betaken
himself, as he had hoped, to a more congenial
soil. Congenial it had, in one sense, proved,
for on his particular claim had been discovered
a mineral wealth, that threatened to become
fabulous, and to place him in a short space
of time, in the first rank of trans-atlantic
capitalists. At this moment he was a man
troubled exceedingly with the responsibility
of it, and he racked his brain, day and
night, as to how such wealth should be best
employed. His thoughts, perhaps naturally,
inclined towards founding a small inland state,
which should be a practical Utopia, and from
this scheme the personality of Roland Tudor
was by no means excluded, although he had
not as yet seriously broached the subject to
him.

The two friends had met hardly at all of late
years, but mutual regard had in no wise waned
and through failure of one sort and another,

St. Maur had retained a confidence in him quite unshaken. " The opportunity will make him," he had always said. " This is the type of the coming man, strong in mind and muscle, of old blood, and good blood, the true gentleman, and with all the true democrat, the man who claims for himself and his class, nothing which he would not throw open to any one, who has it in him to attain an equal position; the exponent of an equality, at least in right, between all men; idealist and materialist, combining the highest aims with the most matter-of-fact exactness of procedure. Sooner or later, such a man cannot fail, unless he stultifies himself, to rise a head and shoulders above his fellows." This had been the substance of St. Maur's reflections, now the time seemed ripe to sound his friend on the project.

In the trivial and contemptible span of human life, spaces of stagnation and of abnormal activity, often alternate for lengths wholly disproportioned. Henceforth the events that crowded in upon Roland, came so thick as to afford him scarce a breathing time. When he reached his rooms that night, a roll of fair copy lay upon the table, and from it fell a letter.

* * * * * *

" You were with us last year, is it too much to hope that you may be here again at Whitsuntide? There are reasons, and I will tell you them. I think poor Guardy has made up his mind to give us the particulars we have both looked for so long. As you know, I have often hinted at it to him, and last night I actually ventured to ask him about my mother—not an unnatural question, perhaps, for her child, who, all the same, shook so, she could scarcely frame the words. But he did not silence me at once, as he has always done, the subject has plainly been on his mind. ' If Roland were here,' he began, and stopped —' When will he be here, child ? He comes so seldom.' I could not tell him. Tell him yourself. I did not press the point, but I heard him repeat to himself, more than once, ' I must do it. I must.' Will this bring you at Pentecost, the feast of gladness, as it once was to us, and it shall be again, if you are here ? Dear love, I am ill when you are absent, and the good gifts, once so bountifully poured upon me, now, one by one, are taken away, through my fault, doubtless, through my fault. I go about, crying desperately with myself. What is it ails thee, oh ! my heart ? Why has the joy gone out of the spring, the gladness from the sunshine, the laughter from the sea, and the colour from the flowers ? What answer should there be ? There is none—and I only know that so it is. Surely, if there is a cure for me, and I feel that the eleventh hour is at hand, it must be through you alone. Heal thy servant as thou knowest. Are these weak fancies ? Then, at least, I have had the strength to tell them, that is something.

*   *   *   *   *   *

" P.S.—If you will bring down your papers, we will not waste the recess."

This letter threw Roland into a state of serious anxiety. It implied something not far short of a break-down on Sybil's part, for he knew of old her courage and the capacity of her endurance, and could conceive what the distress must have been, which could wring from her such an avowal. As there could plainly be no reason for mental anxiety, the cause must lie in her own health, which, he was now more than ever convinced, had been injured by her constant attendance on the invalid. Happily, it was but a week to Whitsuntide, but the whole space of it he was on thorns, to eat, sleep, and work seemed alike impossible. Yet there was no getting away earlier, and not until the eve of the Feast did he reach Sombrewood.

Oh! the intolerable length of the beauteous day, the first gift of the summer! All the long hours, as he travelled down, the young, bright sun rested soft upon the country. All the day a trembling incense rose from the earth heavenwards, and through it, towers, spires, and woods showed as in a mirage, and the streams flowed, dreamlike and noiselessly, away. All day upon the white roads the errant zephyrs danced in little dust clouds, and laughing surely, fluttered into the pale, new foliage of the wayside, where they set a million twinkling leaves a-laughing with them. How merry the world was, and how young, how careless! He watched the quick hedges as they shot past, like the rapid spokes of a wheel. In the lush, flower-gemmed grass of the flitting fields, the cattle stood chewing comfortably, or by the pond in the shadow, with legs immersed, lashed with slow strokes their shining flanks. The myriad flowers that had that morning spread their virgin leaves, were revelling in the glory of young life. Earth was coquetting with her master, but now she drooped to sleep, the evening was at hand.

It was five o'clock when Roland set foot in the well-remembered way and reached the dower-house, nestling in its shrubberies. The doors and windows were open wide; no need for him here, where his very shadow was worshipped, to trouble servants as he entered. The music of Sybil's laugh was the first thing that greeted him, and he stayed and listened, half vexed, half overjoyed; vexed that he should have been, it seemed, unreasonably anxious, overjoyed for sheer love of it. He might have known that, but for his coming, the laugh had been impossible. But there was no one in the rooms.

They of the house were out in the verandah beyond, and, unperceived, he looked out upon them. The shadow and the shade were playing there upon the tea-table, upon the old silver, and the transparent tea-cups, as of yore. The clematis hung motionless in clouds round the slender iron columns, where the aloes were in the tubs, and the slow waters of the lake lapped the steps, which the swans had gathered round expectantly. The depths were flecked milkily, where, here and there, the thick umbrage of the boughs let slip a slanting ray. Beyond, on the other side, the giant elms in their new garments, their base lost in the shades, their leaves agilt and aglow, stood, as ever, a living wall of whispering sentinels, and the scent of the roses was all about.

In his easy-chair sat Mr. Trelawney, looking better and brighter than Roland had seen him for years, and on the rugs at his feet was Sybil, with one, too white, translucent arm cast round the neck of the big blood-hound. The tea-table stood untouched, they were waiting for him. The scene was an idyll of peace and beauty, wherein no trouble might intrude, and the Lord of the Isles stopped a moment on the threshold, ere he declared himself, for it struck his heart with a pang of inexpressible delight. As he did so the chime of village bells fell upon his ear, far distant, like a peal of joy; but the sound fainted away, until only the note of one bell tolling, thrilled in low echoes through the woods.

Then he stepped forward and Sybil flew to his breast, and the old man was shaken with surprise, for the intruder had stolen in like a thief; but, with a quavering gladness in his voice, he welcomed him that he had come in good time, and the big dogs lifted themselves lazily, and swaggered up to greet the new-comer as an old, old friend.

The trio sat for a long time, dreading to break the spell of the hour. No tiniest breeze ruffled the dark mirror of the lake, the incandescent sun sank behind the woods into the oily sea, but the hot air was stagnant, no chill came with the night; and as they sat in the dusk, Roland questioning his true love's hand in his, he resolved that the time had come to ask for the explanations he w s there to seek.

The old man had spoken little, and while the crimson and gold of the sunset had dyed the west, he had turned himself towards it, and sat for a long time looking out into it, his chin sunk upon his breast. Roland's words recalled him, and he nodded slightly.

"Yes," he said, "that is what I want. I have intended this for a long time. It is my duty, both to Sybil and yourself, to place before you certain facts which must concern you intimately. But it's a long story, not that there need be any mystery about it, but at my age—" the withered lips trembled, and the dim eyes grew more dim—"I want courage; but I am glad, boy, right glad you are here, and it gives me strength to see you both." His hands wandered nervously over the fur rug, plucking at it.

"You must first understand, then," he said, raising himself slightly in the chair with an effort, "that I have thought it wise to keep no records or papers whatever about this matter, for fear of their falling into hands they were not intended for. As certain proofs are necessary I will give you the names of the several places, where they are to be found. But before

I begin—come to me, Sybil. I take this opportunity, my dear, dear ward," and he clasped her
hands in his own, " now that Roland is with
us, of thanking you for all your care of an old
and broken man, who is—" his voice grew
husky with tears. "You can never know,
you never will know," he repeated, and the
words came incoherently. But Sybil had flung
her arms about him.

"Dear Guardy," she began, distressed and
kissing his forehead, " never mind to-night."

It seemed as if he took her word, for his
head sank again upon his breast, and he was
silent, but when she looked, she saw that he
had lost consciousness, and, with a cry, she
strove to raise him up.

"Oh! God, it is a fit!" she cried, " and he
has never had one before."

Over the sunken face had crept a sudden
change, and Roland noted in it consternation, as he sprang to her help. It was the
change that comes but once to the face of
man—the change from life to death. Roland
lifted him, out of the chair and bore him
indoors, into the light, to his bed, and
when he had laid him there, he knew full
well that all was over, that the pallid lips
were, henceforth, as voiceless to him and
his, as any that had closed a thousand
years ago. The conviction flashed across
him, that all clue to what he desired most
to know in this world, was gone. This
thought was uppermost with him, but with
Sybil it was otherwise, and when she realized

her loss, it took all her lover's care to soothe her sorrow.

There ensued a dreadful gap in the full, fair days of June, and into it was packed the ghastliness of a funeral week, such as the Englishman loves to make it. The deceased had left no near relatives, and as, if nothing else in life, he had been squire of the parish, the clergyman, whose views were Calvinistic, laid claim to his remains. Noble revenge! Here was a man who had ignored the parson-hood and its pretensions to his latest breath; but there was no doing so beyond, and the parson did as he would: Sybil distressed but non-resistant, Roland grieving that no happier ritual was possible.

The death had, perforce, driven him from the dower-house; he had gone back to his tower, whence he rode over daily. To both the lovers the week seemed unending, and the very beauty of the sunshine, falling steadily through the long calm days, mocked their trouble. There was an infinity of dis-agreeables, in the arrangements that had to be made. The sorting of the dead man's papers —a painful task, and pitiful always—the read-ing of letters dated more than half a century since—love, friendship, plans, prospects—these things appeal strongly to our common humanity; but although they scanned jealously every line, the faded characters gave no token. They had hoped—against hope; that stray fragment of the past, for which they sought, was blotted out for ever.

There followed a descent of lawyers; better these than the undertakers, better than the Calvinistic parson, yet not the friends one would exactly choose for the hour. They brought no unpleasant tidings; for the bulk of the personality was left to Sybil, and the estate of Sombrewood to Roland, on the single, simple condition, that his engagement of marriage should be carried out. So it appeared secure that Sombrewood and the Isles would again become one, and go down to generations of the rightful blood.

On the vexed point the lawyers could throw no light. The dead man had taken a pleasure in baffling the acuteness of his legal advisers; his secret had been well hedged, of Miss Grey's parentage, and of her claims, the men of law knew nothing.

When the evening came round for Roland's return to town, he walked in as usual un-announced, and after some search discovered Sybil in her oratory, upon her knees, absorbed. He had watched her a minute very sadly, she not knowing, and then he had gone up to her and drawn her gently away.

" You pray too much, my darling," he said; " come out with me into the rose garden, for we have a last half-hour to ourselves."

At this she got up and put her arms about his neck.

" Dear love, I will come with you. Oh! my heart, I have already come, and nearer to you than you have guessed. Henceforth your God shall be my God, and so I shall be with you in all things," she said with inexpressible tenderness, gathering his hand in hers; "and you are to me in the place of guardian, father, mother, and brother—all—short only of my God. Swear it to me now before my altar." And Roland swore, and sealed the oath with a kiss, and took her out into the dusk of the garden.

"How is all this?" he asked at length.

"Oh! for a long time, as you know, Roland, I have been thinking over the tenets of the creeds, and for a long time one only has had a meaning for me. The rest are cruel. Last week, for instance, they would not have me pray for my dead; and then only at last, when my one, my dear old friend was taken, did I realize the necessity of it—then a redoubled conviction stole into my heart. I have waited too long. Oh! what shall I do to atone?

"As to our clergyman," she went on, her manner changing; "we have discussed him enough. At other times I have heard you say he is a good fellow, and takes his glass of port like a man. He it was who came to me as I knelt at the bedside, with *his* hand not yet cold in mine, and told me that so the arm of God was shortened, that my prayer was a mockery, that the tree had fallen and so must lie. And he made it plain exactly how it had fallen—for my poor Guardy was never a church-goer." A smile flitted through her tearful eyes.

"'Henceforth ye are apart; he is helpless; but you, for whom he did so much, shall not

help him. God will not hear you. I suppose
I know, if anybody does, what God will hear
and what He will not, and had he not happened
to be squire of the parish, We'" (God and I, that
is) ' " really could not have allowed him Christian burial.'

" It was too ludicrous; most of this he spoke
in the actual words, in manner he certainly implied it all, and rather more.   1 am quite aware
that ' religious ' people generally do this sort
of thing, but in the Catholic Church, there is
at least a foundation over and above private
impertinence."

" Let these things be, my dearest," answered
Roland, and in his voice was a thrill; " it is
enough for me to know, that now there is
nothing to keep you further from me. I can
think of nothing else," and he led her tenderly
to a bench beneath the trellises, where they
sat silent a time, and the roses breathed in-
toxication.

But here some unnamed, speechless, and un-
tellable sorrow of soul again came over her,
and she clung closer to him, resting her head
upon his shoulder, her eyes fixed upon the
constellations, away where they burned in the
zenith—upon the shining sickle of the moon
mowing slowly through the cloud-fields over-
spread; and all the while she took his hand and
twisted the fingers in and out of her own, like a
woman half distraught.

" Astronomy and religion are near akin," she
said at last, " and I have read them together;
the one is the context of the other.   Can any-

thing tell the meaning of religion like the
heavens themselves, or, for that matter, the
earth, which is a part of them, for all its awful
story of travail? Man gropes about it dreaming of nothing else, as though Infinity were not
stretched above his head, and visible to his
eyes if he would only turn them.

"Roland, you have thought of these things,
you first drew my mind to them. You it
was who first brought me to realize what it
was to live, and the mystery of it. And I
have read lately, that the life-period of mother
earth runs away into millions of years on either
hand, into the past, and into the future, so that
you and I stand on the verge between. I like
to think of it all—how the earth lay smiling
before God, and the suns rose and set for æons;
and the great cities and the landmarks of history were not there, but only their places
waiting, waiting, while man, the master that
was to be, was not, or wandered a beast in the
forest, or a fish in the sea; and how, when
the tale of life is told, the dead world shall still
roll in her path through the unchanging years
—an awful corpse with an awful history. Oh!
it is wonderful, and what is the unit *I* in the
face of it? If this is the scale of things, what
is the little fact of one's existence? My own
has seemed shrivelled to a point already past.

"Did you ever try and realize the proportion
of the children's time, compared with that of
the mother that bore them? I have thought
it out, taking seconds as years, to bring some
notion of it to my mind. If the length of the

time, through which life will endure upon the
earth, be put at three hundred million years
altogether (I take a guess from my last book) ;
three hundred million seconds being a little
under ten years, then the proportion of the
longest human life (say, a hundred years) to
this, will be a hundred seconds—not quite two
minutes ; but even in two minutes think of
the good you may do if you are awake to it.
You may give alms, you may pray prayers,
you may make sacrifice, you may see great
things too—the rise of the sun, the bursting
of a storm, the stroke of the lightning. So in
man's little time may be events that are finger-
posts through all history. Oh ! Roland, you
are smiling at me, but my dearest, dearest boy,
can you not see where all this leads, and that
it is a time of tears ? "

She broke down into weeping. Then, as
though she took herself sternly to task, she
went on,—

" This last week, and all that has happened,
has led me deeper into these things. The wonderful tale of human life is brought home to
me. I see the ceaseless crowds hurrying on,
each there, going, as he thinks his own way,
but in reality trampling the one great high-
road smoother for posterity, whether he will or
no. But if there is a something beyond the
mere journeying, if the Good Giver of this gift
of life will accept it for His purpose, if so
great a privilege is attached to such a trifle,
who would hesitate ? Oh ! Roland, this self-
rendering is the law for all things. Do the

trees and the rocks speak to you, I wonder, as they do to me? Shall I show you a living creature chanting its canticle of praise? Do you see that great plane-tree where it stands alone, the stately wave of its dusk-lit branches, the sweep in cadence of its limbs, the play of every leaf, the harmony of its breathing life? It is a thing complete, fulfilling its end, and manifesting its Creator. Nor do I doubt but that the smith at his forge, the cobbler at his last, doing his honest day's labour, or I will say the dog following his master, is manifesting his Maker, even as the angels, clothed in white garments, and with palms in their hands, chanting eternal canticles.

"It is a pity that that last idea has taken root, literally. An Eternity of Psalm-singing! Foolishness prides itself on being literal I have noticed. These parables are for interpretation: the eternal canticles are the strivings and labourings of the creature, towards the Creator, for ever and ever. In this poor world they may take a humble form, as in a higher they will have a nobler, but they are one and the same thing."

And to Roland, as he listened, she seemed inspired. She had drawn apart, and lay back against the rough boughs of the rustic bench; in her eyes was a look of trance, her tears had ceased to flow, and in her face was a transfiguration. Although her neck and heaving breast shone marble-white in the moonlight, the southern blood mantled to life in her fair cheek and full red lips; and in the lightless depths of her black draperies, the fair lines of her fair body were not hid. A chosen child of Nature this, one who would measure things by Her standards—not by those of puny man ; one to whom, in all Her workings, She breathed the romance of eternal truths, while the days flitted by like shadows.

A long time her lover gazed upon her with an almost despairing hunger in his eyes. As she lay reclined before him she appealed to all his manhood, and he noted well the unconscious charms, so slighted by their possessor : the bow of the springing instep, half turned aside, the tapering limbs, the white, light-resting hand, where the fingers curving back, lay against the trellis. He counted it all, and turned a moment aside, that she might not see his face.

His soul, too, was full of an undefined trouble. Had she been fair with him ? Through these long years he had waited on. Surely it was hardly fair upon him, if he considered coldly. Yet to what height had she risen meantime ! No, he would not have her less. Controlling his thoughts, he took her to his heart and whispered,—

" You were always a dreamer of poems, my darling, but the reality is here. Remember that the problem of your life is solved, at least. You and it, are now for my keeping," and there was exultation in his voice.

" That is so," she assented, and murmured to herself, " And by so much, it will be the more to give," and she was quiet a little while, lying in a trance of happiness upon his breast. Then she sprang up again, excitedly.

"Promise me, Roland," she cried, "in this solemn night, before these solemn witnesses, in the face of heaven and earth, that whatever comes, whatever is in store for us—and I fear everything—you will be no less to me. Man and woman do not love as we have done for nought."

She sat up like a mad thing, her grasp tightened upon his wrist, but her hand was cold as ice, her face blanched, so that it shone out white in the night. Then, desperately, she plunged her fair, bared arm among the roses overhead, and plucking a blossom she kissed it passionately and pressed it into his bosom. But her lover, alarmed, and not knowing well what to do, took her to himself, and, lifting her in his arms, bore her through the garden and into the house.

There, seeing she was calmer, he resolved that he had best be gone, and so allowing and speaking no further word, but kissing her again and again, he went out alone into the night, and away. When, some hours after, the old housekeeper went to her mistress, she found her kneeling in dishevelment upon the floor, her face turned in tearful agony to the Madonna and her Child. The poor girl was stricken with a dumb sorrow, she spoke scarcely at all, and was stiffened with long prayer and watching, but she suffered herself to be led quietly from the room.

And when Roland, already afar off, took the

rose from his breast and looked upon it, lo! it
was one old, and long dead and dried, which she
had plucked in the darkness; it was wet with
blood, and salt with tears, but the sweet scent
of it clung still.

*   *   *   *   *   *

The season that year was a late one, a celebrated French lady, an actress (there is hardly
the same sweetness in another name to which
she was equally entitled), had come upon the
Town at the last moment, and, taking it by
storm, she made herself so pleasant in high
quarters, that high quarters stayed and stayed.
Of course there was no going away for low
ones, who enjoyed the hot, dusty August
weather immensely in consequence.   " Odd,"
observed the moralists, " this spectacle of a
city held in chains," but these were curious
times, be it repeated.

Towards the close of the summer Miss Grey
came to Town, and took a suite of rooms at a
private hotel, where she kept up a certain state
which surprised her friends, who had, one and
all, fancied that her tastes lay rather in the
opposite direction. A carriage, horses, and men,
of what seemed, even to Roland, of unnecessary
size and splendour, were the first outward signs
of this new order of things.

Be sure that the world knew all about Miss
Grey, and talked in plenty; her recent 'version
and the death of her guardian, having given the
subject a new spurt.   The uncertainty, too,
that hung about her birth had leaked out, and
with other matters, was made the subject of

various printed paragraphs, in the eccentric taste of the day, and these were venomous, satirical, or patronizing, as the case might be. Even Roland did not escape; reference was made to the unconscionable time during which, without fee or reward, he had worn the fetters of the stony-hearted beauty, and he was vastly commiserated. The custom of shooting editors had not, as yet, crossed the Channel, otherwise undoubtedly one or two would have stumbled in their literary careers about this time. The big carriage became a well-known feature, but, as a lady of rank remarked (be sure, anonymously, and in print), ' it was curious that, although it bowled steadily through the park, day after day, at the appointed hour, rarely indeed could any glimpse be caught of Miss Grey herself—but then it was a close carriage, such a very close carriage, and such a big one for a single lady, and no doubt Miss Grey was busy with her grief on the back cushions.'

There was something in this; the fact was, that while Miss Grey thus projected a simulacrum of herself on the public "retina," her bodily presence was far away, and was to be found in the strangest places, in tramcars, in omnibuses, in slums, and in unsweet districts of which you and I, reader, do not happily, know even the names. She had endured enough persecution in days past, and knew that whatever came, she must be talked about; consequently the carriage and its tremendous appurtenances were set up as a butt, and admirably they served their purpose.

The arrangement was a simple one: she went out in state, and was dropped at a large shop of many entrances, where the carriage called for her some hours later. It would have been difficult to follow her, but there were colonies of nuns living in gloomy convents of smoke-begrimed brick, standing apart in the back-ways of the ten cities of the Thames, who could tell something of her comings in and goings out. And there were other colonies, of which the greater part consisted of dreadful children and still more dreadful elders, where life was one long struggle for bare subsistence, even with the sisters themselves, from morning till night, that could tell more. Many such nur-series had Miss Grey, painstakingly, unearthed; she had started this work years before, when she had first made friends with the "little sister," and was now an old hand at it, but it was a secret work, and even Roland knew nothing of it. To more than one tottering mission she had come as a veritable good angel, and it would be little to say that the sisters worshipped her and the ground she trod on.

Her own name served her very well, she was nobody in particular—this she always in-sisted—and she lived anywhere; but by good fortune she happened to have a number of rich friends, and it was wonderful (miraculous, the good nuns said) how these generous friends would give and give, and give again to their wants—people who could know nothing of them, except through Miss Grey, which proved the confidence and esteem in which she must be generally held. But so terrible a thing is it to commence deceit, that the real donor soon found herself in difficulties, and driven to questionable measures to keep her secret; and gradually a list of fictitious benefactors grew up, for whom the nuns and their poor children and their dirty old men and women prayed night and day. No names were on the list, it is true, but such headings as "A Friend," "An Orphan," "A Well-wisher," "A Convert," "A Lady," "A Soul in Need," made a gallant host in themselves, and many of them being of neutral sex disarmed suspicion; there was no need for more.

Then, too, Miss Grey was so useful, for she would play the organ (usually a harmonium) at Benediction, when often the little congregation would fall to crying as though they would break their hearts; and she would teach the choir, a task of no light labour with the waifs and strays, of whom it was composed. Ever since she had learned to think, the cry of the children of the Great City had rung in her ears. Her whole heart delighted in this service, and went out to the poor little sisters valiantly grappling with heavy odds, in their woman's work of light and mercy, and she came almost to live among her poor.

Had Roland been less occupied with public affairs than he was, he must have been made to feel that there was a difference between now and heretofore, and one not in his favour. As it was, he did not fail to notice her first fervour, and perhaps rather underrated it as such, a thing that would pass away. They could meet but seldom, but when they did, there was nothing of which he could complain; and when he left, though he little guessed it, she would be often prostrated with emotion, and spend hours before her crucifix.

He was growing impatient, but when he would urge that there could be no reason for delay, she would instantly invent a dozen. She would point to Mrs. Brabant, for she had gleaned something of that lady's history, and would ask if that was not warning enough for him; or she would declare, that until all the woman was worked out, none of the sex were of any use or good at all, where a man was concerned, and that she still felt a terrible preponderance of the old Eve. The sexes, she said, in this world stood in natural opposition, and the account at the last day would not be between man and man, but between man and woman. And so she passed from grave to gay, but always with the same purpose.

At last Roland desisted, and went away almost with anger at heart. The old Eve, as she had said, was still there, and this trifling proved it; he found in her an inconsistency, of which there had never been any shadow before, and this was the promise of a bitter pill. What really true woman would turn to weeping, often at the mere sight of him, and yet would so dally with his dearest hopes? Something must be wrong, and there were times when his anxiety overwhelmed him.

He traced back the days of their love, and

remembered how, in the beginning, dreams and fancies had come upon them, and strange events like portents, which, in the joy of his youth, he had laughed to scorn. Their engagement had lasted so long, and their union meanwhile had been so close, that sometimes he felt that they had lived their time together and that it was a thing passed and accomplished. When he realized that for the present, there was no making any headway with her, on the breaking-up of the House he went abroad and took a run through Europe.

For distraction's sake he put in his pocket two campaigns, one of Hannibal's, one of Napoleon's, which embraced a certain tract of country. These he worked out, bit by bit, with a satisfactory minuteness, following the footsteps of the generals on horseback, and arriving at the conclusion that the man of modern times had outstripped him of the old.

It so happened that while he was thus engaged, actual fighting cropped up in an odd corner of the Continent, and thither he turned his steps with all speed. But his mind was unhinged, he could settle to nothing, and one day, soon after he reached the theatre of war, even as he was setting out to view an expected action, he received a letter from Sybil, written in the tenderest terms ever read by lover, but in a vein of almost despair, altogether unexpected. Instantly everything else was forgotten, and though he went on and into action, which he could hardly help, he turned his back upon the field before the day was half over, and while its fortunes still hung in the balance. There was little interest for him in either side, the affair was a puny one ; two armed mobs were scrambling for, an in any case, unworkmanlike victory. He rode out of the business disgusted, and decided, on the strength of the letter, that he would turn his steps homewards at once.

He pushed on with impatience, unable to think of anything else; his life was reduced to an inanity, an empty, idle thing, until such time as he could secure her for himself. Apart from the unique charm which he had ever found in her person, lay the extraordinary range of her mind, which reacted scarcely less powerfully upon his own. It was not that her beauty was of a type which years but ripen, it was the combination with this, of purity, strength, and world-knowledge of the noblest kind, which had worked the spell upon him, and would keep it riveted to the end. Man is incomplete alone; with such a woman at his side, any position that he might conquer must be enhanced ten-fold. He had waited more than seven years, but no patience of Jacob was granted him for another seven ; and from her letter, though it was enigmatic as she herself of late, he gathered something final.

He was stopped on the wrong side of the Channel by the weather, for with this middle of November, the winter seemed to have set in with the greatest severity. Here and there even the railroads were blocked with snow. The few hours that he was kept were en-livened by a brother M.P., a Mr. De la Rue,

who appeared to be remarkably glad to meet
him. This gentleman in himself, constituted a
living temple of the echoes, and was a veritable
epitome of the whispers of the pavement. From
him he learned, on the most undoubted authority, that a change, of the greatest importance to
himself, was in the wind. The Cardinal Archbishop of Pimlico, whose health had for a long
time kept him from active work, was about to
retire, and a certain high-born prelate of fifty,
had been nominated for his place. This
was going a little too fast, but the rumours
were serious enough to Roland. Should it come
to pass, he saw nothing less than the break-up
of his party. He was well aware that if it did,
the man indicated being one who loved power
for its own sake, would never let any of the
reins out of his hands, whether he could drive,
or whether he could not. He was further aware
that this man would be backed by the entire
Catholic " aristocratic " party, whose one idea
was to get trouble and responsibility off their
own hands, and who did not grudge paying
handsomely for the boon ; and that the whole
thing was what he had foreseen the possibility of
long since—a mere Government job, as entirely
as if the appointment had been to Canterbury.
However, with these reflections on the horizon
he thought better to pooh-pooh the notion, and
Mr. De la Rue, finding there was nothing to be
got out of this, changed the subject.

" Saw you breakfasted in Downing Street
before you left town."

" I did; there is much I admire and like in

Lord X—; personally, I have always found him most friendly."

"Perhaps I ought not to mention it, but I'm afraid the baronetcy leaked out. Ha! ha!" and Mr. De la Rue blew a cloud of smoke, under cover of which he directed a keen glance at his hearer.

"Indeed! what baronetcy? It has not leaked in my direction."

"How very good. I see, you don't consider it public property. I always told them they'd have to do it. You're a moderate man, you see, after all; the difference between the Government, and you and your party, is merely one of principle."

"Exactly" (rather drily). "I know nothing, —nothing of the matter."

"Oh!" (much interested) "is that so? Well, I think you were right, 'pon my soul, perfectly right in refusing it. No doubt you see it as I do myself. If you can hold on in your place another ten or fifteen years, they're bound to make it a peerage—bound, sir. Why, look at the thundering duffers" (it was not often Mr. De la Rue spoke so plainly) "they've had to pick out of your people, when they wanted peers from time to time. Not a public man among 'em, hardly a soul outside their own flunkeys knows their names; you're safe—safe as a house, sir. You're a city built upon a mountain, you *can't* be hid."

"Do you think so?" asked Roland, not without some enjoyment of the situation. "Do you really think so?"

" Perfectly—that is if the money is," and here again Mr. De la Rue looked curiously at his brother senator.

Were reports of another sort already about ? Was the world perfectly acquainted with a fact of which he, whom it most concerned, was ignorant ? One of the most irritating points about Mr. De la Rue was, that when he said one thing, he invariably implied half a dozen others—what did he mean now ?

Roland hardly took time to consider, nor did he question him ; the man and his impertinences were beneath notice. Had they not been caught in this storm, he certainly would not have opened conversation with him ; and after hinting that it was very unlikely that he should accept any such offer, even if it were made, he got away and pushed on to London.

He was not in a frame of mind for any subject but one, but with all his eagerness he was unable to reach Sombrewood next day, and was forced to stay his journey and sleep at the tumble-down inn, which was the best hotel in the quaint old City of the Sandhills.

With the morning he remembered that the day was St. Cæcilia's, and the legend came upon him with a secret joy, as a thing of good omen, for the virgin saint ever called up to him the image of his beloved, whom in a few hours he would clasp, never to let her go more. He would bring back the past to-day, he would go to her as he had done in the days when he was but a boy ; and he took the best horse that he could find in the stables of the old posting-house, (for here came no railways,) and setting his face westward he galloped over the light new-fallen snow many bright miles, the whole country-side glistening in the brilliant illumination of the sun.

The leaves were only half fallen yet, but turned by the sudden frost, they gleamed red and russet with scarlet berries against the snow. The day was perfectly still, save for the loud twittering of the birds. The fiery Virginian creeper hung its long strings, motionless from the tiled roofs of the cottages as he passed, and the pale blue smoke of the wood-fires curled like a peaceful incense into the skies.

Never had he felt younger, never more light of heart, as from afar, through the sun-haze, he discerned the giant boles of wood that guarded the domain on the land side, saw the deep blue line lift over the whitened hollows, breathed the fresh breath of the sea, and listened to it, murmurous in the distance. Never seemed earth more beautiful; as he entered the woods his horse's hoofs struck on a golden floor, the long aisles were canopied with a golden roof; and through it and into it, the sun poured indescribable burnishings and glistenings on the hoar and rime of the leaves, and light and shadow swept and trembled over the face of the forest, in a wonderful enchantment. These were the joys of the blessed! What mattered it that spring and summer were gone, and winter was at hand ?—that even now the storm clouds were banking over the haven ?

When he reached the shrubberies, he walked

his horse, drinking in the scene; and he went noiselessly, for the snow had drifted in the paths; there came a strain of music, and he knew again the tuneful pipes of the old Gothic organ. The chant swelled and fell through the sylvan silences, with no words, but with tears in the burden of the song, and it smote him. "This shall not be," he muttered; "she shall weep no more, I will change that note to one of enduring joy." He led his horse to the stable and went forward afoot towards the house, his nerves strung to a painful acuteness. Little things struck and impressed his mind curiously, the tiny track of a bird's feet, the falling of a twig, of a leaf even, the red crest of a pointsettia which the frost had killed, and which drooped upon the snowy coverlet like fierce drops of crimson blood; he noted them and remembered them ever after.

The long window stood, as usual, half opened to the sun; one print of the light foot he knew so well lay pressed there, and, a little turned, it caught the light and sparkled as though an angel had lighted there and passed in.

He flung the casement wide, stepped through, and stood before her. His sudden presence seemed to have turned her to stone.

CHAPTER VII.

SYBIL was standing, leaning her forehead against the quaint carving of the old organ, her slender fingers wandering listlessly over the yellow time-stained keys ; and, as it often happened with her, her thoughts had flown, with her music, to other spheres than this, and she had fallen into a reverie which heeded no interruption.

But here came one who had the right to summon her from her dreams ; and he did so, calling her by that favourite name, which he had used when he first saw her at the instrument in the bygone years—" Cæcilia." And, indeed, she had been but a moment since with that dear saint in heaven, and the tear that rested on her cheek had welled up as, for the thousandth time, she had told her patroness her troubles, and had implored her intercession.

Slowly, she seemed to struggle back to the things of life ; but if this were life, death almost were preferable. The man's heart stood still with a quick spasm and stopped, arrested in its beat, as he witnessed the look of agony that gathered on her face, when her eyes fell upon him.

" Was this their way of meeting at last? Were

they not lovers, and true—ever true—and long
tried beyond all others? What could this
mean?" he asked himself passionately. But
even before she spoke, he knew by intuition;
knew that the mute face of pain, which yet had
lost no tenderness for him, meant nothing else
than that the end was come between them.
That henceforth, through all the long days and
the nights, neither should be any more to the
other than a memory, and a memory of grief
as for the one most dear who is lost—that
henceforth for they two should be no more in
each other council or guidance, love or hope, or
toil onward hand in hand. *This was the end.*

How it was that this flashed upon him, as he
stood gazing at her with eyes incredulous, it
would be difficult to explain, but it did. Hope
took flight utterly. She was not moulded as
many women, this he knew; and that under
all the gentle graces of her nature lay a will of
iron inflexible, so that even he should never
bend it. Pitiful but unflinching, her soft eyes
dealt the stroke; he read his fate in her look;
and as the strong man realized this—he whom
so far no toil or pain had moved—he reeled back
into a chair like one struck, and covered his
face. The sight restored her self-possession.

"Oh! my dearest one," she cried, kneeling
down at his side and raining tears and kisses
upon his hand, "now you are come, forgive me.
'Oh! Valerian, I have a secret to tell thee.'"[1]

[1] St. Cæcilia's words, commemorated in the mass of the
day. The legend will be found in "The Lives of the
Saints."

Then he knew. She was for God, not for him, and he did not answer.

"Ah! dearest," she cried, "you first taught me Cæcilia's story; and you know how, when she told her lover, loving her no less, he gave her to be the spouse of Christ in martyrdom. I would be humble, and not speak of myself with her; but, Roland, this thing has come to me in a like way. You will understand. Oh! my heart, the angel that has been sent to me, is to call me from your side and to martyrdom. Oh! yes, no less. I do not pretend it; and I would it were to the wild beasts, for that would be quick and soon; but this is for our whole lives."

Then Roland put away his hand from his face; but speak he could not, though he would have done so, and his look pierced her heart as with a thousand daggers.

"My soul, my life!" she cried, clinging to the brave and kindly hand that was so much to her, "do you think I love you less because my King calls me away from you, and I live; and shall I not go cheerfully? What do I care, except for this one thing, that you suffer? Oh! it is frightful to have to tell you this, and indeed, indeed I have seen it coming through months and years, but I could not tell how it would be, or how to avert the pain of it. And now there is no help, and it is here.

"Roland, sun and soul of life!" she sobbed, wringing her hands, "speak to me—or where is your faith now? You it is who have led me to the Holy Mount, and you—you know it—lit the sacred fires. You will not grudge the Heavenly Bridegroom so little a thing as this poor bride, who will so love you a thousand times more, and will be more to you through the eternities." She stopped and measured him a space—his goodliness and his strength. A shiver shook her, and she turned to the wan wasted figure, the bowed form upon her crucifix. " Oh! my true, dear lover," she cried, "there is happiness for you—for me—in this world even, and because of each other, if you will promise that you will do no less than this."

But he was silent.

" Oh! my love, have I failed you once through these years?" she gasped pitifully, writhing at his feet. " Say something to me, if it is only to curse me for the curse I have wrought you, or I think I shall die now. I cannot bear that you should look so at me. Oh! Roland, have pity, have pity on me, at least you. A woman's strength is no great thing, and mine has withered away because I should have to tell you this. God help us! "

Alas! for the weak frame rent with emotions. She had fought hard not to give way, but the multitude of thoughts and empty words crowded in, and beat upon her brain like hot hammers, until they drove her mad.

But did the stronger suffer less? He sat as if he could not stir; an ashen hue had crept over his face; the fire of his strong eyes was extinguished. Happy it was for him that, for the minute, his thoughts overmastered outward things; he did not see all her struggle.

How long had he feared he knew not what?—
and now it had taken shape and form in this.

The stroke had been so unexpected, so instantaneous, that there was no coherency in his
thoughts ; but some kindly instinct moved at his
heart, he put out his hand to her, and ran it
tenderly through the massed hair on her forehead, and a balm that was intolerable almost in
its bliss, was poured upon the stricken soul.

He would not then kill her, for to her deli-
rium that stern, set face of his had looked like
the impersonation of death. He was feeling
something for her, was beginning to interpret
her aright. Perhaps ages hence, in the millions
of eternity, he might be led to forgive her " sin "
to him. So the poor brain wandered.

Then at once, and with no warning, he lifted
her in his arms on to his bosom, and whispered,—

" Nay, sweetheart, it is you who are cruel, not
I. But if this is our good-bye, you are still
not less to me, or our love would be a small
thing."

Ah! the pang of joy that shot to her heart
as her ears drank in the words, and she felt his
arms around her, and his kiss. Then in the
mad whirl and questioning of her brain, she
asked herself, doubting, was this her lover's
voice, these hoarse and low accents, this horrible
whisper of renunciation? Even though she
had prayed for it above all things, it was not
like him; the voice was laboured and painful
and harsh, not firm and gentle, as through the
long years of their loving it had ever been ; and
she drew herself up from him a little apart and

looked into his face. No doubt, no doubt the face was his, but it was dreadful to her, for it was changed from all she had ever known it. And *she* had done this, with her own hand she had plucked from him, and destroyed the core of his existence, the best part of his life was even now dead; love, happiness, and all the brightness of it, were blotted out, and even now passing from him like shadows into eternity. No more would he touch any one of these, and through *her*. With some intuition of this, and of the sacrifice of himself which was spoken in his last words, her senses quivered, grasping it a moment; she threw up her arms and fell senseless, like a stone, upon his heart.

This recalled him to himself and to the needs of the minute. He stood up and bore her to the sofa, and, as he laid her tenderly upon it, the matchless grace of her face and form appealed to him most cruelly. Long prayer, long watching, long trouble had written no record there, save in a spiritual delicacy. No line was upon the pale brow, which was of wax, under the waved ripples of her hair. Only deep dark circles lay under the sweeping fringe of her eyelids, which were wetted with her tears; the luminous light hands lay crossed upon her bosom, the lithe limbs at rest.

So she lay at peace, and in her he saw before him once more, the fair child of his boyhood unchanged, as she had lain fainting on the hillside, thrown from her horse. The sight stirred him to the depths, he bent over her and listened for the beating of her heart. She lived. Yes, but not for him, for toil and privation and struggle, to tread the thorniest paths *alone.* Was this right for that tender frame and tenderer spirit, which cried mutely, and appealed to all beautiful and tender things, that the way should be made smooth for feet so fragile. How could they climb by these rough roads, how should this frail frame do a deed of strength that the strongest of earth might shrink from?

Perhaps even now, by his love and his strength, he might snatch her away. He had *the right;* but as he looked, he could not, and to kill the temptation that came over him he paced to and fro, turning his face from her and clenching his hands, as he repeated, "No, I cannot fail her now; I will not fail her now." What was faith, if at such a moment it did not stay with him? What was manhood, if a woman should overmaster him in courage? And as he dared to look again, he marvelled at this weak thing chosen to confound the strong, and he would call no help; himself he waited to tend upon her, and he touched her as a sacred thing already vowed away to God.

And as he waited, he began to read his life backwards, as a man may do if he will, and he saw how all had come logically and strictly out of its antecedent, and how, if he had had eyes to see, he might have discerned this a long time since. For he had never doubted from the first that she, even though she were without any but a natural religion, was a high and holy thing, whom he had striven to make his own,

and to bind to himself and to earth with chains
of flowers. And should he blame her now, that
her spirit yearned back to its natural sphere,
and that she would at all costs leave him, to be
one of that chosen band of virgins whom the
Church in all ages has held up to honour?

He was not what is called a pietist; but to
be a Catholic, meant more than mere profession. He had realized as man or woman outside
the Church never *can* realize, the meaning of
the word "vocation." He knew that with
those to whom it comes, is neither pro nor con,
nor harking backward on the path; that it is
no exaggerated egotism that moves them, but an
overmastering spiritual necessity, even such as
compelled the Apostles of old, when " leaving all
things" they followed Christ. He was a profound
believer in mysteries beyond the illumination
of the altar candle. The religion of the multitude was a childish thing, sufficient perhaps, and
all they were capable of. But he knew that in
the Church were many high and holy souls who
penetrated these forms, these arcana and symbols, and faced the essential truths unveiled. Of
such was the great muster-roll of the saints,
and he had ever felt that prayer, sacrifice, and
well-doing must needs find their full equivalent,
and declare their full meaning, in the ethics of
life.

So long back in the past had this struggling human soul, which now beat imprisoned in the hollow of his hand, been bound
with his own, that when he looked back

upon their two lives they seemed as one, and a shadowy hope crossed him, that even this should not mean dissociation. Despite all difficulties of belief, his spiritual life had been from the first wrapped up in hers, and she, who had then become his true Psyche, might yet live apart this highest life, in a mystical union with him, though all earthly connection were severed between them, could he but overcome the baser nature, which clung so hardly and so sore to her bodily presence, and give her up, a free gift, as she had said. So might he earn his share in the sublimity of her sacrifice.

The shock of this debate within himself was such that, for the moment, faith and reason reeled, but he triumphed. He was, as St. Maur had said, idealist to the heights, materialist to the depths, and in this rare combination lay the strength that carried him through.

He would have been less than man, could he have stood there over his stricken love, in this supreme moment of her self-abnegation, and felt any reproach. As he stood and looked upon her; in the glamour of her virginal grace, in the grave, serene loveliness of the upcast face, he saw not her outer self only, fair though the casket were, but the reflex and expression of that inward beauty so laboriously and toilfully wrought out, until the hour was come to place the crown upon the work.

The crisis of two lives was past.

When consciousness crept back to her, her

eyes opening rested on her lover's bent over her kindly and strong as of old; the storm had gone out of them, her hand lay in his, he was not angry then. Ah! she might have known it, and that he would not be less than the noble lover in the story of her patroness. But had she counted aright, and reckoned all the bitterness?

The joy of this awakening lay in this, that *he* was there. Henceforth, when her soul was darkened, her spirit faint, and her body wearied, he whom she loved would not be there to lift her with his arm; her hand must clasp the air, her eyes look into nothingness. Were there no limits to human pain? She turned her face to the wall, and sometime she communed with herself, praying, even as her Master, "that this chalice might pass away." And it came to her that had the sacrifice been less, it would have been less worthy to lay upon the altar; and she saw the wondrous heights of the spiritual life shining before her, the eternal hills set in a mystical radiance, and she knew that once this worse than bitterness of death were passed, there was nothing to which she might not aspire.

How to tell her lover? This she had questioned with herself day and night, and with yearnings inexpressible to save him the blow. Now it was done—no other earthly tie bound her, she could make light of all else. Now she could go forth joyous, and undaunted to her martyrdom, crying thanks be to God, like her dear patroness. But for him, and the misery she had caused him, she was nigh broken-hearted; and his look, when she had told him, had pierced her very soul—a memory of fresh pain for all time.

Yet such was her thirst after perfection that she would have no less than his sacrifice as well as her own, and it should be a perfect offering, that they should, in their last act together, lay jointly before Heaven. He had promised this, and now she could rise and talk with him of it, as a matter settled. She gathered her forces and sat up, but the effort turned her giddy, and she sank back again into his arms.

" Sybil, Sybil, my poor child," whispered Roland, " be a little merciful to yourself, for my sake. I will bear all. I will do all that you ask, but tell me first how it has come to this, my dearest ; you cannot be afraid to tell me anything."

Then the woman in her overcame the spirit, she buried her head in his breast and sobbed,—

" How can I explain the searchings of my heart, dear ? It has been inevitable ; through a long pilgrimage I have been brought to the Faith and the Church, to the God of my desire. How can I repay this? It seems to me that the mind that once grasps the idea of a God must at once hasten to yield Him everything, even the most precious. And oh ! Roland, I have something that is very dear to me, one thing, only one, that I have treasured, over and

above all, to my heart for years, you know it ;
and I am young still, and I have most of the
good things of this world, and all these are
at their best now at this minute, and now at
this minute I have the power—the privilege!—of laying them all upon His altars,
and, oh, God!" (she had fallen into prayer, and
was unconsciously clasping her hands), "Thou
art so great, so pitiful of us, that Thou wilt not
turn Thy face from this little gift, this poor life
and this poor love," and she threw her arm
round Roland's neck.

"You would go into religion, then, at once,
my darling, is this so?" he asked.

For reply she kissed him, and it seemed as if
she could not keep her arms from his neck, they
were round it again, and she kissed his lips as
if she would die of them; and when he, sore
moved, laid her back a little space on the
cushions, she would not let him go, but drew
him downward and whispered,—

"Oh, my true love, do not think too ill of
me, or that I am seeking only the welfare of
one wretched, selfish soul. For you, I would walk
into hell itself with my eyes open ; but do not
doubt me, dearest—I go, because I *must*. I am
called, and I cannot turn back. These things
are realities for me beyond all else, and I will
ask you one last thing. Will you yourself
give me this day to God, a free gift, and promise me here and now, that you will never look
back?"

"Dear heart," said Roland, soothing her,

" have I ever wished anything but was for your happiness, have I deserved that you should doubt me ? "

" No, you have not deserved it," she cried, " but I, too, do not think that I have forgotten yours. I have studied it always, you will grant me so much, and I *know* that this is the best for you Oh ! I know better than you —I know full well. Your ambitions would have given you no rest ; and even now, because you have failed in many things, you are only spurred to greater—we could never travel together. But though I shall be where I shall never hear your name, or know at all of what passes in the outer world, there is no real severance for us two, dear."

Her wild wide eyes blazed under his as with a supernatural fire. " Where thou goest, I will go. Do you remember, how our spirits clung together in those first fresh days ? Are we less to each other now after so many, many years ? I have drawn sustenance so long from you that I cannot conceive bodily existence for myself in a world where you are not. If you were dead, I could not live. Oh, my true love, I would make haste to follow you ! If you will wait for me a little while, I will not fail to come ; if you will call me to you, oh, then I will not delay.

" And now, Roland, my heart, my soul,—God give me words to ask it you !—will you go away from me now, at once and for all ? " She sank back and covered her face. " Kiss me once again, so you will bless me, and go."

" But, sweetheart, must it be *now ?* " stammered her lover. " I cannot leave you so—we have had so little time together, to settle this, I have heard nothing of your plans."

" I have arranged with the lawyers, and I go to Lady Thomond for a week—I have told her—she will help me to wind up things."

" And I—what am I to do ? "

" You can do nothing now," she said, casting herself upon her knees, " but pray for me ; nothing, nothing. Oh, Roland, do you wish to break me down utterly? Surely you will not stay to see my suffering ? " she rocked herself to and fro, and the anguish of her tones smote him to the heart.

" But, my own dear girl," he said in a broken voice, as he clasped and raised her, " am I to go away from you now, at once, and *for ever ?* "

" Oh, God, no ! " she cried passionately, disengaging herself from him, " for ever ? What faith have you, what constancy, what hope, if you say this ? For ever ? no ! for a few wretched pitiful years, count them in minutes, in seconds, if you like—they are nothing—and after them I am yours, your servant ; your handmaiden for ever, if you will it."

" We know nothing of the relations of the next life," muttered he huskily, " and how can I leave you thus, so weak, so ill, so changed ? I cannot ! "

" Now I will show you," she said, her naturally quiet manner returning, " I have a strength given me which is not my own." She rose and stood before him, beautiful, but cold as any statue.

"What weakness do you see now?" and holding her hands, he knew that her pulses beat slow and firm with the steady flow of health.

"Is there no help?" he asked, his own heart failing. "Is this indeed the end?"

"Nay, dear, there is no help. It has come to the last. We must meet no more; hearts were never strung to this. Dear God, have pity on us! Good-bye! Good-bye!"

He never saw her again.

Mechanically he stumbled into the shrubbery, and to the stable where his horse waited with drooped neck, as though no sore issue of human life were passed meantime. The sun was gone, a winter storm was blowing up from the sea, the leaden skies were overcast, and the fast-drifting snow had turned the day to twilight. His shortest way "home" (name henceforth of ill-omen!) lay through the gardens, and, spurring forward, he took it once more.

Torture, torture, everywhere. A sombre light filled earth and sky, the rushing winds shrieked through the gaunt skeletons of the trees, and rang in the trellises, through the matted framework of dead tendrils as he passed swiftly by the rose garden. Were those living things bending, fighting, cowering in the blast, and these voices that spoke broken sentences in his ears, were they within him, or had he summoned unwittingly ten thousand mocking witnesses?

"Thou hunter after happiness, thou hast had thy fill, now there are husks for thee! Thou wouldst find a heaven, and lo! hell is here waiting for thee. Ha! ha! what wilt thou do now? Thy work is done. Best lay thy bones to rot with thy forefathers yonder in the old charnel-house."

It was as if a thronging host of living beings of whom his spirit was in some way conscious, fled with him through the gardens, stopping him involuntarily now and again. "Here she kissed thee first. Ha! ha! There she lay upon thy breast. Here she promised she would be thine always. Ha! fool, go thy way, now it is over. She would be a saint instead. Ha! ha! and thou art a sinner, and no fit bridegroom, ha! ha!"

Good God, what were these voices in his ears? He pulled up, his horse stood trembling in a sweat, jerking the foam from its bit, and he looked round. Bah! his sorrow had unmanned him. The wind came in furious gusts, and the trees were bending in a witches' dance over his head, waving crooked gaunt arms to the inky heavens. That was all; but surely this was a tale that had been told, and he had played his part in it as now, ages—ages since, and he remembered every jot and tittle of it.

A feeling almost of panic overcame him, and he galloped desperately on through the drenching woods and over the hills, reckless of the storm, the voices still ringing in his head, but incoherent and dying away, little by little, as he went. Meantime his mind was made up. He would never set foot on his hearthstone more. Nay, he would never look upon the old home of his race again. He who had lifted it out of the dust—ah! this was bitter too. And when he reached the gates, he stayed his horse there, and waited while he sent for his foreman to come out to him. Unheeding the driving sleet, he paced to and fro, and all the while the mouldering mottoes mocked him from the carven pillars, " WEL.COM. BETT ᴿ. GON."

As the sleet drove harder, he moved a little into the shelter of the trees, and ere he knew he stood on the banks of the black pool. The spot had been one of hideous memory to him, to-day its parable was read. The sins of his fathers had been upon him. His life, his efforts had been foredoomed to failure; he had been warned long ago.

Shortly the overseer of the works hurried out, expecting some trifling detail of change to be made, but when he saw the Lord Warden's face, his own changed.

The orders were short and deliberate.

" Stop the works at once; dismantle and pull down the new building; replace everything as far as possible in the old grooves. You shall have particulars from the lawyers. Look after the old people, as I shall not be here again. You hear me? "

Then without listening to, or giving further explanation, he turned his horse's head, and, riding away, was lost to sight in the wind and the rain. Once only he stopped on his road, where it trended over the sands far up the haven.

His head had been sunk upon his breast
in despondent thought, when involuntarily he
raised it, and drew a long breath of pain. This
was the spot whence he had first looked upon
the land of promise. That looming on the left
was the thicket, that shaggy, ruin-crested outline
the hill. THEN it was sunrise, and his face had
been turned to it; even now as he looked, the
last light of the wintry day flickered, and went
out behind the ruins. Hardly knowing how,
he stumbled onward in the darkness, and the
conviction came more strongly to his mind that
from the first, he helpless, had been made the
sport of Fate.

So the last of the line went out and away
from his possessions, and the waste, the waters,
and the woodland knew his name no more.

All through the night he travelled on, the
next day he was again in London. He was
met by the news of the appointment of the man
he had feared, to the Primacy of the Church in
England. It was the old story—misrepresen-
tation at Rome from influential quarters—the
real state of things concealed—the Pope persuaded against his better judgment. This had
been tried with disastrous effect in the Irish
Episcopate, but never before in England. An
accredited Envoy had now been installed at the
Papal court (with a Nuncio at St. James's).
The move had come as a necessity. England, who had to govern in person a few
odd millions of Catholics—not all of the most
governable sort—woke up one day to the

conviction, that the greater the governing prestige in her hands, the easier it would be for her. The importance of the post could hardly be over-estimated, but it cut both ways. Secular interference, and advice, as to the selection of the bishops, was the least desirable outcome of it.

The great ecclesiastics, who may be said to have re-founded the Roman Church in England, were gone. Unhappily they had not been replaced by men of equal calibre, and the Church which had been formerly buoyed up by the mere weight of these great names, had sunk deeply in the public estimation, once time had removed them. The present bench consisted for the most part of men, who, on the Continent, would have been termed "reactionaries." One of its most active and promising members, and Roland's chief adherent, was Ridley, whose capacity had quickly carried him through the lower grades, but who on reaching the Episcopate, was appointed to a colony on the other side of the world, and safely transhipped thither.

This last news would have finally decided Roland's course had more been wanting. His conciliatory efforts had failed; between English and Irish Catholics was war to the knife, and it had become evident that the Irish question would only be solved in blood. All the various schemes for giving Ireland autonomy had fallen through, causing the keenest exasperation; he foresaw the failure of his public life, and it hung heavy on him. Stung to the heart by misfortune

he resolved to plunge into a new life. A blank
stretched before him, another should stretch behind, and he set to work deliberately to sever
every link which bound him to the past. He was
detained a space by legal business, the longer
because Miss Grey had nominated him executor
to her estate. However, matters were at last
arranged through one of his old schoolfellows
at Saint Augustine's, whose scruples on the
subject of *Mortmain* were not of a serious
nature.

And she herself appeared no more in the
world of men; but the world talked and
wondered for a week at least, and said many
strange things—said, they had seen it from the
first—said, she had been jilted—said, " Don't
tell me, there *must be a reason* "—said, she was
dying of unrequited love for Lord St. Maur, and
several other men—said, she did it for excitement—said, she was always odd, and intent upon
selfish gratification—said, the Jesuits had done
it to secure her money—said, every wise,
generous, and charitable thing that the occasion
admitted.

Although Roland's political difficulties were
by this time public property, not a little surprise
was created when the announcement of his
resignation was made. Spoken of always as "a
strong man," a " dark horse," and one certain
to " come in well " some day, his retirement
caused a feeling of dismay with all parties, on
account of the extreme difficulty of finding any
of his co-religionists able to replace him, or to
take his leading part in public affairs. There

was at this time not one, sitting for an English constituency, not one, in any public place who could say five words, likely to be listened to by the world, on behalf of that popular Catholicity which, under ten thousand drawbacks, was slowly struggling into life. The drawing-rooms had their spokesmen in the Upper House, but the millions were voiceless.

Many were the efforts that had been made to draw him into the charmed circles. Great men, very great men (in their own estimation), had patted him on the back, and told him to his face what a clever fellow he was; but as he looked for nothing, this patronage rather annoyed him than otherwise. Great ladies had paid court to him, and listened to his dreadful views on Irish affairs and others, with a smile that would not come undone, on their lips. To no purpose. He laughed at the idea of any serious opinion from such quarters, outside the fall of a skirt. What had Society to offer him? It was a ludicrous agglomerate. It was not witty, it was not wise, it was not even well-bred; and as he said so without scruple, it was felt that his case was desperate.

He had hoped to see his Church a shining light on the questions of the day, but he found it likely to be hid and obscured by every species of contemptible fashion, and a factor of no public use or account whatever. Had it been otherwise, or could he have made it otherwise, he would have stayed; as it was, he shook the dust from his feet, and washed his hands of the catastrophe to be.

His farewell letter to his constituents, whom he had learned to look on almost as his children, a family, alas! crying for bread, which it was out of his power to give, ran :—

" MY DEAR FRIENDS,—I regret that circumstances force me to resign the privilege of being your representative. We have struggled onward a little way together ; I am sorry that it has been no farther. I have long since come to the conclusion that no Englishman can represent the legitimate aspirations of your country in the present day. I trust that you may find one among yourselves to fight your battles, unfettered save by those principles of honour and moderation, which mark no less the patriot, than the Christian gentleman.

" Believe me, yours faithfully,
" ROLAND TUDOR."

Without further warning than the publication of this letter he disappeared. It is curiously easy for a man to vanish utterly. One of his type could have but few associates, fewer friends. He had no family ties whatever, but he had a rival or two, and they were glad that he was gone. His career was finished ; he had no interests left ; he had tried everything that was open to him, and had failed. Most terrible of all, the broad tract of life still stretched before him, a blank. He would spend it, perhaps, in travel. Nature had inexhaustible stores for the inquirer, and he had already dabbled in her secrets. He might yet take the sting out of this trouble by severe application, and benefit his race by bringing the knowledge of the East to the thresholds of the West. Some such vague, hopeless hope flitted through his brain as he went away and into the wilderness; but his reflections, and the bitterness of them, were past confessing, even to his own soul.

It was while thus waiting, uncertain which way to turn, that news reached him, indirectly, of the serious illness of his old friend, Brabant, who as a last resource had gone to Algiers for the winter. Thereupon Roland's resolution to cut himself adrift entirely from the past failed him, and taking one of the small steamers that ply along the coast, he set out to join him. There was no difficulty. Mrs. Brabant had carried off her husband (now too weak for resistance) to the liveliest hotel in the town, where she was anxious to make a party, with some of her "set," who had preceded her. It so happened that this illness of her husband's worked in very well with her own wish to winter abroad, and no hardship was made about it. Roland walked in upon him one morning as he sat alone in the big, shaded balcony of his room, and he noted the sunken cheek, the wondrous fire in his eye, the fire that was too surely consuming him. The invalid manifested no surprise, only pleasure.

"Ah! Roland," he said, putting out his hand; "this is friendship. I had hoped you might be here. Have you come to see 'how a Christian can die?'"

And neither said much, for to meet so appealed strongly to them both, and Brabant

had learned his friend's history. Roland stayed
with him. He spoke very little now, but sat
for hours looking out on the glassy sea, though
it was plain from his eyes, that his brain
was as active as ever. Mrs. Brabant looked
in now and then, but she had found so many
people of the "right sort," and there were so
many picnics and parties on hand, that she
could spare very little time to sit in the verandah; and now that Mr. Tudor had appeared,
it was not necessary. Nobody could imagine
how really busy she was, or how sorry that her
time was not her own. So she averred, and she
begged the two gentlemen would excuse her,
which they very readily did.

A week passed without change; the sick
man seemed not ill at ease; sometimes, indeed, he brightened up into his old self, and
told stories and laughed at them with as keen a
gusto as of old. He told how the London
house had been a failure, how everything had
cost at least treble what it should have done, it
being his wife's first essay in housekeeping;
how every waking hour was spent on her
clothes, and yet she had never been fit to be
seen; how the twopenny tea-parties, as he
designated them, had all been duly sent to the
newspapers, until "Society" actually believed
in them; how every scrap of soiled linen was
brought out for public inspection and black-
ened up, until there was not a woman of her
acquaintance who did not commiserate her in
her troubles with her brutal and exacting
husband; how she had an aptitude for uncouth

specimens of the male sex, who wore pins in sailor's-knot neckties, under the impression that such idiosyncrasies meant genius. All this, and much more, he told without a particle of malice and with a sort of enjoyment.

"I'm a thing of the past," he laughed; "it is like telling a good story against somebody else."

His tone struck Roland painfully, and he ventured to say as much.

"My dear fellow," was the answer, "what would you have? I do not believe in piling the agony to the last, that is not Christian hope. I have prepared myself so far as I can, a long time since. I have forgiven the only real enemy I ever had, and go the more cheerfully because life has been intolerable here. All that the Church can do for me is done; but if you think there are no tremors in the uncertainty of this certainty which faces me, then courage has a different meaning to you and to me. It is a hard thing to grow accustomed to the thought that any five minutes may work the great change—that, as you know, is my state. I only wish I could think I had justified my existence. One must look at these things broadly. Something—many things perished that I might have life. I am sacrificed to make room for better. I see—it is not difficult to see—the wider, broader future before the race—even now at hand. I have no place, no part in it. You, I hope, have. Armies of thought are sweeping on to battle; they will be irresistible, everything must fall

before them. But although I see and know all
these fine things, the voice of the man within
me drowns them. When one has been ill before, there has come a change, when one has
begun to grow better. This time it is different.
I mark myself day by day growing worse, and
I can tell, almost to a nicety, how much less I
shall be able to do to-morrow. 'Oh, God!
Delilah shore not hair by hair.'" His face
sank, and he was silent a long time.

But the ruling passion was not dead; he
would devour the English papers when they
were brought to him, and note down remarks
in his pocket-book. Roland found him one
day at his old work of leader-writing, and,
taking the pen from his hand, installed himself
as secretary. Certainly his composition lacked
none of its old fire.

One afternoon they sat smoking as was
their wont, until it grew late. Their talk had
been more serious, and of the future, rather
than the past. The invalid contended that the
popular fancies which obtained in every creed
were absurdly cut, dried, and conventional, and
that no saint or seer had ever taken the plunge
with the slightest conception of the realities
that were before him.

" I once had an experience singularly like
death," he said, sitting up, "singularly. I have
often meant to describe it. I wish you would
put it down, now I think of it. It was the first
time I looked through Van Dam's telescope;
he turned it on the moon, which was just
dawning—(have you got that?) I shall never

forget it. The experience was a sudden, painless transition to another state of existence. In a moment I had passed away from the earth and found myself a suspended Intelligence slung but a few hundred miles (it looked much nearer) above a new world—a scene of the most frightful desolation the mind can conceive. Over it, the sunrise was slowly spreading, revealing on the one side the most minute objects with the intensest clearness, while the other was still wrapped in the mantle of night. Peak after peak, precipice after precipice, emerged from the gloom, and their long shadows shortened as the sun drew high. Without conscious effort I traversed the vast fields of ether. My gaze sprang from range to range, from crater to crater, from desert to desert, across half the globe, which rolled in awful silence below, turning its seamed dead face to the dawning of the new day—a day profitless—one that gladdened no life, ripened no seed, opened no flower—a day like the night of death, a type of all the remainder of the days to come. The sight was horrible in its fascination. My spirit trembled. I was no more of the world that gave me birth. One moment I seemed unable to break the invisible bonds that chained me to this purgatorial region; but even as I looked I was conscious that my existence was like a ship without its anchor. In a dumb terror I was plunging anew into the boundless seas of space. Oh, God! oh, God! whither?"

Almost with a gasp came these last words.

The voice of the speaker was as that of one in the land of shadows. He stopped and laid his cigarette on the table; the ash fell away, glowed a moment, dissolved and expired; he seemed to call. The sudden dusk of the twilight was upon them. Roland, who could see no longer, dropped his pen and stood at his friend's side in an instant.

Even so it was too late. He who had called was gone—the earthly semblance of him lay back motionless, the left hand grasping the little gold cross that hung upon his chain, the right outstretched over the cushions in a last effort of farewell.

At this moment voices and laughter were heard below; it was a pic-nic party returning, the better for a jovial day and free libations of champagne. Roland, with a sense of disgust, closed the windows to shut out the noise, took the dead man's right hand for a moment, and kissed his forehead. He could not grieve, and repeating the " De Profundis," he was moving to the door, when Mrs. Brabant flounced in even more noisily than her wont. She looked flushed and excited.

" I never laughed so much before in my life," she said. " I've just— "

"Mrs. Brabant," said Roland, facing her sternly, "your husband— "

"Oh! yes. I see he's asleep as usual, and nobody's to move hand or foot, I suppose. Here, Warby, wake up! I must tell you, such a lovely thing happened, as—," and before Roland could step forward to prevent her, she had seized the dead man's arm and shaken it roughly; when a piercing shriek rang through the house—another and another.

Mrs. Brabant did not appear at *table-d'hôte* that evening; indeed, while that was in progress, it took all the time of two strong men to hold her down, and it was far into the night before the hysterical paroxysms had ceased, and she fell into a slumber of exhaustion.

* * * * *

It might be expected that her career had been told. On the contrary, it had but commenced. A few words will tell the rest of it.

Within a year she reappeared in London, and No. 100A knew her again. She had decided to cast all upon this particular die, for reasons of her own. The right-hand Marquis was now driven to be much in town; his corns were growing unbearable with age; it might be said that he had come to live for them. As Pallissy burned his bed to heat his furnace, so now Mrs. Brabant threw over and gave up all her worldly possessions, and pinched in every possible way in a last desperate effort, living almost on toast and tea, that she might keep her foothold next door, and be able to garden (she was so fond of gardening) in the most ravishing toilettes in the world.

Heaven knows what the struggle was to the poor woman at this period, and how killing. Day after day, in wet weather and dry, she rouged and squeezed, painted, and attitudinized, on the disgustingly dirty, draughty leads, with all unconscious grace; and in white kid gloves she for ever, potted and unpotted, her darling plants in the boxes. And when it grew warm, she all unconsciously still, slipped off her wraps, and showed the generous beauties of her whalebone, or sat under a vermilion sunshade, just displaying the fascination of a toe fitted with a shoe three sizes too small. Ah! what a thing for effect is a waterpot too, if it is only lifted well up, with a good reach.

But if it was hard work sometimes and she nearly sank under it, how should she dream that an elderly gentleman next door, in a blue frock-coat rather spotted down the front, watched her by the hour together from his study window? The distance was a good one for effect, for this she always felt a thankfulness at heart; for sometimes her face showed weariness, even over her pretty flowers, and she would not have had this known for the world. And the watcher was always at home, for his feet prevented him from straying; it had come to this, that even driving jolted his corns to an excruciating pitch.

But although he was a marquis he was still a man, though a very short-sighted one; he could not watch unmoved the spectacle below him, day by day. She was a "mons'ous fine woman—that's what she was"—and having discovered that she was a widow, with no one belonging to her (he hated men) he decided on his course of procedure. One day when Mrs. Brabant was, oh! so busy with her lilies, who should pop out on the adjoining leads but the little Marquis himself; not that she would have seen him at all, if he had not ventured to say " Good evening."

She was dreadfully coy and proud, he could hardly get a word from her, and it must have been a week at least, before the shy face with its over-voluminous coils of light golden hair, rested one summer night again (all unknowing) on the spotted bosom of the blue frock-coat. But even after this there was a hitch in the negotiations. She would not join the harem— virtuous creature—not on any inducement whatever. A coldness ensued, and for a few days communications were broken off. The Marquis, it has been said, was but a man, an old man doting, and what chance had he against her ? She had happened on the right stage in his existence ; he became as clay in the hands of the potter, and should you ask now the style, title, and lineage of Maria Elizabeth, Marchioness of Pimpington, wife of Jaques Augustus, fourth Marquis, Earl of Sotby, and Viscount Suckleham, &c., &c. ; it would be better that you should desist, lest you be over-dazzled with the glory of it all.

Let her good deeds speak for themselves, her virtues have their reward. She it is who gives the cue in taste and tone to half London ; she lays down the law as to what is right, and noble, and beautiful. She is so shining a light that she has been able to remain a Protestant (as she devoutly prayed to do) and has not had to submit to the tiresome for-malities, and church-goings, expected of people who join the Catholic Church. * * *

When all was over, Roland returned to his headquarters, whence he plunged afresh into the desert, where months passed away before he returned to civilization, months spent in study and research, of a sort which had commended itself most to his attention. Of this study, Force in all its forms was the chief. In the course of his work lay a curious combination of occult and physical science, occult that is in a sense, for he was able in time to resolve all occultism, so far as he pursued it, into physical fact of the most essentially material nature. He laid down a scheme of self-teaching which he pursued relentlessly. While he would spend weeks in the libraries and laboratories of science, verifying facts experimentally, he would then go out for long periods together, into the wilds, accompanied by two or three native servants, where he would observe the phenomena of Nature, down to the minutest particulars, questioning of her face to face.

It is easier to find a desert than is generally supposed. Five days from Southampton will place you in the midst of an African one; and Roland Tudor gathered in these wildernesses many curious fragments of knowledge. Here the Arab stands, unchanged and unchanging, within a stone's throw of civilization. There are wise men among the Moors, who still hold the cabala of that noble and beauteous culture, which once shed so bright a lustre on Southern Spain; theirs are secrets that the world would not willingly let die, and which tend to the elevating and beautifying of life.

The outer world went on with change and counterchange, but he took no share, and although he noted minutely the current of events, he held himself aloof. With one man and one only he never ceased to keep up communication, and that was the solitary student in the marshes, who may be said to have directed his studies at this time. Signs were not wanting, that this extraordinary man's predictions were on the point of being verified, so far as the outer world was concerned; and the manifest tendency of things towards the point he had indicated, probably induced in his pupil a confidence which would otherwise have been wanting. When after a few years Roland took count of all he had gained, he could see plainly that he stood beyond other men, and that should there ever come an appeal to force, in which he should be induced to join, his knowledge of it must stand him in good stead. With all employers hitherto, the blundering, idiotic waste of it, caused by sheer ignorance, had been the main fault; in the conservation of energy lay all potential success. But what should move him again? He had broken link by link every chain that bound him. Sombrewood and the Isles were sold and gone to strangers. What was left for which he should struggle?

One day as he wandered thoughtfully by the tideless shores of an Eastern sea a letter was brought to him. There is a secret virtue in a

letter over and above the range of the post-
office. Instinctively he knew whence it came.
Nothing but love could have discovered him in
this uttermost retreat; and as he looked again
at the handwriting he had known so well, in
which had been bound up all the hopes and
fears of the past—now gone as though they
had never been—a tumultuous flood surged
through his breast. He had thought this was
done with, but the wounds were there, wide
and bleeding afresh. For a space he would
not open it; there was no such thing for him
in the world as good news, and he read and
re-read the address where his name was written
fair and firm, and with no trace of uncertainty.
Slowly he broke the black seal. The sheet was
dated a long time back; no place was named;
she plainly wished to keep it from him.

"Dear Roland," it ran, "to-morrow I take
the final vows of my religious life. This is my
real farewell to the world, and I would make
the same preparation for it as for the hour of
death. So I write these lines to thank you
more than I can say—for all you have done for
me, and for all you have been to me—and to
ask, that if you have ever found me wanting in
anything towards you, you will forgive me;
and for past pain and trial that you will pardon
them, and pray for your ever-loving sister—in
hope of immortality,

"CÆCILIA."

The words went straight to her lover's heart.
Thanks from her, for what he had done. Pardon from him, for what she had left undone.

There was too grievous a pathos in this—it
struck him too hard—and as he walked to and
fro upon the beach, he dashed the tears from
his eyes. What answer could any man make
to such an appeal as this ? and now it was over
and done. She was hence a mere unit in some
poor convent in a London by-way, clothed in
rough sackcloth, a servant of servants, working at the most lowly of tasks for the lowest of
the people. What a fate for her, with whom
beauty and the love of Nature had been a
master passion, and this awful sacrifice of the
definite, for the indefinite, was "in the hope of
immortality."

These words especially rang in his ears as
he went. He too had hoped for immortality,
but in a different way. What was this immortality without the hope of which, no nature of
man or woman could scale the grandest heights ?
As she had taught him, he looked about to the
sea, and the sky and the hills for answer. These,
compared with man, possessed immortal being;
more races had beheld that mountain which
jutted into the waters yonder, than had ever
heard of Cæsar or of Christ.

Around him the shores littered down into
the sea in rocks that were primæval; at his
foot was tumbled a later fragment, in which lay
imbedded on the fresh splintered surface, some
of the oldest of living forms. He struck it
with a stone. Out of its bed sprang from the
rent matrix a perfect shell.

He took it up. What had once been the
living animal shone in crystals, but its fragile

case remained intact and unchanged as in life. How long was it since this creature had lived? Here was an immortality of which no human being had ever dreamed; but this was finite, and, taking a boulder, he crushed the fair shell to dust.

"So ends an existence of millions of years," he thought, "and it is a beggarly thing when it is done." The woman's mind had sprung above his own; immortality lay beyond even the frightful span of the years. How cheap a thing and small, was this mere material duration of existence, which was yet incomparably beyond all human record. If he walked out upon the mudbank yonder, he would be engulfed, sucked under, and held unchanging like the fossil, and nothing short of an earthquake, or the gradual drying up of the seas in the æons of the future, could lay him bare. Even if his corporate form were destroyed, its constituents would remain. And was spirit less imperishable than matter, the vital Ego less than its casket? It was wise in all uncertainty, to take count of this: She had done right to place this first, to follow where the highest lights illumined the way.

That night as he slept, the form of her he had loved so tenderly and so long, haunted him. She was at his side. They were boy and girl again together, and there was no sorrow nor sadness in the world. And in the old way her eyes grew earnest, and she talked of work, of achievement, and of victory—of what was before a man's right hand, of what lay in the

weakness of a woman, and all the lost happiness of life she brought back in her arms with
her; the happiness that woman only holds for
man, man for woman.

Before the morning the vision fled away, but
it left him changed with renewed energies
pouring through his veins. Henceforth the
talent of his strength should no longer lie
rotting in the earth.

CHAPTER VIII.

THE world had rolled into the twentieth century. A terrific convulsion which ran through the entire civilized portion of it, had marked the closing years of the nineteenth. Through half the countries of Europe the scenes of the French Revolution were re-enacted. In Russia, in Poland, in Germany, wherever, in fact, the heel of despotism had been most firmly planted, there, was all Government shaken to its foundations. With a singular uniformity of success, the cause of the people had triumphed along the whole line. Then was made the discovery that this did not mean quite the same thing as in former days. They were not the ignorant savages they had been; education had percolated through the mass, and among their leaders were to be found men of parts, principle, and moderation. As much could not be always said for their opponents. The results of this chain of victories were now beginning to show themselves, in the arrival of a state of compromise, which had in it the elements of a certain finality, for it allowed the plebs to live, under conditions which afforded them a reasonable prospect of comfort and security.

It was not uninstructive to note the way in which the Church had come out of the crisis. In countries where she had been of the people, sharing their labours, and lightening their burdens, she arose like a phœnix. In others, where she had become a fallen thing in the hands of a clique, she was barely able to hold up her head again.

The storm had swept over England, changing the face of the land, laws, customs, dress, architecture, with the strange freaks of such a phenomenon. The monarchy remained, but with greater limitations; the Lords remained, but as an elected body. The Commons rose in redoubled strength, with colonial seats. Imperial Federation was an accomplished fact.

The Church of England remained, disestablished and disendowed, but still promising to be an active and useful body. The cathedrals and most of the churches had been re-claimed by the nation, and were now used for the celebration of service, by all creeds indifferently under certain conditions.

The Church of Rome was struck grievously. When the hurricane passed off, she lay crushed and bleeding in the path. She had come to represent the element most obnoxious to popular rights and freedom, and suffered accordingly. Her establishment throughout the country, with the exception of a few convents and hospitals which the people knew, and consequently respected, had been reduced, to a disastrous wreck.

When the mob had first gathered on Black-heath, the watchword blazoned on their banners had been "Destruction to Popery, Privilege, and Plutocracy." It is possible that had there been at this juncture, a single layman of that creed, popularly known, the danger might have been averted; there was none. A bishop threw himself into the breech, and was brutally murdered. History repeats itself. The infuriated mob this time, a hundred thousand strong, marched on London, and the story of the Gordon riots was re-told on a tenfold scale. Churches and public buildings were wrecked, and for a month London lay divided, the city and central portions in the hands of the Government troops, the suburbs in those of the rebels; the hostile sentries often pacing the pavements on either side of the same street, and refraining, by mutual understanding, from any interference with each other.

It may be just worthy of note, that at this point the Catholic laity of England, to the number of an odd score, and under the auspices of the "Centre," convened a meeting. His Royal Highness the old Duke had some time since departed to his Royal forefathers, and, as a matter of course, the important post of president and leader of the body, had fallen to his son, a boy of fifteen, who accordingly took the chair. The proceedings were exceedingly brief. The Chairman, in opening, said that his experience perhaps was not great (No, no); but he felt a conviction that the time they had so long waited for, the time in fact for *action*, had dawned at length. He thought it an awful pity to allow their bishops to be murdered, and their churches burned over their heads, as had been unfortunately the case last week. Not being able to recollect anything more to say, he sat down. A venerable member here rose, who said that, while entirely agreeing with H.R.H., he must remark that these matters certainly did not come within the "scope" of the Association. A serious discussion ensued, and honourable members being unable to come to an agreement on this delicate point, the majority left the meeting. The party of action, thereupon finding the field clear, and having it all their own way, passed a unanimous resolution "That a *Formal Protest* be drawn up, illuminated on vellum, solemnly blessed and presented to the leaders of the rebellion;" and the meeting, which, as it proved, was the last held by this august body, broke up in a state of self-gratulation even more intense than usual.

The sequence is soon told. The insurgent leaders, being unversed in gothic characters, were unable to read the document when forwarded; but, not being devoid of a sense of humour, they, with some ceremony (having by this time made their way as far as South Kensington), rolled it up into a brand, wherewith to set alight to the new church.

Extraordinary to say, the protest proved abortive, even when put to this modest use, and failed to ignite the pile prepared. Other means had to be resorted to. No more dramatic scene was witnessed during the history of these times, than the storming of the Oratory. The sapient architect of the building, looking to the future as well as the past, had chosen his style (Early English) with a view to such a contingency. Those solid walls, those narrow lancets, that machiolated tower could hardly have been better devised for the purpose. The fury of despair seized upon the congregation barricaded within; and, so gallant was the defence, that after a siege of two days, the mob, finding a backbone in the "Papists" which they had least of all anticipated, and being an English mob, knew how to appreciate, drew off, cheering. The building was spared, and henceforth the current flowed, and spent itself in other directions.

The Democratic movement, which had convulsed the nations of Europe, had meantime crossed the seas, and in the States of America, and throughout the globe generally, it had become a question of People *versus* Privilege.

In the old world the former, for the most part, held their own, and it was obvious that on the comparatively free soil of the new, a soil which perpetuated no tradition either of classic antiquity or feudal despotism, the popular cause must, in the long run, stand an even better chance. It was plain, too, that the gigantic monopolies, which the accidents of a nascent commerce, had placed in the hands of the merchant or monied class, could only flourish for a time, and must eventually yield to the prodigious increment of the people.

For this was a land, the resources of which were limitless for uncounted generations to come, which could support new populations, enlarging without difficulty its habitable area as they doubled and trebled and quadrupled; a land where every healthy man and woman held in his or her right hand potential fortune, by the mere fact of existence; where every child born was a fresh source of wealth; where more than half the conditions of life, as understood in the old world, were exactly reversed. Such a country must, in the working out of the social problem, upset in many ways, what had come to be looked upon as the natural order of things.

It has been stated how a breach between the two great sections of mankind had already shown itself in the West; but so far it had been confined to that part of it alone, where the energies of the great continent centred. It was not to be expected that any marked consensus of feeling would show itself at once over so huge an area, and in South America, owing to its peculiar constitution, it was generally supposed that no such differences were likely to appear. Only in the case of an isolated riot on the Pacific coast had any antagonism so far shown itself, be-

tween capital and labour. On the other hand
a number of distinct Nationalities had grown
up and divided the land among them in huge
slices, and between these, dissensions born of
an intense jealousy prevailed. The wealth of
the interior, as it came to be gradually opened
out, proved so enormous, that a constant
effort was maintained by the more powerful states to annex portions of their weaker
neighbours. At best a sort of armed neutrality prevailed, which effectually prevented
anything like organization among them, for
purposes of mutual advance or defence.

Had an invader dropped from the clouds (and
it did not appear likely, it must be admitted,
that he should come in any other way), the
whole continent north and south would probably have fallen an easy prey to him. Had a
Napoleon with one of the least of his armies
landed upon these shores, there is little doubt
that he might have marched, had he so willed
it, from East to West, from North to South,
his conquest bounded only by the seas on either
hand, and the snows Arctic and Antarctic of
either hemisphere. Looking back upon the
last four centuries, it seemed strange that the
lust of conquest has led no adventurous spirit
of the first water, out of the cabbage gardens
of Europe, into the wide fields of the West.
Even the United States, although they had
waged bloody wars, had never yet drilled or
organized a standing army worthy of the name,
and indeed to have done so would have been in
direct contravention of the principles on which

they were originally founded. It never seemed
to have reached the brain of the nations forming the conglomerate called America that some
Eastern conqueror, some modern Alexander,
fresh from a long tale of victory, instead of
stopping to weep on the confines of the Indies,
might press onward insatiable, and land a
flotilla on their shores, where there was nought
to stay his hand until the vast continent lay at
his feet. The idea had been bruited merely to
be laughed at. Europe had enough to do
in fighting her own battles; such a captain
does not spring up like a mushroom in a night.
It was forgotten that no long time since, a few
weeks transformed a simple officer of artillery
into conqueror of Italy, that a few years again
saw him Lord of half Europe. It was forgotten, that under the hand of such a man levies
spring up, armed, equipped, irresistible, as if
by magic, that his mere words, tossed in air,
are like thistledown seeds of war, and that
where they sow themselves, like the dragon's
teeth of Cadmus, they sprout in crops of fighting men—that, as these are melted away in
the travails of conquest, new ones come up ever
afresh with marvellous rapidity, enabling him
to strike blow on blow, at the most stubborn
defence, and to shatter it at last. No earthly
power will compare, with that wielded over mankind, by the personal magnetism of a great
conqueror. He is as a prophet, and more than
a prophet. Life, death, fortune, are held at his
word mere flea-bites, whole nations will turn
out to follow him ; or, if need be, to bend willing

necks under the tread of his legions, that so they may hasten his chariot-wheels. To him it is given to transform countries, to reconstitute religions, to reframe nations in bonds stronger than those of kin or brotherhood; in the simple necromancy of success lies a power almost divine. As it came about, the conquest of America did not proceed from without, but developed itself from within.

Among the five hundred great reputations which had sprung to light in these world-throes—reputations curious to think of as impossible, but for the accident of the times in which they were made—none stood higher than that of a man whose face and figure had loomed up suddenly, and without warning, upon the political horizon of the West. For some time it appeared that he was no more than his fellows, a waif whom the chances of the struggle had tossed on the top of the wave, only to be dashed into obscurity with the succeeding one; but in a year or two, it began to look as if this man was of the few who compel Fortune, forcing the fickle goddess to her knees, rather than one of the many who, with varying success, day and night woo the favour of her smile. How he came was a mystery; before the call-bell was well rung he had taken the stage, had occupied it, and though other actors had come and gone, he still remained a central figure. When the cause of popular liberty had first shown its head on the Southern Continent, he had espoused it. The outbreak, as it was termed, took place in an insignificant province on the sea-board of the Pacific, and it was not supposed at the time could have other than local consequences. This man, who was a wayfarer, a traveller, with no local connections or interests whatever, one whom chance had brought to the spot, at once threw himself into the struggle. He had money, and apparently influence; at any rate, he raised and equipped a regiment of foot at his own expense. This force, intended rather for defence, than offence, and for the protection of the popular rights, formed the nucleus of a small body, which the oppressed multitude was shortly able to raise by its own exertions. The existence of an armed organization, other than that in the pay of the local Government, proved in itself a *casus belli*. The powers that were, in their endeavours to force a tyrannous system on the necks of the people, had constantly had recourse to coercion, but this being no longer possible in the face of the bands raised for their protection, an open rupture terminated in the declaration of civil war. The force which the new-comer had helped to organize was a rude guerilla body, but not without a certain fighting capacity, which it derived chiefly from the principles at stake; and auxiliary bands were formed of the waifs and strays whom the rumour of battle, no less than the hope of plunder or promotion, attracted to the spot. The struggle on either side wore a constitutional aspect, and was initiated in the name of the Republic. The rebels were by no means led by

men of a low class ; indeed, those who had risen
with the popular wave were, in not a few
cases, of a high type of ability and integrity,
though wanting for the most part in this world's
goods, which accounted very clearly for their
lack of influence in the State. These men were
not long in recognizing their good fortune, in
the advent of the errant stranger who had come
forward to tender his assistance. By degrees
the revolt grew and spread, as did the other
side, until the two forces had gathered their
strength, and stood facing each other in a
lone spot on the immense Pacific coast. The
world cares little for the internal throes of
South American republics on the wrong side
of the Andes, and the state of things may be
said to have attracted no notice whatever.

It was late in the autumn before the two
came to blows, when a series of sanguinary
skirmishes took place, which resulted in the
Government troops being driven inland, and
losing the command they had hitherto held of
the sea-board, so that they were thus deprived
of most of their supplies and munitions of war.
In these engagements the Foreign Legion, as
they were grandiloquently styled, bore the brunt
of the day ; and in the last, which proved so
happily decisive, it was they who delivered the
coup de grâce. In the account of the action
published by the Government, it was stated that
the day was already gained, when a mad gang of
desperadoes had forced the lines at a weak point,
thus causing "an unexpected retirement."
This term was received with proud acclaim by

those at whom it had been hurled; the corps promptly took to itself the name of Desperadoes, a title destined to become famous through all history. This success had been so undeniably due to the courage and discipline of the erst unruly team, and to their manipulation by their commander, that all eyes were turned to see what manner of man was he, who could train and lead raw levies into deeds that a regiment of veterans might have been proud to achieve. It had been imagined that there was hardly such a thing as a real soldier on the peninsula. Here was a man who in six weeks had hewn out of the rough material an entire regiment, employing them with an audacity and tactical ingenuity far beyond their own comprehension, or that of their opponents, but with unvarying success.

To outward appearance he was a man approaching middle age, reserved, silent, stern, and of inflexible will. His aspect with his men was not unkindly, some magnetism attached itself to him, which had the effect of attracting others. In the first hours of a struggle, when all is uncertain, men's eyes and ears are keenly open to those signs and marks of leadership, which time must infallibly disclose among their number. There was no waiting in this case, the look of the man carried conviction with it. Within an hour of the striking of the first blow, the soldiers knew for certain where to follow, and the name of Roland, by which alone he called himself, went

out far over the country-side. It is probable
that even at this early period, the Authorities
gained some inkling of the man they had to
deal with, for an unexpected fact came out—
there were men in the ranks able to identify
him. Not only were there Irishmen who remembered his wearing the British uniform in
Ireland, but there were others.

At the close of the civil war in the south of
Europe, when the troops had been disbanded,
some few had found their way to South
America, where they had friends or relatives,
and, when it came to a question of fighting,
had naturally drifted into the army. Many
a man, finding his occupation gone at home,
had come out hither, prepared to turn his
sword into a ploughshare, when, to his surprise,
he had found work for it as it was. As no
commission in the little force dated more
than six months back, there was not that
jealousy and difficulty to contend with, which
would have existed in the case of regulars.
The best man came to the front, and it
was always open to any one to beat him
if he could. The name of Roland was already
made, it had been one to conjure with years
agone. His story, too, was by no means
unknown in South America; indeed, his
fortune had made him a name beyond his
deserts in those early days. His disappearance and the costly gifts that had reached
his comrades, had made him a marked man
in Iberia, where the popular fancy, always

romantic in a Southern people, had clung to
the figure of their ephemeral hero, and ever
since his name had been crooned in the rude
chants of the mountain peasantry. The new
announcement of it at the present juncture was
received at first with incredulity; but as one
man after another came forward and recognized
him, more than one having actually fought at
his side, all doubt was dispelled, and a furore
of enthusiasm took its place. The legend,
magnified and improved by time, spread abroad;
young men of all nationalities flocked to the
ranks, eager to fight under a chief of reputation; idlers, riffraff, the ne'er-do-weels of a score
of races, ranged themselves under his orders.

The iron was now hot; without waiting for it
to cool, the commander and organizer of this
heterogeneous mass hurled it upon the heads
of the other side. The result was overwhelming.
In the *mêlée* the old Government went down,
never to rise again; its army melted away,
crushed out of being; on the morrow it simply
was not. What had up to this point been
the Rebellion, seized the reins; a Government
was reconstituted on popular lines, and so was
founded anew the young Republic.

A sentiment little short of terror took possession of victors and vanquished alike, when the
full nature of this crushing stroke was understood. The rapidity of the blows, and the awful
loss of human life which had accompanied them,
were matters that appealed to the feelings of
humanity; yet there could be little doubt that a
dragging campaign would have proved even

more disastrous to life and property. But the deviser of the deed stood aloof, giving no explanation, seeking no counsel, a very incarnation of Fate. No attitude could have served him better in such a country and with such a populace. A situation grew up which the new Authorities recognized too late as menacing to themselves, and when matters had presently settled down, an effort was made to relegate the military section, of which the new-comer was the recognized chief, to a more subordinate position, but without effect. The army would not have it; on the question being pressed to an issue, it grew mutinous, and threatened to disband itself, which would have meant no less than annihilation to the newly hatched Republic. Compromise, therefore, was resorted to, and although during the episode the fount and origin of it, held himself somewhat scornfully aloof, his name lost nothing, for it was carried to and fro on the four winds, and his personality loomed greater on the horizon. In a sense it began to attract the notice of the world. South America is not the world, and it was thought condescending of the world to know that there was such a place. The name of Roland was unearthed from the files of bygone years in England, and a particularly enterprising journal not only devoted a leader to the recent events on the Pacific coast, but even mentioned the chain of the Andes, and otherwise displayed local knowledge of an astonishing accuracy. An extract or two will trace the thread :—

" The last days of a recent Continental war, as our readers may remember, witnessed a romantic apparition—a meteoric hero with a name, no doubt assumed, but of classic twang, who flashed through the murky war-cloud, and as suddenly disappeared. This adventurer was stated on all hands to have been an Englishman, and his deeds, which grow no less with time, may now take rank with those of Paladin of old. Such men are rare, and once found, it is a great mistake to let them slip. We are not, therefore, surprised to hear that it has been deemed advisable to resuscitate him, and that he or his double has started on a new career in the troubled waters beyond the Atlantic. The popular party in what once was Chili, have conjured to some effect with his name. The idea has proved a happy one, as the recent settlement of the serious disorders on the coast is attributed greatly to the way in which the local forces, raised and organized by this individual, have been handled," &c., &c.

Another :—

" While Europe has been wrestling in a death-grapple with its own offspring, history has been busy making itself in an almost untrodden quarter of the globe. Ten thousand miles away, where the trackless snows of the Andes look for ever towards the sunset, men are busy with the old task of slaying and being slain. Local giants are afield, and great reputations are won and lost. To-day we hear that a gentleman with an unpronounceable name has framed a State upon imperishable lines, and to-morrow he is forgotten, together with his Constitution, which is chopped into a dozen others. It would be interesting to have an accurate list of these typical republics, and of the various individuals who have swayed supreme power in them during the last half-century. At this hour a local potentate bearing the heroic cognomen of Roland is running away with the honours. One can imagine the supreme importance which this storm in a teacup must assume in the eyes of nations more youthful probably than the reader or the writer of these lines. Some day, no doubt, this Roland will be apotheosized; a couple of thousand years hence he may rank as the Casibelaunus of his ancient State. Such is Fame."

The sneers of the European press notwithstanding, and despite the predominance of the military element, the cause of popular liberty in this far-off land grew and prospered, and the monopolists were driven to make the best terms they could. At this juncture one of the theories of the soldier, who had directed the movement to success, was first put in force, and vindicated itself in the working. At his suggestion a gradually increasing tax was laid on actual income, which at a certain point reached the pitch of preventing further increment. This point was fixed experimentally at a not illiberal figure. The device, which would have been probably impossible, as well as inadvisable, in a long-constituted community, raised a prodigious outcry from the capitalists and their party. Robbery and confiscation were among the mildest terms employed, and it was declared that such a law must directly paralyze all effort. As a fact, it did nothing of the sort; the law was aimed at the gigantic monopolies that had grown up, from mineral wealth and other sources, and the consequent undue aggregation of property in the hands of the individual, to the detriment of the State and the public. It did not, however, apply to the amassing of co-operative capital, which, on the contrary, was encouraged; so that, while it took the reins out of the hands of a score or so of the great capitalists, it placed them in the hands of the community of smaller ones, which virtually comprised the entire nation. Thus it forced the monopolist into partnerships and common enterprise, in which manner his fortune might be indirectly maintained and increased; and capital of all kinds was pushed into circulation. As the really small incomes of the struggling beginners were left untaxed, the measure was an exceedingly popular one; six months' working of it proved its value.

The place and time were fitted for the experiment. For years this vast Southern Continent had been in a transition stage of social upheaval, which had come to be looked upon as chronic. Every state in turn had undergone the oscillations between despotism and anarchy, out of which, by slow degrees, true liberty is born; but as yet nothing permanent had arisen; there was no real stability anywhere. Generally, the grossest systems were paramount in Government, and the jealousy between state and state was intense.

When the air grew thick with war and rumour of war, and the name of Roland was again noised abroad, there was one man in the West who pricked up his ears, a man himself the ruler of a kingdom larger in area than the new State, and at this time held to be the owner of the finest private property in the world. This was Lord St. Maur. The two had been lost to each other, for, with the rest of the good things of life, Roland Tudor had wiped out friendship, as a thing no more to be. He was hardly more capable of it than of love. He was separated by a yawning gulf from the pains, hopes, and fears of mankind. He was no longer as other men; from the position into which he had been forced he looked down upon the world. He had been lifted out of it; he had discerned its inner workings and its way, and saw beyond others whither, and how it tended. Henceforth men were tools, to be used, influenced, bent to his will, but consulted seldom or never. That among such he should take the lead was a matter of course. How should it be otherwise, when he read every man through and through in the face of him? For himself, he was an engine of Destiny, fated to put in motion and keep going for a time a vast machinery. He had taken his life in his hands, a thing valueless and therefore not easily lost; and in his own mind he knew that it would endure until the accomplishment of his work. A rigid fatalism had laid its grip upon him, and though he had succumbed to it, it yielded him a mastery which in no other way could he have achieved. How far this state of things was the result of conscious knowledge, of bodily and mental energy, how far it was hallucination, it is impossible to say. Of the resulting power, there could be no manner of doubt whatever. But if there was one man living to whom some relic of kindly feeling was left in his nature, that man was St. Maur. The latter had heard of the break-up in the life of his former friend, of the ruin of his political prospects and his dearest hopes; yet his confidence in him had never waned, although he had disappeared, leaving no trace. The world was wide. St. Maur had never doubted that time would somewhere disclose him, and in the front rank. This must be the man, on the stage at last where he had most hoped to see him, and St. Maur's delight knew no bounds.

It had long been evident that the contest, between the old ideas and the new, would be clenched on American soil, and that the great change, which growing density of population was forcing upon the world, would be finally inaugurated upon this battlefield. The hour was surely at hand. He waited only to ascertain that there could be no mistake in the reports, and then hurried down South with all the speed possible. That his reception was not as he had anticipated, must be confessed. When the two men met, it was on a different footing to heretofore. In the one had ever been a kindliness, an overflowing of the milk of human sympathy, which the other had as certainly lacked. In all their dealings with their fellows the two men had taken a different course. Where St. Maur fought for the bettering of the people, by gentleness and amelioration, to Roland the ideal had been that of bare right and justice. If he had been unyielding before, he was now inflexible. On his iron features no expression sat more plainly, than unruffled determination to carry through the secret schemes, which lay in his brain, of which justice to all people was the watchword.

St. Maur had found him immersed in preparations which were significant enough of what he looked forward to, and it was plain that he aspired to gather into his own hands the reins of government. When St. Maur referred to the past, Roland sternly told him that the past was blotted out; his career lay in the future, he had but started. St. Maur came away from the interview chilled, repressed. Something like a breach threatened between them. He was angry at this withdrawal of confidence; but henceforth his former friend had neither confidence, nor explanation, for any man. St. Maur went away wavering, and for a considerable time he watched very acutely the lines on which the popular movement was proceeding. At heart he was secretly anxious to fling himself, his vast revenues, and his influence into the scale, and a time came when, with a clear conscience, he was able to do so; but at first sight he feared the part to be played by its new leader, misdoubting, in spite of himself, Roland's motives, and not understanding the unswerving character of the fatalism which led him. Satisfied at length on these points, he cast himself into the cause with a characteristic generosity, giving thereby a spurt and solidity to it which proved invaluable. Certainly the same objections did not apply to war on this continent, as upon the old. There, every shot fired was at the risk of destroying some priceless relic of the past; here, each was the laying of a foundation-stone of a new civilization.

The preparations proved not to have been without reason. The new Republic was too insignificant, and its success upon fresh lines was too marked, not to arouse the jealousy of its neighbours. Here was an upstart half-fledged State, south of the equator, out of the pale of humanity almost, airing an original Constitution, and impregnating the atmosphere with pernicious and socialistic doctrines. It was not to be borne. A coalition was formed by two or three of its big neighbours, who agreed to walk over the ground and divide it.

It is impossible to do more than indicate a few points in the extraordinary drama, of which this was the opening. On all sides preparations were made by stealth, any idea of hostilities being still an open secret. Happily for itself, the new State lay along the sea, and possessed a good harbour, for much of the war material had to be imported; although manufactories of cannon and small arms, together with great laboratories, had been established in the Capital, under the supervision of the General; while Europe was hunted over for engineers, scientific men, chemists, astronomers, and a thousand likely and unlikely personages. It was found, at the commencement, exceedingly difficult to procure those of anything like the first eminence, but men of science were sometimes poor, and it began to be whispered, that the baits held out by this insignificant State, were of a substantial character. Indeed, throughout this couple of years of preparation, its name stood exceedingly well, on the books of many of the great firms in London, Birmingham, and elsewhere. Meanwhile, however, the jealousy within its own boundaries, had grown to be hardly less than the jealousy without, and even the genius of the director, would probably have been unable to cope with the situation, but for the windfall of ready money, consequent on St. Maur's accession to the cause, on the strength of which he was able to negotiate heavy loans for the public treasury. Thus, while nominally in a subordinate position, he became the figure-head of the vessel.

As the war-clouds began to lower, all attention was merged in the anxiety that was felt for the State itself, the very existence of which was threatened. One council after another was held; it became evident that the man who held the reins could not be spared from his place, and that when the army took the field, it would have to be without him. He himself made the announcement; the necessity of it was generally

allowed, and although the troops rose with one
voice, he was inflexible. In a speech at a
review held for the purpose, he briefly informed them that nothing short of a disgrace
to their arms could take him to the front. He
had no doubt whatever of the issue, and he
promised them, that the campaign should be
won at his desk. This statement, made in
the most circumstantial way, as if it were a
thing already foregone, had its due effect.
There was now a considerable number of brave
men and able officers in the force, which was
quite capable of taking the field. Happily, by
this time, Roland was surrounded by an efficient
staff, whose confidence in him was boundless,
and any one of whom, would have gone
through fire and water to serve him. Foremost
among these was St. Maur, who, accepting the
inevitable, had come to act as his confidential
secretary. Now that the new footing was
understood, difficulties had vanished, he had
even regained something of his old intimacy,
based on conditions of which the foremost was
that the past was not.

On the day of the actual declaration of war,
while the city was ringing with the news
and in a turmoil of confusion, the General was
seen walking down the main street arm-in-arm
with St. Maur. He was dressed in mufti—a
loose linen suit, and was smoking a cigar.
Neither appeared to have anything particular to
do. They sauntered along leisurely, under the
trees, and eventually sat down for a mixture at
a street *café*. But here the mob gathered so

thick and uproarious, that they were forced to make their escape, which they did through a by-street, hurrying back to the War Office, where the pressure of work was overwhelming. The conception was no trifle, probably it was equivalent to five thousand extra troops in the field. The people and the army caught the infection of confidence, and the *morale* of the men was raised to the highest pitch. It was seldom that the autocrat vouchsafed any word of explanation, even to the one man who might still claim to call him friend; something perhaps in the popular enthusiasm had touched him, and as they entered the office he said with almost a smile,—

" That half-hour was not altogether wasted. Now I know how the enemy mean to come, I shall be ready for them. I beat two of them as we went down the High Street, and I think I see my way to the third. The difficulties all lie within this space," and with his compasses he pricked the map before him. " Here, you see, is army No. 1 defeated; and here No. 2, also defeated, but making good its retreat behind this range of hills. No. 3 is at sea, and here I hope to leave him."

St. Maur set down the words as those of an oracle. He had never forgotten the strange incident that had marked their first meeting years before; there seemed to dawn a meaning, the fulness of time was surely at hand. He had a confidence that there was work before the man with whom he was associated, which would not be confined within the narrow limits of nations, but would spread in world-wide benefit. It was in the vindication of a great principle that he had unsheathed the sword; through these nascent struggles lay the road that must perforce be travelled.

The event was precisely as predicted. The two invading armies were divided by a ruse, and beaten off separately, with conspicuous ease; but the case of No. 3 presents incidents worth notice. This was a budding naval power which, with a couple of ironclads and half a dozen submarine torpedo vessels, held command of the sea. By this means it had succeeded in seizing the frontier town of the coast, an important place, where the young Republic had its dockyard, which had been fortified in a way hitherto unexampled on that continent. The main difficulty lay in this, that in order to relieve it, the troops must proceed by the only practicable road, one which lay along the shores, exposed for the whole distance to the fire of the enemy, where they would be without a shadow of shelter or the faintest hope of retaliation.

A forced march of several days proved so harassing, and the loss inflicted was so considerable, that a fresh scheme was telegraphed from headquarters. In accordance with this, by day the army broke itself up, and dispersed in little companies all over the wide sides of the mountains, stretching from the sea, each individual securing such shelter as could be found, of rocks, and trees, and scrub. With nightfall they rapidly closed in upon a given point, re-formed themselves, and the march was proceeded with. Though the enemy were not unaware of this, and searched the coast indefatigably with powerful lights, the difficulty of ascertaining their exact whereabouts, with sufficient accuracy for aim, was so great that the casualties henceforth proved insignificant.

Arrived at last before the fortress, the wearied forces gave themselves little time to rest, investing it as far as possible as they came up, on the land side ; and here a new feature made its appearance on the stage of war, and one which was destined to prove almost as essential as gunpowder itself.

Some years since, while the Commander-in-chief was still sitting in the British Parliament, pursuing at odd moments his scientific investigations, Professor Van Dam had brought to his notice a certain gas, the buoyancy of which exceeded by many times that of any previously known. He had further placed in his hands the secret of its composition. By means of this a man might be lifted from the ground, and sustained in mid-air by a four-foot bag. With the help of light sheets of iron, buckled like shields to the arm, it was found that he could propel, and even steer himself, and by presenting with these a broad or narrow surface of resistance to the air, retard or accelerate his flight; or, dropping his wings, he could poise himself at rest, being really slung in a sort of hammock from the bag above. Roland had spent both time and money in perfecting the idea, the importance of which he foresaw. He devised large flappers of tin, which, while very light for use, would, when let down, so as to meet under the feet of the aeronaut, form a veritable shield both to himself and the bag, thus inclosing him in a wedge as seen from below, which was evidently the best shape, to protect him from missiles directed at him from the earth. These ballunets had already caused considerable annoyance and confusion among the hostile fleet ; they had been employed, when the wind allowed, at night, in dropping explosives upon the decks, so avenging to some extent the sufferings of the force on shore.

They were now sent out at once, and posted all round the city in mid-air. Upon the discovery of this, confusion prevailed within the walls and throughout the camp, for it was plain, that there could no longer be any secret as to the details of the defence.

But the time afforded for consideration was short ; an event took place which put an end to speculation, and brought out the specialist knowledge of the director of the campaign, in the strongest light. Regarding the scientific nicety necessary in his operations, he had himself trained a number of picked men, out of his own Desperado Regiment, as specialists. He had combined with these certain chosen spirits, from his corps of Engineers (a corps in which he had made a high pitch of actual scientific knowledge a *sine quâ non*), and to these, under officers who were again picked men, he intrusted the entire conduct of the ex-

plosives, a branch which had in this day come
to mean the core and substance of all warfare.
The invention of dynamite had made it possible
for a determined man to carry in his pocket
the wherewithal to breach any ordinary wall;
but the investigations of the professor, and of
his *clientèle*, had improved upon the original
dynamite, until they had produced a destructive compound, as much superior to the original
as the original had been to gunpowder. It had
been decided to try the effect of this, in breaching the fortifications on arrival, and before the
enemy could have any idea that an offensive
movement had been planned. So great was
the number of men who volunteered for this
desperate business, that they had to be chosen
by lot, and those who stood at the head of the
list were accordingly marched off as soon as
darkness came on, carrying their implements
with them.

The night was favourable, and the party were
successful in making their way undiscovered
up to the very ditches, into which at measured
intervals they carefully dropped the spheres,
each of which contained the charge and machinery for firing. The great difficulty, however,
had yet to be overcome; in order to secure the
desired effect, it was necessary that some at
least of the bombs, should be placed against the
inner walls to insure their destruction. These
were for the most part timed by clockwork to
explode simultaneously; but in the centre of
the position, through which it was intended to
deliver the attack in event of success, it was

thought necessary to guard against any loop-
hole of miscarriage, and here it was decided to
connect the spheres with wires, and to fire
them by electricity. The service of placing
the machines and laying the wires was one of
extreme danger. In parts of the *enceinte*
the nature of the ground made it impossible;
but the main energies of the party being directed to the one spot, the scheme was at length
carried to completion; thanks in great measure
to the defective look-out kept from the walls,
above which the dim forms of the ballunets
hovering high in the air and discharging lightless squibs, undoubtedly served to divert attention. The night was still, but clouded, what
little breeze there was, blowing towards the
party, and often as they waited, carefully laying the charge, the tramp of the sentry could
be heard upon the ramparts overhead, and
even the words of the challenge as the rounds
passed.

Before it grew light, the officer in charge
had finished his task and managed to retire
his men, all with the exception of one, who
for a hundred pounds to be paid to some
address in Rotherhithe, within a given date,
agreed to stay to finish the night's work. It
would be interesting to know something more
of this type of individual, never wanting to
such a place and time, but the history of his
ethics is a secret one. The outside only is for
the eye. This fellow, a hale man in his prime,
whispered a careless farewell to his comrades, as
they stood paraded to march back, and then as

carelessly, he turned in the opposite direction.
He had plucked a gorse-bush as he went, and
now he planted it in a corner of the fortification, where he lay under it, concealed as far as
possible. Here he waited quietly enough (being
an ex-British soldier) for the hour when he
should tumble his horizon in ruins about him.
If he regretted one thing, it was by no means
his past life, it was that he could not smoke.
From where he lay he could see more than one
of the canisters, disguised in their rough cork
casings, dabbled with moss and green paint, as
they lay all innocent in the tufted grass. In
one not far off, he could even hear the steady
ticking of the clockwork, which by some accident had been set in motion. There was no
stopping it now. He looked at his watch—
five minutes more—it was going to be a fine
day, the sky was reddening in the East. He
re-examined his wires, and his little hand-bat-
tery. All was well, as the sentry above had
just informed him. He was cramped and
chilled; he stretched himself and shook his
bough; it was prickly and uncomfortable; he
had not thought of that when he had gathered
it. Three minutes. "Life is short," he mused.
He took out his pipe, and with great deliberation lit it. Before the smoke could reach the
nostrils of the fellow who tramped overhead,
there would be something else to think about,
and he chuckled. But he was mistaken. In
the intense stillness, the striking of the match
caught the ear of the sentry, who, leaning over
the parapet, detected a moving bush in the angle

below; not being a British soldier, he did not think it necessary to report to headquarters, but instantly covered it with his rifle. It was a case of touch and go. The quick ear of the man in the ditch noted the cessation of the sentry's step, and looking up, he saw the pale light of the dawn gleaming along the barrel as it covered him. Instantly he moved the finger of his dial, turning on the current, and simultaneously with the flash from the battlements, a prodigious roar went up, sounding and rebounding along the face of the *enceinte* like ten thousand thunders. The massive masonry was literally lifted into the air, then fell in crumbling ruins, and thereupon uprose again in mountainous rolling clouds of dust, ascending slowly higher and higher into the pale sky. The destruction was terrific. Of the actual masonry for many hundred yards, hardly a stone rested on a stone. The force travelled in the most eccentric directions—here upward, tossing the ballunets like cockleshells; there downward, digging out great craters; and in other cases in zigzag lines or concentric circles. What but a few years before would have taken months of mining and trenching, the bringing up of a siege-train, the erection of batteries, together with a sacrifice of blood and treasure incalculable, had been accomplished from beginning to end, by a score or two of men at the end of an exhausting march, with a few pounds of material, and at a loss on the side of the assailants of a single life! At such a velocity had science advanced! The area of destruction, however, it was remarkable, was not extensive; in the actual vicinity of the bombs nothing had escaped, but the fluid expended itself in the pulverization of what may be said to have been immediately in reach. Beyond this, within the town itself, the damage was slight, and chiefly confined to windows, doors, and chimneys. Those who had watched the development of explosives were not altogether unprepared for this result. Fortunately for the defence, the walls had not been manned at the time, no immediate assault having been anticipated, for in this case the force would have been annihilated.

Now at one blow the city lay defenceless; it was impossible for the Officer Commanding to fling himself with effect into a breach which extended across half the face; but with rare skill he at once organized the panic into an orderly retreat. Leaving a rear-guard with a few guns to make some pretence of covering it, he withdrew his men out at the back, and so with all arms, and carrying his baggage, ammunition and stores, he marched out, and took up an excellent position on the hills commanding the town to the north-east. Although this operation was at once perceived from the ballunets, and telegraphed to headquarters, it was too late to intercept him, and the city with its ruined walls alone, remained a trophy in the hands of the victors.

Upon the same day a naval engagement took place. Two powerful gunboats, watching the coast like bull-dogs, and detached from the fleet, fell upon a small wooden frigate, which was almost the only vessel of war boasted by the young Republic. She was, however, manned by a crew selected by the Chief himself. She was commanded by a man, who had won his laurels at blockade running, and had been specially nominated for the present service, which was that of laying torpedoes. Her captain had been grievously disappointed at being unable to place them in time to prevent the enemy's fleet from harassing the march; but he fancied that he understood the manœuvring of a vessel, and burning to retrieve his ill-fortune, he engaged his two formidable assailants without a moment's hesitation. Such was the superiority of his seamanship, that in the combat that ensued, in the course of a couple of hours, he had silenced one vessel, and driven the other ashore. Fortunately, the ponderous shot of the floating batteries never struck the frigate's hull, though it played sad havoc with the spars and rigging; had but one of these missiles gone home, there would have been a different story to tell. The young navies of the Pacific, unused to the handling of complicated war-vessels, learned the lesson that they were worse than useless, when the trained crews to man them were wanting. As it was, the feat stood unrivalled of its kind.

These successive blows proved of too crushing a nature to be withstood; the weather also came to the aid of the expedition; it turned cold and wet. The enemy who had taken refuge on the hills, being without tents, devoid of many necessaries, and unable to operate with any chance of success, were forced to lay down their arms and capitulate. Thus victory crowned the arms of the rising State, by sea and land, along the whole line, and thus ended the first act of the great tableau.

CHAPTER IX.

EUROPE at this particular period had her own fish to fry, and was much engaged in the process, but notwithstanding, the events just detailed attracted universal attention, and the three days' war, as it was called—in consequence of the actual fighting having all taken place within that time, when the power of three States had been broken, both by sea and land—was discussed everywhere, and by every man who pretended to the least judgment on military questions. Not only were the means novel and startling, in which lay the secret of its rapid success, but the arts of concentration and organization had been carried to a wondrous pitch, and this, in a most difficult country where railroads were almost unknown, and even the highways were often impracticable for the movement of troops. Yet the blows—and they were crushing ones, taken separately—were struck simultaneously, and the eyes of those on the look-out for the signs and portents of the coming time, were turned upon the soldier of fortune, in whose brain the campaign had originated, and who had carried it through without hitch to its successful conclusion.

The public fancy was taken by the picture of
this impassive, inscrutable figure, in civilian's
garb, who, smoking perennial cigars, and
seated before a map, in a whitewashed timber
shanty a hundred miles from the field, visualized
every necessity of time and place, and who,
hour by hour, led his men on, to almost
bloodless victories, at the end of a skein of
electric wires. Something, no doubt, was due
to his lieutenants, in the choice of whom a
peculiar fortune had attended him. In an army
half volunteer, half pressed, such as this was,
the conditions of choice were not fettered as in
others, and it appeared as if he possessed some
extraordinary instinct which enabled him to read
character at a glance. How otherwise should
he have singled out men, who might have been
actually created for the posts to which he preferred them? As time went on, this quality
developed itself, until it was marked as absolutely
unerring. He had searched far and wide for
his tools, and as a rule was able to find those
he required. When it was not so, it was
noticed that he left it in no dubious hands,
but did the work himself.

But we anticipate. By this time his identity
was no longer in doubt, and Englishmen
proudly laid claim to him as one of those,
whom for centuries past the country has sent
out, rough hewers of new worlds, framers of
nations and of empires.

He had been so well known, in London
in former days, that his name rapidly became a household word; but what exercised

the popular mind still more, was the fact of his friend, Lord St. Maur, the man with the palace in Park Lane and the inexpressible income, being associated with him in a subordinate position. The true old British Tory, whom no revolution could move on, thought comparatively little of the strategic fireworks of the new Carnot; but the picture of the phenomenal peer of the realm, slaving in a stifling office, and spending his time, his health, and his money, in a local squabble between half a dozen semi-savage races, appealed most powerfully to such intelligence as he was blessed with.

"If St. Maur wanted something to do, why the doose, sir, didn't he come and drive a four-in-hand in Hyde Park, and do his dooty by the country as a gentleman should? This nigger business was by no means fit for a man of his rank, though it might serve a west country squire to make a name with." For the fossil always saw in a lord a microcosm of his country's greatness and dignity, and was consequently very careful of him. "Nigger business" was the phrase that went about, and was thought sufficiently precise, for anything South American; but as a fact, the races concerned were of a hundred hybrid stocks—a mixture of every known people under heaven, but chiefly of European descent. This, while in some unaccountable way it produced a bounteous crop of rowdiness and ruffianism, yet supplied a magnificent material out of which to mould armies.

It will hardly be surprising to those who have studied the history of the South, that a whisper went round, on the return of the victorious forces, " the General for President."

The honour was a barren one. Since the formation of the State, power had been vested in a Council, which was felt likely to be the more permanent institution of the two—Presidents in those parts exhibiting a chronic tendency to collapse every few months. Possibly laughing in his sleeve at the extent of the dignity, Roland acquiesced. The provisional Government thereupon passed a vote, cautiously investing him with the office for one year, a term which could be extended at will, should his fame prove to have sufficient vitality. It appeared to be now at its zenith, and by all precedent should be shortly on the wane. He had achieved military success unheard of in that hemisphere, he had risen from a private individual to the head of the Government in less than three years; and his tactical knowledge, his mastery over every subject he handled, his old English name, the money at his back, his face, his figure, all contributed to single him out as a popular idol.

It was not wonderful that, to the uneducated soldiery, he appeared something more than human, and wild stories went afloat about him. He seemed to have the power of ubiquity, his hand far-stretching beyond that of others; and there were not wanting men in the ranks who swore that they had seen him lead the way in person, as they marched in to take

possession of the conquered city, when all
the world believed him to be miles away
at the base. Putting aside these tales, however, it was universally felt that here was
the Heaven-sent genius, who alone might pilot
the crazy bark of the new State through the
troubled waters, and before long it became
evident that the choice had been the only
possible one.

The renewed successes of the upstart Republic were not to be borne with equanimity,
and after some short haggling of preliminaries,
most of the older States joined in a coalition
for the purpose of making a descent upon it.
What the President thought of the situation
was never exactly known, for he took counsel
of no man. Whether he felt any faith in the
vague omens and prophecies so often reiterated,
it is hard to say, or whether these very things
urged him on. But it is scarcely probable
that the full magnitude of the enterprise on his
hands dawned upon him until now, when he
was driven to the conception of resisting the
forces of almost the entire Continent, by
seizing the western sea-board, and operating
thence from behind the natural frontier of the
Andes.

Again, it is impossible to particularize. With
the declaration of war the President assumed
the title of Dictator, and having by this time
organized all his work at the base, and placed
it in the hands of his own chosen coadjutors,
he himself took the field with a large force
equipped exactly to his mind, and overran

with ease the entire strip from end to end.
By this means he may be said to have
secured the whole Pacific coast as a base, and
the difficulty of attacking him on land, it will
be seen, thus became almost insurmountable.

The passes of the Andes are not pleasant
campaigning grounds for forces that must be
brought hundreds and thousands of miles
through forest and desert and plain. A
first pioneer expedition which penetrated as
far, perished to a man, leaving its lifeless
carcase on the steppes, to be preserved by
the wonderful air of those regions, intact
and entire as in life, an awful legacy to the
future. The disaster to this ill-fated force,
effectually prevented any further spasmodic
efforts of the kind, but in no wise mitigated the
hostility of the belligerents. After some desultory action upon the coast, which continued for
months without leading to any particular
result, it became evident that this war on the
Pacific was changing from a defensive to an
offensive one, *Delenda est Carthago.* There
was not room for the new dominion and the
old, and having once realized this, the Dictator
who had gathered at leisure, stores, provisions,
and munitions of war in depôts along the
entire line, poured his forces with unexampled
rapidity through the more practicable of the
seventeen passes of the barrier range, and
advanced upon the great Continent throughout
its immense length simultaneously; while the
world paused to watch, for it was hardly

doubted that this time he must accomplish his aims.

There was some talk that England, France, and Holland, the European nations concerned, should equip an expedition to the aid of the threatened Republics, and to protect their own borders. But so strong was the admiration excited by the rising of this new occidental star, and the confidence inspired by his invariable moderation, that it was a common opinion that Europe would coincide in any boundary to which he might push his conquest, if only stability and a sure government could be secured, desiderata from which the South American States seemed further off than ever.

When his plan first became apparent, a curious spectacle presented itself, and the multiplication of his armies was like the miracle of the loaves and fishes, division on subdivision took place, and each part was as large as the first.

For many years much of Europe, and more especially England, had suffered from a plethora of population, owing to the prevalence of the idea, that the number of children in a family was the affair of the gods, and that parents were mere irresponsible agents, whose sacred duty it was to bring as many as possible into the world, whether there were any rational hope of supporting them or not. This mania, which was destined eventually to break up Europe, had already caused incalculable misery, and overwhelmed all the great towns with pauperism and vice, before it culminated in the late revolution. However, religion, as it was then understood, taught that it *was* a sacred duty, that even the prudential check was anathema; which was much like teaching that because a man cannot live without drinking, therefore he should go to bed drunk every night! When duty and pleasure are found marching together hand in hand, it is not to be wondered at, that the majority hasten to take advantage of it; so the iniquity spread, crying aloud to Heaven for that vengeance which was in due time to come. The Revolution had cleared the air, but it had not solved the problem. Meanwhile here was a temporary respite—an opening out of fresh fields to the overplus, and the name alone of Roland had become a talisman.

The heart of man yearns towards human greatness. It is idle to say it is a small thing intrinsically. We are measured man with man, not with gods nor with angels; it is the barleycorn of measurement for human kind. Gathered about the Conqueror's standard, came twenty times ten thousand vagrants from all the byways of the world, and as the war continued they poured in from every quarter, and were formed into great reserves whence, when drilled and equipped, he was able to draw off supports for the front, as the loss and waste of the campaign demanded. Young Englishmen, ready at any hour of the day or night to break a neck for a wager, found here sport something bigger than at Melton, or on the Moors, and flocked in hundreds. Younger sons, sons of younger sons, and scions of stock, as well as men of grit and backbone from the middle classes. Nowhere do reputations grow as on the battle-field; nowhere is Fortune swifter with her wreath of laurel or of cypress, and ere long the lieutenants of the Conqueror, bearing such names as Pulteney, O'Bryan, Devigne—names which told their own tale—were scouring the Continent and carrying his ensigns through territories wider than many Europes. So through a series of campaigns lasting several years, and conducted with a success almost unbroken, the master spirit moving the enterprise from point to point, from victory to victory, until at length the enormous Continent was subdued, and lay prone at the point of his sword. From the frozen Horn, and the ice-bound Straits, where the bleak Terra del Fuego still flamed under the southern snows, and northward across the prairies, whither the conquest had spread, crossing them slowly, a pillar of cloud by day and a column of fire by night, the armies of the Dictator had marched, still spreading until they sweltered under the fierce suns of the equator, and sheltered in the pathless forests of Brazil. Nor did they stop until they rested on the narrow bridge of the isthmus which divides North America from the South, and here still facing northwards they sat down.

A paused ensued; the world breathed again, and men began to look round.

The old landmarks were gone; the old states had died hard in many bloody battles, for they also had been able to gather large armies to repel the invader, but to no purpose. Through this prodigious campaign, prodigious whether looked at in detail, or in its results, there was hardly a single action which appeared in the light of a reverse. There had been failures of course, but it was remarkable, that these were invariably where the undertaking had, by some chance, fallen from one subordinate to another. In no single instance did the hand of the great Leader himself fail to snatch back the laurel wreath from the unwilling Victory; and never man deserved it better, for he had wooed her from the first, and mastered in long study all her ways. He had pursued and chased and pressed her, laughing at her frowns, stoutly demanding of her smiles, and clinging to her skirts, nor would he let her go until she blessed him.

The struggle had been fiercest in the beginning, and the loss in men, horses, and material by forced marches, and accidents of place and climate, had been very great. And when, after vanquishing the tremendous difficulties opposed by the defiles of the Andes a descent was effected into the Pampas, the lack of forage and water proved a drawback of the first magnitude, resulting in a frightful waste of life. In these early days, the Indians, splendidly mounted as they always were, perpetually harassed the line of march, and succeeded in driving off the live stock which accompanied the armies, until the entire force was threatened with actual starvation. To meet this, a special corps of mounted riflemen was organized, equipped for the purpose, and equally well horsed with their assailants, on picked steeds of the desert. This succeeded in effectually breaking the back of their resistance, but not until several of the tribes had been annihilated; when the remainder not only submitted, but finding their territory guaranteed to them, threw in their lot with the victor. Henceforth, they formed a guerilla corps under his ensigns, where they proved themselves an invaluable and untiring scouting force, always to be found in the van, and far out on the flanks of the advancing armies.

With the progress of the new Empire which grew under their eyes, and in which they thus shared a part, their reverence for its founder and builder grew until it almost extended to worship. He was known among them as " the child of God," but the superstition that prevailed towards him, was hardly less in the ranks of his regular forces.   Over and over again these had been witnesses of hairbreadth escapes on his part, and feats of strength and endurance altogether, as it seemed, beyond the range of man; it was a jest that he could be in two or more places at once, and it was universally believed that he bore a charmed life.   The first-fruits of his success were a crop of attempts at assassination, all of which came to light, mysteriously addled in the hatching.

It happened once that the man deputed for the business reached his presence, where he sat alone at a writing-table and unarmed.

But the scoundrel declared that the instant the eye of the Dictator fell upon him, he felt his purpose read through and through, and that his arm was paralyzed so that he could not strike; dropping his knife, he fell on his knees and confessed, saying he was ready to pay the penalty. The head of the armies looked up from his writing which he had not stopped.

"Go," he said, "give me your life when I require it, on the field of battle."

But if the man into whose hands an almost universal power had come, could thus show clemency of occasion, he knew how to strike terror by the severity of his punishment, if the need arose. On one occasion marching to the relief of a town, when the safety of the whole force was endangered by the misbehaviour of a single corps, although every hour was of importance, he halted the entire column of march, forming it into an immense square, a manœuvre hardly possible on any other ground than the prairies. He caused the officers of the mutinous regiment to be marched as prisoners, to a slight eminence in the centre, whereon stood a stunted and solitary tree. There, with no word of explanation, and without any pretence or pretext of trial, he gave orders that the ringleader should be executed by being flogged to death. This in the space of ten minutes was accomplished, and the mangled and dripping form was hoisted into the air, in sight of some fifty thousand men of all arms, who were drawn up around. The body was left to the vultures; the rest of the officers were dismissed

back to their corps, which was deprived of its
arms, and transformed into porters for the
baggage-train. Amidst loud murmuring, the
order was then given to re-form column and
proceed. Before the army lay down to sleep
that night, they had delivered battle and carried the place by storm.

The story of this Nemesis did much to
remove the Dictator from human kinship;
it struck a chill through the civilized world.
The humanitarians raged. Yet it was justified
by results, for it utterly uprooted a growth that
must otherwise have resulted in the loss of
thousands of lives, before its futility had been
demonstrated. Had the act stood alone it
might have condemned the perpetrator, but
looked at by the side of his usual care and fore-
thought for his men, and his tenderness to the
wounded, which would often cause him to lose
hours, and even days of precious time, in order
to spare them, it went far to prove that it was
carefully calculated to the urgency of the moment. But henceforth the Dictator stood alone,
he had distanced even his oldest friend, and
he moved in a sphere wholly apart. St. Maur
himself, hard-headed but soft-hearted, who was
with the expedition, dared no word of remon-
strance. With the army it cannot be said to
have diminished his popularity, the thing seemed
secretly worthy of all admiration, to the swash-
bucklering ruffianism that composed the bulk
of the soldiery; and the superstitious pointed to
the victory of the day, as a proof that the God
of battles had blessed the deed.

Now that the conquest of the Peninsula was virtually complete, a gigantic federation had been formed, to which state after state as it had fallen had been admitted. This, while it secured local autonomy, insured a common bond between all, and knit them together in the common interest of mutual development.

Assemblies, elective and representative, in each, controlled the internal affairs, subject only to the central authority at present vested in the person of the Dictator, whose aim appears to have been, thus to instruct the youthful peoples in the principles of self-government. So he hoped to build up a scheme of constitutional liberty, which should contain the elements of permanency. And although it was not found practicable to enforce the somewhat Spartan restrictions upon income previously projected, a new feature was introduced in the matter of land, with regard to which the State reserved to itself absolute and ultimate control, granting, however, long leases, which for all purposes of improvement might be considered the equivalent of freehold. By this means it was hoped to obviate the most monstrous evils of the old European system.

There was little upset in all this, the wealth of the country lying almost exclusively in land, and that in large tracts of country, not in small parcels of town; on the settling down of affairs, the influx of population was such, that the increment of wealth in a short space was something fabulous. Instances were not uncommon where a plot of land, bought for five pounds, was sold a year or two after, for five hundred. Happily, too, this prosperity was not built on a substratum of struggle, poverty, and distress. Nature had spread a feast bountiful for all.

Never had conqueror before held out such prizes to his followers; there was no one man of energy among them who might not, if he chose, found a family and an estate, which should be historic in the great empire of the future, for the potential increase of the soil was practically limitless. Four centuries it had lain torn by conflicting interests, and waiting for the chance of Fortune, which might happily weld them into one. No better machinery could have been devised for the development of such an empire than an enlightened despotism. And here was a despot who, besides being a great soldier, strong to take and hold, was a man possessing an unrivalled talent for concentration and organization, one who had dipped deep below the surface of human things, and one accustomed to pursue every subject to the fountain head.

In the course of his career, he had gathered round him the most eminent names in science, philosophy, politics, and art, and with due result, but it was no doubt, the extraordinary and happy combination of accidents which he represented, which made his achievements possible. His name itself was a happy chance, his surname too, though for many years it had lain lost in the ranks of the British squirearchy, was one which had arisen in the middle ages, and glittered through the mists of history. His training, his religion, his misfortunes, the transition state of the world to which he sprang, and on which he brought to bear his peculiar gifts, all contributed to make ready for him the place he filled.

The conflicting ideas of the day in their struggle had approached a compromise, in which the principle of live, and let live, formed the basis, guaranteeing a future of uniform progress, wherein the poor should share to a certain extent, if to a limited one, in the well-being of the rich. If such an experiment, and one on so large a scale, could be successfully carried through, the world must follow in the wake. It was towards this end that all the efforts of the Dictator tended, and it was perhaps because this was clearly perceived, that his rule found ready acceptance with the conquered peoples. But it was not to be supposed that the world outside looked on with indifference.

It would be difficult to give an idea of public feeling in the United States during this period. So long as possible the new light and his work were ignored, but as his star rose steadily in the Heavens until it shone like the mid-day sun, fear, anger, and amazement held them spell-bound. An impossible, outrageous, old-fashioned thing had come to pass, on the sacred soil of the Americas. An hysterical outcry arose from the class which arrogated to itself the title of privileged.

Why was he not stopped? Everybody had told

everybody else how it would be from the first. But it was the old question of belling the cat. He was not stopped, and there were other phases of feeling which had to be reckoned with. There were sections of the community, in which admiration was largely mixed with other sentiments, and in which the Yankee love of a "big thing" proved a powerful factor.

Were the States really threatened? What if this man were a despot? His despotism lay in the enforcing of federation and self-government upon the conquered peoples, and they from their position, must necessarily take the first place in any incorporation. Their liberties would not suffer. Facilities of communication by sea, land, and now it seemed likely, owing to late discoveries—by air, necessitated an expansion of boundaries, and made possible and even pressing, a unity, the idea of which had previously been ridiculous. It was a real big thing this, and their wisest plan might be to throw themselves into the movement, and identify themselves with it.

Not less remarkable was the aspect of public feeling at home. The last page of history had not taken by surprise the philosophical thinkers of the day. To politicians, economists, and soldiers, the signs of the great movement which was now culminating in the West had been apparent for some time, and the necessary man had stepped into his place when the hour struck. But it was in the religious world, which was a world governed by laws which human capacity had as yet failed to tabulate, that the greatest commotion was perceivable.

At Exeter Hall—a place where the highest type of Christian piety was always to be found, it was publicly given out, that here was Anti-Christ at last. It was well known among the elect that the end of the world was at hand, hitherto the only missing link had been this very Personage. Of a certainty this was He. What supplied proof positive was, that out of his name, could be twisted in black and white, the number of the Beast. There were inherent vitalities in Exeter Hall, which promised its survival through a score of revolutions, should such present themselves. A series of meetings which was to have aroused all England, and to have been the forerunner of a war of extermination, however, fell flat; the English instinct was too strong in the country, its sympathies were with the conqueror.

But if there was fanaticism on one side, it was not wanting upon the other. There was a strong party, who shall be nameless, who declared that this was the dawn of the millennium.

At length, the Deliverer was come upon them, the true eldest son of the Church, who would support her material authority at the point of a million bayonets. He would, no doubt, after establishing the Holy Catholic Church dominant, and absolute, in Southern

America (with a good working Inquisition), turn his steps to Europe—conquer England, as conquest appeared to be a mere bagatelle with him—re-establish the ancient Church upon her ancient throne, abolish Protestantism and the sects by Edict, so securing at one happy stroke the entire conversion of England.

After this he could do no less than cross to the Continent, exterminate the rascally Liberals from off the face of the earth, restore the States of the Church to the Holy See, with the addition of all Italy in compensation for past losses, and bring every European sovereign on his knees before the Pope, with an oath of fealty and allegiance; and after this? Well, after this he might be allowed to die a natural death, in order to hurry his canonization!

Oh! who shall know the mind of God, and who shall be His counsellor? The question is answered every day—the bigots of all creeds, the chosen of Heaven, the children of Christ.

For the myriad rumours as to his intentions, which, at this interval, vibrated on every telegraph-wire throughout the planet, the Dictator cared not a straw, nor turned one hair-breadth from his path. In the re-founding of the South American States, the Church was given no advantage over the veriest conventicle of ranters. He had been heard to affirm that the progress of faith must be from within, not from without, that advancement of other description must necessarily be specious and false—that in a fair field the truth must prove itself, and could stand at no odds.

It was at this time—an interval of peace between the two deadliest struggles the Western Continent had witnessed—that the election of the Cardinal Archbishop of New York, a native-born American, to the See of St. Peter, took the world by surprise. A new departure appeared to be marked by this event, the importance of which it would be impossible to over-estimate. Its immediate effects in the South were of the happiest description. With religion and government restored upon a fixed basis, came confidence and prosperity; the new states were shortly flourishing, and began to exhibit refinements of civilization before unknown. The astonished hemisphere witnessed Art new-born, shoot up into a strong and vigorous plant; so with Literature.

But the most noticeable feature of all, was the extraordinary opening out and development of new regions hitherto looked upon as sterile, barren, and utterly unfit for human habitation. In the course of the investigations, made by the scientific army which followed on the heels of conquest, an invaluable discovery had been made with regard to the utilization of sun power. Not only were men enabled by means of it, to drive engines, and apply it to purposes hitherto entirely monopolized by steam, but the possibility, long suspected, of extracting electricity from its rays, followed immediately upon the earlier discovery. The process was simple and inexpensive once demonstrated, and its results it would be difficult to describe in words. The reservoir was inexhaustible, the reserve of power boundless.

Henceforth the inhospitable steppes, the deserts, the vast equatorial plains, unconquerable in their wildernesses, were to give up their secrets, to blossom like vineyards under the toil of the husbandman, transformed into gardens for the supply of the world. The prodigious loans which the Dictator was able to effect almost without further backing than his name, were chiefly laid out upon the soil—a soil which, for the most part, scarcely needed the proverbial scratching to yield a hundred-fold, and in which everything planted seemed to be subject to a miraculous multiplication.

A finance of an exotic and semi-fabulous character marked the first period of settlement. Towns planted in the wastes sprang up like mushrooms, sowing fertility around them. Before a year had elapsed, there arose groups of streets and public buildings, filled with such appliances and conveniences of civilization, as put to shame European cities centuries old. To this process there appeared to be no end. Town was planted on town, city on city, as the great exodus from the old world continued growing in force and intensity. And the increased facilities of communication, tending always to the obliteration of distinctions and widening of boundaries, made possible a unity and a oneness in government and interest, for which, under former conditions, it would have been idle to look.

The Dictator was untiring in his work, his gifts of foresight and ubiquity had never been surpassed by man born of woman. The enormous command of labour which lay ready to his hand, enabled him to direct the energies of the entire Continent to any one portion which appeared to demand it most at the moment. Owing to the troubles in Europe, and the new opening afforded across the Atlantic, South America at this time may be said to have absorbed half the floating capital of the globe—to say nothing of the migratory capital of labour which followed in its wake.

By the original constitution of the new Empire, the federal councils of the several states were responsible, and subordinate to, the General Council (which was recruited from their numbers); this again was virtually responsible to the man who had erected them and all the machinery of government. But the arrangement as it then stood not presenting sufficient permanency of form, an elective Presidency was proposed by the Dictator himself.

This office, against his own ideas and principles, he was eventually prevailed upon to accept for life, with the understanding that a limitation of ten years should be placed on the tenancy of his successors. It embodied to some extent the principles of a constitutional monarchy, but was free from its defects, inasmuch as the office was not hereditary, and its representative must necessarily be the elected of the people. In spite of the democratic temper of the head of the Empire, there appears to have

been a desire to establish a recognized aristocracy in his system, with the temporary sovereign as the fount and dispenser of honour. A
man so versed in human nature could hardly
feel otherwise. The sentiment shortly found
expression in the institution of two orders of
nobility, a higher and a lower, both of which
were elective and non-hereditary in character.
The chief distinctions of the time were necessarily military.

The success which had attended the first
welding of the states into one, was so enormous
that few difficulties were thrown in the way of
these further developments.

The South American Empire was now
formally recognized by the leading European
Governments, one and all of which had been
incalculably, if indirectly, benefited by the
establishment of it, and there was a general
wish for its permanency. Only from the
United States came the cry of bitter and prolonged hostility.

It was not to be expected that America
proper should view with equanimity the up-
rising upon its borders of an Empire with an
area considerably greater than its own, and
one which, within the space of a few years,
should miraculously develop resources hitherto undreamed of, and this under a military
despotism, the parallel of which had not
been told in history. Had the lost continent of Atlantis suddenly reared itself from
out the face of the waters, the daze in
men's minds could hardly have been greater.

The United States lay absolutely defenceless.
It was impossible, with a brand-new Empire
as their next neighbour, which had already
spread like a wild fire over the prairie, to leave
their frontiers unguarded as of yore, and the
irritating tax of large armies, was added to a
people wholly unused to the support of such a
burden.

But the States would have been less than
themselves, had they allowed that they were
beaten in anything; superhuman exertions were
made, conscription was resorted to, opposition
was howled down, and in the course of no
long period the "North" was announced to
have the finest army in the world. In the
beginning, there were great difficulties as to
generals to command the forces, not from any
want of them, but because their quality was
unproven. "Money will do it," said the States,
"guess we'll buy the best general in the Universe." Eventually, the chief commands were
given to men who had already won their spurs,
and were red-handed from the late battle-fields
of Europe. The unique example of the conquest of the South had spread a military furore
abroad, and a race of hard-headed, hard-hitting
heroes had arisen, who were ready out of mere
professional instinct to carve their way through
any fortune.

CHAPTER X.

FOR a space of time the now unified "North" and the new "South" lay cheek by jowl like a couple of giants, armed but sleeping. A hushed expectation was in the air ; for it was no secret that ere long must ensue a herculean struggle, which would be for the possession and the loss of half the globe. So vast a tableau would not have been possible in an earlier age. For some time—such was the activity of the peace and arbitration societies, which had then grown into considerable importance—it seemed unlikely that any decent pretext would be found as a ground for the commencement of hostilities; and the fire-eaters on either side were despairing, when the little breeze arose which was to fan the smouldering embers into flame.

The difficulties first reached an acute stage in the negotiations concerning the respective rights of the contending Empires in the canal dividing the Isthmus of Panama. The first decisive step was taken on the side of the North, by its forcible stoppage of the works of a new one, at the moment in progress, pending the settlement of the questions at issue. This in itself

was tantamount to a declaration of war, and as
such was accepted on both sides. Both were
ready and burning for the fray; both were
equipped and armed as to men and material
as no armies ever seen before on earth,
and the almost fabulous resources of recent
scientific discovery were equally at the disposal of both commanders. It was felt that
under these circumstances the struggle could
be of no long duration. A word and a blow,
or a blow without the word—these throughout had been the tactics of the Southern
Conqueror; and it was plain that if he was to
be beaten, it would be by reading him a leaf out
of his own book. He had revolutionized the art
of war to a greater extent even than Napoleon:
he may be said to have raised it to the dignity
of a fine art, which his Prototype with the
coarse butchery and brutality of his strokes
never did.

Roland was the first who realized what
science had done for the soldier, what scientific
warfare might mean in the hands of the man
able for the conduct of it. A specialist himself
in some of the main branches of scientific knowledge, he had gathered up into his own hands
every speciality likely to prove of use in the
advancement of his aims, and at his elbow
were the leading scientists of the day.

"Had Napoleon had my advantages," he was
wont to say, "he *must* have conquered the
world."

There existed always this possibility: that
another, trained in his own school, should arise

and defeat him with his own weapons. But the advantages of long practice lay on his side, and out of long custom he had so refined the game of war that, to the eye of the onlooker, it had become like a game of chess. He gave his adversary checkmate in the smallest possible number of moves, and there could be no doubt whatever as to its finality. A protracted struggle was thus avoided, although before this came to be understood, there was long and bloody wrestling against what appeared to his bewildered adversaries like a stroke of fate.

"The wars of science—the wars of the future," he had often declared, "will be swift and catastrophic. And although the sword and the bayonet, in some shape, will probably survive as long as man himself, battles will not be won with them among civilized races. When the day is gained they will be wanted to finish it. In the field itself, electricity, automatic machinery, and explosive will do the work; and the brain most capable of combining and directing these will prevail. Great masses of men will often be not only useless, but a positive weakness to their side. Corps of experts, highly trained in their respective branches, will be the Commander's first desideratum."

Such, in great part, was the army he had built up in the course of his campaigns. Its actual numbers, large as they were, were small compared with that of his adversaries. Yet he had always worked miracles with it, and already it had been given to him to take up and accomplish, under happier auspices, the secret aims of the great Napoleon ;—those wild visions of conquest, to which all that he had effected in the old world, was to be but a stepping-stone on the way.

The gathering of armies to the Isthmus was a spectacle for gods and men, and in proportion to the magnitude of the stake at issue. The forces which the twentieth century put into the field were ordinarily on a colossal scale, but these eclipsed any that living man had ever wielded before. For miles on either side the country was one vast camp; but the unhealthy nature of this fever-stricken district prevented the actual occupation of the field of operations until the last moment. When at length delay was no longer possible, a descent was made into the lowlands, and the campaign opened with two or three unimportant skirmishes, in which a few thousand men only, of either side, were engaged. These had no particular result, the victory being claimed by both.

It almost seemed as if the South had been taken in a state of unreadiness. The Dictator was at the base and either not willing or not able to stir, his arrangements being apparently incomplete; and he contented himself with strengthening his lines of defence, without pushing forward as was his wont. In consequence of this inaction the first strategic move of note was made and won without difficulty by the enemy. This consisted of the seizure, in its entire length, of the unfinished canal. The importance of this could not be gainsaid. The North, already possessed of the old canal, which lay behind parallel to it, in many places and at no long distance, poured in their transports and gunboats. In a few hours the dry bed of the new, with the earth already thrown out and heaped in breastworks which it took little labour to perfect, presented superb and unbroken lines, which, when strengthened in the ordinary way, and backed as they were by ships' batteries, often within a few hundred yards, might well be considered impregnable. The actual bed of the future canal, which formed this huge shelter trench, was, so far as it was completed, dry, hard, and firm, and formed a road upon which every arm could be moved with speed and facility, and in almost absolute security.

The northern bank was forthwith sloped in easy grades at fixed points, and so permitted of the ingress or egress of heavy guns and material, with little delay or danger.

The sympathies of the world, speaking broadly, were not with the American nation for various reasons, and it stood amazed and aghast at this beginning. It seemed incredible that this should have been allowed to take place unresisted, and the fame that accrued to the Commander-in-chief of the American armies in consequence of the manœuvre, and of the manner in which it was executed, rose to so high a pitch, that it was confidently averred that here was a man at last who had proved himself equal to the unique strategist with

whom he had to deal. This surely was the first
sign of the waning of that terrible star. Rumour, too, leaked out—whether authenticated
or not it was impossible to say—that the Dictator's health was failing; that his strength of
body was not what it had been (he was now
past middle age); and that he suffered from
the effects of former hardships and exposure,
and from the intense strain implied by the preparations of the last few years. Be that as it
might, he made no immediate effort to repair
the mistake.

For some days, grotesque as it must sound
to the ears of the reader, the operations were
confined to upper air, among the ballunets
—a newly-invented curse to an army, hostile
or friendly, and a greater than was ever special
correspondent. Nothing could be hidden from
these prying eyes; nothing was safe. The
machinery could be packed into such small
compass, and set in motion so easily, that there
was no limit to the numbers that made their
appearance. Once up, nothing could touch
them from the earth; and, although their
weight-carrying capacity was small, their opportunities for harassing the foe by casting
dejectiles into their works, and espying their
slightest movements, were unbounded. The
only thing they had to fear was from each other.
To one another they were fatal. The man or
the apparatus once injured, a few seconds
brought them to earth as surely as a bird that
had been riddled with shot. This certainty
of destruction, if a false step were made, in-

duced a degree of caution to be exercised in the
aerial manœuvres, which was unknown on the
surface of the earth. The real struggles on
both sides were for the best points of sight;
and when two hostile armies were bivouacked
face to face, it was not unusual that the floating
outposts, like those on the field below, came
to a tacit understanding, as to the range and
extent of their respective beats.

A week elapsed, and it was evident that a
general engagement could no longer be deferred. The ballunets reported that the preparations for an advance from the Northern
lines appeared to be complete. For this the
Dictator had apparently been waiting. He decided to take the attacking into his own hands,
and orders were issued for a general advance
upon the entrenched positions of the enemy
at daybreak.

The bald, brief outline of this tremendous
day, which is unfortunately all that can be
given the reader, will, it is to be feared, fail to
convey to his mind the intensified character of
the wrestle between the two vast continents;
but it must suffice. In the shock, the fate of
half the world was to be decided, and where
was the Champion of free peoples to stay his
steps?

Morning broke slowly, it seemed, and reluctantly; the heavy cloud-screens rolled away
before the light. There is ever a strange
solemnity in the hush of the dawn that ushers
in the day of battle. The livelong night had
been one long tumult of preparation. Now all

was in readiness, and there was a breathing spell of rest.

Two men were standing apart a little, on a low hill that dominated the scene for many miles. Around was one huge ant-hill of human beings, whose presence was only indicated by a low murmuring that possessed earth and sky. The two were the Dictator Roland and St. Maur, the companion of all his victories. The former stood silent awhile, as he surveyed the camp. His arrangements were completed. There was nothing now to do but to wait. He turned to his friend.

" Bear me witness, St. Maur," he said, " that this has been none of my seeking. It has been forced upon me from the first."

In his face were signs of emotion, almost of tenderness.

"Posterity will judge us," answered St. Maur. " Your wars—our wars—have been those of humanity. They were a necessity of its history and progress. We have fought out the battle of man against man. We have established his rights, I trust, for ever. It has been the victory of principle, and must spread until it conquers the world. We have proved, I think, that in the future there is no room for monopolists or sham aristocracies."

The Dictator did not answer; but after a minute he spoke again, passing his hand across his face, like a man who would tear away a veil that obstructed his sight.

" St. Maur," he said, " have we dreamed this? Am I mad or sane? Do I stand here at this moment, the arbiter of the destinies of millions unborn? Is it I who have brought these vast armies face to face? Or are they a shadow as I am myself? Yesterday I was a boy at school; and on whose shoulders now will fall my mantle?"

In the years that he had followed him, St. Maur had never known his Chief visibly affected by external events. He had been the man of iron pursuing his way, relentless as Destiny herself. This sudden sensibility at what needs must be the culminating point of his career filled St. Maur with doubt and alarm. He controlled himself to answer; but a sudden movement in the field recalled the Dictator to himself. The latter waved off the reply, for the hour had struck and the forces were already in motion.

Without hitch, hurry, or confusion, the movement began. Division after division, brigade after brigade, his beloved legions swept past the hill, below him, orderly and self-possessed, with the elastic spring of confidence, as though marching out to the gala parade of a gigantic field-day. He stayed impassively, saluting each as they passed onward, until his own favourite and favoured corps came by. Then he went upon the brow of the hill, uncovering his head until they were passed. These were the very pioneers of battle, the rough hewers of the work; where they cleft a way the thousands followed. It would have been inconsistent with the discipline and traditions of the regiment to have uttered a sound; but it may be conceived that this token of his feelings for them provoked irrepressible enthusiasm in the ranks. The confidence that was spread through the whole army was shared by one and all alike, in spite of disparaging comments outside, and the apparently insurmountable difficulties that confronted it. A passage in the orders of the day probably went far to contributing to this. It ran:—

"Soldiers, we have burned our ships. From this point there can be no retreat, and you will understand why the Leader you have followed so long and so far has considered it unnecessary to prepare for any such thing to-morrow."

Sphynx-like, he betrayed no secrets, and his actual plan of operations was unknown even by his chief lieutenants, until the moment when it was justified by its success. The soldier loves such. He asks few questions, makes few comments, knows little—the private soldier nothing —of the very work he is set to do. But for the chief, with whom, when the smoke and din are cleared away, he finds that he, the horny-handed, has grasped the laurels of victory; there is no service that man can render man that he will not do.

Not for the first time in history the engagement began by going against the Dictator. The breaching effected by the dynamo and other explosive shells flung into the enemies' works proved ineffective and insufficient. Batteries of automaton guns, smokeless, soundless, but for the whirr of their machinery, pushed well to the front, played steadily from either side, while sheets of lightning from the electric

field-pieces swept the intervening space.
Hour after hour passed in an artillery duel,
followed by a general advance on the side of
the South. By noon, owing to the enormous
strength of the North American positions, the
left and centre of the attack had been beaten
off and driven back, and were withdrawn
sullenly out of action in the effort to re-form,
which was rendered possible by the failure of
the North to leave their trenches and prosecute
their advantage. On the extreme right the
South appeared to have gained a footing, and
were holding their own steadily and well. Meanwhile, torrents of rain had commenced to fall,
blotting out the details of the action. Roland,
who had hitherto remained on the hill where
he had first taken up his place, hardly stirring,
found it necessary to move down. Ordinarily,
his faculty of grasping a bird's-eye sense of
the position (the first of military talents, he
maintained), seemed to serve him in lieu of
and better than actual vision, but to-day he
appeared restless, and as if doubts were crossing
his mind. As he went message after message
reached him.

The attack on the left had failed utterly.
Devigne's division was destroyed. Spencer's
was giving way; fresh supports were urgently
needed. On the right Pulteney was holding
out, but with difficulty, and if reinforcements
did not come, he, too, would be driven back.

To all, the same answer was returned, "Fight
on."

Came four colonels, whose regiments had

been annihilated. "Then, gentlemen, fall in with the ranks," and to the messenger from the right, "Tell General Pulteney to hold on at all costs." The Dictator snapped his watch. "Almost before you reach him he will be relieved." Suiting the action to the word, he gave the order for the instant advance of the Reserves.

There was a thunderous sound from the trembling earth for a space; then, launched simultaneously, the blows struck the enemies' lines on their entire length like a tempest. The sodden atmosphere which hung above the field was quickened into an awful life, and filled throughout its spaces with the tearing, screaming, hurtling of shot and shell, as if ten thousand fiends had been together let loose upon it. So dense, so continuous, so unbroken was the fire and the hail of missiles, that the onlooker stood rooted, as if under a spell, feeling that to move out hand or foot must result in the limb being torn away.

In the dull red glow beneath, it is visible that this last spurt has had the effect of causing a recoil on the part of the enemy,—but only for a few minutes. Slowly they recover their ground, and where the Southern host has penetrated into the trenches on either flank they are now rolled back and back hopelessly. The reeling ranks lose all cohesion. Victory totters and trembles in the balance. Nay, the day is surely decided. Nothing can cover this; that long line of sabres that flash together in a futile effort are mown down, even as one looks, like hay before the sickle. Another, and another, it is idle—worse; they are heaped high, body on body, it is no longer possible even to ride over these writhing hills. There are no Reserves now to speak of, and step by step the wreck is being huddled to its fate.

The North, already nerved by the spell of victory, are straining every muscle to follow up their advantage. From the flanks, east and west, the flying guns are flogged towards the centre, and dash rocking to and fro like weight-less things, rebounding from the ground over the living, over the dead; now everything must be sacrificed, man and horse; for this is the supreme moment, this the one that changes defeat into rout, a beaten enemy into one that, as such, no longer has existence at all. The new positions gained, the batteries are able to pour their concentrated fury upon the centre which still stands. But it can stand no more. Death ploughs in dreadful furrows through and through the midst, and lo! the harvest is there reaped, ready and overflowing. At such an instant the eye mentally beholds each army as a unit, a sentient, breathing creature. On the one hand, crushed, bleeding, disabled, recoiling in slow helpless pain. On the other, a monster bristling triumphant, irresistible in its advance, in its eye exaltation, in its stroke death, in its crest Victory.

When, invading the horrible din of battle, comes a strange sound and a different, a murmur hoarse and low in the beginning, rising, swelling, spreading, until it absorbs all else, and the cannon are drowned. It rings upwards, piercing the skies, the cry of tens of thousands perishing at once—the death-rattle of an army in the throes of dissolution.

Over the field was flung a transformation, as of magic. Where the serried North had stood since morning, undaunted and invincible, was a chaos of destruction; horse was flung on man, waggon on horse; a raging torrent, a vast wave, like a moving wall, tore its resistless way through the valley; the whole struggling, surg-- ing mass of living things was borne along powerless before it, the very lines were swept away. The still rising water, after filling the new channel, burst outward upon the banks, for miles the lowlands were covered with the stragglers in wild stampede. Those who had not been actually within the lines and carried away in the first rush, made for the gun-boats in rear, for the most part in vain. In their struggles the maddening crowds trampled each other to death—a holocaust, such as had not been since the days, when Pharaoh and his armies were whelmed in the Red Sea depths.

The Staff, who had been gathered round the Dictator but a minute before in an agony of apprehension, scanned his face, but it had sunk to its old stony immobility.

"Water! water!" The word was repeated stupidly, and they gazed from one to another, like men stricken of their senses. In effect, the secret work entrusted to a band of the Des- peradoes, that of breaching the banks of the upper channel at a point far down by means of an electro-explosive mine, had been carried out. The Atlantic was pouring in unchecked.

"What next?" muttered a veteran, as he realized the fact; "what next?"

"New York," answered a voice.

The Dictator turned about. "Come, gentlemen," he said, in his ordinary accents; "my work is done," and closing his field-glass he rode forward, leading the way down the hill.

To have followed Cæsar and his fortunes in this hour, was a thing to mark a man to his race for all time. The Staff closed about him. The rain still poured heavily. The wonder-worker spurred a little in advance on the black charger, which had carried him through many battles up till this. It was noticed that his head was bent upon his breast, that his features were set with a sternness, strange even in his stern face. What hopes, what thoughts, must fill his brain, in this the supreme hour of such a life? He had distanced human kind. His long-tried followers who knew him best, even they were stunned, as they beheld in a moment the uplifted blow, averted and turned back redoubled, crush their already victorious foe to atoms.

The storm beat pitilessly about their heads, and as they went the black horse swerved. It may have been a sudden gust which drove across the plain, or the flash of a near battery which, recovering from the stupefaction of its first astonishment, had recommenced its work upon the havoc below. In the confusion none knew; a very hell was raging round about. The swerve was followed by a stumble, horse and rider were flung together down the steep.

What was this? What last event had crowned this crowning moment in the history of the Nations?

The maker of the times, he who had wrought the work, had left it—the achiever—the Colossus who had bestridden his world, the man among the men of his years—was dead.

* * * * *

Far away in another hemisphere, there stands hid in the midst of one of the great wildernesses of humanity—a lowly house of religious. Within it news of the world's doings—of war and rumour of war hardly reaches—nor touches at all their lives whose watchword is " peace." Only the sisters amid their works pray for those who are called to these things, and this day, unknowing, they are at prayer.

And there is among them one scarcely to be singled from the rest, but that she carries in her face the traces of a great beauty, and there is added to it something over and above beauty, which this world does not give. She is bowed a little, like a lily that is fading, and when the rest go out she still stays praying—praying as if she, poor soul, alone upon her knees, would stir God for the great world. But she will always thus, and of old they have had to order her from the altar ere she will go. So presently they come and tell her that it is time, but she does not hear. Her face is sunken in her hands, and though they touch her she does not look up. Then they carry her out, and to the poor cell which has been her home through the long years. It is the dawn of day.

Another sun is rising for the toiling millions, but for this toiler the sun of earth shall rise no more. At length, at length, the boon is forced from the reluctant heaven; the slow limit of endurance has been reached, the golden bowl is broken. She—our sister—is not here.

And Thou, oh Christ—the man with whom it is given to us to speak, as man with man, who hast not disdained to walk the ways of the world, to mark the heights of man's sacrifice and the depths of his suffering;—Thou who, even unto these days of unfaith, dost illumine thy chosen ones with a burning light, wherein they walk, and wherein all other philosophies grow dim,—remember Thou thy promises. A faithful servant, clothed in the robes of her virginity, and bearing in her worn hands a gift, stands before Thee trembling, for the shadows are passed away and the reality is upon her.

Beyond the portals of the daybreak, receive thy spouse within the gates of Life.

GILBERT AND RIVINGTON, LIMITED, ST. JOHN'S SQUARE, LONDON.